"ROBSON DELIGHTS US. . . .

She revels in the language and reveals the Japanese as a poetic, witty people."

The Washington Post Book World

"Engrossing . . . Re-creates the colorful people, stunning landscapes and arcane customs of feudal Japan . . . Robson keeps the story moving deftly through the separate worlds of courtesans, warriors, priests, peasants, poets and actors, with an eye to the complex rules that govern them all."

San Francisco Chronicle

"THE TŌKAIDŌ ROAD has an authority of detail and atmosphere that can only come from careful, extensive research and a lively historical imagination. Cat is an intriguing character [and] many readers will enjoy following her travels."

JEANNE LARSEN
Author of *Silk Road* and *Bronze Mirror*

"Lucia St. Clair Robson, who has captured a loyal following with her American historical novels, now turns her considerable talents to an actual incident in Japan in this absorbing novel. . . . Robson has added her special creativity to her superbly detailed research and written an unforgettable novel."

Rocky Mountain News

Please turn the page
for more praise for
THE TŌKAIDŌ ROAD

"CAPTIVATING AND TRANSPORTING . . .

What is to us an unfamiliar world comes absolutely alive."

Cosmopolitan Magazine

"Excellent . . . A fast-paced, rousing adventure tale skillfully interwoven with one of Japan's great stories: the early eighteenth-century vendetta of the forty-seven *rōnin* or masterless samurai. Robson is well informed about Japan and Japanese history and . . . she maintains a sound historical framework for her tale."

PAUL VARLEY
Professor of Japanese History
Columbia University

"A grand tale for anyone with a fondness for rich adventures . . . A real gift to those who know and are continually intrigued by Japan, its people and their history . . . THE TŌKAIDŌ ROAD is replete with detail and colorful images that offer wonderful insights into the ways of ancient Japan. It is a skillfully woven tale that is captivating and thoroughly entertaining."

Annapolitan Magazine

"THE TŌKAIDŌ ROAD is an engrossing novel. Its main characters are complex and believable; its minor characters offer wonderful insights into feudal Japan. Most astonishing is Lucia St. Clair Robson's grasp of detailed aspects of life in the early Tokugawa Period. A *Canterbury Tales* backdrop to an *Eye of the Needle* suspense story. I read it in one sitting!"

ROBERT OXNAM
President, The Asia Society
Author of *Cinnabar, A Chinese Mystery*

"A SUMPTUOUS, EXTRAVAGANT, AND EXOTIC SENSUAL FEAST . . .

A sweeping tale of vengeance, mystery, adventure, intrigue, and love set in early 18th century Japan . . . Filled with a myriad of accurate and colorful historical details, THE TŌKAIDŌ ROAD is a lush, picturesque read. Readers will feel as if they have been steeped in Japanese tradition, language, and poetry. . . . Masterful."

Rave Reviews

"A richly detailed saga . . . The experience of the road, with its quixotic encounters, exquisite verbal images and vibrant sights, and sounds and smells, grows almost as significant as the journey's goal—making this a charming, unusually memorable adventure. Earthy, humorous, lively—and a veritable encyclopedia of the ways of old Japan."

The Kirkus Reviews

"Replete with hand-to-hand battles, rooftop chases, and perilous escapes, their adventures are also rich in details of customs, attire, ritual, and terrain, punctuated with poetry. This depiction of an era commands interest. Recommended."

Library Journal

THE TŌKAIDŌ ROAD

A NOVEL OF FEUDAL JAPAN

Lucia St. Clair Robson

BALLANTINE BOOKS • NEW YORK

Copyright © 1991 by Lucia St. Clair Robson
Maps copyright © 1991 by David Lindroth

All rights reserved under International and Pan-American Copyright Conventions. Published in the United States by Ballantine Books, a division of Random House, Inc., New York, and simultaneously in Canada by Random House of Canada Limited, Toronto.

Library of Congress Catalog Card Number: 90-93213

ISBN 0-345-35639-X

Manufactured in the United States of America

First Hardcover Edition: March 1991
First Mass Market Edition: May 1992

For Brian, my companion on the Road.

ACKNOWLEDGMENTS

I would like to thank Dr. Yoji Kondo for his advice in the writing of this story. His knowledge of the complexities of Japanese history and culture and of the vicissitudes of fiction were invaluable. If errors remain in the text, the author takes sole responsibility for them.

Friends in Japan have also encouraged, aided, and sheltered me while I researched the tale of the forty-seven *rōnin*. In 1970 the Nakatsu family of Iwakuni allowed me to live in the tea house in their enchanting garden where I could not help but fall under the spell of Japan. In twenty years, that spell has only grown stronger. Also in 1970, Shizuko Osaki, doll-making *sensei* extraordinaire, tried her best to steer this outlander through the intricacies of Japanese society. She's been a true friend and mentor ever since and I owe her a special debt of gratitude.

In Otake, my old friend Masaaki Hirayama and his family took me into their home. Masaaki helped me find information and drove me to places hard to reach even on Japan's marvelous rail system.

For all these friends' continuing generosity of spirit I can only give inadequate thanks. Likewise, the Japanese who have befriended me on my travels are too numerous to name, but their kindness to a stranger will always be remembered.

PRONUNCIATION OF JAPANESE WORDS

Japanese vowels are pronounced as follows:

"a" as in father
"e" as in weight
"i" as in ink
"o" as in open
"u" as in due

Syllables are given equal stress, with each vowel being pronounced separately. For example, the word for "no," "iie," is pronounced ee-ee-ay. O's and u's with a macron over them (ō, ū) are given a slight emphasis. Tōdo would be pronounced to-o-do.

NOTE

In feudal Japan days were divided into twelve periods, six for day and six for night. The lengths of the periods were adjusted to the seasons but generally coincided with two of our hours. Each "hour" was named:

> Midnight to 2:00 A.M.—the hour of the Rat
> 2:00 A.M. to 4:00 A.M.—the hour of the Ox
> 4:00 A.M. to 6:00 A.M.—the hour of the Tiger
> 6:00 A.M. to 8:00 A.M.—the hour of the Hare
> 8:00 A.M. to 10:00 A.M.—the hour of the Dragon
> 10:00 A.M. to noon—the hour of the Snake
> Noon to 2:00 P.M.—the hour of the Horse
> 2:00 P.M. to 4:00 P.M.—the hour of the Ram
> 4:00 P.M. to 6:00 P.M.—the hour of the Monkey
> 6:00 P.M. to 8:00 P.M.—the hour of the Cock
> 8:00 P.M. to 10:00 P.M.—the hour of the Dog
> 10:00 P.M. to midnight—the hour of the Boar

The hours were often marked by the ringing of the temple bells. Midnight began the "ninth" time, 2:00 A.M. the "eighth" time, 4:00 A.M. the "seventh" time, until the end of the "fourth" time at noon when the series started again.

In this story, units of time are measured by the old Japanese system. Two and a half hours, therefore, would be about equal to five of our hours. The first quarter of the hour of the Rat would be 12:30 A.M.

Distance was measured in *ri*, which equaled about 2.44 miles. A *cho* was about 352 feet. Because a *shaku* measured just over eleven and a half inches, the English term *foot* has been used to indicate that length.

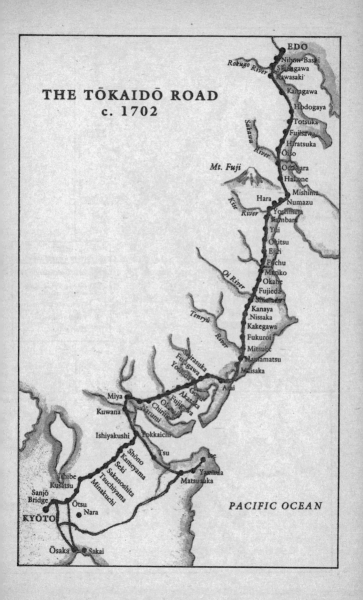

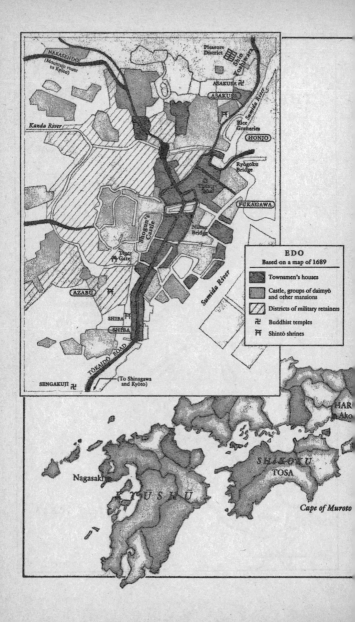

EDO
Based on a map of 1689

- Townsmen's houses
- Castle, groups of daimyō and other mansions
- Districts of military retainers
- 卍 Buddhist temples
- 鳥居 Shintō shrines

NAKASENDO
(Mountain route to Kyōto)

Pleasure District

Saké Godowns

ASAKUSA 卍

ASAKUS

Kanda River

Sumida River

Rice Graneries

HONJO

Ryōgoku Bridge

Shōgun's Castle

FUKAGAWA

Nihon Bridge

Nihon Road

Tiger Gate

AZABU

Sumida River

SHIBA

SHIBA

TŌKAIDŌ ROAD

SENGAKUJI 卍

(To Shinagawa and Kyōto)

HAR
Ako

SHIKOKU
TOSA

Nagasaki

KYUSHU

Cape of Muroto

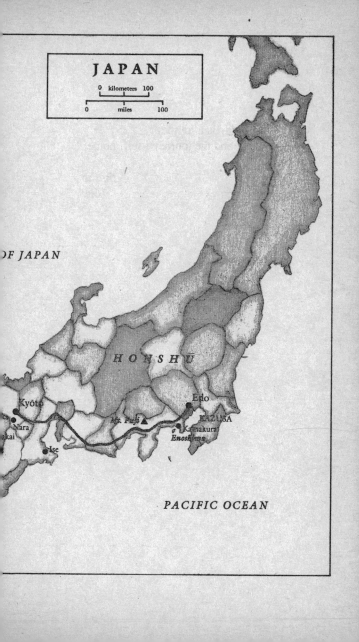

Each day is a journey
and the journey itself, home.

Bashō
1689

THE
TŌKAIDŌ
ROAD

*Genroku 15, the Year of the Horse
(1702)*

CHAPTER 1
BEWARE THE STOPPING MIND

Next to Cat's room in the House of the Perfumed Lotus a game of Naked Islanders was in riotous progress. Five of Old Jug Face's third-rank courtesans were dancing to the thin, rhythmic whap of a hand drum and the staccato notes of a *samisen*'s catgut strings. When the music stopped the women froze. Anyone who moved had to take something off.

As the jars of rice wine emptied and were refilled by silent attendants, the dancers found it more difficult to stay motionless during the drum's silences. Around the women's feet, their silk robes and underrobes and their long brocade sashes swirled in a shimmering lake of color. Their stiff, white, split-toed cotton socks floated like ducks on top.

The game had reached the point where the guests joined in. Apparently one of the men was dancing with an undergarment draped over his head. Cat could hear its owner's giggles and playful slaps as she tried to retrieve it.

As Cat knelt, watching her own guest die, she heard the merrymaking as she would have heard a distant waterfall or a windstorm. She was still wearing her thinly quilted lavender silk robe and a heavy brocade sash. Over it she wore a full, plum-colored satin coat embroidered with peacocks and crimson maple leaves. It kept her warm in the chill of the eleventh month. Its heavy, trailing sleeves were folded neatly across her thighs, as though she were a guest at a tea ceremony.

The soft light of the floor lantern outlined the long slope of Cat's neck rising into the glossy black loops and wings of her hairdo. The collars of her robes were set far back to reveal the most alluring part of a woman's body, the sensuous, vulnerable curve of spine and nape. The rush light glowed on Cat's face, delicate and slender as a melon seed. The gold of its flame was reflected in the dark brown irises of Cat's eyes.

Cat had swallow's eyes, long and curved. Her feathery black eyebrows arched high and symmetrical as a silkworm moth's

3

antennae. She had brows that physiognomists said belonged to someone who made plans and carried them out. Her narrow, high-bridged nose and the full lips of her small mouth cast shadows across her chalky-white cheek.

Cat was as cultured as she was beautiful. She was the secret daughter of a *daimyō*, Lord Asano, and his outside-wife. She had been trained in music and literature and art. She had never thought she would use her skills in a house of assignation in Edo's pleasure district, but then she couldn't have foreseen the tragedy that had brought ruin and disgrace to her mother and father.

A year ago Cat, whose real name was Kinume, Golden Plum, had arrived here on foot. Palanquins were not allowed in Edo's pleasure district, the Yoshiwara. She had hidden herself under a striped travel cloak and large-brimmed hat of woven sedge. Two of her dead father's former box bearers had followed single file with a large wicker chest slung on a pole between them. The chest had held Cat's remaining silk robes and sashes and her favorite books and scrolls, her matched, lacquered cosmetic set, her writing box, and a few precious keepsakes.

Cat herself had signed the contract with the owner of the House of the Carp where she would live. By the time her grief-stricken mother learned what she had done, it was too late to change her decision.

When Cat's high wooden pattens clattered across the slate paving of the House of the Carp's entryway, she had been struck by doubt so sudden and intense, she had almost turned around and left. But Cat's nature wasn't to quit what she had begun. She had hidden her fear and grief and loneliness behind a lovely, impassive mask ever since.

The usual custom was to give oneself a new name when starting out on an important enterprise. A different name was especially vital in Cat's case, to keep her real identity a secret. Her friend Plover had begun calling her Koneko, Little Cat.

Plover used the nickname affectionately, and it caught on. Others began calling her Cat because she was as graceful and aloof and unpredictable as her namesake. But Golden Plum couldn't replace her sorrow the way the nickname Cat replaced her old name and identity. She could only do her duty as the daughter of a lord and a warrior and endure her fate without complaint or self-pity.

She moved through her duties in the assignation house called the Perfumed Lotus with the grace and reserve of her class and breeding. She already had attained the second rank here, but she preferred to act the part of *tayū*, grand courtesan—to dazzle her guests with her wit, to stand on ceremony, to talk little, and to be hard to please.

She'd often been known to refuse to grant her favors, a luxury only the *tayū* enjoyed. And always, Cat's guests had to spend a long time charming her before she would consent to undo her sash. So it had been this evening. Now it seemed she would be spared the necessity of politely spurning this guest.

With her legs demurely under her and the toes of one white-clad foot overlapping those of the other, Cat sat back on her ankles. The cool, tight weave of the thick, rigid *tatami* mats covering the wooden floor gave slightly under the pressure of her toes and knees. Cat leaned forward almost imperceptibly to study the guest.

At first she had thought, with relief, that he had passed out from drinking too much of Old Jug Face's watered *sake*. That would have been fortuitous. He was one of those guests in whom unconsciousness was the most desirable trait.

Cat had planned to leave him there, sprawled on the thick mattresses piled three deep on the *tatami*. But that was when she had assumed he would awaken the next morning with a headache, nausea writhing like a tangle of squid in his stomach and a rueful realization that he would have to pay a great deal for the privilege of feeling so bad.

The heavy robe of wadded yellow cotton bearing the crest of the House of the Perfumed Lotus was bunched up under him, revealing bowed, hairy legs that sprawled carelessly. Saliva oozed in a froth from his half-opened lips and dangled in a thin rope from his chin. His wiry black topknot was askew. His eyes were open.

Without rising from her knees, Cat moved closer. She laid two pale, slender, impeccably manicured fingers on his neck. Nothing. Not a flutter of a heartbeat. The customer had left his homely body, never to return. The next occupants would be small, white, and legless. Already a hardy fly, an émigré from the privy, was circling solicitously.

Cat felt panic rising from the seat of her soul, behind her navel. She drew several deep breaths. She needed to be calm. She needed to think.

Soon the watchman would strike midnight, the hour of the Rat, on his wooden clappers. At midnight Centipede would close the small door in the Great Gate. He would lock the corpse into the pleasure district and into Cat's company until cock's crow.

Cat was sure the guest had been murdered. The murder weapon, or what was left of it, lay on the lacquered tray that also served as a table. The blowfish had been cleaned carelessly for a deadly purpose.

Only a single slice of *fugu*, blowfish, remained. It was paper thin and transparent enough for Cat to see the deep blue waves painted on the porcelain platter under it. Unless cleaned correctly, a speck of the poison in the fish's ovaries and liver could kill a person.

As the numbness spread through his body, the guest had been able to think clearly but unable to talk. He probably had known he was dying when he'd lost control of his arms and legs and then his lungs and sphincter.

Kira, Cat thought. *He won't be content until he's killed me.*

Tomorrow was the fourteenth, the monthly anniversary of her father's suicide. Lord Kira Kozuke-no-suke Yoshinaka had been responsible for that suicide. Maybe Kira feared Cat would do something rash on the fourteenth. Maybe he thought she was plotting revenge. Maybe he merely had decided to ensure that Cat bore no children to threaten him in the future.

With a chopstick Cat poked the last slice of *fugu*. Not often did death arrive in such a lovely package. The filmy slices of pale flesh had been artistically arranged in the form of a flying crane. It was the sort of ironic gesture Lord Kira would make. The crane was a symbol of longevity. But *fugu* was also a powerful aphrodisiac, which was why the customer had eaten with such gusto. A pinch of death was spice for fornication as well as for food.

Except for the inconvenience his corpse caused, Cat wasn't sorry the guest was dead. He had recently come into an inheritance and had been scattering it like rice chaff about the Yoshiwara. He was a clerk in the government finance office, a bannerman with ambitions.

He had bad breath, a face like a pickle jar, and his poetry was trite and contrived. Cat regarded him as she would a slug that had invaded her rooms and left a trail of slime behind it. His remains would cause a great deal of trouble to Old Jug Face, the auntie of the Perfumed Lotus, but he was still inconsequential. The important problem was that Lord Kira was trying to kill Cat.

As Cat knelt on the wheat-colored *tatami* in the pool of pale golden light thrown by the night lantern, she withdrew into herself.

> We lock infinity into a square foot of silk;
> Pour a deluge from the inch-space of the heart.

The ancient poem calmed her. Behind her closed eyelids Cat could see the ink-laden brush drawing it out in bold, black strokes. For a moment she dwelt in the inch-space of her heart, the core of her being. She didn't stay there long because in his *Water Book* Miyamoto Musashi warned to beware the stopping-mind. Cat knew she had to act.

Slender and graceful as an iris, she rose in a murmur of silk and glided across the elegant room, her purple satin overrobe billowing behind her. She slid aside a panel of the paper wall and slipped into the small dressing room. It was as homey and cluttered as the entertaining room was bare.

Cat's toiletries lay scattered about the freestanding black-lacquered shelves. The mirrors, the combs, the jars and boxes and brush handles, matched the shelves. All bore, in mother-of-pearl, the Asano family crest of crossed feathers. In a corner, a big orange cat slept on a second set of shelves that held books and the long-necked *samisen* Cat had been learning to play.

Cat moved to the screen standing in the opposite corner. The steep black ravines and gray clouds, the prickly pine trees and silver swirls of mist painted on the screen looked inviting. Cat wished she could walk into the landscape and disappear among the pines.

"Butterfly." Cat knelt beside the pallet behind the screen. She gently shook the child sleeping under a pair of thin quilts.

"Earthquake?" The girl sat bolt upright, then fell back with a thud against the pillow stand when she realized the roof tiles weren't chattering in the throes of a tremor.

"Get up."

"What hour is it, mistress?" Butterfly mumbled.

Cat glanced at the slow-burning incense joss on the book-shelf. It was perfuming time as well as marking it. "Almost midway through the hour of the Boar. Centipede will lock the Great Gate soon. We have to hurry."

"Where are we going?" Butterfly was confused. The hour was too late to promenade or to run an errand. And she had not gone outside the walls of the Yoshiwara pleasure district since her distraught and impoverished mother had sold her to a procurer two years before, when the girl was seven years old. As far as Butterfly knew, her mistress, Cat, had left it only a few times. Almost none of the white-necked ones left the Yoshiwara unless they were dead or dying. Was her mistress dying?

"I need you to comb out my hair," Cat whispered over her shoulder as she brought the rough earthenware jug of water from beside the shelves.

Butterfly hastily wrapped an apron around her wadded cotton sleeping robe, tied back her sleeves, and pondered this latest surprise. Cat never drew her own water. Old Jug Face employed a small army of maids and servants and apprentices to do that sort of work.

Cat obviously wasn't going to explain anything, and the child dared not ask more questions. She knelt behind Cat, who sat in front of the big round mirror on its lacquered stand. While Butterfly untied the hidden paper ribbons that held the tiers of coils and falls of Cat's hairdo in place, Cat scrubbed the white makeup from her face.

"How shall I fix it, mistress?" Butterfly asked softly. The soft, glossy mass of hair lay across her palm, and she continued combing it almost reverently.

"Simply tie it."

Butterfly wound a flat, red paper ribbon around the hair, catching it just above Cat's waist in a style no longer in fashion. It made her appear archaic, like a lady of the royal court.

When Cat finished washing the layer of powder off her face, neck, arms, and hands, she dipped a brush into the jar of black paint and thickened her arched eyebrows. With her heavy eyebrows and the few freckles scattered across her nose, Cat looked like a demon, a very beautiful demon.

The festivities next door had grown more boisterous. They were having so much fun, in fact, that the party on the other side of them slid back a section of the paper-paneled wall between the rooms and joined them. A guest had pulled the bumpy skin of a sea slug over his erect *ano mono*, "that thing." One of the women had drawn a face on it with her teeth-blackening paint. Now it was preceding its owner, leading them all in a game of Follow the Leader. The drum beat steadily, and the paper walls vibrated as they danced in a long, tipsy, naked line around the enlarged room.

"Help me drag him out of here." Cat pulled the big, soiled

quilt around the customer as efficiently as if she were changing dirty linen.

The quilt was shaped like a large *kimono*, and Cat brought the bottom edge up between his spraddled legs and put it together with the sleeves. It formed a bulky sling with the customer's skinny shins sticking out in opposite directions. With his staring eyes and his open mouth, he seemed about to protest the indignity.

"I might wake him." Butterfly inadvertently touched his hand. It was as rigid as a bamboo back scratcher. She squealed.

"Only the Beloved Amida, Buddha Himself, can wake him now." Cat rapped Butterfly lightly on the crown of her head with a folded fan to recall her from death's distractions. "He certainly doesn't care what you do. And I didn't kill him. The *fugu* wasn't cleaned properly."

Butterfly looked in horror at the flimsy tissue of blowfish whose edges were curling up slightly as it dried. A dead fly lay on it.

When Cat and Butterfly dragged the body off the pile of mattresses, it landed with a thud and knocked over a tall iron candle holder. Trapped gas escaped in a noisome explosion from the guest's bowels. Butterfly giggled nervously into the palms of her hands. Cat looked around in alarm.

She needn't have worried. Against the ranks of sliding paper wall panels receding into the brothel's dim interior, the writhing shadows and rustlings of professional courtship went on unabated. The laughter and drumming continued. Distant music cascaded from a *samisen*.

"See if anyone is in the storeroom." Cat was much stronger than her slender body looked. She dragged the bundle across the slick *tatami* to the opening through which Butterfly had just disappeared. She peered into the narrow servants' corridor. For once, she was glad Old Jug Face had spitefully assigned her these rooms at the rear of the house.

Butterfly scurried back, her feet snapping the hem of her robe. "It's empty."

"Now find a candle on the shelf next to the books. Light it and bring it."

"Will you hide him in there?" Butterfly nodded toward the dark doorway of the storeroom.

"I'm going to pickle him like an eggplant."

CHAPTER 2
A STATE OF CONFUSION

Cat slid the quilt sling and its stiff cargo along the cherry planks of the hallway. The wood was smooth, with a satiny patina buffed by forty years of daily rubbing with damp cloths. A single candle on an iron stand shed a dim light. The body bumped over the threshhold and onto the raised wooden walkway across the dirt floor of the storeroom. Cat let her breath out slowly and waited for her eyes to adjust to the gloom.

The storeroom was a wild disorder of goods and tools stacked as high as the dusty rafters. Five hulking cedar barrels bound with hoops of twisted bamboo splints were stacked in a far corner. Old Jug Face transferred *sake* from the distilleries' smaller casks into them so she could water it. The barrels were almost as tall as Cat was. This wouldn't be easy.

Cat knew she would have to put the body into the top rear barrel, which should be about half-full. The servants regularly siphoned off the *sake* from that one, figuring Old Jug Face wouldn't notice. Cat was sure the mistress of the Perfumed Lotus charged the customers extra to cover the loss. That was easier than trying to stop the larceny.

When Butterfly returned, Cat set the candle holder on a small shelf. Then she boosted the child onto the first row of barrels. "I'll push while you pull."

Cat and Butterfly hauled the body up the side until the customer's waist was balanced on the rim. Cat grasped each foot and shoved the corpse the rest of the way. She put the wooden pry bar on top of the casks, then climbed up a stack of bales of rice and onto them herself.

She pried open the rear lid and slid it off. She and Butterfly wrestled the body into position and eased the customer headfirst into his last bath. Cat had to lean on his feet to crumple him enough to fit.

The *sake* covered the guest's soles. He wouldn't begin to smell until the servants drained off enough wine to uncover him. Cat set the lid back on. She climbed down, scooped up a handful of fine dust from the dirt floor, and sifted it onto the cask lids to cover the evidence of activity. With a small broom Butterfly swept away their tracks in the dust behind them as they and the quilt retreated to Cat's dressing room.

The guest's clothes hung on a wooden rack in the small reception room that led into the sleeping chamber. Cat regarded them with distaste. The *shōgun*, Tokugawa Tsunayoshi, banned his officials from frequenting the pleasure districts. The ban was ignored, of course, but those affected by it generally wore disguises. Cat's guest had favored the clothing of a common laborer.

Cat left the long strip of cloth the guest wore as underwear in his travel box sitting behind a low screen in her dressing room. She found another length of cotton cloth in her own big cedar chest. She stripped off her robes, folded them neatly, and put them in the chest.

She stood perfectly still while Butterfly wound the cloth around her hips, pulled the end into the cleft of her buttocks, passed it between her legs, and tucked it into the front of the belt. When she finished, Cat was wearing the loincloth sported by men of the laboring class.

Next Cat held one end of another long piece of cloth against her abdomen while Butterfly walked around her, pulling it taut as she wrapped it around Cat's abdomen and chest.

"Tighter," Cat whispered.

The cloth was called a *haramaki*, and commoners wore it around their stomachs for warmth and to protect their navels, the seat of their emotions, from the mischief of the Thunder god. Her uptilted breasts were small, but they were taut, and the nipples were large and firm. The *haramaki*, wrapped higher than usual, would flatten and hide them.

Cat pulled on the blue drawers with their tight legs and baggy seat and tied them at the waist. Then she slipped into the light undershirt. Butterfly held up the dark blue wadded jacket with narrow sleeves. The number ten had been embroidered in white floss inside, indicating the clothes had been rented for this occasion. Cat flinched when the rough hemp cloth settled on her shoulders.

It reached to her knees and had "Nakagawa Freight Company" and "Felicitous Service for Fifty Years" emblazoned in bold white characters down the back. Cat overlapped the front edges and held them while Butterfly wrapped the wide, stiff sash three times around her and tied it in back. The child arranged the sash high on Cat's hips and rakishly low in front.

Cat pulled the jacket up to shorten the hem hanging around her knees and expand it above the sash. It made her look bigger and provided hiding places for the things she would need on the road.

Finally Cat knelt in front of her mirror again. She held her hair out taut, sucked in her breath, and, with her shears, cut it off just below her shoulders. Butterfly moaned. A woman's hair was her pride.

The three-foot-long hank of hair was still tied with the paper ribbon. She coiled it and folded it into a sheet of pliable rice paper. She tied the packet inside a blue silk scarf decorated with the Asano crest of crossed feathers stenciled in white. She put it into the front of the jacket, under her sash. No sense leaving behind any clues as to how she looked when she escaped.

She pulled her hair together at the crown of her head and tied it into a man's topknot. She draped the guest's thin blue cotton towel over her head and knotted it just under her lower lip. The customer had worn it that way for the same reason Cat did, to hide his face.

Butterfly watched with dread and fascination. Her mistress was a shape-shifter. She was one of the enchanted cats who disguised themselves as beautiful women to cause trouble for men. Cat certainly had caused trouble for the man who right then was sole deep in more *sake* than he'd ever dreamed of having.

With her shears Cat cut off her long fingernails and wrapped them carefully in one of her embossed paper handkerchiefs. "Give them to Plover to sell for you." She handed them to Butterfly.

Butterfly knew how valuable they were. A courtesan would cut off a fingernail to give to a patron as a pledge of faithful and exclusive love. However, she often made the same pledge to several men. Since more than one short fingernail on her hand would expose the trickery, she bought extras.

Cat hid the scissors inside her coat, under the sash. They might prove useful in the days ahead. She had decided to take revenge.

"Mistress . . ." Butterfly sucked her knuckles nervously while Cat rifled the customer's small travel box.

"Look down at your feet, child. Are they covered with rice

paddy mud? A courtesan's little sister doesn't suck her fingers.''
Cat felt a sharp pang of remorse. She might be endangering the
child. ''The less you know about this the better, little Butterfly.''

''But, mistress . . .''

''Bring my travel cloak.''

Cat didn't know what to pack for a trip. Servants had always
packed for her. In fact, servants had done just about everything
for her.

She rolled a thin cotton towel and draped it around her neck
as commoners did. Inside her jacket she stowed her flat wallet
of paper handkerchiefs and the bag containing her long-stemmed
pipe with its tiny brass bowl. With a straw cord she hung from
her sash a bamboo container that held wine but could be used
to carry water. She considered taking along the collapsible pillow stand but decided it was too bulky.

She found the guest's wallet, opened the drawstring, and
peered at the money inside. The three rolls of a hundred coppers
each had been strung onto straw cords and the ends knotted to
hold the coins tight against each other. A smaller roll was made
up of silver coins.

Cat wasn't as naive as the noblewoman who thought a roll of
coins was a huge caterpillar. Cat had seen money, but she had
rarely held it. She folded back the opening of the wallet and
touched the hard metal. She stroked the rough, round edges and
wondered what these would buy. Then she pulled the draw-
strings shut and tucked the sack inside her jacket, too. Old Jug
Face would have separated the guest from his money in the
morning anyway.

Cat was wondering what else to take when she heard Old Jug
Face shriek. She was so startled that she almost slowed down.
Her father would have said she almost stopped the sword in its
deadly arc. That was always a mistake, usually a fatal one.

''Lout! Radish!'' The auntie wasn't shrieking at Cat, though.
A customer must have urinated against the paper panels enclos-
ing her office near the entrance of the Perfumed Lotus. Now
and then a drunken guest, too lazy to walk to the privy, missed
the edge of the veranda and hit the paper panes.

''What about the auntie, mistress?''

Cat sighed. When she made her decision to sell herself into
the Yoshiwara, she went to the House of the Carp, where her
nurse's niece, Plover, lived. Plover had told Cat about the Carp's
kind mistress and friendly atmosphere. But Cat had been ignorant of the customs of the pleasure district. She hadn't realized

that the house where she and Plover lived was not the one where they would work. They met their guests in the Perfumed Lotus, and Old Jug Face ruled the Perfumed Lotus.

"I'll sneak past her," Cat said. But she and Butterfly both knew that wasn't likely. Old Jug Face employed brawny peasants and out-of-work *samurai* as shopmen, inside men, bed men, overseers, bath men, and downstairs men, not to mention the people Lord Kira had sneaked in as spies. They all took turns as nightwatchmen.

Confusion. Cat reviewed the advice in Musashi's *Fire Book*. "Induce a state of confusion in the opponent."

She scooped up the orange cat still sleeping on her bookshelf, his stomach and legs hanging over the edge. She had named the scarred old warrior Monk for good reason. He maintained a meditative tranquillity in the midst of all this late-night activity and shape-changing.

"Please deliver Monk to Little Dragon's room." She handed the cat to Butterfly. "Then go to Mistress Plover's room and stay with her. Tell her I asked that she say you were with her all night." Cat glanced at the joss stick's wooden holder. The sandalwood had burned almost to the notch marking midnight, the watch of the Rat. "Tell Mistress Plover I'll miss her."

Butterfly slung the inert Monk over the crook of one arm. With her free hand, she poked under her mattress until she found a small brocade sack closed with a drawstring. When she handed it to Cat the copper coins inside clinked cheekily for such a piddling sum. They were her secret fund, the tips customers had given her for running errands.

"No, little Butterfly," said Cat. "Keep your tea money. One day, if a rich, handsome man doesn't marry you first, you'll save enough to buy your freedom."

"Mistress, forgive my rudeness, but this is a good-bye present." Butterfly gathered the courage to contradict Cat. "You'll need money to eat and sleep out there."

Butterfly had almost forgotten what "out there" was like, but she had overheard the guests' stories. Out there people had to struggle for their daily rice and a roof. Bandits and demons and tax collectors lurked out there.

Tears brimmed in Butterfly's eyes. Lady Cat had been a good mistress. She sent warmed *sake* out to her box bearers on cold nights. She hushed up the maids' indiscretions. And if, during a long night of entertaining, Butterfly fell asleep on the job, she didn't scold.

Lady Cat was haughty, that was true. But Butterfly knew hauteur was to be expected in a woman of a *samurai* family. And she sensed that Cat's eyes mocked the world so no one would pity her. Only Plover and Butterfly had seen, in Cat's rare, unguarded moments, the grief in her dark eyes.

Butterfly also knew that Cat was old. She would turn nineteen at the celebration of the New Year. Nineteen was a most unlucky age. The characters for nineteen also meant "repeated sorrows." Cat had had more than her share of sorrow.

"The Lord Buddha will watch over me." Cat knelt so she could look into Butterfly's face. She put her best jade comb into the sack with Butterfly's tea money. "Please accept this trifle in thanks for all you've done. As one more favor I ask that you deliver Monk." Cat smiled conspiratorially.

Butterfly slid the wall panel open just enough to slip through. Cat picked up the guest's rented hat, shaped like a wide, flat, shallow bowl. She slipped the inner woven cap onto her head and tied the paper cords under her chin. The name of the rental shop was painted on the brim. The hat too was designed to hide a face.

Cat went to the open wall panel and waited. She didn't look over her shoulder at the rooms where she had earned her living for the past year. Most of her books and her ornate chests full of the sumptuous robes of her new profession were in the room she shared with Plover at the House of the Carp.

Cat didn't have to wait long. Butterfly knew the brothel's maze of narrow back hallways well. She silently slid aside the thin wooden panel of Little Dragon's rear wall. Little Dragon was entertaining her guest with the erotic tricks her small dog, Chin-Chin, could perform. From the darkness outside the room, Butterfly slung Monk back in both hands and heaved him inside as high and as hard as she could. When Monk landed he was irritated.

Chin-Chin's plumed tail stiffened over his back like a battle banner. Yapping hysterically, he scrambled up the length of his mistress's prone, naked torso, leaving claw tracks on her stomach and chest. Getting a purchase on the foothills of Little Dragon's hairdo, Chin-Chin launched himself at Monk, who was ricocheting off the folding screens and shredding the paper walls. Monk sounded as if he were being skinned and gutted to make a *samisen*. Against Chin-Chin, Monk had the edge in weight, speed, reach, and volume.

Little Dragon's naked customer fell seat first into the glowing coals of the firebox sunk into a well in the floor. His howls of pain, Little Dragon's screams, and the crash of mirror stands and *sake* jars and folding screens caught Old Jug Face's attention. Cat could trace the auntie's progress by the rise and fall of her shouts as she ignored corridors and charged straight through adjacent entertaining rooms to save time.

In his hurry to get to the excitement, a drunken three-hundred-pound wrestler plunged through a wall into the game of Follow the Leader. Floors and walls shuddered under the impact. Someone began screaming, ''Earthquake!'' From all over the house footsteps and shouts converged on Little Dragon's rooms. Cat could hear Monk's battle cries above the din.

Soak in, Monk. Close with your enemy and strike quickly. Cat thought about the *Fire Book* again. Monk was like any good warrior. He was meditative in peace and formidable in war. He was capable of taking on the entire assembly if necessary.

Cat smiled grimly to herself. There was no turning back now. The boat had been boarded, as the old saying went.

CHAPTER 3

AIM FOR HIS WEAK POINT

Cat sat on the large flat rock that served as a stoop at the side entrance and selected a pair of straw sandals left there by the guests' servants and box bearers. The rough straw weave began to abrade her tender feet the moment she put them on. From inside she heard Chin-Chin's howl deteriorate into tormented yipping. Monk had soaked in. He had closed with his enemy.

As Cat stood in the narrow passageway between the two-story Perfumed Lotus and the House of the Spring Fan next door, her metaphorical sword hesitated briefly in its course. Cat suddenly understood Old Jug Face's ancient parrot.

The parrot was bald on top, but for one tattered feather. He looked as if his mistress regularly dusted hard-to-reach corners with him. He brooded malevolently in his cage, his stubby gray head lowered and swinging in tiny arcs, like a snake preparing to strike. He lived only to eat rice, swill *sake*, and tenderly

nibble Old Jug Face's pendulous earlobes. He bloodied any finger that strayed within range. He was a moth-eaten tyrant until
his mistress let him out of his cage. Then he cowered until she
put him back.

Cat put a hand on the rough, weathered timbers of her own
cage. Had she escaped the dragon's mouth, or was she walking
into it?

No matter. She hadn't escaped anything yet. She still had to
pass under Centipede's ravaged nose.

The back alleys of the pleasure district were quite different
from the lovely gardens and serene front rooms where guests
were received. The narrow passage was crowded with buckets
and tools, broken barrows and strings of braided barrel hoops.
Cat scuffed the reeking stew of alley mud onto her smooth, pale
feet. She pulled the hat brim lower over her eyes and drew her
slender, manicured hands into her sleeves. Abandoning the hip-
swaying gait of the courtesan, she walked with the deliberate
care of someone drunk trying to pass for someone sober.

She moved smoothly into the unsteady stream of men who
hadn't the money to stay until dawn with their "one-night
wives." Groups of them laughed and sang and composed poetry
to the white-necked ones and to rented passion. Cat walked
among them as though in a dream. As though she were looking
down on herself and on the tipsy throng around her.

Both sides of the main thoroughfare were lined with round
paper lanterns hanging from the first-story eaves. As the Yoshiwara emptied, sleepy servants lowered the lights on the ends of
long poles. When snuffed, the wicks gave off a strong odor of
whale oil that settled over the street. Almost directly overhead,
the moon, which was almost full, looked like a lantern they
couldn't quite reach.

Most of the beggars and musicians and peddlers had moved
outside the gate to importune the men as they exited. Servants
were sliding the heavy wooden shutters across the open fronts
of the tea shops and assignation houses. Soon they would present
a uniformly blank face to the customers who had spent their
silver and were of no further use. The "ground-tea harlots" no
longer sat behind the wooden grills in front of the lower-class
brothels. They had gone to work or to bed, which amounted to
the same thing.

The gay district called the Yoshiwara covered eighteen boggy
acres enclosed by a high wall. Besides the massive two-story
houses where the courtesans lived or met their guests, there were

hundreds of tea shops called "introduction houses" where arrangements were made for evening trysts. In the tea houses near the Perfumed Lotus, a list of Cat's accomplishments was included on the menu of second-rank courtesans.

Cat was one of those known as "midway starters." Because of her upper-class upbringing she had become a courtesan without having gone through the usual apprenticeship. If Cat had stayed in the Yoshiwara, she surely would have been elevated to *tayū*, courtesan of the first rank.

In the pleasure districts *tayū* were royalty of sorts. They selected their patrons from among the richest and most refined men. Their beauty, grace, and accomplishments were admired throughout the country, and they set not only fashion, but style. There were only four *tayū* in the Yoshiwara.

If Cat had stayed, her earnings would have assured a comfortable life for her mother. Providing for her mother was why Cat had sold herself in the first place. She had done it even though she knew that would make it easier for Lord Kira to spy on her. Even though her beauty and talents were filling Old Jug Face's brass-bound money chests with the lozenge-shaped gold coins. When Lord Kira and Old Jug Face discovered Cat was missing, the search for her would be thorough and extensive.

Thousands of courtesans, waitresses, apprentices, cooks, scullery help, and maids lived here. The Yoshiwara was a city of women, constant and pliant, perplexing and accommodating. Men flowed in and out like the tides. Now, as the hour approached midnight, the tide was ebbing. The flow was constricted at one narrow outlet, the small door in the Great Gate, guarded by Mukade no Gonzo, the man everyone called Centipede, but not in his hearing.

As Cat drew closer she saw the old man standing, small and wiry and intense as a hummingbird, at the gate. Near by, his assistants took the wooden tickets men handed them in exchange for their weapons. The long swords and the occasional bows, halberds, and spears were stored by type on wall racks in the small gate house. It wouldn't do to have a *samurai*, deep in his cups, decide to dice a paying customer. Guests were required to check their weapons at the entrances to the various houses. Some men, however, preferred to leave their arms with Centipede.

Centipede was seventy. Old scars cleaved the dark, wrinkled leather of his nose and parted the bush of his left eyebrow. Each year, as his hair receded, he had to shave less of his head to maintain his warrior's topknot. But he was still lean and tough and resilient as the steel of his two swords, heated, folded, and hammered repeatedly in the forge of adversity. His eyesight and memory were as keen as his blades.

The small door in the fifteen-foot-high gate was brightly lit with lanterns. Centipede studied every person who passed through it. He would remember the unremarkable customer in the shabby blue Nakagawa Freight coat even though the press at the door grew more frenetic as midnight approached.

For a man without money to be locked into the Yoshiwara was humiliating at best and often disastrous. He would have to seek shelter in a house that would extend him credit. Knowing a man was at their mercy often resulted in exorbitant expenses for one night's lodging. Toughs from some of the lower-class establishments had been known to move into a defaulter's home and wreak havoc on his domestic life until the debt was paid.

As Cat neared the periphery of Centipede's buzzard stare, she wandered out of the traffic and into the shadow of a stack of fire buckets at the head of an alley. She sneaked the bamboo cylinder from her coat and decanted it. She spread her feet, cocked her hips, and tilted the cylinder under her coat hem. While the stream of wine splashed into the dust, she stared contemplatively out over the throng. She wore the usual look of a man astonished yet again that pissing was such a thoroughly soul-satisfying act.

As she shook the last drops from the cylinder, Cat finished her survey of the crowd. Her means of escape was somewhere among the guests and servants, the messengers, jugglers, procurers, shills, cutpurses, and food vendors with their portable shops balanced on bamboo poles across their shoulders. Cat's means appeared as though on cue.

He was a person of great importance, which was why he was dressed as a peasant. Forbidding bureaucrats to visit the Yoshiwara was like forbidding a tidal wave to hit the shore. Thousands of men were required to run a government based on intrigue and pervasive suspicion. They were the Yoshiwara's most valuable customers.

This one was a *metsuke*, an inspector and an official gatherer of intelligence for the *shōgun*'s junior council of elders. He was a ponderous blotch of a man who had drunk too much *sake* to make the journey to the Great Gate unaided. Two huge, shaven-headed servants of the House of the Winged Mountain sup-

ported him between them. The weaving course the servants
steered indicated they had been drinking, too.

The *metsuke* wore a big bamboo hat and straw sandals. Even
though the night sky was cloudless, he wore a raincape made of
thick layers of rice straw tied around his neck and waist. It
thatched him from his trio of overlapping chins to his bulbous
calves. He looked like a straw stack with feet. Cat recognized
him.

Thank you, Kannon-sama, she thought. The thousand-armed
goddess of mercy had sent the perfect man for Cat's needs.

During the mornings and afternoons the Yoshiwara was empty
of guests. A languorous tranquillity settled over it then, the more
precious because it was transitory. The young apprentices swept
up, and servants cleared away the night's debris or watered down
the dust in the streets. Trusted go-betweens delivered ''next-
morning-letters.'' Maids gossiped at the district's new well.

In the mornings men emptied the contents of the privies into
long buckets and carried away the precious cargo to fertilize the
outlying fields. Paperers came with their rolls of heavy rice paper, glue, and laths to repair panels mangled in the night's revelry. Farmers carried on their backs towering wooden frames
piled with lotus roots and cabbages and huge white radishes.
On the corner of Yedo-cho and Ni-cho-me streets, greengrocers
and fishmongers hawked their wares.

The courtesans gathered then for dance or calligraphy or *samisen* lessons in the large, uncluttered *tatami* rooms behind the
closed shutters. They discussed the latest permutations of the
hairdo fashions while the blind shampooers plied their trade.
They talked endlessly of love and the possibility of some rich
patron freeing them from the Yoshiwara. They bathed together
in cedar bathtubs big enough to soap down a horse. They joked
about the guests.

Their laughter found its way through the cracks in the wooden
shutters and rippled throughout the Yoshiwara. When this one's
name was mentioned, the jokes turned bitter.

This one's juices flowed only when he inflicted pain. But Cat
hated the man for more than his casual cruelty. He was a distant
cousin of Lord Kira.

Aim for his weak point, Musashi advised. *And with your body
rather floatingly, join in with his movement as he draws near.*

As he approached her, Cat put her small pipe in her mouth
as though she were going to take a few puffs. She separated one
of her paper handkerchiefs from the folded stack of them in her

wallet and twisted it. She lifted the oiled paper shade of a square
street lantern and lit the end of the twisted napkin. She shielded
the guttering flame with her sleeve as she swiveled smoothly.
She bent and, hidden by the bulk of the servants' backs, held it
to the bottom of the straw-thatch raincoat as the *metsuke* passed.

The flame spread noisily outward and upward, toward the
peak of the official's rented, conical straw hat. The layers of
straw in the raincape curled and blackened behind the fire, exposing hairy calves and the folds of an expensive silk brocade
kimono tucked up into the man's sash.

The *metsuke* sniffed in alarm. A strong smell of smoke always
made people nervous. Fiery holocausts swept the city so often,
they were called the Flowers of Edo.

The servants flailed at the blaze with their cloaks but only
succeeded in fanning it. The *metsuke* clawed at the cape's ties,
knotted at his neck and waist, while the flames reached up
around him, embracing him. He began to scream. Cat could
smell burning hair and burning flesh at about the same time.

The watcher in the fire platform atop the tea house nearest
the gate began tolling the big bronze bell. Men and women, in
dishabille and carrying whatever they could grab, spilled into
the streets. The *metsuke* decided that if he couldn't get the cape
off, he would run away from it. As he raced, shrieking, back
into the Yoshiwara, people scattered in front of him. The wind
of his passing only made the blaze hotter. Sparks billowed and
pranced upward.

"*Shire mono!* Idiots!" Centipede elbowed through the crowd,
trying to clear a path for the fire brigade.

When Cat ducked through the low door, no one followed her.
The government had devised a variety of inventive public executions, but seeing a man immolated alive was a rare form of
entertainment. No one wanted to miss it. Cat was almost pushed
back by those outside rushing in to see the spectacle.

Cat threaded her way through the deserted palanquins parked
outside the gate. She passed the small shrine to Inari-sama, the
Rice God, and the Colt-Tethering-Pine-Tree near it. She passed
the tiny kiosks that sold guidebooks to the pleasure districts.
And she hurried by the stands that rented clothing and hats. In
the morning they would no doubt send a man to try to collect
the price of the clothes and hat from the dead guest.

Cat walked down Dressing Hill, where men adjusted their
clothing before going home to their wives. At the Gazing-Back-
Willow she turned to look at the high wall. Behind it, the spy

was transmuting into greasy smoke, dark and ominous against the pale moon. Cat could hear people shouting, but the spy's screams were weakening. She waited until they stilled. The bronze fire bell stopped ringing, but its booming voice resonated in Cat's ears.

The watchman's wooden clappers struck the hour of the Rat. The rectangle of light in the Great Gate disgorged a gout of men before it narrowed, then darkened. The Yoshiwara was closed for the night.

One man pulled away from the group outside the gate as though the others had stopped to chat. Centipede's courier had tucked the rear of his *kimono* up into his sash at the small of his back. He held a tall spear vertically in one hand. It was his badge of office.

As the courier passed the Gazing-Back-Willow at a dead run, Cat could see the taut muscles in his powerful legs. The thick fringe of horsehair ringing the top of his long spear quivered and jounced. He disappeared down the raised causeway that threaded through the marsh surrounding the Yoshiwara.

It has started, Cat thought.

Through the coarse skirt of her jacket coat, Cat hitched up the unfamiliar waistband of her loincloth. She pushed the wide sash lower on her hips.

In her year as a courtesan Cat had learned to converse with men. She knew their slang and their rhythm of speech. She was used to taking boys' parts in impromptu dances and dramas for the entertainment of more favored guests or for the amusement of the other women.

Without much effort she shed almost nineteen years of training as a paradigm of feminine grace and subtlety. She trotted into the darkness with the peculiar, flat-footed, light-footed, splay-footed gait of a peasant used to scurrying at his superiors' beck.

"Shire mono!" she grunted. "Idiots!"

CHAPTER 4
THE BURGLAR IN THE HOUSE

Cat dodged through the late-night foot traffic. The roadway was crowded with entertainers and with *samurai*, beggars, hawkers, holy men, and sightseers. This was the teeming neighborhood between the pleasure district and the city of Edo itself. It and the Yoshiwara made up what had come to be called *Ukiyo*, the Floating World. Life here was of the moment, lovely and perishable as cherry blossoms.

Commoners came on foot, and the aristocracy arrived in the privacy of closed palanquins. Merchants and mountebanks had settled here to cater to them. There was no demand, however trivial, not met by some entrepreneur.

Beyond the marsh and rice paddies surrounding the Yoshiwara, the high, packed-dirt road was hemmed in by open-fronted shops of dark wood. The crooked alleys that wandered among the two-story buildings were wide enough for only two people to walk abreast. They were festooned with paper lanterns painted with advertisements.

White cotton banners hung almost to the ground and fluttered in the winter wind. In bold, black characters they announced each shop's specialty. Laundry hung on the bamboo poles that laced together the wide, second-story eaves above the passageways.

At this hour many of the shops were shuttered, but not all of them were. Some still displayed souvenirs and guidebooks to the pleasure district or hand-colored prints of actors and courtesans. Food and *sake* vendors still called out to passersby.

The short curtains strung across the tops of the open fronts forced people to duck to see what was offered. The theory was that if the head could be lured inside, the rest of the customer would follow. The merchants here were determined that no denizen of the Yoshiwara should be left with a single copper in the bottom of his wide sleeve.

The smell of noodle soup and roasted rice dumplings coated

with sweetened soy sauce, the odor of fried fish and fresh garbage, made Cat's head reel. She hadn't eaten since long before the customer had devoured the serving of blowfish, and her stomach ached with hunger.

In her year in the Yoshiwara, Cat often had sat at night on the second-floor balcony of the House of the Carp and looked out at Edo. From that distance the Eastern Capital had seemed a fairyland of colored lights. Currents of music and laughter had drifted on the wind across the dark carpet of marsh grass.

Up close, the enchanted city was a confusion of alleys and slums. The poor houses, set side by side, were so narrow they were called "eel beds." Many neighborhoods were sealed off with barriers that were closed at night because of rice riots in years past. In a hundred years the five Tokugawa *shōgun* had turned a swampy fishing village into their capital city, a metropolis of more than half a million inhabitants. As she walked, Cat considered the task of finding her way around in it.

Cat had been raised in Edo, but she had only seen its streets from between the narrow slats of the blinds covering the windows of a palanquin. If she had been able to locate the house where she grew up, there would be no point to it. It had been confiscated along with Lord Asano's town mansion and second villa in the suburbs. The *shōgun* had given them to someone else.

Cat's mother was living in a shabby house in the drapers' ward, but Cat didn't know how to find her, either. Even if she could locate the house, she would only carry disaster through the gate.

She did know that after Lord Kira's retirement he had moved to his new villa across the Sumida River, but she didn't know where. The city was full of the government's informers, and Cat could hardly go up to strangers and ask for directions. She realized that if she was going to avenge her father's death, she would need help and information from someone.

She went through the possibilities. Many men were besotted with her. The small rosewood casket in her room at the Carp was full of their letters. Whenever the box became too full, Cat had paid a discreet servant to transform the poetry and passion into smoke. But Cat knew she could expect the least help from those who claimed to be most smitten by her.

They certainly wouldn't help her escape from the Perfumed Lotus and their own grasp. Even those who had proposed setting her up as their outside-wife were only offering her another sort

of cage. Besides, they were all too cowardly to risk the wrath of
Kira's third son, the powerful Lord Uesugi.

Cat knew of one man who might help her. She even knew
where to find him. She stepped to the side of the road, pulled a
playbill from inside her coat, and studied it. Somehow she had
to reach the heart of Edo, the Nihon Bridge.

Nihon Bridge was the commercial center of the city. Most
people considered it the center of the country. All distances were
calculated from the middle of its high, crescent span. All high-
ways, including the great Tōkaidō, began there. The theater
district lay nearby.

Cat had visited the theaters three times, but she hadn't crossed
the city to get there. She and the other women of the Carp had
traveled by boat down the Sumida River to Nihon Bridge. Because *kabuki* plays started at dawn, they had had to board at the
hour of the Ram, when most of the world slept.

The excursions had been the only times Cat had felt at peace
in the past year. She and Plover and the others had drunk *sake*
until they were giddy. They had sucked the sweet flesh of grilled
river trout from delicate bones. Accompanied by Plover on the
samisen, they had sung sad ballads, their voices floating out over
the river. On the way home the next evening they had heatedly
discussed the merits of the actors and the details of the plays and
the costumes.

Cat remembered all that as she rolled the playbill and stuck
it into the front of her jacket. If she could find the Sumida, she
could find the Nihon Bridge and the theaters. She could find
someone who might help her.

"A true inhabitant of Edo never keeps a coin overnight in his
wallet." The voice sounded, loud and hoarse, at Cat's elbow,
and she jumped.

Its owner was hidden by the short, divided curtains hanging
from the front opening. The curtains were dyed dark blue with
white caricatures of octopi wearing short coats and towels,
twisted and tied around their heads as sweatbands. A purple-
veined hand snaked out from between them and clutched the
hem of Cat's jacket. Another hand pulled aside the curtain.

Cat looked down at a mass of wrinkles, interrupted by the
broad, concave delta of a nose. From the center of the weathered
landscape gleamed two black eyes, shiny as beetle carapaces.
They glowed with points of colored light, reflections of the paper lanterns.

Like those on either side of it, the shop's dirt floor was below street level. The old woman sat cross-legged on a tattered cushion on a platform that she shared with a small, rectangular iron grill. The grill was covered with eels that had been sliced open, spread out flat, and threaded on skewers.

The coals underneath were so hot that the old woman had pulled her skinny arms out of her ragged sleeves. In spite of the tenth-month chill, her patched wadded cotton robe hung over the sash around her waist, leaving her chest and back bare. If she hadn't been careful when she dressed, she would have caught the empty sacks of her breasts under her sash.

"Handsome, most honorable customer, try our delicacy." She tugged at Cat's jacket tail, which was taut because Cat was pulling away from her. "Our eels are guaranteed to make you fertile, Your Honor." The eel vendor had lost so many teeth, she had forgotten how her own wares tasted. "O-Inu-Kubo-sama, Honorable Dog *Shōgun* himself, eats them."

Cat knew that was a lie. Tokugawa Tsunayoshi was called the dog *shōgun* because he forbade the killing of animals, although seafood seemed to have escaped his notice.

Keeping her grip on Cat's coat, the old woman selected a stick from among those slowly turning to charcoal on the grill. The eel had roasted to a dark mahogany color, and its odor was overwhelming. She held it up tantalizingly. Cat wanted it.

But Cat had never paid cash for anything. When merchants brought their wares to her mother's mansion or to the House of the Carp, she never had to ask the price. Everything was charged to the clandestine account her father had set up for her mother, or to the Carp. In the latter case Cat's debt was taken from her earnings. Even now she couldn't bring herself to discuss something so vulgar as money.

She bowed to the level proper for the owner of the clothes she was wearing. It was a very low level. "I have the empty wallet of a true Edokko. I shall borrow a few coppers from my friend and come right back."

"You wouldn't trick an old woman who shares her wretched hovel with the god of poverty, would you?"

"I assure you, I shall return shortly and bring my hungry friend with me. He's waiting for me at the Sumida River. Can you tell me which way it is?"

The eel seller considered a moment before pointing the eel eastward. She knew very well this particular fish would swim away and not come back, but there were other fish, and bigger.

"You!" She waved the skewered eel at a shaggy, emaciated

black bear and his bearded Ainu handler. The eel had the bear's complete attention.

"Step right up, Your Honors," the old woman cajoled. "Try our delicacy. It'll make you fertile." With a round paper fan she blew the coals under the grill as though she were preparing to temper steel.

"Tell me," she said conversationally. "Which of you hairy barbarians is carrying a purse?" The eel seller broke into a storm of laughter that set her wrinkled breasts to quivering. But since neither the bear nor the Ainu understood her language, the joke was lost on them.

Cat melted back into the crowd with the eel seller's laughter still in her ears. Was the old woman an informer? Would she wave a hand at Cat's retreating back? Would Cat find a pack of Edo's policemen, solid and impassive as stone monuments, blocking her path?

Cat felt as if she carried her father's crime and her own blazoned across her hat, the way religious pilgrims painted the names of their hometowns on theirs. But when no one ordered her to halt, when a slender shaft of steel didn't intrude under the sloping eave of her hat, her heart slowed. She had been perspiring with fear, and it felt cold on her brow in the winter air. She took several deep breaths and headed in the direction the eel vendor had pointed.

The route took her down silent streets fronted by the high walls and massive gates of the mansions of the *daimyō*. Cat felt small and lost and alone walking past them. Dogs barked at the sound of her footsteps echoing off the walls.

The *shōgun*'s decrees strictly defined the size and ornamentation of the gates each lord was allowed. The classifications were based on the number of *koku*, or bales of rice, raised on the *daimyō*s' estates. These gates all belonged to men who, like her father, rated fifty thousand to seventy thousand *koku*. Her own father's mansion, or the one where he ended his life, might be nearby.

Cat wondered if her father traveled down this very street, to spend his final hours as a prisoner in Lord Tamura's house. He had been dressed in shabby hempen robes. He had been carried in a *kago*, the flimsy open-weave sedans used by commoners. The guards had thrown a net over it and paraded him through the streets like a criminal. Cat's face grew hot even now at the shame of it.

She left the residential neighborhood and walked until she

came to the government's granaries lining the Sumida's banks. During the day this was a bustling place. Men hauled bales of rice through the noisy traffic of handcarts. Lighters crowded the wharves. But now the rows of huge, white-plastered warehouses were silent and ghostly in the moonlight.

When Cat reached the broad Sumida she stood on the stone embankment. The full moon was almost directly overhead. It threw a shirred ribbon of light across the water. It seemed to hang so low that Cat felt as though she could reach up and touch it.

A moon this full and bright had the power to illuminate the past. As Cat stood in its spectral light, she remembered the last moon viewing in the garden of her mother's house. It had been in the second month of the year of the Dragon, a month before her father's suicide.

Cat remembered her father's arrival in the plain palanquin he used for discreet visits to his outside-wife. As always, the house had been cleaned thoroughly. As always, Cat and her mother, with the servants in ranks behind them, had kneeled on the veranda and bowed in welcome. When Lord Asano stepped from the palanquin, Cat had felt the thrill she always did. He was so handsome and so obviously in love with her mother.

The moon viewing had been a quiet affair, with only Lord Asano's Chief Councilor, Oishi Kuranosuke, and a few close friends. Lord Asano's official wife came from a powerful family; and though the marriage had been arranged only for political connections, Lady Asano was not happy about her husband's outside-wife and child.

Lord Asano's simple, countrified moon parties had been less extravagant than those of the city *daimyō*, but they had been admired nonetheless. The gardeners had built a high mound of pure white sand, a cone as smooth and graceful as Mt. Fuji. Servants served humble food on plain lacquered trays to remind everyone of the vanity of ostentation. Tasteful presents had been exchanged and graceful poetry composed about the loveliness of the moonlight on the sand.

The silvery light of that full moon had made Cat's mother and father appear as young as teenagers. They had laughed together and shared looks of furtive passion. And Lord Asano had told them of his decision to legally adopt Cat, over his wife's objections. Cat couldn't remember ever seeing her mother look so happy. She had been as radiant as the moonlight.

There had been other news, that night. Cat's father had just learned that he and a young lord from the province of Iyo had been selected to receive the imperial envoy at the *shōgun*'s court. Lord Asano knew he would have to pay for food and drink and entertainment for the envoy, as well as buy silk court costumes for himself and his retainers. The expense would be extravagant, the ritual complex. But the high councilor had assured him that Lord Kira, the *shōgun*'s master of ceremonies, would instruct him.

Lord Kira. The name had meant nothing to Cat then. Now she could think of little else. She looked across the moonlit waters to the trees on the far shore. Somewhere over there was Lord Kira's new villa, the one he couldn't afford.

Kira was a bannerman, one of Tokugawa Tsunayoshi's own retainers. The position was prestigious but not well paid. Kira had built this mansion with presents he had demanded from other lords.

He expected much more than the traditional package of dried bonito in exchange for instruction in court etiquette. Cat knew her father was austere and schooled in the old ways. He was quick to anger. Among the free-spending folk of Edo he was said to be frugal to the point of parsimony. He would not spend great amounts of money to obtain what was Kira's duty to provide. As a result Kira refused to teach him the intricate moves of court ritual.

Cat squeezed her eyes shut to keep from crying. She knew it was useless to resent fate, but she could not stop herself from going over those tragic events again and again. If only her father's advisers had secretly given Kira the presents he expected. But they hadn't. If only Lord Asano's chief councilor, Oishi Kuranosuke, had been in Edo instead of at the family estate in Akō. But he wasn't.

Instead, the situation deteriorated until Asano couldn't ignore Kira's insults any longer. Asano drew his sword in the *shōgun*'s palace and attacked Kira. It was a terrible mistake. The penalty for such an act was death.

Cat could see it all in her mind's eye as surely as if she had been there. She knew her father's headstrong nature.

"Stop, Father!" When she said it out loud her own voice startled her. "Please stop."

Her only reply was the comforting murmur of the river as it flowed past her on its way to the sea.

The story of Lord Asano's death soon leaked out and became the subject of gossip. The folk of Edo were outraged at the injustice. Tokugawa Tsunayoshi didn't punish Kira for his part in the feud, but he did make him move out from behind the moat surrounding his palace and grounds.

Lord Uesugi was Kira's son. He had put his shrewd councilor, Chisaka, in charge of his father's defense. Chisaka had sent extra warriors to guard Kira's more vulnerable new mansion, and all of Edo speculated. After all, one could not live under the same sky with the slayer of one's lord or father. When would Lord Asano's men, the warriors of Akō, take revenge?

"Are you afraid, Lord Kira, shut away behind your walls?" Cat whispered. She wondered which lights shining among the thick growths of pines marked her enemy's villa. She stared until the lights and the sound of the river's current almost sent her into a trance.

She followed Musashi's advice and imagined herself as Lord Kira. Kira was the burglar whom Musashi wrote about. Everyone thought of the burglar as a fortified enemy. But what did the world look like to the burglar in the house?

The burglar who is shut inside is the pheasant, Musashi wrote. *He who enters to arrest the burglar is the hawk.*

Now you are inside, Kira, Cat thought. *And I am outside.*

CHAPTER 5

A BEGGAR'S BAG

The full moon had almost dropped beyond the edge of the roofless area over the center of the theater, but its spectral light still illuminated the empty hall and the stage at one end. As Cat walked across the hard-packed earth of the pit, her presence seemed to stir the emotions that always hovered there, waiting for a body, a vehicle to inhabit. Cat felt a ripple in the air, a ghostly echo of shouts and music and the tock of wooden clappers signaling scene changes. A cat's-paw of sound in the stillness.

Cat thought she saw a fan flutter in the deep shadows of the roofed boxes along the theater's sides. But the boxes were empty, too. The hair stirred on the nape of Cat's neck as she found the narrow backstage stairs and climbed to the mezzanine floor.

"Shichisaburo-san," she called softly. Because of one of Nakamura Shichisaburo's usual peccadillos, the *shōgun* had forbidden him to leave the theater's premises. Cat had been certain she would find him here.

"*Mmmmph!*" A loud, dull thud followed the muffled grunt from the dressing room on the second floor.

Cat backed slowly down the stairs. She picked up a tall candle holder from the row of them at the rear of the stage. The iron spike that usually stuck into the base of the candle suddenly looked menacing. Cat took off her clumsy sandals, and with the long, heavy rod held ready to strike, she prowled back up the stairs.

"*Baka!* Fool!" More thumping and a loud crash. "You board across a ditch! Radish!"

Cat peered into the actor's dressing room. By the light of the floor lantern she could see a large, sturdy square basket of the type that usually contained corpses. It was rocking back and forth.

"Shichisaburo-san?"

"Get me out of here."

Cat put down the candle holder and untied the straw cord holding the lid on. Nakamura Shichisaburo was curled inside like a chick in an egg. His wrists were tied with a soft, blue silk cord, knotted artistically and finished off with thick tassels. Cat untied them and helped him out of the basket.

"Did they ask you about me?" Cat took off her hat and towel so Shichisaburo could see her face. "Did they torture you to find out where I am?"

Shichisaburo stared at her as though at a ghost. He looked behind her for the usual escort of Old Jug Face's servants.

"You're a pony from a wine gourd, Miss Cat. Your Ladyship. Kinume-san." Perplexed, Shichisaburo rubbed the faint stubble on the shaved front portion of his head. Was the young beauty Cat the courtesan, or Golden Plum the gentlewoman and illegitimate daughter of the late Lord Asano?

The complex rituals of proper behavior depended on everyone staying in their place. Cat was most definitely displaced. She had thrown the comfortable, predictable rules of etiquette into disarray.

"Why are you wearing that . . ." Words failed Shichisaburo.

"That." He waved his fan at Cat's shabby hempen coat and trousers.

"Lord Kira tried to poison me, so I fled. Didn't his lackeys tie you up? Haven't they been here looking for me?"

Shichisaburo clapped his pudgy hands and laughed, delighted that life was presenting him with a drama at least as fine as any he acted on stage.

"That new apprentice, that insignificant wretch of a boy, was teaching me the art of 'squeezing-out-of-a-basket,' " Shichisaburo grumbled. "But he must have gone off to rumple a mattress with Ichikawa. The two of them have had their minds between their buttocks since they first laid hands on each other."

Shichisaburo adjusted the front opening of his robe and made a futile effort to tuck stray ends of hair back into his oiled topknot. Then he sat cross-legged and gathered his enormous black silk robe about his thick ankles and square feet. The cleavage of his plump breasts was visible in the diagonal plunge of his neckline. His robe was embroidered with persimmon-colored crayfish swimming upward from the hem among rolling, silver waves sewn in metallic thread.

His thrashing in the basket had tinted his fat cheeks a vivid pink. He was a mild, rotund little man, affable and effete, with bulging, grasshopper eyes. He hardly looked the part of the dashing young lover, the roles that were his specialty.

"We plan to use the trick in the next play." He nodded at the basket. "As my esteemed colleague Sakata says, 'The art of an actor is like a beggar's bag and must contain everything.' "

"Isn't he the same one who says an actor should even know how to lift purses?"

"Yes." Shichisaburo smiled. He poured two cups of tea from the kettle simmering on the brazier. He handed one to Cat and sipped daintily at the other.

"We constantly have to devise ways to entertain the riffraff in the pits." *And in the galleries, too,* Shichisaburo thought, though he didn't say it.

As a whole, the *samurai* of Edo were a coarse, swaggering lot. They preferred Ichikawa Danjuro's less subtle *aragoto* style of acting, the "rough stuff." But Shichisaburo knew Cat came from a military family, and so, for once, he kept his opinions to himself.

Shichisaburo's dressing room was cozy. One entire side was lined with low, battered lacquered shelves containing built-in compartments and drawers. Posters advertising past triumphs decorated the sepia-colored rough plaster walls. Costumes were draped over freestanding racks whose lacquered surfaces were chipped. Scattered helter-skelter in the corners were stacks of the latest presents, still in their wrappings, from Shichisaburo's fans. The small wooden lantern on the *tatami* spilled light around Cat and Shichisaburo and threw shadows over the rest of the room.

Cat was suddenly exhausted. Shichisaburo's voice sounded hollow and far away. As though he were in another room, talking to someone else. Talking about someone else.

Cat shook herself. Her chest itched under the tightly wrapped *haramaki*, and she longed to scratch it.

"Are you cold, my lady?"

"No. Just tired."

"I should think so. Tried to kill you, did they?"

"With *fugu*."

"Forgive my rudeness, Your Ladyship, but perhaps you should have accepted the adoption arranged by your father's chief councilor. Kira couldn't threaten you so easily in Kyōto."

"They would have expected me to marry their son."

Shichisaburo grimaced. The family that had agreed to take Cat in after the scandal was among the wealthiest in the country. The son, however, was reputed to be lacking in physical, social, and intellectual graces.

"At least you would have been safe and well provided for."

"A woman's wisdom only reaches the end of her nose." Cat stared at the floor as she sipped her tea. In spite of the self-deprecation, her silence said much more.

Like Cat, Shichisaburo was adept at conversing in silences. He knew that in this particular pause Cat was remembering all the factors that had gone into her decision to choose life in the Yoshiwara over marriage to a foolish boy. Cat knew that Kira or his son, Lord Uesugi, would certainly send men to spy on her at the House of the Carp, but all of Kira's spies wouldn't amount to the surveillance of one mother-in-law. Even though Kyōto was closer to Akō, Lord Asano's fief, Cat thought she would have a better chance of finding someone to help her take revenge than if she'd been shut away in the isolated women's quarters of a mansion.

And there was her mother. With Oishi far away in Akō, Cat's mother had had no one to defend her in those terrible days after Lord Asano's death. She had been stripped of home, privilege, and possessions. Lord Asano's wife came from a powerful family. Her steward had taken it upon himself to see that his mistress's rival was ruined completely. Cat's mother was proud. She said nothing of the unjust treatment. She shaved her head and became a nun.

Now she and Cat's old nurse lived in a small house of two rooms. Her former servants, themselves out of work, came by to visit and sweep the bare yard, to fill the water jars at the communal well, and to bring vegetables and small gifts. Cat was consumed by the shame of not being able to provide better for her mother. But to attract patrons a courtesan and her apprentices had to dress extravagantly, although the sumptuous clothes brought Cat no joy. And after Old Jug Face and the owner of the Carp took their percentage from her earnings, not much was left.

On top of all the other humiliations Cat had felt the added shame of ingratitude when she'd refused the adoption offer. She remembered Oishi's visit to the House of the Carp shortly after she had fled there. He had come alone, disguised as a priest to avoid the gossip his presence would cause.

The interview had been a torment. If Oishi had raged at her, if he had ordered her to go to Kyōto, she could have become angry in return. She could have set her jaw and stared icily at him, a technique she had perfected as a child in contests of wills with her nurse. But of course he didn't give her the chance.

In all the years Oishi Kuranosuke had been her *sensei*, her teacher, in the arts of the warrior, she had never seen him lose his temper. She remembered his calm voice, so familiar, as he asked her to consider her family's honor. He was asking her to fulfill her duty as Lord Asano's only child and bear sons to pray for his soul for generations to come. Cat's duty to both her parents, the one who had died and the one who still lived, had been the most difficult part of her decision.

Cat hadn't been able to look into Oishi's eyes. With head lowered she had whispered, "I will not." As evening shadows gathered around them in the House of the Carp's large, bare reception room, they had sat in silence, both of them trapped by tragic circumstances beyond their control.

Cat had felt another sorrow added to their shared burden of grief. Oishi had always seemed invincible, infallible. He had always been a man who could command any situation. But he had been managing the Asano estate in Akō, a hundred and fifty-five long *ri* southwest of Edo, when the quarrel erupted.

Of course he couldn't have prevented it himself, but he knew his master's frugal nature, and he knew what sort of man Kira was. He should have foreseen Kira's demands and Asano's refusal. He should have instructed Asano's advisers to give Kira extravagant presents, behind their master's back if necessary. But he hadn't.

Nor could he provide for the woman who had been his lord's greatest love. He had paid off creditors. He had given as much money as possible to the three hundred and twenty former Akō-Asano retainers and their families, who were now without prospects. He had bribed officials in an attempt to reinstate the family name. All of that had drained away most of the estate's resources.

Now he could not even assure his master's daughter's future. This was the child Lord Asano loved and had planned to make his heir. This was the child Oishi had taught since she was old enough to clutch a miniature halberd, a *naginata*, in her tiny hands. And she was defying him.

He knew she was silently blaming him, too, not only for allowing her father's death, but for turning over the family castle in Akō to the *shōgun*'s officials without a fight. He knew she considered him a coward for not taking revenge or at least following his master by committing *seppuku*.

His shame had resonated, pulsing imperceptibly like the lantern's light in the dim room. He had risen and bowed low, just slightly too low for his station. Cat's tears had blurred his image as he left, but he had looked old. He had looked defeated. Humiliated.

Now, as Cat listened to Shichisaburo, her face burned and her ears rang with fatigue and shame.

"Have you heard any recent news?" Cat's calm voice gave no hint of what she was feeling. In a graceful, flowing motion she set the small teacup back on its tray.

"Child, I know only what all of Edo knows."

Shichisaburo picked up an abacus from the tumble of objects on the shelf next to him. In the silence he clicked off beads with his chubby index finger, as though he could quantify tragedy. As though he could add and subtract the betrayals and deaths and sorrow and arrive at an answer for it all.

"You must have heard that your father's younger brother has been sent to Hiroshima to live with his cousin there."

"Yes." Cat also knew the implications. After a year the *shōgun* finally made his decision to strike the Akō-Asano name from the list of *daimyō*. A vendetta would no longer imperil

Lord Asano's younger brother's future, since he could not assume the title in any case. But in the five months since then, Oishi and the former Akō retainers had done nothing to redeem their dead master's honor.

Shichisaburo debated telling Cat the latest rumor. She might have heard it already, and if she hadn't, it would only make her more unhappy. Still, it was a most succulent morsel of gossip. Shichisaburo relished gossip more than sex, and he relished sex a great deal. His enthusiasm for sex, especially sex with forbidden partners, had put him in Cat's debt, which was why she could come here for his help.

"Have you heard about Oishi's divorce?" he asked finally.

"No!"

"Rumor says he divorced his wife, abandoned his children, and is enjoying a heroic debauch in Kyōto. They say he hasn't been sober or had his sword out of a woman's scabbard since your uncle was sentenced to life in Hiroshima last summer."

"I don't believe it." Cat was stunned. No one had dared tell her this. Surely there was some mistake. Oishi loved his wife and treasured his children.

"Perhaps the stories are only lies." Shichisaburo was sorry he had brought it up.

"Shichi-san, I need your help."

"Ah, child, how can I help you? The government calls me a riverbed-beggar and confines me to this shabby quarter." But Shichisaburo was only stalling. He owed Cat a debt, and he knew she was here to collect on it.

"How is our friend?" Shichisaburo figured he might as well get the subject of Plover out in the open.

Cat had pretended to accept Shichisaburo as her guest at the Perfumed Lotus so he could sneak in to see his real, if temporary, love, Plover. Part of Plover's allure was that a certain highly placed official was infatuated with her, too. He was very powerful and very possessive, which made the ruse necessary and the affair piquantly dangerous.

"She has not been feeling well lately."

"Affairs have kept me busy. But I must go see her soon."

If Shichisaburo had a fault, it was self-indulgence. He didn't mention that an illicit exchange of love letters with one of the attendants of the *shōgun*'s wife was what had distracted him. Shichisaburo was straying closer to the mouth of the tiger's den.

"Just how did you slip past Centipede?" The improbability of Cat's escape finally occurred to him.

"Someone's straw raincoat caught fire and caused a diversion."

Shichisaburo smiled wickedly and quoted the poet Bashō. " 'How does the firefly see the path ahead, when it's his own ass that's alight?' " He added tea to Cat's cup. "Who caught fire?"

"Kira's cousin, the *metsuke*."

Shichisaburo whooped with glee and spewed tea all over the *tatami*. He mopped at it with a paper handkerchief. "Kira's cousin! The one who bites off women's nipples?"

"Yes."

"Kira will perfume his underwear when he hears his cousin's been grilled like a sweet potato. He's terrified that Oishi will come after his head, you know. Rumors say he hasn't been able to satisfy his wife or his mistress or his new boyfriend since the . . ." Shichisaburo hesitated. "Unfortunate incident. His bodyguards follow him into the privy and check the hole before he squats."

"Shichi-san, I must get to Kyōto." Cat had no more time for socializing.

"You're planning to travel the Tōkaidō alone?"

"Yes. I need a disguise. I need papers to take me past the barriers."

"Not easy." Shichisaburo guessed that Cat intended to find her father's councilor, Oishi Kuranosuke. This could mean big trouble indeed. Very exciting. Helping her with this would definitely wipe out his debt to her.

Shichisaburo studied Cat's pale, lovely face. Now that she was a fugitive and a danger, her beauty started a sensual throbbing in his loins.

"I haven't time for that, Shichi-san." Cat knew him well.

Shichisaburo sighed. Lady Asano's small ears were as perfectly shaped as the winkle shells on Suruga Beach. Even without rouge her full lips were red as a persimmon bud. High on her smooth forehead, her hairline formed a lovely inverted peak, like the silhouette of the sacred mountain, Fuji. And her toes, ah, her toes.

It was said that beauty and luck rarely went together. If that was so, Lady Asano would have no luck at all.

No, this wouldn't be easy. Shichisaburo got up suddenly and began rummaging through the costumes in the big chest nearby.

"So, let's see what we can find in our beggar's bag, for a stray Cat."

CHAPTER 6
ENDURANCE AND NO DEFECTS

With her heavy, striped paper travel cloak pulled over her, Cat lay curled up behind the stone dais in the small chapel to Kannon-sama, the goddess of mercy. The chapel stood among the trees of Sengakuji, Spring Hill Temple, less than a *ri* from Shinagawa, the first of the government's fifty-three post stations on the Tō-kaidō Road.

Cat's short sleep had been harried by sinister dreams. Not until the black sky above the growth of ancient pines began to fade did her mouth stop twitching, her face become serene. Cat's dreams had taken her home.

Others might have thought that Lord Asano was overly concerned with his account books, but he had always been generous to Cat and her mother. The garden at their modest mansion had been his greatest joy. Cat's happiest times had been there.

Now she dreamed she was standing in a flurry of fragrant white cherry blossoms at the edge of the biggest pond. When her shadow fell across the water, hundreds of carp swarmed to meet her. The sun glinted on their golden scales.

Cat knelt on a silken cushion and tossed crushed acorns into the turbulence. She dipped her fingers in the water to feel the nibbling of the fish's hard mouths and to hear the chuffing sounds they made. But the cherry blossoms turned to snow and piled up around her. An icy wind began to blow. Cat tried to pull her thin spring robes closer around her, but they shredded under her fingers and fell away.

She heard loud voices and the heavy tread of men's feet in the quiet corridors. She turned to see that the paper panes of the door panels beyond the garden veranda were ripped. Their torn edges flapped in the sudden wind. Tall weeds had sprouted among the flat gray stones of the pathways.

As Cat slept, she drew her knees up tighter and jerked in a spasm of terror. She tried to scream but could only whimper.

She awoke with a start and lay there, orienting herself and remembering.

She remembered the stifled sobbing in distant rooms, as the servants hurried to empty the storehouse and pack the household goods. The *shōgun* had granted them only a day to leave the house that had been Cat's home since birth. By the time Cat's father committed *seppuku*, in a distant garden, the house had been turned over to government agents.

Forgive me, Father. I wanted to bid you good-bye.

Cat hadn't been allowed to watch him carry out the *shōgun*'s sentence, but she knew the ritual well. He had dressed in the white robes of death that every *samurai* kept ready. He had knelt under the cherry tree with blossoms blowing around him. A trusted swordsman, blade poised, stood behind him. He had pulled his arms out of the wide sleeves and tucked them under his knees so he would fall forward instead of sprawling in an undignified way. He had reached for the dagger on its tall, ceremonial tray and held its paper-wrapped hilt steadily in both hands, the blade turned toward himself.

Cat couldn't see what followed, though. Even if she had been present, the act would have happened too swiftly for the eye to see. The sword descended in a flash of light. Cat could only picture her father's head hanging from the piece of skin the swordsman left so it wouldn't bounce away. To keep from crying out, Cat bit down hard on the heel of her thumb.

Everything that happens in life is reward or punishment for what we have done. Only the ignorant resent their fate. Cat's mother had said it often. It had been her soft admonition throughout Cat's rebellious childhood. But Cat did resent the cruelties of fate. That was why she hadn't become a nun as her mother had. She could not sit in a small room copying *sutras* for the rest of her life. A hunger for revenge was gnawing at her soul. Religious piety wouldn't satisfy it.

Still shivering with the cold, she stood stiffly. In the cramped space she tried to brush out the wrinkles in the baggy hempen trousers of her priest's costume. She straightened the tattered, belted overcoat whose frayed lower edge reached just below her knees. The pale hem of the short priest's robe showed below it. Then she walked around in front of the statue.

She put her palms together, fingers pointed heavenward, and draped Shichisaburo's rosary over them, holding it in place with her thumbs. She bowed her head and asked the goddess, Kannon-sama, to bless her. The statue was ancient, carved from a camphor log in some forgotten time by some forgotten hand. The gilt paint that had covered it had mostly worn away.

This particular image of the thousand-armed goddess had only four hands. Two were folded in prayer. One was raised toward heaven. The fourth held a lotus blossom. Kannon-sama's lovely face looked no older than Cat's own. She smiled down so serenely that Cat almost smiled in return.

Cat looked out from under the dripping eaves of the small chapel. A gray veil of mist twined through the grounds of Spring Hill Temple, as though the old stone monuments themselves were dissolving. Jewels of dew covered the dark green moss on the crowds of monuments and statues and the tall stone lanterns.

The sky was as gray as the mist and the breasts of the pigeons flying about the wide eaves of the main temple building. The dawn bell began ringing. Night was opening. Cat had overslept.

She took deep breaths to push back a momentary panic. This was where her father was buried. The police and Lord Kira's men would certainly search here for her. She had to hurry.

Close to Cat's shelter was the stone marker of her father's grave. His last poem had been incised into it. Cat had memorized it, but through her tears she read it anyway.

> Far more fragile than
> Tender blooms, so soon scattered
> By the fresh spring winds,
> Must I now bid you farewell
> And leave gentle spring behind?

Oishi Kuranosuke had made arrangements for erecting this monument to his lord. He had contributed the funds to assure that the priests here performed the rituals for Lord Asano's soul at the proper intervals. The grave was covered with fresh cedar boughs, a fragrant expression of grief. Someone had set out offerings of persimmons and rice. Cat could see the stubs of hundreds of joss sticks burned in her father's memory.

The temple bell continued tolling, its booming notes following one on the other like waves against a rocky shore. With a heart so full of grief that Cat feared it would break, she picked up the bamboo ladle lying on the stone basin. She filled it and rinsed her mouth to purify it. Then she poured more water over her hands and over the grave. She put her palms together and rubbed the beads of the rosary as she bowed her head and chanted a scripture for the repose of her father's soul.

In front of the statue of Kannon-sama lay a heap of wooden strips. Mourners had painted on them the names of dead loved ones. Cat had none for her father, but at least she could leave something.

She took out the paper-wrapped coins from the dead guest's purse and the blue scarf with its coiled hank of her shorn hair. This was the last money she could give her mother. Cat didn't expect to live to see her again.

She looked for a place to hide them and decided on the squat brass censer with its lid perforated in a design of autumn grasses. Cat recognized the urn. It had sat for years in the ornate altar cupboard in the main reception room of the inner apartments of her father's mansion. Oishi had said it belonged to him so that Lord Asano's wife would allow it to stay at the grave.

When Cat emptied the ashes and blew out the residue, their aroma reminded her so strongly of home that she became disoriented for an instant. The incense was called Smoke of Fuji, a blend of camphor and sandalwood and secret ingredients mixed by the master, Wakayama. The subtle, magical smell had pervaded everything belonging to Cat's mother. It had permeated her clothing and the *tatami* and bedding and screens of the inner chambers where she spent her days.

As Cat breathed in the lingering traces of Smoke of Fuji, she breathed in her mother's essence. She heard her soft voice, her laughter, like delicate wind chimes in another room. Cat longed to see her. Just a glimpse, a word. She could bear any danger then and any hardship. She could bear even the loneliness.

As she was laying the scarf and the coins inside the censer, a clamor of bells and voices and small hand drums sent the pigeons flapping in all directions. Out of sight in the courtyard behind the temple the monks were kneeling in a line on square mats. They had begun their morning devotions. The time had come to start for Shinagawa, and the barrier set up to regulate travel.

Cat reached into Kannon-sama's chapel, picked up the flat brass bell lying there, and slipped the hemp cord over her head so the bell hung at her chest. Next, she pulled out a tall, bulbous cylinder of a basket with a section of latticework woven in. She settled the inner frame onto her head, tied the cords, and adjusted the hat so she could see through the open weave. Her face was unrecognizable behind it. The basket made her look taller than she was.

Dressing Cat as a *komuso*, a priest of "empty nothing," was

Shichisaburo's solution to the problem of a disguise. *Komuso* were mendicants, often former *samurai*, who traveled alone. At times they engaged in sorcery and exorcism. The fact that people expected them to behave strangely might cover the mistakes Cat was sure to make on the road.

Shichisaburo had ransacked his theater's costumes and props and had been rather proud of the result. Cat's cropped hair was pulled into a shaggy horsetail near the top of her head. Even belted, the short white hemp robe and black coat were so big and shabby that they disguised Cat's body. The bottoms of the rough, straw-colored trousers bloused out at the knees, below which they were gathered into black canvas gaiters and black *tabi* that buttoned up the back. The *tabi* socks hid her aristocratic feet and cushioned them from the chafing of the ties of her straw sandals.

Best of all was the six-foot-tall bamboo walking staff that had been a prop from one of Shichisaburo's plays. It contained the slender oak shaft for a halberd, a *naginata*. Holes had been bored through the solid joints of the bamboo. The rigid partitions at the joints held a *naginata* shaft in the bamboo's hollow center and kept it from rattling around. A wooden stopper fit tightly into the opening at the top. Fastened over it was a cap of ornate iron filigree in the shape of a paulownia leaf. Three iron rings hung from each side loop.

Housed in a leather sheath, then swaddled in cloth, was the long, gracefully curved blade that attached to the *naginata* shaft. The government forbade the use of metal in stage swords, but Shichisaburo's troupe had skirted the law by rationalizing that a *naginata* wasn't a sword.

Cat would have preferred to carry a weapon she didn't have to stop to assemble, but this was far better than nothing. The *naginata* was unadorned, but solid. Musashi would have approved of it. He wrote that just as a horse must have endurance and no defects, so it was with weapons.

The *naginata* was the weapon of choice of women of the *samurai* class. Several of them had hung over the front doorway of Cat's mother's house. In these times of peace neither Cat nor her mother would have been required to defend the mansion against invaders, but the *naginatas* hung there anyway. They were symbols of the days when the women of a *samurai* household were a castle's last defense.

Shichisaburo also had given Cat a priest's wicker backpack with the bamboo framework extending below the bottom to form feet. Usually such packs were filled with religious articles, but Shichisaburo had ransacked the actors' dressing rooms for useful items and stray food that hadn't been nibbled by cockroaches.

Cat's pack contained the *naginata* blade, spare straw sandals, a rain cloak of paper soaked in persimmon juice, an extra coat made of heavy paper, and a well-worn pair of *tabi*. Packed on top of the clothes was a dried bonito wrapped in oiled paper, a comb in a charm bag, a peck of uncooked hulled rice, and most important, a packet of powder that Shichisaburo had assured her would discourage fleas.

Cat also had five silver *mame-ita*, the smallest denomination, and the string of a hundred copper *mon* that Shichisaburo had given her. They were all that he had had on him. He had offered to get more for her when his banker opened his shop in the morning, but Cat had dared not wait for that.

Cat put her arms through the woven straps and adjusted the straw pads under them where they dug into her shoulder. She bowed and once more chanted a prayer to her father's memory.

"You! What do you want?" Spring Hill Temple's new assistant abbot was so fat, he rocked from side to side as he rumbled down the steep stone steps of the temple's main hall.

Cat figured this was as good a place as any to try begging. She held out her cracked wooden bowl and thumped her walking stick, jangling the iron rings on top.

"*Namu Amida Butsu.* Homage to Amida Buddha," she droned through her nose. "I ask a small donation in the name of the All-Loving Buddha for the temple we are building to honor the god of ten thousand good fortunes."

"Begone!" The assistant abbot ran out of breath halfway down the steps. He wheezed like a pair of wet sandals and waved his sleeves at Cat.

"Buy a talisman of the Thousandfold Blessing," she said. "It will banish the danger years. It will make you fertile." Cat held the bowl out farther.

"Begone!"

"Who is it?" The head abbot stood in the temple's doorway.

"Some wretched, thieving 'abandoning-priest.' " His assistant trundled back up the stairs toward the clangor of the monks' bells.

Even though the head abbot couldn't see Cat's face, she lowered her head and retreated. Spring Hill Temple was near her former home. The abbot had been an old friend of her father's.

He had given Cat and her mother religious instruction. Unlike his new assistant, he was a kind man. Even if he thought her no more than a mendicant priest, he might have invited her in for morning tea and a talk.

Cat paused before passing through the gate, though. She turned and looked back toward her father's grave, surrounded by the hundreds of other gray monuments, the ranks of the dead.

"I will not forget you," she whispered. "Not even for an interval as short as those between the notes of the bells."

CHAPTER 7

THE JOURNEY OF
A THOUSAND *RI*

A tall pole stood near the fence leading to the barrier in Shinagawa. One short crosspiece was lashed near the bottom of the pole and a longer one farther up. A naked man hung with feet braced on the bottom crosspiece and arms outstretched and tied to the top one.

All his blood had drained from the ragged gashes torn in his sides by a spear blade. The ground under the pole was black with it. The executioner had been clumsy or careless or cruel. He had stabbed the man several times before puncturing enough organs to finish the business.

The dead man had been caught trying to sneak around the barrier. His body had been hanging here for three days as a lesson to anyone with similar plans. Men of the *eta*, the outcasts, leaned on their shovels and puffed on their tiny pipes and joked around the open hole where the body would be thrown. The soil of the mass grave was studded with bones, hair, and teeth.

In spite of the stench, only Cat seemed to notice. While they waited their turn, pilgrims and travelers and porters sat on their luggage near the corpse. They chatted as they munched on the rice cakes and pickles and sweet potatoes they had retrieved from their packs and big cloth bundles. Whether they considered themselves too worldly to notice another public execution or whether they were really afraid, Cat couldn't say.

The Tōkaidō Road wove through Shinagawa like a river meandering through a low wooden canyon. Here the highway followed the line of hills on one side and the bay on the other. Shinagawa's role as a way station for people headed somewhere else was clear. It was famous for its restaurants and its audacious "rice servers," women who, for a fee, delivered more than rice.

At the end of the commercial district stretched a forbidding wall. It funneled all the foot traffic, for no wheeled vehicles were allowed on the Tōkaidō, through one narrow gate. Government officials checked the travel papers of everyone passing through it.

Cat's nerve almost failed her when she saw the early-morning crowd of travelers bunched at the barrier. A group of *samurai*, each with a pair of swords stuck through his sash, guarded the gate. They were separating out the women and escorting them into a nearby building.

To keep the restive *daimyō* under control, the first Tokugawa *shōgun*, Ieyasu, had devised a form of loyalty-by-hostage called "alternate attendance." The lords were allowed to spend time on their fiefs scattered about the country; but they had to leave their wives and children in Edo as a guarantee of their good behavior.

If a *daimyō* could smuggle his family out of Edo, he could foment rebellion without fear that their heads would decorate Edo's execution grounds. So women, especially women of the nobility, were watched very closely. Cat knew the women were being stripped and inspected by female examiners. If they didn't match the detailed descriptions on their permits, they would be detained or sent back to Edo or punished.

Cat wished she could stop at one of the busy, open-fronted tea houses and spend an hour or so over a steaming cup and a bowl of rice and vegetables. It would give her time to observe the barrier and the procedures there. But to drink tea and eat rice she would have to take off the basket covering her face.

Beyond the narrow alleyways between some of the buildings, Cat could see the quartz-and-sapphire glitter of the bay. Boats bobbed on its surface. Gulls dipped and swooped overhead, unaffected by man-made barriers. Cat envied them.

Shichisaburo had said that priests and nuns and holy men didn't need travel permits. But what if he were wrong?

Cat read the notices painted on strips of wood and hung on the big, roofed-over board standing outside the gate. She found only the usual admonitions to the lower classes to work hard, avoid frivolous pastimes and showy clothing, and honor one's superiors. There was no mention of a murder or two in the Yoshiwara. No word of a runaway courtesan.

For the first time since her escape from the House of the Perfumed Lotus, Cat would have to face government officials. She would have to speak to them. And if they discovered she was in disguise, they would arrest her.

In situations like this Musashi advised seizing the initiative. Cat jangled the iron rings on her staff. Those at the rear of the crowd jumped. They were less indifferent to the specter of death by crucifixion than they seemed.

"Namu Amida Butsu," Cat droned.

People glanced up in annoyance and moved away. A few pressed their hands to their sashes or the fronts of their jackets where they kept their purses. Cat approached the roughest men she saw.

"Buy a talisman of the Thousandfold Blessing!" She draped the mendicant's cloth over her hand and held out her begging bowl to a group of *kago* bearers. They were sprawled in a patch of morning sun, drinking warm *sake* and swapping lies.

"Try this talisman's virtues," Cat said. "It will cancel out the danger years. It will banish warts. It will make you fertile."

One of the men had a dragon tattooed the length of his arm. With his round, woven-bamboo fan he scooped up a pile of dog excrement and dropped it into the bowl. His friends doubled over with laughter.

Cat bowed low. "The Buddha will remember your gift, kind sir," she said. *And I will remember your face,* she thought. *And if we meet under different circumstances, I will separate your head from your shoulders.*

Ignoring their laughter, she moved on through the crowd, begging her way toward the head of the line. By the time she reached the gate she had emptied the bowl of the *kago* bearer's contribution, but nothing else had taken its place. The people of Edo seemed to have no time for charity or religion.

With heart pounding she passed between the guards and walked to the open-fronted building where the government's officials sat. White bunting decorated with the three hollyhock leaves of the Tokugawa crest hung from the eaves of the porch.

The magistrate hardly glanced at Cat when she stood before him. He sat cross-legged on a cushion on a *tatami*-covered dais and leaned on an elbow cushion. His assistant sat at a low writing table covered with sheafs of paper and ink pads and stamps.

Behind him, on a lower level, the captain of the guard and three of his men sat back on their heels.

Cat had rehearsed her story, but the magistrate didn't even question her. His assistant waved her past.

Cat's knees felt weak as she walked through the opposite gate. Beyond it was the broad Tōkaidō, the great road called the Eastern Seaway. While Cat leaned on her staff to calm her racing heart, a pack train passed. The bells on the horses' bridles jingled merrily. Just ahead of Cat walked a group of pilgrims who also wore bells. They were singing and clapping time and improvising dance steps as they went. Their straw sandals kicked up little explosions of dust.

"Holy man."

Cat jumped when the old man tugged at her sleeve.

"Holy man, please accept this unworthy donation for your temple." The man was bent and worn, and his clothes hung about him in tatters. The ten-*mon* piece he held out must have been most of what he had.

"You need this more than I, grandfather," Cat said.

"Excuse my rudeness, but you would honor me by taking it. It will bring me the blessing of Buddha." The old man bowed low and hobbled off before Cat could say anything else.

Cat stood in the center of the busy traffic and looked down the wide road. Its raised, hard-packed earthen surface was unmarred by ruts. Wheeled vehicles weren't allowed on it. Rebel armies could be fed and armed with the contents of wheeled vehicles.

On both sides of the Tōkaidō, huge pine trees provided shade. The brown mosaic of rice paddies and irrigation ditches of the plain of Musashi came right to its verges. At the other end of the Tōkaidō, one hundred and twenty-five *ri* away, lay Kyōto, the Western Capital of Peace and Tranquillity. According to Shichisaburo, Oishi spent his nights in Shimabara, Kyōto's pleasure district. Cat's hopes and all her prospects of avenging her father resided there.

Musashi wrote that the journey of a thousand *ri* began with the first step. A stranger in her native country, Cat drew a deep breath of chill winter air and took the first step.

CHAPTER 8
THE WHITE WAKE

The parrot perched on a thin cotton towel spread across Old Jug Face's shoulder. As usual when he was nervous, he searched under the second cloth tied around her head as a kerchief. When he found her pendulous earlobe, he nibbled it and murmured to her.

"Centipede says you're the best." Old Jug Face's dubious expression was understandable. Hanshiro didn't look prosperous. He didn't even look solvent. He grunted noncommittally.

"The best is required for this situation," Old Jug Face hastened on. She didn't want to offend him. Centipede said he was particular about the jobs he accepted. She shuffled along, close on his *tabi*-clad heels as he crossed the room where Cat had entertained her last guest.

"People in high places want her kept here. Out of the way," Old Jug Face whispered. She knew that servants, both her own and a few sent by Lord Kira to spy, were listening intently in the nearby rooms.

Hanshiro grunted again. Kira was at quite a disadvantage. The *shōgun* disapproved of him. Members of the upper class ridiculed him. The rabble despised him.

If the mistress of the Perfumed Lotus was telling the truth, Lord Asano had had an outside-wife and child. Kira must fear that the daughter would coalesce a vendetta among Asano's former retainers. The fact that Asano's daughter had disappeared on the monthly anniversary of her father's death must have Kira agitated.

Hanshiro stood in the doorway between Cat's small dressing room and the bedchamber. They were both tidy. The soiled quilt and the blowfish were gone. After Hanshiro had inspected the single slice of *fugu* and its garnish of dead flies and cockroaches, servants had cleared it away.

Hanshiro read the titles of the books on Cat's shelf. They

consisted of classics and all five volumes of Musashi's *Book of Five Rings* instead of the usual bawdy romances.

Pretensions of intellect, he thought. He unrolled a scroll and studied the calligraphy. An exceptionally good hand for a woman. The characters were drawn with a boldness that was almost masculine.

"Is she *kurage*, a change of saddles?"

"No, she's not a habitual runaway. This is the first time she's disappeared. All her clothes are still here and at the Carp."

Hanshiro was bored. He had heard this story many times before, with only the slightest variations. Women had no sense. They ran away with the first man who rolled his eyes, waved his cucumber of love, and pledged his everlasting devotion. As soon as he lured them out of the Yoshiwara, he resold them elsewhere.

The dressing room was elegantly furnished, but that was to be expected. According to what the mistress had reluctantly divulged, the courtesan named Cat had come from a good family. Her mother's people had been of noble stock, sturdy of arm, strong of spirit, but empty of purse. She was probably pampered. Spoiled. Vain.

"I don't know how this happened." Old Jug Face was still frantically sorting through possible ways to avoid blame for the disaster. "Centipede says he saw Lady Asano's guest near the Great Gate at the hour of the Rat, but he didn't see her. Of course there was an unfortunate accident at the gate last night."

Hanshiro didn't even bother to grunt. He had drawn both arms inside the capacious sleeves of his rumpled, dusty-black jacket and crossed them over his taut stomach. He poked one hand through the frayed diagonal of the neck opening and scratched the dark stubble on his cheek. The beard, streaked with a few wiry gray hairs, blurred the angles of his high cheekbones and strong jaw, but his dark, brooding eyes glowed clear and sharp and with an intensity that bordered on the savage.

He obviously hadn't been to a hairdresser in a long time. The wide strip of scalp from his forehead to his crown was supposed to have been shaved. Instead it bristled with a half-inch pelt. The long black hair around it had been caught up into a shaggy whisk at the crown of his head and carelessly wrapped and tied with a cord of rice straw.

He was slightly taller than average and solid, with muscular arms and shoulders and big hands. He was forty-one, born in the year of the Tiger. In a lifetime of adversity he had learned that he could depend only on himself.

Hanshiro didn't like to ask questions, but now and then they were the quickest if not the best way to get answers. He didn't want to waste any more time on this job than necessary. He was tired of cases involving runaways. He had taken this one because the story of the young woman's downfall had piqued his curiosity.

"Your servants have checked everywhere?"

"Oh, yes." Old Jug Face's parrot muttered to himself and scanned longingly for his cage. "She's not in the district."

Hanshiro put his arms back through his sleeves. He was left-handed, and as he knelt, his right hand moved reflexively to his side. He intended to push his long-sword's sharkskin-covered hilt down so its tip would swing upward away from the *tatami*; but his long-sword was in Centipede's care.

Hanshiro's blunt index finger and thumb closed delicately around a few black silken threads lying on the dark green binding where two mats met. When he held the hairs up, they hung down a foot and a half on each side of his fingers. Old Jug Face stared at them as a mouse would watch a snake. Her own stubby fingers were interlaced under the light mauve apron she wore over her brown checked robe. Her hands were clenched so tightly that white ellipses formed at the knuckles.

Old Jug Face was almost thirty-nine in a profession where the foot soldiers were dismissed as middle-aged at twenty-five. She had struggled to fortify herself a comfortable redoubt here. She made a hundred *mon* in squeeze from every *ichibu* a customer spent on food. She made a percentage on the maids' and servants' tips and the courtesans' fees. Now she was terrified that Lord Kira would have her turned out, as she herself had turned out women too old to attract trade.

"The woman's guest probably didn't leave," Hanshiro said.

"But Centipede saw him, just before the *metsuke* . . ." The possibility of a link between Cat's disappearance and the fire that had consumed Lord Kira's cousin hit Old Jug Face. She looked like a crow that had just flown headlong into a wall.

In a daze she plucked the parrot off her shoulder. When she cradled the bird in her arms he struggled briefly, sneezed, then subsided. Hanshiro could tell that his latest employer was staring straight into the leer of her own mortality. He wasn't given to jocularity, but he almost smiled at the look on her face.

Hanshiro went to the rear wall panel and slid it open. He looked up and down the back corridor. No woman, especially none of Cat's rank, cut off three feet of her hair unless she intended to become a nun.

"Was she religious?" he asked without turning around.

"Not particularly, although she read the holy scriptures each day."

"And the *fugu*, the blowfish?"

"A terrible accident."

"You had an unusual number of accidents here last night."

"Nothing like that has ever happened in the Perfumed Lotus before. My *fugu* man is a qualified fish surgeon. Never in his . . ."

Hanshiro held up a hand to quiet her. He wasn't concerned with what was probably a murder. He wasn't being hired to solve that. Nor did he want to be. Missing people weren't usually very interesting, but they were more interesting than dead ones.

"No one else was with her?"

"Her little maid slept in another room last night."

Hanshiro prowled the narrow back corridor toward the dark doorway to the storeroom. He walked with a straddle-legged swagger and a slight limp. If the long, divided, pleated skirts of his *hakama* had been new and crisp, they would have flared almost to the wall on either side. But this *hakama* was limp and faded from black to a streaked bluish gray. The hems had raveled into a pale fringe. Even the tips of the fringe were frayed.

Behind him Hanshiro heard the rustle and squeak of women. He knew the maids were fluttering like radiant butterflies behind the paper walls, trying to see and hear. He could picture them whispering behind their sleeves. For a morning, at least, they had more on their minds than hairdos.

Hanshiro stood in the doorway of the storeroom and tried to conjure up the image of Cat, the woman who was to have been Lady Asano. He tried to form her from her handwriting and from the scent that lingered in her rooms. Was she a fugitive or a victim or a murderer?

The sun shone through cracks in the wall and painted gilt stripes on the sacks and barrels. Dust motes frolicked in the sunbeams. When his eyes adjusted to the gloom, Hanshiro saw the traces of Butterfly's broom and the trail of the quilt. He saw the freshly scattered dust, lighter in color than the rest, on the *sake* barrels. Cat's white wake, left in her flight.

He thought of the old poem.

> To what shall I compare
> this world?
> To the white wake behind

A ship that has rowed away
at dawn.

Hanshiro rapped the sides of the *sake* barrels with the pry bar. He opened the rear one and peered inside. The corpse was naked. Was Lady Asano wearing the guest's rented clothes?

"Here," he grunted.

"The woman we seek?" Old Jug Face's blocky silhouette filled the lighted doorway.

"No." Hanshiro felt something that was almost admiration, but not quite. After all, she couldn't have done this herself. She had an accomplice.

He crossed one possibility off the list. She might be a fugitive and/or a murderer, but she probably wasn't a victim. Yet.

When Old Jug Face looked inside the barrel, she gave a strangled scream and pressed her hands to her painted mouth. She looked around in panic, trying to figure out how she could hide this from the authorities and knowing she couldn't.

Without another word Hanshiro strode toward the back door. The madam had given him a list of Cat's regular guests. He would start with them.

Old Jug Face scurried after him. "Find her before she bothers Lord Kira, and I'll pay you extra."

And add the cost to Lady Asano's debt, Hanshiro thought.

When he reached the back stoop, the Perfumed Lotus's sandal man appeared on the run around the corner. Lowly as his job was, he was a master at it. He carried Hanshiro's tattered, muddy straw footgear without a hint of distaste. Hanshiro stood on the back stoop while the sandal bearer tied them over his worn *tabi*, then bowed repeatedly and disappeared.

The broad eaves of the two brothels almost met overhead. Hanshiro looked down the gloomy alley to the ribbon of sunlight at the end, to the slice of bustling street life visible there.

It was happening as it usually did.

Hanshiro was always alert; but once the chase started something stirred and stretched inside him. Something yawned and flashed long, ivory fangs and a pink predator's tongue. Something sniffed the odors on the eddies of the wind and rumbled hungrily far back in its throat.

When he was twenty-five Hanshiro had joined the ranks of unemployed *samurai* called *rōnin*, which meant, roughly, "men adrift on life's seas.'' In the fifteen years since then he had earned a precarious living in the shifting, elusive field of endeavor called the Water Trade. The Water Trade was made up of gamblers and procurers, of *sake*-and-bathhouse proprietors, aunties, courtesans, prostitutes, and entertainers.

Hanshiro found lost things—people, treasure, honor. Enough people, treasure, and honor were misplaced in the Yoshiwara to keep him busy full-time. He didn't often have the sums of money necessary to patronize the assignation houses, but he was a familiar figure here nonetheless.

Hanshiro went directly to the Great Gate, where he planned to exchange his numbered wooden ticket for information as well as for his weapon. Centipede's assistant knew better than to retrieve Hanshiro's sword. He stood back, bowing, while Centipede himself accepted the ticket and went into the gate house.

Even though Hanshiro's Kanesada blade was in its scabbard, Centipede carried it on a silk cloth laid across both palms. He bowed low over it when he held it out. The bow was more out of respect for the curved, slender, two-hundred-year-old length of silvery-blue steel than for its present owner. Mortals passed into other existences, but the spirit of a sword like this endured forever.

With the trailing edge of the silk cloth, Centipede lovingly polished the horse roundels of mother-of-pearl inlay on the copper-and-gold-flecked lacquered ground of the scabbard. The crows circling the round brass hilt guard represented the New Shadow school of strategy.

Centipede sighed. ''The inferior new blades can't match those of the Kotō masters.''

Hanshiro grunted. He knew that if he kept silent, Centipede's curiosity would do most of his work for him.

Centipede had acquired his nickname in his youth when he had been so fast with two swords, he'd looked as though he had extra arms. Like Hanshiro, he was a *rōnin*. His master had died in the bed of a famous *kabuki* actor during the great Fire-of-the-Long-Sleeved-Garment forty-five years ago. The ignominy lay not in the fact that the lord had died with *ano mono*, ''that thing,'' splitting the melon of another man, but that he had died in bed instead of in battle. The tragedy had given rise to a lot of sly poetry about the heat of his passion.

A true warrior observed a quota of one lord per lifetime, and the government forbade loyal retainers from following their masters into the spirit world. Besides, the country had been plagued by peace since Tokugawa Ieyasu had taken power a hundred years ago. Warriors, especially unemployed ones, were as welcome as fleas in a low-class inn, and about as plentiful. Since the gay life in the Yoshiwara had always suited Centipede, he had decided to make a career of his hobby.

Now his hobby was accumulating rumors. He had quite a large collection of them, but he shared it with very few people.

Centipede left his assistant in charge of the gate. The district was deserted by all but merchants' clerks and service people at this hour anyway. He invited Hanshiro into the tiny gate house for a cup of tea.

As he poured, Centipede drew air in through his teeth with a hissing noise. He was concentrating on finding the best way to start the conversation. He was mortified that his carelessness had allowed Cat to disappear. He even felt responsible for the accidental death of the *metsuke*, and he suspected the two events were related somehow.

He decided on noncommittal. "There was some excitement here last night."

"So there was." Hanshiro was a master at noncommittal.

The two sipped in silence for a while.

"She'll have a difficult time hiding," Centipede observed. "She's very beautiful."

"A bell cricket is kept in a cage because of its song."

"The bannerman must be worried." Centipede couldn't resist mentioning Kira's lower rank.

"Keisei," Hanshiro said, and Centipede laughed.

Beautiful women were called *keisei,* "castle falling in ruins," because they often led to the destruction of men and kingdoms. One had destroyed Hanshiro's young lord in Tosa fifteen years ago. The young man had squandered his portion of his family's fortune for the favors of an arrogant, fickle courtesan. His father had posted an act of disownment. Humiliated, impoverished, cut off from his family, the young man had shaved his head and become a mendicant monk. And so, indirectly, a beautiful woman had ruined Hanshiro also and changed the course of his life.

By the end of the hour of the Dragon, Hanshiro had learned a great deal. He had left just enough rumors with Centipede to pay for the information. More important, he had listened to the old man's reminiscences of the times long past. He had shared with him the anomie of living among *samurai* obsessed with money and the acquisition of goods.

Finally, Hanshiro stuck his long-sword's scabbard into his sash at a precise angle to the right of his short-sword. He passed silk cords through the loops of the scabbards and secured them to the sash. He bowed and left Centipede brooding over his fifth cup of tea.

Hanshiro knew which people to talk to along the route into the city. He met with success at the fifth try.

When he reached the eel seller's stall he bowed low and actually gave a flicker of a smile. He had sought information here often, and he knew that this one required more than money. To get full value from her he had to show he shared her sense of cosmic irony. "Did you see a slender commoner in a Nakagawa Freight uniform pass here last night? A little after the hour of the Rat?"

The old woman stared at him blankly, her eyes wide as an owl's. "My hearing is bad, Your Honor."

Hanshiro added ten paper-wrapped *mon* to the pile in his palm. The eel seller slipped them into her sleeve. Then she went back to tending her rack of charring eels. "I might have. My sight is not very good, either."

Hanshiro patiently added ten more coins.

"Ten more would help my memory." She smiled fondly at him as he wrapped the coins. She smiled at him the way a cat smiled at the hand holding the fish entrails.

"Yes, I saw her. A young woman dressed as a dirt-eater. Very convincing. But she smelled of camellia oil, and she reached up to arrange hair that was no longer on her head. Also, her hand was uncallused."

"Who was with her?"

"No one."

"No one?"

"No one." The old woman grinned toothlessly at him. "But for the insignificant sum of ten more coppers, my memory might improve enough to tell you where she went."

Hanshiro complied.

"When she left here she was reading a playbill."

"Which theater?"

"Alas, coppers enough to choke a priest wouldn't improve my rheumy old eyes that much."

Hanshiro bowed low and gave her ten more coins, for luck. She handed him half a section of bamboo heaped with rice and with a savory eel lying across the top. He ate as he headed for the theater district.

"Tosa-san," she called after him. When he returned she spoke in a much lower voice. "There's one you should beware of."

"One of Uesugi's men?"

"No, although Kira's son's toadies are on the prowl after your pretty dirt-eater. This is a young westcountryman. A *rōnin* like yourself. From Akō, judging by the accent. He's been asking questions."

Hanshiro paused a moment. The westcountryman was probably from Asano's estate in Akō, or one of Asano's neighbors, perhaps hired by Kira because he knew what Cat looked like.

Hanshiro left the eel seller with something better than coppers. He smiled at her. She probably appreciated the rarity of the gift.

He went to Shichisaburo's theater, the Nakamura-za, first because Shichisaburo was on the list given to him by the mistress of the Perfumed Lotus. Also, Centipede had told him the actor wasn't actually matching his bird to Cat's nest when he arranged assignations with her. Something was amiss in that.

Besides, Shichisaburo was a versatile actor, and Hanshiro liked his style. He hadn't adopted the vulgar new "rough stuff" method of acting so popular with Edo's merchants and *samurai*. Hanshiro agreed with the theater critic who said Shichisaburo was like patent medicine, good for everything.

CHAPTER 9
TO CROSS THE EXPANSE

Cat was strong, but she wasn't used to walking. By the time she reached the village of Kawasaki, a mere two *ri* and three *cho* from the Shinagawa barrier, her feet and legs ached. The pack's straps were digging painfully into her shoulders.

She stopped at a shop displaying a stack of plump rice balls, each wrapped in a sheet of dark green, iridescent seaweed. She gathered her resolve. She would have to engage in the vulgar exchange of money for goods, or she would starve. She pointed to the rice balls and held out two precious coppers.

The shopkeeper looked astonished, then angry. "Please accept this as a humble donation." As he put a ball into Cat's begging bowl, he bowed with excessive courtesy. The bow was so exaggerated, it was unmistakably insulting.

Cat could see that the rice ball had been dropped in the dirt. "May the merciful Buddha bless you," she said.

"Two coppers for a rice ball!" he muttered as Cat walked away. "Does he take me for a fool?"

Cat was so hungry that she brushed off the dirt and slid the ball under the rim of the basket so she could eat it. It was stale and brittle, and it tasted like chaff in her mouth. Cat did not like the view of the world from the other side of a begging bowl. Her hand trembled in humiliation and rage.

Cat's indifference toward commoners was hardening into a tight knot of loathing. She would have given her life to assemble her *naginata* there in the crowded, dusty road and to pin the rice ball vendor like a fly to the wall of his shop. But her life was not hers to give. The stakes were much higher than that.

Even after eating the dry rice cake Cat felt dizzy with hunger. She limped to a spot of sunlight against a wall that blocked the cold wind. She leaned on her staff for support and watched the cheerful traffic stream by.

She realized that she would face problems that hadn't occurred to her when she thought she could reach Kyōto in ten days. She didn't know what food or lodging cost, or the price of a bath or the ferry across the Tama River on the other side of Kawasaki. She couldn't even do something as simple as buy rice.

"Are you thirsty, holy one?" A young tea seller, perhaps nine or ten years old, stopped in front of her.

His spindly hips were draped in a loincloth worn thin as gauze with age. His torn paper jacket was belted with the straw cord from a rice bale. His conical rush hat advised people to visit Mitsui *sake* shop, where there were "Cash sales" and "No fancy prices." Even in the chill of early winter his feet were bare.

Two wooden water buckets, almost half his height, hung from the pole he carried across his right shoulder. Balanced on top of the front bucket was a two-tiered tray with wooden slats forming its high sides. It held four chipped bowls, a lacquered tea canister, and bamboo utensils. On top of the lid of the rear bucket perched a tiny iron charcoal brazier and kettle.

"How much is your tea?" Cat felt more comfortable discussing money with a child.

"No charge." The boy studied Cat. "Are you still hungry?"

"Yes."

"How many coppers do you have?"

Cat searched through the pocket formed by the seam that closed the bottom two-thirds of her jacket sleeve opening. She held out the ten-copper piece the old man had given her at the barrier and five *mon*, all she had managed to beg.

The boy raised his eyebrows at the fiscal incompetence of this priest. Then he took the money and disappeared into the crowd. Cat was beginning to berate herself for letting him rob her when he returned with two fat, fresh rice cakes wrapped in bamboo leaves artistically formed into tetrahedrons, and a small packet of pickled radish. He handed them to her, then set down his buckets.

"Nosewater," he shouted to a passing noodle seller.

Cat flinched. The last thing she wanted was attention. She took off her pack and sat wearily, cross-legged, on the ground.

"You owe me a fist, remember? For the *sake*," the tea seller said.

"Suck it, Jōshū," the other boy replied amiably. Strapped on his back was a high box whose narrow shelves contained bowls of buckwheat noodles. "I only owe you four fingers."

"A fist. But give me two bowls and we're even."

The noodle vendor reluctantly handed over two bowls of cold buckwheat noodles and stood waiting for Jōshū and the priest to empty them.

Cat would have to take off her big hat to eat. Next door, however, were the stables and courtyard of Kawasaki's post station. The office building itself was set back from the road so the porters, messengers, and horses gathered there wouldn't snarl the foot traffic. In the courtyard, *kago* bearers, hostlers, and off-duty couriers lounged in the sun.

On the *tatami* mats inside the low, open-fronted transport office sat a flock of clerks in identical robes. One of their main occupations was keeping tabs on the likes of Cat. With their ink stones and brushes and rolls of paper they were as dangerous, in their way, as the police and Kira's retainers.

Cat turned away from the transport office and took off the tall hat. When she shook her high-set tassel of hair, dust flew from it. If someone recognized her, so be it. She couldn't reach the Western Capital if she starved to death first. She held out her hands for the bowl of noodles.

If the boys noticed Cat's delicate features, they said nothing.

They had seen too many strange goings-on to comment on the foibles of a *komuso*, a priest of empty nothing. Most of them were mad to begin with, and not a few were fallen aristocrats and dangerous men.

Jōshū handed Cat a pair of chopsticks, and she didn't even look to see if they were clean. She didn't worry that someone of her rank didn't eat in the streets like an ill-bred commoner. She devoured the noodles and gave the vendor back the bowl. Then she ate one of the rice cakes and the pickles. She wrapped the other in her thin towel and stowed it in her sleeve to eat later.

"Tell Suruga I'm looking for him," Jōshū called as the tall noodle stand bobbed back into traffic.

Jōshū wiped out a narrow teacup with the dangling end of his loincloth. Squatting in the dust, he used a tiny bamboo ladle, hardly bigger than an ear pick, to measure out the coarse dried black leaves and stems of the cheapest grade of tea. He set the small kettle onto the brazier to warm.

"It would be most fortunate to meet someone who could see the future." Jōshū artfully arranged his request into a polite oblique as he waited for the water to heat.

"Reading events to come is not my talent." Cat saw disappointment skim across the boy's face. "Why do you need to know the future?"

"My parents died while we were on pilgrimage. I want to know if I'll ever see my village again."

"Do you have six coppers?" Cat wiped her fingers on her dusty robe and held them out. Jōshū dipped water from his bucket and poured it over them. Reading the future was holy work. It required purification.

Jōshū laid down one of the wooden lids for Cat to work on. His purse hung from a long cord around his neck. He pulled it up from the depths of his paper jacket and separated six *mon* from the string of them.

"I haven't the eight diagrams, so this will be only a simplified reading." Cat shook the coins in her closed hands.

Like all the women who lived in the House of the Carp, Cat had had her future read often by the blind masseuse who doubled as a diviner. She knew the simplest of the more than eleven thousand combinations, and in any case, she was determined to make up a bright future for Jōshū.

She laid the coins out in a vertical line on the lid, and the boy leaned closer. He was trying to see happiness, or at least a

thatched roof and a daily bowl of rice, in the combination of the
coins' stamped and plain sides.

As Cat studied the results she sucked in her breath, hissing
with pleasure. All the coins had landed with their stamped sides
up, a rare combination. She would not have to lie to him.

"Will it be a good life?" he asked anxiously. A few people
stopped to look over his shoulder. Then a few more.

"This is a pairing of two Heaven combinations. Very manly."
Cat was so intent on the message in the coins, she didn't notice
the small crowd of people craning to see.

"Extreme happiness will follow sorrow." Cat was astonished
at her own elation over his good fortune. "A dragon rising to
Heaven is your symbol. Even if you're not doing well right now,
your worries and troubles will diminish. But you must work hard
for success."

"Ma!" Jōshū murmured. "You don't say!"

When Cat scooped up the coins to return them, he held up
his hand, refusing them. He gave her a hempen cord and showed
her how to thread it through the square hole in the center of each
copper, then knot them in place. It was a small accomplishment,
but it gave Cat the sudden, heady feeling that she could learn
the arcane ways of commerce. She could survive in the world
of merchants. She smiled as she put the small string into her
sleeve.

"Do me the kindness of reading my future, holy one." A
woman set down the two huge cloth-wrapped packages she carried and squatted in front of Cat. The child who rode on her
back and shared her oversize coat peered out from the big, loose
collar. The woman held out six coins.

"I am weary," Cat said. "Let me rest a few minutes." She
was having trouble keeping her eyes open.

"Go on." Jōshū shooed them away. "The holy one has traveled far. Can't you see he's exhausted?"

Reluctantly, the crowd dispersed.

From the direction of Edo a jangle of bells approached. The
tips of two messengers' spears, with their thick black fringe of
horsehair, bobbed above the traffic. Travelers moved toward the
side of the road, and a pair of couriers panted into the yard of
the transport office.

They weren't the regularly scheduled runners, and Jōshū
smelled intrigue. Intrigue was more than just entertainment for
him. From time to time he was able to exchange his knowledge

for coppers. "Will the honorable holy one do me the august favor of watching my shop?"

Without waiting for an answer, Jōshū abandoned his water buckets and tea tray to Cat's care. The last Cat saw of him were the blackened soles of his feet as he wriggled through a well-worn hole under the post station's plastered wall.

Cat leaned her lower back against her own wall, crossed her arms on her raised knees, and rested her head on them. The sun felt warm on the top of her head. The noise of the Tōkaidō faded and surged and echoed around her. Worms of light swam in front of her eyes.

Jōshū found her sleeping there a few minutes later. He studied the top of her head. The priest was pretty enough to be the one the authorities sought. But if he were the woman, surely she wouldn't be napping here like a chicken in the dust next to the government office.

"Holy one." Jōshū shouldered his pole and adjusted the buckets to balance. "I have to sell the rest of my tea."

Cat tried to force her eyes open against the fatigue that weighted the lids. "What message do they carry?" she asked.

"A courtesan ran away. They think she may be heading for the west country." Jōshū was disappointed that the news had been so uninteresting.

"Is she wanted for any crime?"

"No." Jōshū considered her a moment. "There's a place where you can sleep, holy one, away from noise and curious eyes."

He led Cat between the buildings to the beach beyond. He maneuvered his pole and buckets among the nets and drying racks and boats until he stood in front of a half-rotted hull. It was turned upside down, with one gunwale in the sand and the other propped up by a broken rudder.

Cat lay down gratefully on the raveled mat Jōshū spread out under the boat. She cradled the walking staff in her arms. A tattered scrap of a quilt and a few broken utensils were wedged up into the thwarts overhead. Jōshū took down the quilt and spread it over her.

A pair of wooden tablets with Jōshū's parents' death names written on them were fastened to the ceiling formed by the boat's broken floorboards. Stubs of incense sticks bristled from the sand. A bowl of cooked rice with chopsticks stuck into it and a thimbleful of water were mute evidence that Jōshū had been faithfully providing for his parents' well-being in the spirit world.

"Buddha of the Boundless Light will bless you, child," Cat murmured before she fell asleep.

She slept through the hours of the Snake and Horse. She slept through the rainstorm that produced a flowering of bright, water-repellent paper umbrellas and big straw rain hats along the road and sent unprepared travelers scurrying for cover. She slept until the moist crunch of feet in the sand woke her. Without changing the rate of her breathing, she slipped her hand into her sash and found the scissors.

"Holy man." The voice was gruff. Cat tightened her grip on the scissors. "Jōshū says you're a diviner."

In spite of the introduction, of sorts, Cat almost stabbed the face that peered under the dripping gunwale. The man's vein-laced nose had been broken two or three times. The bulbous tip of it slanted toward the lumpy left ear growing like a fungus on the side of his head.

He had shaved his eyebrows, exposing the thick ridge of bone over his bulging eyes. His bristle of black hair poked out from under a towel, rolled into a narrow tube, wrapped around his head, and knotted above his left ear.

At first glance Cat thought his head was being swallowed by a snake. A snake's distended jaws had been tattooed along his own jawline. The lower and upper fangs bracketed his puffy-looking lips. A forked red tongue flicked across his nose. A pattern of blue scales covered his chin and ran down his neck.

"What do you want?" Cat asked.

"To beg a favor of you. In return, to offer you food and lodging."

"And a bath?"

"My wretched hovel has few amenities, but certainly you can bathe there."

Musashi wrote that to cross the expanse one must assess the perils, the directions, the obstacles. Cat realized, with a heavy feeling in the pit of her stomach, that she didn't know what the perils and obstacles of the Tōkaidō were. She didn't know whom she could trust and whom she must fear. As she crawled out from under the boat, she saw that this was certainly a man to fear. She decided to trust him.

He was squat, with long, powerful arms. The thick calluses on his shoulders marked him as a *kago* bearer. The snake tattoo that started at his face wound in thick coils down his neck, across his chest, and around his torso. The tail disappeared into the pouch of the loincloth that was his only clothing. Cat suspected that the tip of the tail ended at the tip of *ano mono*.

He hissed politely as he bowed. "For reasons obvious to all but a blind man, these stewed tea loaf fools call me Mamushi no Jiro, Viper." He gestured at the world in general. It was the sort of name a bandit or gambler would adopt, and Viper seemed pleased with it.

He motioned her toward a flimsy bamboo *kago* sitting on the sand. Another bearer squatted beside it. As Viper slogged off through the sand, he hitched up his loincloth and tightened it for the work ahead. Cat stared, fascinated, at the golden-and-black-striped tiger face covering his bare, tightly muscled buttocks.

The narrow white roll of loincloth partially obscured the pink nose at the point where his nether cleavage began. The huge eyes glowered from either side of it. The tiger's cheeks followed the contours of the nates, and when Viper walked, his great cat seemed to be chewing thoughtfully.

Cat knew that to cross the expanse she would have to trust her own instincts. Her instincts told her Viper was offering her more than shelter. He was offering her sanctuary.

"What do you want of me?" She pulled her staff and pack from under the boat.

"To speak to the dead."

CHAPTER 10
THINGS LATELY FASHIONABLE

Hanshiro's posture marked him as a true swordsman. And for the eye untrained in such subtleties, his two swords were usually warning enough. The hem of his baggy, thigh-length coat rode up over the scabbards. They formed the distinctive silhouette that identified him as a warrior and a man to avoid. But bearing and a pair of swords didn't always ensure respect, certainly not here in Edo's theater district.

Hanshiro ignored the acrobat who trotted along on his palms beside him. He had wrapped his feet around his neck and held a begging bowl in his agile toes. He jingled the few *mon* inside it beguilingly. Safe in his haven of imbecility, he tilted his head sideways to grin up at Hanshiro.

"Read your fortune, honorable sir?" asked a heap of paper rags. The diviner inside them sat on a small square mat. His divining sticks were laid out in front of him.

He was blind and couldn't see Hanshiro's scowl or his swords. The scowl deepened and hardened. It was a look that usually guaranteed Hanshiro wouldn't be bothered, but in the theater district bothering people was the principal occupation.

Hanshiro joined the crowd of theatergoers and sightseers, peddlers, street entertainers, and beggars, holy and profane. The narrow roadway was lined with fifteen-foot-tall poles. The white banners that hung vertically from them were painted with the actors' crests and bold black ideograms announcing the plays.

Shops and tea houses, built side by side, fronted directly on the street. Posters of the actors in their most famous poses covered the walls. Strings of spherical, red paper lanterns decorated the first- and second-floor eaves. From the balconies, people called down to their friends passing below. Drums sounded continually as touts tried to attract attention. The noise of people hawking everything from firewood to love amulets reverberated off the walls, making it difficult to hear anything below a shout.

Even though the opening dance had started at dawn and the actors were well into the first play, the river imps were still at work here. Like the *kappa*, their demon namesakes, they plucked at the sleeves of likely customers and tried to draw them into the theaters.

"Come to the finest show in Edo." They bowed and wheedled and circled their victims. "Witness the tragic story of the courtesan Oshu. Your tears will saturate your sleeves."

"Buy a program. Buy a program." Younger boys wore foot-tall wooden pattens called *geta* and waved the booklets over their heads so they'd be seen in the press of people.

To get their money's worth, country folk had left their homes at two in the morning, the hour of the Ox, to arrive in time for the first dance. They had long since rented small mats to sit on and had settled into their places, packed shoulder to shoulder with the Edokko on the bare earth of the pit. They had spent the morning eating cold rice from their wooden lunch boxes, smoking their tiny pipes, nursing babies, chatting to each other, and calling out criticism and encouragement to the actors. The pit was redolent with tobacco, pickles, and urine.

Those who rented the expensive box seats were more urbane. They thought it fashionable to come late. Rollicking parties of them brushed by Hanshiro. They wore *geta* to keep their travel cloaks and the hems of their bright robes out of the dust. They twirled parasols painted with flowers and poetry.

Their servants followed with rattan boxes swinging from poles over their shoulders. The boxes contained supplies for a day at the theater—makeup and changes of clothing, playing cards, books, tobacco, and pipes. And most important of all, paper, ink stones, porcelain water containers, and brushes for poetry contests and love notes. Employees from the tea houses hurried alongside, bowing and soliciting business.

The latecomers bought programs and clattered into the slate-paved entryways of the tea houses. They would spend most of the hour of the Snake eating and drinking and discussing the plays. Before going to the theater they would change their street robes for elaborate *kimono*. It would be the first of two or three costume changes they would make before darkness ended the day's performance.

As Hanshiro watched the bright crowds swirl past, he wondered what made people mad for the latest nuance of sash knot or sleeve length. The zeal with which people pursued such absurdities mystified him. Fashions changed, but the mania for being fashionable endured the ages. The theater district always made him think of a song written almost five hundred years earlier.

> Things lately fashionable in the capital:
> Painted eyebrows, hairdos, hairpieces,
> Saltwater bath robes, women in men's clothes,
> And not a nun who doesn't have her *naginata*.

"Here you are, here you are!" One of the wicket *geisha* beckoned to Hanshiro. On a long bench next to the theater's doorway he danced and shouted enticements to the crowd. "Buy a ticket and see the famous Shichisaburo perform in the tragic story of Oshu. See the spirit of the famous courtesan rise from the flames of her lover's letter. Step inside. Step inside."

The wicket *geisha* wore a woman's robes and a blue towel draped over his head and tied under his chin. The towel was dyed with Shichisaburo's crest. The *geisha* stalked the length of the bench in Shichisaburo's soft-stuff style. He flourished his open fan over his head, cocked his other elbow, crossed his eyes, and struck a *mie*, the particular pose Shichisaburo had made famous. Then he squatted to be at eye level with Hanshiro.

"You look like a man of fine sensibilities, *rōnin*." He shielded his mouth with his fan, as though sharing a secret. "The new impersonator, Dragonfly, from Osaka, acts the part of the doomed courtesan. He's very sensual. Irresistible."

Hanshiro hardly spared him a scrap of his glower. He strode through the stacks of cake and clothing boxes and *sake* barrels, gifts from adoring patrons to their favorite actors. Many of them bore Shichisaburo's crest.

Hanshiro turned into the alleyway, behind Shichisaburo's theater, the Nakamura-za. Casually, as though only passing time, he used the butt of his old parasol to scatter the heap of trash there. He didn't expect to find anything, but from what people threw away he could reconstruct entire lives.

At the bottom of the pile he found the charred remains of a blue hempen coat. The white characters for Nakagawa were still visible. With hundreds of secondhand stores and pawnshops in the city, no one threw away clothing unless they had a good reason.

Hanshiro was waiting for Shichisaburo when he made his dramatic exit. The agitated clacking of wooden blocks signaled the climax of the first act. It was accompanied by shouts of "That's the way, Shichisaburo!" from the audience.

A pair of black-clad, masked, hooded, and stockinged assistants followed Shichisaburo. They had hovered about him on stage, adjusting his sixty pounds of layered, weighted, gold-and-silver-embroidered robes each time he moved. They continued to do it here.

Beyond the black curtain Hanshiro could hear the rustle and murmur of people stampeding for the passageways to the nearby tea houses. The tea houses had privies. The theater didn't.

"I haven't time to chat." Shichisaburo was preoccupied.

His lady love had sneaked out of the *shōgun*'s palace and into the city. She was waiting for him in a back room of the tea house next door. As a pledge of her affection she had sent her fingernail clipping in a tiny jade box. Anticipation had Shichisaburo in a fevered state.

Hanshiro held out the handle of the parasol with the charred jacket dangling from the end of it. Shichisaburo blanched under his thick crust of rice powder makeup, but he put on a brave show. Earlier that morning he had convinced Kira's retainers that he was ignorant of the young Lady Asano's whereabouts. Shichisaburo was, after all, an actor. The simple westcountryman from Akō had fared no better with him.

"I've already told Lord Kira's rabble I know nothing of the matter." Shichisaburo looked around for help as Hanshiro, stifflegged, silent, and somehow much larger than the physical space he occupied, crowded him toward the stairs to the dressing rooms.

The mob of Shichisaburo's female admirers shouted their offers of love and/or marriage and/or a brief dalliance from a safe distance, a tribute to the ferocity of Hanshiro's demeanor. Ordinarily they would have crowded close to press flowers and gifts and middling but fervent verse on their idol.

The shadowy stage assistants prudently disappeared, leaving Shichisaburo to tussle with his costume and the surly stranger. As he climbed the narrow stairs, the long train of his heavy robes tangled with his feet. The sleeves of his huge outer coat were four feet square and stiffened with bamboo splints. The bamboo caught on the door frame and bent backward. When they released and sprang back into shape, one of them bruised Shichisaburo's hand. He was rubbing it dolefully when he reached the upstairs dressing room.

Hanshiro spread a silk cloth on the *tatami* and laid his longsword on it. With his left hand he deftly slapped the baggy hem of each *hakama* leg out of the way as he crossed his legs and sat down.

When he was comfortably seated he regarded the actor with a chilly smile. "Now, honorable riverbed-beggar, tell me what you know."

CHAPTER 11
NOT AT HOME

Fragile skeletons of half-finished umbrellas crouched like giant insects in the corners of the room. The smell of glue was almost overpowering. Hanshiro's contemplation of his new, red oiled-paper umbrella was interrupted by crockery hitting the other side of the thin wooden wall.

"Cockroach!" a woman shouted. Another bowl crashed.

The old umbrella maker hammered on his side of the wall with a length of loquat wood. His workshop was so tiny that he didn't have to leave his seat to do it. Plaster had fallen away from the many such beatings the wall had received.

"Be a man," he shrieked at the woman's unseen husband. "Beat the fox demon! Drive her away! Find yourself a handsome boy to love!"

"*Chikusho!*" she screamed back. "Four-legged beast!" Another crash.

"The fool is spread under a woman's buttocks." Still muttering, the umbrella maker concluded his business with Hanshiro.

He bowed until his forehead rested on the floor, and Hanshiro inclined his head slightly in return. When the old man took Hanshiro's paper-wrapped coins, his fingertips were hard and shiny with dried glue. Hanshiro imagined his heart encased in the same impervious stuff.

For fifteen years Hanshiro had come to this dark Edo alleyway for his umbrellas. For fifteen years he had pushed aside the same dusty bamboo blind. He had seen the same clutter, each item of which appeared in exactly the same place it had been on his first visit. He had waded through the fluttering drifts of colored paper scraps on frayed *tatami* so old it was soft and sunken in places. He had sat cross-legged among the bamboo parasol skeletons and sipped weak tea with the old misogynist.

For his regular customers, the umbrella maker always kept in stock a few parasols made of tough loquat wood rather than bamboo. They were the only kind Hanshiro bought.

As he left the shop Hanshiro looked around him gloomily. Except for a more pronounced stoop to the umbrella maker's shoulders and an ever-sharper loathing for women, the old man hadn't changed in the years Hanshiro had known him. His tiny shop was still squeezed between a seedy bathhouse and a store whose faded banner promised a remedy for unwanted hair. But the neighborhood around his shop had altered considerably, as had Edo itself. The changes weighed on Hanshiro's spirit.

As always, shabby, dark pine shutters shielded the merchants' houses from the dust and noise of the narrow street. But behind them the rice brokers and hardware sellers, the wholesalers of tea and clothing, *sake* and lacquerware, lived in forbidden splendor. After each of the fires that swept through Edo, the merchants rebuilt their houses larger than before. Hanshiro scowled as he stalked past the illusory poverty.

None of the five Tokugawa *shōgun* had been able to prevent the despised merchant class from accumulating great sums of money; they could only forbid the flaunting of it. Tokugawa Tsunayoshi allowed no cedar doors, no frieze beams or fine woods, no openwork or lacquering. But as with the restrictions on travel and clothing, the townsmen found ways around the edicts.

They threw lavish parties in the pleasure districts that were officially off limits to the upper classes. Under their drab hempen robes flashed brilliant silk linings in crimson or plum or green the color of a cicada's wing. On the walls of their inner rooms hung rare works of art. Behind the grimy, soot-darkened facades of their houses were sumptuous palaces of fragrant cypress and cryptomeria wood, and white-plastered storehouses stacked to the rafters with chests of silks and lacquerware and porcelain.

The world was topsy-turvy here. The natural order had gone awry. Lowly exchangers of goods and that most vulgar of commodities, money, lived like princes. Worse yet, while the emperor, the descendent of O-Amaterasu the Sun Goddess and rightful ruler of Japan, languished in faded splendor in Kyōto, the Tokugawa usurpers ran the country.

Each succeeding *shōgun* had recruited more men from outside the ranks of the classically trained warriors. Now they brawled in the streets with the lower classes. They swaggered about Edo wearing the two swords of *samurai* while the real warriors, the *bushi* like Hanshiro, wondered where they would get their next *koku* of rice.

Hanshiro hadn't taken long to prepare for this trip. The umbrella was the last necessity. He had bought his favorite brands of tobacco and tooth powder in the shop next to the umbrella maker's, the one that also sold the remedy for unwanted hair. He had visited the apothecary and replenished his supply of ginseng, bear's gall bladder, and oil of toad.

In the two-*tatami* room he rented on a noisome back alley, he rinsed out his thin cotton towel. He put on his black *tabi*. He tied his faded black canvas gaiters around the wide skirts of his *hakama* to keep the hems from the dust and to make walking easier. He slipped his travel permit into the flat wallet that contained his paper handkerchiefs and put it into the front opening of the loose, faded jacket that had lost its shape at the shoulders.

He stuck into the back of his patched sash the heavy war fan with the sharpened iron ribs.

When he had stowed each of the journey's modest necessities into its accustomed place, he rolled his other wadded cotton coat and his old paper rain cloak inside a thin mat woven of rushes. He tied a long straw cord around each end of the mat and slung the resulting loop across his chest so the mat rode high on his back.

He had tried to find one of the books portraying the famous courtesans of Edo. The young artist Masanobu had included Cat's portrait in them. But all the copies had mysteriously disappeared. Lord Kira probably had ordered them bought up. He would want to keep Lady Asano's picture from the avid public. If word got out that Lord Asano had a daughter and she had been employed in the Yoshiwara, gossip about the entire affair would be revived.

In fact, Hanshiro suspected most of the books had been bought as keepsakes. The folk of Edo, high class and low, followed the fashions and gossip of the Floating World. A small army of messengers had left the pleasure district that morning to spread the news of the odd contents of the *sake* barrel in the House of the Perfumed Lotus, the accidental immolation of Lord Kira's cousin, and the disappearance of the lovely courtesan named Cat.

Hanshiro hefted his new umbrella in his hand, testing the balance of the heavy, lacquered cording on the butt of the handle. He opened it, taking a somber delight in the crimson of the oiled paper, clear and translucent as poppy petals. He spread his damp towel across the convex surface to dry, rested the handle on his shoulder, and rocked it back and forth gently so the towel wouldn't fall off.

For Hanshiro joy and sorrow were frivolous indulgences, unworthy of a man of his calling. But now that he was leaving Edo, a diffuse aura of pleasure put a bounce in his step. No matter that the job was a trifling one. He felt buoyant as a fifth-month paper carp swimming in the currents of the wind above the rooftops. For Hanshiro the warrior's Way was most easily traveled on the road.

He turned off a *ri* before the barrier at Shinagawa. He tied the towel around his wrist and closed the umbrella. Then he walked down the double row of ancient maples, almost bare of leaves now, and through the ornate, roofed wooden gate of Spring Hill Temple. A group of children played among the tombstones in a far corner. The ringing of small bells and the muffled chanting of priests emanated from the temple's main hall.

A shabby palanquin, its wickerwork torn, lay toppled and abandoned under a large willow near Lord Asano's grave. The bearers and attendants obviously had fled. At the grave itself, four men surrounded a small figure wearing over her head the large white scarf of a Buddhist nun.

The men wore nondescript clothes, but even without seeing the crest of three paulownia leaves, Hanshiro was sure Kira had sent them. He would be trying every means possible to find his enemy's daughter before she incited the Akō men to revenge. But he would be discreet. He was already in enough trouble.

The fugitive called Cat must have exchanged Shichisaburo's monk's disguise for a nun's, but Hanshiro saw that he had guessed right. She had come to her father's grave to pray for his soul. Kira's men had caught her. Now all Hanshiro had to do was take her from them. He was disappointed. He had allowed himself to look forward to the chase.

Two of the men shoved their captive toward the palanquin, and the scarf fell away. The woman's eyes were calm, remote, as though none of this had anything to do with her. Even with her head shaven she was beautiful, but she certainly wasn't young enough to be Asano's daughter.

Hanshiro leaned his umbrella against a tree. Fanning himself casually, he stepped into the open.

"Move, stray dog." One of the men tried to push past him while a second held the woman's arm and the other two drew their swords.

Moving too fast to be seen, Hanshiro snapped the iron fan closed and drove it into the closest man's neck, just under his ear. He fell like a stone down a well and lay unconscious. From his ineptness Hanshiro judged him to be a hireling and not one of Uesugi's well-trained retainers.

The one holding the woman shoved her aside, and he and the other two circled, carefully. They weren't very skilled, but they weren't stupid, either. They could see that the rōnin was faster than anyone they'd faced. They knew that if they attacked him at once, they would most likely end up slicing each other.

As always when in battle, Hanshiro fell into *mushin*, "no-mind." His mind and his body were one. His body and his weapons were one. He and his opponents were one. He could react, without conscious thought, to their moves, just as he could react to the fingers of his own hands. Hanshiro could tell from his opponents' stances that being-not-being was a state they talked about, bragged about, strived for, and had never attained.

Hanshiro raised the fan into the path of the second sword as it swept downward toward his skull. So far, the contest had been almost silent. Now steel rang against iron, and the sword snapped. The broken end clattered onto the paving stones.

The children stopped their play and lined up to watch from behind the tombstones. Pain from the impact of the sword on the fan ran like an electrical current up Hanshiro's arm. The man drew his short-sword but warily kept his distance. Hanshiro could tell from his eyes and his posture that he was considering flight. He was beaten already.

Hanshiro's graceful dance of thrust and parry continued as he used the New Shadow school technique of ''circling crows'' to avoid his opponents' strikes. The fact that he didn't bother to draw his long-sword enraged the other two. They knew they were being mocked.

Holding his sword raised in both hands, the third man attacked from the rear. Hanshiro whirled, ducked, and dropped sideways to one knee, his other knee bent and his foot braced in front of him. His lunge brought him up between the man's two arms and his sword. He shoved his shoulder into his opponent's groin and raised his other arm, pushing the fan up under the man's chin, paralyzing his windpipe. The *samurai* dropped onto all fours, gagging and trying in vain to suck in air.

The fourth shouted his name and charged an opponent who was no longer there. He screamed in pain as Hanshiro slammed the fan onto his fingers, crushing bones against the sword hilt.

The first man was still unconscious. The second sheathed his short-sword, turned tail, and fled. The other two were no threat. The woman had disappeared, probably taking refuge with the monks, who were also prudently absent.

As Hanshiro turned to go, he saw a knotted, blue silk scarf dropped by the nun. Printed in the center were two crossed feathers, the Akō-Asano crest. The nun had been either Lady Asano or Lord Asano's outside-wife.

When Hanshiro untied the knot, the four corners fell away and hung over the edges of his big, outspread hands. In the center of the scarf lay a shiny black coil of hair. Hanshiro raised it to his face and smelled it.

Sandalwood. Musk. The camellia oil with which the shampooer had dressed Cat's hair. The sensuous aromas brought back Cat's rooms, complete in every detail, except one, her face. Hanshiro retied the scarf and put it inside his jacket, next to his travel papers. The wind chilled the sweat on his face, and he wiped it with his sleeve.

He realized he was slightly short of breath. His fingers were numb from the sword blows to his fan. Sparks, like tiny fireworks, exploded in front of his eyes.

Hanshiro wondered what his *sensei* would think of his performance. *Not much*, he thought. He almost smiled at the memory of entering the gate of the No-Sword school and challenging the master.

By the time Hanshiro had been sixteen he could beat anyone in a street fight. And brawls were common between the Yamanouchi family's peasant recruits and young warriors still loyal to the old order. At sixteen Hanshiro was already strong and fast and fearless. He had been absolutely sure he could beat the old man in spite of his reputation.

As he remembered what happened, Hanshiro actually allowed himself the briefest of grins. "Come at me any way you want," *sensei* had said as he stood with hands empty.

So with a shout, Hanshiro attacked. He felt the blow on his chest that rattled his teeth and knocked the breath out of him, but he never saw it. The hardwood floor flew up and hit his back, and his sword slithered across it.

Sensei had looked down at him, no trace of amusement or triumph in his mild eyes. "Try again."

Hanshiro did. He tried all day, until evening shadows darkened the practice hall and Hanshiro was so exhausted he could barely pick himself up from the floor. *Sensei* looked as rested as when he started. "The Way of a warrior," he said, "is a road of the mind, not a road of the body."

Hanshiro remembered every detail of that day. It had been raining when he left the school, and his arms had been too tired to open his umbrella. But he had reported at the gate of the No-Sword school before daybreak the next morning to sweep the grounds and clean the floor. He studied with *sensei* for nine years, until he could fight challenger after challenger, for days if need be.

Five years ago a fight like this wouldn't even have caused him to sweat. He thought of the old poem that had meant so little to him five years ago.

> If only, when one heard
> That Old Age was coming
> One could bolt the door,
> Answer "Not at home"
> And refuse to meet him!

Not at home. Hanshiro rumbled an old drinking song far back in his throat as he set off toward the Great Eastern Seaway, the Tōkaidō Road.

CHAPTER 12

SIDETRACKS

As Viper trotted toward the foothills west of Kawasaki, his song blew back in great gusts around Cat.

> What I like to lie beside,
> The body of a young girl.
> Her flesh is smooth
> And firm as bean curd.

Sitting cross-legged, Cat clung to a strap hanging from the carrying pole running across the top of the flimsy contrivance. She had ridden many times in palanquins, but she had never had a ride like this one. Cat weighed so little, the *kago* felt almost empty to Viper and his companion, Hiyameshi no Jimbei, whom Viper referred to as Cold Rice.

> Sleep with her one night,
> And you're mixed up seven days after.

Viper and Cold Rice sang ditties that the family servants wouldn't have dared repeat in Cat's presence; and they sang them lustily.

> The body of the young girl
> Is beau-u-u-tiful!

Cat's mother's palanquin had been a lacquered wicker coach three times this size, with silken cushions and gilded interior. Now Cat sat on a dirty straw mat infested with fleas. Her flea powder was in the pack strapped to the carrying pole.

This was a mountain *kago*, built as light as possible for carrying up steep slopes. It was only a large, shallow circular basket hanging from the carrying pole by triangular woven panels at front and back. A flat, rectangular mat served as a roof. The entire contraption squeaked and groaned rhythmically to the beat of Viper's bare feet. Cat's staff was tied alongside the *kago*'s carrying pole, and the iron rings jangled loudly.

As Cat bounced along she felt as though her organs were being wedged up into her chest. For what seemed hours, Viper and his partner had headed toward the line of blue-green hills to the west. They were following a raised path through the brown rice paddies that covered the southern edge of the broad plain of Musashi. Cat looked out at the farmers thrashing rice or measuring it under the watchful eyes of the government's tax collectors.

She watched the tiny hamlets pass, one after the other. They all looked alike to her—ramshackle huts and small garden plots perched on higher ground, surrounded by brown, stubbly fields and irrigation ditches. The women sat in their dooryards spinning yarn or cranking small rice hullers. The dusty, half-naked children stared at Cat as she passed.

In his *Wind* book Musashi warned that to all Ways there were sidetracks. "If you follow the true Way and diverge a little," Musashi wrote, "this will later become a large divergence."

This was becoming a large divergence. Cat was about to shout at Viper, to tell him to stop, when he turned onto a precipitous track hacked from the side of the first high hill. Cat fell against the flimsy back of the *kago* as the front of it tilted upward abruptly.

She had a terrible headache, and with each bounce pain chipped away at the backs of her eyeballs. Hunger and the jostling had unsettled her stomach, and she tasted bile rising in her throat. How did one tell, she wondered, if one's present situation resulted from *karma* or merely a stupid decision?

"Go on, go on!" From the rear of the palanquin, Cold Rice called encouragement to his partner. "Are you asleep up there?"

"You're the one who sleeps," Viper shouted good-naturedly over his shoulder. "I hear that while you're away your wife powders her face with rice flour. She waits with her rolled mat under the Bungo Bridge and services the bargemen.''

"Your old woman consorts with badgers and grave diggers."

At the next jolt, Cat's head hit the carrying pole. Her teeth snapped shut on her tongue, and pain coursed through her mouth. She tasted blood. She was furious.

She held on to the bamboo frame and leaned out to berate Viper's bare buttocks and soles, the only parts of him visible, and she stared over the edge of the footpath and into a deep, boulder-choked ravine. Hastily she pulled back inside. This was not the place to get into an argument with *kago* bearers. *Kago* bearers had been known to dump irascible or stingy customers off the sides of mountains and laugh about it afterward, over their teacups full of *sake*.

"*Ekkorasassa!*" Viper hissed as they rounded a sharp turn. It was the signal to set the *kago* down.

Cat heard the clack of the men's stout oaken sticks as they transferred the carrying pole to them and lowered the *kago* to the ground. A *samurai* stood, arms akimbo, in the middle of the trail. He was a small man, which may have been why he wore a *kataginu*, a formal sideless vest with shoulders quilted and stiffened to stand out like triangular wings. His partner waited at the chess board set up on a stump outside their thatched shelter.

Like most fugitives, Cat assumed everyone was after her. She draped her towel over her head to hide her face. She began rubbing the beads of her rosary and droning the Lotus *sutra* as though deep in meditation. Her staff was tied along the carrying pole, so while she chanted, she assessed the distance to Viper's heavy oak stick.

"Whom do you carry?" The *samurai* used the guttural, clipped speech of men either used to authority or bent on acquiring it.

"We carry only a mad priest to cure a worthless stone-woman." When Viper bowed low, the tiger tattooed on his buttocks seemed to smile at Cat.

"Lord Katsugawa wants no madmen or beggars depleting his resources or spying." Lord Katsugawa's retainer walked closer to inspect the tall hat hanging next to Cat's staff. Priests of empty nothing were often employed as spies.

"The holy one will perform the necessary exorcism, then be on his way, Your Honor."

"Your papers." The *samurai* was so close, Cat could see the dust in the weave of his leggings.

Viper produced his travel permit from the pouch that hung from the carrying pole. The *samurai* studied it for what seemed an eternity. Finally he handed it back.

"Pass." As parting proof of his rank, he rapped the top of the *kago* with his staff.

Viper and Cold Rice picked up the pole. *"Ho-yoi-yoi,"* they shouted as they settled it on their callused shoulders. Except for grunting the nonsense syllables *"Ho-yoi-yoi"* in time with their footsteps, they didn't speak until they were safely out of hearing.

Viper signaled to set the *kago* down. There was a short silence, and then Cat heard the sound of a stream of water hitting a rock. " 'Lord Katsugawa wants no madmen and beggars on his lands.' " When Viper finished urinating he hawked and spat and tightened his loincloth.

"All the madmen and beggars are in Katsugawa's employ," he said. "I happen to know that that fool standing in the road like a *ri*-marker is the third son of a millet farmer. Did you see him inspect that paper, Cold Rice? Solemn as a clam. And the idiot can no more read than a toad can dance."

A stone-woman, Cat thought. A woman who could not bear children. Of all Viper's cheerful obscenities, this was the only one that shocked Cat. It was a phrase women never spoke aloud.

Viper had said he wanted Cat to speak to the dead. Was the stone-woman dead? Was her soul in Stone-Woman's Hell, condemned for eternity to dig bamboo shoots with a lamp wick? Was her spirit the one to which Cat was supposed to speak? Or was she alive and her barrenness caused by a homeless ghost?

When Cat left Edo she had been prepared to fight mortal enemies. She hadn't considered immortal ones.

Even so, the hissing *"Ekkorasassa!"* was welcome when Viper and Cold Rice finally set the *kago* down. Viper hurried around to untie Cat's pack and hat and staff. Even in the cold air his sturdy body glistened with sweat as he bowed Cat out of the basket.

"Welcome to our humble village." He gestured cheerfully. "It's three *ri* from a wine shop and two *ri* from a bean curd shop."

Cat stood stiffly and leaned on the staff, waiting for the sensation to return to her legs. The lower end of her spine felt bruised from the jolting, but the cold air revived her. The pain in her head subsided. She looked around.

Twenty or thirty small houses were scattered on several levels of a hillside that was covered with bushes and tall trees. The houses' steeply pitched thatched roofs almost reached the ground at the eaves. The walls of unpainted timber and pressed earth had weathered a dark brown. Straw thatch covered enormous wood piles.

Bamboo pipes caught water from the many rivulets and tiny waterfalls and directed it to stone pools and cisterns. The sound of running water was constant. The low mountains were neatly terraced with fields carved into the slopes.

The women stopped their spinning and their hulling. The men put down their flails and their square measuring boxes. No one looked directly at Cat, but she could feel their suspicion. The place had an air of foreboding.

The headman stepped forward. He was not old, but his face was furrowed with care. Concentric, semicircular folds of skin hung under his eyes. He beckoned Viper to one side, but Cat could hear the murmured conversation.

"What news do you bring, nephew?" he asked.

"This priest has kindly consented to cure my foolish wife. He will speak to the troublesome ghost."

"One trusts he's not a cheat, like the last with his mossy skull of a so-called saint and his demands for contributions."

Under the villagers' surreptitious scrutiny, Cat felt young and inept and a contemptible mountebank. She was also angry that Viper had taken her so far out of her way and made such extravagant promises on her behalf.

Still, Kira's men weren't likely to look for her here. Maybe they would press ahead in their search, leaving her to follow them. She would feel much safer behind them than in front of them. As for the stone-woman's barrenness and the homeless ghost, she would do what she could.

She pounded the butt of her staff on the ground, jangling the iron rings on top of it. Everyone bowed a little lower but peered at Cat obliquely.

"*Namu Amida Butsu,*" she intoned through her nose. She rattled the rings again. "After I have bathed and purified myself, I shall question the woman," she announced. "I shall speak to the spirit."

"I've tried all the cures." Viper's wife, Okyo, lay under a faded quilt with matted gray cotton wadding escaping from the torn seams.

Her closed eyes were sunken into hollows the color of ripe eggplant. She was so thin and wasted-looking, Cat jumped when she spoke. She had thought she was dead. As for Okyo, when she turned her head and looked at Cat, she was surprised to find that the priest was a boy, beardless and beautiful.

In the kitchen Viper sat with his back stolidly toward this small sleeping room. He and Sakuta, the village headman, were discussing Lord Katsugawa's latest assessment added to the sixty percent taxation rate the farmers were already paying.

"I made a pilgrimage to Shojuin Temple and left a statue of the sainted Jizō-sama there." Okyo hadn't the strength to speak much above a whisper.

The damp night air was cold, and she shivered under the quilt. Cat rose onto her knees and moved across the plank floor to the cupboard. Balls of dust and lint nested in the corners. Okyo had been ill a long time, and her young maid had no one to supervise her.

Inside the cupboard Cat found another coverlet in as poor condition as the first. She shook it out and laid it over the woman. Then she sat back and fingered her beads. Cat's flea bites made her frantic to scratch, but she forced herself to listen quietly.

"I burned incense and prayed to Benten-sama," Okyo said. "I asked Kannon-sama for help. I slept in the room with my husband's sister, who has given birth to three children. I jumped over the birth sacks of the last five babies born here." She paused to catch her breath.

"I've asked my husband to divorce me." A single tear spilled over her eyelid and coursed slowly down her hollow cheek. "If I live, I shall wear a pilgrim's bell and roam the earth. I cannot stay here. The people of this village believe I'll cause all the wombs to wither. They think I'll cause all the women to become no-life-women like myself." Okyo reached under the cover and held up a doll made of straw. "This was found nailed to the oak in the center of the village. Someone put it there to lay a curse on me."

"Maybe it was meant for another."

"It was meant for me."

"Your husband believes the bones unearthed in the new field have caused your barrenness."

"He doesn't want to admit the real reason."

"What do you think is the real reason?"

"Ours was a love marriage," she murmured. "Not one of duty. We have been self-indulgent, reckless with our feelings.

This is our punishment. I will have no children to make offerings when I die. But my husband can remarry and have children by a worthier woman.''

''I will ask the spirits the true reason.''

Cat had seen diviners at work. She knew the procedure, if not the sorcery behind it. And if she wasn't a priest, she was at least a bat in a birdless village. She would have to do.

She held out a bowl of water and a slat of wood on which she had written Okyo's name. Okyo dipped the wooden tablet in the water and sprinkled Cat with it.

Cat leaned her elbows on a box and rested her forehead in the palm of her hands. She heard no voices from beyond, but then she hadn't expected to. However, the wave of grief and loneliness that swept over her took her by surprise. She felt a terrible, aching pity for the time-ravaged bones unearthed by strangers in a field.

''I'm hungry.'' When she finally spoke her voice was strained by grief and sounded alien in her own ears. ''I'm lonely. I'm frightened. No one cares for my soul as I travel the Three Paths.''

Okyo's eyes grew wide.

''Bury my bones properly.'' Cat knew, as clearly as if the owner of the bones had spoken to her, what she must do. ''Say prayers over my remains. Burn incense. Feed my spirit, and I will haunt this woman's womb no longer.''

CHAPTER 13
TO MOVE THE SHADOW

Cat sat near the small stone shrine to the village's tutelary god. Next to her was the mossy boulder that would serve as a seat for the restless spirit. In front of it Cat had planted a wand of anise wood with diagonally folded white paper strips and a lock of Okyo's hair attached. On the other side of the boulder knelt Okyo. The villagers sat among the moss-covered tombstones and tall wooden funerary stakes of the cemetery.

''I'm only a priest of inferior rank.'' Cat could hear the blood thumping in her temples. "My prayers may not be of much use."

In spite of her disclaimer, a purl of alarm spread through the villagers when she rubbed her rosary beads together with a loud clicking noise. The beads were sure to rouse the malicious ghost. A baby cried at the rear of the crowd.

Cat began chanting lines from a *Nō* play in which a spirit was summoned. She was quite sure no one here would have heard it before.

Pure above and pure below. Pure inside and pure outside. Pure in all six Realms. Gallop here now on your big gray horse.

A sudden wind shook the pine overhead, and Cat thought she smelled the odor of stagnant water, the effluvium of a ghost. Okyo moaned. Her eyes rolled up in their sockets, and her head fell forward, then lolled from side to side.

Cat stopped in alarm. What if the poor woman had a seizure in front of the entire village? What if Cat really did call up something hideous and demonic? But she'd gone too far with this act to stop now.

She rubbed the beads harder and began to shake violently. Maybe she could distract Viper's wife and transfer the tension to herself.

"Hear me." Again Cat's voice sounded like a stranger's to her, though she knew it was only the strain of the act she was putting on. She remembered to take loud, deep breaths, another sign of a shaman's trance.

"My name is Saemon of Izumo. This is my sad tale." She began her account of how the mouse-gnawed, amber-brown bones had come to lie in the recently cleared field.

"Many years ago I fell in love with a beautiful courtesan. To pay for my carousals, I sold my house and all my possessions. My children had to beg for grains of millet to ease the pangs in their shrunken bellies. My loyal wife drove a knife into her breast and expired while our little ones wailed around her."

Cat was gratified to see her listeners wiping their eyes on their sleeves.

"This woman who had bewitched me was no ordinary being." Cat lowered her voice to draw them further into her tale. "The ravishing creature who nibbled my earlobe and trailed her fingers down my naked spine . . ."

When the audience sucked in its breath and leaned forward as one, Cat remembered she wasn't entertaining guests in the Perfumed Lotus. The villagers wanted demons and lust, but they wanted them disguised as a morality tale.

"The woman I loved was a demon cat with eyes like coals and teeth like razors. It had ripped open the throat of the gentle, lark-voiced beauty and had drunk her blood. It had dragged her body under the porch and scratched out a grave with its claws. Then it took her form.

"I began waylaying drunken passersby at night, stealing their money and selling their clothes to pay for the favors of my beloved. My friends suspected supernatural mischief, so they hid behind a screen and waited until my lover and I entered. Again and again she demanded that I satisfy her, until at last I lay as though dead. When she began to suck my soul out through my fingertips, my friends knew she was a demon.

"They fell upon her and stabbed her. With a shriek she trembled and contorted. Her nose broadened and her eyes widened to the size of hand drums. Whiskers and fur sprouted on her face. Her ears grew pointed. She snarled and hissed. Then, lashing her long black tail, she ran out the door, leaped onto the roof, and disappeared.

"When I had regained my strength I went in search of my children. But they lay in unmarked graves at the dry river bottom where executed criminals are exposed."

The nose blowing grew louder, and when Cat paused for breath she heard weeping.

"As penance I vowed to crawl the length of the land. When I reached here, I was waylaid by bandits who stole the rags from my back and left my bones to molder."

Cat leaned forward and rested her face in her hands. She was shaking and weary. The people around her sat absolutely silent. Finally she sat up straight.

"Saemon regrets that he has caused the *kago* man and his good wife such grief." Cat spoke in her usual voice, but it was thick with fatigue. "When we have chanted the proper prayers over his remains, he will become a Buddha. If you continue to leave offerings to feed his spirit, he will trouble you no more."

As the villagers rose quietly, Cat stared straight ahead. She prayed that the bones would not trouble her, either. She worried that her sacrilege had imperiled her own soul. Each of her thoughts and deeds in this world affected her *karma*. Evil bred evil. Good bred good. Cat hoped that her efforts to put a troubled spirit to rest would be considered good.

Cat tried to sleep on the hard pallet stuffed with rice husks, but the coarse hempen covers abraded her skin. She had put aside the block of cedar that was to serve as a pillow and cradled her head in the crook of her arm. She felt under the edge of the mattress for the reassuring touch of the four-foot-long stave she had hidden there.

She had pleaded exhaustion and excused herself early from the feast. The strain of the exorcism and burial and the gratitude of the villagers had worn her out. All afternoon women had whispered to her as they passed, asking her to pray for ailing children or aged parents. Men had taken her aside to request amulets to ensure virility.

Cat knew that if she didn't leave at first light, the elders would have her march through the fields on the mountainside, asking the gods' benediction. These were people capable of staying afloat in life's capricious current, but they could hardly be blamed for grabbing on to a raft if one appeared.

Cat drew up her legs to ease the cramp knotting in her stomach. The food had been plentiful that evening, but not of the sort she was used to.

To provide this room for Cat, Okyo had gone to stay with her sister-in-law. In the only other room of the house, Viper and headman Sakuta and the older men of the village were continuing the party around the hearth. They had draped their arms across each other's shoulders and were swaying from side to side as they sang. Viper put a towel over his head, tied it under his chin, and flipped open a fan.

As the men clapped time he began a burlesque of a courtesan's sensual dance. Cat could feel the thud of his feet vibrating through the floor and the thin walls. The men's laughter filled the small house. When he finished he sat down in a storm of applause.

"Did I bring you a fine holy man or did I not?" he shouted.

"You did." Sakuta's voice was a bit slurred. "Never have I seen a priest so wise and so young. Some are saying he's the holy O-Daishi-Sama himself, walking among us in disguise."

"We can raise subscriptions and build a temple here," someone said. "People will come from everywhere to worship. Women will flock to leave offerings to rid themselves of the curse of childlessness. Our village will become a center of piety."

"We'll build an inn and tea shops and souvenir stands," a more practical mind added.

"What's the use. He'll take what we earn."

Suddenly the talk grew much quieter. They were discussing Lord Katsugawa's extra tax levy, and what they were saying was treasonous. Lord Katsugawa's profligate ways had placed a heavy tax burden on the people of Viper's village. As headman, Sakuta was responsible for either producing the added *koku* of rice and millet, and watching his people starve, or protesting the injustice. Since the penalty for protest was death, neither alternative was appealing.

Talk of taxes meant little to Cat, so the men's low voices lulled her. She remembered a song her mother used to play on the silk strings of her *koto*, her long, horizontal harp of paulownia wood. The notes had fallen like drops of water into the still black pond of night. Cat sang the words silently to herself as she lay in the darkness of the shabby room.

> So lonely am I
> My soul is a floating weed
> Severed at the roots.

From somewhere out on the plain of Musashi below, a temple bell tolled as though to guide lost souls through the darkness. Before its mournful call finished sounding in the still air, Cat was asleep.

The wispy touch of fingertips on her shoulder jolted her awake. In an instant she was out of bed and across the small room, the heavy stick raised in attack position. The night lantern had burned out, leaving behind the stench of whale oil. Cat strained to distinguish her assailant in the darkness.

"Don't kill me, most noble shining prince!" The serving maid held the quilt in front of her while she groped for her discarded sleeping robe. "I hoped you would grant me your favors. Pillowing with you will ensure that I have children."

"Go away, child."

Cat knew that rumors were flying around the village. Everyone said the handsome young exorcist was more than he appeared, but they couldn't agree on his real identity. Some insisted he was the illegitimate son of a court noble. Others thought he had failed in a suicide pact with his lover, leaving her to journey to the Western Paradise alone. Some even suggested he was the ghost of the tragic young lord Yoshitsune, still fleeing his murderous brother.

When the maid scurried out Cat replaced the stick and crawled back under the covers. She slept until just before dawn when Okyo, looking much better, brought in a tray of food. She asked after Cat's health, then bowed her way out. Cat dressed and sat cross-legged in front of the tray. She morosely surveyed the meager heap of pickled vegetables and the cup of hot water flavored with parched millet.

She almost called Okyo back. She almost complained about the meal. Then she remembered the feast of the day before. Cat didn't doubt that Viper and his wife would give her the best they had. After yesterday's extravagance this was all they had.

"Good morning." Viper came in, bowed deeply, and sat cautiously, as though he feared his eyeballs would fall out and roll away if he jostled his head too much. He busied himself with his pipe as Cat picked up the chopsticks and the bowl of vegetables and began to eat.

"I apologize for the wretched accommodations, holy one," Viper said. "My poor house is not worthy of someone of your stature and piety. I hope our drunken foolishness last night didn't offend you or keep you awake."

"I slept very well." Cat captured the last fragment of radish and ate it. Then she sipped the hot water.

"My partner and I will take you back to the Tōkaidō today. I'm very sorry to have delayed you from your mission."

"Thank you."

"We'll take you to the Yaguchi ford."

"But there's a ferry. . . ."

"Local people use the ford. If a man had enemies, he would be less likely to meet them there. Maybe one or two enemies would be stationed at the ford. No more."

"Take me to the ferry." Cat wondered just how much Viper knew and why he was talking of enemies.

No matter.

It's time to move the shadow, Cat thought. *It's time to strike the enemy and make him respond so I can identify him and learn his strength.*

"Of course, holy one." Viper bowed. "One as young and virtuous as you certainly wouldn't have enemies." He reached into the front of his coat and drew out a small cloth sack. The contents clinked when he held it out to Cat.

"The wretch of a *kago* man with the dragon tattooed on his arm sends his most abject apologies for so gravely insulting you at the Shinagawa barrier. He offers you these few miserable *bu* as a gift for your holy work. And he sincerely prays for your forgiveness, though he knows he deserves none."

"But how . . ." Cat was astonished. She hadn't even mentioned the bearer who had dropped feces in her begging bowl. Viper gave a deprecating wave of his hand.

"The road stretches many *ri* in front of you, holy one," he went on. "Every crossroad is haunted by foxes and demons and cutpurses, all bent on mischief. Perhaps this will be of use."

He handed her a small bundle wrapped in a cloth. She unwrapped it to find a stick a bit longer than her hand and about as thick as her wrist. It was carved of soft sandalwood with a large knot at each end. It looked innocuous, but it was a weapon.

"What makes you think I would know how to use a *yawara*?"

"You speak the language of the *bushi*, the warrior, holy one. I assumed you would know how to use it."

"And what are you doing with this?"

"Ah . . ." Viper bowed to hide his smile, which was directed at himself, not to her. "Even dirt-eaters have secrets."

CHAPTER 14
THE WAY OF DEATH

Cat felt as though she had been pleated like a fan, stuffed into the tiny *kago*, and shaken thoroughly. She had tied her towel across her mouth and nose to keep out the worst of the dust. She knew that if she could stand the journey, Viper and Cold Rice would cheerfully carry her all the way to Kyōto in their *kago*.

She also knew that if the two *kago* men were caught at the government barriers with a fugitive, their heads would be cut off and set out like melons in the marketplace. Besides, strong as they were, without fresh teams to spell them they would soon become exhausted. And even if they made it safely, Cat had no funds to pay them. They would lose almost a month's worth of income that their families desperately needed.

Cat had been taught that part of her duty as a member of the ruling class was to be benevolent, protective, and just toward subordinates. She wanted no innocent blood on her hands. She didn't want to cause hardship to those who tried to help her. So she was content to ride only as far as the Tama River just beyond Kawasaki.

Viper and Cold Rice trotted past a covey of pilgrims and a line of plodding pack ponies. They bowed and called out irreverent greetings to each pair of *kago* bearers who trotted toward them. When they passed a farmer's wife shoveling horse manure off the road and into a basket, Viper slapped his rump and offered to make a donation. In a hail of indelicacies they evaded the pair of bald-headed nuns who offered to entertain them in exchange for a donation to their temple. When they outpaced a merchant dozing on a rented horse, the road ahead was clear of travelers.

Beyond the rice paddies, Cat saw the first of Kawasaki's handful of shops and ramshackle houses. She called out loudly enough to be heard over Viper's singing and the rhythmic jingle of the rings on her staff, which was strapped alongside the carrying pole.

"This is as far as we journey together."

"We're still half a *ri* from the ferry, holy one," Viper said.

"I've inconvenienced you too much already. Please take me into the grove. I'll get out there and be of no further bother to you."

Viper and Cold Rice turned onto a narrow path through a stand of pine trees and a head-high thicket of bushy bamboo. The path ended at a huge pine loosely girdled by a thick rope of braided rice straw. The rope and the diagonally folded white paper streamers that hung from it set this tree apart as sacred. At the base of the pine lightning had formed a long, sinuous, elliptical opening. The elements had sculptured the creases and folds of the wood around it into what looked like a woman's secret gate.

Hundreds of small red wooden *torii* gates were stacked in front of it. A haze of incense rose from the bundles of joss sticks stuck into the sand. Papers containing women's prayers for love or children or protection from venereal disease had been folded lengthwise and tied around the twigs of the nearby shrubbery.

When the basket settled, Cat levered herself out. She rolled her head to relieve the aching cramp in her neck.

"Thank you for the ride. Buddha will bless you." She bowed to Viper and his partner, who both bowed back.

But Viper made no move to untie her belongings. Instead he threw himself to the ground and pressed his forehead into the forest loam. Cold Rice did the same. Cold Rice was bewildered but curious to know what turn this strange affair would take next.

"Untie my belongings," Cat commanded. If Viper recognized her, it didn't matter. The worst he could do was inform on her and collect whatever reward Kira was offering. She was about to confront Kira's men anyway.

"Consider me an unworthy successor to Benkei, O most illustrious general." Instead of obeying her Viper brandished his *kago* stick. " 'Cleaver of Rocks' and I will stand with you."

Benkei? Cat stared at him. Benkei. So the fool thinks I'm the ghost of Minamoto Yoshitsune.

"Your youth, your beauty, the monk's disguise . . . I've suspected from the first." The fact that Yoshitsune had been hunted by his ruthless brother and forced to commit *seppuku* more than five hundred years before made no difference to Viper. Moreover, he fancied himself as the young hero's loyal companion, the great, irreverent, brawling monk Benkei.

Shire mono, Cat thought. *Idiot. I should let you be destroyed for meddling in the affairs of your betters.*

And why not? Commoners were expendable. A peasant's fate was to serve and to die and to hope for a better lot in the next life. Then Cat thought of Viper's frail wife and the smile on her face that morning as she'd waved the *kago* out of sight. She thought of her father's instruction in the manner of treating one's servants.

"I go on from here alone," Cat said. "You've repaid me for any service I might have done you. There's no need to entangle yourself in my affairs. I ask you again to untie my belongings."

"Fools, like scissors, will work. It only depends on how they're used."

"I have no need of fools or scissors." Cat forced herself to be patient. She wasn't used to arguments from commoners.

She waited for Viper to retrieve her things, but when he untied the pack he upended it as though by mistake. The lid fell off and the wrapped *naginata* blade tumbled out at his feet, along with the box of food Okyo had packed, spare sandals, the flea powder, the dried bonito, and the paper rain cloak.

"I'm such a clumsy oaf, my lord." Viper grasped one end of the cloth wrapping and lifted it, causing it to unwind and to tumble the big blade onto the ground. Cat had it unsheathed and the tang in her grasp before Viper had half bent over to pick it up. Holding the blade's curved edge at his throat, she backed him up against the pine. Incense smoke twined around their ankles like cats.

"Do not toy with me, peasant," she hissed. "You take foolish advantage of my good nature. I spare your life only out of regard for your unfortunate wife." Still furious, she lowered the blade slightly. "Now get out of my sight, you insolent wretch."

"My lord . . ."

"Begone!"

Viper edged around Cat and threw himself to the ground next to the *kago*. It was a fragile shield at best, but Cold Rice had already put it between himself and the inevitable beheading of his reckless partner by a ghost. He too was as close to the ground as he could get without using a mattock.

"My lord, trying to curb my mouth is as impossible as wrestling with a shop-front curtain," Viper said. "If you will not accept my humble offer to fight for your cause, honor me by releasing me from the travail of this mortal path."

Still prostrate, Viper bared his neck to Cat's blade. He and his partner waited for the death blow. If the young priest were of noble or warrior birth, as Viper suspected, he would have the right and the inclination to behead the two commoners right there.

Cat sighed in exasperation. The peasant's impudence and obstinate loyalty were causing her annoyance and delay. "I'll make a bargain with you." Her voice was still sharp with anger.

Viper remained kneeling with his neck bared.

"This involves some risk."

"I will happily risk all to serve you, lord."

"You have only to risk that device of torture you call a *kago*."

She held out the bag of silver coins and the strings of coppers Viper had given her that morning. When he didn't take them she dropped them onto the matting in the bottom of the *kago*.

"I cannot take payment from you, lord."

"This is to pay for the *kago*. You will abandon it at the ferry."

Cat detached the iron cap and scrollwork from the top of the staff. She slid the shaft out from inside and inserted the tang of the blade into the slot cut for it. Then she searched through her pack for the twine to wrap around it.

"My debt to you is too great to accept money also." Viper looked at the coins in consternation.

Cat stopped wrapping the cord around the shaft's head and stared at him coldly. Her nostrils flared in fury. "If you do not take the money, I shall curse you with impotence, you impudent radish."

Viper opened his mouth, then closed it. He sidled over to the *kago* and picked up the coins.

They were all the money Cat had, but that was the least of her worries. Musashi said that the Way of the warrior was the Way of death. Cat knew that to fight well she must be more than just prepared to die. Life and death must be matters of indifference to her. *Killing a man,* Oishi had once said, *is only difficult if you want to keep yourself alive.*

When Cat had given Viper and Cold Rice their instructions and they had trotted off with the *kago* between them, she sat cross-legged by the tree. She breathed deeply, drawing in *ki*, the life force, and filling the hollow vessel of her body with it. When she breathed out she felt her breath pressing against her diaphragm, concentrating her strength in her belly.

Her thoughts sank to her abdomen and calmed. Aware of everything around her yet unaffected by it, she felt as though she were being held aloft like a feather on her own breath.

CHAPTER 15
TYING A LINE OF FISHES

Kawasaki wasn't situated where travelers were likely to spend the night. Usually all they left behind them was dust from distant provinces and contributions in the farmers' wayside conveniences.

A one-legged beggar sat on a frayed square mat across the road from the open-air tea shop near the ferry. He kept up a steady racket, beating with a mallet on the flat bell lying in front of him. He had been droning *sutras* since before Viper and Cold Rice arrived.

"I'm terribly embarrassed about the poor quality of the tea."

The tea shop's owner arrived with the tray held over her head so her breath wouldn't contaminate the contents. She set it down between Viper and Cold Rice. "The typhoon ruined the crop."

"This is tea to make a palate rejoice." Viper held up the cup and admired it politely.

He and his partner dangled their feet from the wide bench outside the shop. Their *kago* stood between them and the open shed that sheltered the ferry's waiting passengers. A pair of dusty mats had been thrown over the *kago*'s carrying pole.

"May I bring you anything else, Boss?" Viper was Oyabun, Boss of the brotherhood of *kago* bearers for this section of the Tōkaidō.

"Can you serve us some fresh news, Kiku-san?"

"I can indeed!" Kiku, Chrysanthemum, was so small that she had to double her blue-and-white tie-dyed cotton robe twice under her sash to keep from tripping on the hem. She was also shy, but she lit up at the chance to relay gossip.

"A pack of rascals passed through," she said in a low voice. "They waited a day at the Full Moon Inn. Then they left three men behind and continued on. The three have been squatting there like toads ever since, drinking all the Full Moon's *sake* and complaining endlessly."

"Who are they waiting for?"

The waitress beamed from behind her tray. This was the best part. She looked around, leaned closer, and lowered her voice even more.

"A terrible brigand." She was elated that a terrible brigand might pass through Kawasaki. "Travelers from Edo say the Eastern Capital is buzzing with stories about him. He single-handedly fought off a horde of enemies and burned down half the pleasure district. They say he's extremely handsome and he may even be disguised as a woman."

"Who are his enemies?"

"I don't know. But I hear they're wicked. I hear the lone warrior intends to annihilate them and give all their gold to the poor."

"Is that so?"

"That's what I hear."

"Thank you." Viper bowed and smiled. "We'll finish our tea and trouble you no more."

"No trouble at all, Boss Viper." She bowed as she backed away. In her tall *geta* she clattered back to the domed clay stove where her kettle simmered.

Viper thought of the mysterious young lord as he had last seen him, a slender, stoic figure in dusty priest's robes meditating in a cloud of incense smoke at the foot of the pine tree.

"This whole affair is a fire across the river," Cold Rice muttered into his teacup. "It doesn't concern us."

"It's entertaining, my old friend."

"The boy-lord's orders were to leave the *kago* near the ferry, then disappear." Cold Rice persisted in his attempts to dissuade Viper from folly, even though he knew it was hopeless.

Viper just smiled into his teacup. He counted among his friends members of Edo's *otokodate*, gangs of commoners who fought against the depredations of *samurai* and bannermen. He had been in more street brawls than Cold Rice could count.

"Arguing with you is like driving a nail into bran." Cold Rice was exasperated.

"Which of them do you suppose are the spies?" Viper studied the assortment of people sitting on the benches under the thatched roof.

"How should I know?"

"There," Viper said. "Our young lord approaches." He felt around next to his bare legs to make sure his oaken *kago* stick was close by.

Through the square of open mesh in her hat, Cat saw Viper about the same time he saw her. "Idiot!" she muttered.

She was furious that he would defy her. So be it. If he was determined to become a Buddha, she wouldn't stop him.

Clutching her staff, Cat walked slowly past the dusty weeds and dry, brown rice paddies west of Kawasaki. She had tied back her sleeves to be ready for action. From inside her big hat she surveyed the few wretched hovels that fronted directly on the roadway. Except for the activity at the ferry, the village seemed almost deserted.

The passengers who had just arrived from the other side of the river were dispersing. Some rested in the shade of the tall trees along the river or stopped at the shabby tea houses. Others continued their journeys. Cat gave a start when a merchant strode up to Viper and demanded to hire his *kago*.

"You're too fat," she heard Viper say. "Walk. The exercise will do you good."

Cat left Viper to argue with him and watched the two-horse pack train that was delaying the loading of the ferry. The flat-bottomed boat could only hold one animal at a time, and neither horse was cooperating with the driver. While they waited, the travelers chatted or rooted in their cloth bundles for radishes and rice dumplings. Children selling sweet bean cakes and straw sandals and toothpicks swarmed around them.

The boy Jōshū was selling tea from his portable stand. When he saw her, he looked worried. Several surly men from Edo and a formidable *rōnin* from Tosa had been asking about the handsome young priest of empty nothing. They might show up at any moment. Jōshū had told them nothing, of course. He owed the young priest a great debt for the wonderful future he had read in the six copper coins.

The beggar stopped his chanting and bell ringing. He hung the cords of the mallet and bell around his neck. He emptied the coppers from his begging bowl into his sleeve, slid his rosary onto his wrist, and tucked his mat under his arm. He hauled himself up on his staff, hiked the hem of his long robe up into his sash, and hopped off on his one leg.

The spy, Cat thought. Now she only had to wait until the beggar alerted his employers.

The travelers waiting at the ferry were the usual sort. The pack horse leader. A pair of dry-goods clerks with their pilgrim's scrolls slung on their backs. A panderer for harlots at ten percent. A pawnshop owner. A ditch cleaner with his broom and rake. And the retinue of two prosperous rice brokers from the bustling Kitahama commercial district in Osaka, where, it was said, money flowed past the wharves and strolled in the streets.

There were also three women going to the vast temple complex dedicated to Kōbō Daishi in the forest on the opposite side of the river. And a young artist, a westcountryman, who painted folding paper lanterns with pictures of Benkei on the Gojo Bridge. He had set up shop on an overturned tub.

The artist seemed to be seventeen or eighteen, a year or so younger than Cat. He wore his towel over his head with the sides folded across his cheeks and tied under his lower lip. Peasants covered their heads that way, and so did men who wanted to obscure their faces.

Jōshū wandered casually up to Cat. "Tea, Your Holiness?"

"Thank you," Cat answered.

"Beware." To cover his voice Jōshū rattled the wooden ladle against the side of the water bucket. "Several men are looking for a priest, and they mean him harm."

"Thank you for your kindness to a stranger." Cat bowed and accepted the small cup of tea. She drank it as though nothing were amiss.

When Cat didn't retreat Jōshū followed her at a distance. He scanned the river's broad dry bed and the treeline for enemies. He jumped when Cat pounded the butt of her staff on the ground, jangling the iron rings.

"Allow me to read your fortunes, gentlefolk," she said. "Your future is written in your face."

The rice merchants ignored her. They sat on their travel boxes, smoking and discussing the recent fortuitous typhoon. The storm had created food shortages around Edo and made them both wealthy men.

"Permit me to read your face." Cat stopped in front of the painter of paper lanterns. The cloth of his *hakama* was the orange and blue and yellow plaid common to the area around Akō. She wanted to make him speak to see if his accent confirmed her suspicion about his origins. "You, sir, have a long-life eyebrow."

The artist waved his sleeve peevishly at her and tried to avoid her gaze, but she persisted. "Note how his eyebrow is wide, and the hairs are longer at the tail than at the head."

The three women and several of the children crowded close to look. Jōshū set down his big water buckets and watched from a distance. The artist became increasingly agitated, but he said nothing. He stood up suddenly and knocked over his water pot and scattered his brushes in the sand. He tied back his sleeves with a long cord and knelt to collect them.

"Please do me the favor of reading my future, holy one," one of the women said. She and her two friends giggled behind their sleeves as if life itself were a wonderful joke. They were merry with the intoxication of travel and the freedom from responsibility.

Cat took off her hat and leaned her staff and pack against one of the shed's corner posts. She studied the woman's face. "You have a long head and a wide chin. You're a fire person."

"Is that good, holy one?"

"You are polite, but you have a hot temper."

"That's you!" The two friends laughed.

From the corner of her eye Cat saw Kira's three retainers hustling across the trampled beach toward the ferry landing.

"Your clear voice and thin body mean you're combined with wood," Cat went on. "Success and fame will probably come to you after age thirty."

Jōshū hissed a warning, which Cat didn't seem to hear. She bowed low as she accepted the woman's donation of ten coppers tossed into her begging bowl. While the other two congratulated their friend on her good luck, Cat moved out to meet Kira's retainers.

"Allow me to read the future in your faces, kind sirs."

The men were startled. They had expected her to run or at least to be frightened. But Cat was following Musashi's advice. She was making her fear transferable. By appearing calm, she was transferring restlessness to her enemy, the way one transferred sleepiness by yawning.

"You, sir . . ." Cat pointed her staff at the leader. "You have a small gray ear. Not a good sign."

"Come with us." When the leader and his two companions drew their long-swords, the passengers, the children, and the ferryman ran for the tea shop. Only the young artist remained, holding his paintbrushes.

Cold Rice stood back to belly with the others under the shop's eaves, as though sheltering from a sudden and violent storm. Viper stayed where he was, sitting on the bench with his legs dangling. He held his *kago* stick ready, but he suspected that his young lord wouldn't need much help.

"A gray ear means you can't be trusted to keep a secret." Cat threw back the matting over the *kago*'s carrying pole. She unloosed the slipknots and released the six-foot-long *naginata* from alongside the pole.

"And your nose . . . modern diviners never pay enough attention to noses, in my opinion." Holding the *naginata*'s shaft loosely in her hands, Cat circled to the left.

Cat had studied many aspects of the warrior's Way, but she had worked hard at only one endeavor in her life. She had practiced with the *naginata* from the time she was big enough to hold a small one. She had begun serious training at the age of seven.

The *naginata* was a heavy weapon and required great stamina to wield, but the weight of it felt good in her hands. The year away from it seemed only an instant. She remembered Oishi's calm voice as he coached her in *Ten-no-michi*, Heaven's Way. She was glad now that he had insisted she use a variety of *naginata* so she didn't develop a preference for one.

Cat held her chin high and looked straight ahead. Her nostrils flared as she felt vigor flowing up into her scalp. She had a three-foot reach on the swordsmen, and they were cautious. But Cat could tell they didn't consider her dangerous.

"You have an eagle's nose." She turned to the leader to divert the others' attention as she moved to keep the sun on her right.

You must drive the enemy together as if tying a line of fishes, Musashi wrote. *And when they are piled up, cut them down without giving them room to maneuver.*

With a sudden cry and using her lead hand as a fulcrum, Cat whirled, hissed, and snapped her rear hand upward. Because strokes with the *naginata* were made not with the lead hand, but with the rear one, it slashed faster than a sword and didn't signal its movements. And so, when the long, curved blade swooped down, the second man didn't move quickly enough.

Cat clearly saw, as though time had slowed, astonishment streak across his face when the blade sliced deep into his right shoulder. He dropped his sword. Blood spurted from his ripped sleeve. Cat flipped the blade up and felt the slight tug as it disengaged from his flesh. She was beyond all conscious thought now, or fear or elation.

With quick, small steps she lunged and swirled in a blur of motion. Her long blade described flashing circles in the sunlight as she parried and feinted. She slid her hands easily along the smooth shaft, snapping it downward, then reversing her grip to bring it up again in deadly arcs. She made low, horizontal sweeps at the men's shins, keeping them hopping to avoid amputation.

From the corner of her eye she saw the painter of paper lanterns run toward her with a sword he had hidden in his rolled sleeping mat. Too fast to see, she reversed the *naginata* shaft and smashed the butt of it sideways into his nose as he came abreast of her. She heard a crack as the oak crumpled the cartilage. The artist's eyes widened in surprise and chagrin before he sprawled in the sand and lay still.

Cat severed the third man's sword hand at the wrist. People scattered as he stumbled into the tea shop. With his good arm he knocked the kettle to one side and plunged the bleeding stump into the glowing coals. It hissed and steamed and sent out an odor of charring flesh. Backed up against the back wall, the waitress screamed steadily.

"*Ma!*" Viper tucked his feet under him, sucked on a straw, and watched raptly.

When the leader tried to dart into sword range, Cat swiveled the curved blade downward again and sliced his ear off at the skull. Demoralized, he turned to run, and she swept the blade low, severing both ankle tendons.

"Ancient Chinese diviners wrote," she called after him as

he crawled away, "that 'a man with a nose like an eagle's beak will peck at another man's heart.' "

Cat threw the ten coppers the woman had given her onto the wide, flat prow of the ferryboat. She didn't know if the amount was enough, but it would have to do. She turned toward the tea house where the ferryman cowered. Viper and Cold Rice and their *kago* had wisely disappeared before the authorities could arrive. Viper must have realized that the young priest didn't need his help and that staying there would surely mean trouble.

Cat stood her *naginata* upright and hung on to it, panting. "Ferryman," she shouted. "Take me across."

CHAPTER 16
COLD EVEN TO HIS GUMS

Hanshiro sat cross-legged in the shelter of the straw mat he had thrown over a bamboo pole propped up by a forked stick. Upriver from Kawasaki, he shared the grove of bare willows at the Yaguchi ford with a big bronze bell hanging under a wooden roof with upswept eaves. The willows didn't stop a cold wind from blowing in off the river.

Now and then dusty travelers stopped to dip water from a small stone basin in front of the bell. They rinsed their hands and mouths, purifying themselves for a small act of worship. They pulled on the cord that swung the horizontally suspended log into the bell. The low-pitched tolling vibrated in Hanshiro's chest.

He could have stayed at the shack that served as an inn here at the ford, but he knew it was infested with fleas. And when possible he preferred to keep watch himself instead of hiring someone to do it. So this lean-to under the rustling, bare branches of the willows had been his home for the past three days. Frankly, as the old saying went, his teeth were itchy. He was impatient and irritable.

Hanshiro was impatient with his impatience. *Time is an illusion invented by the mind,* he reminded himself.

The past didn't exist. The future didn't exist. The only reality was the moment. But the moment was cold.

He leaned over the river embankment and dipped a broad section of green bamboo into the fast-moving water. He fed willow twigs into the tiny fire he had built between three flat rocks. Then he balanced the bamboo container on the rocks and drew closer for the warmth. While he waited for the water to heat, he mended a torn *tabi*.

He used his thumbnail to push the needle through the seam in the canvas. He knotted the cotton thread, bit it off, and wrapped the remaining length around the needle. He stowed it among the packets of ginseng and bear gall and powdered horn in the *inro*, the set of small nested lacquered boxes hanging from his sash. He put the *tabi* back on and tied his straw sandal on over it.

He measured tea leaves into a small cup. Using his towel to insulate his fingers from the heat, he picked up the bamboo pot and poured water over the leaves. He let it steep, holding the narrow, cylindrical cup in his big hands and enjoying the warmth emanating from the porcelain. He stared out at the parade of humanity.

In the middle of the deep ford four porters were demanding more money to carry an enormous wrestler across. Hanshiro could hear them complaining about his weight. They were threatening to tip the platform on which he rode and spill him into the icy river.

It was an old ruse; and given the fact that the collected intellect of the five would not have filled a *sake* cup, it was comical. But Hanshiro was not amused.

With a willow withe he drew a circle in the sand. It was lopsided. The circle was a test of clarity of mind, and Hanshiro had just failed it. He sighed.

This woman was interfering with his rhythm, with his concentration. Where had she gone? How could she vanish in less than two and a half narrow *ri* of road? Losing her was like losing an ant on a bell rope.

A detour west across the mountains was unthinkable. They were precipitous and uncharted and infested with brigands. Maybe she went by sea or hired a boat to cross the river, although he knew Kira's men had been questioning all the fishermen between here and Edo. No one admitted to seeing her. And if Kira's men were inept at swordplay, they were very able at intimidating the lower classes.

In fact, they must have visited Nakamura Shichisaburo again, and Shichisaburo's memory must have improved. Kira's agents were now asking about a *komuso*, a priest of empty nothing.

Hanshiro knew Kira's men hadn't taken Cat. Three of them were waiting near the ferry, and two of them were here, lounging in the shade of a roofed well on the approach to the ford. They scratched themselves frantically as they squatted over dice. They had been staying at the inn.

Hanshiro continued his methodical analysis. He was trying to slip into the body and mind of the small fugitive as he had just slipped into his own *tabi*. He was finding it much more difficult than usual.

Hanshiro had a young informant at the ferry, and so far he hadn't reported seeing a wandering priest of Cat's description there. Maybe she had changed disguises. Maybe a procurer had kidnapped her or lured her back into service. Maybe she had been sold and now sat in one of the lath cages in the maze of brothels back in Edo, but Hanshiro doubted it.

Hanshiro was used to looking beyond appearances into the essence of a matter, and he had revised his initial opinion of the runaway. This woman was surrounded by mysterious deaths and disappearances. She had a *naginata*, and she would not, he was sure, allow herself to be captured without a fight. Any such incident would have been a prime topic of conversation among the travelers and denizens of the Tōkaidō.

Both Shichisaburo and the old woman who sold grilled eels had said she was alone; but maybe they were wrong. Maybe unknown accomplices had hidden her. Hanshiro decided that was the most logical explanation.

He took the blue silk scarf from his jacket and untied it. The coil of black hair inside was still glossy. He raised the scarf to his face and breathed in. The hair no longer had an aroma. After three days of separation from its owner, it had lost her essence. It was neutral and uninformative. He wrapped it up again and returned it to his sleeve.

With the willow twig he began tracing characters in the sand. He was amused by the cynical old verse that came to mind. It described three impossible things.

> Sincere courtesans,
> Square eggs, and a fat full moon
> On the month's last day.

Even the act of writing such a foolish verse calmed Hanshiro. It gave order to what was turning into a disordered affair. He drew another circle, much more symmetrical this time.

The wind plucked at his sleeve and funneled down the neck of his old coat. He erased the verse and wrote one of Bashō's.

> The salted bream
> Looks cold even to his gums,
> On the fishmonger's shelf

He felt like that bream, cold and waiting on a shelf.

"Tosa!" A boy dodged through the travelers gathered in small knots to haggle with the river porters. He raced across the sand and into the willows. He carefully avoided the poem Hanshiro had just drawn. He dropped to his knees and bowed low. "Tosa, the priest came to the ferry landing. Four men attacked him."

Hanshiro rubbed the stubble on his chin and stared out at the river. He had given Lady Asano too much credit. She had walked into Kira's men's trap.

"He beat them, master," the boy said.

"Alone?"

"Yes."

Hanshiro hissed, maybe in surprise, maybe in warning. The boy had never lied to him before. Was he doing it now?

"He's a *naginata* player." The boy jumped to his feet. He made whistling noises as he flung his arms about, imitating Cat's fighting style. "They're calling him the Devil Youth. They say he's the ghost of Yoshitsune and he studied with the mountain demons."

The boy had been enthralled by a lad, not much older than he, beating three *samurai* and one sword-wielding lantern painter.

"Maybe he was a different holy man."

"I think he was the one you seek, master. The whole village is as excited as a madman stung by a hornet. The magistrate is shouting about all the reports he'll have to write."

Hanshiro ducked out from under the mat and began to roll it up, along with the one on which he had been sitting. "What happened?"

"He was splen . . ." The boy hesitated. He didn't want to insult Hanshiro by praising another. "He defended himself well enough for one so young. But of course a *naginata* is a woman's weapon. It gives the wielder an unfair advantage."

Hanshiro tied a cord around the ends of the roll of mats, leaving a long loop in the middle. He put the loop over his head and adjusted it across his collarbone.

"Where did they take him?"

"He escaped." The boy grinned. "They were too busy picking up the ears and hands the Devil Youth left scattered about."

"Is that right?" Hanshiro stared hard at him. Was the boy teasing him?

"It's true."

Hanshiro held out a packet of coppers, and the boy bowed and accepted them. "Where did he go?"

"I don't know, master." The boy was apologetic. "No one rode across in the ferry with the mad priest, except the ferry-man."

Within three or four minutes Hanshiro had packed his meager gear, buried the fire, and turned to leave.

"Let me go with you as sandal bearer, master." The boy dreamed of being Hanshiro's disciple in the Way of the warrior, but he dared not ask for such a privilege. "I'll serve you well."

"I want no one trailing after me."

"Please, master. I ask nothing. Not even that you teach me."

Hanshiro knew that that was exactly what the child did want. But he didn't have the temperament to be a teacher. He felt no need to pass his skill and knowledge to others, certainly not for money. Besides, the country was full of out-of-work *rōnin* setting themselves up as masters of this school or that.

Hanshiro had watched many of them and had decided that if they were masters of swordsmanship, dragonflies were birds.

"I cannot take you with me." Hanshiro turned to go, then relented. " 'While riding the ox the boy looks for the ox,' " he said. "When you can explain this, come find me."

"Yes, Your Honor." The boy was rigid with concentration but hardly able to contain his excitement. He knew the task Hanshiro had given him might take him years, and he was eager to start.

Hanshiro gazed across the river. Then, with the toe of his sandal, he rubbed out the circles and the poem. He put his swords into his sash, hitched up his *hakama*, and settled the roll of mats on his back. He took off his sandals and *tabi* and tied them with a straw cord to his sash. Then he waded into the icy water.

CHAPTER 17
SEEING THE ESSENCE

Cat crouched in the deep shade of the towering cedars near a small statue hall on the temple grounds across the river from Kawasaki. She began to tremble uncontrollably, and tears streamed, unnoticed, down her cheeks. She had wounded men of *samurai* rank in daylight, in front of witnesses.

With her father dead and the rights and privileges of his rank stripped away, Cat assumed she would be punished as a commoner instead of as a member of the upper class. There would be no official remonstrance and comfortable seclusion at home for her. The authorities would arrest her, execute her over the blood-pit, and expose her head by the roadside. Cat wasn't afraid of dying, but she was mortified by the form it would take.

She didn't remember how she came to be here. She didn't remember the ride across the river with the boatman watching her warily from the stern as he poled. She didn't remember walking across the dry floodplain and into the woods. All she remembered was the sword with a hand still clutching its hilt in the sand and a man crawling away, blood unreeling like a crimson satin sash behind him.

Cat gripped her elbows, trying to control the shuddering tremors. She looked around cautiously. No one was in sight. The temple grounds dedicated to the sainted Kōbō Daishi were extensive and boasted fifty or more buildings. Although Jizō-sama was a very popular bodhisattva, this small hall devoted to him apparently was not.

Cat stared at the bloody *naginata* leaning against a tree. She had to get rid of it. She carried it to the far side of the weathered wooden building. She leaned it against the wall while she climbed onto the barrel that held water in case of fire. She stood on tiptoe on the lid and laid the blade and the staff into the bamboo rain gutter along the chapel's eaves.

She put her hands together, bowed, and said a prayer for both of them. They had served her well. Then she walked to the front of the hall. In the depths of the room, in the darkness behind the statue of Jizō, she could see a shadowy jumble of gilt and painted carvings—gods and blue-faced guardian kings, huge lotus flowers, monkeys, and lions—all thrown together and forgotten.

Cat reached through the barred window and as an offering to Jizō-sama left her rosary near one of the lamps. Jizō was clad in the usual red bib and beret. He carried his pilgrim's staff with iron rings to warn insects of his approach so they wouldn't be stepped on. His stone smile was reassuring, and his eyes seemed to follow her as she backed away.

Cat was still crying reflexively. Musashi's admonition that one must always take up the long-sword with the idea of cutting down the opponent was easier to accept in the abstract. The straw dummies she had practiced on as a young girl hadn't bled. The mutilation of one hadn't meant sure and terrible punishment.

A small stream flowed from a waterfall splashing down the side of a hill. It had been channeled into a bamboo pipe that diverted it to a big granite basin under the trees. With the bamboo dipper lying on top of it, Cat scooped up the cold water and rinsed her mouth and hands. Only then did she notice that her hands, grown soft over the past year, were red and abraded from the *naginata* shaft. She drank and splashed water on her face and arms.

Cat's pack and tall hat were gone. In her distracted state she had left them at the ferry landing. She tried to remember what was in the pack. She couldn't think of anything that would implicate Shichisaburo or Viper or Cold Rice. The hat wouldn't do her any good now, anyway. Her enemies would be looking for the priest who wore it. Even so, she felt exposed without it.

She took off the black overrobe and the priest's baggy trousers and white underrobe. Shivering from cold, she stuffed the white robe into a crevice in the face of the hillside and raked dried cedar needles over it. She put the faded black outer robe back on and belted it. She used her scissors to cut off the hem, turning the robe into a jacket. With fingers still trembling she clawed at the raw edge, raveling the coarse cloth to disguise the freshly cut material. Then she tore the trousers into strips and wrapped them like leggings around her tall *tabi*. She held them in place with the cloth ties from the trousers.

She turned away the bamboo pipe that splashed water into the basin. When the surface became still she used it as a mirror.

She untied her disheveled hair and bent over, throwing it forward and combing it with her fingers. She wrapped the same dirty cord several times around the base of the bundle of hair. She grabbed it above the cord and used her shears to cut it off above her hand. When she let go, it bushed out in a tuft, a boy's jaunty tea whisk style.

She trimmed the hair around her face into bangs and long sidelocks. When she inspected herself in the water, she was surprised by the handsome urchin who looked back at her. Then she noticed the splatter of blood across the front of her black coat.

She pulled her arms out of the sleeves, leaving the coat belted at her slender waist. Her upper body was bare, except for the *haramaki* that was still tightly wrapped around her abdomen and chest. She held the coat under the water gushing from the pipe and rubbed the stain, rinsing out the worst of it.

"Washing one's clothes without undressing. It must save a lot of time. I should have thought of it."

The quiet voice startled Cat so badly, she almost screamed. She plunged her hands into the sleeves and pulled up the wet coat, adjusting the front opening. She whirled to face the speaker.

Like most Buddhist lay monks, this one had shaved his head entirely, although his hair had grown out into a shadowy fuzz. He carried a staff, and he was dressed for traveling, but he was walking backward. He squinted nearsightedly at her from over his shoulder as he approached her.

The rear tail of his old black robe was tucked up into his sash, exposing bowed calves clad in brown leggings. A bronze pilgrim's bell and a rosary of heavy black beads and fat red tassels hung around his wrist. His conical sedge hat rode on his back, over a closed paper parasol, a rolled mat, and one cylindrical brocade case for his bamboo flute and another for his pilgrim's scroll. He wore a small white towel draped on his head, a white prayer stole on his left shoulder, straw sandals, and a smile.

He passed Cat and walked, still backward, up the uneven stone steps of the chapel. He turned, bowed, and muttered a short prayer.

"One hundred," he said then. He threw a twisted straw into the box on a stand by the window through which Jizō-sama peered out benignly.

He picked up the box and walked down the steps, frontward this time. He nodded at Cat, who bowed deeply.

"These days I call myself Musui, Dream Besotted. I'm visiting old friends and older temples and seeing the historic sites."

Cat almost blurted out her recognition of him. Of course she had heard of Musui and his poetry, but she remembered, just in time, that she was about to pretend to be ignorant of both.

Musui took a fistful of straws from the box and handed them to her. "You're so good at saving time, what with washing your clothes while you're wearing them," he said amiably. "You can save me time by helping me count these." He sat on the bottom step, rested the staff across his knees, and began tallying the rest. "*Hi, fu, mi, yo* . . . One, two, three, four . . ."

Famous or not, Cat was infuriated by his complacency. She was about to be beheaded and her corpse gibbeted, hung out like laundry, and he acted as though nothing were out of the ordinary.

"Please." He waved the back of his hand at her, encouraging her to start.

She squatted beside the neatly raked path. Now that she was dressed as a boy, behaving like one came easily to her. She rather enjoyed being feckless and common. She would have enjoyed it more under better circumstances.

"*Hi, fu, mi, yo.*" She laid each straw on the ground between her feet as she counted it. The act was curiously calming.

"Forty-six," she said finally.

"Fifty-three." Musui sighed. "Fifty-three and forty-six is ninety-nine. How is that possible? I counted the straws out beforehand. We shall just have to do the Hundred-Times-Worship again."

"I must be leaving, Your Honor." Cat bowed and backed away.

But Musui held out his hand, fingers down, and opened and closed them rapidly, the signal for Cat to come with him. "If you're going to be my page, you'll need better clothes." He started down the path as though the matter were settled. "My companion became ill and returned to Edo two days ago," he called back to her. "Now the Beloved Amida has sent me another."

Cat started to say that she couldn't make his journey with him, then stopped. The two stared at each other a moment, shrouded and dwarfed there in the deep shade of the majestic cedars.

Musui had a gentle look, but Cat had the feeling that *tatamae*, what she showed others, didn't fool him. He was a man capable of seeing the essence.

His skin was the color of tarnished bronze. One corner of his wide, thin-lipped mouth curled up, the other down. His mouth, jowls, and jaw canted forward from a flat nose and flared nostrils. They gave him a look of simian impishness. In spite of his nearsighted squint he had an air of intelligence and nobility as well as humor. He had wrinkles above and below his large, bright eyes. He had elephant eyes.

Cat knew that people with elephant eyes were popular. They were kind and creative. A person with elephant eyes could be trusted.

Musui could get into trouble for helping her, of course, but he was of noble birth. And famous besides. If he were caught, his punishment would be far lighter than that meted out to a commoner like Viper. Cat had been taught to be protective of subordinates, but superiors didn't need her protection.

If there is a god who forsakes, she thought, *there is another god who helps.*

"Forgive my rudeness, Your Honor, but I have no money for clothes worthy of such an exalted position." Cat gave Musui a chance to extricate himself from the trouble he had blundered into. In spite of Musui's fame he didn't look as though he had funds to outfit a servant.

"When one has friends one doesn't need money. His Reverence the abbot is an old friend of mine." As he walked, Musui waved in the general direction of the long, low building that housed the monks. "I have trouble making out temple inscriptions and road signs along the way," he said. "Can you read?"

"I'm the ignorant offspring of a poor widow, Your Honor. I go in search of a teacher."

"You search for a teacher. A teacher finds you."

As they left the grove of trees Musui nodded toward the five men gathered at the door of the abbot's quarters. "And I wonder for whom they search."

Cat almost shrank back at the sight of them. In their sashes they wore their badges of office, the long forked steel rods that if skillfully used could snap a transgressor's sword in two.

"Police?" she asked.

"They have the appearance of police."

Musui gave a shallow nod. The men bowed low and backed down the steps while Musui called on Amida Buddha to bless them.

The abbot stood in the doorway and watched them until they were out of sight among the trees. Then he bowed to his old friend Musui and nodded to his old friend's new apprentice.

"They're looking for a brigand who wounded three *samurai* and an artist at the ferry this afternoon," the abbot said. "They say he was dressed as a *komuso*. I don't wonder one of them is behaving like a mad dog, attacking civilized folk." The abbot disapproved of the sect's methods. A *komuso* had passed through recently selling amulet bags that he said had been made from Kōbō Daishi's robes.

"I told the police to search the grounds. We harbor no miscreants here." The abbot glanced at Cat. "I see that your companion has rejoined you, Musui-*sensei*. Are you feeling better, lad?"

Cat looked quickly over at Musui, who continued to smile as though he hadn't heard the question. "I am feeling well, Your Reverence," Cat said.

" 'In travel, a companion. In life, sympathy.' " The abbot intoned the old proverb as though he had just invented it.

He said everything as if it were valuable information his listeners should note and remember. He was big enough to be one of the fierce warrior-priests who had defended the huge temple complex on Mount Hiei in the old days. But muscle had given way to fat.

He waited while they sat on the raised floor of the reception area and removed their footwear. Then he led them through cool cherrywood corridors to his inner room and to the tea and smoking accessories laid out on the *tatami*. The door to the inner courtyard was open, and a tiny waterfall splashed in the garden there. Three fat ducks snoozed at the edge of the carp pond. The sound of distant chanting of the Lotus *sutra* soothed Cat. She felt as though she were being ushered into Paradise.

CHAPTER 18
MAKE EMPTINESS YOUR PATH

"Musui, my old and tender friend, you said your companion had become ill, but you didn't tell us he was so handsome." For all his pompousness, the abbot was a bluff, good-natured fellow. He appraised Cat by the soft light of the floor lanterns. "Paint black eyebrows on him and blacken his teeth and he could be Lord Yoshitsune's lover Shizuka in her disguise as a pageboy."

Ready to refill and relight her new master's tiny pipe every few puffs, Cat was kneeling on the *tatami* behind him. She bowed low, acknowledging her unworthiness of the abbot's compliment. She was also trying to hide the fact that she could be a woman in disguise more easily than the abbot imagined.

At least she felt scrubbed and fed and civilized for the first time in days. The clothes she wore had been handed down through generations of boys serving at the temple. The cotton cloth was softened by long wear, the collar of the loose coat frayed. But the clothes were clean, and they harbored no fleas or lice.

Over her loincloth Cat wore full gray breeches tied and bloused at her knees. Over that she had put on the quilted, black-and-yellow-striped cotton robe. She had pulled the wide black *hakama* over both and tied it low on her hips. The breeches and the robe showed through the long slits down the *hakama*'s sides. Its stiffened rear panel stood up jauntily against the small of her back. She wore white *tabi*. Her hair was dressed in the tea whisk style but tied now with a scarlet paper cord.

"He's handsome enough to be a *gohodoshi*, a messenger of the gods and retriever of lost souls." The man who spoke had large overlapping front teeth that looked like the yellowed ivory vanes of a fan. He was one of five monks of higher rank who had come to spend an evening with the famous poet. The sullen acolyte attending him glared at Cat. He didn't like the presence of a good-looking rival in the abbey.

"If I were to stray into the spirit world," the monk leaned over and whispered at Cat, "I would want you to escort me home, *Gohodoshi-san*."

Cat ignored him and the acolyte's jealous glower and the abbot's look of disapproval. She stared instead at the bit of paper glued by a spot of blood to the back of Musui's pale, smooth skull. Cat had been charged with shaving her master's head. She'd never shaved a head before or anything else, for that matter, and her hand had slipped. Now she was afraid that someone would notice the bloody scrap and embarrass Musui, but she dared not call attention to it by picking it off.

A wrestler named Arashi, Mountain Wind, filled one corner of the twenty-four-*tatami*-mat room. The broad shaven strip from his forehead to his crown bulged between the oiled banks of his hair. His clubbed topknot rested on his bare pate like a lizard sunning. He wore a quilted cotton robe big enough to cover a double mattress. He sat cross-legged with his feet tucked under his massive, lumpy thighs like small, well-fed creatures sheltering there. He leaned on an ironwood elbow stand that creaked under the pressure.

He was still fuming about his dousing in the river that afternoon when the larcenous river porters had tried to extort more money from him. And he was irritated that the poet was sitting in the place of honor and receiving all the attention. The poet wasn't going to wrestle the local strongmen in a charity performance for the temple the next day. Mountain Wind was.

One of the monks had just asked Musui why *haiku* poems were composed of seventeen syllables when the door slid open and an initiate spoke from a kneeling position on the corridor floor.

"Your Reverence, a gentleman wishes an audience with you." The youth moved out of the way.

Hanshiro knelt in the doorway and bowed. He entered without rising, gliding along by putting his left foot out, drawing himself forward on it, lowering that knee to the floor, extending the right foot, and repeating the process. When he reached the humblest location in the room, nearest the door, he slapped his *hakama* hems out of the way, knelt again, knees slightly apart, hands on his thighs, and settled back on his heels.

"Tosa no Hanshiro." He bowed as he introduced himself. "Your Reverence, forgive the discourteous intrusion while you're entertaining such an honored guest."

Hanshiro absentmindedly reached inside the neck of his ancient jacket to scratch a *moxa* scar on his shoulder. Those sitting nearest him assumed he had fleas and edged away. He had bathed in the river and had retied his topknot, but he still seemed a scruffy thistle among the pruned and cultivated monks, all of whom came from noble families.

Cat stiffened. She might not know the price of a rice cake or a ferry ride, but she recognized danger, even if it had left its long-sword politely at the door.

"You're quite welcome here," the abbot said. "We amateurs were only chatting about poetry. But we are indeed honored to have among us Musui-*sensei*, a disciple of the master, Bashō himself."

"Maybe you can answer our question." Musui smiled innocently at Hanshiro. "Why does a *haiku* poem usually consist of seventeen syllables?"

It was a test, of course, but Musui had no intention of embarrassing Hanshiro. He was sure the newcomer knew the answer. He was arranging for Hanshiro to earn a respected place in the gathering, although he also was sure Hanshiro of Tosa didn't care if he were respected or not.

"My knowledge of the arts is trifling." Hanshiro looked at Musui, but he surveyed the room from the corners of his eyes.

Cat felt the cold, hard edge of his gaze brush her. She shivered inside her big jacket and *hakama*. That the clothes were borrowed must be obvious. Cat could almost hear them crying out, "Imposter!"

"I would say that Bashō-*sensei* composed poems of seventeen syllables because they can be read in one breath." Hanshiro bowed gravely in thanks when an acolyte set down a tray of smoking utensils. "The poet's thought can be grasped in an instant. The expression of his enlightenment approaches the point of no-time. Of no-mind. Of no-being."

Musui beamed. He had been right about the unkempt stranger.

"What of poets like Ihara, who create dozens of poems a day?" The monk who spoke was sitting next to the wrestler.

His voice startled Mountain Wind, who had settled his chins onto the overstuffed cushion of his chest for a snooze. Mountain Wind dutifully sat up straighter, ready to regale them all with a listing of the forty-eight falls. When he realized they were still discussing poetry, he went back to sleep.

"*Sensei* said that he who creates five *haiku* during a lifetime is a poet," Musui said. "He who completes ten is a master."

"And which of the master's poems is your favorite, Hanshiro?" the abbot asked.

Hanshiro cleared his throat and stared straight ahead. He looked beyond the gathered monks and beyond the abbey walls to Tosa, the wild, remote land of his birth. He stood at the end of the world, on the high black promontory of Cape Muroto. He heard the roar of the surf, felt the cold salt wind on his face.

> A winter moon's light
> Silver-crested waves rising
> To knock at my gate

His reciting voice was deep and resonant and sent a chill through Cat. Everyone sat silent, appreciating Bashō's genius. The waterfall in the garden seemed loud in the stillness of the room.

The poem was well chosen. It was in keeping with the coming of cold weather and expressive of longings for a distant homeland. Cat was grudgingly impressed.

"And what brings you so far from the coast, where waves knock at your gate?" The abbot had finally gotten to the business of Hanshiro's visit.

"I'm looking for a fugitive who wounded four men," Hanshiro said. "That one may be dressed as a wandering priest. That one was seen headed this way." The language's pronouns didn't distinguish male from female, so Hanshiro didn't have to reveal that the fugitive was a woman.

Cat feared she would faint. All that stood between her and destruction at the hands of this coarse ruffian was the affable shield of her master's smile.

"A-so. The unfortunate affair at the ferry." The abbot already had dispatched underlings to find out as much as possible about the fight, just as Hanshiro knew he would.

Hanshiro also knew the abbot was appointed by the emperor, one of the few official functions left to him. He had little loyalty and less love for the *shōgun*'s upstart government in Edo. Locally the abbot had power and information, without the legal obligation to ask Hanshiro the kinds of questions the authorities would have asked. That was why Hanshiro had come here.

"We have not seen him. Have any of his opponents died?" The abbot's question wasn't an idle one.

To save themselves the bother of dealing with nosy officials, the local folk were in the habit of depositing the corpses of unidentified travelers on the temple steps. Since the unauthorized burial of persons who had died under unusual circumstances was a punishable offense, the abbot was stuck with each decaying body until the matter could be straightened out. A proportion of the *sake* donated to the temple by wealthy patrons went toward preserving the malodorous evidence in such cases.

"No, they didn't die." *Although they probably wish they had died,* Hanshiro thought.

At least the shame of being beaten by one small woman would keep Kira's men from making much of a fuss about it. They were like men who stepped in dog dung in the dark. They would be quiet about the entire affair.

The abbot ran a hand over his satiny skull. This brawl at the ferry would surely bring him problems.

"A thick-livered fellow, that priest," said Musui. "Four to one, you say."

"His opponents were small-livered, cowardly, and unskilled."

Unskilled! With her head still bowed Cat sent a smoldering sideways glance Hanshiro's way. She looked down quickly when her eyes met his. Unskilled!

She was outraged. Didn't the filthy hired killer have a high nose. Didn't he have a good opinion of himself, though. Unskilled, indeed.

"Might this be connected with the Akō-Asano affair?" In the dim light Musui didn't seem to notice Cat's hands shake as she poured his tea. "I've heard many stories about it lately."

"They say a lone warrior is gathering an army to avenge the death of Lord Asano," said the man sitting next to Mountain Wind.

"The fugitive is only a wandering lunatic," said Hanshiro. "But there are those in Edo who want this nonsense cropped while it's a tender shoot, before it grows into something requiring an ax."

"And you are certainly the shears to prune it," murmured Musui.

"In the village, the well-side talk is that Lord Asano had a daughter who has fled the capital. She's now in hiding, and this warrior-priest is her champion," said the abbot.

"I was there," Mountain Wind said.

They all turned to stare at him.

"I was in the House of the Perfumed Lotus the night the wench disappeared, the one they say might be Asano's child."

Cat was sure they could hear her heart, loud as storm surf in her head. Except for Musui's bamboo flute, there was nothing close at hand to serve as a weapon. If only she had her scissors with her. She could at least have driven them into her heart before the hired killer took her. She vowed that if she lived through this night, she would keep the scissors honed and would always carry them with her.

Make emptiness your path. The words from Musashi's *Book of Emptiness* calmed her. *Make emptiness your path and your path is emptiness.*

"What does Her Ladyship look like?" Hanshiro asked casually. He was already sitting bolt upright, but Cat noticed his spine stiffen a bit more.

"I didn't actually see her. It was my first visit to the Perfumed Lotus. And my last." Mountain Wind was happy finally to have the group's attention. "I had wrestled the champion, Mr. Long-Way-from-Nostril-to-Nostril, at the Green Jade Hall that afternoon. He beat me with the dragonfly twist, but—"

"Excuse me . . ." The abbot had spent evenings with wrestlers before. "What happened in the House of the Perfumed Lotus?"

"Nothing we'd want to know about." The long-toothed monk gave Cat's sleeve another seductive tweak.

"It was an unpleasant evening," Mountain Wind said. "The vixens there had forced me to drink a bit of *sake*. Four half-night whores were taking turns sucking on my scepter when an army of men attacked."

Mountain Wind waved his bulky arm as though flourishing a sword. "They were probably Asano's retainers, come to rescue their dead master's daughter. There was much screaming and running to and fro. I think there was an earthquake, and then the fire bell rang. I had to dash into the night air naked. The whores scattered like spider young. I left unsatisfied."

As the talk of what was called the Akō-Asano affair continued, Cat passed through fear and into a detached serenity. She walked the path of emptiness.

She kneaded her master's shoulders when he complained of stiffness and in the process managed to remove the bloody scrap of paper from his skull. She poured his tea and emptied and refilled his pipe, although she was careful not to perform too gracefully.

Cat was not too detached to notice that the *rōnin* from Tosa was a willow in the wind. He bent before questions so that they blew over him. The *rōnin* had tiger eyes, eyes with golden irises. People answered the questions of those with tiger eyes. He spoke little, but he skillfully nudged the conversation along, setting it back on course when it strayed from the subject of the feud between Asano and Kira.

By the end of the evening he had extracted all the available information. He had surrendered almost none himself. Cat was relieved to hear that the available information added up to very little that was correct, more that was incorrect, and a great deal that was pure foolishness. The word had gotten out, though, that Lord Asano had a daughter.

"Do you play the flute, Tosa-san?" Musui picked up the flute from where it lay next to him.

"Very badly," said Hanshiro.

"Perhaps you would honor us with a song to end this most pleasant evening."

"Forgive me, but I lack the skill to perform for such an august company." Hanshiro bowed to blunt the rudeness of his refusal.

"Please honor us by passing the night with us here," said the abbot. "Our accommodations are austere, but I trust you'll find them adequate."

"Thank you, Your Reverence."

As the monks prepared to retire to their tiny rooms, Hanshiro debated paying a night visit to the page who had glanced at him with such a flash of passion in his eyes. He was a comely lad. Graceful. And clever as a woman at pretending to be shy and virtuous. After that first signal he hadn't met Hanshiro's gaze again. Very appealing.

In fact, every time Hanshiro looked at him he felt a warm, tingling confusion, like that produced by the first few sips of *sake*. As the evening progressed the confusion had taken the form of desire.

But a tumble with him would divert Hanshiro from his purpose. And the boy might already be the lover of the master Musui. In any case, he would probably find the lad's bed either empty or doubly occupied.

Besides, Hanshiro's experience with boys had been unsatisfying. Even the most beautiful of them couldn't escape the impediment of being young and inexperienced and much too worshipful in the light of day. Hanshiro didn't relish being teacher as well as lover, which was what boys required.

Hanshiro preferred second- and even third-rank courtesans, and the older, plainer-looking ones at that. They were as skilled but not as devious as the *tayū*. Their fees didn't drive a man to the money lenders. Unlike the haughty *tayū*, they didn't taunt him or keep him waiting in the reception room with giggling apprentices. They didn't make petulant demands for expensive presents and fawning love letters.

"*Sensei.*" Hanshiro gave a slight pull on Musui's sleeve as he passed on his way to the door.

"Yes."

"I wish to make a presumptuous request."

"Anything you like, my son. It was delightful to hear the views of one as cultured as you."

"May I borrow your flute?"

The night had turned chill, and thunder rolled like waves onto a distant and desolate shore. A wind rattled the bamboos in the abbey garden. Cat lay under a thin quilt on the narrow pallet assigned her. Many of the thin pallets in the acolytes' crowded quarters were empty, however. The boys who should have been occupying them were warming the beds of their masters.

O-Jizō-sama of the Six States of Existence, Cat thought. *Tomorrow I will make an offering and send up incense and prayers to you for protecting me this night.*

Then she surrendered her attention to the mournful music coming from the stormy garden outside the abbey.

Musui said that each bamboo flute had a soul and a voice of its own. He said it only waited for a kindred human spirit to release its song. Now his flute was singing through Hanshiro. Its song was the moan of lonely winds through high, wind-scoured mountain crags. It was the cry of seabirds hovering above waves crashing on huge rocks.

If Cat hadn't already seen the *rōnin*'s hard, implacable face, she would have thought it the song of a man lonely and longing for love. The deep minor-key tremolo set up a resonance of longing in Cat herself. She yearned for the company of women, even the women of the House of the Carp.

In the past year Cat had endured the maulings of the men who paid for her company. While they plunged and grunted she had consoled herself by thinking of the money Old Jug Face would send to her mother. But now she missed lying under the satin quilts with Plover in the moments they had managed to steal together.

She missed the whispered talk, mouth to ear, of Plover's hopes for the future. Like most of the women of the Floating World,

Plover dreamed of a handsome, rich, kind young man who would pay her pillow fee and make her his separate consort. In the pleasure districts love, not sex, was forbidden.

Cat missed the warmth and security of Plover's arms around her. She missed her gentle laugh and her accomplished caresses. While the flute's notes floated down around her and the bamboo whispered to the wind, Cat spread her legs under the quilt. She ran her hand across her breasts and down her belly, seeking the hidden kernel. She imagined that her own fingers were Plover's as she slowly, sensuously, consoled herself.

CHAPTER 19
THE DISCIPLE IS THE THREAD

What was taking him so long? Musui was such an amiable, unaffected sort, hardly the type to suffer from constriction of the bowels. Cat stared at the head-high thicket of bamboo screening the roadside privy in the hills above Kanagawa. She stamped impatiently and splattered mud. This was her fourth day on the road, and she hadn't even reached the third post station.

Rain dripped steadily from the brim of her hat. She shivered in the raw wind. She stamped her feet again, this time to relieve the cramp in her calves.

Cat was offended. She didn't want Musui to recognize that she was the daughter of Lord Asano, of course; but she expected him, somehow, to realize he was in the presence of a peer. Musui, however, seemed unaware of his own privileged birth, much less hers.

He had left Cat standing in the road, in the cold rain. The muddy stream of rainwater washed over her sodden straw sandals and soaked her *tabi*. Her toes were numb with the cold.

Far below, at the bottom of the hill, a group of pilgrims in bamboo hats huddled like mushrooms under a bead tree. Otherwise, the road was empty. Sensible travelers had all sought shelter.

Cat carried Musui's big cloth bundle, his *furoshiki*. The knotted ends cut into Cat's chest, but she dared not take it from under her raincape. It would have been soaked immediately. Cat had never had to carry her own things, much less someone else's. The indignity of it bothered her more than the effort.

The bundle had seemed light enough when she started, but it had grown more burdensome with each step. She felt like the greedy woman who tricked an enchanted sparrow into giving her a basket of riches. The basket had grown heavier and heavier as the woman carried it. When opened, not riches but demons tumbled out.

Cat was wearing the yellow-and-black-striped jacket and the gray breeches given her at the temple. The bottoms of the breeches were tucked into her old black canvas leggings. When she walked, the rubbing of the wet cloth stridulated, measured and imperious as a cricket's call.

She had to hold on to her hat or the wind blew under it, causing the straw cord under her chin to choke her. Rain fell from the edge of the brim and sluiced down the rectangular cape of woven straw. The cape refused to compromise with her body. It stood out from her back and flapped like a broken wing. The sandals and wet *tabi* had rubbed raw places on Cat's feet. Those feet had carried her only two *ri* today, and she felt they couldn't take another step.

She and Musui had left the broad plain of Musashi behind. The hills had become increasingly precipitous since leaving Kawasaki. Rags of mist drifted among the trees on the steep slopes. The Tōkaidō followed the coastline where possible, but at times it was forced up and over the stubby green fingers of headlands poking into the surf. As the road wound upward it passed beneath ancient pines, twisted by the ocean's salty breath.

After a long climb Cat and her master had reached the crest of a high tor. A large stone phallus, covered with moss, stood nearby. A pile of rocks as tall as Cat stood next to it. Each rock was the offering of some traveler who had gained the top.

To the southwest Cat could see the thatched roofs of Kanagawa rising from a lake of mist. The village was wedged into the crotch of two steep headlands. It backed up to a bay that was pale under a gray sky. A glow at the horizon, like a row of floor lanterns behind a screen, promised better weather.

"What a splendid privy!" Musui was still adjusting the tucked-up skirts of his robes as he emerged, beaming, from the thicket of bamboo. "It qualifies as *Daibenjo*, a Great-Convenience-Place."

Like Cat he wore a clumsy raincape and a wide hat on which

was written "We two, pilgrims together." The second pilgrim referred to was the long-dead priest, scholar, artist, educator, humanitarian, and builder, Kōbō Daishi. Musui also had on a short white underrobe and a black outer one and muddy brown gaiters. His prayer beads and bell hung around his wrist. On top of his raincape rode the roll of his sleeping mat with his pilgrim's scroll and flute inside.

He opened his umbrella and smiled his lopsided grin at Cat. Musui was so suffused with good spirits that Cat found it hard to stay angry with him, but she managed. She lowered her head so the hat hid her scowl as she hurried through the wet bamboo to the privy. In the past four days she had had more experience with commoners' toilets than she wanted.

But Musui was right. As roadside privies went, it was exceptional. Some enterprising farmer had made additions to lure travelers into passing up other privies in favor of his, thus providing more fertilizer for his fields.

A waist-high screen of supple bamboo shielded its occupant while allowing a fine view of Kanagawa's roofs, like peaked, straw-colored waves, and the bay lapping at its back doors. The floor around the hole was of fragrant, newly cut cypress. The farmer had fastened two blocks of pine, cut in the shape of feet, on each side of the hole, to help the weary traveler adopt the best position. A thatched roof sheltered it all. Wisteria vines climbed the support posts.

With his piece of charcoal Musui had written a poem on the tight weave of the bamboo screen. Cat wasn't surprised. He had been leaving poems on the sides of storage houses, on gates and fences and rain barrels. The rich merchants of Edo, eager for the furtive status derived from acquisition, would have paid stacks of thin gold coins for samples of Musui's poetry and his sinuous calligraphy. Yet if the rain washed off the words as soon as Musui drew them, it seemed to make no difference to him. The privy's roof, however, kept this one dry.

> Flocks of silver birds
> Shift and veer toward coming night,
> And do not heed me.

Cat balanced herself on the raised footprints and watched through the doorway as gusts blew the rain westward in undulating lines across the hard-packed earth. When they hit the ground the drops splattered, sending up twin sprays that did look like the wings of the birds in Musui's poem. Cat became mesmerized by the erratic flights of the phantom birds. They exploded into life, then vanished, to be replaced by others, blown along in front of another gust.

Cat took as long as she could at the privy. She was grateful to be out of the rain and wind. Grateful not to be climbing interminable hills and sliding in the mud. But she knew she mustn't keep her master waiting long. She sighed and trudged out to the road.

"A farmer with the heart of an artist." Musui held the umbrella so it sheltered them both. Then he and his bamboo staff splashed off through the water, and Cat had to hurry to keep up.

"Daishi knew the importance of commoners," Musui said. "He preached that one can't make a delicious meal with one flavor or a beautiful song with but one note."

Maybe the Honorable Daishi never had a commoner drop a turd in his begging bowl, Cat thought.

"The next village looks like a pleasant place to eat." Cat was trying to maneuver Musui into resting.

"I had hoped to have a talk with that gentleman from Tosa." Musui was not to be maneuvered. "But he seemed to be pressed by urgent business."

He's no gentleman, Cat thought. *And his buttocks are in the fire all right, until he has me in his flea-cracking grasp.*

She was glad Musui had delayed so long at the temple that morning. By the time he had chanted the entire Lotus *sutra* and he and Cat had completed the Hundred-Times-Worship, backward, Hanshiro had been gone for many hours.

The Hundred-Times-Worship had taken more time than usual because the temple grounds were teeming with the faithful, come to worship and to cheer for their favorite wrestlers. Musui and the abbot had shouted encouragement as one after another, the local aspirants entered the ring and tried to get a purchase on Mountain Wind's unaccommodating bulk.

The challengers had wrapped their arms as far around him as they could reach. They had clung to his broad leather loincloth in desperate embraces. But he had waddled them over the ring of rice bales faster than they could name their home villages.

"Hanshiro is from the Cape of Muroto." Musui seemed unaware of the murderous thoughts his disciple was harboring for the taciturn *rōnin*. "Daishi-sama achieved enlightenment there, you know. I wonder if Hanshiro has seen him. Perhaps we'll meet up with him on the road and I can ask him."

"A *torii, sensei*." Cat was eager to change the subject.

"Where?" Musui squinted into the lush, sodden undergrowth. Almost hidden among the trees and up a slope, an old wooden gate leaned forward precariously. It marked the entrance to a shrine.

Musui stopped at every roadside temple and shrine. Small shrines and temples dedicated to local deities abounded, and members of the Shintō and Buddhist pantheons were often mixed together. Shintō or Buddhist, Musui worshiped at them all. He rinsed his hands and mouth, dropped a coin in the slatted wooden box, and rang the big bronze bell if there was one. He burned incense. He clapped his hands, bowed his head, prayed, and chanted. When Cat finished her much shorter rituals, she waited.

At first Cat had been impatient with Musui's delays. But as the road grew steeper and the rain drummed on her hat and she slid in the muddy streams flowing past her feet, she began to look for chances to stop. She preferred the monuments with roofs where she could get out of the weather, but any rest was welcome.

The narrow trail to this almost forgotten shrine was overgrown. As Cat pushed through the wet bushes, more water showered down on her. Mossy stone steps, all a-tilt, staggered up the wooded hillside. They led to a small shrine to Hachiman, the Shintō god of war.

Sharing his roof was the Buddha Fudo-sama, a ferocious figure surrounded by carved flames and sitting on a lotus flower. That Fudo-sama was here was an especially propitious omen. He represented unshakable resolve and invincibility. He was the patron saint of warriors.

Cat pictured the ideogram for "desperate." Its ancient meaning was "to risk one's life for a place on this earth." Cat was certainly desperate, but she didn't expect to find a place on this earth.

Her father's name had been abolished and disgraced. The family's fortunes had gone to provide for its displaced servants and retainers. Cat knew that to change that would be like trying to put spilled water back in a basin. But she was prepared to lie, dissemble, and kill to reach Oishi.

Cat thought about all that as she bowed before Fudo-sama. The blue paint had long since worn off his face, but he still brandished his wooden sword and rope and scowled fiercely. Fierce Fudo in his cloak of flames cheered her a little. Fudo,

Buddha of the Unmoved and Immutable, frightened away evil spirits. And perhaps he would bless her quest.

The chapel, an odd mixture of Buddhist and Shintō styles, was neglected. The paint had peeled away from the ornate diaperwork around the ceiling. Moss and weeds grew on the rotted cedar shingles of the roof. The scent of mold, like the musty odor of chrysanthemums, pervaded the dark interior. But behind the building was a small waterfall whose splashing was cheerful, even in the rain.

Musui filled the small altar lamps with fragrant rapeseed oil. He lit the lamps and a bundle of incense. Sitting cross-legged on the warped wooden floor in front of the statues, he chanted the Lotus *sutra* and confessed to the sins of the six senses. Finally he intoned an invocation to Amida. By the time he finished, the sun had set.

"Please lay out our sleeping mats," Musui said. "We'll spend the night here."

Cat started to protest but stopped herself. One didn't argue with one's master. If you would have retainers, the old proverb went, first you must be a retainer.

She opened the mats out on the veranda under the wide eaves of the hut. She set the wet cloth bundle, the *furoshiki*, between them.

Musui said he preferred a *furoshiki* to a wicker travel box, because the cloth could be tied around just about anything. And if one wanted to be free of material effects, one could just throw them to the winds, fold up the cloth, and stick it into one's sleeve. So it should be with one's material things as one grew older, he said. By the end of the journey one should have nothing.

Cat's stomach growled. Musui was taking too much to heart his own philosophy of having nothing. The day's only meal had been breakfast at the temple. It had been a pitiful affair of cold rice and a few pickled vegetables. Cat had saved part of it to offer to Jizō with a request that he keep watch over her father's spirit.

"Do you think we need to bathe?" Musui peered out into the darkness and the steady rain.

"If bathing under an icy waterfall makes one holy, *sensei*," she said, "then we are truly the holiest of the holy."

She held up her hands. The pads of her fingers were wrinkled by the day-long soaking. Musui's laugh was so infectious, Cat laughed, too, in spite of herself. Like children, the two of them sat on the edge of the narrow porch and wiggled their toes as they held their bare feet under the cascade off the eaves to wash away the mud.

By the light of the altar lamps, Musui searched among the contents of the *furoshiki*—his writing box, jars of oil, packets of incense, scrolls of *sutras* and other religious paraphernalia. He found two towels, two pairs of chopsticks, and a flat wooden box tied with a cord.

Cat almost cried with relief when he opened it. The abbot had included a meal with his good-bye gifts. Inside the box nested six fat balls of rice, wrapped in crinkly strips of dried seaweed. Tucked neatly around them were pickled plums and coils of boiled gourd peels, all garnished with a spray of pine needles.

When they finished eating Cat packed away the box with a pair of rice balls left in it for breakfast. She cupped her hands, caught the runoff from the eaves, and drank. Then, while Musui played his flute, she watched the curtain of rain fall from the roof.

Cat had heard flutes played often, of course; but here, in the forest at night with the rain falling, the song was eerie. It seemed to be calling to the restless spirits that surely must inhabit such a dark, brooding place.

When the song ended Musui handed the flute to Cat. It was cool and glossy and slightly curved in her hands, as though falling away from her grasp. It was made from the section of the bamboo nearest the root. The walls of the long joints were thickest there, and the natural bore became narrow, making high notes possible.

"Mountain bamboo is strong, yet delicate," Musui said. "It bridges the earth and the sky. Its roots are planted firmly in the ground, yet clouds nest in its leaves."

Cat took a deep breath and blew into the flute as hard as she could. Only the harsh whistle of air emerged from the other end.

"Emptiness is the necessity," Musui said softly. "The universe is an empty shell in which your mind plays. Think of your body as an empty room with walls of skin. Look at a bowl without seeing the sides.

"The walls of the flute do not sing." His voice was hypnotic. "Nor does the fire that cures it, nor the lacquer that glazes it, nor the string that binds it. The emptiness sings. Hold in your hands the emptiness that is the flute. Play not with your fingers but with your abdomen, your soul."

Cat held the flute through the hour of the Cock and into the hour of the Boar. The lamps had long since burned out. The rain slowed to a diffident tread on the roof, then stopped. Fragments of a waning moon, misshapen but as fat and white as the rice balls, glowed through the branches of the pines. Musui sat silent near her in the darkness.

Stand in sound as though under a waterfall. Cat heard the words, but she was sure no one spoke them. *Hear the sound of sound.*

Cat put the mouthpiece to her lips and merged the pulsing emptiness in her skull with that of the flute. She was rewarded with the hint of a tone, like that of a wind blowing across the moist mouth of a jug. But try as she might, she couldn't make it sound again.

"Maybe tomorrow it will sing with you."

"Where are we going tomorrow?" Cat handed the flute back to him.

"Does the cloud ask where it's going? Does the river?" Musui lay down on his mat and draped his spare robe over him.

" 'The teacher is the needle and the disciple is the thread,' " Cat murmured.

"And who has taught you the words of the sword saint, Musashi?"

"I must have heard them somewhere. 'Even boys hanging about the temple gate learn to chant *sutras*,' as the old saying goes."

"And do they learn to count, too?"

Count? Cat turned hot, then cold. He had tricked her into counting the straws for him that first day. Perhaps he was not as guileless as he seemed. "One must count to survive, *sensei*. Counting is not reading or writing." Cat couldn't tell by the silence that followed whether Musui believed her or not.

"You must have a journey name." He seemed unconcerned about whether she had lied to him. Or what her background was. His lack of curiosity unnerved Cat. She had been auditioning and rehearsing various stories about herself, but he had asked for none.

"As you say, *sensei*."

"Your name shall be Shinobu, Endurance."

"You honor this miserable person too much, *sensei*."

Shinobu. It was a girl's name, but boys were sometimes given girls' names to mislead the demons of disease and bad luck. Shinobu meant more than endurance, really. It had an under-meaning. To hide oneself. To live in concealment. It was a good name.

CHAPTER 20
A TRUE WARRIOR

Cat awoke to a washed and sparkling morning. Through the dark green branches of the pines she could see shards of a winter sky pale and lambent as porcelain. Musui stretched, yawned, and wandered off into the bushes to urinate and to scrub his teeth at the waterfall.

Cat rolled her mat. Then she made a small offering of rice cake and prayed for her father's soul. As always when she thought of her father, she wished she had had a chance to speak with him before he died. But actually Cat spoke more with her father now that he was dead than she ever had when he lived.

When she was growing up he had visited only rarely her mother's house. As soon as Cat was old enough to understand, her mother had explained that her father's many duties required him to be elsewhere. When he did visit he often quoted Lao Tsu, who said one should govern people as one would cook fish, poking as little as possible. Lord Asano seemed to have the same attitude toward raising children, as though fatherhood were a government post to which he'd been appointed.

Cat was fiercely proud of him, though. She thought him the handsomest man born. As a child she had wanted his approval more than anything else, which may have been why she trained until the *naginata* shaft rubbed her palms and fingers raw and glistened with her blood. Her mother said she had inherited her father's obstinacy, but Cat did it to make up for the shame of being born a girl when she knew he wanted a son. And for the slight nod he would give when she pleased him.

Now Cat laid everything out on the big cloth, the *furoshiki*, brought the corners up to the middle of the bundle, and tied them. Then she hung the brocade bag around her neck. Inside, wrapped in the waterproof sheath of a bamboo culm, was her new travel permit.

The abbot had seemed pleased to be able to thwart the *shō-gun*'s law by issuing illegal papers. He had sorted through a stack of them while Cat knelt with head bowed. They all had been made out for pilgrims, authorizing them to visit the holy places. They had been signed and stamped by the local magistrate and by the abbot himself, as head of the home temple.

Musui had been apologetic about the bother, but the abbot had waved a languid hand. "Don't worry. Pilgrims arrive here every day with no more notion of permits than seaweed has when it washes up on the shore. Or they have a thousand excuses for losing theirs."

The abbot had mimicked the terrified grimace of a peasant. " 'Forgive this miserable fool, Your Most Illustrious Grace.' " His voice had quavered as he imitated the exaggerated trembling of a peasant faced with authority. " 'My paper fell down the privy hole while I was squatting.' Or, 'The river *kappa* grabbed it when the ferry sank.' Or, 'It burned up in the inn where I was staying.'

"Sometimes the heretics who pose as holy men convince the faithful to boil their permits and drink the broth as an elixir."

The abbot was feeling particularly vexed with itinerant holy men that day. In the midst of the temple's festival a gang of them had set up housekeeping in a corner of the temple compound. They had proceeded to ring their bells and chant unceasingly and at full volume.

With brush inked and poised above the heavy rice paper, the abbot had looked at Cat. "Name?"

"Ichiro." Cat had answered without hesitation. It meant "Firstborn Son," and it was her father's pet name for her.

"And are you indeed the firstborn?"

"Yes, Your Reverence." That at least was true.

After Kanagawa, Musui took a side road into the hills in search of a temple that claimed to have a sample of Daishi-sama's writing. But the small, run-down building had an abandoned air about it. It was closed up, and Musui could find no one to open it for him. Cat could tell he was disappointed. She herself was annoyed by the useless delay.

By the time they returned to the Tōkaidō the sun was well on its way to setting behind the mountains that crouched in purple ranks to the horizon. The rain had brought warmer weather, and the road to Hodogaya was crowded with travelers. The bay below reminded Cat of a cloak dyed with mountain indigo. A line of surf undulated like a white thread along the shore. In the distance to the southwest, Mount Fuji towered above them. Its smoke-blue slopes swept heavenward in graceful folds.

When Cat had been much younger she and her mother had accompanied her father on the yearly trips to Akō. A lord's official wife couldn't leave Edo with her husband, but an outside-wife, "a noblewoman of the province," could. While her nurse napped, Cat had hung from the window of the big palanquin. She had watched the sacred mountain grow as the procession of retainers and porters, sandal bearers, servants, maids, and palanquins approached it.

Cat remembered how carefree those journeys had been. Her father's standard-bearers had cleared the road ahead of them. The staffs of the best inns had been lined up and waiting to make them comfortable. Cat had stepped from the palanquin directly onto the floor of the entryway, and her feet never touched the road. As they traveled Cat had slept or read or listened to her nurse's songs and stories.

Cat wished she were in that palanquin, napping while the road flowed by, traversed by the efforts of others. And she missed her nurse, who in a way had been more familiar to her than her own mother.

Maybe the group of women who passed reminded her of her nurse. They were rice hullers. They shook the bran dust from their aprons and massaged their stiff shoulders and arms.

When Cat and her mother were forced out of their house and the money set aside for them mysteriously disappeared, Cat's nurse had gone to an employment agency. The only work available was as a rice huller in a government granary. It was exhausting work. Cat remembered her coming back to the tiny house late in the evening, her clothes covered with bran dust. She had developed a racking cough from the dust. Cat worried that it would ruin the old woman's health, but she insisted on doing it so she could add her few coppers to the household funds. Her uncomplaining sacrifice had been part of Cat's decision to seek a contract at the House of the Carp.

As Cat and Musui walked onto the arc of the bridge outside Hodogaya, Musui lifted his staff so it wouldn't tap on the planking. "We mustn't disturb the Daishi's sleep."

Cat leaned over the railing to look underneath. Bundles of belongings were stacked against the big stone pilings where the bridge spanned dry land. It seemed that someone, if not the Daishi, was sheltering there.

"In his wanderings the Daishi was once refused lodging and

had to sleep under a bridge,'' Musui said. ''He wrote a poem about it.''

''What was the poem, *sensei*?'' She knew the poem already, of course, but was maintaining the pretense of ignorance.

'' 'They refuse to help a traveler in trouble,' '' Musui recited. '' 'One night seems like ten.' ''

Musui smiled and bowed and called out greetings to everyone he passed. Musui was a traveler. He had been up this road many times. He could probably answer any question Cat had about the Tōkaidō. And Cat had lots of questions.

She wanted to know how closely the *daimyō* scrutinized travelers passing through their lands and how quick they were to flog or crucify those who displeased them. Which rivers boiled with rapids, and how did one bargain with river porters? What was the cost of a night in a respectable inn? Of a bowl of rice or a bath? Did bandits really lurk in the mountains? Most important, where was the next government barrier?

''*Sensei* . . .'' She thought it best not to appear too curious about details. ''What is the road like ahead?''

''The Path?'' Musui's expansive embrace included the bay, the hills, Mount Fuji, and the terraced brown paddies following the contours of the slopes. He beamed at the colorful stir of travelers that swirled around them.

''Everyday life is the Path. To ask about it is like the birds asking what is air; or the fish inquiring as to the nature of water.''

Cat sighed. This would be difficult. She tried an oblique approach. ''Have you made many pilgrimages, *sensei*?''

''Ah, yes. Three times I've circled Shikoku, visiting the eighty-eight temples associated with the Daishi. I've been to his burial place on Mount Koya. I've been to the Land of the Eight Clouds Rising.''

Musui bowed to a huge stack of brushwood creeping along on a pair of legs as thin as the iron chopsticks used to transfer live coals. The old woman underneath was bent at a right angle, her chest parallel to the ground. She walked with the aid of a gnarled branch.

''Auntie, let me carry that for you.''

She stared suspiciously up at Musui from under the load. When he tried to lift the frame the wood was tied to, she veered, tugging it out of his hands. She was astonishingly strong, but when Musui let go of the load its weight carried it off in the opposite direction. The old woman had to skip a few steps to get control of it again. *"Baka,"* she muttered under her breath.

"I have no plans to steal your wood, auntie."

"A gentleman like you shouldn't bother with the likes of me, Your Honor." She continued to stare up at him like a rat cornered in the woodpile. She was trying to analyze this madman's scheme to trick and rob her.

Cat was appalled. Surely *sensei* wasn't considering carrying wood like a peasant. She was even more appalled by the possibility that he would expect her to carry it in his stead.

"Please, auntie." Musui smiled at her beguilingly. "Allow an unworthy pilgrim the honor of bearing your burden a short way. For the sake of O-Daishi-sama."

Reluctantly the shoulder-burden-auntie lifted the woven straw carrying strap from across her bony chest. Even more reluctantly Cat helped Musui heave the heavy wooden frame onto his back.

Having her load removed made no difference in the old woman's posture. She still walked bent double at the waist, as though searching for something dropped. She had to hold her head at an angle that made her chin jut out. With one hand she clung to the staff. She held the other arm straight behind her for balance. Her bare feet left long scuff marks in the damp earth.

Musui slowed his pace to match hers. Cat closed her eyes and took several deep breaths. She silently chanted a *mantra* for serenity. At this rate she would never reach Kyōto.

"Is Your Honor going to Ise?" The old woman peered sideways up at Musui.

"The gods alone can say, auntie. The Path matters. The destination doesn't." Musui was off on his favorite subject. "My disciple and I follow the instructions of the Daishi to roam about until exhausted, then drop to the ground, and in this dropping be whole."

"I could tell you pudgy city priests a thing or two about dropping from exhaustion." Now that the shoulder-burden-auntie had recovered from her shock, her basic nature was reasserting itself.

She swiveled her knobby head to look up at Musui. Her hair was gray and feathery as lint. Below it her skull looked as though thin leather had been sewn tightly over a collection of edged objects.

"I have advice much more valuable than that." Her beady eyes glinted with the malice spawned by a lifetime of grievances.

"Keep your money in your belt. Don't pull your knife on a drunkard, and don't show your daughter to a monk.

"Or in your case, pretty boy . . ." She shook her walking stick in Cat's direction. "Don't turn your back on one. They'll hop into your drawers faster than a flea."

"I'll add that wisdom to the Daishi's rules of the road." Musui's equanimity seemed to disappoint her.

"What are Daishi-sama's rules, *sensei*?" Cat asked. Maybe Kōbō Daishi had some practical advice for travelers. Cat could use any advice she could get.

" 'Do not wish for riches or acclaim or gratification of the flesh,' " Musui said. " 'Do not kill, steal, fornicate, drink, or talk idly.' "

"Might as well stay home," the old woman mumbled at her feet.

" 'If you meet a highwayman, give him everything,' " Musui continued. " 'Don't haggle over the cost of an inn or a ferry. Give alms to beggars. Never ride a horse or *kago*.' "

"Why is that?" Cat immediately discarded most of the advice, keeping only the part about not haggling with ferrymen and innkeepers.

"One travels the Path humbly, without outside aid. When you feel the desire to break these rules, stop your journey and go home."

The woman resumed her load when they reached the edge of Hodogaya. Without saying "Thank you" or looking back, she trudged off and was soon lost to sight down a side street.

"Ungrateful," Cat muttered.

"He who knows kindness is a true warrior."

Cat's face burned at the gentle reprimand. Oishi had often said the same thing when as a child, Cat had lost her temper with the household servants.

"Hold out your begging bowl." Musui drew his own wooden bowl from the front of his robe and extended it. "Homage to the Daishi who impels our earnest pleas," he chanted to passersby.

Cat clenched her teeth and did likewise. Of the many virtues her parents had taught her, humility was the most difficult.

In Hodogaya the begging bowls served two purposes. The waitresses in their thick white face powder and blue aprons dodged around Cat and Musui. They went in search of wealthier travelers to drag back to their inns and tea houses.

By the time Cat and Musui had passed through the village

they had collected forty coppers, a few handfuls of uncooked rice, a dried fish, and an offer of lodging in a hovel that a rat would have avoided. The afternoon was late, and Cat was ready with a refusal, in case Musui were mad enough to accept the offer.

The hut sat on a barren piece of rocky ground at the edge of the village. It was made of panels of woven bamboo lashed between posts, with cast-off mats thrown over for roofing and held down with rocks. The mat that served as a door was thrown back to reveal the furnishings, a heap of bamboo leaves in a corner.

With a bundle of brush a gaunt old woman was sweeping the earthen floor at her doorway. She wore a tattered paper robe and a faded rag over her head with the front corners tied at the nape of her neck.

"Honor our miserable house by staying here, kind pilgrims." Like the shoulder-burden-auntie, her back was permanently bent, but she bowed lower. "Bring the Daishi's blessing to us with your presence. I have only gleanings from the millet fields for your supper, but I shall fetch fresh river grass for you to lie on. And I will massage your weary feet."

"We must journey farther before stopping for the night," Musui answered her gently. "Perhaps on our way back we can enjoy your generous offer. In the meantime, please do us the honor of accepting this meager trifle for the Daishi's sake." He gave her a small wooden tablet with an invocation and a picture of Kōbō Daishi stamped on it. "It comes from Mount Koya. It will protect you and your loved ones." He added the rice and the fish they had been given and all the coppers.

Clutching the treasures, the old woman wept and bowed and called her thanks until they rounded a curve in the road. When they were out of sight, Musui sat down abruptly on a rock. His eyes sparkled with tears.

As Cat stood staring down at him, grief and shame overwhelmed her. She saw the old woman curled in the pile of straw with snow drifting in through the gaps in the roof and walls and covering her frail body. Cat shuddered. She crouched next to Musui, buried her face in her sleeves, and began to cry as though her heart would break.

"Here now," a young woman shouted. "Everyone dies in the end. So while we're in the world let's be merry."

Cat glanced up and saw the group of young women standing in the roadway, but she couldn't stop crying any more than she could have said why she was doing it. The tears flowed from some dark spring hidden inside her. They stemmed from despair that someone as kind as the old woman should suffer before being released by death and born into a better life. She cried in fear that her own mother would die poor and alone. She wept for her nurse, who no longer had a home or a livelihood worthy of her.

"There, there, Shinobu." Musui became concerned. "We must have endurance, Endurance." He handed Cat a towel to wipe her eyes. "I shall ask the abbot to find a simple job for her and a place to live on the temple grounds. In her next life she will certainly be born higher on the wheel."

Musui handed her a paper handkerchief. As she was blowing her nose Cat felt the playful tap of a fan on her head.

"Such a pretty boy and such a red nose." The six young women, all dressed in identical pilgrims' hats and robes, stood in a semicircle around her. Behind them stood a trio of porters, almost invisible under their loads of boxes and bundles.

"Jizō-sama has sent us to cheer you." The speaker for the group had a round, plain face and a merry smile.

"Ah, the seven sages have left their meditation in the bamboo grove." Musui helped Cat up under the weight of the *furoshiki*.

The women laughed. Everyone knew the ancient story of the seven Chinese sages who left the frivolity of court life to meditate and drink and compose poetry among the bamboo. The joke was that the ideogram for "seven sages" was pronounced the same as "seven prostitutes." In spite of their plain white robes, their pilgrims' bells, and the pious slogans on their wide bamboo hats, Musui had recognized their profession.

"You flatter us, Your Honor," said the leader. "We are but simple bathhouse girls, off on a pilgrimage to Ise."

"Our holy gift to pilgrims is to make their road seem shorter," one of them said.

And they did. The leader thumped time on her hand drum and Cat sang the "Song of the Tailless Ox" and other, more vulgar ditties. For most of the two *ri* to Totsuka, the seven sages laughed and clapped time and danced.

CHAPTER 21
KARMA PILED UP

A young man sat in an unsavory drinking establishment on the outskirts of Totsuka. He was dressed in a threadbare dark blue hempen laborer's jacket. His legs were bare. His high, shaved forehead was divided horizontally by a faded blue towel, twisted into a roll and tied in front. Clear, artless eyes shone from under the dangling ends of the knot.

He watched an old couple shuffle by as the divergent tides of the Tōkaidō surged around them. They were dressed as pilgrims, but their unpatched robes were cotton, not paper. The square bamboo pack the husband carried was shiny and new.

The young man rose to his feet, settled his sash lower on his thin hips, slipped his toes through the thongs of his straw *zoris*, and sauntered after them.

His smile was affable and polite. "Grandfather, allow me to carry your pack. It will earn me merit on the Great Wheel."

"Thank you, my son. How kind of you. Thank you so very much." The old man's exhaustion made him effusive.

The teakettle and the small pot tied to the pack jangled when he took it off. His wife squatted, panting, in a patch of late-afternoon sun.

"We're on our way to Ise to ask Amaterasu-sama, the Sun Goddess, to cure my old woman's ailment." The man's face was as circular as a soup bowl. His features were rounded and flattened, as though weathered by the elements. His sparse eyebrows arched high above slightly bulging eyes, giving him a faded, startled look. His wife resembled him remarkably.

"The trip is difficult for her," he said. Actually the couple looked too frail to walk to the public bath, much less make an arduous trek across wild rivers and over mountains.

"My beloved, devout mother journeyed to Amida's Land of Pure Light last year." The young man's smile shifted to grief. "I have sworn to help any old people I meet. I myself am on

132

my way to Mount Koya to bury her ashes and to pray for the repose of her soul.''

''Buddha has sent you, and He will bless you.'' The old man helped his wife to her feet and put an arm around her waist. She clung to him as she laboriously slid one foot in front of the other. ''We were about to seek lodging at an inn,'' he said. ''It's getting dark, and my wife cannot travel farther today in any case.''

''I know a fine inn, grandfather.'' The young man was earnest. ''It's run by a pious woman who charges a pittance for pilgrims. But it's a bit off the trampled road.'' He gently herded them onto a narrow path along the dike between the rice paddies.

The path led into the hills just west of town. The man followed his prey patiently. ''Just a little farther,'' he called cheerfully. ''The inn has a splendid view of the town.''

To take their minds off the deepening twilight and the extra distance, he described the simple, wholesome meal that awaited them. He praised the hot bath the mistress of the inn would draw for them. He promised to massage their feet himself.

When the path passed the last farmhouse and entered a towering, whispery grove of bamboo at the base of the hill, he decided they'd gone far enough. He started forward to close the space between them and himself, but although his feet continued to move, his body stayed where it was. He reached back to free the pack straps of whatever was snagging them. He touched warm flesh.

His yelp startled a flock of crows into the air. He twisted, trying to see what had such a firm grip on the pack and his sash. His companions swiveled, as slowly as two stranded sea turtles, to see what was happening.

Still holding the thief helpless, Hanshiro put his mouth close to his ear and spoke in a low voice. ''Do not reach into your coat. Remove the pack. Take off your coat. Then lie on your stomach and do not move.''

''Here then! What are you doing?'' The old man brandished his staff. ''Cullion! Bandit!''

When he saw the two swords in Hanshiro's belt, he folded stiffly to the ground, pulling his wife with him. ''Spare the lad, honorable sir,'' he cried. ''Kill us. We're old. But the boy was only trying to help.''

''Take everything.'' Wearing only his loincloth, the thief lay sprawled facedown in the loam of the grove. ''I'll show you where you can hide their bodies. I'll work for you.''

Hanshiro pulled a straw cord from his sleeve.

"Come here, grandfather." He quickly tied the thief's wrists.

He looked up to see that the old man was still prostrate on his knees, his body and arms flung forward. He trembled so hard that he rustled the dry bamboo leaves. His wife was chanting the Mantra of Light to dispel evil *karma*.

The thief recited a garbled lament that included his widowed mother and six starving siblings, ailing grandparents, a deserted sister and her brood, a typhoon, a fire, a plague, the malice of neighbors, and an ancient curse. When that failed to get him any pity he offered Hanshiro the sexual favors of his widowed mother, his sister, all of his younger siblings, nieces, nephews, and himself.

"Come here, grandfather." Hanshiro's impatience didn't sound in his voice. He had paid a boy to watch the road for him, but he knew that while he tarried, his quarry might be passing through Totsuka. "I won't hurt you."

The old man struggled to his feet and crept toward him, as though Hanshiro were a poisonous snake. Hanshiro held the man's bound hands up for inspection. "Do you see calluses?"

"No." The old man peered at the soft palms and long nails.

"Yet he wears the clothes of a laborer." Hanshiro rolled him over. The knife was stuck into the back of the waistband of his loincloth. "He planned to kill you with that, uncle."

"But all we have are a few coins, the stamps and amulets from the temples we've visited, and the spare clothes in the pack." The old man was bewildered.

"It's easier for a hawk to attack a morsel of mouse than a meal of wild boar." Hanshiro gestured toward the village of Totsuka. "Take his coat and sash. You can sell them and get something for the trouble he has caused you. Go back to the main road. When you pass the stables and the *tatami* maker's shop, ask for the Bamboo Inn. It's on the street of the medicine-box makers. Tell the mistress that the *rōnin* from Tosa sent you. She's honest."

Hanshiro didn't bother lecturing them to be less trusting. Dishonesty wore so many masks on the Tōkaidō, he could never list them all. As the old man led his wife away she was still chanting the *mantra*. Hanshiro's rescue had only convinced her further of its efficacy.

Resting his weight on his heels and his elbows on his thighs, Hanshiro crouched near the thief's head. The man's topknot had come loose, and his stiff, oiled hair fanned outward. He had

drawn his knees up to his chest and his chin down to meet them.
He was weeping and pleading incoherently now. His tears mixed
with the black soil and muddied his face.

"I am Emma, lord of Hell," Hanshiro said quietly. His victim drew into a tighter coil and sobbed and babbled louder.

"Listen to me." Hanshiro poked him with the cold iron ribs
of his fan. "I stand at the gateway of Hell, and I am in a hurry.
Tell me where the bodies are, and I may turn you away from my
kingdom this time."

The thief made a prodigious effort to control himself. He had
already soiled himself. Three long shudders rolled through him
before he could speak. "In a small cave. In the side of the
mountain at the edge of the grove. By the big pine."

Hanshiro hauled him to his feet and shoved him forward. The
thief led him to the cave's small opening, hidden at the base of
the slope by rank growths of wild azalea and rhododendron. It
was covered by a wall of stones that looked like a rock slide.
With a second cord he tethered the man's feet so he could walk
with tiny steps but couldn't run. Then he untied his hands.

"Pull away the stones," Hanshiro said. "And remember that
Emma, the king of Hell, has more important business to attend
to. If you delay him, you irritate him."

When the thief pulled down the first few stones the stench
expanded outward from the opening as though it were inflating
like the bloated corpses inside. Hanshiro almost gagged.

"Faster." Hanshiro tied his towel across his nose and mouth.
He could see that this was not a cave, but a small cavity in the
face of the hill. The faded light of sunset illuminated patches of
the tangle of rotting limbs and bare bones jammed inside. The
ominous, relentless buzz of flies seemed to be the chanting of
sutras for the abandoned spirits of these dead.

Hanshiro thought of the poem written eight hundred years
earlier.

> *Karma* piled up from long ages past
> keeps us coming and going in these bitter lives.

When the man had pulled away most of the rocks, Hanshiro
retied his wrists. He pulled the thief's towel off his head. He
unknotted it, tore off a strip, and stuffed the rest into his mouth.
He used the strip to tie the wadded cloth tightly in place.

He picked him up and stuffed him into the opening, on top
of the charnel pile. The softened flesh gave way easily under

him. Hanshiro wedged him in so he couldn't work his feet loose and kick away the stones. The flies and ants that swarmed over the heap began climbing over him.

The gag muted his screams, but Hanshiro could hear them as he methodically piled the stones up again, walling the thief inside with his victims. He left one rock ajar so he could breathe.

Without looking back he reentered the cool, green-and-silver-and-russet twilight of the bamboo grove. The bamboos' sleek grace and the creak and rustle of their culms and leaves calmed him. As he walked among the shiny stalks, Hanshiro agreed with the Chinese poets who said a bamboo grove was the best of all places to get drunk. He decided that getting drunk was a good idea.

When he caught up with the old couple on the thread of a path dividing the rice fields, they slid down the side of the dike. They clasped their hands and bowed, their foreheads resting on the edge of the path.

Without a glance, Hanshiro stalked by them with his splay-footed gait. He was annoyed with them even though he understood why they made these pilgrimages to the great shrine of the Sun Goddess at Ise.

They had years of blessings to give thanks for and paltry sins to atone. Now that the current lifetime was drawing toward the end, they thought more about how they would spend the next one.

Hanshiro considered their kind the bane of the Tōkaidō. Serene in the unswerving belief that their piety would protect them, they clogged the road. They slowed traffic. They filled the inns. They interfered with commerce. And like the annual summer hatching of mayfly nymphs with dampened, crumpled wings, they encouraged swarms of sharp-toothed pike to feed on them.

Hanshiro wanted to turn on them and shake his fan at them. He wanted to admonish them to stay home and let their sons support them, their daughters-in-law wait on them, and their grandchildren crawl over them. But that would have been disrespectful. And he would have had to listen to their apologies and their self-recriminations and, worst of all, their thanks.

CHAPTER 22
GETTING DRUNK AND WEEPING

Hanshiro walked along Totsuka's crowded main street, past the government office and the big, roofed board out front with the latest of the government's notices. He stopped to see if anything had been posted about the Asano affair or the fugitive holy man. The only placards hung up, however, were the usual platitudes that everyone had memorized by now. They admonished families to be harmonious, servants to be faithful, and masters to be just. For good measure, they exhorted all citizens to be frugal, industrious, and mindful of their stations in life.

Hanshiro heard the clatter and squeal of wooden shutters being slid across doorways in the darkening alleys. Flocks of children ran laughing down the narrow streets. They darted through the openings left before the last heavy panels were slammed into place. Hanshiro smelled the mélange of odors from a hundred evening meals. From the upper story of a house he heard the hesitant notes of a *samisen*'s strings being strummed by a beginner.

Totsuka's inns and tea houses and rice shops were just rousing for the evening's business. Hungry travelers clustered around the itinerant peddlers of noodles and tea and rice cakes. Totsuka was fourteen *ri* from Edo, and it was where people usually spent their first night. It was bigger than the other villages. It had more inns and restaurants and back streets. More places for a fugitive to hide.

Hanshiro passed the street of the medicine-box makers. He would not be enjoying the light-hearted favors of the Bamboo Inn's mistress or the soothing skill of her nimble fingers. He shook off the waitresses who darted out from the doorways, begging him to sample the hospitality of their establishments.

He walked to the Wisteria tea shop, a large, open building in a less crowded part of town. Rice paddies reached almost to its rear door. The tea shop and the inn behind it were built near a marshy stream. A granite column stood next to a stone lantern at the foot of a wooden bridge over the stream. It marked the turnoff for Kamakura to the southeast.

The place was bigger, busier, and costlier than Hanshiro would have preferred, but it was located where he could watch the crossroad. Besides, five or six of Kira's men were staying here. If they should catch Cat first, Hanshiro wanted to be nearby so he could take her from them.

The front of the tea house and the side wall nearest the stream were open to the weather, with tracks for the wooden shutters that closed it off at night. The view there was obscured only by the double sets of posts. They supported the second story and the narrow roof extending from the first floor to keep rain from blowing in on the customers.

The front part of the tea house was earthen-floored so travelers in a hurry didn't have to remove their sandals. It had five long, low, scarred tables for them to sit on. In the rear was a raised area of *tatami* mats for those who wanted to dine with more style and leisure. At center front the open kitchen formed a square, steamy island. Bream splashed with soy sauce were grilling, and a huge pot of red bean soup simmered fragrantly.

A squat, perspiring man performed at the stove. The sleeves of his brown cotton jacket were folded up over his shoulders and the collar opened wide. He had tied a knot in each of the four corners of a small square white cloth and now wore it as a cap.

He snapped his big round paper fan with a rhythmic syncopated popping as he fanned the flames under the fish. At the same time he tossed noodles in a huge pan over a flame that roared and leaped. As he worked he carried on an irreverent banter with the customers and the waitresses. The sizzle of the noodles and fish blended with the waitresses' cries and the hum of conversation. Whenever a customer left, the staff sent him off with shouts of ''Good luck!'' and ''Good-bye!'' and ''Thanks!''

A line of *kago* bearers waited to discharge their passengers at a narrow gate between the far wall and the bamboo fence that extended out from it. Travelers who wished anonymity could exit from the *kago* through the gate. Without being seen from the road they could walk through the garden behind the fence to the inn's rooms in back. Today, however, a pair of policemen checked the passengers before allowing them to pass.

Hanshiro dipped a ladle of water from a bucket at the well and rinsed his mouth and hands. Then he sat on a small platform while a waitress washed his feet. But he still smelled decay over the aroma of the noodles and grilled fish.

A large bench was positioned on the other side of the room so one end of it stuck out beyond the eaves. A bowing, perpetually smiling waitress stood next to it and welcomed mounted customers. Two merchants were using it to climb stiffly down from their rented horses while the postboys held the reins.

Hanshiro chose a wide, low bench near the open-sided front corner. He laid his short-sword next to him and sat cross-legged on one end and glared at the merchants when they tried to sit at the other. They bowed and muttered apologies, then moved on. They lowered themselves gingerly to a rear table's wooden surface. They weren't used to riding horseback.

"*Irasshaimasu*. Welcome, honored guest." The waitress spoke in the falsetto chirp so beguiling and indispensable to her trade. She bore above her head a footed tray of tea things, which she set down in front of Hanshiro. She poured an aromatic, straw-colored tea into the cup. "What would you like, Your Honor?"

Hanshiro grunted and studied the list of house specialties and prices posted above the flaming stove. "*Sake*, if you please. And writing materials."

"Shall I bring you *sake* at thirty-two coppers, or at twenty-four?"

"Mix them half and half."

Hanshiro's appetite had deserted him. He felt as though the stench of old death clung to his clothes and the lining of his nostrils. It coated the inside of his mouth and throat. To wipe out the taste of evil he would need quantities of *sake*, the stuff called "hot water of transcendental wisdom."

He decided that when the outside lanterns were extinguished and he could no longer see the passersby, he would take a bath. He would have the attendants scrub him until he was as red as a boiled lobster. Then he would soak in the steaming water through the hour of the Dog. He would soak away the clinging odor of death and deceit.

Since leaving the temple across the river from Kawasaki, Hanshiro had spent two days in fruitless questioning. He had canvassed Totsuka thoroughly and discreetly. He had heard many versions of the exploits of the *naginata*-wielding priest, but no information.

The rainstorm the previous night had driven to shelter even those travelers who were on grass-pillow journeys, who camped along the way. The only roof available had been pilgrims' lodging at a small temple that claimed miraculous cures. Rather than lie elbow to elbow with the diseased, the raving, and the lice-infested, he had slept on a roofed-over woodpile behind a potter's shop. So far this had been a tiresome, grass-pillow journey for Hanshiro, too. He was ready to spend some of Old Jug Face's money on a proper bath, clean bedding, and a room shared with no one.

A servant arrived carrying a small brazier with a kettle of *sake* warming on it. The waitress brought a long-handled tray of smoking supplies and set down a second tray containing an ink stone and a bowl of water, a small bamboo mat with two brushes rolled inside, and several rolls of heavy, pliant paper. "Do you want me to prepare the ink for you, sir?"

"No. But bring me another jar of wine. And tell me, are the police looking for that fugitive priest from Edo?"

"Yes, sir." The waitress glanced toward the police and the line of *kago* whose bearers were complaining loudly about the delay. "But you needn't concern yourself. This is an honest establishment. There are no criminals here. Although . . ." She leaned down to whisper. "The young westcountryman at the third table over, the one with his head bandaged, he actually fought with the rogue priest." The waitress bowed and retreated to the kitchen area.

The artist was sitting by himself also. Like Hanshiro, he had left his long-sword on the rack in the entryway. His pole, festooned with collapsed pleated painted lanterns, lay under the bench on which he sat.

Not much of the man's face was visible through the swathing of bandages, but his eyes and nose were dark purple. He was using a reed to take his nourishment in liquid form, fermented bean paste broth and a lot of *sake*.

From the corner of his eye Hanshiro studied him. He had fought with Lady Asano, if the mendicant priest had indeed been she. By now Hanshiro had his doubts. He was beginning to think she really was in hiding and the priest was just another madman loose on the Tōkaidō.

With deliberate, circular motions of his wrist, Hanshiro rubbed the block of pressed black powder against the moistened, polished slate. While the ink collected in the trough at the end of the stone, he composed his letter to the police at the government office.

A murderer lies with the evidence of his crimes. Pass through the bamboo grove behind the distillery. Look for a cave in a thicket of azaleas by the big pine tree at the foot of the mountain. The cave entrance is covered by rocks.

Not very poetic, Hanshiro thought. He didn't mention the old couple who were the intended victims. They wouldn't want to become involved with the police. No one wanted to become involved with the police. Tsunayoshi's justice had a way of turning and biting those who sought to set it on someone else.

Death by horror. *Karma* piled up. Maybe the thief would be alive when the authorities found him, and maybe he wouldn't. His trip to hell would be unpleasant in any case. Perhaps his fate was to return as a maggot, Hanshiro thought, to spend another lifetime living off the dead.

Hanshiro folded the letter. Then he balanced two small silver coins in the palm of his hand. They weren't worth much since Tokugawa Tsunayoshi had debased the currency to pay for his eccentric extravagances. But one of them would still be more than the waitress earned in two or three days. He laid the coins inside one of his paper handkerchiefs, twisted the ends, and gave both to her.

"Pass the letter to a servant to deliver to the police station," he said. "Divide the contents of the other paper with him."

"Thank you, Your Honor."

"Tell the servant that a traveler gave you the message, then continued his journey toward Edo. You don't know who he was."

"Yes, sir."

When she left, Hanshiro unrolled a second strip of paper. He anchored the top corners with the polished river stones supplied for the purpose and renewed the supply of ink. With firm strokes he drew the characters, spelling out part of an ancient poem. The words had been rattling in his head for two days.

> I call myself
> a man of spirit,
> but on this journey,
> grass for a pillow,
> my thoughts keep going back.

But his thoughts went back only two nights, to the abbey and to the boy and to the look that had started an aching warmth in his loins. Hanshiro was chagrined to realize that the heat was spreading to his heart. It was ridiculous. He was too young for infatuation with boys. He completed the poem.

> And like the fires that burn
> when fishergirls of Ami bay
> boil down their salt,
> these memories burn
> deep within my heart!

The waitresses were lighting the small lanterns inside and the big square ones outside when Hanshiro heard music approaching. It was a courtesan's song. And a very old one at that. The melancholy of courtesans went back a long time.

> Things that pierce the heart:
> night travel, boat travel, being on the road,
>   a roadside inn,
> a voice reciting *sutras* from a mountain temple
>   in a dark wood,
> a lover who leaves you before you're tired of him.

The lanterns outside cast an artificial light on the facade of the buildings across the way and on the street between. They gave the Tōkaidō the appearance of a stage. The travelers were extras entering and exiting. Dancers were about to open the program.

When the seven women passed, drumming and singing and dancing, several of the tea house customers applauded. Musui had taken off his big hat, and it hung against his back. His page's face was still covered by his hat, but Hanshiro recognized his clothes and the lithe body inside them. He took deep, slow breaths until the merry caravan passed and the music and laughter faded.

It was time to forget about boys. It was time to see who the bandaged painter of lanterns really was. Hanshiro picked up his kettle of *sake* and affected the exaggeratedly upright manner of someone drunk trying to appear sober. He wove a tipsy course to the bench where the artist sat brooding.

" 'To keep silent and act wise,' " Hanshiro recited, holding up the kettle.

" 'Still not as good as drinking *sake*, getting drunk, and weeping.' " The artist finished the poem through clenched teeth. He was in pain from the blow inflicted by the butt of Cat's *naginata*.

Hanshiro introduced himself as the Cup No Man Can Finish, *rōnin* and underpaid fencing instructor for the spoiled brats of minor nobility. The westcountryman confided that he was called Mumyosai, Nameless, *rōnin* and underpaid painter of Benkei on the Gojo Bridge.

As the evening progressed Hanshiro and Nameless drained a few more jars of *sake* and drank toasts to the old days. They were waving their bowls in rhythm and chanting ancient Chinese poetry about overflowing wine when the inn's servants closed the big front shutters. They were still chanting when teams of waitresses heaved them to their feet and half carried them, half led them to the steaming bath.

CHAPTER 23
MEETING A BUDDHA IN HELL

" 'I'd like to be called a traveler in the mist . . .' " As Musui recited the opening of Bashō's famous poem, he bowed to the group of men shuffling on their knees across the *tatami* of the reception room of the Four Heavenly Kings Inn in Totsuka.

Again lodging under sasanqua from place to place. Cat silently finished the famous verse.

She didn't care that the men had interrupted her calligraphy lesson. She despised having to make crude, wobbly strokks with the brush. She found it difficult to look blankly at Musui when he recited poetry she knew as well as her own family lineage. Several times she had almost blurted out the classical references that were the sign of her breeding.

She especially missed her books, bound in rue-scented silk covers to protect them from insects. She longed for the authors in whose company she had spent so many pleasant, solitary hours. After she moved to the Yoshiwara she had treasured them for the escape from loneliness and sorrow they had provided her.

This evening, Musui's visitors included three more innkeepers, the manager of an employment agency, and an ancient cloud dweller, as the nobility were sometimes called. This one had been a courtier to an emperor long retired. The nobleman now eked out a living teaching calligraphy and the art of distinguishing scents. There was also a manufacturer of high-grade hair oil, a fish broker, and a maker of brocade borders and ties for mosquito nets. Each one carried his lacquered writing box and a scroll of his own poetry.

The margins on most of the scrolls were filled with commentaries made by Totsuka's professional literary critics at one copper a verse. The hair oil magnate carried a much thumbed recent edition of the five-hundred-year-old text, *Good Poetry of Modern Times*. Besides examples of superior poems, it listed poetic phrases that could be used frequently with impunity. In composing poetry, creativity was not admired nearly so much as the ability to incorporate the classics into one's verse.

The innkeeper bowed apologetically to Musui. "My friends heard you were honoring us here, *sensei*. They beg your candid opinion of their attempts at verse."

You mean you sent servants on the run to inform them, thought Cat.

She watched closely, to be sure the host showed the proper respect for Musui in the seating arrangements. In their efforts to appear cultured, many of the townsmen foolishly hired mountebanks to instruct them in the Ogasawara school of etiquette. As far as Cat was concerned they had no more idea of refined behavior than a chicken. But the host gave Musui the seat of honor in front of the *tokonoma*, the tall niche for displaying flower arrangements and scroll paintings. The others settled back on their heels and arranged their robes and writing materials.

Musui smiled graciously through the introductions. This happened almost everywhere he stayed, which was why he hadn't minded spending the previous night in the abandoned chapel.

"Would you be so kind, *sensei*, as to forgive my presumption and inscribe my fan with a few words?" The fish broker folded at the waist until he touched the *tatami* with his forehead, then slid the paper folding fan toward Musui.

"You honor me." One of Musui's seemingly endless supply of rules of the road was "Never refuse a request for calligraphy, but never offer it unless asked." He dipped his brush into the ink and quickly, effortlessly, wrote:

The joy of meeting,
longer than a lover's sash
in bed at midnight

Everyone gasped with pleasure as the fish broker passed it around. Cat knew that from now on he would find a reason to display it to every person who entered his house. He would boast of this night until, when his friends saw him approaching, they would remember urgent business on the other side of the street.

Maids hovered with jars of warmed wine and plates of rice dumplings and raw sea bream with a searing horseradish sauce. Other maids broiled strips of abalone on a hot stone. After the men had sat around hissing and sucking bits of food from their teeth, after flattery and self-deprecation had taken up a quarter of the hour of the Dog, the host raised his hand for attention.

"I propose a contest of linked verse."

"*Hai!* Yes!" They all had drunk enough *sake* to be bold. They didn't require much. "What topic shall we pick?"

"Not frogs," said the mosquito net trimmer. "We're simple country folk. We could never equal the poetry of Bashō's famous frog match. You were there, were you not, *sensei*?"

"I was." Musui smiled at the thought of it. Bashō and nineteen of his disciples had recited away the spring night and raised the dawn with frog poems. Toward sunrise they had been so tired and tipsy that the last few matches had been undecided. But the poems had been collected into a book that was widely read.

How Musui missed the master. Bashō had refined linked verse and given it a humorous, gentle serenity all his own. He had taken it from the intellectual snobs and the nobility and had made a present of it to everyone.

"Shall we compose serious verse or *haikai*, the comic stuff?"

"I propose *haikai*," said Musui. "Let our topics be the crane and the pine tree."

"We must have a judge," said the manager of the employment agency.

"Musui-*sensei*! Musui must judge."

"I shall record the poems." The innkeeper motioned for his servant to bring his writing kit.

The other men began laying out their ink stones and brushes, water containers, mats, and felt pads, lining up everything precisely. With small figures carved of ivory or jade or wood they weighted down the long strips of mulberry paper on which they would write their own copies of the poems and the commentaries. In an evening with Musui they would receive free instruction worth many silver *chogin*.

The eight earnest poets paired off. One of each pair would compose the first part, or the *hokku*, of the poem. The other man would add the *wakiku*, the second part, using linked associations or pivot words or word-plays. Musui would decide the winner of each match.

As the honored guest, Musui opened the performance. He arranged a graceful compliment to the host into the requisite three lines of five, seven, and five syllables. The innkeeper linked it to a self-deprecatory second part of two lines of seven syllables each. Then the match began in earnest.

The cloud dweller, the old nobleman, was an adequate poet, but his mental faculties weren't what they once had been. The townsmen were slow, and their efforts were clumsy at best. The performance was interrupted by laughter and the loud hissing of a man in the throes of creation and by the clapping of hands and cries of delight at a particularly agile phrase.

In games like this, the wit and the quantity of the verses counted more than their aesthetic quality. But as far as Cat was concerned, she and her friends in the House of the Carp had performed better. Linked verse required training and intense concentration and cooperation. The performances had complex rules of subtle word associations and categories, and Cat listened carefully to Musui's comments and corrections. He deserved his reputation as a master.

"Shinobu, Endurance," Musui whispered to Cat while the fish broker was pondering his line and muttering and sucking his breath loudly through his large front teeth, "please fetch my tobacco."

Cat rose in the discreet swish of her *hakama* and bowed. She slid the carrying stick through the wire handle of a small floor lantern and padded down the hall. The laughter and murmur of voices from the poetry circle faded. Cat heard the ubiquitous sound of chopping from the kitchen and men's wheedling voices. The poetry guests' sandal bearers were trying to cadge wine and fleshy favors from the scullery maids.

As Cat entered the dark hall next to the inn's entryway, she heard talk of a more serious nature.

"Have you seen this woman?"

She set the lantern down at a distance so she would be in

darkness. She eased up the paper wall screen so it wouldn't squeak in its track and slid it open a crack. Through the slit she saw two of Kira's men standing on the flagstones next to the raised wooden flooring of the entryway. They held up a copy of Masanobu's *Portraits of Courtesans of Edo*.

The book was opened to the stylized drawing of Cat. From his higher position on the raised floor, the head steward peered down at it by the light of the lantern a servant held.

"Forgive my abysmal ignorance and inability to help, but there's no woman here who looks like that." The steward was punctilious and apologetic and absolutely uncooperative. He was adept at recognizing the lowborn trying to impersonate the high-born.

"Of course there isn't. She's in disguise." Both men were irritable by nature, and their days of futile questioning hadn't improved their dispositions. Also, Lord Kira was sending them increasingly petulant and threatening letters via courier. "We must speak to the master of the inn."

"It's my most regrettable duty to inform you that the inn-keeper is unavoidably indisposed now. But if you'll follow that homely, foolish little maid, she'll try her unworthy utmost to make your most honorable persons comfortable at our humble establishment whilst you await him."

With courtesy so exaggerated it could only be disdain, the steward bowed the two into an inner room. He would keep them there as long as possible. He would see that they were well supplied with food and drink and entertainment. Then he would present them with an exorbitant bill for it.

Cat walked quickly and silently through the maze of inner corridors to the small room she shared with Musui. She hung the lantern on the wrought-iron stand and trimmed the wick as low as she could. Musui had been so kind. Even if it meant peril to her, she couldn't leave him thinking her ungrateful.

She cleared the tea things off the tray. With a teacup she scooped sand and ashes from the firewell onto the tray. She smoothed it with a chopstick and sprinkled water from the tea-pot to dampen the surface. Then she held the chopstick poised over it. She hadn't the nerve to compose a poem of her own for a poet of Musui's stature, so she decided on one he would be sure to recognize.

> If I could do as I wish
> I would acknowledge more profoundly . . .

"Ungrateful slut!" The voice that interrupted her came from behind the sliding panels separating Cat's room from the one next to it.

Cat jumped at the suddenness of it. She saw a man's pacing shadow loom large, then recede, then grow against the paper panes. She didn't have to hear much to realize that the speaker was a procurer unhappy with his strumpet.

"I rented you this robe and a scarlet crepe underskirt, a brocade sash, and a silk floss veil at ten *momme*. Not to mention the travel cloak for three *momme* extra. I paid three hundred *mon* to have this room alone in a high-class inn." The man's voice was low and menacing.

"I paid the old hag of a go-between two *momme*," he said. "I paid the shampooer and the hairdresser one *momme*. I hired a *kago* and cushions and two bearers at three *momme*, thirty *mon*. . . ."

The procurer hadn't added the cost of this night's food and drink to the tally. He and his commodity wouldn't be here in the morning when the bill was presented.

The procurer planned to collect the rest of the fee when the merchant finished his business with the woman. Then he would sneak her out the rear gate and continue on to Edo where he would sell her to a bathhouse.

"Stop sniveling!" he muttered. "The customer is a rich man. If he weren't afflicted with a slight problem, he wouldn't have settled for the likes of you. And his cock is not so badly diseased. You won't notice in the dark, anyway."

As soon as Cat realized the conversation didn't concern her, she ceased hearing it. She finished writing the poem.

> If I could do as I wish,
> I would acknowledge more profoundly
> the sorrow of departing in winter.

She knew that at any moment Musui might send a servant to look for her. She hurriedly changed into the tattered leggings and the old black jacket that once had been her priest's robe. She folded the borrowed page's clothes neatly and laid them on top of a camphorwood chest, along with her travel papers.

They were useless to her now. The inn's steward wouldn't interrupt his master during the linked verse contest, but the innkeeper would see Masanobu's album of courtesans eventually. When he did he would certainly notify the authorities. They would be on the alert for someone wearing Cat's clothes and carrying her papers.

Cat prayed to Kannon-sama that Musui wouldn't get into serious trouble; but after spending a few days with him, she was rather sure he wouldn't. Trouble seemed to wash off Musui like water off a frog's face, as the old saying went.

Cat stuck her few possessions into her sleeves and the front of her jacket. Carrying only what she had had when Musui found her, she turned to go.

As she headed for the door, she brushed against Musui's flute, which jutted out over the edge of the wall shelf. It was inside its brocade bag, but it hit the floor with a thud that coincided with a silence in the other room. Cat was bending to pick it up when the procurer shoved aside the dividing panel and rushed in.

"What did you hear, boy?" He grabbed for her. As though making a graceful, sweeping dance movement, Cat swung the bamboo flute up and back in both hands and then slammed it into his head. The flute was designed to double as a club. Its dense, thick wall made a sharp cracking sound even through its cloth bag. The procurer slumped at Cat's feet.

She hissed in exasperation. She didn't have time for this. She snuffed out the lantern, grabbed the procurer's ankles, and dragged him into the other room, closing the panel behind her. She hardly noticed the young peasant woman huddled in her tawdry finery against the far wall.

Cat untied the procurer's loincloth and trussed him up quite artistically with it. She had learned the art of knot tying at the Perfumed Lotus. There were customers who fancied being helpless for the "trembling silk" of foreplay and the "bursting fruit" of orgasm.

This particular pattern of binding would strangle the procurer if he tried to struggle. There was a system of knots for each social class. The one Cat tied now was reserved for beggars.

Cat used one of the inn's thin cotton towels to gag him. She opened the bedding cupboard and heaved his torso, then his legs, inside. She closed the sliding door and turned to her next problem.

The peasant was still crouched against the wall. She was about sixteen, two or three years younger than Cat. Her eyes were wide with terror, and she looked even younger.

She clutched a torn wicker pack to her chest. She had been through terrible troubles, and the pack had become her only link

with the past, with herself. Cat was strong, but it would have
taken someone even stronger to wrest it from her.

Irritated, Cat considered her. The homely piece of white
goods would almost certainly spread the alarm. She would have
to come along.

"Put on your sandals." Cat grabbed the young woman's arm
in a hard, tight grip and yanked her to her feet. "If you make a
noise, I'll gut you like a herring."

She dragged the peasant behind her, out the room's rear exit
and into the dark passageway. Cat had already located the rear
exit. She was learning to plan for escape.

By the light of the moon Cat dragged her captive, stumbling
in her long, confining robes, through the inn's rear yard. They
felt their way among stacks of roofing tiles, bamboo scaffolding
poles, and big wooden tubs. Cat rolled several of the tubs up to
the wall and made the peasant help her stack them into a pyra-
mid. She could see the dark triangles of iron spikes set into the
top of the wall, but she would get over them somehow. The
problem would be hauling the peasant baggage over them.

She unwrapped the long cord from the woman's sash and
knotted it around her wrist. She would take her to the outskirts
of town, tie her up, and leave her for someone to find in the
morning.

"Master . . ."

"I'll go over the wall first." Cat ignored the peasant's timid
murmur. "Tuck your skirts into your sash and follow me. If you
even squeak, it will be your last."

"Master, the procurer left the gate unlocked." The young
woman cringed, expecting a blow for her insolence.

The peasant knew that one master had been exchanged for
another; but she had been thrown into the company of such
scoundrels that, for all his threats, this one didn't seem so bad.
At least he was young and handsome.

She doubted she was meeting a Buddha in hell, as the saying
went. She hadn't found a protector. But the wretch who had
mistreated her was now tied up in a closet. She didn't believe
her fortune had taken a turn for the better. It had just taken a
turn.

Halfway through the hour of the Boar, Musui reached for his
pipe and realized that his disciple hadn't returned.

"Dear friends," he murmured, "forgive my rudeness." He
knew they would assume he was visiting the place-for-business.

As the tea and wine took effect, there had been many such interruptions. The only exception was the cloud dweller. He followed the custom of those who had participated in interminable court rituals. When his bladder filled, he signaled his equally ancient servant, who held a bamboo container so the old man could relieve himself in place.

Musui visited the privy. Then he went to see if his disciple was in their room. He lit the lantern and saw the clothes folded as a woman would fold them. He knelt by the tray and read the poem.

> If I could do as I wish,
> I would acknowledge more profoundly
> the sorrow of departing in winter.

May the Lord Buddha protect you, Lady Asano, he thought. *I shall do my best to mislead them.*

CHAPTER 24

A LANTERN ON A MOONLIGHT NIGHT

The first-story eaves of Totsuka's shops and tea houses almost met over the narrow roadway brightly lit with hundreds of lanterns. They formed a tunnel of light and color and smells in the cold night. The market booths were set one up against the other, with no space between them. The street swarmed with people who had to duck and weave among the bird cages and baskets, hair ornaments and fans and toys, hung up for display.

"What is your name?" Cat muttered.

"Kasane, Your Honor. Gillyflower."

"Dig out your earholes and listen well, Kasane," Cat growled. "Try to escape and I'll gut you."

Kasane was too frightened to answer. She hurried after Cat, trying to maintain the customary three steps' distance of a wife who dared not step on her husband's shadow. She walked far enough behind to appear respectful, but not too far to get herself killed for trying to run away.

"Here's your fine bream!"

"Come along. Don't be nervous. Have your fortune told."

"Hokkori! Hokkori!" The sweet-potato vendor stood behind his portable brazier and juggled three steaming samples of his wares. "Eat 'em while they're hot!" He had to shout to be heard in the confusion of the night market. Without missing a beat in his performance, he caught the paper-wrapped coppers a customer threw him and tossed a potato in exchange.

All around Cat and Kasane, silver and copper coins rattled in the money changers' scales. The din of hand drums was constant as touts tried to entice customers.

Bands of men wore their inns' identical hempen robes and quilted jackets. Some had draped the inns' small patterned towels rakishly on their heads. Others had rolled them and wore them as headbands. The tall slats on the bottoms of their *geta* supplied by the inns allowed the wooden platforms to tip forward and hit the ground with each step. The resulting tattoo sounded like the fire watchman's clappers as the men clattered from tea house to tea house.

"Stop here! Stop here!" The waitresses tugged at their sleeves.

Cat slowed her headlong flight and stared at a bookseller's inventory in the wooden box on his back. On top of the box sat a large model of an assignation house. The model was so detailed, it included the curtain across the top of the door and, on the roof, the big barrel of water for fires. Cat recognized it as the Spring House near the Yoshiwara's Great Gate.

For a moment Cat had a vivid memory of the broad avenue awash in light from the lanterns strung along the second-story eaves. She remembered herself promenading in silks and satins and brocades and flanked by maids and servants from the Perfumed Lotus. Was it possible that that world existed and that she had left it only a handful of days ago?

Cat looked through the prints of courtesans and actors the vendor carried hanging from a slender pole. She was relieved to see that her own picture wasn't among them. The rest of his stock consisted of books stacked in the wooden box. There were bawdy novels, guides to the pleasure districts, and ghost stories luridly illustrated on flimsy sheets of paper folded, then sewn between heavy paper covers. Among them Cat saw one she wanted. She held it up.

"How much is this one?"

"A good choice!" The bookseller swiveled to see which one

she was holding up. "Our guidebook is indispensable, Your Honor. It lists the sights and savors of the great Tōkaidō."

"How much?" asked Cat.

"One hundred *mon*. A bargain at twice the price. It also tells you where to find the most accomplished women and the best-looking boys."

Cat took the short, knotted cord of coppers from her sleeve and counted them. There were forty-five. She replaced the book and started to move on.

She felt a shy tug at her sleeve and whirled around. She had almost forgotten about her hostage. Kasane held out a square brocade purse on a long cord. It clinked.

Cat grabbed it from her, dragged her into a dark alleyway, and pulled her down behind a big two-wheeled cart. "Don't wave money around, you rice bale."

"I'm sorry, master."

"Where did you get this?"

"My last master stole it from a gambler in Hiratsuka."

"And you stole it from him?"

"He's a black-bellied man, master. He's evil."

Cat smiled to herself as she emptied the lumpy silver coins and the strings of a hundred *mon* into the tail of her jacket. The peasant wasn't as stupid as she looked. Cat counted the coins. She tucked the silver under her sash and the copper into her sleeve. She stuffed the purse into her other sleeve. The coins were anonymous, but such an ornate purse embroidered with its owner's crest would be recognized.

When the procurer was discovered in the closet, someone would come looking for his trollop, if only to recover the gaudy rented robes. Cat had to get rid of them.

"Have you other clothes in that pack?"

"Yes, master."

"Put them on. Be quick. I'll keep a lookout."

"Here?"

"Where do you think?" Cat was so exasperated with her unwanted captive and her harsh country accent, full of extra syllables, she wanted to pull the child's ears.

Sniffing back tears, Kasane stooped so the cart hid her body from the nearby street. Fear and the unfamiliar complication of the clothing made her clumsy. She wasn't used to intricately tied sashes and sleeves that dangled past her hips.

With trembling fingers she tore at the knot in the long, wide ornamental sash, then the undersash and the tightly tied cord beneath that. She pulled off the lined *kimono* and the loose undershirt and shivered. Bare-chested, the hard tips of her dark brown nipples taut from the cold, Kasane struggled with the cord holding the scarlet crepe cloth wrapped around her as an underskirt. Cat forced herself to wait patiently. The sooner she was rid of this country simpleton, the better.

Cat was surprised to see that Kasane's own clothes consisted of a white pilgrim's robe. Even though the robe was torn and stained, Cat could tell it was new.

While Kasane was tying the cheap sash around her, Cat folded the rented clothes and stuffed them behind the cart. Then she wet her towel in a nearby water barrel and scrubbed off most of the white powder and the rouge.

"Do you remember what I said about trying to escape?"

"Yes, master."

But Cat still kept a suspicious eye on her as she returned to the book vendor.

"I'll give you forty coppers and this fine purse for the guide-book."

"Stolen?" He held the purse up to the light of the street lantern.

"Do I look like a thief?"

"Yes." The vendor handed her the guidebook and gave a perfunctory nod of a bow.

For some reason being mistaken for a miscreant pleased Cat. She felt free and independent and dangerous. She had watched Musui in his dealings with innkeepers and tea shop owners, and she had gotten the hang of it. She was elated by the sound of silver and copper jingling in her sleeve. The prospect of asking the price of things, of counting out the coins and handing them over, excited her.

As she browsed she kept her eyes open for weapons but found none for sale. Only members of the noble and military classes were allowed to carry long-swords and *naginata* and spears. The makers would be situated discreetly on a back alley somewhere. Cat dared not attract attention by asking about them.

Her first purchases were a large, dark blue cloth to use as a *furoshiki*, a stout walking staff, and a wide-brimmed bamboo hat. To hide her face, she wore the new hat instead of carrying it slung on her back. Musui's writing on her old one made it too distinctive, and she had left it at the inn. She regretted having to abandon the calligraphy "We two, pilgrims together" that he had painted on it for her. It would have been a valuable keep-sake.

From the clusters of sturdy straw sandals dangling about an old woman's person, Cat selected eight at ten coppers each. She started to put them onto the *furoshiki*, but Kasane held her hand out to take them and the cloth bundle, too. The world was back to normal. Someone else was carrying Cat's burdens.

Next Cat shopped for food for the journey. She hadn't the least notion how to cook anything, but she had learned that the kitchen staffs of inns would prepare food supplied by the guests, thereby cutting down on lodging expenses. The variety of food for sale here was bewildering.

"Our confections were celebrated by the august tea master Sen no Rikyu himself, Your Honor."

"Here, here. The renowned prawns of Totsuka. Take them back to the folks at home."

Kasane was even more bewildered than Cat. She had never seen so much food. She couldn't read, so she didn't know what was in the artistically wrapped and labeled packages of local delicacies, the "Name-things" for which Totsuka was famous. She did know that they were expensive. She watched in amaze-ment as her new master bought pickled ginger and Totsuka's prawns, as well as small dried flying fish plaited horizontally into a straw cord and rice dumplings stuffed with sweetened bean jam and wrapped in the papery sheaths of bamboo shoots. Cat did buy tea and raw rice, but only the most expensive type of each.

When she bought tooth powder and a willow twig toothbrush, the woman selling them bowed low and presented her with a tiny packet of toothpicks as *omake*, a bonus.

"Luck to the seller," the woman said. Cat was as pleased by the modest gift as by any expensive present she had ever re-ceived.

Next she bought an ink stick and stone in a plain wooden writing case and brushes in bamboo tubes. She added a flint, a tortoiseshell comb, and a crisp, dark blue loincloth.

She bought four coppers' worth of Willow brand tobacco, a packet of cheap paper handkerchiefs, and a heavy paper folding wallet in which to put them. She chose a hempen travel cloak and a paper raincoat permeated with persimmon juice to make it water-repellent. She smiled when the merchant threw in a small towel for *omake*.

Cat tied her final purchases, two sleeping straw mats, on top of Kasane's pack. By the time Cat finished, the *furoshiki* had grown so big that Kasane could hardly be seen behind it. Kasane was astonished. She had never seen such extravagance. Her new master was the sort to carry a lantern on a moonlit night.

Vendors and merchants were packing their stock into bags and baskets and extinguishing their lanterns. Cat heard the squeal of wooden axles as farmers wheeled their unsold goods away in their cumbersome barrows. The market was taking on an abandoned air.

The crowd was thinning. The beggars were leaving with their straw cushions under their arms. Street entertainers were gathering up their instruments and props. Soon all the stands would be screened with mats or boarded up or dismantled. Not enough people would be left to provide cover for Cat and her silent, unwelcome companion.

Cat knew she dared not stay at an inn. Kira's men and the book with her picture in it had probably visited them all. Kira's son Lord Uesugi had enough retainers to send one or two to each of the fifty-three government post stations between Edo and Kyōto. And he would still have men left to maintain his father's bodyguards at home.

The black ribbon of sky between the eaves of the buildings was spangled with stars. No rain likely. Cat and the peasant could sleep somewhere on the grounds of the local temple, in an abandoned building or chapel or under a roof sheltering a bell.

Cat glanced at Kasane. She looked young and tired and frightened. Cat could tell from her callused hands and her new pilgrim's robe that she hadn't been whoring long. "You didn't sell yourself to the flesh broker, did you?" Cat asked.

"No, master." Kasane spoke so low, Cat could hardly hear her.

"Kidnapped?"

"Yes, master." Kasane hesitated. "The others were killed," she murmured.

"What others?"

"From my village. Thirteen of us were traveling to the great shrine at Ise." Kasane stopped in confusion. She hadn't meant to draw attention to her plight.

Cat turned away to discourage further revelations. She didn't want to find out any more about the dirt-eater. She might feel obligated to help her, and she didn't need anyone else's troubles. She already felt guilty about taking the money the child had had the foresight to steal from her captor. Cat soothed her conscience by reasoning that she would arrange for her to be found in the morning. Then she would be someone else's problem.

Cat bought a cheap lantern with a carrying pole, a collapsible paper shade, and a few extra rolled paper wicks. Then she stopped at stacks of round wooden tubs filled with various types of oil. The oil peddler stood among them and scratched his back with the long handle of his sieve.

"Where's the nearest temple?" Cat asked as he measured out whale oil into a bamboo container.

He waved his sieve toward the west. "You'd be better off at the shrine on the main road to Edo, though," he said. "It's dedicated to Daikoku and his magic mallet. The fat businessmen flock there to clap their hands before his image and bargain with the god of wealth for a bountiful crop of gold and silver.

"On the other hand, the temple has fallen on hard times. It doesn't even have a bonze. The Shintō priest changes his robes and goes there now and then to chant the Buddhist services."

Impatiently Cat started to bid him good night. Then she thought better of it. "Is the temple deserted?"

"Only by the living." The oil seller grinned and wiped oil off his hand and onto his heavy black apron. "In my grandfather's grandfather's day it was famous for its warrior-monks, adept at the art of the spear. The graveyard is full of the tombstones of the foolish young students of the warrior's Way who journeyed there to challenge them."

"Thank you." Cat bowed and backed away. When she was out of sight she doubled back behind the buildings and headed for the deserted temple.

CHAPTER 25
GHOSTS AND GIRLS

As she walked along the dark road, the expression on Kasane's plain round face was stoic, but she had no illusions about her future. She knew that her new master might be intending to take her to a deserted place and rape and kill her, but she doubted it.

Kasane was a shy child and a virtuous one, but in the past few days she had come to think of herself as merchandise.

She had been kidnapped at sea by a pirate masquerading as an honest boat captain. He had sold her to the procurer, who had peddled her to innkeepers twice and then restolen her. He would have done it again if the mysterious, ferocious young stranger hadn't interfered. Now this latest master would undoubtedly go into business, too, with Kasane as his stock. One didn't waste anything that could be exchanged for money.

Before leaving for the pilgrimage to Ise several days earlier, Kasane had never been beyond the call of her village drum. Since then she had seen only the worst of men, but this one was nothing like the pirate and the procurer. For one thing, he was very young. And he was certainly extravagant. Even though the moon was only beginning to wane and was almost directly overhead, he had lit the lantern.

Kasane carried the baggage and the lantern too along the deserted farm road. She walked in front and held the lantern's pole to the side and behind her so it lit her new master's way. She glanced back over her shoulder only once. The light and shadow had transformed Cat's glower into a hideous mask. She looked to Kasane like Lord Emma, the king of hell.

The temple grounds were beyond the fields, among the steep folds of the high hills west of Totsuka. A heavy mist swirled low to the ground there. In the darkness of a grove of trees, Cat almost missed the slender granite marker indicating the turnoff onto a badly maintained path.

As she and Kasane moved forward cautiously, the trees and bushes closed in around them. A fox barked. Something rustled in the black depths of the undergrowth. Kasane stopped so abruptly, Cat almost bumped into her.

"A goblin," Kasane whispered.

"Keep walking, simpleton."

In the stillness of the night Cat's own voice sounded harsh to her. She thought of Musui's kindness and felt small and mean. She remembered his gentle admonition. *A true warrior knows compassion.* Cat decided to leave the child some money when she abandoned her.

In the moon's bright light, tears glistened on Kasane's cheeks. Her lips trembled as she felt her way along the dark, rocky path. A gust of wind blew, and both she and Cat heard a rattling, like bones.

Kasane gave a small cry and shrank back when something

tall and thin loomed from the ground fog. She felt rather than saw more shapes in the darkness under the trees.

"Tombstones." Cat lowered her voice and took a firmer grip on her walking staff.

Hundreds of tiered stone monuments rose up from the fog and crowded the slope of the hill. A forest of tall wooden funerary laths, some new, some old and neglected, clattered against each other in another gust.

Cat and Kasane walked past granite columns and slabs, carved with snarling lions and the ferocious faces of Buddhism's guardian kings. In the mist the grave markers looked like a silent army turned to stone.

The lantern had been burning low. Suddenly it guttered and went out.

"He said it held enough oil for two hours' light." Cat was furious that the oil vendor had cheated her. She knew he had long since closed up for the night and decamped; but she wanted to march back to Totsuka, rap him on the head with her staff, and demand her money back.

Kasane shrank back against her and clutched her sleeve.

"Don't be a fool." But Cat herself spoke in a whisper. "When our eyes grow accustomed to the darkness, the moon will guide us."

Kasane didn't dare point out that the massive cedars were now shutting out most of the moon's light. Still clinging to Cat's sleeve, she strained to see around her. "Did you see that?" she whispered.

"Yes," Cat murmured. Suddenly Kasane's presence was a comfort to her.

A flame flared in the distance, then softened and broadened into the glow from a lantern. It lit portions of the gravestones around it and in places left angular sheets of night.

Three huge shadows stooped and reared against the granite monuments. Each shadow sported a pair of pointed fox's ears.

"Where?" The word drifted, like a fragment of a lost conversation, through the gravestones.

"Over here." The voice was nervous and subdued.

"Bring the light, you bucket of night soil."

"Two of them in one night." The first speaker sounded as though he had fortified himself with strong drink, home-brewed sweet-potato wine, probably. His dialect was too coarse to belong to someone who could afford *sake*. "What luck."

Cat heard the rhythmic *kachunk* of wood striking stones and saw the curved shadows of two mattock blades rise and fall on the monument. She thought again about returning to Totsuka but dismissed the idea. The inns would be tightly shuttered. Even if she could have found shelter in a shed or chapel in town, she would have had the problem of avoiding Kira's men in the morning. The idea of sharing her night's lodging place with this sort of riffraff made her skin crawl, though. The only solution was to evict them.

With both hands gripping the staff lightly, she held it up as though it were a long-sword, parallel to her body and with the tip slanted outward. Her pulse thrummed in her ears as she started forward, crossing each foot in front of the other in the buoyant scissor gait of a sword player.

She was concentrating on centering her thoughts and breathing properly when she felt a hard tug at her sleeve. She whirled, dragging a heavy weight with her. She struck down and behind her with great force but stayed her hand at the last moment. When the staff landed on Kasane's side, it was painful but not damaging.

Kasane shut her eyes tight and held on to Cat's sleeve with both hands. She had decided she would rather die of a blow from her strange new master's staff than release her grip.

"Let go of me, you idiot!" Cat whispered as she tried to disengage her. "Wait here."

"Don't leave me, master." Kasane spoke in a tiny, strangled voice. "Kill me, but don't leave me in this haunted place."

Cat could see the hysteria rising in the peasant's contorted face. She shook her hard by the shoulders. "I'll be back. I'm only going to see who they are."

"They're demons or ghosts."

"I doubt it. I think they're human, and they're up to no good."

Cat pried Kasane's rigid fingers loose. She brandished her staff and started forward again, using the gravestones for cover. She lifted each foot deliberately and set it down as softly as a leaf landing. She thought they were mortal, but she wasn't certain.

Kasane stood in the gloom and watched the only being who might possibly be human desert her. From the corner of her eye she thought she saw something stir in the well of night behind a tombstone. The roots of her hair tingled at the nape of her neck. She tucked her robe's skirts up into her sash. Crouching, she crept after Cat.

Kasane wanted to scream to drown out the noise of the mattocks and the rustlings and squeakings and the liquid hooting of the owl in the darkness. She could only whimper far back in her throat. She remembered the old proverb, "Ghosts and girls are best unseen," but it was no comfort.

"When were they buried?" The man's voice sounded so close, it startled Kasane. It distracted her from the sharpening odor of rotting flesh.

"The other one's only a few days old. This one's been here almost a week."

The light of the lantern was close enough now to make the darkness around Kasane complete in contrast. But at least she could see the beings that were casting the shadows. She could see that the fox ears were formed by the stiff knotted ends of the towels tied around their heads. She also could see that these demons were wearing filthy loincloths and collections of paper rags.

Kasane crouched behind a marker and watched Cat approach the men. She put a hand down to steady herself, but instead of earth, she felt the cold, rubbery skin of a woman's breast. It gave strangely under her fingers. The stench of death hit her in the face.

Kasane shrieked. She shrieked again. She kept on shrieking.

CHAPTER 26
NO HOME IN THE THREE WORLDS

At Kasane's shriek, Cat whirled to stare into the darkness. "Idiot!" she muttered. "I should have left her in the closet, too." But Cat's skin prickled, and her heart raced at the horror in Kasane's cries.

At the start of a battle, Musashi wrote, *shout as loudly as possible. The voice is a thing of life.*

Cat took a deep breath, gripped her staff tighter, and gathered her courage. "Ei-i-i-i-i!" she screamed as she charged through the gravestones toward the lantern light.

No one was there. When Kasane's screams descended to gurgling sobs, Cat heard the men running headlong through the underbrush. With her staff at the ready and her heart still pounding, Cat picked up the abandoned lantern and prowled the area. When she was sure they were alone, she called to Kasane.

"There's a dead person here, Your Honor." From the darkness Kasane's voice shook with fright.

"There are hundreds of dead people here, you bucket of dirt." Cat was so enraged that she forgot her parents' careful instruction on proper conduct and terms of address. Kasane's scream had unnerved her and completely disrupted her concentration. "Peasants have no sense," she muttered to herself.

"This one isn't buried," Kasane said. "Maybe it's a homeless spirit."

Cat walked among the tombstones to where Kasane crouched, her arms crossed in front of her and her hands clutching her own shoulders. Her eyes were wide in terror.

Cat stooped to inspect the body. "She's gone in the white scarves of death." She knew she was only affirming the obvious. "But someone bothered to bury her for those dung beetles to dig up. She must have relatives to pray for her soul. In any case, we can't do anything for her." Cat stood. "It's late. We have to find a place to sleep."

"Here?" Kasane dared to question her new master. Her encounter with the supernatural had made him seem relatively harmless by comparison. Mad, certainly, but not homicidal. "The demons might come back."

"They aren't demons." Cat held Kasane's wicker pack while Kasane arranged the woven straps over her shoulders. Then she tied the rolled mats on top of the pack and held the *furoshiki* on top of the mats while Kasane adjusted the knotted ties across her chest. The burden towered over Kasane's head.

"They're men so poor they steal from the dead." Cat handed her the lantern. "They fear the executioner's blade in this world and the wrath of the gods in the next. They won't be back."

"Must I go first, master?"

"Yes." Cat prodded her with the staff to start her moving.

"What were they stealing?" Kasane spoke in a hushed voice. She was fearful of disturbing the corpses and angering her master; but she was more terrified of a silence broken only by the anonymous rustlings of foxes and monkeys and owls.

"A corpse's hair and fingernails are easily pulled out. The thieves sell the hair to wig makers. They trim the nails, then sell them in the gay quarters. The women give them to their patrons as pledges of love. That way a woman can fool many men into thinking each is the only one she loves.''

''Don't the women know where the fingernails come from?'' Kasane shivered at the thought of touching a corpse's fingernail. Being kidnapped by pirates and almost violated, being dragged into the night by a fierce stranger, finding opened graves and plundered corpses, they were all too much for her. She shook so badly that the lantern's light trembled along the ground.

''We . . .'' Cat caught herself. ''The women don't think about it. Go-betweens buy the tokens from the robbers and sell them. The buyers never see the scoundrels who did the deed.''

Coffin carriers, priests, and merchants have found a way to profit even from death, Cat thought. She remembered the delicate, half-moon-shaped nails she herself had bought, and wondered, for the first time, from whose hand they had been taken.

Through the canopy of leaves Cat saw a slope of silvery moss and weathered cedar shingles glinting in the moonlight. A well-worn path led to a plainly built, open-sided chapel set back among the trees and bamboo and underbrush. She rapped Kasane's pack with the staff and pointed to it. ''We'll sleep here.''

Near the place of death was one of life. The small, wall-less building was festooned inside with wooden ladles with the bottoms missing. They had been blessed by the Shintō priest who also served as a Buddhist bonze. Then they had been carried home by pregnant women. After successful deliveries, the women had written their names and ages on the handles and returned them.

''Lay out the mats,'' Cat said.

''Yes, Your Honor.'' Kasane was relieved that at least he didn't seem inclined to kill her. She hurriedly unrolled the mats and laid one on top of the other for double thickness.

''You can sleep on one,'' Cat said gruffly. The chapel's floor was of packed earth and quite cold. As angry as Cat was with Kasane, she couldn't bear the thought of making her sleep directly on it.

''You're very kind, master.'' Kasane knelt and knocked her forehead repeatedly on the ground. Then she scurried around, filling Cat's small brass pipe and lighting it with the flint. While Cat smoked and stared out at the dark forest, Kasane took her brother's paper travel cloak from her pack and laid it over her master's mat. She spread Cat's new cloak on top of that as a coverlet.

She lay down on the other bare mat. She drew up her legs

and tucked the hem of her robe around her icy feet in a futile attempt to warm them. She pillowed her head on her arm, closed her eyes, shivered with the cold, and thought of home.

The thatched hovels that made up Matsu-mura, Pine village, would all be dark by now. Kasane knew that her parents and her grandmother would be asleep on their frayed straw mats in the single room of their tiny house there. They wouldn't even be worried about her. As far as they knew, she and her younger brother and seven other pilgrims were in the care of the leader of Pine village's pilgrimage club and were on their way to the great shrine at Ise.

Kasane was sure that fate wouldn't allow her to see her family again. She was also sure that was just as well. Her parents had engaged a go-between to arrange a marriage for Kasane with a young farmer, a stranger from a neighboring village. Kasane's trip to the Sun Goddess's shrine was to be the traditional pilgrimage of a bride-to-be. But the pilgrimage had gone dreadfully awry.

Now Kasane felt sullied beyond redemption. Even though she had not lost her virginity, she knew that no man would have her as a bride. She knew that if she returned to Pine village, she would bring terrible shame to her family. She would live out her life single and the object of endless gossip. Tears burned her eyes and nose as she buried her face in the crook of her arm.

The procurer had snatched Kasane from the inns where he had sold her each night and had kept her on the run for days. She was so exhausted that even her grief, the cold, and the terrors of the graveyard nearby couldn't keep her awake. By the time Cat finished smoking and brooding about the journey ahead of her, Kasane was asleep.

Kasane looked so young and innocent and helpless that Cat felt a pang of shame at treating her so badly. She draped the shabby paper cloak over her. Then she wrapped herself in her own cloak, laid her staff next to the mat, and drifted into uneasy sleep.

Because the temple had no priest, no dawn bell rang to waken Cat. The hour of the Hare was half over, and the sun had risen when she opened her eyes. Cat stared up at the clusters of dusty wooden ladles dangling from the broad beams of the chapel's ceiling. Each represented a child brought into the world. Cat wondered what all of them were doing this morning.

She glanced at the other mat. It was neatly rolled and tied and set next to the dirt-eater's pack and the *furoshiki*.

"Idiot!" she raged at herself. If she had slept so soundly she didn't hear the peasant escape, she wouldn't have heard enemies creeping up on her, either.

Cat knew she had to leave immediately, before the child brought the authorities. She tied up the *furoshiki*'s ends and settled it on her back. She studied the abandoned pack. Surely the peasant didn't want it, or she would have taken it. Inside, there might be something she could use as a disguise. Cat put one arm through the pack's straps and hoisted it onto her left shoulder.

She was tying the cords of her hat under her chin when Kasane appeared. The hem of her white robe was tucked up, and her bare feet and legs were covered with black loam. She carried several dirt-covered bamboo shoots in her arms. They were about as long as her forearm and pointed at each end.

"I brought the bamboo's children for you to eat, master." She put them down and washed her hands and feet in the nearby stream.

Cat took off the hat and the *furoshiki* and the pack. When she sat cross-legged and rummaged in the bundle for her pipe, Kasane lit it. Then Cat watched in astonishment as Kasane pulled a large, sharp knife from inside her robe. Where had she gotten it? Cat was appalled at her own carelessness.

Kasane was staring humbly at the ground, but she caught the look. "It belonged to my last master," she said.

She deftly split a large section of bamboo that was dead and dried to a silvery brown. She carved a narrow slit in the back of one of the halves. She filled the hollow in the piece beneath it with bamboo shavings.

When she rubbed a strip of bamboo across the first half, sparks flew from the silica in it. The hot powdered residue fell through the slit into the tinder below. Kasane blew gently on it through a slender bamboo tube. She had a fire going in about sixty heartbeats.

She fed the tiny flames with dried cypress needles and twigs, then larger pieces of wood until the fire crackled and burned steadily. She arranged five flat stones around it. On them she balanced three sections of green bamboo with bottoms formed by the nodes. While the water in them boiled she used the knife to peel, trim, and slice the shoots. The rice, the bamboo's children, and two of the dried flying fish were cooked about the same time. Kasane used the water in the third container for tea.

Kasane dished the food onto bamboo sheaths and served all of it to Cat. Then she retired to the far side of the chapel. She sat back on her haunches, folded her hands in her lap, and bowed her head.

The shoots were white and crisp and sweet. When Cat had eaten the two fish and half the rice and shoots, she pushed the bamboo sheath with the remainder across the dirt floor to Kasane.

"Thank you so very much, kind master. You honor this miserable individual." Kasane bowed several times before eating the warm rice. She savored the rich, unfamiliar taste of it.

The *shōgun* had decreed that peasants weren't to eat rice, but Cat decided to defy the law. She wasn't happy about the necessity of tying up her captive and abandoning her. She was buying her conscience off cheaply.

"What village do you come from?" Cat asked. If it turned out to be convenient, she would send word to the peasant's people.

"Matsu-mura, Pine village, in Kazusa province."

"I have to tie you up and leave you here."

"Please, master, don't leave me." Kasane flung herself forward in a supine bow. "I beg of you, please don't leave me here. This is a haunted place." She imagined being tied up when night fell and the robbers returned to pull out her fingernails.

"You'll tell the authorities where to find me." Even as Cat said it, she wondered why she was bothering to explain her actions to a peasant.

"I promise I won't tell anyone." Kasane was weeping so hard that she was practically unintelligible. "No one will find me in this desolate place. Night will come. Demons will come." She clutched at Cat's jacket. Her tears left dark spots on the faded black cloth. "Take me with you. I'll be your servant. I'm strong. I'll carry everything. I'll massage your feet and cook your meals."

"Don't be a fool. In the next town I'll tell someone to notify your people. You can go home."

"I can't return to Pine village, master. I've been disgraced."

"I have enemies," Cat said. "Traveling with me would be dangerous."

"If I stay here, the old master will catch me." Kasane's voice trembled, but she stopped crying. This was to be her fate. She must accept it. "He'll beat me and sell me again, but there is no help for it. A woman has no home in the three worlds."

The old saying had originally alluded to the three realms of Buddhist existence. Among country folk, ignorant of Buddhist philosophy, it had come to mean that women must live first in the homes of their fathers, then their husbands, then their sons.

Kasane opened her pack and dug into it. "This will protect you on your journey, Your Honor." She held out a cheap wooden amulet in a tiny brocade bag. It was dedicated to the god of travelers, and the headman and president of Pine village's Ise club had presented one to each pilgrim. Then she handed Cat a packet wrapped in cloth and oiled paper. She treated it as though it were as magical as the amulet.

"My brother's travel permit."

"How do I know you won't inform on me?" Cat stared at the packet. "How do I know the authorities won't be looking for this permit?"

"I promise, master."

"What good is a peasant's promise?" Cat was ashamed of the sympathy she felt for this commoner.

"Even an inch-long worm has a half-inch soul, master," Kasane said softly.

Cat winced. Kasane's words struck her like a side blow that slipped through her armor. She remembered Musui's kind smile. This whole business was bothering her far more than it should. She was becoming weak and foolish. This peasant's trifling problems were interfering with her purpose.

Cat stared at the travel permit. It would be of great use, but she had good reason for not wanting to take it. To accept it would burden her with *on*, a debt of gratitude. *On* could be a very heavy load indeed.

Cat took the permit and paced with it. Through the cloth and the oiled paper she felt its sharp, crisp edges. Ahead of her lay the mountains of Hakone and the most formidable government barrier of them all. The permit might get her through it.

"I'll take you as far as Fujisawa, the next town," she said. "From there you must make your own way."

"Thank you, master. Thank you. May the gods smile down on you." Kasane bowed low again. Then she hastened to clean up and pack.

CHAPTER 27
THIS FIRE OF LOVE

Everyone in Fujisawa seemed to be celebrating, except Hanshiro and his drinking companion, Nameless, the painter of paper lanterns. Hanshiro had to concentrate to keep from wincing every time someone in the boisterous throng jostled him. The pain in his skull throbbed in time with the huge drum. It exploded anew with each beat of the drumsticks, thick as a man's wrist. Then it pulsed with the reverberations.

His stomach churned, and he belched up bile. Nameless's face was still bandaged, and he seemed to be sunk at least as deep in misery as Hanshiro. Fujisawa was usually bustling with worshipers on their way to the sacred island of Enoshima across the tidal flat. But this was the annual festival coinciding with the Fowl Market, celebrated on the day of the Cock, of the eleventh month. Today, especially, Fujisawa was no place for two men with hangovers.

Hanshiro could no longer distinguish the boom of the drum from the pounding in his head. The drum was only one of thousands being played in Fujisawa, but it was by far the biggest. And it was much too close.

It sat in a massive wooden cart pulled by a patient ox. At least Hanshiro assumed it was on an ox cart. He could see the great humped curve of the drum, like a diving whale, moving slowly through the sea of people and banners along the waterfront. The ox, however, was invisible. The drum and the drummers seemed to be borne on the shoulders of the noisy worshipers.

The red-and-black crest painted on the drumhead dwarfed the two drummers, who wore only loincloths and headbands. They stood facing each other in the cart and alternated their strokes, keeping up a booming cadence, measured and primal as a heartbeat. The expressions on their spare, angular faces were remote, as though they were hypnotized by the pulse of their own making. Sweat glistened on their naked bodies. The muscles of their backs quivered with each stroke.

The drum was accompanied by the clangor of bells, the keening of flutes, and the piercing, nasal chant of thousands of pilgrims. Most of the faithful were beating on small drumheads stretched across circular frames and held by handles, like round fans. More people lined the second-floor balconies of the houses and shops facing the bay and rained noise down on Hanshiro's aching head.

The crowd was following the ornate gilt portable shrine as it moved ahead of the ox cart. The shrine's carrying poles were shouldered by a host of young men. They chanted as they careened from one side of the road to the other. They plowed through the press of people, tilting the shrine precariously and causing the purple silk draperies to wave and flap. Hanshiro could follow its course by the scattering and contracting of the crowd and by the graceful, gilded phoenix on top.

Hanshiro and Nameless slowed their pace, allowing the procession to surge around them. When they had almost reached the rear of it, Hanshiro raised his folded fan above the press and pointed it at a tea house, the Fuji-Viewing shop. He and Nameless began maneuvering toward it through the thinning crowd.

They pushed aside the short curtains that hung from the open front of the shop to just below eye level. They took off their sandals and stepped up onto the raised floor. Hanshiro spread a silk cloth out on the *tatami* and laid his long-sword and scabbard on it, close to hand.

Nameless leaned his pole of painted lanterns and his travel kit against the side wall. Then he too laid out his sword. The two men moved with great care, so as not to exacerbate the pounding in their heads. They lowered themselves slowly to sit cross-legged at a low table.

From their position on the *tatami* they had a view of the sparkling blue water of the bay and Enoshima island's high sheer cliffs with a dense green carpet of trees and bushes spilling over them. In the distance, the soaring, misty serenity of Mount Fuji's slopes made everything else seem insignificant. A powdering of snow covered its peak. It looked like a white-capped wave, frozen at its crest.

The procession turned a corner, and the clamor became muted. Hanshiro and Nameless could still hear the crowd's roar rise and fall as the shrine moved through Fujisawa's back streets. It would spend the day traveling the surrounding countryside with frequent breaks for rest and refreshment for the bearers.

Three *samurai* occupied a big bench on the hard-packed earth at the front of the shop. They were talking and laughing over cups of tea. They did not wear Lord Kira's crest embroidered on the sleeves and on the backs of their jackets, but Hanshiro knew they were Kira's or Uesugi's men. He could tell by their Edo accents and by their bearing and the cut of their clothes.

Hanshiro hadn't come to this shop by accident. He had managed to leave Nameless long enough to ask where he might find Edo *samurai*. He hadn't had much trouble learning where they were. Even in a town as crowded as this one, the Edo warriors and their purpose here were the subject of gossip and speculation.

"*Irasshaimasu!* Welcome!" The waitress appeared as if conjured from the air. She kneeled and bowed.

"Tea, if you would be so kind," Hanshiro said. "And noodle soup."

"The same," mumbled Nameless. Now that the effects of last night's *sake* had worn off, his broken nose was throbbing again under the bandages. He closed his eyes at the approaching sound of a drum.

This one had a high, insistent beat, like some large, angry insect. It was being played by one of a pair of dancers under a green hempen cloth painted with an elaborate, stylized orange-and-red flame design. The cloth was attached to a ferocious lion mask of red-lacquered papier-mâché. The man in the rear played the drum while the one in front sang and worked the mask's hinged jaw. As he and his partner danced he raised and lowered it and shook it from side to side to set the stringy rope mane tossing wildly. All that could be seen of the men were their sandals, their gaiters, and their baggy green pantaloons as they cavorted.

They stopped a few doors down and lifted the costume over their heads. They set it on a bench in front of a tightly shuttered building. The black characters on the vertical white banner out front said it was a bathhouse and that, like most bathhouses, it would open two hours later, at the hour of the Monkey. That didn't discourage the dancers.

With the confidence of longtime customers, they pushed open the small side door and called inside. "Auntie, we've come to drink your *sake* and climb two of your prettiest mountains."

Hanshiro and Nameless could hear the muffled voice of the proprietress shouting from the rear of the house. "Go away, you drunken ne'er-do-wells. We're closed. The girls are sleeping."

The two men disappeared inside anyway and didn't come

back out. Their costume lay on the bench like the skinned trophy of a fanciful hunt.

"Where will you go from here?" asked Nameless.

"To my home country."

Hanshiro's casual questions about the artist's broken nose had elicited only evasions. The westcountryman seemed preoccupied, but he claimed to know nothing about the monk he had fought at the ferry, except to admit, grudgingly, that he was skilled. Hanshiro would have thought him an Asano retainer, except that if he were, Lady Asano would have had no reason to break his nose.

Hanshiro had told Nameless nothing of his own commission. He wasn't about to divulge that he planned to capture the *naginata*-wielding priest before he reached the Hakone barrier. If Lady Asano passed it, bringing her back through would be a great deal of trouble. If she didn't fool the guards, she would be arrested, and since Hanshiro couldn't deliver her to Old Jug Face, he would lose the final installment of his pay.

Hanshiro didn't expect Kira's men to take Lady Asano. She had evaded them handily so far. In fact, Hanshiro's annoyance with her was giving way to admiration and a certain sense of anticipation.

"Is there work in Tosa?" Nameless interrupted Hanshiro's thoughts about the elusive Lady Asano.

"No. But I would rather starve in Tosa than feast in Edo."

The artist grimaced morosely. He suspected the Tosa *rōnin* was lying about the purpose of his trip, just as he himself was. But he recognized the sentiment as sincere.

"I too am weary of the soft, false ways of the Eastern Capital," he said. "The townsmen have raised vulgarity to a high level. And the cowardly rascals who call themselves *bushi* . . ."

Nameless glanced at Kira's men and fell silent. To even speak of the swaggering Edo *samurai* sullied his tongue. He sipped his tea as though to wash away the taste of them. The two men settled into a pensive, cautious silence.

"Tosa." One of Kira's men recognized Hanshiro's accent. He leaned over and hissed in an attempt to get Hanshiro's attention. "Hsst. Tosa."

Hanshiro didn't glance his way. He sipped his tea and stared across the water, past the island of Enoshima to the mountains on the curve of the mainland beyond the bay and to Fuji, rising like a prayer in mist like a cloud of incense.

"Hsst, Tosa." The man was as persistent as he was foolish.

His eyes were red-rimmed. When he laughed he exposed a wide gap where his front teeth used to be. He had not been a *samurai* for long. He still had the odor of rice paddy manure about him. Killing him would not be worth filling out all the official papers his death would require of Hanshiro.

"Is is true that travelers to your country are so glad to leave it that they make a special offering when they pass the barrier?" The other two laughed uproariously, encouraging him to dangle one foot over hell. They were acorns comparing their statures. "Is it true they squat and add to the Dung Monument at Pine Tree Ascent?" The man waited a bit for a reaction. "Hsst. Tosa," he said when he got none.

The word *Tosa* began a resonance inside Hanshiro, not in his head, but in the center of his spirit behind his navel. It spread outward in a shudder of longing for his homeland. He remembered the stunning view from the barrier at Pine Tree Ascent. Green mountains, azure sea, waves washing among the roots of the gnarled pines along the shore far below. He remembered surrendering his exit permit there. He remembered the intense ache of being set adrift from the country of his birth and upbringing, the home of his ancestors.

Hanshiro seemed as unaware of Kira's loutish young retainer as the retainer was of the sudden and messy death he had almost called down on himself. But to have to suffer nausea and regret and fools, all in one morning, made Hanshiro melancholy. Maybe the time had come to stop doing battle with the world and face his fiercest opponent. Himself.

When he finished this job maybe it would be time to withdraw into a life of seclusion and contemplation. To return to his homeland and play out his days meditating in one of the plangent seaside grottoes of the tumultuous Cape of Murato. Perhaps the sea's steady roar, which Hanshiro thought of as the voice of the universe, would soothe the insistent whine of his own petty thoughts.

Hanshiro picked up the soup bowl in his right hand and hooked his thumb and forefinger over the rim. It was a warrior's gesture, used whether an attack seemed probable or not. Nameless ate the same way. The simple ploy was designed to protect against an enemy who might try to slam the rim of the porcelain bowl into the bridge of his nose while he drank.

The bland broth and noodles settled Hanshiro's stomach. The agony in his head subsided to a throbbing ache, although the regret at his fall from moderation the night before lingered.

He sucked at his teeth to dislodge any seaweed garnish that might have clung there.

He was sucking and running his tongue over each tooth and staring fixedly at Mount Fuji when Cat saw him and Kira's men. Kira's men were too engrossed in their jokes to notice the peasant lad under the big sedge hat, but Cat was a savant of Edo dress and manners. She knew immediately who they were.

She also realized Hanshiro must have sensed her presence even though he was looking the other way. She only hoped he didn't know her in the shabby clothes she wore. The artist's face was hidden beneath his wrapping of bandages. Cat didn't recognize him from the fight at the Kawasaki ferry.

She whirled to find a pair of policemen lounging on the corner of the almost deserted street. She turned back again, her heart pounding. She could fight Kira's men, but not Hanshiro and the policemen, too. She took several deep breaths to calm herself.

"What is it, master?" Kasane whispered.

"Follow me." Keeping her chin down so the brim of her hat hid her face, Cat walked to the bench where the lion costume lay. She slowed as she approached it.

"When I say to, slip under the cloth," she muttered. "You have to work the mask so I can sing."

Kasane had several objections to that plan, but she dared not voice them. When Cat was alongside the costume she turned casually so she faced away from the tea house. She took the *furoshiki* from Kasane and slung it on her own back. She loosened the cords across her chin and slid the hat down over the *furoshiki*.

"Now!" She lifted the cloth up over her head. She watched Kasane settle into the mask ahead of her and tuck her skirt up into her sash so her legs were bare. "Are you ready?" Cat asked.

"I don't know what to do, master."

"You must have seen a lion dance before, you radish. Grip the bar with your hands and clack the mouth open and shut. Shake the head around while you dance up the street."

"I can't."

"Then I shall turn you over to the police and tell them of the money you stole." Cat counted on the peasant's being too simple or too timid to point out that Cat seemed to fear the police, too. She also counted on the costume's owners not returning and on the *rōnin* from Tosa being too uninterested in the peccadillos of peasants to involve himself in this particular theft.

Kasane clicked the jaws gingerly.

"Harder." Cat ground her teeth in fury at Kasane's timidity.

Kasane pulled hard on the bar and slammed the jaws shut with a loud clack. Cat began the lion song, stamping her feet in time and pushing Kasane forward with the butt of her staff. The mask's eyeholes were a hand's length away from Kasane's eyes, and she moved forward cautiously, using the exaggerated kicks and leaps of the dance to cover her uncertainty. But by the time she drew alongside the tea house she was shaking the heavy mask with vigor, if not enthusiasm. Cat chanted the lion dance song lustily.

Hanshiro and Nameless watched them pass. When they had disappeared around a corner, Nameless tugged on the cord around his neck to retrieve his flat square purse on the end of it. He pulled the purse up from the depths of his jacket as though he were landing a squid on a jig line.

"I must be on my way." He counted out twenty coppers for the soup and the tea, then dropped the purse back down the neck opening and pushed it under his sash.

Hanshiro grunted.

"May the seven gods of good fortune smile on you," Nameless added.

"And on you." Hanshiro bowed. He was relieved that the westcountry *rōnin* had chosen to go his own way. That saved Hanshiro the necessity of making up a story to rid himself of him.

Nameless complimented the waitress on the soup and bowed again. He stuck his long-sword back into his sash, put on his sandals, shouldered his pole of lanterns, and sauntered casually off in the wake of the lion dancers.

As Hanshiro resumed his contemplation of the mountain, a poem lingered in his mind. It had been written long ago, when Mount Fuji rumbled and spouted smoke and fire.

> No ways are left me now to meet my beloved;
> Must I, like the lofty peak of Fuji in Suruga
> Burn on forever
> With this fire of love?

CHAPTER 28
THE THICKNESS OF A PLANK

After Cat and Kasane turned the corner and threw off the lion costume, Cat led the way through the back streets of Fujisawa until she was sure neither the police nor Hanshiro nor Kira's men were following her.

Cat stopped at the intersection marked by a large red *torii* gate. From there a road branched off to the beach, where hundreds of people were preparing to wade across to the island of Enoshima. The worshipers intended to pay their respects to Benten-sama, the Shintō goddess of art and music and eloquence; but they were also heading for the collection of souvenir shops and brothels, inns and *sake* shops, clinging to Enoshima's steep hillsides.

"We part company here," Cat said.

"It's as you say, master."

Kasane helped heave the *furoshiki* onto Cat's back. It was heavy, but not as heavy as the bundle Cat had carried for Musui. Of course, Musui had walked slowly and stopped often. Cat, on the other hand, was in a hurry.

Cat gave Kasane a small towel with two strings of a hundred coppers each wrapped inside. They weren't much, but she didn't have much money left herself. She was alarmed at how quickly the procurer's coins had dwindled, consumed by the necessities of the trip. She also begrudged Kasane the money because she had a feeling the simpleton wouldn't be able to hold on to it long. As far as Cat was concerned, the child had no more sense than a gnat.

"Go to Benten-sama's shrine and ask to see a priest," Cat said. "He'll help you." But she knew the advice wasn't much good.

Enoshima's shrine to Benten was among the richest and busiest in the country. The priests there would be much too busy selling fortunes and amulets and special litanies to pay attention to one lost peasant woman. Still, Cat might have been able to walk away from the dirt-eater if she hadn't glanced back.

Cat turned and saw Kasane standing where she had left her. She seemed oblivious to the throng of noisy, happy people brushing past her. She clutched the towel and the coppers to her breast and stared fixedly at Cat. Her narrow, upslanted eyes glittered with unshed tears. Her face was impassive, set in the stoic hopelessness of the victims of life's cruelty and indifference. She had the look of a waif who had fallen overboard in a stormy sea and was watching the boat sail off without her.

Even as Cat watched, a man approached her and tugged at her sleeve. Kasane shrank away from him, her eyes still pleading with Cat.

Cat blew out her breath in exasperation. She had just learned another of life's lessons: the master was also the servant of those he would rule.

Brandishing her staff, she strode through the crowd, scattering everyone between her and Kasane. She was two-thirds the weight, height, and age of the man, but the ferocity and suddenness of her charge discouraged his suit. He melted into the crowd.

"Oiso!" Cat ground the word out between clenched teeth. "I'll take you to Oiso and no farther. We can hire a place in a boat that will carry you to Kazusa province."

Cat dumped her *furoshiki* at Kasane's feet. Kasane hoisted it onto her shoulder, balancing it with her pack and the rolled mats.

"You're as hard to get rid of as head lice," Cat muttered as she stalked off.

Cat was in a hurry to leave Fujisawa. She imagined she saw Hanshiro's glower at every turn. Finding him in the same tea house with Kira's men had confirmed her suspicion that he was one of them, hired by Lord Kira or his son to catch her or kill her.

She remembered the *rōnin*'s tiger eyes, his golden irises and unwavering gaze. A person with tiger eyes had power over people. The Chinese physiognomists said that those with tiger eyes led difficult, lonely lives; but that wasn't much consolation.

Cut off by mountains and water from the rest of the country, the men of Tosa were reputed to be exceptionally proud, tough, and skilled at swordplay. Cat had no doubt that the *rōnin* called Hanshiro was all of that. He was a man of considerable arm, as the saying went. He was the only one Cat really feared.

With her hat brim hiding her face, Cat sauntered by the Fujisawa transport office where the *kago* bearers and postboys lounged with their palanquins and horses. "I'm on my way back home, young gentleman," they shouted at her. "I'll take you cheap for this stage."

The prospect of riding was tempting. Cat was rehearsing how she would ask the price and how she would haggle when she noticed the man sitting on a box under the willow in the middle of the trampled yard. He was obviously the retainer who had lost the draw and had been assigned this duty instead of drinking *sake* with Kira's other three men.

He was checking the identity of everyone who engaged a *kago* or a horse. Lord Kira's men assumed Lady Asano would not walk if she could ride.

They think I'm stupid. For some reason, that angered Cat as much as their dogged pursuit of her.

Cat struck out for Hiratsuka, but she didn't take long to realize she was being led from behind. Kasane followed meekly the usual three paces back, but she was walking so fast that Cat was obliged to increase her own speed, in spite of her aching feet. Cat knew Kasane was hurrying so she couldn't be accused of slowing her master down. She was determined to give no excuse for Cat to abandon her.

Cat studied the guidebook as she walked. She could arrive in Oiso by early afternoon, hire a boat, and launch the peasant woman. Once rid of her she could walk to Odawara, almost four *ri* farther, and arrive well before sunset. She would find an inexpensive but respectable inn. She would bathe, eat, and rest up for the arduous climb through the Hakone mountains. She would prepare to face the barrier at the high pass there.

Her heart thumped faster when she thought of the Hakone barrier. The officials there were said to be able to identify a person's village by the nuances of dialect. If Cat carried the travel permit of Hachibei, the peasant woman's younger brother, she would have to speak with his accent. She had almost discarded the one person who could instruct her in it.

So far Cat's companion had spoken as little as possible. That was commendable in a peasant, but Cat realized she had to hear Kasane speak so she could imitate her. She wondered what she could possibly talk about with a commoner. Certainly not art or drama or literature. Cat slowed and took up a position just ahead of Kasane's right elbow.

"How did you come to have your younger brother's papers?" she asked.

"He put most of his things in my pack so he wouldn't have to carry so much."

"Where is he now?"

"Gone." Kasane stared at her feet as she plodded doggedly along under her burden.

"Tell me what happened to him." To ask such a direct and personal question was rude, but Cat was desperate.

"I should not bore your estimable person with my insignificant troubles, master."

"It doesn't matter if you bore me . . ." *You gourd,* Cat thought. She resisted the desire to beat conversation out of Kasane with her staff. "To fool the guards at the barrier I have to speak like your brother, Hachibei, from Pine village. Tell me everything that happened, in great detail, so I can study your accent. Do you understand?"

"Yes, master." Kasane took a deep breath. "Several days ago nine of us left our village—my only brother and I, the president of the Ise club, and the six people who won the lottery."

"The lottery?"

"Yes. Each month members of the Ise club pay a few *bu* into the club fund. Each year those who win the lottery use the money to pay for their trip. When we left, there was a great celebration with speeches and gifts."

In fact, at the time, the leavetaking had been the most exciting event of Kasane's life.

"The president chose to travel at this time of year because the inns' rates are lower. And the geomancer promised unusually warm weather. We spent the first night at a poor inn, and someone . . ." Kasane hesitated again. She blushed a deep pink.

"Go on." Cat tried to be patient.

"In the dark, on the way back from the convenience, someone thought my bed was his own. When I told him he was mistaken, he hurried off."

In spite of herself Cat had to smile. Pilgrims were supposed to put aside all carnal thoughts. But away from the watchful eyes of family and neighbors, pious journeys often turned into frolics.

"Some rough-looking men were staying at the inn, too, and I was frightened. I took my pack and slept in the empty closet where they store bedding. When I crawled out the next morning

I discovered that the president of the club had run away and taken the treasury with him.''

Cat almost laughed out loud. So far it was a tale worthy of a stage farce. "Why didn't you all turn around and go home?''

"The others had a few coins set aside, and they decided to beg along the way to eke them out. Then a boatman offered us a ride across the water to Oiso. He said it was his pious gift to pilgrims. He even left a seat for Funadama-sama in his boat.''

Like everyone else in the fishing village where Kasane was born, she had heard the faint tinkling sound that came occasionally from the beached boats at night. She knew then that Funadama-sama, the lovely goddess of fishermen, was moving around in them.

"And the boatman turned out to be a pirate." Already Cat was adopting the peculiar rhythm and pronunciation of Kasane's speech.

"Yes.''

Kasane's voice sounded strained. Cat glanced around and was surprised by the anguish on her face. Cat was embarrassed that she had caused such a public display of emotion. She moved farther ahead of Kasane and asked no more questions.

Behind her, Kasane walked as if in a trance. She was remembering that terrible boat ride. "One thickness of a plank . . .'' went the fishermen's proverb about boats. "Below, hell.''

Once again Kasane cowered in the bow as the captain stood at the huge sweep in the stern. His hair had come loose from its queue, and long tendrils of it whipped like eels around his head. His face was contorted, as though the storm raged in him as well as in the the waters of the bay.

The men of Pine village knelt in the center of the open boat and held on to the boom. They fell against each other as they tried to follow orders and undress in the pitching vessel. With his long knife the pirate made a sweeping gesture toward the leeward gunwale. Brandishing knives and staves, his crew rushed the naked pilgrims. Kasane's brother cried out as he was pushed overboard with the others.

"Pray for me, elder sister," he shouted. "Do not let my soul become a homeless ghost.''

Kasane watched, helpless, as he sank below the side of the boat until only his hand was visible on the gunwale. Then someone smashed it with a stave. The fingers became shorter as they slipped, then disappeared. Kasane continued staring at the splintery wood where they had been.

One pirate held up a stained, waterlogged pilgrim's robe. "Country people. They wear cheap goods."

The others laughed as they rifled the men's packs. Kasane tried to listen for her brother's voice, but over the flapping of the sail, the roar of the storm, and the pirates' laughter she couldn't hear the cries of the drowning men.

She pressed as deeply into the angle of the bow as she could and stared down at the black bilge water in which she sat. She didn't look up when the captain's bare feet filled her view. He grabbed her hair and pulled her head back. She went rigid and mute with shame and terror as he knelt on one knee, reached up under her robe, and probed her with his finger. "This one's homely, but unspoiled," he shouted. "We can sell her. Tie her up."

As a crewman pulled Kasane's hands behind her and the rough straw rope cut into her wrists, Kasane heard a faint tinkling sound. It wasn't lovely Funadama-sama, the goddess of fishermen. One of the pilgrim's brass bells was rolling back and forth on the pitching floor.

Now, as Kasane walked behind Cat's straight, indifferent back, she wiped her eyes with the thin towel Cat had given her and blew her nose into it. In the days since her brother's death Kasane hadn't even been able to pray properly for his soul, and the tinkling of the bell on a passing pilgrim sent a shudder of grief through her.

CHAPTER 29

A CUDGEL FROM A BAMBOO BUSH

Just before Hiratsuka, the Tōkaidō became a raised causeway through the brown rice paddies that covered a broad plain. On both sides the paddies came up to the huge pines that lined the road. The mountains of Hakone that hunched against the ashen sky to the southwest were the same dark gray as the clouds closing in overhead.

Raveled strands of lightning flicked at the mountain peaks. The branches of the pines stirred fitfully. A *kago* bearer trotted by with his empty conveyance strapped to his back. As a pack horse driver hurried his animals past Cat and Kasane, the bells on the harnesses had an urgency to them.

Cat stopped at a stand selling religious accessories to those going to the small temple in the grove of ancient pines nearby. She bought two bundles of slender incense sticks, two small bowls of rice and tiny cups, and a pair of deep orange Mino persimmons. She chose the persimmons with care, picking the largest, so ripe and swollen with sweet juice that they seemed about to burst.

Cat divided her purchases with Kasane. "For your brother," she said gruffly.

Kasane tried to thank her, but she was too overcome to speak. She bowed low over the things in her outspread hands.

Together they rinsed their mouths and hands at the chapel's big stone basin. They put the bowls of rice and cups of water in front of the altar. They lit the incense in the coals of the brazier kept there for that purpose. Then they each put their palms together and bowed their heads. Cat prayed for the repose of her father's soul and Kasane for her brother's.

They resumed their journey in silence and were just entering Hiratsuka when the first large drops splattered on the brim of Cat's hat. A gust of wind tore umbrellas and blew people's clothes about them. It set the pines to lashing, and Cat and Kasane had to lean into it to walk. The few remaining travelers ran for shelter.

"Stop!" The cry came from the stable next to the government transport office. It was loud and imperious, and Cat heard it, of course. She shifted her grip on her staff so she could use it as a weapon and kept moving.

"Halt, you!" Two men moved away from the stable.

As the rain began falling in torrents, Cat dodged into an alley. She tucked her chin down, pulled her elbows in, and ran, splashing mud all over herself. She darted at random down one narrow passageway, then another.

She was trying to lose the peasant woman while she was at it. Being caught with Cat would mean trouble for Kasane. But Kasane had been ill used by so many people, she had come to think of Cat as a champion of sorts. She was determined not to be left behind. Burdened as she was, however, Kira's men soon passed her.

Cat could hear the men gaining on her. When she saw the back door of a bathhouse slightly open, she slipped inside and slid it shut behind her. She ran down the dark back hallway while the wind rattled the heavy wooden shutters across the front of the building and rain drummed loudly on the cedar shingles of the roof.

Cat almost collided with an off-duty attendant on her way to take a bath herself. She was wearing an unbelted cotton robe with a small towel draped over one shoulder. She screamed and threw up her hands, and the toiletries flew out of the basin she was carrying. She charged through a sliding screen to avoid being trampled by Kira's men.

Cat found the maneuvering space she needed in the large, high-ceilinged room of the bath itself. A square cypress tub with sides as high as Cat's waist stood in the center of it. It was big enough to accommodate eight or nine bathers. Round wooden buckets for washing were stacked in pyramids against the walls. Wooden grates covered the long drains that ran around the edges of the room. One wall near the entrance was covered with broad shelves for clothing.

Two more attendants were taking advantage of the off-hour leisure. Naked, they gossiped as they scrubbed themselves with small bags of rice bran. They had been anticipating a long soak in the bath. They had slid off the wooden lid so that one edge rested on the floor and the other against the rim. Steam rose from the water.

They stared, with mouths open and bran bags poised, as Cat rushed in. When they saw the expression on her face they screamed and fled, leaving their clothes behind on the shelves. Cat whirled to face the door. She raised her staff in a fighting stance and poised her weight on the balls of her feet. Kira's men followed with their long-swords drawn.

Cat backed up until the side of the tub almost grazed the backs of her legs. The steam rising from it enveloped her, giving her a ghostly appearance. When outnumbered, take the offensive, was Musashi's advice. With a cry she charged. She maneuvered toward the left, pressing their off sides and keeping them in front of her. She thrust and blocked without the interference of conscious thought, sensing the men's moves before they made them.

She knew she couldn't hold out long against the two of them. She wasn't well trained in the use of the staff, and in any case it lacked the reach and menace of the *naginata*. Her only advantage was desperation and the fact that Kira's men had been ordered to capture her if possible and kill her only as a last resort.

Kira didn't want to be linked to a murder he couldn't claim was an accident.

Musashi taught that a warrior must strike slow and hard, like the flow of deep water. Cat must feel the strength welling up within her. She must strike from the muscles of the abdomen and swing into the blow with her entire body. Cat's staff resounded each time it blocked a steel blade. The shock of the blows numbed her fingers. Cat knew she was barely holding them at bay, and she was beginning to flag. Soon they would close and disarm her.

From the corner of her eye she saw Kasane enter the room. Kasane had taken off her pack and the *furoshiki*. As she raised one of the heavy wooden washtubs high over her head, the sleeves of her pilgrim's robe fell back, revealing the sinuous muscles of someone used to hard work. Kasane heaved the bucket at the man closest to her.

He saw it coming, but not soon enough. He hadn't been expecting a cudgel from a bamboo bush, an attack from a peasant. The tub hit him squarely on the side of the head. He toppled facedown into the bath, with his legs sticking out over the side. Other than the waving of his sleeves in the turbulent water, he didn't move.

Kasane stared at him with a dazed look, as though her hands and arms and shoulders had acted without the permission of their owner. As though their imprudence were likely to get her into a great deal of trouble. Cat took advantage of the diversion to strike.

With a crunching sound, the staff connected with her opponent's skull. Cat felt the give of bone through her fingers and up into her arms. As the man's sword clattered to the floor and he crumpled, Cat whacked him across the back of the shoulders for good measure.

"Help me put him in the water." With numb fingers and throbbing arms, Cat grabbed him under the armpits. Kasane picked up his legs. Together they swung him into the tub. Water cascaded over the sides and rushed across the floor and into the drains along the walls.

"Go check the alley," Cat said. "Hurry. The police are surely coming. I'll be right behind you."

As soon as Kasane left, Cat heaved the first man's legs into the water, too. Then she pulled the heavy lid up over the tub. It was designed to fit snugly inside the pale cypress walls and to float on the water. It pressed the men under. Maybe they would be rescued before they drowned, but Cat didn't care if they weren't.

She looked longingly at the fallen swords but left them. Even one of them would be too hard to hide and too likely to be traced. Instead she scooped up a robe and sash left on the shelf. She grimaced to herself as she thought of the old saying, ''A liar is the beginning of a thief.'' In her case, a murderer was the beginning of a thief.

Only a short time had passed between Cat's darting into the bathhouse and her reemergence into the empty alleyway. She put the stolen robe in Kasane's pack. Then she took the *furoshiki* from her and settled it onto her own back. Relieving Kasane of half her burden was small thanks for saving Cat's life.

Beyond the end of the covered alleyway, Cat could see the storm raging. Trees whipped to and fro. The rain fell so heavily that she couldn't see the building across the street.

Cat knew she and Kasane couldn't stay in Hiratsuka. The police would be searching for her and for Kasane too if anyone had seen her hit the *samurai*. They would surely set up roadblocks and post notices. Oiso was only three-quarters of a *ri* away.

Cat put a spare cord over her hat and tied it tightly under her chin. Kasane did likewise. They both put their raincapes on over their packs and belted them around the waist to keep them from shredding in the gale.

When Cat reached the end of the alleyway's shelter, she bent over to shield her face from the sting of the wind-driven rain. Leaning into the storm, she set off for Oiso. Without a word of complaint or protest, Kasane pulled down her hat brim and followed.

Hanshiro decided to seek shelter in Hiratsuka until the storm abated. He was sure Lady Asano wouldn't be traveling in weather like this. When he saw the people clustered under straw mats and raincoats in the downpour outside the bathhouse, he went to investigate.

The crowd parted to make way for him and his swords. He could hear the high, shrill babble of women's voices inside. He found the room where the cedar tub was and stood quietly behind the police and Hiratsuka's magistrate, the bath's manager, attendants, and servants.

He was startled to see the two corpses laid out on the floor.

They were still bright red, parboiled by the bathwater, which had heated up considerably under the wooden lid.

Hanshiro almost smiled. He had to admit the wench was a woman of arm. She had persistence, length of heart. But if they connected her with this murder, she was doomed.

"He was a ghost!" One of the women who had been washing when the fight started now clutched a loose bathing robe about her. Her hairdo was disheveled, and she hadn't even bothered to put on makeup. "I saw right through him."

The second attendant disagreed. "He was a demon. He had horns. He had the face of a fox and the ears of a badger."

Hanshiro listened a while longer to make sure no one here would be able to describe Lady Asano to him. But she was close, probably hiding somewhere in Hiratsuka. Finding her would be like searching for a thing in a bag.

Lady Asano had turned her flight into *musha-shugyo*, training that took the form of a journey. A warrior went on a pilgrimage of sorts to challenge other sword players and sharpen his own skills.

Hanshiro was amused by the thought that he would have to exercise some care in capturing her. This would be more entertaining than he had anticipated.

The tiger's loose in the market, he thought as he hitched up his raincape around his shoulders, pulled down his hat brim, and walked out into the storm.

CHAPTER 30

A DEVIL TIED UP IN DARKNESS

The room Kasane was to share with the seven sages at the See No Evil in Oiso looked as though a typhoon had passed through. Combs, cosmetic brushes, and lacquered boxes of powders and tiny jars of hair oil lay scattered among tangled combings of black hair on the crude straw mats. Robes and underclothes were strewn in every corner. When the seven bathhouse attendants went on pilgrimage, they left tidiness behind, along with their other obligations.

The mess was hardly noticeable in the See No Evil. Usually clutter in an establishment like this was found in the servants' hall. But the See No Evil was a chaos of broken furniture and rice mortars, parts of looms, tools, lumber, mildewed account books, stacks of dusty tubs and earthenware jugs and torn straw matting. Swags of blackened cobwebs hung from the high beams.

Cats perched everywhere, and the odor of their urine pervaded the place. The ceilings were water-stained. The fine latticework on the round windows and the carved openwork over the doorways were coated with grime. Most of the paper panes in the sliding door panels were ripped. The See No Evil seemed determined to sink into ruin despite the desultory efforts of the antique manservant who dozed by the door and the three young maids from the country.

The plaster on the wall out front had fallen off in large slabs, revealing the packed mud and straw underneath. The monkey carved on the faded sign over the roofed gate may have had its hands over its eyes in chagrin. The See No Evil had started as a respectable establishment, built sixty years earlier to elegant proportions. It had slid considerably since then.

Its open corridors were ranged around the ruins of a tiny garden. Only a few wiry azaleas and durable ferns were left in what was now a pond of mud. Wooden washtubs sat atop the garden's three decorative boulders.

In sunny weather laundry dried there. Today however, beyond the doorway of the seven sages' room and the open corridor, rain was still falling. The cascade of water from the eaves created a steady roar under the sages' banter.

When Cat and Kasane had arrived, soaked and shivering, at the See No Evil, the sages had been delighted to see Cat again. They remembered her as Musui's handsome acolyte, Endurance, but they accepted the fiction that Cat was Kasane's younger brother, Hachibei. If they noticed that Cat's accent had grown thick and rustic in two days, they said nothing. Stranger things than that had happened along the Tōkaidō.

They had made a fuss over Cat. They renamed her the Mountain of Love. With playful slaps and tickles, the sages had offered to strip off Cat's wet clothes and rub her dry. Cat had barely managed to towel off and slip into Kasane's brother's baggy-seated peasant trousers and tie the sash around his spare jacket before the sages had come looking for her.

Laughing and teasing, they had dragged her into their room

to keep them company while they passed the rainy afternoon. Cat was there now, feeling the warmth of the tea flowing into her stomach. The chipped porcelain cup felt wonderfully hot between her numb hands.

The sages wore only their unbelted underrobes as they sat in front of their mirror stands and arranged each other's hair and makeup. O-Taka, Hawk, the leader of the sages, had already dressed Cat's wet hair in a boyish style—a short queue atop two full side folds with the back section drawn up tight and tied with a red paper cord. When Hawk had finished she beckoned Kasane to sit in front of the mirror.

"I'm far too homely for you to trouble yourself with," Kasane murmured.

Hawk laughed. "White hides seven defects." She held up a box of face powder. "And even a devil is pretty at seventeen."

"I was once maid in charge of the front service of Lord Hanobo's mansion." Sea Wave, the proprietress of the See No Evil, lounged by the door. She watched Hawk divide Kasane's damp hair into three parts and rub camellia oil into it.

As Cat sipped tea she too watched Kasane intently. She worried that Kasane would forget to call her Hachibei instead of "master." She worried about what the peasant woman would do when she finally realized she had attacked a *samurai*. It was a crime that, given Kasane's low status, would earn her a gruesome death. But Kasane sat still as a statue, as though bewitched by the gentle touch of Hawk's kindness.

"Lord Hanobo's mansion was a fine place, I can tell you." Wave puffed contentedly on her small pipe. She was long-waisted and sturdy, and she wore a blue-and-white cloth tied around her disheveled hairdo. She had shrewd eyes, a child's voice, and the build of a rice mortar.

"My lady had a fawn-colored traveling outfit of eight-roll silk, with flaming maples embroidered on it," Wave went on. "When we promenaded, we all wore the same color robes with my lady's crest on them. She made us dress like country bumpkins with our sashes tied behind, while she wore her sash high and her sleeves open in the masculine way that was all the rage. I received a yearly salary of a hundred and twenty *momme* and clothes for the four seasons."

Hawk smoothed the rear section of Kasane's thick hair and folded it into the hanging hairdo called a seventeen *shimada* because it was worn by seventeen-year-old women. She sculpted it to lie in an outwardly curving loop along the nape of Kasane's neck. She held out her free hand, and Bamboo, the youngest of the sages, gave her a flattened black paper cord to tie it in place.

"Why did you leave the lord's service?" Hawk poked a wooden skewer into the coil and used it to ease the hair into a fuller contour.

"My lady became jealous. I was thought by some to have slightly better than average looks, though you would never guess it now." Wave caught a cat that sauntered by, headed for the tray of broiled bream. An animal crossing a room was bad luck. "Please excuse me," she said to it as she turned it around and boosted it out the door.

"My lady became cruel toward me," Wave went on. "She refused to renew my contract."

"You should have stolen her husband to spite her."

"The ladies of the inner apartments seldom catch a glimpse of a man, much less smell the perfume of a loincloth." Wave smiled slyly. "For their pleasure they must court their middle fingers. But as I was in the front service I saw my lord every day. He became quite taken with me. Our pillowings were so tempestuous, we caused the sliding doors to rattle in their tracks."

"Why didn't he keep you?"

"His wife's family was influential, and she had a high nose. He was spread under her buttocks. Besides, I was born in a Fiery Horse year. When my lady dismissed me, he said nothing in my defense. I was a wisteria without a pine to cling to."

The women hissed in sympathy. Women born in a Fiery Horse year were usually too spirited for marriage. Fiery Horse women were inclined to kill their husbands. Not many men were willing to risk extended liaisons with them.

When Hawk finally finished, the women exclaimed on the transformation. Kasane tried to hide her powdered and painted face in her hands.

For the rest of the afternoon she rubbed Cat's feet and back. She served her tea and lit her pipe while Wave and the sages gossiped. Now and then she reached up cautiously to pat the thick clubbed topknot of her *shimada* as though it were a pet cat with an inclination to claw. She sneaked glances at her painted face in the big round mirrors propped on their stands.

Toward the middle of the afternoon the old servant appeared and whispered in Wave's ear. Wave excused herself. She came back excited.

"Murder was committed in Hiratsuka. The police were here

asking if anyone suspicious had checked in. They looked through my guest book.''

"A murderer!" The sages were thrilled.

Kasane dropped the canister of tobacco. "Please, excuse my stupid clumsiness." With trembling fingers she brushed the spilled tobacco back into the jar.

"Forgive my fool of a sister." With her folded fan Cat rapped Kasane hard on the shoulder. "She's stupid and clumsy by nature; but fear makes her doubly so." Cat looked at Wave with wide, guileless eyes. "Imagine," she said. "We came from Hiratsuka this very afternoon. The killers may have been on the road with us. How many were there?"

"Only one." Wave was disappointed that the police would part with very little information for her to pass on. "Witnesses say he was huge, with red eyes and a fearsome expression."

Cat was relieved. No one had seen Kasane use a wooden tub to drop the *samurai*.

To Cat's and Kasane's relief, the talk left the present and meandered off among stories of past murders and suicides and illicit affairs. Wave talked of her decline from maid of the front service to the ranks of "nighthawks," older women who solicited trade in the darkness under bridges. As a nighthawk she had consorted with men who didn't even carry paper handkerchiefs to clean up after themselves.

Not many who sank so low rose again, but Wave had become the beloved mistress of the owner of the See No Evil. When he died he left behind no wife or relatives to dispute Wave's claim to the inn.

Bamboo had poured a bit of *sake* into her teacup. When she rose to entertain them all, her robe fell off one shoulder, exposing a small white breast. She fluttered her fan coquettishly at Cat and danced a few mincing steps.

"I think I'll wash my testicles with care." As she danced she sang with exaggerated innocence. "For as the old saying goes, 'If you don't polish a ball, it won't shine.' " She ended in a suggestive and definitely masculine pose.

The sages' laughter and their simple songs and tales made them seem carefree and innocent in spite of their profession. Cat imagined the sages back in the unlicensed brothel that masqueraded as a bathhouse. She knew that after their customers had bathed, dressed, climbed into their wooden *geta*, and clattered off into the night, the attendants who had made engagements to meet men at their inns ate a quick meal and prepared to go out.

They would probably borrow a sash or a veil or paper hand-kerchiefs from the women who were staying home. Those who had made no assignations would share the bathhouse's scant bedding and wadded nightclothes. They would lie hip to hip and talk of actors and of their home villages and of the latest fashions worn by the courtesans of the Yoshiwara.

The day's light was fading when the See No Evil's ancient seneschal came to tell Cat the bath was ready. The tiny size of the inn's dark bathroom with its round, one-person cedar tub saved Cat from having all the sages offer to crowd in to scrub her down. To be safe, she tied the door closed with a straw cord. She washed from the basin on a stand in the corner, near a flickering wall sconce. She barely had room to climb the step to the platform that held the tub and get in.

She heard the old servant's knees creak as he stooped to poke twigs and leaves and wood scraps into the tiny furnace opening on the other side of the thin wall. As Cat soaked in the scalding water, with the nape of her neck resting on the rim and her knees drawn up to her chest, she savored one of the prime benefits of being male, the right to be first in the bath.

Finally she stepped out of the tub and dried off with her damp cotton towel. She was struggling into her stiff new loincloth, and bumping her elbows in the cramped space, when Kasane yanked on the door and broke the cord holding it. She stood silhouetted in the lighted doorway. She carried a wadded jacket loaned by Wave for the boy the sages now called the Mountain of Love.

"Mas—" Kasane stopped in midword. She stared open-mouthed at Cat's small, taut breasts, turned a bright pink by the hot bathwater.

Cat grabbed her arm and yanked her inside. She pulled the door closed and used her sash cord to tie it shut again. The time had come for a heart-to-heart. A talk with their knees drawn together. Cat would have to act out two fictions at once.

With Kasane almost chest to chest with her, Cat put on Ka-sane's brother's old jacket. Then, to maintain the level of superior above inferior, she sat on the edge of the tub platform. Kasane knelt on the tiny square of floor. She faced at an angle to one side with her eyes downcast, as courtesy required.

"Do you know who I am?" Cat whispered.

"No, master . . . Hachibei . . . mistress." Kasane was trembling so badly that she would have collapsed had there been room. She had stumbled onto a devil tied up in darkness, as the old saying went. She was trapped with a demon shape-changer. A fox or a badger or worse.

"I am Usugumo, Pretty Cloud." Cat remembered the popular stories about love suicides, and she improvised as she went along. "My lover was banished to the southern island. I'm traveling in disguise to meet him there. We plan to sink together so we can sit on the same lotus flower before Amida's throne in the Western Paradise."

Kasane was ashamed to think how she had pitied herself and lamented her own petty problems. "I will serve you faithfully on your journey, mistress," she whispered.

"Stop talking such foolishness." Cat held her temper. Kasane had saved her life. Cat owed her a debt she couldn't repay in several lifetimes. The least she could do was treat her civilly.

"My lover's enemies think I go to offer him the aid of my family. You've seen what they're willing to do to stop me. Now I'm wanted for murder. Surely you know the punishment for that."

"I do, mistress. But please take me with you."

No wonder peasants had a reputation for being blockheads. Cat took a deep breath and started again. "You must not come with me. A foot ahead all is darkness. The Beloved Amida alone knows what fate awaits me."

"Forgive my rudeness," Kasane whispered. "But none of us knows what fate awaits us. Take me with you. Please . . . Hachibei." Kasane had already sorted out Cat's various identities and arrived at the appropriate one for the occasion.

"In the morning I'll hire you the best boat on the beach," Cat said. "I'll send you back to Pine village in grand style."

"Fate has rowed me far offshore already."

Cat smiled sadly at her. Kasane had indeed been through all the dangers implied in the old phrase. "We'll see how the world looks in the morning," she said.

"Thank you. Thank you." Kasane bowed until the oiled club of her *shimada* grazed the floor. "Thank you."

Kasane probably couldn't have explained why she preferred traveling the Tōkaidō with a fugitive to returning to Pine village. She didn't know what dangers lay ahead on the road. She did know that if she returned to Pine village, her parents would blame her for the death of her younger brother, their only son. She would have to live with their grief and silent recriminations.

Her neighbors would consider her soiled goods. They would gossip about her until she died.

Kasane raised her head and looked directly into Cat's eyes. "You need have no worries about me." She said it with astonishing dignity and passion. "Should your enemies cut me up and salt me, I won't betray you."

Lovelorn cats howled and moaned in the darkness beyond the See No Evil's front reception room. Before an audience of guests and servants, the seven sages were acting out the story of the Sakai sisters. It was a popular story, known to everyone.

At twelve, one of the sisters had sold herself to a brothel to provide money for her impoverished family. She rose to become a famous *tayū* in the Yoshiwara, but she dreamed of returning to care for her parents in their old age. Her younger sister came looking for her to tell her that their father, a *samurai*, had been killed for defending the farmers of his district from unjust taxes.

The seven sages acted out the scene where the younger woman, ridiculed by the courtesans for her rustic accent, was recognized by her older sister. After a tearful reunion the younger sister told of their father's tragic end. Tearfully Hawk and Bamboo clutched each other and declaimed, in song, their vow to avenge their father's death. The scene played to a chorus of snuffling and nose blowing from the audience. By the time Hawk delivered the last lines, not a dry sleeve was left.

The merchant of scrolls, the wallpaperer, the itinerant pot polisher, the young farmer on pilgrimage, and the mantis-thin cloud dweller were dabbing at their eyes. Cat had been studying the last two guests with particular care.

The farmer was powerfully built and had an innocent, earnest expression. But he was traveling alone, an unusual circumstance on the Tōkaidō, and Cat was suspicious. He hadn't been paying attention to Cat, though. In fact, he had been casting shy glances at Kasane.

The old courtier had been one of the poets with Musui the night Cat had fled the inn in Totsuka. But neither he nor his aged servant, who was almost blind, recognized Cat. In fact, a serious distraction had been added to the cloud dweller's usual befuddlement. His lord, the former emperor, was dying. Stricken with grief, the old man was trying to reach Kyōto to wish him farewell.

He sat straight as an arrow in the back of the room with his servant just behind his right shoulder. It would have been hard to guess from the old nobleman's bearing that he had hardly enough coppers to make a clinking sound in his sleeve. His robe with the cloud and lightning design was of Tozan silk, long out of fashion. The neck of his second-quality hempen undergarment was frayed. The patches on the servant's robes were patched in turn. Cat was sure that each spring the old courtier pawned his one winter jacket and robe and redeemed his summer clothes at twenty percent interest. Each fall he reversed the process.

The old man had already taken each male guest aside. In a low, cultured voice he had offered them a sample of his calligraphy, either an original work or a poem of their choice. Of course no mention of payment was made; but Cat had given him a silver coin, ostensibly to bring her good luck.

As Cat was contemplating the sad fate of the nobility in this time of vulgar mercantilism, a particularly lustful cat yowled in an agony of passion.

"Sir Mountain of Love," Hawk called out playfully, "sing for us."

Cat bowed politely. She stepped behind the screen where the sages had left their props and chose a gaudy robe to drape around her. She pinned a small scarf into her hair, to cover the area just above her forehead. It was a ploy used by the *onnagata*, the male *kabuki* actors who specialized in women's roles. The scarves hid the fact that the crowns of their heads were shaved like a man's, in compliance with government orders.

When Cat reappeared she hitched the collar of the robe provocatively away from the nape of her neck. She fluttered her fan in front of her face and minced across the stage, trailing the robe's hem behind her. She imitated a peasant boy burlesquing a city woman. She sang the courtesan's song in a falsetto.

> With no care for duty or people
> or strange looks,
> or the opinion of other cats,
> one cat striped and the other white
> climb to the ridge of the roof.
>
> Driven by the need of love
> which is stronger than death.
>
> One day the wind of winter shall come
> and they will not know each other.
> My soul, I envy the love of cats.

When she finished, everyone called out compliments.

"Ka-sa-ne-san." Hawk began the chant, and the other sages took it up. Kasane tried to hide behind Cat, but she pushed her forward.

"This is a poem I learned from my mother." Kasane looked as though she were about to cry from embarrassment. She turned her head and cleared her throat.

Kasane glanced up at the pilgrim. He held her eyes prisoner for the briefest of moments, before she looked down again. "Fog clings to the high mountains," she recited in a trembling voice. "My eye clings to him. . . ."

CHAPTER 31

A ROPE WOVEN FROM A WOMAN'S HAIR

"A beautiful woman is an ax that cuts off a man's life." But even as he said it, Gobei the gambler studied the portraits in the album with care. He turned the heavy, pleated pages slowly. The wrestler Mountain Wind looked over his shoulder.

The rest of the card players crowded around. The fifteen-year-old artist Okamura Masanobu hadn't included just any women in this collection. These were twelve of the most beautiful courtesans of Edo's Floating World. Masanobu had caught each in a gesture, in a moment stolen from time and fixed for eternity. They were gazing into their mirrors or lounging with robes draped carelessly. They were walking in high lacquered *geta* through new-fallen snow or smoking a pipe on a riverside balcony and staring pensively out over the water.

"Which one ran away?" someone asked.

"Number seven."

"I was there the night she escaped." Mountain Wind pointed a thick finger at the page and began again the tale of his experiences at the Perfumed Lotus.

Hanshiro could hear the men's loud conversation through the floor of his upstairs room. He knew that his prey, the young Lady Asano, was in the album of Masanobu's women. It was a copy of the book Kira's retainers had been discreetly showing to innkeepers, *kago* bearers, and postboys all along the road.

One of those retainers had bet it and lost it to Gobei two hands ago. He had gone out into the rainy night with his shoulders bunched against the cold and his thoughts written on his face. He was trying to invent a lie that would save him from the unpleasantness of disemboweling himself to appease his irascible lord.

Hanshiro had disdained to approach any of Kira's lackeys, so Cat's picture had eluded him. He refused to join the crowd now. He stayed where he was, alone in the small room at the back of the house. The gambler Gobei had been dealing cards in the room beneath him since the hour of the Cock.

Hanshiro knelt with spine straight and with his legs folded under him. He held a paintbrush poised, resting lightly between the tips of his thumb and index finger. He seemed entranced by the sheet of white paper on the low writing stand in front of him. To draw bamboo he knew he must see it first in his mind. Then he must transcribe what he saw as quickly as the hawk stooped on the hare. He was so engrossed he barely heard the *shoosh, shoosh* of Gobei's stockinged feet on the polished boards of the corridor floor.

"*Isogashii?*" Gobei called politely from the doorway. "Busy?"

"*Irasshai.* Welcome."

Gobei entered and sat on the other side of the clay-lined firewell. The coals in the well spread a welcome heat into the damp chill of the room. Both men sat sideways to the door, so that neither would have his back to it.

Gobei crossed his legs, bringing his feet under his baggy yellow *hakama* stenciled with dark blue ginkgo leaves. He laid the folio, its cardboard covers tied shut with gold silk cord, on the *tatami*.

Hanshiro drew in a deep breath. His hand dropped suddenly, and he drew the bamboo with swift, sure strokes—strokes called by names like "goldfish tail," "startled rook," "stag's horns," and "fishbones." He was using the technique called "flying white," painting with a fairly dry brush so that the paper could be seen underneath. He worked unperturbed by Gobei's presence.

Gobei shook back the sleeves of his quilted silk jacket and poured himself tea. "Aren't you done dabbing at that paper yet?" He added more tea to Hanshiro's almost empty cup.

"Confucius said a work is finished not when the last thing has been added, but when the last thing has been taken away."

"As one whose business it is to take away the last thing, I can only agree with Confucius." Gobei shifted his toothpick from one side of his mouth to the other. He had full lips nestled in a black beard, a high, narrow nose, bushy brows, and eyes that were little more than slits in his broad face.

"Have you finished taking away the last things from the unfortunates downstairs?" Hanshiro asked.

"I left them the hair in their anuses and their manly organs." Gobei grinned wolfishly. "Peasants are not called the 'great august treasure' for nothing. It is their fate to give, mine to take."

He reached for the tobacco canister on the wooden, boxlike tray the waitress had set beside him. He packed the bowl of his oversize pipe and lit it with an ember from the firebox on the tray.

He held the big pipe horizontally in the palm of his hand, with his fingers folded diagonally over the stem. Brigands carried large pipes and held them this way, and it was an affectation of Gobei's.

"You can work with me, you know," Gobei said. "My offer stands, old friend. You can be a rich man and live with a fan in your left hand."

Hanshiro's mouth twitched in a shadow of a wry smile as he bowed. His nod expressed refusal, but with just the proper balance of sincere regret, irony, and condescension.

He added an elegant tracery of characters down the upper right-hand side of the page, a poem of his own composing. He should have been offended by Gobei's effrontery, but he had known him too long for that. And he found him amusing.

Besides, Gobei was the head of the gamblers' syndicate. His word was law along the Tōkaidō among the hundreds of men who were considered members of the guild. Some of the men in the guild made their livings by more nefarious means than dice and cards. Taking issue with their leader would have gained Hanshiro nothing and could have put obstacles in his way.

Gobei leaned over to inspect Hanshiro's ink painting of bamboo bent before a wind. " 'When calm, paint iris.' " He quoted the ancients. " 'When angry, bamboo.' "

"Anger is like breaking wind in a typhoon," Hanshiro said. "It provides temporary relief but avails little."

"This fleeting world is temporary; but temporary is better than nothing at all. As the poets say, 'Enjoy life! Tomorrow we may end as sea wrack on the rocky shore of Oya-Shirazu, Not-Knowing-Parents.'" Gobei lifted the large folio to his forehead with exaggerated courtesy, then bowed as he held it out to Hanshiro.

"I brought you the book," he said. "But you need not leaf through it by the light of the night lantern while you bedew the palm of your hand. Self-pleasure is like scratching your foot through the sole of your sandal. Allow me to show you Odawara's garden of night-blooming flowers. I will introduce you to Lotus." Gobei molded the air sensuously with his hands. "Her buttocks remind one of a ripe peach."

"Another time, Gobei-san." Hanshiro laid the unopened folio aside. At least with Gobei Hanshiro didn't have to bother with punctilio.

"From your interest in young Masanobu's art, I assume you're hunting the *yakko*, the *samurai* courtesan, and not the boat-swallowing fish who's been reducing the population of late." Gobei leaned forward and grinned across the firewell. "I hear that rascal made soldier soup of two Edo men in Hiratsuka." Gobei laughed in delight at his own pun on the words for soup stock made of dried bonito and the word for soldier.

"I'm hunting the impossible, a night's sleep in a dry bed free of fleas and cutpurses."

Hanshiro cleaned his ink stone. He washed out his brush and laid it on a silk pad. He emptied the dirty water from his gourd-shaped porcelain container into the wide-mouthed jug placed there for that purpose. With a silk cloth he wiped each item in his writing case and replaced them in their proper compartments.

"You needn't have rushed to Odawara through that tantrum of a storm in the dark of night. This story of the Asano wench's escape is a ruse, Tosa-san." Gobei lowered his voice. Sound carried through paper walls. "Kira had her kidnapped from the brothel. He has dispatched her spirit to the Western Paradise and her body to the burning grounds at Hashiba. You're chasing her smoke, my boy. Kira's conducting this hoax of a search to allay suspicions. Everyone knows it."

Gobei knocked the dottle from his pipe into the bamboo container in the tobacco box. "Do you really think a woman would be foolish enough to attempt the Hakone barrier," he continued, "to tread on the tail of the tiger?"

"I have no pressing engagements. I shall wait by the road and see who passes."

"Have a care, my friend. This murderer has the authorities in an uproar."

"Thank you for the warning, Gobei-san."

"And now I shall pay a visit to the white-necked ones. I stayed away from the House of the Wisteria several days last month when I was ill with stomach pains. When I returned, my sweethearts there held me down and threatened to cut off my topknot for neglecting them."

"If that's the worst they threaten to cut off, you have nothing to fear."

"Would you honor a miserable wretch by allowing him to add this magnificent painting to his collection of works in the Tosa school?" Gobei bowed. When Hanshiro handed him the rolled paper, he stowed it carefully in the gap where the left side of his jacket overlapped the right.

Gobei rose and shut his fan with a clack of farewell. As he left he opened it again, gesturing with it in the slow dance of the *Nō* drama. With his other hand he slapped his rear end to keep time. He took the part of Ono no Komachi, an old woman possessed of the ghost of a former lover. The words to his song, however, were of his own invention.

"I . . . am . . . the . . . Devil . . . farting," he declaimed in the nasal singsong of *Nō*. The technique made the words sound stretched and distorted. "I am the ba-a-a-stard child of the god of swi-i-indlers."

As Gobei disappeared down the hall, Hanshiro could hear his singing and slapping and tongue clicking in imitation of wooden clappers grow fainter. The maid appeared to lay out the bedding, trim the lamp wick, and lower the wooden nightshade over the lantern. Then she bowed and wished him a pleasant rest.

When she had knelt in the corridor and closed the door in front of her own bowing face, Hanshiro sat alone in the shadows a while longer. He listened to the night crier clapping his wooden blocks and warning against carelessness with fire. He watched the slow undulating pulse of the lantern's shadow on the wall.

Finally he untied the cord and opened the folio. He turned the pages slowly and stopped at the seventh portrait. It carried the red, gourd-shaped seal and the words "From the genuine brush of the Japanese artist Okamura Masanobu."

Cat was posed in front of a latticework bamboo fence covered with wisteria flowers. Her body was half-turned toward the right edge of the page, but she was glancing over her shoulder to the left. Cat's sumptuous robes and sash were hand-colored in heron's-egg-green and rose tints.

She was holding a half-opened paper umbrella at an angle off from her left shoulder. She wore a man's headband rakishly tied at the side in a large, flat knot. A wind was blowing her robe against her left hip and thigh and lifting her hem to reveal the men's gaiters that women of fashion were sporting in the Eastern Capital.

Masanobu had spared no detail of Cat's dress. Her face, however, was difficult to distinguish from the others in the album. Masanobu had given all the women the stylized features considered most desirable. He had painted Cat with brows thin as black silk thread, tapered eyes that were little more than slits, a long hooked line for a nose, an impossibly tiny mouth, full cheeks, and a round chin.

But Masanobu had captured something in Cat's face that none of the other women had. As she stared over her shoulder, the look in her eyes was defiant. It was the pose and the look Musui's handsome young disciple had given Hanshiro the night he'd discussed poetry with the monks at the temple near Kawasaki. It was the look he had mistaken for lust. Suddenly Hanshiro realized why the boy had seemed familiar. He resembled the nun he had seen near Lord Asano's grave at Spring Hill Temple.

The heat that reddened Hanshiro's face was as much chagrin as a surge of desire mixed with admiration. The young Lady Asano had made a fool of him, just as she was making fools of Kira's men. Hanshiro didn't like being reduced to the level of Kira's men, but he had to admit the Lady Cat was very good. Perhaps she had mastered the art of *saiminjutsu*, hypnotizing her enemies.

Hanshiro closed the book and retied the cords around it. Then he took from the front of his jacket the flat brocade case like the one in which he carried his paper handkerchiefs. Inside was the silk cloth with the crossed-feather crest. He unwrapped it and held it in the palm of one hand. With his fingers he stroked the coil of Cat's hair, black and glossy as a leopard flower seed.

Now he could combine the perfume of the incense in her room and the cool sleekness of her hair with her face and her form. He could construct her from memory and his own heart's yearning. Like the image of the bamboo he had just painted, Cat appeared in his mind's eye.

He could imagine this length of hair flowing in a cascade down her slender back. He pictured it lying along the curve of her haunch. He saw it swaying as she walked in the "floating step," the hesitant, hip-swinging gait of the courtesan on promenade.

Hanshiro felt as though a loop were tightening around his heart. A rope woven from the locks of a woman's hair, the old poem went, would bind a very elephant.

What was he to do? Lady Asano's quest was madness. She would surely be caught, and even if she weren't, she could accomplish nothing. No vendetta had been registered in her father's name. Her uncle was in exile. The Akō retainers had scattered. Their leader, the Councilor Oishi Kuranosuke, had sunk in a mire of debauchery. Lady Asano would be shamed and executed for her folly. Hanshiro saw, suddenly, this lovely hair crusted with blood.

He decided to start a rumor in the morning to throw Kira's men off the trail. He knew he would have to find Cat before she reached the Hakone barrier. But he also knew he could do it. He now knew what she looked like.

He would return her discreetly to the Perfumed Lotus before she was connected with the attack at the ferry and the murders in the bathhouse. Some rich merchant or lord would redeem her. She could start another life as an outside consort or a *daimyō*'s pampered woman of the province.

Hanshiro convinced himself that what happened to Her Ladyship after he returned her was a fire across the river. It was no concern of his. Even so, a woman's laughter in another room set his heart to pounding.

CHAPTER 32
THE BALL OF DOUBT

Northeast of Odawara the Tōkaidō wound upward into steep hills. At the top of a high ridge, Cat sat cross-legged on a moss-

covered boulder. She had stopped to rest and to wait for the
dawn. Kasane had fallen asleep curled among the roots of an
oak. She and Cat had left the See No Evil inn in Oiso while
everyone still slept. They had traveled by the light of a waning
moon in a star-strewn sky.

Cat looked out over the dark valley to the southwest and to
the mountains of Hakone on the other side of it. In the darkness
the mountains weren't visible, but she felt their presence.

Cat was frightened. Her stomach churned at the prospect of
facing the Hakone barrier. How stupid she had been, to think
she could fool the officials there with her mimicry of a peasant
boy. She could almost feel their rough hands on her as they led
her away.

Unnerved by her own fear, Cat considered the possibility that
she wasn't capable of the task she had set for herself. She had
had few moments of uncertainty in her life. This one made her
think of the old Chinese poem:

> Lodged within my heart
> A ball of doubt as big as
> A wicker basket.

To calm herself she stared into the darkness as though she
could see her father's west country lands more than a hundred
ri away. The estate of Akō had been the home of her father's
family for almost sixty years. Until seven years ago she had
spent every summer there. But when she turned thirteen Lord
Asano's request for travel papers for the child listed as his servant's daughter had simply not been granted. Nor had a permit
been issued to leave Edo since then.

No explanation was ever given, but Cat and her mother
guessed the reason. Cat had come to resemble strikingly both
her father and her mother. Government officials had discovered
her real relationship to Lord Asano. In a way, the government
too was tacitly recognizing Cat as his daughter and heir.

So over the years Akō had become fixed in Cat's mind as a
haven, always warm and green and safe. It was a paradise scented
with salt breezes and with the blossoms from the groves of sweet
oranges. Cat longed to wander the forested hills and shining
headlands of Akō again.

She had reveled in the freedom of country life. With Oishi's
son, Chikara, who was three years younger, she had explored
the high turrets and balconies of her father's graceful, many-

gabled keep. They had looked down on the roofs of the retain-ers' houses below. Cat had luxuriated in the prickle of grass under her bare feet. She had fenced with the plainspoken sons of her father's west country retainers. Best of all, she had studied the warrior's arts with Oishi almost every day.

On hot summer evenings Cat and her mother and nurse had gone for boat rides on the Inland Sea. They had sailed among small islands of rocky cliffs and gnarled pines. They had laughed and sung and composed poetry about the beauty of the moon-light on the water. The fishermen had lit fires in the metal bas-kets hanging from the prows of their boats. Rocked by the gentle swell, Cat had watched the distant lights swoop and wink in the darkness.

Cat and Chikara had caught fireflies on the bank of the river. They had put them in gauze-covered cages and used them as lanterns to light the way home. Cat's nurse released the fireflies into the rippling, room-size tent of silk gauze that served as Cat's mosquito net. Their twinkling had amused her until she fell asleep.

Cat's mother told her the fireflies were the spirits of the dead, come to light the way for loved ones left behind. *The spirit,* her mother had said, *can travel a thousand* ri *in a day.*

Cat drew a bundled towel from inside her jacket and un-wrapped Kasane's knife. She pressed her thumb hard against the blade. It was sharp.

As she held the knife in her lap, Cat remembered the old tale Oishi had told her that summer long ago. He told it during a game of a Hundred Supernatural Stories. As each person told a ghost story he or she extinguished one candle. The party had started in the eerie light of a hundred candles covered with blue paper hoods. By dawn only one had been left. Oishi had snuffed the last light and they all sat in darkness as he told of the warrior who traveled a hundred *ri* in a day.

The warrior had left his home near Akō to travel to Izumo on the other side of the country. He promised his brother he would return on the ninth day of the ninth month. He arrived almost at the end of the appointed day. Everyone had gone to bed except his brother, who waited for him at the front gate. The two men had a joyful reunion, and the returning warrior told of being imprisoned by the cruel lord of Tonda castle.

As Oishi told the story he took both parts.

" 'Until today,' the warrior said, 'I could find no way to escape.'

" 'Until today!' his brother exclaimed. 'But Izumo is a hundred *ri* away.'

" 'Yes.' The warrior looked at him sadly. 'Fortunately I was allowed to keep my sword and so could make the journey here in time. Say good-bye to our mother.' With that, he disappeared.''

Cat remembered the heat of that summer night and the cool itch of salty tears on her cheeks as she had listened to Oishi's low, resonant voice in the dark. "He had killed himself," Oishi said. "So his ghost could travel a hundred *ri* and keep his promise."

Cat opened the neck of her jacket and laid the flat of the cold blade against her breast. She closed her eyes and concentrated on the hard, smooth feel of it as it took on the warmth of her body. It too could release her spirit and allow her to reach Oishi in a day. Her ghost could enlist his help.

Cat sighed. The story of the two faithful brothers was a tale told to amuse children. Belief in ghosts was for servants and peasants and the very young.

Cat would have to stay alive. She would have to continue walking along a road that seemed to have no end. She would have to face the officials at the Hakone barrier.

She pulled her jacket farther open and felt under her ribs for the place where the knife's blade would enter if she were to commit suicide as her father had. With eyes still closed she turned the knife so she was holding the handle in both hands, the blade poised. She sat like that a long while, breathing deeply and trying to imagine her father's last moments, his last thoughts.

Finally a cold gust from the sea caused her to shiver. When she opened her eyes she saw that dawn was just spilling out from the seam where the bay met the sky. As she watched, the pale blue of the water became streaked with iridescent turquoise and lavender and spangled with fire from the rising winter sun.

The loops and folds of the Sakawa River trailed across the landscape below like a discarded length of metallic thread. Beyond the bare fields and the town on the other side of it were the mountains. At the mountains' base the tiered roofs of Odawara castle, with their upswept gables, floated on the dark green canopy of firs and pines. The shadows among the trees' branches looked like shreds of night still caught there. A flock of crows separated from the shadows, cawed, and rose into the sky.

Cat put away the knife. She took slow, deep breaths of the cold air as she stared at Mount Fuji rising pale as a cone of mist beyond the dark mountains. The sight of Fuji calmed her fearful spirit. She realized she had become distracted by the details of her journey. The feverish tally of *ri* and *cho* and towns and days had been clicking in her mind like the beads of a merchant's abacus.

Cat had studied Zen with her mother's mentor, the abbot of Sengakuji. She had sat long hours in meditation; but now, although she tried to eliminate extraneous thoughts, Musui's mischievous, lopsided grin intruded. His presence was as unstoppable as the sun that would soon appear and brighten the day.

Sensei, Cat thought, *the disciple you named Endurance wants nothing except to behead a man.*

"*You must eat the fruits of your own deeds.*" Cat heard Musui as clearly as if he were standing at her side, fingering the beads of his rosary and enjoying the fine view. "*Don't worry yourself about life. The world is but a traveler's inn. The Path is not the means to an end. The Path is the goal itself.*"

Cat let her breath out until she felt empty and light. She paused before drawing more air in. For an instant she felt as though she had no need of breath. She was serene and unafraid.

"Thank you, *sensei,*" she murmured.

She climbed down from her perch on the boulder and crouched next to Kasane, who was still asleep. She looked so young, so innocent, that she reminded Cat of something Bashō had written. In his travels he had met a pink-cheeked farm girl, a "darling named Kasane." "Kasane," he wrote. "A curious, sweet name."

Watching her, Cat realized that Kasane too had lost her home and a loved one and had been pursued by enemies. Cat vowed to make amends for her own meanness of spirit.

"Elder sister," she said.

Kasane jerked awake. She jumped up, grabbed her pack, and began struggling into the straps. "I'm sorry to delay you, mistress. Please forgive me, though I don't deserve your forgiveness." In her haste Kasane fumbled with the roll of mats. Cat helped her fasten them in place.

"While I slept and wasted time your gentleman waits for you in the south country."

"Don't worry yourself. We have time." Cat settled her *furoshiki* on her back, then retrieved her staff from where it leaned against the boulder. "*Dewa mairo?* Shall we go?"

They hadn't walked far along the deserted road when Cat felt a shy tug at her sleeve.

"Forgive my rudeness. . . ." Kasane held out a round white paper fan.

Someone had written on it in a simple, masculine hand using *hiragana*, the syllabary of women and the poorly educated. Cat was relieved to see that the writing held neither threat nor warning.

"Where did you get this?"

"I found it in my pack." Kasane crowded close to look over Cat's shoulder. "Who wrote it?"

"It's a poem." *And an unpolished and presumptuous one at that,* Cat thought, but she held her tongue.

Cat was rather amused by the flawed but heartfelt attempt at eloquence of a young man caught up in the romance of the road. She read the poem aloud.

> The last maple leaf,
> blasted by an icy wind,
> turns crimson and falls.

"What does it mean?"

"You must have an admirer. He probably paid a servant to slip this in among your things."

"*Dame!* Impossible!" Kasane blurted out. She covered her mouth in horror at her own rudeness.

"Maybe it was written by the handsome young man who was staring at you last night in the See No Evil. I think his poem means that your cold glances wounded him."

"Is that so?" Kasane was rattled. She turned her face away and waved her hand, as though to scatter such a preposterous notion. But when Cat gave the fan back to her she held it reverently and stared at it before sticking it into her robe and under her sash.

"No one ever sent poetry to this unworthy person before," she confessed shyly.

Wisps of hair were already escaping from the *shimada* hairdo Hawk had created on her the day before. Kasane had wrapped a blue-and-white cloth around it and tied it at the base of the thick looped club of hair. The kerchief made her look again like the commoner she was. She wore her big straw pilgrim's hat over it. She wore mud-spattered cloth gaiters and straw sandals over bare feet. She had tucked the skirt of the pilgrim's robe into her sash at the small of her back.

Her brother's pilgrim's robe had gone overboard with him, so Cat had traded his wadded jacket for a pair of used white robes from Wave, the proprietor of the See No Evil. Wave probably had everything she had ever acquired stored somewhere in the inn. She had led Cat to a small storage room and ransacked the trunks there. She had thrown clothing about until she'd found the white robes. They'd been left by two unfortunate pilgrims who had died, and Wave was glad to be rid of them and the bad aura that accompanied them.

Cat was grateful that fate and Wave had provided two robes. A brother and sister wearing a mismatched pair would have aroused suspicion. Still, she had inspected the style of the weave closely. The cloth had been made in Edo. It was possible that two pilgrims from Kazusa could be wearing it.

For walking Cat too had tucked up the hem of the robe, revealing Kasane's brother's tight-fitting breeches. She also wore his old *tabi* and gaiters. She and Kasane had tied their spare sandals to their sashes. They carried walking sticks and wore travel cloaks against winter's cold. To a passerby they did look like brother and sister.

Cat, however, was still wondering how she could convince Kasane to leave her. If Kasane were caught with her at the barrier, the punishment could be terrible. Cat decided to coax her into talking about her family and the fishing village where she was born. Maybe she would grow homesick enough to agree to return there. In any case, Cat could hear more of her accent.

"Elder sister, tell me about Pine village."

"Excuse my rudeness, but there's nothing to tell. It's a poor, dull place."

Cat knew Kasane was right, but she tried to think of something she could ask that would start Kasane talking.

"I have a book." Kasane spoke in a voice so low, Cat turned around to make sure she hadn't fallen behind. Kasane rested the pack on a low wall and found the book. She blushed a charming pink as she held it out to Cat.

It was one of the cheap editions of "spring pictures" bound between heavy cardboard covers. Peddlers sold them throughout the countryside. The wooden blocks from which it had been printed had worn down until even new, the pages were barely legible. The hairdos were months out of style, but the book's twelve foldout panels contained detailed illustrations of men with penises the size of mackerel copulating acrobatically with women. The books of "spring pictures" were customary presents for brides-to-be.

Cat leafed through it with amusement. "Was this an engagement gift?"

"Honorable Go-Between gave it to me." Normally Kasane would never have talked about this with someone of Cat's class, but Cat's insistence on asking personal questions had suspended the rules of proper behavior.

"My parents hired her to arrange a marriage for me with a gentleman from another village," Kasane went on. "The go-between said that even though I'm homely, I'm strong and healthy and there is no insanity in my family, so she made a good match for me. We were going to be married after the trip to Ise. His mother wanted me to be there for the spring rice planting." Kasane's blush deepened. "I never saw him, and now I never will."

CHAPTER 33

A MOUNTAIN AND SEA CHANGE

The black tile roofs of the castle of the powerful Okubo clan of Odawara towered over the low roofs of the town below like a lord over his obeisant subjects. Odawara was a major port and an industrial center of about five thousand tile-roofed houses. It had a large complement of carpenters, paperers, plasterers, tilers, and coopers. It also boasted three dyers, five blacksmiths, ten sword sharpeners, two lacquerers, six silversmiths, and a hundred and three *sake* brewers.

When Cat and Kasane entered the town midway through the hour of the Hare, its streets were filling with peddlers and bearers laden with boxes and bales. Children carrying trays of homemade snacks for sale wandered out of the small side doors of their tenements.

With a rumble and clatter apprentices were opening the heavy shutters at the shop of the bean curd maker, exposing the boiling vats and the rank, steamy bustle inside. Fishmongers touted

their bream and herring. Coins jingled in the scales of the exchange shops. From one side alley Cat could hear the steady
clink, clink of sword makers' hammers. From another came the
frump of the weavers' mallets as they pounded cloth to soften
it.

Maids were taking advantage of the unusually warm weather
to wash clothes in big tubs in the courtyards behind the front
gates of inns and houses. Others stretched long, wet rectangular
panels of disassembled *kimonos* onto frames hung horizontally
between trees. Still others leaned from the second-floor windows to lay bedding out to air on the first-story roof overhangs.
They called teasing invitations to Cat, and she pulled her hat
farther down over her face.

Cat led the way through the twisting streets. At the crossroads
on the outskirts she stopped to study the small forest of wooden
and stone road markers. Then she turned west onto the broad
track of the Tōkaidō as it led into the foothills. Just beyond the
city, past the Sanmai Bridge, as though they had been discarded
there, were small stands selling tea and souvenirs.

The most plentiful items for sale were slender paper lanterns
with wire handles. When not in use they could be collapsed into
their round bamboo rims and tucked into the front of a robe.
They were the specialty of Odawara, and small groups of pilgrims clustered around the stands selling them. The road to
Hakone was long and precipitous, and the sun set early behind
the high peaks. Night in the mountains was very dark.

Kasane lagged behind to inspect the garlands of sedge hats
dangling from the beams and corner posts of one stand. When
Cat looked back Kasane beckoned to her. "Hachibei . . ." Kasane caught hold of Cat's sleeve and drew her away from the
stand. "Our hats don't match," she said in a low voice.

"I could say I lost mine."

"Of course." Kasane dared not contradict her mistress by
pointing out that that would draw attention to them. That it
would necessitate more discussion with the barrier guards. Cat
figured it out for herself. She traded in the old hats and some
coins for two new ones. She handed one to Kasane.

"Forgive my rudeness, but they should have marks." Kasane
stared at the ground and flushed at her own impertinence.

"Marks?"

"A charm. To protect us."

Cat sighed. Kasane was right. Pilgrims' hats always had some
pious sentiment painted on them.

She found a calligrapher. The old man was laying out his faded cushion and setting up his lacquered writing stand under a roof of torn matting thrown over a rickety frame. Cat kneeled on the small straw mat he had laid down for his customers.

"Oh, honorable Five-Brush-Monk . . ." She bowed low. "Our pilgrims' hats were lost overboard in yesterday's storm. Will you honor us by inscribing a suitable phrase on these unworthy surfaces?"

"I am honored that my inferior abilities may be of use." The old man settled a pair of wire-framed spectacles onto the sharp bridge of his nose. "Since you're my first customer, I'll give you a discount."

He spoke a refined dialect in a whispery voice, tinged with irony. He was charmed by Cat's comparison of himself with the great calligrapher Kōbō Daishi, the Five-Brush Monk. He was further charmed that she chose to share with him the secret that she was not, in fact, an uneducated peasant.

As he laid out his brushes and ink stone with spidery fingers, Cat noticed the slight droop of his left shoulder. It indicated a man who had carried the two swords of a *samurai* most of his life.

"How much, most venerable sir?" It embarrassed Cat to have to ask the *rōnin*, reduced in circumstances though he might have been, the price.

The old man waved a hand, as though payment were of no consequence. "Ten coppers," he murmured.

Cat laid the hats on the frayed mat next to him. She settled back on her heels to wait.

"Hachibei," Kasane said, "I'll be back soon."

"Where are you going?"

"To buy rice for your meal tonight." Kasane bowed and hurried into the crowd at this small morning market.

The old man added a few drops of water to his stone and methodically ground his ink stick on it. When the water became black and thick he added more, washing the ink into the small trough at one end of the stone.

Apparently oblivious to Cat's presence and to the noise of people hawking their wares all around him, he continued the methodical, circular grinding for a long time. Then he took up one of the hats and turned it in his hand. He tilted his head back to study the brim's wide surface through his spectacles. Two more customers arrived and squatted on their heels to wait, but he ignored them also.

He sat for several more long moments with his hand poised over the brushes in the earthenware container. Finally he chose one with a bamboo handle and a fairly broad tuft of badger hair. He dipped it gently into the ink. For his ten coppers he painted his words on the cheap hat as painstakingly as if he were fulfilling a commission for the emperor.

Kasane arrived as Cat was putting ten coppers, plus five extra for luck, into the center of a paper handkerchief. She twisted it so the ends spread out into a shape like the petals of a flower. He bowed when she presented the package to him.

Cat gave Kasane her hat and led the way to a small open-air tea stand. With their feet dangling, the two sat on the wide bench in front while the waitress fixed their morning tea.

"What did the honorable writer put on our hats?" Kasane studied the thick black characters as though if she looked at them long enough, they would make sense to her.

"The words say, 'Before the first step is taken the goal is reached.'"

"How splendid!"

Kasane didn't understand the phrase, but she continued to stare at the miracle of writing. Cat watched the travelers stream by. Already the road was crowded. Even though this time between harvest and the New Year's celebrations was not the season for pilgrimages, the tinkling of pilgrims' bells was constant.

"Did you find food?" Cat asked.

"Yes." Kasane held up a small cloth tied around a handful of raw rice and shook it. "I held out my pilgrim's bowl and begged. A kind woman gave me enough for us to eat tonight. Someone else gave me forty coppers."

Kasane pulled a pair of cloth arm guards from her sleeve and handed them to Cat. They were shaped like long, fingerless gloves of the sort worn by laborers. Kasane had gotten them from a used-clothing peddler. They had seen hard wear, but she seemed pleased with them. "I used some of the coppers to buy these."

"We haven't money to spare for such things."

"They only cost twenty coppers." Kasane lowered her voice. "They'll help to hide your hands."

When Cat tried one on, a wide flap continued from her wrist across the back of her hand and down to the first row of knuckles. She put on the other one. They did obscure the fact that she hadn't the hands of a fisherman. "Thank you," she said.

Then Kasane gave Cat the crude straw gaiters she had bought.

They were itchy, but they disguised the slender curves of Cat's legs. Next she showed Cat how to wear her cotton towel as a peasant man might. She draped it low on Cat's forehead, folded the ends over, brought them down across her cheeks, and tied them under her chin. The towel hid her face somewhat and finished her transformation into a fisherman.

Kasane and Cat hung their rosaries of a hundred and eight prayer beads on their wrists and tied their brass pilgrims' bells to their sashes. Then they put on their hats and packs. Fortified by the hot tea and leaning on their staffs, they joined the stream of traffic.

When at an impasse Musashi recommended a mountain and sea change. If one's opponent is expecting the sea, give him mountains. Cat was now prepared to give the guards at Hakone barrier a loutish peasant lad named Hachibei.

As the Tōkaidō wound up and around the side of the mountain, they could look over the edge and see the hamlets and paddies in the narrow valleys far below. The sides of the mountains were covered with hardwoods, all woven together with wisteria and azalea and saxifrage.

Young women from the mountain villages hawked sweet dumplings and tea by the side of the road. Occasionally Cat passed a priest or nun begging. Rich merchants plodded by on rented horses led by postboys. Porters and *kago* bearers exchanged good-natured insults as they passed one another. Groups of pilgrims sang ditties from their home districts or chanted the praise of Buddha. Pairs of couriers jogged by shouting nonsense syllables, *"Ei-sassa, ei-sassa, korya, korya, sassa, sassa,"* in time to their pounding feet.

As Cat and Kasane climbed higher, however, the tall cedars closed in over them, shutting out the sky. The small statues of Jizō-sama, who protected travelers, became more frequent. Clusters of them, each wearing a small red bib, stood in niches carved from the granite boulders lining the road.

People grew quiet. Even the *kago* bearers were saving their breath for the ascent. Cat heard her own gasps over the muffled clop of the horses' straw-shod hooves on the rocks and the tinkling of bells. In the chill mountain air she began to sweat, and she took off her travel cloak.

The road became a rocky, narrow trough passing between two rows of towering cryptomeria trees. As it rose toward the clouds, the Tōkaidō twisted and turned on itself in short switchbacks. It was bordered by high banks and sheer drop-offs. It

was flanked by stands of bamboo and tangled heaps of fallen
trunks covered with moss and ferns.

The trees were immense. The undergrowth was lush and
dank. Silvery waterfalls catapulted down granite cliff faces into
the deep, green crevices of valleys. The plumb faces of the
mountains rose in hazy blue ranges as far as Cat could see.

As Cat rounded a sharp turn she saw a small figure stumble
just ahead. The child was burdened with a load of straw-wrapped
bundles tied to a wooden frame and thatched with straw. The
frame reached above her head, and it caused her to lose her
balance. When she pitched toward the cliff's edge, Cat grabbed
the nearest side pole of the frame and hauled her to safety. The
fall was three hundred *cho* to a river raging over boulders.

The child staggered and collapsed onto her hands and knees
on the rocks of the roadway. Her chest was heaving, and she
was gasping for air as she struggled to rise again. She looked
about eleven or twelve years old.

"Wait." While Kasane held the frame, Cat lifted the broad
straw-padded strap from its place just below the child's collarbone. Then she helped her up, led her to a boulder by the side
of the road, and sat her down. Kasane steadied the ladderlike
frame and leaned on it patiently.

"Where are you going?" Cat asked.

The girl only stared at her with wide, desperate eyes.

"Where are your people?"

Nothing.

"Where do you live?"

The girl gestured to her mouth.

"You cannot speak?"

The child was deaf and mute, but her eyes were eloquent.
She was dressed in the rags of a paper shift tied with a wisteria
vine. She was barefoot. Her arms and legs were thin as hairpins.

Cat remembered her father's mother admonishing her once
for helping a servant. By helping her Cat had raised the woman
above her proper station and threatened her orderly rebirth in
the next life. But Cat also remembered Musui carrying the old
woman's burden of firewood.

"I'll carry it." Kasane reached for the frame.

"You have the pack to carry, and the bundle." Cat put her
pilgrim's bell and her rosary into the *furoshiki*. Then she handed
it to Kasane.

Kasane held the frame, and the child arranged the thick woven straw pad on Cat's back. Cat lifted the strap over her head

and arranged it under her collarbone. She steadied the load while Cat stood up under it and shifted it to balance it. The frame forced her to wear her hat slanted forward and down. It restricted her vision to the stony patch of ground under her feet.

Its weight bent her over. She tried to imagine what it must have been like for the child. She beckoned to the girl to follow. Then, leaning on her staff, she began trudging up the narrow road.

CHAPTER 34

JUMPING OFF KIYOMIZU TEMPLE

As Hanshiro sat on the tea house balcony jutting out over a narrow chasm, he had to admire the sagacity of the mad bandit priest. The view from this crag was spectacular. Hanshiro could see all the way to the sparkling waters of the bay of Suruga, but that wasn't its main advantage. From here he could also see travelers, on their way to the Hakone barrier, toiling along the switchbacks both up and down the mountain. When they passed directly below, they were out of sight of those above and below them on the road. It was an ideal place for an ambush.

The bandit had been wise in his choice of roosts, but not in his selection of victims. Fifteen years earlier, the crag where this tea house now stood had been the highwayman's lair.

He had lived in a cave in the face of the cliff, and he had waited here until likely prey appeared. With his staff and its iron rings and spear's head strapped on his back, he would swing across the chasm on a retractable rope bridge. In the guise of a mountain priest soliciting donations he would rob travelers of their clothing, their goods, and their money. Then he threw them, still alive, into the abyss.

Thus he disposed of both evidence and witnesses. And he might have been operating here yet if late one winter afternoon he had not made the mistake of selecting a lone man heading eastward, down the snowy mountain. The traveler had been a seedy-looking individual with rustic written all over his shabby sandals, snow cape, hat, and leggings, all of straw. The bulky cape had hidden Hanshiro's pair of swords, which were about all he had to his name when he'd left Tosa to find employment in the Eastern Capital.

When the mad priest, red-rimmed eyes wild and staring and topknot all a-bristle, had loomed up in the road, Hanshiro hadn't sullied his blade on him. His walking staff had sufficed. The priest had joined his victims. The bottom of the crevice was a long way down, giving him time to reflect on his misdeeds before he landed.

"Is there anything else Your Honor desires?" The girl bowed low.

"Everything is splendid." Hanshiro smiled at the child.

She was the very image of Snow, her mother, whom he could hear giving frantic orders in the kitchen. Hanshiro had asked Snow not to go to any trouble, but he knew the request was futile. He knew Snow had whispered instructions to her fifteen-year-old son as soon as Hanshiro appeared. Even now the boy was speeding down the mountain to buy fresh bonito in Oda-wara.

When he returned Snow would toast the fish over a fire of pine needles. She would beat the fillets lightly with straws so the flavor of the smoke would permeate them while they turned a golden brown. If Hanshiro was still there when they were done, she would serve them with soy sauce and garlic. Bonito cooked that way was a specialty of Tosa; and if bonito was available, Snow always prepared it for Hanshiro.

She would refuse payment, of course. Hanshiro never paid for anything here. He was responsible for Snow and her husband owning this tea house, although the mad priest was also their unwitting benefactor.

After he killed the priest Hanshiro hadn't looked for the treasure he must have hidden away. He had been much younger then, and naive. Money of all kinds was distasteful to him. Money tainted with death was anathema. But events turned out as they should on the Great Wheel.

Another *ri* down the mountain Hanshiro had found Snow and her husband destitute and in rags. They had been begging in the snow by the side of the road. Their newborn son had been bundled up and asleep on Snow's back. Hanshiro had assumed that they were the ones who were fated to receive good from the priest's evil.

Because the sun's light had been fading fast, Hanshiro had given them his lantern. He had told them to search in the cave on the jagged precipice that blocked most of the sky above the road. In a way it was Hanshiro's test of their courage and determination. Because of the priest's depredations and the mysterious disappearances of travelers, stories abounded about that promontory. The mountain people whispered that demons lurked there, swooping down off the crag to crush the bones of hapless victims and suck the marrow.

The couple braved the terrors of the accursed place. They found the neatly tied packets of heavy oval gold coins and the sacks of silver and copper in a basket hidden under matting at the rear of the cave. An army of priests marched up the mountain to exorcise the site and the money and to accept a generous donation for their services. Another army of tax collectors arrived to claim the government's share. A phalanx of officials arranged for them to have the use of the land and received their "thank-money" in turn. With what was left the couple built this tea house.

They named their aerie Gentle Haven. They added a red-lacquered arc of a bridge over the chasm. They lined the path to their front gate with stone lanterns that glowed cheerfully, welcoming travelers caught by nightfall. They built small shrines to Jizō and Benten. They prospered.

Over the years they had learned not to inquire into the reasons for Hanshiro's visits. So now, except for a steady flow of tobacco and tea, hot towels, select tidbits, and the sweet *sake* for which Hakone was famous, no one bothered him. He had sat, straight and still, looking down the Tōkaidō, since shortly after dawn. There was no evidence on his face of the emotions scuffling behind his navel.

He watched the long procession of a *daimyō*'s entourage wind past. He inspected each person trudging up the slope, each bald-pated nun and peasant, each merchant, clerk, pilgrim, and itinerant pot polisher. He even scrutinized the couriers with their wooden letter boxes bouncing on their backs. Lady Asano would be deranged to try to pass herself off as a messenger, but he didn't put it past her. She already had proven herself audacious and inventive. And deadly.

The Tōkaidō was so steep and treacherous here, most post-boys were reluctant to rent their horses for this leg of the journey. The horses wore out the straw sandals quickly on the rocks, and their feet became tender. The way was littered with discarded horse sandals. As a result there were more of the light, open, mountain *kago* here than along the coast. A few of them had mats thrown over them to obscure the occupants. Hanshiro knew his quarry might be hidden in one of those, but he doubted it. Kira's men were checking all *kago*.

Hanshiro watched the approach of the peasant family, the ragged child, and the woman in the dirty white pilgrim's robe. He saw their companion's wide-brimmed pilgrim's hat, gloved hands, and *tabi*-clad feet in tattered straw sandals and dirty white gaiters. They were the only parts visible under the stack of goods. Something was odd about the three as a group, though, and Hanshiro studied them as they made their slow progress up the mountain.

Pilgrims didn't usually carry such heavy burdens, but they often did behave strangely. A journey to a far country had a way of changing people. Virtuous farmers and obedient housewives turned frolicsome and licentious. Harlots and scurfy knaves became religious fanatics, determined to crawl the length of the country or wash the feet of every leper they could find.

Hanshiro suspected that the peasant under the load was performing a self-indulgent penance for petty sins. Maybe he had made a fool of his neighbor's wife in the communal storehouse. Or diverted a few *momme* of silver from the tax collection. Or mixed in extra handfuls of chaff with his own tax portion of rice.

Once the three had passed, Hanshiro transferred his attention to the approaching group of merchants with their bearers and servants. And not far behind them the west country artist, and Hanshiro's drinking partner, Nameless. Hanshiro watched him until he was out of sight.

Then he settled back to wait. The day was new. He was sure that by the end of it he would have Lady Asano.

"What is our lord's name?"

"Tsuchiya, lord of Kururi."

"Who is the magistrate?" As they walked, Kasane helped Cat memorize the names of the functionaries of their home province. The officials at the barrier might ask them such questions.

"Yamashita," Cat panted.

"How many *koku* of rice does our lord command?"

"Seventy thousand."

The child interrupted the drill. She tugged at Cat's sleeve and pointed upward.

Cat turned her head sideways, peering out from under the load and up the steep slope. The trail through the huge boulders and the dense tangle of bushes, ferns, and trees was almost invisible. "Do you live up there?" she asked.

The girl pointed again and pulled at the frame. Kasane helped Cat draw her arms out of the straps. The child tested the straw cords holding the stack of goods together before she let them transfer the straw pad and the frame to her back.

"You can't carry such a load up a path that steep." Cat mouthed the words and gestured, but to no avail. The girl was already on her way.

With her toes she sought purchases in the rocks and grabbed the bases of bushes to haul herself up the incline. It looked as though the load itself had acquired arms and legs and were crawling up the mountainside. Cat and Kasane watched her until she was out of sight in the luxuriant vegetation and drifting mist.

May Amida protect you, Cat thought. Then she and Kasane resumed their own journey.

Without the child's load on her back Cat felt light-footed, able to run up the mountain. But soon she was gasping for breath again in the thin, biting air. A new weight seemed to press down on her. More weight dragged at each foot as she moved it out in front of her.

Snow lay in patches on rocks and outcroppings, but Cat was sweating. She passed men struggling up the slope under loads as tall as they were, or resting by the wayside, eyes bulging, muscles quivering with the strain.

About the middle of the day Cat and Kasane stopped to sip cups of hot water from the kettle on a boy's portable brazier. They bought skewers of rice dumplings from a shy young woman who stood by the side of the road. They trudged silently past tiny hamlets clinging to the mountainsides.

As they climbed higher their afternoon shadows lengthened behind them. Without being aware of it, they drew closer together as they neared Lake Hakone. At the lower end of the long, narrow stretch of water was a saddle in the basalt rock. Straddling it was the fenced compound of the government's control post.

Bordering Lake Hakone was a thriving town of inns and tea houses. Shops and baths and a small, insouciant pleasure district lined the main thoroughfare. The women in the souvenir shops offered bowls and boxes decorated with elaborate cherry- and camphorwood inlay.

The inns' maids importuned travelers. Touts shouted the advantages of the sulphur waters of their hot springs spas. Dozens

of ferries and pleasure boats bobbed at anchor along Lake Hakone's shoreline. It was a cheerful place, but at the other side
stood a government guard. Each traveler who passed him had
to be bareheaded. Those on horseback or in *kago* had to dis-
mount. As Cat passed by him she felt his gaze assessing her.

The short stretch of the Tōkaidō beyond the town was particularly lovely. The roadbed was more level as it followed the
ridgeline and passed between an avenue of silent, towering cryptomeria. The huge trees muted the noise of the couriers and the
kago bearers and the pilgrims' bells. Their grandeur didn't ease
Cat's dread. And she was reproaching herself for leading Kasane
into such peril.

Cat saw the crowd of travelers waiting to pass the barrier
about the same time she saw the four severed heads. Each head,
with black hair unbound and hanging loose where the men's
shoulders once had been, rested on a narrow shelf fastened atop
two posts. The four shelves were lined up parallel with the road
and at eye level. Each head sat in a ring of blood-soaked cloth
that held it upright.

Stuck into the ground beside each was a narrow plank with a
square plaque nailed to it. The plaques were inscribed with the
crimes of the heads' owners. As they walked slowly past them
Cat read the plaques to Kasane.

"This one killed a bird." Cat considered the irony of Tokugawa Tsunayoshi's law making the killing of any living thing
punishable by death or exile. "This one tried to sneak around
the barrier."

"Why does the third one have a doll's head with it?"

"He was a wandering puppeteer. He was suspected of being
a spy."

Cat read the fourth plaque, then she read it slowly again. The
fourth man had been beheaded for the murder of two *samurai*
in Hiratsuka and a merchant in Odawara. Was that a coincidence, or had he paid the price for Cat's crime?

Kasane whimpered as she moved closer to Cat. She once had
seen a man decapitated in her village. He had been caught trying
to bribe the assessor to overlook his newest field. She had passed
the exposed head each day, and she had studied it as though it
were an artifact. Now she realized she might suffer the same
fate.

Cat sat down under three huge cedars growing from a grassy
hillock near the flight of stone steps leading to a temple. She set
the bottom of the bundle on the slope behind her and leaned

against it. She spread her legs in a most unladylike way and rested her forearms on her knees.

"What will happen to us, mistress?" Kasane spoke in a low voice as she massaged Cat's calves. They were knotted and quivering with the strain of the climb.

Cat reached out and tilted up Kasane's chin so she could look into her eyes. "Turn back now, elder sister." Her voice was low and intense. "I'll say you took ill and returned to our village."

"They'll find me on the road. They'll execute me anyway."

"Don't be silly. They don't know the whereabouts of every peasant." But Cat knew she would never convince Kasane of that.

Kasane was sure the government's spies kept it apprised of the comings and goings of each of its thirty million subjects. She assumed the *shōgun* knew to a grain how much millet the people of her village harvested from their tiny fields and how many fish they caught. It knew the decisions made in each meeting of each of the hundreds of thousands of groups of five heads of households in each of the thousands of villages scattered throughout the land.

If it hadn't taken her into custody yet, that was only because it hadn't cared to. That made her determination to try to fool the barrier guards even more astonishing.

"I will stay with you, mistress."

"Then we have jumped off Kiyomizu temple." Cat could tell that Kasane had no idea what she was talking about. "Kiyomizu temple sits on a mountainside near the Western Capital," Cat said. "It has a sheer cliff in front of it. To jump off the terrace of Kiyomizu temple means one has done a rash deed and cannot turn back."

Cat used her round fan with "Souvenir of Totsuka" written on it, to brush the dust off her trousers. "The official at the barrier will demand our permits. I'll give them both to him. Say nothing unless he asks you a question. A woman may take you aside and search you, but they don't usually pay much attention to peasants."

Cat took a deep breath and closed her eyes briefly. Sitting down had been a mistake. Her body rebelled at the thought of getting up and walking again. She used her staff to haul herself to her feet.

"Dewa mairo?" She smiled at Kasane. "Shall we go?"

CHAPTER 35
NEITHER GATE NOR INTERIOR

Four of the barrier guards were warming their hands at a brazier beside the roofed gate in the high picket fence. Cat envied the carefree travelers coming out of that gate. They had passed the barrier and now were headed down the mountain toward Odawara. Beyond the gate was the compound with its outbuildings, guard barracks, and the long, low wooden structure where the officials were.

Through the openings between the fence slats Cat and Kasane could see travelers, scribes, couriers, and flocks of minor officials scurrying to and fro. Pack drivers reloaded baggage that had been checked. Postboys fed and curried their mounts.

The gate guards wore broad white headbands tied in the center of their foreheads, just below their shaved crowns. They looked identical in uniforms of dark orange *hakama* and persimmon-colored *kimono*, each with a broad white stripe across the chest and the hollyhock crest of the Tokugawas.

The men at the brazier talked in low voices while the deputy guard, in black *tabi* and a knee-length black-and-white *hakama* over a black *kimono*, sorted out the travelers. He allowed official messengers and members of the upper class to pass without waiting, then priests, pilgrims, and farmers. Merchants, artisans, beggars, and entertainers were held until last.

"Your passes." The deputy guard glanced at the permits Cat held out. "Over there." With his fan he motioned Cat and Kasane toward the pilgrims and farmers waiting in the cedar grove.

Some of the travelers were eating food they had bought in Odawara. Others were massaging their sore feet. A few had fallen asleep, sprawled on the ground with their travel cloaks wrapped around them and their heads leaning against their travel boxes or packs. Four or five young men, dressed as pilgrims, were playing cards. Another pilgrim was rattling his rosary and praying loudly.

Nearby, the *kago* bearers traded boasts of their sexual exploits. Their bone-sore passengers walked around to loosen stiffened muscles and joints. One of them was suffering from *kago* sickness. He vomited into the bushes while the bearers made jokes about him. A line of people waited at the shed housing the privies. Peddlers of tea and rice cakes circulated among the crowd.

Cat lowered her heavy bundle to the ground. Kasane set her pack on its short legs. She unrolled one of the mats for Cat to sit on, then she took off her tattered sandals and stepped onto the far end of it. She knelt and sat back on her heels. She pulled her paper travel cloak tight around her and twisted her fingers in it so their quivering wouldn't be so noticeable. She stared at the swords bristling from the guards' sashes.

Cat thought about taking her guidebook from the front of her jacket and distracting Kasane by reading from it, but she reconsidered. A fisherman who could read would be noticed.

"Won't you try my mushroom tea? It's the very finest." The old man crouched, set down the portable brazier and the heavy wooden water bucket balanced on his carrying pole. "Only five coppers, Your Honor." He tucked his head under his arm and sneezed into his sleeve, which was tied back with a straw cord.

"We're fine, thank you." Cat politely avoided the ugly word *no*. She would have liked a cup of hot tea, though. Now that she had stopped walking, the wind was chilling the sweat on her body. But she knew to a copper how little money they had left, and she knew she must spend it frugally.

When the old man had taken up his burden again and trotted off, Kasane looked around, then tugged surreptitiously at Cat's sleeve.

"He gave me a folded paper, mistress," she whispered.

"The old tea peddler?"

"Yes. I think it's from that same young man."

"The one at the inn last night?"

"Yes. He's at the tea stand across the way." Kasane glanced up obliquely. "He's waving his sleeve at me. What should I do?" She was agitated, but at least her mind was off the ordeal facing her at the barrier.

"This is an intrigue between the two of you," Cat murmured without looking up. "Hide the letter in your sash and don't let on you've told me."

Cat didn't need this foolishness distracting her from the problems ahead, but still she had to stifle a smile.

"Bring the fingers of your right hand to your lips," she said.

"Then reach over and lightly touch your left shoulder. Dip your sleeve gracefully as you return your hand, very, very slowly, to your lap."

"What does that mean?"

"You're acknowledging that you received his letter and will give it attention as soon as you can."

"Hurry up!" The guard waved the farmers and pilgrims toward the gate.

The command was unnecessary. People grabbed their bundles and rushed to be first in line. Cat and Kasane ran barefoot to the fence and put their sandals on while they waited to enter. One *daimyō*'s small procession had just passed, which was the reason for the delay. If a large one were to arrive, they could all be stranded here for another day while hundreds of retainers were cleared.

As Cat entered the compound she saw the last of the upper-class travelers. The woman was dressed in a shabby paper robe rented from the tea shop just outside the gate. Two guards and a woman hired at the tea shop to serve as a go-between were escorting her toward a small building. Cat glanced over at Kasane's pale face. She had seen her, too.

"They only inspect women of the upper class," Cat whispered.

The line edged slowly toward the squat building. The broad swags of white bunting hanging from the wide front eaves snapped in the wind. The draperies were emblazoned with the Tokugawa crest, and they formed a sort of corridor. The gently pitched roof was weighted with stones to keep the cedar shingles from blowing off in the fierce mountain storms. The wooden shutters were slid back to reveal the large room inside.

"I'm frightened," Kasane whispered.

"You're a peasant. They expect you to be frightened. But I expect you to be calm."

Cat could feel her heart pounding as she moved with the line of travelers crossing the noisy compound. What if her act didn't fool them? What if they took Kasane away for a search and frightened her into exposing Cat? What if they found the *yawara* stick in Cat's sleeve? It seemed like years ago that Viper had given it to her. The guards would recognize it as a weapon.

In this world, if you go into the mountains and decide to go deeper and yet deeper, you will emerge at the gate. Cat thought of Musashi's words. *In my school of the long-sword there is neither gate nor interior. There is only the spirit.*

When she and Kasane reached the checkpoint they held their pilgrims' hats in their hands, and with heads bent respectfully, they entered the chill shade under the eaves, behind the draped curtains. They knelt on the wide bench that ran the length of the building and bowed low. The bench put them below the raised floor of the room. They faced at a properly obsequious angle to the captain of the guard. The guard himself knelt below the three officials who sat on a *tatami*-covered platform.

Now that the upper-class travelers had passed, the officials were relaxing. One leaned on an elbow cushion and smoked. With chopsticks the other two picked tidbits off the plates set on lacquered stands in front of them. Off to one side, the scribe sat at his low writing desk. His brush was poised to enter Cat's name, age, district, and village on the register.

"Your papers." The captain waited for his assistant to take the travel permits from Cat and give them to him. "Have you funds enough to support you?"

Cat gave him the cloth sack she had tucked inside her jacket. The captain loosened the drawstring and spilled the silver and strings of coppers into his hand.

"I suppose you plan to beg to eke this out."

"We were told we could depend on the piety and generosity of those kind souls we meet along the way." Cat knocked her head abjectly on the bench.

"Simpletons." The captain tossed the sack back to Cat. "Don't try selling your sister to cover your expenses. Pass quickly through this province. If you're caught spying or disobeying the law, you will be punished."

"Yes, Your Honor."

While the scribe entered the information on the permits into his ledger, Cat listened to the conversation passing among the three officials. She almost panicked when she realized they were talking about the man whose fate was to be beheaded in her stead.

"Which one is it?" The man who was smoking had just arrived.

"The last head," said the younger man.

"The ugliest one," said the older.

"Fast work." With brass chopsticks the smoker picked an ember from the brazier and relit his pipe.

"Witnesses saw him kill a merchant for his purse outside Odawara last night. The police arrested him at a low-class brothel in Miyanoshita. After the torturer applied the 'lobster,' they only had to show him the investigation whip. He began crowing like a cock. He confessed to the two murders in the bathhouse in Hiratsuka.''

"How did one peasant manage to kill two *samurai*?''

"He said they were drunk. He told a very funny story just before the executioner barbered him. We were all amused.''

Cat was concentrating so hard on the conversation that she didn't hear the captain of the guard say, "Next." He rapped his fan sharply on the *tatami* when Cat didn't respond. "Move along.''

"Forgive me, Your Honor.'' Cat retrieved the permits the assistant held out and scrambled clumsily off the bench.

She purposely moved too slowly to avoid the assistant's rod. When he brought it down across her shoulders the pain surged down into the small of her back and up her neck, where it spread out behind her ears. She yelped and scuttled off, sideways, bowing as she went.

Cat and Kasane walked across the compound and through the gate. They hurried past the *kago* men who rushed to congratulate those who had passed the barrier and collect the coppers the relieved travelers gave them for luck. Cat, however, had no coppers to spare.

She and Kasane paused at the chapel to Jizō and gave thanks for their safe passage. Then they walked quickly past the shops and tea houses. In spite of the pain throbbing in her back and head and shoulders, Cat felt like laughing. Passing the barrier had been easier than she had dared hope. Being a faceless peasant had its advantages.

Once beyond the village Kasane spoke first. "I'm sorry he hurt you. I'll rub your shoulders when we stop tonight.''

"Pain is a matter of indifference.'' This pain, in fact, proved that Cat had fooled the guard. He would never have hit her had he known she was of a *samurai* family. She whirled to face Kasane and walk backward down the trail. "I don't see your young man behind us.''

Kasane turned to look.

"Give me the letter.'' Under her wide-brimmed hat Cat still wore the towel Kasane had tied under her chin, and she grinned out from it. The smudges of dirt Kasane had rubbed onto Cat's face made her look young and mischievous.

Kasane gave Cat the letter. "You were very good at the barrier, younger brother,'' she whispered.

Cat unwrapped the heavy outer paper and took out the soft

pliable sheet folded inside. The folds were well done, simple, yet with a certain rustic elegance. Kasane's suitor was a peasant with artistic sensibilities.

" 'If the wind blows . . .' " Cat read. " 'And bends the temple willows; won't you bend too, in love's wind?' " Cat looked up in mock disapproval. "He's a bold fellow!"

"He's only a farmer." Kasane defended him diffidently.

"It is said that a curse will fall on anyone who refuses to gratify the love of another." Cat gave the letter back to Kasane. "It is said that if a person suffers obsession of the heart and is not relieved, his or her spirit will return after death to take vengeance."

Kasane was unable to find in her limited experience anything to say about such a complication. She was terrified of ghosts in general. The idea that one might have animosity for her personally almost paralyzed her with fear.

"I think this is just an infatuation of the road." Cat took pity on her and stopped teasing. "Maybe he wants a marriage not entered into the book at the temple. Do you want to discourage him?"

"I don't think so," Kasane said almost inaudibly.

"Then we'll send him an answer tonight." Cat was amused by this flirtation, but she was wary of it, too. It could put her and Kasane in jeopardy.

Cat also felt protective, brotherly, in fact. Kasane was so naive. So inexperienced. A man could easily make a fool of her.

Cat was composing a poem to send to Kasane's suitor when she saw a man and woman struggling by the side of the road. The attacker had a hand over his victim's mouth so she could make only muffled cries.

The few other travelers in the vicinity hurried past; but Cat brandished her walking staff and advanced, stiff-legged, toward them. The thief saw her coming and shoved the woman into her. Then he ran into the thick undergrowth and disappeared.

Kneeling in the road and sobbing incoherently, the woman clung to Cat's waist. She looked middle-aged and quite respectable, although she was hysterical and disheveled by the attack.

"Calm yourself, auntie," Cat said. "He's gone now." She was pleased to see that Kasane still clutched her own staff in a fighting position. *She wouldn't be the first peasant to become a* samurai, Cat thought.

Cat helped the woman to her feet. "Do you live nearby?"

Still sobbing, the woman pointed up the mountain. She bowed

repeatedly as she backed toward a narrow path. Cat and Kasane continued down the trail with her thanks following them.

"You're a brave one, Kasane."

"I was frightened, but I knew you could beat him."

Cat turned off onto a side trail, screened by bushes.

"Plant your feet like so." She demonstrated a fighting stance. "Hold your staff up."

Kasane stood as she was told, and Cat did a reverse grip spin. She cracked her staff against Kasane's, not with full force, but hard enough to send a shock up her arms.

"That's the basic strike. Now you try it. Use the force of the spinning shaft to knock me over."

Kasane hit at Cat's staff timidly.

"Hard."

Kasane hit a little harder.

"As hard as you can."

Cat felt the beginning of the tingle that meant Kasane was applying force, but she knew she had a great deal of strength she wasn't using.

"We'll practice later," Cat said. "While we walk we can play the priest game."

"How is it played?"

"You carry both our packs until you see a priest. Then I have to carry both of them until I see one, and so on."

"It distresses me to see you carrying one pack. It wouldn't be right for you to carry two."

"I'm a strong lad. I can carry a horse's load."

"May I use the knife?"

When Cat handed it to her, Kasane cut a pole from the stand of bamboo growing along the road. She slung her pack on one end and the *furoshiki* on the other. She lifted it and balanced it easily on her shoulder.

She bounced the pole once to settle the burden. "Let's go."

A setting sun as red as madder root burnished the mountainsides the color of old copper as they hurried along. A cold wind pushed them from behind. The steep descent caused cramps to knot the muscles of their calves and drove their feet forward into their sandals. They had to change into new ones that rubbed their feet raw, but they hardly noticed.

Their pilgrims' bells jingled merrily. They laughed and talked and switched off loads whenever one of them spotted a priest's bald head. *Kago* bearers shouted out propositions to both of them as they passed.

Night fell before they left the mountains, but they reached Mishima by the light of the moon and the big lanterns hung from the outlying shops and tea houses.

"The guidebook recommends the Trout House," Cat said. "It says it's inexpensive and clean."

They found the Trout House on a quiet side street and sat wearily on the raised floor of the entryway. They had been walking since before dawn that morning.

"Welcome." The maid bowed low. She lined up their dusty sandals neatly with the toes pointed outward so they could climb into them easily in the morning. A second maid hurried in with towels draped over her shoulder and a basin of hot water to wash their feet.

"Wait!" Cat patted the front of her jacket.

"What is it, younger brother?"

"Our money," Cat whispered. "Our money is gone."

CHAPTER 36

THE DIVINE FAVOR OF THE THOUSAND-HANDED KANNON

The tiny house sat by itself next to the forest at the outskirts of Mishima. The latticework showing under its cracked mud plaster and its crooked window bars of peeled branches reminded Cat of a cricket cage. She and Kasane stood on the hard-packed earth of the narrow entryway.

"Fifteen coppers each." The proprietress wore a hempen robe, made mostly of patches, that reached the middle of her bare shins. It was held shut by a straw cord wrapped around her waist. Her graying hair was tied in a rag knotted above her forehead. "Bath and food and fuel for cooking are extra, of course." She spoke loudly to be heard above the wailing of the baby inside and the shrill quarreling of his parents.

Cat peered around the woman and into the single, smoky room. The knee-high wooden platform that formed the bare floor was crowded with people and their belongings. The only light came from a rush wick burning in a pottery bowl on a shelf and the flames in the firewell in the center of the room. The unpleasant smell of whale oil permeated everything.

Cat leaned back to see the wooden plaque nailed to the outside of the door sill. "Pilgrims' Inn," it read. "Inexpensive rates."

"Enter or leave," the innkeeper snapped. "You're letting in the weather."

Cat was so cold that she could hardly move, and she heard Kasane's teeth chattering. She turned and slid the plank door closed behind her. She regretted the decision immediately. A foul stench overpowered the smell of the whale oil. It came from an aged nun whose bald head was covered with festering sores.

"We were robbed." Cat was too weary to go elsewhere. She was disheartened by her search through Mishima for lodging she could afford. And she couldn't bear to force Kasane to walk any farther. "We have only twenty *mon*." She jingled the coins she and Kasane had gleaned from their sleeves, small change the cutpurse had missed.

"Anything to barter?"

"We carry only necessities."

The woman studied them through narrowed eyes. She obviously considered twenty coppers preferable to the nothing she would get if she turned them away. "All right." She gestured toward a heap of filthy quilts in the corner. The pile seemed to quiver with the six-legged life infesting it. "The bedding is extra."

"We'll do without." Cat set down the *furoshiki*, then sat on the edge of the platform herself. She untied her sandals and took off her muddy *tabi*. Her wet feet were blue and numb with cold.

The woman brought a basin of cold, murky water. Kasane scooped out the cockroach floating in it. Then she and Cat dipped their towels and washed their feet. They stood up and picked their way among the pilgrims and their goods. The baby had not stopped shrieking. His parents were still bickering.

Cat's plan was to get as far from the nun as possible. She made her way past the couple with the unhappy baby and an old man and a young woman, probably his daughter, whose back was curved like a fern shoot. She must have been struck by the mysterious illness that deformed the spines of its victims. The two were probably on their way to Ise to ask the Sun Goddess to cure her.

The master of the house sat near the fire. He seemed oblivious to the noise and the smell. He had anchored two loops of rice straw cords over the long, callused toes of his right foot, and he was plaiting a sandal around them. Without even asking his pardon, Cat stepped rudely over his sprawled leg.

She wasn't just annoyed that she hadn't found a better place to stay. She was furious with herself for allowing her sack of coins to be stolen. Only nightfall had stopped her from turning back to hunt down the thief. The woman who had pretended to be attacked must have pinched it when she'd clung to Cat.

Baka! Fool! It was a vulgar word that Cat never would have used, but Kasane's brother would have. As she had stalked through the silent, muddy streets of Mishima, past the shuttered houses, she had muttered it over and over, savoring the small explosion it made as it left her lips. *"Baka!"* she muttered to herself now.

The only clear space was in a rear corner, near an old woman who was sleeping curled on her side on a scrap of matting. The corner had the added advantage of being next to the back door. Cat and Kasane set their loads against the wall. The fleas launched an immediate attack on their ankles, and Cat regretted the loss of Shichisaburo's flea powder at the Kawasaki ferry.

"The roaches are big enough to pull an ox cart." Cat swatted one with a spare sandal.

The insects swarmed on the strings of dried fish hanging from the log rafters. They crawled across the floor. Their droppings littered the basket of millet on a shelf nearby.

Kasane stamped her feet to scatter them and unrolled the mats. "Maybe we should bargain with Locked Fist for her bedding," Kasane said in a low voice as she rubbed Cat's feet with her towel to warm them.

Cat stared at her as though she had gone mad.

"Then we would be blessed with the divine favor of the Thousand-Handed Kannon." Kasane's expression was solemn with only a hint of a twinkle in her dark eyes.

Cat had to chuckle. She looked warily toward the bedding. "We would need a thousand hands to scratch the holy Kannon's blessings."

When the baby stopped wailing to draw breath, Cat heard a tearing noise outside. It sounded as though someone were ripping the low-hanging thatch from the roof.

"Chikusho! Beast!" The innkeeper opened the front door and shrieked out into the night. "Take your filthy animal away and feed it!" She picked up rocks from the pile she had stacked

by the door and flung them at the hungry horse and the postboy who was allowing it to eat the inn's roof.

" 'Fleas, lice,' " Cat recited in a murmur for Kasane's benefit. " 'Horse pishing by the pillow.' "

"Did you write that poem, younger brother?"

"No. Master Bashō wrote it." Actually, Cat was cheered by the poem from Bashō's famous travel journal. The master himself had stayed in an inn as bad as this one.

"I have to go somewhere," Cat told Kasane. "Watch our things."

Cat wouldn't feel at ease until she had checked out the back exit. She lit her night lantern, and the landlady eyed it greedily. Cat knew she would demand it in the morning as partial payment for the lodging.

Cat stood on the rotting back porch and snuffed the lantern. She waited for her eyes to grow accustomed to the darkness and studied the tiny, cluttered backyard. It was a morass of mud from the recent rains. It sloped toward a ravine, a ribbon of black at the edge of the mud. Cat found a short, stout stick and set it next to the heavy wooden storm shutters. Then she put on the worn-down privy *geta*. Even with her eyes closed, the privy would have been easy to find.

When Cat returned she found that the rice gruel bubbling over the firewell belonged to the couple with the child. It had finished cooking, and the mother was feeding it to the boy. He had fallen blessedly quiet while he ate.

Kasane had hung her small pot on the iron hook over the flames. The handful of rice she had begged that morning was cooking inside it. Thick slabs of mushroom were grilling on bamboo skewers. They had appeared in the mountains as if by magic, a result of the rains and the warmer weather they brought. Kasane had gathered them, washed them in a clear stream, and wrapped them in a bamboo sheath. Now she dabbed them with soy sauce she had bought in Odawara. The aroma canceled out the other smells and made Cat's stomach grumble.

Even so, Cat stared morosely at the turmoil around her, trying to ignore the hunger in the faces of the other pilgrims. She soon realized why this corner had been vacant. An icy wind blew steadily through the wide cracks between the warped boards in the door. It carried the privy's scent with it. Also, people would be passing constantly on their way outside. Every time they opened the door the steady breeze would turn into a blast of cold air.

The woven bamboo ceiling that was the floor of the loft over-head creaked as some unseen member of the household walked on it. Grit sifted down onto Cat from the straw mats up there. She wrapped her travel cloak around her and shivered.

"How did you get old Locked Fist to part with the charcoal to cook the food?" Cat muttered when Kasane knelt and set two small bowls of rice topped with the dark slices of mushroom on the mat in front of her.

"I gave her the book." Kasane sat back on her haunches, waiting for Cat to finish before she started eating.

Cat held the bowl a long moment, savoring the warmth and the solid curve of it in her hand and the aromatic steam issuing from it.

"You gave away your spring pictures?" she said between mouthfuls. The mushrooms and hot rice were delicious.

"It won't be needed." Kasane spoke to the floor. "No one will ever have this miserable person as a wife."

"Don't be so sure." With her chopsticks, Cat motioned for Kasane to eat. She knew she must be ravenous. "I've thought of a poem to send to the pilgrim."

"You're too kind." Kasane blushed and bowed low over her bowl.

"I'll write it down when I finish eating."

The old woman lying next to them suddenly rose up on one scaly elbow. Shadows pooled in the hollows of her cheeks and eyes and her toothless mouth. Kasane jumped as though she had seen a corpse rising from the grave, which was understandable. The old woman did resemble someone long dead.

"You know how to write." It wasn't really a question. "Write me a letter." She rose to a sitting position and reached for her pipe and tobacco. "This is what you must say."

Without waiting for Cat to answer, she launched into her dictation. " 'Beloved Nephew. Send me money immediately or I will curse you and your offspring for eternity. Praise Buddha.' Sign it 'the saintly pilgrim, Springtime.' "

A knock at the door interrupted anything else she might have had to say. Even as the innkeeper made her way across the room to open it, Cat knew that the knock was about her. It had the ring of a sword hilt to it.

Cat prepared for flight. No purpose would be served by fight-ing here, in this confined space with so many people about. With so many witnesses. With luck she and Kasane could flee out the back and escape in the darkness.

"We might have to run." Cat gulped the last of the rice and stuck the bowl and chopsticks into the *furoshiki*. She quietly put her staff within easy reach. "Take your pack outside and wait for me," she whispered. "Be careful! There's a steep drop-off just beyond the porch, and the ground is slippery."

Kasane disappeared out the back door just as the innkeeper slid open the front. Two men stood framed in the opening. They closed the door behind them and wrinkled their noses at the smell in the room. Distaste replaced boredom on their faces.

They didn't expect to find Lady Asano here, but their leader insisted on a house-to-house search through Mishima. Besides, the latest couriers, direct from Lord Kira's mansion in Edo, bore letters promising a large reward for the ones who found her.

"We're looking for a thief," said the tallest of the two. "He stole money from his master and ran away from the place of his employ. Anyone found harboring him will be punished."

"Anyone who turns him in will be rewarded." The shorter man glowered around the dim, smoky room that, except for the crackling of the small fire, was absolutely quiet for the first time that evening.

"Stop!" the taller man shouted at Cat's retreating back. The young mother screamed, and people scattered as the two *samurai* drew their swords and leaped from the stone step up onto the floor. They arrived at the back door in time to hear the rumble of the heavy wooden storm shutter closing outside.

"Get her!" the tall one shouted through the matting over the outside of the barred window.

"Run!" Cat wedged the stout pole between the door frame and the edge of the shutter. It would give her and Kasane a few extra seconds.

Kasane grunted, and Cat turned to see a man grappling with her in the dark. Someone else crashed into a pile of empty tubs and fell with a splash into the mud. One or two or maybe three of Kira's men must have been hidden in the junk near the back door. The first two were undoubtedly on their way around to join them.

The area behind the inn was filled with tools and stacks of firewood, broken baskets, and millstones in a slimy morass. Cat slid perilously close to the edge of the ravine as she tried to reach Kasane. The sticky mud clung to her bare feet, weighing them down. The moon had just risen, and it came out from behind the clouds, shedding a pale light on the yard.

Cat braced herself against a barrel and squinted into the

shadow cast by the privy. She managed to pick out which figure was Kasane and slam the other one in the small of the back with her staff. As he fell Kasane shoved him. He staggered backward, into Kasane's pack. Both he and the pack toppled into the ravine.

Cat felt the staff wrenched from her hand. An arm circled her neck from behind. She reacted with the reflexes of her training. She gripped the forearm with both hands, dropped to one knee, and shoved the arm around and up. She used it as a lever to force its owner to his knees, then facedown in the mud. She bore down with her knee between his shoulder blades and threw her weight into the arm. When it broke with a loud crack, the man screamed in pain. Cat pulled her staff from his other hand as he tried to struggle to his feet and hit him with it.

Even as Kasane was being dragged away, she called out softly, so as not to attract more attention: "Help me."

When Cat stumbled toward her, two dark forms closed in on her. She dodged, but she felt their hands clutching at her. She elbowed one in the stomach and heard him grunt, but the one behind locked her arms and her staff at her sides. She kicked at the second one who was trying to maneuver a sack over her head.

She heard another loud *thwack*, the sound of wood on bone. A third assailant must have mistakenly hit the man holding her. His grip loosened, and he slid down Cat's back. His weight knocked her off balance in the slippery footing, sending her into the one with the sack. By this time her eyes had adjusted to the darkness, and she saw the third figure loom up, his arms raised and a staff poised to strike.

She fell to the ground and crawled behind a woodpile. From the hollow thump and the grunt, Cat knew the man with the staff had hit his comrade in the chest.

Baka! she thought. Kira had hired a pack of fools who were knocking each other out. She crept around the woodpile, ready to finish off the last man. He had disappeared. "Coward!" she muttered.

The innkeeper poked a pole through the bars and pushed up the matting hung over the outside of the window. She was shrieking at full volume.

"Be quiet!" Cat barked. The woman fell abruptly silent, and the matting fell back over the window.

With her staff Cat pushed the man curled up and gasping for breath into the ravine. His two unconscious companions followed. Cat was incensed. Kira's retainers had driven her back out into the night and gotten her covered with cold, slimy mud besides. She regretted pushing them over the side before she had hit them a few more times, just to make herself feel better.

"Hachibei!" Kasane was wrestling with the last attacker, who had her pinned against the wall of the privy.

Cat drew the *yawara* stick from the folds of her sash. She held it loosely in her palm, settling her fingers into the grooves of the shaft between the two knobbed ends. She rapped one of the knobs lightly on the nerve just behind the knuckles of the hand grasping Kasane's wrists. The hand's owner yelped in agony. His fingers flew open. Cat pressed his thumb against the grooves of the stick and applied pressure, increasing it until the man stopped struggling.

"It hurts." The pain raised his voice to a whine. All the pain ever created was concentrated in the thumb. It wiped out memory and ambition, all thoughts of past and future, all other feelings.

Cat led him by the thumb to the edge of the yard. "Jump," she said.

"Please," he quavered. She squeezed his thumb harder against the stick.

For all he or Cat could see, the ravine might have been a few feet deep or it might have been bottomless. He shrieked and leaped into the black wedge. Cat listened for the thud. It came fairly quickly. The ravine wasn't very deep.

Cat was feeling around for her *furoshiki* when she heard shouts and footsteps running toward her. The noise of the fight and the landlady's shrieks had roused the neighbors. Cat left the *furoshiki*. With only their staffs and cloaks, she and Kasane darted, barefoot and muddy, into the dark forested foothills beyond the inn.

They ran blindly through the rain-soaked bushes. As the terrain tilted upward, they clawed at roots and rocks. They blundered into boulders, waded icy brooks, and crashed into trees. They pulled brambles from their clothes and flesh and pushed on desperately until they reached a ridge where the underbrush became too dense for them to go any farther.

Hemmed in, panting, they crouched on a patch of sodden moss, in blackness that was almost total. A wild dog howled in the distance. Several more took up the chorus. A monkey shrieked.

They had lost everything except the staffs, their travel permits, the guidebook stuck in the front of Cat's jacket, the twenty coppers they were to have given the innkeeper in the morning, and a few other small items stowed in their clothes. Twenty coppers wouldn't even pay the ferryman to take them across the next river. Tears of despair welled up inside Cat. She took deep, shuddering breaths to fight them back.

Kasane brushed against her, and Cat felt her quaking. Then she realized Kasane wasn't just shivering. She was crying, silently, desperately.

"Little Kasane . . ." Cat spread half her travel cloak around Kasane, put an arm around her shoulder, and pulled her closer. "What do you think of this poem for your young man?"

CHAPTER 37
SINCE I LOST THE BRINDLE CAT

About the middle of the afternoon Hanshiro saw, walking up the mountainside, the person who was surely Lady Asano. Her disguise as an intinerant entertainer was clever. The huge red papier-mâché demon mask was familiar to Hanshiro. It was the type carried in shrine processions in Tosa. It reached from above her head almost to her waist. Its long nose distorted her silhouette. Imagining a beautiful face behind it was difficult.

Hanshiro left Gentle Haven inn and tea house, crossed the red-lacquered bridge, and waited out of sight behind the tall bushes at the side of the road. When Lady Asano passed he moved out behind her. As he followed her he was amused by her stride. It was jaunty, even on the steep slope of the mountain trail.

Dressing and acting in a mannish fashion was all the rage among the courtesans and upper-class women of the Eastern Capital. Hanshiro had always thought the style beguiling. He was charmed to find that Lady Asano was adept at it.

Even though her legs and feet were swaddled in dirty leggings and *tabi*, he had to admire them, too. With his eyes he followed her slender heels and ankles to her calves, then to the hollows behind her knees. Above them his view was blocked by the frayed hem of the long baggy coat of wadded cotton. Before he

could rein in his thoughts, however, they had strayed where his
gaze couldn't.

Hanshiro imagined the celestial intersection where her thighs
met the firm curves of her haunches. He pictured the secret cleft
with its soft black copse of hair nestled in the depths of that wild
country between her legs. He pictured parting the hair with
gentle fingers and touching, ever so lightly, the recumbent lilac
folds hidden under it. He pictured, in fact, more than he ought
to have. His loins ached as he stared, mesmerized, at the subtle
churn of slender cheeks under the tail of the patched, dusty
jacket.

He blinked and raised his eyes to the *samisen* tied across her
back. But its bump and sway in rhythm with her boyish stride
caused his heart to thump faster in spite of his resolution to
remain detached. His face grew hot. His chest felt constricted,
making each breath more difficult in the mountain air.

Idiot! he thought.

Hanshiro rehearsed what he would say when he confronted
her.

Do not fear me, Your Ladyship.

No. That wouldn't do. To begin with, he suspected she didn't
fear him. The look she'd given him at the abbey that night hadn't
been one of fear.

I'm here to protect you from Kira's rabble.

Insulting. She had proven to be capable of protecting herself.

I must ask you to come with me.

Too abrupt.

I mean you no harm, Lady Asano.

Better. But best not to say her name aloud. Hanshiro moved
quickly around in front of the masked beggar, who came to an
abrupt halt.

"I mean you no harm." Hanshiro lightly held his umbrella
across his body to block the way. "Struggling will serve no
purpose."

"Robbing me will serve no purpose, either." The boy took
off the mask and grinned up at Hanshiro. "I spent my last coppers on a ground-tea harlot at Sanmai Bridge." He waggled the
mask's long nose suggestively forward and back.

For a heartbeat Hanshiro was perplexed. The face under the
mask wasn't beautiful. It wasn't Lady Asano's. It wasn't even a
woman's.

"I mistook you for someone else," he said.

"How about a few coppers for the fright you caused me,

general?'' The lad was a brash one. "You terrified me so badly I soiled my loincloth. I'll have to buy a new one.''

Hanshiro didn't go so far as to smile at the jest, but he did toss him a five-*mon* piece. While the boy bowed with exuberant courtesy and called blessings down like a summer cloudburst upon Hanshiro's children and the children of his children, Hanshiro retreated.

He returned to the high balcony of the Gentle Haven to ponder this particular turn of fate's wheel. The landlady's son was waiting for him.

When Snow sent her son down the mountain after bonito, Hanshiro had given him an additional charge. The boy was to read the notices on the board outside the government post station. He was to inquire, circumspectly, among the couriers, the postboys, and the *kago* bearers at the transportation office. He was to report unusual events.

"Any interesting news?" Hanshiro asked.

"Yes, honorable uncle." The boy was at that stage in life when his arms and legs were too long for his small, slender body. His hands and feet were too big and too far away for him to manage gracefully. "The authorities caught the murderer of the two *samurai* in Hiratsuka.''

"Is that right?" Hanshiro continued to gaze calmly out over the valley, but he heard the rest of the boy's report as though he were inside a big bronze temple bell that someone had just tapped with a wooden mallet.

"He was dressed as a priest. They captured him in a bawdy house in Miyanoshita. He killed another man in Odawara. He was very drunk, and they had to hem him in with ladders to take him. They say he's the one who was in that fight at the ferry at the Tama River.''

"What does he look like?"

"Headless, I would imagine. The police took him directly up the mountain, in the black of night. I hear they executed him at the barrier at first light this morning. His head is on display.''

"Did you hear anything else?"

"No, Your Honor.''

"Thank you.''

"I've been studying the moves you taught me, Your Honor.'' The boy dared not directly ask Hanshiro to play *go* with him, but he glanced at the game board set up on a low table. His ambition was to be accepted at the *go* academy in Edo.

"The road is long," Hanshiro said. "The hour is late.''

The boy knew that was Hanshiro's way of saying he could not play with him today. He bowed and withdrew. Hanshiro sat alone.

Hanshiro had no family. His mother died giving him birth. When Hanshiro was six his father was killed in a dispute with a gang of *gōshi*. *Gōshi* were peasant warriors recruited by the Yamanouchi family, descendents of the Tokugawa allies who had usurped power almost a hundred years earlier.

The orphaned child was taken in by his father's master, a minor lord of a fiefdom worth only fifteen thousand *koku*. Hanshiro and the lord's only son had been raised as brothers. It was only natural that as soon as he was of age, Hanshiro pledged his sword to his young master.

The lord retired to Edo and left the running of the estate to his son, but the boy squandered his inheritance on the favors of a beautiful courtesan. The lord's retainers were turned out. The money lenders took the proceeds from everything the family had left to sell. The rice crop was mortgaged to creditors. Tokugawa Tsunayoshi granted the estate to a scion of the Yamanouchis.

The young lord's father publicly disowned him. Dressed in the rags of a mendicant priest, he set out to do penance. When he bade farewell, Hanshiro thought the sorrow too great to be contained. Now he was ambushed by grief much more unexpected and almost as fierce as that.

Since I lost the brindle cat . . . The words of Kanzan, the Mad Poet of Cold Mountain, came unbidden to mind. *The rats walk right up and peer into the pot.*

Within a few heartbeats of hearing of Cat's beheading, the rats of Hanshiro's discontent had become very bold indeed. By the time he had gathered his few belongings and politely said good-bye to Snow and her family, he had made his decision.

He would verify that the head exhibited at the barrier belonged to the beautiful, ill-fated woman he had been hunting. He would pray for her spirit's well-being. Then he would continue his westward journey.

The authorities must have discovered that the body of the executed killer was a woman's. They must have identified her as the illegitimate daughter of Lord Asano; but they hadn't made the information public. Maybe they intended to keep the disgraceful affair a secret to avoid the inconvenience of a scandal.

The Akō retainers deserved to know the fate of their lord's daughter. Hanshiro would carry the word to Lord Asano's councilor, Oishi, whom gossip said was carousing in Kyōto. When he had done that, he would walk to the coast. He would hire a boat to take him across to Shikoku. He would retire to that grotto by the sea. He would not think of Lady Asano again.

When he arrived at the Hakone barrier at dusk, he walked slowly along the line of four stands and the heads, placed conveniently at eye level. He read the writing on the square wooden plaques set on upright poles next to each one. He reached the last stand, turned, and walked back slowly.

He looked at the staring eyes, the open mouths, the bluish skin. He studied the texture of the shaggy, unbound hair and the condition of the teeth, bared in the grimace of death. Then he stood for a long time, gazing past them to the fence and the guards and the building where the officials sat.

A shadow of a smile crossed his face. He had underestimated her again. She must have walked under his very nose sometime that day. His face was stoic; his heart soared like a dragon kite in a second-month wind. He thought of the old proverb: "You cannot catch the wind in the meshes of a net."

Hanshiro presented his travel permit at the barrier. On the other side he found the tea house frequented by the guards and the barrier scribes. As he sipped hot tea and watched the steady, light rain that had just begun, he methodically reviewed all those he had watched pass on the road.

It had been the usual Tōkaidō parade—pilgrims, clerks, brokers for the big merchant houses, priests, peripatetic laborers, porters, pack train drivers, peasants carrying all manner of goods. And Nameless. West country warrior. Painter of Benkei on the Gojo Bridge.

Nameless. Hanshiro paused with his cup halfway to his mouth. He didn't notice the steam tickling his nose. He almost heard the whisper of a smooth *go* stone sliding across the heavy wooden game board. The polished, black slate disk was small, a convenient size to hold loosely between thumb and forefinger. He heard the crisp click of it being snapped down on its new place at a nexus of grid lines. Black game pieces converging, surrounding the round, polished white clamshell disk of the opponent. The key was Nameless.

Despite his broken nose, Nameless could have traveled much farther along the Tōkaidō in the days since the fight at the ferry. Instead, his progress so far had matched Lady Asano's. Whom had he been following today?

Hanshiro eliminated all the travelers except the unseen creature struggling along under the stack of goods. Even then he found it easier to believe that Cat hadn't traveled the road to Hakone at all that day. Something told him, however, that she had been that faceless peasant.

Astonishment was one more emotion in which Hanshiro rarely indulged; but he was astonished at the idea of Lady Asano hauling a load like any shoulder-burden-auntie. He could imagine the pampered daughter of a lord setting out on a foolhardy journey alone and in disguise. He could imagine her fighting her enemies and even killing them. He could not imagine her submitting to the humiliation of serving as a beast of burden.

More than any other evidence of her endurance and her determination to reach her father's lands, this was the most poignant. As the tea house filled with the boisterous laughter of the off-duty barrier guards, Hanshiro sat motionless.

He remembered *sensei*'s words, *The Way is not difficult, if you do not make choices.* Hanshiro realized that he was not making a choice. He was only acknowledging, finally, what he had been meant to do from the time Old Jug Face's messenger appeared at the door of his room. He vowed silently to do more than just protect Lady Asano in her quest. He pledged himself, heart and spirit, arm and sword, to her and to her cause.

Now all he had to do was find her. He looked over at the rear corner where the government scribes usually sat. Two were there now, drinking *sake*. They would know the names on the permits of the hundreds of travelers who had passed them that day. In all likelihood they would be able to match those names with faces. That was their job.

The skills of the warrior were diverse and inventive. Hanshiro had learned the cord-tying art, the sword-drawing art, the arts of treading water in armor and swimming with arms and legs bound. He had learned to deflect flying arrows with an iron fan and to spit needles into an opponent's eye. Now he needed the one art for which there was no school, no known master. That was the art of getting a man just drunk enough to remember what Hanshiro needed to know and too drunk to remember the next morning what he had said the night before.

CHAPTER 38
RAT'S HEAD, OX'S NECK

Cat and Kasane found an abandoned woodcutters' hut at dawn after a long, cold night huddled in the open. Kasane used the knife to cut bushy, low-growing bamboo for a bed. Exhausted, soaked, and shivering, Cat and Kasane curled together for warmth and slept on the mattress of leaves until the sun was above the trees.

Then they went foraging for food. Cat had no idea where to start, but Kasane led the way to a grove of bamboos whose feathery tops showed above the persimmon and cedar trees.

"Listen with your toes." Kasane frowned in concentration as with her own feet she kneaded the rich loam of the bamboo grove.

"Here's one!" Cat felt the hard lump of the bamboo shoot in the ground under her bare foot. She was excited, but she kept her voice low. Shouting would have been more than merely stupid and dangerous. It would have disturbed the murmuring green peace of the grove.

Cat knelt in the dry leaves. For the first time in her life she began digging with the knife and her bare hands. She scooped a heap of the black dirt into her palm and crumbled it between thumb and fingers. She lifted her palm to her face and breathed in the musty perfume of it.

When Kasane realized she couldn't dissuade her mistress from dirtying her hands, she instructed her not to bother with the bamboo's children that had already pushed aboveground. They would be fibrous and unpalatable. Now she was teaching Cat how to use her feet to find the hidden ones.

"The bamboo's children will be small because no one heaped dirt on them as they grew." With the knife Kasane hacked at the packed dirt and sliced the exposed base of Cat's find where it narrowed and attached to the rhizome. "But the shoots of Kanzan-sama are good to eat any season of the year."

"Did you know this bamboo is called Kanzan after the Mad

Poet of Cold Mountain?'' As she talked Cat noted where and how Kasane severed the tapered shoot, encased in its yellow-brown sheath. ''He usually appears with his friend, the Foundling.''

''Are they the ones with the brooms?'' Kasane placed the sprout onto the pile she had gathered.

''Yes.''

''Is that why they call these bamboo Cloud Sweeper?'' Kasane glanced up at the delicate silvery underside of the canopy whispering above her.

''I suppose so.'' Cat sat back on her heels and looked around the open grove with its hundreds of slender culms. ''Confucius says that without meat, people become thin; but without bamboo they become vulgar.''

''That's true,'' Kasane murmured.

The thin-walled culms were hard and shiny, as though they had been painted dark green, brushed with silver and emerald and purple, and then lacquered. They swayed sedately in a breeze that rustled the leaves above Cat's head. The culms creaked as though pressed by the weight of the sky.

With the knife, Kasane hacked down a young bamboo and sliced it off where it began to narrow, about shoulder height. She buried the blade in the top of the culm, and tapped it, pushing it down and slicing off a thin strip. She repeated the process until she had a supple pile of splints. She bent them into a circle, overlapping the ends, and tied them. Then she slung the coil over her shoulder.

She loaded the shoots into the tucked-up skirts of her robe. Cat brushed her hands off on the front of hers. Both robes were stained with mud from the fight the night before. The sound of falling water grew louder as the two of them walked back to the woodcutters' hut.

A small waterfall cascaded over thick mats of glistening moss and through tiers of ferns growing from crevices in the dark granite outcrop. It splashed into a pool in the bedrock. The woodcutters had diverted water from the pool through bamboo pipes to a basin chiseled from a boulder near their hut. A steady stream poured from the mossy end of the pipe into the hollowed rock. The overflow had carved its own channel down the rocky hillside.

The windowless hut was spacious, although in disrepair. Its plank roof and sides were covered with vertical sheets of cypress bark held in place by saplings lashed horizontally. Inside, an earthen passage ran lengthwise from the front to the back door. The hearth was in the center of it. A tree limb with a branch whittled off to form a hook was suspended from the smoke-blackened beam over the charred remains of past fires. A rusty iron pot hung from the hook.

On each side was a low platform of wide, rough-cut boards where the woodcutters slept. On the floor next to the fire was the small pile of lotus and burdock roots, watercress, nuts, and mushrooms Cat and Kasane had gathered. They had found a tree that still had several ripe red-gold persimmons hanging from its bare branches, and Cat had boosted Kasane up after them. They had eaten them immediately.

"Show me how to start a fire with bamboo, elder sister." Cat looked up at the sun, now straight overhead. The day wouldn't get much warmer than it was now. "While the food cooks we can bathe and wash our clothes."

The water in the pool where they bathed had begun as melted snow. It hadn't warmed much on its journey down the mountain. Immersion in icy water in wintertime was a form of religious asceticism but Cat had bathed quickly. She didn't want to be caught naked by some wandering local.

Now Cat and Kasane sat on the lowest of the three log steps leading up to the door of the hut. They were sitting in the warmth of the sun, but their hair was wet. Their clean damp robes felt clammy on their backs.

Kasane had whittled them each a pair of bamboo chopsticks, and Cat used hers to reach for the last slice of bamboo's child on the bamboo sheath that served as a platter.

Kasane was deftly weaving a wide-brimmed hat of papery sheaths and the pliable splints she had weighted with a rock and left soaking in the pool that morning.

"Do you think someone will come?" Kasane asked.

"I don't know." The icy bath had invigorated Cat. She felt more than just clean. She felt as though she had left in the muddy yard in Mishima not only her few paltry belongings, but the worst of the past. With a long bamboo twig she began drawing characters in the dirt.

"Forgive my rudeness, but what does the writing say?" Kasane finished the hat, set it aside, and started another one.

" 'A pale moon waning.' " Cat pointed to each character as she read it. " 'Wisp of cloud shadow passing. It is. Then is not.' "

"My poem."

This was the gift Cat had recited to her the night before, to comfort her in the dark and rain-soaked forest.

"Would you honor this unworthy person by telling its meaning again?" Kasane never tired of discussing this poem.

"It means you think his regard might already be waning. It might be a passing fancy. Like the shadow that crosses the moon's face." Cat shook the twig in the direction of the Tōkaidō to the east and to the unseen bustle of the world there. "One can never be too careful with men, elder sister."

"Maybe I'll never see him again."

"One cannot control one's fate. Sleeve touches sleeve because it's predestined to do so."

"What does this one mean?" Kasane leaned over to place her finger under the first character.

"The writing is *onna-de*, woman's lettering. Each mark stands for a syllable, a piece of a word." Cat pointed with the twig. "These three spell 'waning.' "

"*Ma!* Imagine that!" With the tip of her finger Kasane hesitantly drew an awkward character in the dirt.

"Curve the tail in more, elder sister." Cat closed her hand around Kasane's and guided her finger.

Kasane giggled. "I'm too foolish to learn to do this."

"No gem sparkles unless polished." Cat demonstrated the strokes of the *hiragana* character. "Try again."

Kasane hurriedly finished her own hat. Then with a broom of Cloud Sweeper leaves she cleared the bare ground in front of the hut. Cat drew each of the forty-seven characters of the *hiragana* syllabary, and Kasane began copying them. As Cat watched her she understood Kasane's exhilaration. She was unlocking the great treasure chest of writing. A hidden world was unfolding in front of her. Cat remembered her own fervor.

When she was young, the ten-day period between each visit of *sensei*, her calligraphy teacher, had always seemed interminable. An hour ahead of time she would line up her brushes, ink stone, ink stick, and water pots on the low, lacquered writing desk. Then she would sit, waiting for him in the wide, sun-filled room that opened onto the garden of her mother's mansion.

The room had been lined with shelves of books. The poem scroll hanging in the *tokonoma*, the alcove, had been changed with the seasons. In honor of *sensei*'s visit, special incense always burned on a teakwood stand near the low writing desk.

Someone else lived in the mansion now. Someone else's

scrolls hung in the alcove. The books were gone. But the room and the anticipation Cat had felt there existed in a fragile bubble of memory.

During her lessons, Cat had lost herself in the strokes and curves, in the silent voice of the ideographs. Unlike most girls, Cat had learned the Chinese writing used by men and scholars. She had learned the layers of meaning and allusion in each of the thousands of characters.

Even in the depths of winter, when her fingers had been almost too numb to hold the brush, she had sat on the *tatami* through the hour of the Ram and halfway into the hour of the Monkey. She had sat with her legs under her, her *tabi*-clad feet turned so her toes pointed inward, her back absolutely straight.

Once she had blundered. She had leaned almost imperceptibly forward for the briefest of instants. With deep regret *sensei* had looked at her across the low writing table.

"The young mistress is not ready to study today." He had risen in a rustle of silken gray robes. He had bowed to her sorrowfully and left. She had sobbed inconsolably all evening. She had never slumped again.

To sit alone in the lamplight with a book spread out before you—Cat thought of the old poem, her teacher's favorite—*and hold intimate converse with men of unseen generations—such is a pleasure beyond compare.* Cat shook her head to burst the memory of that room until she could re-form it again at a time of leisure.

"Elder sister . . ." Cat regretted interrupting Kasane's lesson. "We have to return to the road."

"Couldn't we sleep here? We could keep a fire burning to frighten away demons." Kasane was beginning to think of this hut as a haven. As a home.

" 'What shall I do? What shall I do?' " Cat quoted the Mad Poet of Cold Mountain. " 'Take this old body home and hide it in the mountains!' "

"Yes!"

"We could be Kanzan and the Foundling." For a moment Cat indulged in the dream. "The madwomen of the mountain."

"We could, mistress!"

Cat sighed. The fancy was a tempting one. She too dreaded the Tōkaidō and its dangers. To return to it was like immersing herself once more in the icy waters of the pool. She envied Kanzan his aerie on Cold Mountain. She remembered his description of it.

Where I spend my days
Is farther than I can tell.
On the naked trees
Clouds hover in place of leaves. ·
Touch of rain, the mountain quakes.

"The woodcutters might come back," Cat said finally. "You can stay, elder sister. It would be better for you if you did. But I have to continue my journey."

"Of course. Please forgive my stupidity." Kasane was mortified that she had forgotten her mistress's lover, waiting for her on the southern island.

With her broom of bamboo leaves Kasane swept away the writing in the dirt. Cat filled two bamboo canteens with water from the pipe. She plugged their ends with carved wooden stoppers. She gave one to Kasane and tied hers to her sash with a strip of bamboo. She put on the hat Kasane had made her. She passed a rolled strip of cloth, torn from the hem of Kasane's robe, under her chin, then through the bamboo loops around her ears. She twisted it around itself to keep it from slipping and tied the ends in the hollow under her bottom lip.

"One's life is like the morning mushroom." Cat pulled the hat low so it hid her face. "It springs up at dawn and shrivels away before nightfall. We must do what we can with the small amount of time allotted us."

"Yes, mistress."

Cat settled her sash on her hips and picked up her staff. She took a deep breath and led the way down the woodcutters' steep path toward the Tōkaidō.

She and Kasane passed the outlying farms and fields as night was falling. They stood under an ancient pine at the margin of the road and watched the evening traffic as people hurried to reach shelter before darkness caught them. After the solitude of the mountain the scene had a fantastical quality about it. Cat felt as though she had come into a theater in the middle of a performance.

Across the road stood a beggar with the matted beard and hair and the tattered robes of a mountain ascetic. He was leaning on two forked branches padded with straw and propped under his armpits. His torn, frayed trousers were tied up high, exposing legs as twisted and knobbed as blackthorn limbs. He had placed oil and a twisted grass wick in the palm of his hand and had set it alight. With mad eyes blazing, he chanted *sutras* while the wick burned and the oil heated in his bare palm.

Cat hesitated. She had planned to give the money to someone who was obviously in great need, not a certain madman and a possible mountebank. But the idea was to rid herself of the last of her resources.

Dodging the porters and *kago* bearers, she walked deliberately across the highway. She drew her hand into her sleeve, pulled out the twenty coppers, and dropped them into the holy man's begging bowl set in the dust. He didn't stop chanting. He didn't acknowledge Cat or her gift, but behind her she heard Kasane gasp.

"It wouldn't have bought us enough to matter, elder sister. We must remember the rat's head and the ox's neck."

"To eat?"

"No." Cat smiled at the idea of rat-head-and-ox-neck soup. "We have to stop worrying about insignificant details like what we'll eat or where we'll sleep."

"Yes, younger brother." Kasane sounded dubious. Her stomach was inquiring anxiously about supper.

"The great swordsman Musashi wrote that when we're preoccupied with details our spirits become entangled with them. We have to enlarge our spirits. We have to think of the ox's neck as well as the rat's head."

"It's as you say, younger brother."

Cat turned westward, into the last pools of sunset color silhouetting Mount Fuji's graceful cone. She set out for Numazu.

They reached the outskirts of the village in half an hour. Both she and Kasane looked longingly at the big temple gate as they passed it. It promised a roof and a hot meal and kindness to weary pilgrims.

"We can't stay here," Cat said. "The priests might report us to the authorities." Cat studied the road as it passed through the lit streets of Numazu. "The guidebook says that near the temple there's a bridge over the Kise River. We can sleep under it."

They took a side road and soon saw the dark curve of the bridge against the paler gray of the sky. They could also see the glow of a few small fires on the dry riverbed under the bridge.

Cat and Kasane climbed down the open-weave bamboo crates full of huge stones that shored up the embankment. They walked across the sandy bed toward the fires. When they approached close enough to see the huddled shapes sheltering under the huge, diagonal crossbeams of the bridge, Kasane shrank back in horror. She held up the four fingers that meant four-legged beast.

"*Hinin!*" She whispered the dreaded word. "Nonhumans!"

CHAPTER 39
A SORELY PRESSED BIRD . . .

Even after she had sat for a while, holding her hands and feet to the flames to warm them, Cat couldn't tell how many *hinin*, outcasts, were at the other two fires on the dry riverbed under the bridge. Dark forms sat around them, but their number was obscured by the huge wooden piles supporting the diagonal struts. However many there were, Cat assumed they were all members of the despised caste called nonhumans.

Behind her tangled, dirty hair the woman sitting near Cat was young. Hunger and hardship had made her loveliness even more haunting. There was a waxy translucence to the skin stretched across her angular cheekbones. She wore the straw matting from a *sake* cask draped across her shoulders.

With one hand she massaged her blind grandfather's stooped shoulders. She held her baby in the other arm, shielding her from the cold wind blowing off the river. The baby was nursing at her breast, exposed where she had pulled aside the front opening of her torn paper robe. Her small son, naked but for a loincloth, was asleep curled on a scrap of matting with his head on her lap. Both children had two spots of soot on their foreheads to fool demons into thinking they were dogs.

"My husband disappeared five days ago." She stroked the sleeping boy's thatch of black hair, cut like a bowl around the top of his head. "On New Year's eve we had no money to pay the landlord or the grocer or to buy bean paste and millet. To pay our bills at the previous midyear we had pawned an umbrella, a teakettle, my only sash, a measure box, and a pair of pottery bowls. They were the last things we owned."

The young woman spoke in a calm, light voice, as if her troubles were just minor inconveniences. To do otherwise would have shown an overweening regard for herself and her personal problems.

"At New Year's our hearth was cold. We sat in the dark while the creditors pounded on the door and called insults through the shuttered window."

A horse clattered across the wooden roadbed overhead, setting up a thundering din below. The young woman waited until the noise died, then went on.

"Even though we had no one to care for the babes, I told my husband I would sell myself so they could at least have food. But the boy began to cry. He begged me not to leave him. My husband became even more despondent.

"That night, while we slept, he sneaked out. He waylaid the bailiff's drunken assistant returning late from a tea house. He knocked him down and robbed him.

"When he came home the next day he brought New Year's rice cakes with a pinch of burdock, and a kite for the boy. He brought me a new green sash of hemp. He brought Grandfather a sack of tobacco. He brought a picture of Ebisu-sama to set on the empty god shelf and bring us wealth in the coming year. For an hour at least, we had a merry time. Then the police knocked on our door."

Cat had hardly slept at all in the last two days. She was exhausted and dizzy with hunger. As she listened to the young woman's tragic story, she felt light, as though her flesh and bone and blood had dissolved. The hollow was filling with grief for outcasts.

What distilled the grief were Cat's memories of her own New Year's celebrations. She remembered the frantic stridulation of abacuses from the wing where the man sent by her father settled the year's accounts in the big ledgers. The accompanying tinkling of the bill collectors' tiny metal mallets on the balances of their money scales had been a merry sound. They had rung in a new year, cleansed of debt.

For days, servants had pounded out the glutinous paste for rice cakes in huge vats. In New Years past Cat had feasted on chestnuts and lobsters and delicacies of the season. The servants, dressed in her mother's gifts of new clothes, had decorated the eaves with sprigs of pine. They had put huge pine branches on each side of the front gate to insure long life to those inside.

But the New Year had always been a disappointment to Cat. She had watched the palanquins of merchants and happy visitors crowd the street outside the gate, but they were going to the other houses with their gifts and good wishes. Very few people visited Cat's mother's small mansion set inconspicuously on a side street, even though on New Year's eve the neighborhood had been bright with pine flares and raucous with the sound of laughter and scurrying feet. Cat had had no one to play battle-dore with in those days except her nurse's niece, Plover.

"What happened then?" Cat shook her head to clear it. She was ashamed of all the times she had pitied herself as an outcast of sorts.

"My foolish husband was judged as a criminal ought to be. The magistrate decreed that he wear a red sash."

Kasane gasped. The red sash marked him as an exile to whom no one could speak. He was excluded from the companionship of his fellow beings. It was the most hideous of punishments. At least if one were executed, one had a hope of being reborn into another body. Banishment was death in life.

"We had to leave our house." The young woman sighed. "We had to leave the village where we were born. We became *yadonashi*, those without a lodging." The young woman sighed. "Better than a feast elsewhere is a meal of hot water and millet at home."

"Such a pity." Cat knew her words were useless, but she didn't know what else to say.

Those without lodging were not registered with the government. They had no recourse, no legal existence. This young woman had done nothing wrong, not in this life, at least. Her children, her grandfather, were all innocent. Yet they were being punished cruelly. Such was their fate.

"Worse than four hundred and four illnesses is the disease of poverty," said the grandfather.

"For almost a year we have begged for our food," the young woman went on. "We have slept under boats on the beach and eaten fish entrails thrown down for the dogs. We have slept in pine groves, or under bridges or temple porches.

"Five days ago my husband earned a few coppers burying a corpse. Even though I begged him not to, he went to buy wine with them. We haven't seen him since. I've asked everywhere in Numazu. No one knows where he went. Have you seen him? He has a red, gourd-shaped mark on his cheek."

"No," Cat said. "We haven't seen him."

"If he doesn't come back tomorrow, grandfather and the children and I will start up to the Western Capital. We'll ask Kannon-sama at Kiyomizu temple to have pity on us."

"I'm sure she'll help you," Cat said.

"Do you think so?"

"She once helped a young woman who believed in her." As Cat began her story, the heaps of matting at the other fires stirred and moved closer so the people huddled under them could hear better.

"At a time now past there was a small shrine to the goddess of mercy at the top of a mountain." Cat spoke in the guttural, drawn-out rhythm of the storyteller. It turned the telling of this old tale into a performance.

"A young wife who lived in the valley worshiped Kannon-sama devoutly. Every evening, when she finished her work, she went to the shrine to pay homage to the statue of the goddess. The young woman's husband grew suspicious of her nightly trips. He was sure she was being unfaithful. Jealousy gnawed like a rat at his soul until he could stand it no more. He took his sword to be sharpened.

"One night, after she had left, he hid in the dark woods by the path. When she passed on her way home he swung his sword at her, cutting deep into her shoulder."

By now the various pieces of matting were sitting upright. They framed dark faces with shaggy black hair. The outcasts were listening raptly.

"He wiped the blood from the blade and went home, satisfied that he had punished his wicked wife and sent her to be reborn much lower on the Great Wheel. When he arrived at his house he was astonished to see there the woman he thought he had hacked to death. He took a lantern back to the place where he had ambushed her and found drops of blood in the road.

"Then he went home again and asked her, 'Didn't you feel something strange when you passed the eight-limbed pine tree at the stream?' 'Yes,' she answered. 'For a moment my blood turned cold in my veins.' " Cat lowered her voice to a husky whisper.

Her audience drew closer to the comfort of the fire.

"When the husband went out the next morning, he found a trail of blood from his house all the way up the mountain to the shrine. The statue of Kannon-sama had a long cleft on her shoulder, in the exact place he had struck his wife the night before." Cat paused eloquently. "So the tale's been told, and so it's been handed down."

"Ma!" A murmur rose from the listeners.

"The merciful goddess substituted herself to save the faithful wife." The young woman seemed to find comfort in the story.

"That's right," Cat said.

After a short silence the grandfather spoke. "Why are you two young people alone on the road?" He looked at Cat with milky eyes that seemed to see through her.

"My sister and I are the children of poor but loving parents." Cat spoke in the same detached voice as the young woman, as though her story had happened to someone else. "Our mother and father rose before dawn and worked until long after dark to provide for us.

"Because our father was the farmers' representative, he was responsible for delivering the five-families' assessment to the headman. He discharged his duty punctually, but he absent-mindedly left without getting a receipt for the rice.

"The next day the headman claimed the rice had never been delivered. He accused our father of stealing it. Our father protested his innocence. He begged the headman to clear his name, but to no avail.

"While we and our mother were in the yard, heckling what little rice was left after four *koku* out of every five had been taken for taxes, our father threw a rope around a beam in the kitchen. He tied one end to a pillar and put the other around his neck. He stood on a bucket, then kicked it out from under him. We found him hanging there when we returned at nightfall."

Kasane wiped her eyes on her sleeve. She knew Cat was making up the story, but she was crying anyway.

"Our mother went mad with grief." Cat sighed sadly. "She shaved her head and disappeared."

Cat regretted lying to people whose own troubles were so great, but she had no choice. In any case, her father truly had been betrayed and had killed himself. Her mother had shaved her head and become a nun.

"We have vowed to visit every temple until we find her."

"May Amida Buddha help you," the young woman murmured. She held out a small packet wrapped in a bamboo sheath. "I was saving this for the morning meal, but we can always beg more." She saw that Cat was about to protest. "As a holy gift, Your Honor."

One could not refuse a pious gift to pilgrims. Tears stung Cat's eyes as she bowed low and took the package. She opened it, split the crisp, toasted rice cake inside and gave half to Kasane.

The most ferocious-looking of the men knelt in front of Cat and bowed. The wadded cotton of his ancient jacket showed through the huge rips in it. "A token of gratitude for the story of the substituting Kannon-sama." He held out a short cylinder of coppers wrapped in a scrap of grimy paper.

"Thank you." Cat was so affected by the kindness, she could hardly speak. It wasn't just that he had given her money when he obviously had almost none himself. He had not given her the coins naked, as one would toss them to a beggar.

"Amida bless you," she said softly. "As you travel, may no wind stir the pine trees along the road. May those you meet be polite and generous. May ferrymen not overcharge. And may the young and the blind walk safely alone."

Cat took off her travel cloak and draped it over the sleeping child. "My sister is tired," she said. "We're going to sleep now." She pressed her comb into the young woman's hand. It was one of the few things she had had on her when she and Kasane had fled Mishima.

"You're too kind to the unworthy, Your Honor." But the young woman smiled as she tucked the cloak around the boy. Then she began running the comb through his hair. "*Oyasuminasai*," she called softly to Cat. "Rest well."

Cat joined Kasane, who was trying to make herself comfortable on the bare, cold gravel. She had left her torn paper cloak laid out for Cat to sleep on, but Cat gestured for Kasane to lie on it. Cat curled up behind her, with her back to the river and her face toward the direction of possible attack.

She fitted her body to the curve of Kasane's back and hips and legs. She laid her staff alongside Kasane, where she could reach forward and grab it in an emergency. She pulled the rest of the cloak as far over them both as she could, but she felt the cold air blowing in from the river. Her feet were icy.

For a time she lay with her head pillowed in the crook of her right arm and her left arm along Kasane's hip. She listened to the river murmuring over rocks. She tensed at the hollow sound of running footsteps overhead. When they diminished in the distance, she relaxed. The feet probably belonged to a courier on an urgent mission that sent him on through the darkness.

"Do you think we're too close to the water, younger brother?" Kasane could see the moonlight sparkling on the ripples. She flinched when something splashed.

Kasane was right to worry about *kappa*, river imps. Fishy-smelling and naked, they came ashore from time to time at night to steal cucumbers and melons. They also raped women, sucked the blood and livers of horses through their anuses, and dragged people into the water to drown.

"We have no cucumbers, older sister," Cat teased. "Or are you hiding some that the river imps might be after?" She tickled Kasane, who giggled and twisted to avoid her fingers.

"One mustn't laugh at *kappa-sama*," Kasane said softly. "It annoys them."

"Have you ever seen one?"

"No. But many years ago a man and woman in my village did."

"What did he look like?"

"As *kappa* usually look. He was small and green, with a long nose and a dishlike head and a tortoise shell on his back."

"Where did they see him?"

"The wife of the most prosperous man in the village was very beautiful. One night when she went to the privy she felt a cold touch on her buttock."

"Is that so! He grabbed her in the privy?"

"Yes." Kasane giggled again. "But she was the daughter of a masterless *samurai*, and not one to be trifled with. She shouted, 'Scoundrel,' and saw a shaggy little man run away.

"The next night she took her short-sword with her to the privy. When he grabbed her in the same spot, she cut off his hand. He ran away shrieking. The woman took the hand to her husband."

"Was it webbed?"

"Yes. Her husband told her the *kappa* must have fallen in love with her. He kept the hand until the next night when the *kappa* came and begged him for it. Before he would give it back he made the imp sign a pledge promising never to harm the people of Pine village."

"Did he keep his promise?"

"Yes. It's said that the man's descendents still have the paper stored with the scrolls of their ancestors. But we children were cautious. Whenever we went near water we said, 'Mr. Kappa, we belong to Pine village. Please, don't play tricks on us.' " Kasane fell silent for so long, Cat assumed she was asleep.

"You're so beautiful, mistress," Kasane whispered at last. "Be careful when you go 'somewhere.' "

"I'll always take a weapon into the privy with me, elder

sister.'' Cat smoothed Kasane's hair. ''I'm sorry I couldn't find a better place to spend the night,'' she murmured.

''There's no help for it and a sorely pressed bird isn't choosy about branches.'' Kasane snuggled up against Cat. *''Oyasumi-nasai,''* she said. ''Rest well.''

''Oyasumi-nasai.''

CHAPTER 40
ARTS FOR SALE

Cat had purposely picked a quiet spot on the teeming grounds of Numazu's main temple. She had set up her booth near a small door in the temple's side wall. The door had not been used in such a long time that kudzu vines had covered it.

The priests' kitchen had been destroyed recently by fire, and they had set aside this day to solicit donations for its rebuilding. The faithful had flocked here from Numazu and from the hamlets scattered for several *ri* around. Farmers dragged small carts loaded with grain while their wives, many of them with babies strapped on their backs, pushed from behind. Others carried coils of rope, fardels of bamboo poles, and rolls of cloth.

The usual vendors of tea and dumplings, fans and willow withes, of lurid papier-mâché masks and paper birds, had gathered, and the occasion had turned into a fair.

''You have a mouth as big as a stew pan!'' Cat spoke in the explosive, guttural syllables and fierce nonsense words of the *aragoto* style of acting, the ''rough stuff.'' She was taking both roles, which required her to prowl back and forth behind her booth made from a plank laid across two upturned tubs.

To emphasize the moment, she rapped one of a pair of oaken blocks down on the plank. She paused, then hit the two blocks alternatively again and again. The intervals between the sharp sounds grew shorter until she was beating a frantic tattoo, a flurry of ratcheting clacks that signaled high drama just ahead.

She left the blocks on the plank and posed with her right arm held stiffly outward and her hand clenched into a fist. Her left hand rested on the butt of the stick stuck into her sash as a sword.

She stuck out her left leg with her toes pointed upward and rolled her head, ending by looking over her right shoulder. She crossed her left eye in the direction of her imaginary opponent and froze in a burlesque of Ichikawa Danjuro's dramatic *mie*. The *mie* wasn't called for in this comic interlude, which made it all the more ridiculous.

"That's what we've been waiting for!" Someone shouted out the usual *kabuki* encouragement. The audience roared with laughter, luring more people away from the competition in Cat's vicinity.

Cat had cut a wide strip from the bottom of Kasane's black paper travel cloak and had wrapped it around her head. Another long piece covered the lower half of her face. It was the usual disguise of someone who didn't want to be recognized. Bandits wore them, but so did illicit lovers, priests, and *samurai* when they frequented the gay districts. Cat knew a host of stories—romantic, comic, tragic, and terrifying—that required her to wear a mask.

She was playing both of the bumbling bandits in the old farce *The Literate Highwaymen*. She had reached the part of the play where they attacked each other.

Cat turned away from her audience. She wound one arm up around her neck and the other across her side, gripping at the small of her back. "The way we are grappling must be a wonderful sight." She twisted and swayed so it appeared as if the hands belonged to someone else and she was struggling with him.

"If we should die, no one would see this heroic scene," she shouted over her shoulder. "And who would notify our wives?"

"We could leave a note." She assumed the guttural growl of the second bandit. "What do you think?"

"We can't write a note." Cat wrestled ferociously with herself. By now the laughter caused people to come running from distant parts of the temple compound. "Our arms are locked."

"Let's count 'One, two, three,' and at 'three' we'll both let go at once."

The sword swallower, the diviner, and the magician glowered at Cat. The blind lute player bowed gracefully to circumstance and went off in search of a quieter corner.

Cat hadn't intended to draw undue attention to herself. She only wanted to earn a few coppers for the day's food. At most she had hoped to make enough to pay the ferryman to take her and Kasane across the Kano River.

Kasane was doing her part, too. She had cajoled a bamboo ladle from a shopkeeper and was now circulating through the grounds, begging with it. Cat knew that begging was an honorable and virtuous activity, but she hated doing it. She suspected that the old saying might be true—one who had been a beggar for three days could not stop. She preferred entertaining. Of course, entertaining was considered a form of begging and was neither honorable nor virtuous. And Cat suspected Musashi wouldn't have approved.

In his *Earth Book* he deplored the trend toward "arts for sale," men thinking of themselves as commodities. But he had been referring to those who advertised their schools of martial strategy, selling their prowess for profit. Cat was merely selling her wit.

She had fabricated her mask, using the scissors that had been with her through seven falls and eight rises, as the old saying went. She had scrounged the materials for her booth from the construction site at the charred kitchen and had gone into business. Now she was regretting her success and the attention it was drawing.

She would have regretted it more if she had known that Hanshiro stood at the edge of the crowd. He had come to make a donation to the temple and, while he was at it, to ask discreetly if a certain brother and sister had sought pilgrims' lodging. Instead he waited behind a tall, moss-covered stone lantern and listened.

Hanshiro was now in disguise himself, not because he thought he could fool Cat, but to be less conspicuous. He wore a blue cotton towel over his head and tied under his chin. He wore the wide bamboo hat, loincloth, fringed short apron, and belted padded jacket of a *yakko*, the lowest ranking of a lord's retainers. When a mischievous wind blew up the tail of his jacket, it revealed a matched pair of bare, muscular buttocks.

Hanshiro had rolled his long-sword into the mat strapped across his back. He wore his short-sword in his sash and his iron fan tucked out of sight inside his coat. He carried his few belongings in a small *furoshiki* slung from his staff.

He had cozened the barrier scribe into revealing the names on Lady Asano's and her companion's travel papers, but he knew he would have to proceed cautiously. Alarming Lady Asano would undoubtedly cause a commotion that would be disastrous for all concerned.

Mistress Cat was continuing to cut an astonishing swath

through her enemies and managing to remain anonymous while she did it. According to Hanshiro's usual informants at the transport office in Mishima, a dangerous pair of thieves was on the loose. A young peasant and his sister had attacked and bested five Edo *samurai* at a low-class guest house two nights before.

They had beaten the men senseless and thrown them into a ravine. The *samurai* had suffered broken bones and bruises. When questioned by the authorities, they were mysteriously vague about the encounter, and the local magistrate was holding them in custody until the matter could be looked into.

The actual battle had been shrouded in night's black cloak. However, plenty of witnesses and lanterns had been on hand when the men were pulled from the ravine. Even so, Hanshiro found it almost impossible to believe that one small woman and a peasant accomplice had overcome five of Kira's retainers.

Whatever had happened behind that wretched inn, Lady Asano was certainly complicating Lord Kira's life. He must be bowel-locked in fear.

Hanshiro smiled inwardly at the thought of it.

"Thank you all." When her performance was over Cat bowed into the applause and the shower of coppers. She stood back until the last of the coins had fallen on the plank, then she began collecting them. Her audience drifted off to see the magician exhale bees.

Keeping the tall stone lantern between Cat and himself, Hanshiro backed away, turned on his straw-clad heel, and melted into the throng. Now he knew what voice the Lady Cat was using in her disguise as Hachibei of Pine village in the province of Kazusa. He retired to the small pleasure district hard by the temple's main gate to drink tea, allow his heart to slow to its normal pace, and ponder his next move.

"Hachibei . . ." Kasane set her ladle on the plank of Cat's booth. It contained thirty-seven coppers. She was flushed and out of breath. "I saw him!"

"Who?" Cat was seated on an upturned tub, but she pulled her staff closer and studied the milling crowd for enemies.

"The young man. The pilgrim. Please write the poem for me."

Cat counted out some of the precious coins. Love, after all, was more important than food. "Buy a bit of ink, a brush this thick . . ." She held up her little finger. "And two sheets of paper. *Honsho* paper if you can find it." Cat added more coins for a better grade of paper. Kasane deserved it, and besides, in worshiping love one should not distinguish between the highest and the lowest.

Kasane darted off.

"Forgive my rudeness. . . ." The voice was husky and musical. Its owner spoke with an Ōsaka accent. A pale, graceful hand laid two silver coins called "little drops," wrapped in scented, lavender-colored paper, next to the coppers Cat was counting out on the rough board. "Are you interested in employment?"

When Cat looked up she saw a lovely white mask with a high arched nose, rouged cheeks, and a poppy-red pucker of a mouth painted in complete disregard of the actual contour of the lips. The teeth were blackened. The eyebrows had been shaved, and new ones, thin as a three-day moon, had been drawn halfway up on the forehead. The *onnagata*, the female impersonator, was wearing black-lacquered *geta* a foot high.

He also wore a heavy unbelted silk brocade coat that looked black until sunlight revealed it to be the deep purple color of the black dragonfly. It was embroidered with huge gold-and-silver dragonflies. The iridescent green-gold lining of the rolled, padded, and weighted hem would have trailed in the dust if not for the *geta*. The *tabi*, white as a crane's down, fit like a second skin.

A lavender scarf was tied to two of the long, jade-tipped hairpins in the actor's elaborate coiffure. The scarf covered the top of his head and dipped onto his brow. It hid the fact that a large circle on the crown of his head was shaved as the government required of actors who impersonated women. The *onnagata* was flanked by a box bearer, an attendant for his pipe and tobacco, five servants, almost invisible behind their loads of parcels, and a boy apprentice also made up and dressed as a maid in bright scarlet.

A flock of adoring women had gathered behind them. Out here in the provinces people rarely saw the fashionable elite of the Eastern and the Western capitals. They had to make do with books of theater news and pleasure district gossip. They studied the cheap woodcut prints of famous actors and courtesans. And they lamented the fact that styles changed so quickly in the capitals, the prints were usually out of date by the time they saw them.

So these women clutched their writing boxes in hopes the exquisite *onnagata* would inscribe a poem on their fans or their copies of the theater guide, *Three Cups of Sake on a Rainy*

Night. They discussed in earnest whispers the latest convolutions of his hairdo. They calculated the exact width of the brocade sash that covered his chest from his groin almost to his chin under the long, trailing coat. They speculated about the subtle messages in the enormous, superimposed folds of the bow tied in front in the style of the courtesans.

"What kind of employment?" Cat asked suspiciously. She didn't intend to encourage someone who was shopping for a catamite.

"Ah." The actor flipped open his fan and tittered behind it. "I was so entranced by your performance I forgot my manners entirely. My name is Hashikawa Hatsuse. But I prefer to be called by my art name, Dragonfly." With his fan, Dragonfly brushed nonexistent dust from the enormous insects embroidered into the front of his coat. "Our troupe is touring, and we have need of strong lads to help with scenery and costumes. What is your name, if I may be so rude as to ask?"

"Hachibei," Cat mumbled. "From Kazusa province."

"Well, you are the mysterious one, Sir Hachibei, with your horrid little mask." Dragonfly used his fan to lift the bottom corner of the long paper cloth that covered Cat's face and chest. Cat drew back and turned her head just enough to disengage the fan.

"Ah, the bashful rustic." Dragonfly peered impishly over the fan. "I shall tell the theater chief to expect you. We're staying at the reception rooms next to the priests' quarters."

He made a slight gesture, and the box bearer produced ink and a brush. Using the box as a desk, Dragonfly wrote a poem on his fan and presented it. A wistful sigh rose from the women.

> That the season has begun
> Is decided by the appearance of
> The red dragonfly.

"Show this to the stage manager. He'll admit you." Dragonfly adjusted the six collars of his layered robes to expose more of the shaved, white nape of his neck while his apprentice hastened to open the parasol. Dragonfly was tall, and the *geta* raised him well above the crowd. His young page had to wear very high *geta* to hold the umbrella over his huge hairdo.

Walking in foot-high pattens was difficult even for the practiced. For balance, Dragonfly kept a languorous hand on his page's shoulder as he swept off through the press, his slender hips undulating in the "floating step" of the courtesan on promenade. And like a courtesan, he gave way to no one.

His entourage of admirers parted to let him pass, then closed in and trailed behind him. The sunlight on his dark silk robes sent off shimmers of subtle yet intense color. Long, sinuous, and radiant, he did indeed look like a dragonfly among crickets.

Openmouthed, Kasane watched him go.

"Do you plan to make a living like that fraud over there?" Cat nodded toward the magician.

"What?" Kasane transferred her attention to Cat.

"Do you intend to belch bees through that ugly gap under your nose?"

Kasane closed her mouth and blushed.

"If you want to attract a husband, you'll have to learn refinement."

Kasane hung her head and sighed. "You can't make a crow white, even if you wash it for a year," she said sadly.

"Maybe not. But we can dip you in white paint. By the time your suitor finds out you're not a crane, he'll love you for your inner virtues."

"He's nearby." Kasane blushed. "At the stall of the comic gentleman selling tea."

Kasane was afraid the young man would leave before she could have her letter delivered to him. She was more terrified that he wouldn't. She laid the brush, the paper, her ladle filled with water, and the small bamboo container of liquid ink on the plank.

"Pick those things up and lay them down again, elder sister," Cat said. "Hold them as though they were a hummingbird's eggs in the palm of your hand. Set them down as gently as a leaf landing on a windless day. A person's breeding shows in how she handles objects."

Cat's interest in improving Kasane's market value wasn't exactly selfless. If Kasane's allegiance were to be transferred to a worthy man, Cat could travel on alone. She could act unencumbered by the fear of exposing an innocent to peril.

Kasane kept glancing over at the tea stall while Cat wrote out the poem.

A pale moon waning,
Wisp of cloud shadow passing
It is. Then is not.

When the ink had dried Cat folded the paper in a simple, slightly dated, but tasteful style. The fold's message was that the sender was a thrifty, wholesome virgin of traditional values. Cat put the letter inside the second sheet, which she folded lengthwise until both formed a narrow strip. She looped one end around the other until she had tied a flat knot in the middle. She dry-brushed ink along the creases.

"Why are you doing that, younger brother?" Kasane asked.

"To ensure secrecy. If someone undoes the knot, they won't be able to tie it exactly as it was. The brush strokes will not match."

"Ma!" Kasane despaired of ever learning the tricks of love.

"Bring a piece of kudzu vine from the wall," Cat said.

Cat used her scissors to trim the vine, then twined it around the letter. Her deliberate motions were maddeningly slow.

"At a time now past," Cat said as she worked. "A princess fell in love with a lord, and he loved her in return. Their passion was deep, but they kept the affair secret so the lady's reputation would not be eaten by worms."

Cat frapped the ends of the vine to hold it in place. "When the princess died, the lord's love became a kudzu vine and clung to her grave. So the tale's been handed down."

She studied the effect of her handiwork. Sending a first poem wrapped in a vine with such an erotic history was a brazen move. *Shame is thrown aside when one travels,* Cat thought. And the sooner Kasane eloped with her lover, the better for everybody.

"Now what do we do?" Kasane asked.

With the knife Cat slit the end of a slender bamboo pole and held the cleft open with the blade while she wedged the letter into it. "What is he wearing today?"

"The same white pilgrim's robe and black leggings. And a short cloak of blue-and-white-striped pongee. And he has a mole at the outer corner of his left eye."

Cat studied her choice of messengers in the throng of fairgoers. The one who delivered the poem must set the correct tone. She beckoned to a girl of about seven carrying her baby brother in a sling on her back. She would strike the right note of innocence, a delicate contrast to the kudzu vine.

The girl could tell from the letter wedged into the cleft bamboo cane what was wanted of her. It was the usual way to carry messages.

"Five coppers to deliver this to the young gentleman in the

pilgrim's robe sitting at the tea stall. But wait until we're gone before you do it.''

''Yes, Your Honor.''

''Come along, elder sister.'' Cat held up the paper-wrapped coins Dragonfly had given her. ''As soon as I see a riverbed beggar about work, we're going to the used-clothing dealer. You can't attract a suitor dressed like that.''

Kasane did look shabby. If fate had rowed her far offshore on a sea of troubles the past few days, the pilgrim's robe had traveled with her. Cat didn't worry about the ragged condition of her own clothing. The more tattered and stained it was, the safer and more anonymous she felt.

Still wearing her mask, Cat led the way past the drum tower and the main temple, then through the rear courtyard to the low building housing the reception rooms and the priests' quarters. A novice intercepted her warily on the veranda. Cat looked as though she harbored fleas, at the very least. And her mask was ominous.

Cat started to ask to see the *kabuki* theater chief. Then something in the periphery of her vision registered. She waved Dragonfly's fan at the huge stack of travel boxes that were being carried into the side door of the building.

''Where is the troupe from?'' Cat recognized the crest, but Hachibei the peasant boy wouldn't be likely to.

''This is the famous Nakamura-za, of Edo.''

''Is that right? What is the theater chief's name?''

''The renowned Nakamura Shichisaburo, of course. The greatest of the Eastern Capital's 'soft stuff' actors.''

CHAPTER 41

SHARPEN THE TWOFOLD GAZE

The fact that the theater chief of the Nakamura-za knew Cat required her to change her plan. For an interview with Shichisaburo she would have to see him alone. To do that she would have to look more presentable. With her bamboo hat pulled low and her staff in hand, she took Kasane to the used-clothing dealer just outside the temple gate.

They took off their sandals, pushed aside the short blue curtains, and stepped up from the street onto the *tatami*-covered platform of the shop. The owner and clerks all shouted greetings as they sat. Cat smoked while a clerk served them tea. Another employee fanned the coals in the porcelain brazier to warm the chill in the open-fronted shop.

"I'm not worthy of such kindness, younger brother," Kasane murmured.

"Yes, you are." Cat waved toward the women's robes that the shopkeeper's wife held up for Kasane's approval. "Pick what you like from those."

Then Cat considered each of the men's garments. Since everything was about the same size, fit was no problem. But the shop's owner sent the stock boys on several trips back to the storeroom before she decided on an outfit.

Kasane wasn't used to being waited on. Tears sparkled in her eyes as she whispered behind her sleeve to Cat. "I've never bought anything for myself."

Cat could tell that. She could tell that this pathetic collection of peasant castoffs was unimagined luxury to Kasane.

Cat had thought to save money by renting clothes. She intended to return them the next morning, after her interview with Nakamura Shichisaburo and after Kasane had impressed her young man, even if only briefly. But as she watched Kasane's face set softly alight by the used-clothing dealer's meager stock, she changed her mind. She instructed the shop owner's wife to take away the rentals and bring out the better robes. They were a bit faded and worn at the collars, but they had no patches.

Dragonfly's "little drops" bought Kasane a pair of dark indigo peasant's trousers, gray leggings, black *tabi*, and a wadded robe of deep blue cotton with huge white chrysanthemums. Cat mentally computed the cost of the clothes plus the loincloth, wadded jacket, trousers, and leggings she had rented for herself. Then she added a sash of orange-and-yellow tile design to Kasane's things.

She used the remaining coppers to buy two pair of new straw sandals and two big squares of cotton to use as *furoshiki*. The shop owner retired to his desk behind a low slatted partition to weigh the coins and enter the items and amount of the sale in his ledger. While he worked, Cat and Kasane changed behind the screen at the back of the shop.

Cat helped Kasane tie the sash low on her hips and tuck up the back of the hem of the jacket in boyish fashion. She redid Kasane's hair in a tea whisk style. The effect was charming and all the rage among women of Edo. Cat was sure Kasane's suitor would approve. And since women were forbidden in *kabuki* companies and in the reception rooms of the priests' quarters, Kasane would blend in better.

They left to shouts of "Thanks for your continued favors!" from the owner, his wife, and every clerk and stock boy. When they entered the temple grounds again carrying their old clothes in the *furoshiki*, Kasane could hardly contain her delight. She brushed away motes of imagined lint so she could stroke the robe and sash, whose textures had been softened and their colors deepened by wear.

Cat draped the black paper cloth around her head again and replaced the mask covering her nose and mouth. The mask was hardly noticeable among the other costumed entertainers, and Cat felt safer behind it. Besides, she didn't want Shichisaburo to recognize her right away. He might turn her away without hearing her out. He had, after all, thoroughly discharged his obligation to her.

Cat and Kasane sat with their legs dangling off the edge of the veranda of the temple's reception rooms until the sun was setting. When the novice finally came to fetch Cat, she left Kasane sitting in the twilight and followed the boy inside.

The austere cherrywood corridors were cool and dark and serene. The distant chanting of priests seemed to cleanse the air of impure thoughts as thoroughly as the novices cleansed the corridor of dust. Each morning a row of them, bent double at the waist, their skirts tucked up and with dampened rags pressed to the floor, ran hip to hip along the corridors' boards, polishing them until they glowed faintly.

When Cat entered Shichisaburo's crowded room, the actor was admiring a severed human head on a round wooden box lid. It was resting on thick paper, between the sheets of which was the usual cushion of rice bran and ashes to absorb blood. The head's shaven scalp had been colored a livid purple by the blood that had pooled in it. The bulging eyes were fixed in a death stare.

"What do you think of it?" Shichisaburo gripped the topknot with one hand to steady the head and with the other jovially held the lid up for Cat's inspection.

"It resembles you remarkably, Your Honor."

"It does indeed!" Shichisaburo rotated the lid so he could study the wooden likeness from all sides.

He lifted it to look at the bottom of the neck, which had been carved and painted to simulate the sliced skin, sagging muscles, trailing ligaments, and spinal cord and windpipe. He beamed at the young man in formal black *hakama* and *haori* coat who knelt with knees slightly spread and hands on his thighs.

"Your master is a genius," Shichisaburo said. "It's so lifelike I hear flies buzzing around it. And he used paulownia instead of persimmon wood."

"Only the best for the greatest, most honorable sir." The young man bowed low. "My master sends his abject apologies for keeping you waiting. I hurried as fast as I could."

The young man looked peaked. Riding in a jolting palanquin for two days and a night hadn't agreed with his digestive system. Sensation was just returning to the hand that had gripped the palanquin's looped ceiling strap.

"Your master could hardly be blamed. I left the capital precipitously. The road called."

Actually, Shichisaburo had left Edo just ahead of serious trouble. Kira's men had returned. They had refrained from applying painful methods of persuasion. Torturing a celebrity like Shichisaburo would have created a scandal, and scandal was what Kira was trying to avoid. But they had mentioned a certain attendant to the *shōgun*'s wife, the woman with whom Shichisaburo was having a dalliance. Shichisaburo had confessed to discovering a missing priest's costume but had assured them he hadn't seen the fugitive.

The theaters usually closed down for the eleventh and twelfth months anyway. Everyone in Edo was making preparations for the new year and had less time for frivolities. The *kabuki* companies used the lull to prepare plays for the next season. Shichisaburo had decided it was a good time to disappear for a while.

He handed the head to the young man, who swaddled it in a large silk cloth. He placed it reverently in the nest of silk floss in a fragrant cylindrical head box emblazoned with the woodcarver's crest.

"The likeness arrived at a most propitious time," Shichisaburo said. "Today we begin rehearsing *The Revenge of the Soga Brothers*. When this is produced in the last scene, the audience will be stunned."

Shichisaburo lifted the lid for one last look before the young man tied the red silk cords around the box. He nodded first to the wood-carver's employee, then to his own assistant. "This gentleman will show you to the stage manager's room," he said. "He'll see that this masterpiece is properly cared for."

When the two men had gone Shichisaburo turned his attention to Cat, who knelt facing at a respectful angle. She bowed low and placed Dragonfly's fan and poem on the *tatami* in front of her. If Shichisaburo had been alone, Cat could have revealed her identity then, but of course the theater chief of the Nakamura-za wouldn't be alone. Attendants hovered around him here just as they did on stage.

One arranged his layers of silk robes whenever he moved. One poured tea. One tended his pipe. One took dictation, and another ground ink. One sat ready to carry messages and perform any other chores Shichisaburo might need done. Others bustled in and out with letters, gifts, invitations, flowers, and miniature presentation casks of *sake*.

"The mysterious masked youth of Kazusa!" Shichisaburo smiled artlessly as he balanced Dragonfly's closed fan on his own and handed it back. "Hashikawa says you have some talent."

Cat felt a rush of affection and relief. At last she was in the presence of a friendly, familiar face.

"I'm but a stupid fisherman, Your Honor, whom fate has rowed far offshore." Cat knew of Shichisaburo's impartial attitude toward sex. She knew that in Edo he frequented both the women's pleasure district and the boys'. She intended to use his impartiality to get him alone.

She had no trouble flirting from behind a mask. She even used it to advantage. A man as jaded as Shichisaburo would appreciate the dash of intrigue. She flipped open Dragonfly's fan ingenuously, but her eyes flashed seduction above the black cloth. The fact that she sat at an angle meant she could turn her head slightly and look at him sideways. It was a thoroughly beguiling pose.

"You look familiar." Shichisaburo knew he was being enticed, and he was enjoying it. "Where might I have met you?"

"Forgive my rudeness, Your Honor, but nowhere, I'm sure. My master"—Cat emphasized "master" just enough to hint at a connection beyond business—"was taking my sister and me to Ise. But he departed for the far shore, sent from this burning house of a world by a brain hemorrhage. It was brought on, the doctor said, by an overindulgence in wine and passion. Now we're trying to reach the holy shrine alone.''

Cat twisted her towel sensuously around her fingers. The gesture could be either an expression of grief or a form of invitation.

''Your master left you beached and broke, did he?''

''Yes, Your Honor.''

''And now you want to become a star of the stage, I suppose.''

''No, Your Honor.'' Cat lowered her radiant eyes, then raised them in sultry entreaty, staring out through long black lashes.

The look had always worked before, and it worked now. One of Shichisaburo's painted eyebrows arched in admiration. When he drew in a deep breath, his plump chest expanded, as though filling to capacity with desire.

''I would never aspire to put my mud-stained feet on the boards trod by a celestial talent such as yours.'' Cat bowed until her forehead, still swathed in black cloth, brushed the *tatami*. ''I'm such a clumsy oaf, I have trouble keeping my sash tied.''

Cat could hear the attendants' disapproval in the loud rush of air through their nostrils as they inhaled collectively; but Shichisaburo smiled at the boldness of the overture. Cat continued to stare at the floor as the scribe and the servants excused themselves. The last one to go trimmed the wick of the floor lantern and lowered the wooden openwork night hood over it.

The resulting shadows enhanced the allure of Cat's vaguely sinister disguise. They etched planes and angles into Shichisaburo's bloated face. They masked the effects of time and overindulgence on his features. The rustle of his silken robes was sensual. The very darkness was charged with his erotic enthusiasm.

A novice appeared with a pedestaled tray full of covered bowls and tea things. He replaced the half-empty tobacco canister with a full one and fanned the coals in the brazier.

''Shall I make up the bed?'' he asked.

''If you would be so kind.'' Shichisaburo lifted the lids from the bowls and inspected the contents of each. He found only vegetables and boiled millet, the usual fare of Buddhist priests. If he was disappointed, he gave no indication.

''Shall I tell the masseur you request his services?'' the novice asked.

''I'm exhausted from a long day of travel. I prefer not to be disturbed.'' With his chopsticks, Shichisaburo picked up a gray, slimy lump of pickled eggplant and held it out for Cat. "Try this. It's the specialty here."

"Will there be anything else?" As the novice bowed, his shaven pate gleamed pale in the darkness.

Only solitude, Shichisaburo thought. *That cheap commodity that can't be bought at any price.* "You've all been very kind," he said. "Please express my gratitude to His Reverence."

When the boy had knelt in the corridor and slid the door closed, Shichisaburo sat staring past Cat's shoulder until the great bronze temple bell stopped tolling its evening song outside.

"Where have you and your sister and your late master slept at night, Hachibei?" he asked at last.

"In poor inns, Your Honor. Dirty places, most of them, and frequented by the lower orders. But I can assure you I have no fleas nor lice nor carbuncles."

"If the meanest of beggars can scrape together the price, he can rest his head on the pillow of a roadside inn." Shichisaburo sighed. "But I, the toast of Edo, am not good enough to sleep in public accommodations. The government fears I might contaminate the lower classes with sumptuous notions, you see."

Shichisaburo motioned for Cat to eat, but she declined politely. She was touched that Shichisaburo would treat a peasant boy with such consideration. But she thought of Kasane, alone, cold, hungry, and beset by night with its attendant ghosts and ogres and demons bumping about in the darkness under the veranda. Best to hurry this along.

"Is that why you're staying here, Your Honor?" Cat feigned ignorance of the laws concerning actors.

"It is." Shichisaburo slurped fermented bean paste soup from one of the bowls. "The priests take us beggars in. And we in turn draw the faithful into their web of cant. We also donate large sums to their coffers.

"But alas, this is not one of those temples smelling of meat and fish," he said. "The priests have not become obligingly gluttonous and carnal. One finds no compliant nuns here to relieve the tensions of a long, dusty journey." Shichisaburo sighed wearily. "I could visit the pleasure district, of course, but it's so inconvenient. The fans mob me and create public commotion."

"Perhaps one of the handsome young initiates would do as well," Cat said.

"Acolytes treat sex as if it were a religious obligation." Shichisaburo finished off the last of the eggplant, drew a paper from the wallet at his side, and wiped his mouth daintily. He crumpled the paper into a tiny ball and slipped it into his sleeve, leaving no unseemly litter. "They become tiresome."

"Forgive my rudeness, Your Honor. But surely they're awed by the magnificence of your presence."

"Do you think so?" Shichisaburo looked positively demure, but Cat knew he was excited by the prospect of groping in darkness with a young, veiled lover.

Cat could imagine his imaginings—a boy's sturdy, smooth thighs. Thin, hard buttocks that would resist the pressure of impassioned fingers. Round, pliant testicles wobbling evasively in his grasp and a slender, throbbing cock to fondle and lick. Cat was almost sorry she would have to disappoint him so completely, although she hoped he would be charmed by the danger she would offer as consolation.

When Shichisaburo helped her escape from Edo, he had settled his accounts with Cat. Now she would have to put herself in his debt. She didn't relish it. To receive a favor was to sell one's liberty; but she knew she had best get it over with. She had one more errand to run this night.

She rose onto her knees and moved so close to Shichisaburo that she could hear him wheezing softly with lust. She could smell the aloeswood with which he censed his sleeves. She could smell the pickled radish with which he had cleansed his palate.

When he put a heavy arm around her shoulder and reached out to tug playfully at her sash, she took off her mask. She smiled up into his face.

"Sharpen the twofold gaze of perception and sight, old friend," she said in a low voice. "What you fish for may not be what you catch."

It was a credit to his acting ability that Shichisaburo's expression didn't twitch. "Unlike the clear-eyed Musashi," he said with amused dignity, "my business, like yours, is bewilderment."

"I need a job, Shichi-san." Cat teasingly tapped his chest with her fan.

"A job!" he murmured. "Don't be absurd, my lady. Silk brocade doesn't make a good mop."

Rain cascaded from the edge of the bridge above, splattering loudly when it hit the shingle of the river bank. Kasane held the lantern up so Cat could see the faces of the people huddled around the blowing fires among the pilings. Cat recognized none of them.

"Have you seen the old blind man and his family?" Cat asked. "The young woman and her two children?"

"They left this afternoon." The old woman's face was invisible in the shadow cast by the square straw hood over her head.

"Do you know where they were going?"

"No more than I know where the wind blew the dust of the road today." The woman didn't even look at Cat, and her tone was hostile. The comradeship born of shared adversity under this bridge was gone. Cat was now an outsider with a lantern, a waterproof umbrella, a new straw raincoat, and probably a dry bed.

Cat had convinced herself that she wouldn't be interfering with the young woman's fate if she gave her the food in the *furoshiki* and the three silver coins she carried wrapped in paper and tucked into the *hara-maki*, the cloth wrapped around her stomach. It was part of the money Shichisaburo had given her, and it was to be a pilgrim's gift for the young woman and her family.

Cat had always known generosity to outsiders as a form of commerce. It was the buying and selling, on credit, of obligation or future favors or divine blessing. But she was discovering that the joy of giving without expectation of being repaid was much greater than the satisfaction of receiving.

When she realized the young woman was gone, her disappointment was so bitter it almost overwhelmed her. She took deep breaths to stop the sobs rising in her chest. She hitched her straw raincoat up around her neck, pulled her hat down, opened the umbrella, and stepped out into the downpour. The cold, blown rain immediately dispelled the heat of the tears on her cheeks.

CHAPTER 42
A FLOCK OF SPARROWS

The performance of Shichisaburo's company at Kambara's temple was open-air. The "theater" was defined by large straw mats hung from bamboo palings. From the wings of the temple's outdoor stage, Shichisaburo looked out over the house, or rather the yard.

Kabuki audiences were always boisterous, and Shichisaburo had the small bruises faded to a purplish yellow on his calves to prove it. The bruises had been inflicted by overwrought fans in the pit, the place-for-packing-them-in. They had reached up and pinched his legs when as the villainous character Lord Kudō he had strayed too near the edge of the stage.

Even so, this audience made Shichisaburo uneasy. The people sitting on temporarily roofed platforms along the two sides were decorous enough. They were in the expensive seats, after all. But the ten-*mon* ticket holders, the farmers and servants and merchants' clerks, were crowded into the three center sections—the place-for-packing-them-in, the great beyond, and at the very rear, the deaf gallery. They sat on the ground on bundles of grass or on rented thick, rigid straw cushions that looked like half a *tatami*. They seemed to be in even more of a ferment than usual.

Most of the farmers had never seen a *kabuki* performance before. Their hamlets were too far from Edo or Kyōto or Ōsaka for them to travel to the theaters there. In any case government decrees forbade their attendance.

The government held that *kabuki* would waste the farmers' time and fill their heads with extravagant appetites. They would start using hair oils and tying their topknots with paper cords instead of straw. They would demand umbrellas and barbers, public baths and pawnshops, all of which would surely mean the downfall of the nation. But as with most of the admonitions posted on the government's bulletin boards, this one was being honored more and more in the breach.

272

People shouted their orders to the purveyors of boxed lunches and tea and *sake* as they hawked their wares through the tightly packed crowd. With mouths full of vinegared rice and raw fish, the fans gossiped and discussed the performance and called out encouragement to Dragonfly on stage.

Shichisaburo noticed that the vendors were selling a lot of *sake* and *shochu*, a potent brew of sweet potatoes. The farmers were drinking especially heavily.

"A big crowd." The stage manager peered around the huge, stiffened sleeves of the outer robe Shichisaburo wore for the role of Lord Kudō. "We'll have difficulty clearing away the corpses from the last scene."

"How many cockroaches?" Shichisaburo asked.

"Only twenty or so of the abbot's relatives. Most are paying customers." The stage manager bowed and hurried off to chastise a writer who thought his ideas should take precedence over the leading actor's. He shook his head at the general state of moral decay that could produce such a preposterous notion.

Shichisaburo had other worries, however.

The Danjuros of the pit will go out on their ears today, he thought.

When young swells of the lower classes got drunk they imitated *aragoto*, the "rough stuff" acting method of their idol, Ichikawa Danjuro. Brawls sometimes erupted, and the police had to drag the combatants away by their topknots.

Because Danjuro had fallen ill ten days ago, Shichisaburo had been obliged to take over some of his roles and adopt his acting style. Shichisaburo suspected Danjuro had feigned illness long after he was better so he could stay behind in Edo and continue his clandestine affair with a young guardsman.

Shichisaburo knew that ignorance was what made a man resent his fate, but he wasn't happy to be playing the villain. The "soft stuff" style of the romantic heroes was more to his liking. The swooping blue-and-black-and-purple lines of the "rough stuff" makeup Shichisaburo had painted onto a white powder base were designed to throw his pug nose and well-padded cheekbones, forehead, and chin into high relief. They had transformed his pudgy face into the hideous mask of the evil Lord Kudō. Lord Kudō's scowl mirrored Shichisaburo's mood.

Even with four or five men to hold up the train of his layered robes and the enormous square, shieldlike sleeves, Shichisaburo's costume weighed him down. He gestured, and an attendant slid a tall stool under him so he could sit back on it and still appear to be standing. It was a device used often on stage to give the actors relief during long scenes.

Normally Shichisaburo would have been napping in the small dressing room curtained off for him, but he couldn't relax today. He had to see Lady Asano in her first appearance in this dance interlude between acts of *The Revenge of the Soga Brothers*.

Even though the temperature of the air was brisk, moisture formed where the thin copper base of his huge wig and horned headdress rimmed his painted forehead. He made another subtle gesture, and a hand and towel shot forward to dab delicately at his brow.

Shichisaburo had good reason to perspire. He was taking a tremendous risk inviting Lady Asano to stay on. At the very least he would be reprimanded for allowing a woman to work in his company. And if he were caught harboring a fugitive, his theater would be closed permanently and he himself banished to a place where his acting talents would not be appreciated.

But Shichisaburo enjoyed the intoxication of risk. And he couldn't just give Lady Asano the money she needed and turn her out as she had suggested. Under Shichisaburo's fierce makeup was a bland, world-weary visage that in turn belied a tenderness of heart. He couldn't bear to think of Cat braving the perils of the Tōkaidō with only that foolish young peasant woman for whom she had developed such an irrational attachment. Besides, Shichisaburo was so short-handed that he was desperate for reliable help.

He needn't have feared that Cat would betray him by a misstep. Dragonfly had been right. She was a master of bewilderment and a very fast learner. She had had only a few hours' rehearsal before this performance, but with confidence and grace she now made her debut by way of the musicians' and stage hands' small "coward's door."

As a *kurogo*, a "black man," she was to assist the actors and make sure props were where they should be. She was perfectly obvious to the theatergoers, of course, but she was as invisible as a shadow. She was swathed in the *kurogo*'s black costume from the top of her head to the toes of her *tabi*. Her face was covered by a black veil. Because black was the color of nonexistence, Cat didn't exist.

Cat's heart was pounding as she ducked through the low door at the rear of the stage. She walked behind the three singers seated in a row and behind the flute and *samisen* players and the three drummers, all of whom were absorbed in their music.

Beyond them stretched the stage. It wasn't a large stage, but to Cat it looked vast and empty and lofty. Even though Dragonfly was dancing at the other end of it, Cat felt as if, far below, every eye in that sea of heads was watching her. With heart pounding, she crouched in her assigned place near the backdrop and waited for her cue.

Dragonfly was acting the part of a shy waiting maid who had been ordered to rehearse the lion dance. Left alone with the lion mask on a stand, she danced hesitantly at first. As the mask began to exert its power, however, her eyes were drawn more and more often to it.

Finally she went to the stand, knelt, and took the lion head in her hands. Tentatively she clapped the hinged jaws a few times. Then, holding it out in front of her, she began to dance with it in time to the flute and *samisen* and the chanting of the singers.

Slowly the lion head took control of the young woman. Dragonfly's tremulous movements became stronger, more powerful. He tried desperately to rid himself of the heavy mask, but he couldn't. It began leading him around the stage.

Just as the mask had bewitched the waiting maid, so Dragonfly bewitched Cat. She was so mesmerized by his lithe, strenuous performance, she almost missed her cue. When it came she picked up the long flexible rod from which dangled a butterfly of bright red silk stretched over a frame of bamboo slivers. Cat took a deep breath and stood up slowly. Holding the butterfly out in front of the mask, she began her own dance in simple counterpoint to Dragonfly's elaborate one.

Hanshiro was in the audience, and he was as drawn into Cat's spell as she was into Dragonfly's. He stood with arms crossed at the rear of the deaf gallery, near the main entrance, the "rat gate" under the drum turret. He had taken his long-sword from the rolled mat and stuck it back into his sash. His umbrella and his iron fan were at hand.

He had already identified seven men who were probably Kira's retainers scattered through the crowd. An informer at the temple must have discovered Cat's presence and alerted them. Hanshiro knew there were informers. One of them had identified Cat's job on stage for him.

One of Kira's men wore a towel sling supporting his broken arm. He had ended up in the bottom of the ravine behind the pilgrims' inn in Mishima after Cat had disabled him. Hanshiro assumed he had been brought along to identify Lady Asano when they captured her.

In spite of the certainty of trouble, Hanshiro concentrated on the small, lissome figure in black. As he watched Cat dance with the rod, he thought it fitting that she should be the butterfly enraging the lion. It was a part she was playing well in the interlude that was life.

The beat of the drums became louder and faster and more insistent. The *samisen* sounded alarmed. The mask reared and swooped in Dragonfly's hands as the lion chased the butterfly on the end of Cat's rod. The wooden blocks rattled, increasing in speed with the swelling music and the drums' tempo until the tension seemed unendurable. Then, as the clappers gave a resounding crash, Dragonfly turned his back to the audience. Cat crouched unobtrusively again.

Two other black-clad *kurogo* moved up next to Dragonfly. Each one pulled a thread in the shoulder seams of his robe. The pale purple silk with its drifts of clouds and flights of magpies dropped open. One of the assistants unfastened the wide sash, which also fell away.

Underneath was a dragon's-blood robe emblazoned with huge gold flames and silver lightning bolts. Another assistant slipped off Dragonfly's wig while two more replaced it with the lion's wild white mane, the train of which dragged on the stage floor. A *kurogo* held a mirror while Dragonfly, still on stage and in a matter of moments, repainted his makeup.

When he turned back around he had become a ferocious lion spirit. The crowd went wild.

"You're as good as your father!" they shouted. "We've been waiting for this!"

Cat hardly heard them. She and Dragonfly moved as though connected by a taut, invisible cord. Time and again Cat whisked the butterfly out from under the lion's nose. She teased him with it until Dragonfly was whipping his long white mane about his head in a frenzy.

"Sun!" The crowd was delighted. "Light of my life!"

When Dragonfly chased Cat into the wings the audience applauded wildly. People in the pit threw flowers onto the stage. They called out Dragonfly's clan name, family name, and art name. The elite in the box seats extemporized poems to his genius.

One by one, Kira's retainers, using the uproar as cover, closed in from the sides. They reminded Hanshiro of a line from an old poem, *"A flock of sparrows raises quarreling voices . . ."* He followed casually at a distance. The men were obviously planning to catch Cat backstage.

Cat didn't stay backstage long, though. She was to assist for the last act of the Soga brothers' famous epic. Kasane, now dressed as a boy herself to avoid the theater's ban on women, quickly handed Cat a towel. Cat lifted her black veil and wiped her sweaty face with it. Her heart was pounding with exertion and excitement.

"Did you see your pilgrim?" Cat whispered.

"Yes!" Kasane's eyes sparkled. "He's sitting near the front. He sent another poem." She put a hand to her waist where the letter was hidden under the sash of her jacket.

"I'll help you read it when the performance is over." Cat ducked back through the "coward's door" and crouched at the rear of the stage again while the turmoil died down.

Now that she had finished the most difficult part of her duties, she could look out over the crowd and see individuals instead of a noisy blur. The first individual she saw was Hanshiro.

"Burei-mono!" she muttered. "Impudent clod!"

Once she discovered Hanshiro she wasn't surprised to see his cronies, Kira's retainers, flanking the stage. Their robes were tucked up, and their sleeves were tied back for action. The pairs of swords projecting from their sashes marked them as *samurai*. Various affectations, such as the patterns on their jackets, the knots in their sashes, and the way they wore their headbands, identified them as residents of Edo.

Cat also recognized the man with the broken arm, and she was sure that more of Kira's lackeys were stationed behind the theater to cut off her retreat. In the middle of it all sat Kasane's pilgrim, enrapt and oblivious.

"Daikon! Radish!" A roar of disapproval met Shichisaburo's entrance. During the first two acts the pit had formed a strong dislike for the villainous Lord Kudō.

Shichisaburo gamely declaimed his lines, although he was drowned out by cheers when the gallant Soga brothers appeared. The cheers turned to more shouts of "Radish!" and "Turnip!" when Kudō motioned imperiously for his guard to arrest the brothers.

"This play is no good!" A hulking farmer stood up in the third row. "Those two brave young men can't fight against so many. I, Buhei, am strong." He pushed up the sleeves of his coat to show the corded muscles of his arms. "I'll help them."

"Yes, help them!" the farmers shouted. Their fury at Kudō's villainy spread to the rest of the fans in the pit, many of whom were primed by *sake* for a diversion anyway.

"Help them!" The cry was taken up as far back as the deaf gallery, where people weren't even sure what was going on.

Someone threw a heavy straw cushion at Shichisaburo, who ducked. The cushion landed with a smack on the wooden floor of the stage. The *kurogo* tried to fend off the mats that followed, but the musicians crowded through the "coward's door."

Shichisaburo hiked up his skirts and fled for the wings in a hail of mats, wooden lunch boxes, soft persimmons, and chopsticks.

Women started screaming. The farmers stormed the stage. The pilgrim, fearing for Kasane's safety, began laying about him with his staff, and a brawl broke out in the pit.

In his haste to escape, one of the musicians knocked a round box off a stand just inside the wings. Shichisaburo's wooden head fell out of it and bounced across the stage. Buhei reached it first and held it up triumphantly by the topknot. The people in the deaf gallery cheered and surged forward.

Cat saw Kira's men shoving through the crowd. They would reach the wings before she could. Hanshiro was close behind them.

The last singer was at the nearby "coward's door" pushing the man ahead of him into the one ahead of *him*. Cat grabbed him by the back of the sash and whirled him away. He collided with the first of Kira's men climbing onto the stage. They tumbled over the edge and into the farmers.

As Cat ducked through the low door, she scooped up a chopstick. When the *samurai* who was following her cleared the low lintel and raised his head, she swung the pointed end upward. She gave it the full force of her arm, stabbing it through the back of his chin. As the chopstick drove into his palate, it impaled his tongue against the roof of his mouth. He dropped to his knees in the doorway and made squealing noises in his throat as he clawed at the short, protruding butt of the stick.

Cat couldn't see Hanshiro using his fan and umbrella to dispatch her enemies in the mêlée on stage. " 'A flock of sparrows,' " he chanted to himself as he sent another man sprawling, " 'raises quarreling voices for a place to sleep.' "

He was interrupted by the sudden appearance of Nameless, who attacked Hanshiro with the stout stick on which he had carried his lanterns. Hanshiro was surprised to see Nameless, but he wasn't surprised to find him a challenging adversary, even for one so young. The two of them were fencing with umbrella and stick when the police entered the rat gate and people began scattering through the matting along the sides.

"What's happening, younger brother?" Backstage, Kasane was wide-eyed with fear.

"Ruffians!" Dragonfly ran shrieking toward them. "Save me from the uncultured beasts." When he clutched at Cat she felt the weight of a packet of coins drop into her sleeve. "Follow my son," Dragonfly whispered.

He started screaming hysterically again, and he kept on screaming. He was screaming when he brought a stool down hard on the first of Kira's men to find his way through the dark maze of backstage corridors, piled with scenery, curtains, and props.

The boy slid open a closet door under a stairway and pulled away the pile of bedding stored there. He had washed off his makeup, but he still wore his red maid's robes, *geta*, and wig. Cat and Kasane crawled into the closet as Dragonfly's son's head disappeared through a trapdoor in the floor and down a ladder.

Kasane scrambled after him. Cat followed and closed the door over her, leaving them in darkness. She could smell the dust of centuries in the passageway. It must have been built for escape when bands of warrior-priests and monks from rival temples attacked and counterattacked in the ancient wars. Cat heard a rat's squeak and the skitter of small toenails across the plastered wall. She jumped when she felt the boy's gentle touch on her arm.

"Exchange clothes with me," he whispered. From overhead came shouts and the heavy tread of running feet.

Feeling slow and clumsy in the dark, confined space, Cat stripped off her black head covering, the veil, her black jacket, trousers, and *tabi*. Going by feel, she handed them to the boy and received his robes and *geta* and wig in return.

"Continue along this passage." As he whispered he put on the *kurogo*'s costume. Kasane buttoned the *tabi* for him while he tied the sash. "It will bring you out in a chapel to Jizō-sama in the cedar grove. There's a small door in the wall there."

"What will happen to all of you?" Cat asked.

"Shichisaburo-san will talk us out of this. He has before." The boy didn't have to say that without Cat and Kasane there to incriminate them, the official inquiry would go much better.

He started up the ladder again. "Father says to tell you to be careful of Satta Pass,'' he whispered over his shoulder. ''It's dangerous. But the view is the most beautiful in the world.''

Cat and Kasane saw his slender form black against the wedge of light when he opened the door. Then he closed it, leaving them in total darkness again.

CHAPTER 43
TO SPIT AGAINST HEAVEN

Just beyond Kambara's outlying fields, the Tōkaidō became steep as the skirts of the mountains swept precipitously to a towering, pine-fringed escarpment above the sea. Along the top of the cliff snaked the road over Satta Pass. Cat and Kasane had walked almost to the bottom of the long ascent that would take them over it.

Cat kept looking back over her shoulder for pursuers, but all she saw were a pair of postboys and their shaggy mare.

''Hitch up your underwear and speed away. . . .'' The two men were singing off key as they ambled up behind Cat.

One led their pony, and the other rode her. They were barelegged and dressed in belted, blue cotton wadded jackets. They had draped blue-and-white towels over their heads and knotted them under their chins. Their large, conical hats dangled on each side of the horse's haunches.

''Forty coppers for both the hats,'' Cat called out.

''Thirty each and they're yours.'' Both men bowed deeply and sardonically.

''Fifty for the pair.''

''Sold.''

When the man who was afoot moved to untie the hats, the horse laid back her ears and drew her lips over her teeth. She sidestepped daintily and kicked out with her rear hooves. The postboy ignored her.

As he exchanged the hats for the string of coppers, the hostler gave Kasane and her scarlet robe and wig an appraising look.

''How much do you charge for her?'' he asked.

"More than you can afford," Cat answered.

As they trotted away the two men started their song again.

> Hitch up your underwear and speed away;
> We'll spend the night at Mitsuke.
> Whatever happened to Hachibei?
> The horses ate him along the way.

When Cat heard Hachibei, the name on her travel papers, her hand tightened on her staff. She relaxed only when the horse's rump disappeared around a bend, and she remembered that Hachibei was a common name among the lower classes.

Cat was now dressed in the boy's clothes she had bought for Kasane. Kasane was wearing Dragonfly's son's wig and red silk robe. She had tucked the long skirts into her sash, but the *geta* made keeping up with Cat a struggle.

Kasane was in high spirits in spite of the rough road. She read aloud the signs of the roadside stands. She had been infected with the excitement of the theater, and she was anticipating rejoining Shichisaburo's troupe in Okitsu. She had been backstage when the fight broke out, and she didn't realize that the mêlée at the performance had been more than the foolishness of farmers. She didn't know that she and Cat were in more peril than usual.

Also, she was enjoying the feel of the red silk dress. She was vaguely aroused by the cloth's soft cling and by its subtle shifting of colors in the sunlight. She didn't know that Cat intended to put her back into cotton at the first opportunity. A peasant in silk could attract the attention of officials as well as hostlers.

As for her suitor, Kasane wasn't very upset about leaving him behind in Kambara. This game of cat and rat seemed only to fan the fires of his passions, and she was sure he would find her again. Kasane preferred the chase because it postponed a decision as to the disposition of her virtue.

She touched her sash where the pilgrim's latest letter was hidden in an oiled paper under her robe. He had addressed it to "the Floating Weed" and signed it "the Traveler." Something his hand had touched was touching her bare body. Kasane's face warmed at the thought. Part of her elation was due to the fact that, with Cat's help, she could now read the Traveler's words.

"What happened to the Soga brothers?" Kasane asked.

She had been particularly taken with the younger brother, Gorō, in the *Revenge of the Soga Brothers*. The actor's dramatic pose, with his outer robe flung off his shoulders and the map to

Lord Kudō's hunting camp clamped in his teeth, had made her dizzy with a romantic fever.

"They avenged themselves on Lord Kudō for the death of their father." Cat was understandably distracted. She glanced back again, expecting to see the unkempt *rōnin* of Tosa closing in on her. "Jurō-san was killed in the fight."

"And Gorō-san?"

"He was captured and condemned to be beheaded with a dull sword."

"That's not fair! Wicked Lord Kudō killed their father! Jurō-san and Gorō-san registered their vendetta legally." Kasane was outraged. "That play is foolish. The farmers were right to protest."

"The play is only a mirror reflecting life. One cannot change one's fate. Jurō and Gorō killed Lord Kudō. They avenged their father. They died satisfied."

Cat thought of Lord Kira, safe in his mansion while she pursued what might prove to be a fool's undertaking. She would have considered it a bargain to have her head sawed off with a blunt sword in exchange for the privilege of beheading Kira. She pictured the long, glittering curve of a *naginata* blade slicing as easily through his neck as a honed knife through bean curd. She imagined the feel of it, the resistance his spinal column would make.

If she were to execute him, she would not even try to leave a piece of skin intact. She wanted to see his head, lifeless eyes still bulging in terror, bouncing across the ground.

"Something's happened ahead." Kasane nodded toward a group of people standing in a circle in the middle of the road.

In low voices they were discussing a pale gray river rock, a bit larger than a man's fist, which sat in the dust. A black cord was tied around it. It was a path-barring-stone. It said, "Go no farther."

The two small feathers fastened to the cord carried an additional message. Their shafts had been laid at right angles to each other and lashed with thread. Many families used variations of crossed feathers as their crests. Banshu-Akō was one of them. Cat assumed the warning was meant for her.

A few people turned back. Most joined together into larger groups for protection in case the stone's warning was genuine. They all had heard the stories of bandits at Satta Pass. The travelers tied back their sleeves, pulled their loincloths tighter for the climb, and started up the treacherous slope.

Cat sauntered off the road to a shed housing a traveler's convenience. She needed time to think.

As she loosened her loincloth and squatted over the hole, she stared at the simple lines of an opened umbrella carved into the wall in front of her. A woman's name and a man's name were incised in flowing, vertical characters, one on each side of the umbrella's shaft. A man and woman sharing an umbrella was an old conceit. It meant they were lovers.

Cat sighed. As far as she was concerned, lovers were of a different species. She couldn't imagine being in love. She couldn't even imagine sleeping through the night with a quiet heart.

She was suddenly overwhelmed by despondency again. Her enemies were everywhere. How long could she avoid them?

Who had known she would pass this way and had left the stone for her to find? If she must stop to fight for every foot of ground between here and Kyōto, how could she ever reach Oishi? And how often could she engage her enemies before she was caught and punished?

"What does the stone mean?" Kasane whispered through the open top half of the shed.

"It means we're not going over the pass."

"Where are we going, then?" Kasane was bold enough now to ask it of Cat when she came out of the shed.

"To Okitsu."

"But—"

"We're going by the lower route. By way of 'Not-knowing-Parents.' "

Cat was too impatient to wait for the tide to ebb completely. The surf was still crashing when she and Kasane made their way down the overgrown path and through the tumbled boulders to the base of the cliff.

Kasane took off the cotton cloth wrapped around her waist as an underskirt and laid it on the ground. She put the wig and *geta* in the middle of it and knotted the ends around them so she could sling the bundle over her shoulder. Then she hitched up her skirts. She was ready to follow her mistress into whatever calamity the Tōkaidō might provide.

"According to the guidebook, 'Not-knowing-Parents' is only twelve *cho* across," Cat said. But she could see that reaching the other side of the great stone barrier would be difficult.

The strip of boulder-strewn beach had been aptly named. In

fleeing the tiger's den, they had entered a dragon's hole. Cat tried to imagine lines of travelers passing this way fifty years earlier, when "Not-knowing-Parents" was the only route.

Some of the boulders rose three or four times higher than Cat. Waves crashed against them, sending up geysers of salt spray that stung their eyes. Before Cat and Kasane had gone twenty steps, they were soaked to the skin and shivering with cold. Flat swags of glossy brown seaweed twined around their ankles. The dark, wet-slick stones that paved the narrow beach rolled about under their feet.

Cat and Kasane splashed through tidal pools. They clambered over the branches and tree trunks and flotsam snagged among the boulders. Barnacles cut them when the larger breakers pushed them against the rocks, then tried to drag them out to sea.

About halfway around the vast bulge of the escarpment, Cat stopped suddenly as she was passing between two huge boulders. She braced herself with each hand pressed against one of the rocks and stared ahead.

"What is it?" Kasane asked.

"Fuji-san."

Cat reached out to steady Kasane over a particularly rough stretch, then stepped to one side so she could see. The two of them held hands in the shower of cold spray, with the waves surging around their legs, and stared at Mount Fuji.

"It's splendid," Kasane said at last.

"So it is." Cat regretted being cheated of the view from the pass. If it was this beautiful here, it must be magnificent from above.

The mountain was framed by the jagged, glistening black crags of "Not-knowing-Parents." Its backdrop was a blue sky, so clear it seemed to pulse. Snow had fallen on Fuji during the night, cloaking the graceful slopes in a gleaming white mantle. A cap of cloud hung over the volcano's cone.

"Do you see a dragon's form in the cloud?" Cat asked.

"A dragon, mistress?"

"A dragon in the clouds above Fuji means success."

Kasane stared intently. "I think I see one. There. That's his nose and that's his tail."

"I see it."

Twenty waves roared in and crashed against the rocks before Cat finally broke the mountain's spell. She started forward again, then stopped when she heard Kasane's cry. She turned in time to see her twist and pitch sideways, her foot caught in a crevice between two rocks.

"Sister!" Cat scrambled back to help her up before the next wave washed over her.

"It hurts," Kasane said softly.

"Put your arm around my shoulders." Cat put her own arm around Kasane's waist and supported her weight as Kasane limped forward.

"I'm so clumsy." Kasane was sobbing, not with pain but with remorse at slowing Cat's progress toward her love, waiting, she thought, among the ferocious southerners of Satsuma. "I'm so stupid."

"It's my fault, dear Kasane." Cat held her close as though Kasane were a child in need of comforting. She cried, too, stung by her own remorse. "I was too impatient to wait for the ebb tide. I'm sorry."

Together, they struggled toward a large tangle of debris. Kasane winced each time she had to put weight on the injured ankle, but she made no complaint.

Cat was helping Kasane over the slippery trunk of a fallen pine when they saw the naked body. The man's fractured arms and legs were wrapped at impossible angles around the spokes of the tree's upturned roots. Cat and Kasane stared down at him.

"He hasn't been here long," Cat said.

"The *kappa* must have caught him and pulled his liver out his anus."

"Bandits, more likely." Cat laid her head back, trying to see the trail at the top of the rough gray wall towering over them. A fish hawk swooped from its nest in a crevice and soared out over the bay.

"They stole his money and his clothes and threw him over the side," Cat said. "Even the poor are not safe."

"Was the path-barring-stone a warning about bandits?"

"Probably." Cat knew there was more to the warning than bandits, but she saw no use in making Kasane unhappier than she already was. A blind person feared not the snake.

When a wave lifted the man's head, Cat noticed the red, gourd-shaped mark on his cheek. "Do you know who this is?"

"Who?"

"The husband of the outcast under the bridge."

"That's right." Kasane rested against the trunk as she considered the implications. "His family must not know he's gone on to travel the Three Paths."

"No."

"Probably no one but us knows."

"That's right."

"He's a homeless spirit." Kasane shivered from dread as well as from cold and pain.

"We'll burn incense and pray for him at the first temple we come to."

Of the many forms Cat had seen death take, this one was the saddest, to lie broken and forgotten, discarded like a worn-out umbrella on a rubbish heap.

"And then we saw you," Cat recited.

> Pillowed upon your shaking beach,
>   Using those wave-beaten rocks
> As if the coast were spread out for your bedding;
>   On such a rugged place
> You have laid yourself to rest.

"That's a sad poem, mistress," Kasane said. "Did you write it?"

"It was written long ago by someone who found a body on a beach like this. The end of the poem is saddest of all."

> If I but knew your home,
>   I would tell them where you sleep;
>   Your wife would come searching for you.
> How she must be waiting,
>   How anxiously now longing for you,
>   She the dear one you call wife.

Kasane knew that the outcast had spit against heaven and must suffer the retribution he deserved. But she had a tender heart. She gave a small whimper of a sob and wiped her eyes on her sleeve, which didn't do much good since her sleeve was soaked.

With Cat supporting her Kasane started slowly toward the far end of the cliff; but she kept looking back, as though the homeless ghost might be following her, drifting along just above the beach like some hideous supernatural flotsam.

"We children found a man on the beach once," Kasane said.

"Was he someone you knew?"

"It was impossible to tell. The crabs had eaten his face."

Kasane was struck by a sorrow and a fear from her childhood. She remembered the nights she had looked out over the black

water, searching among the many fishermen's lights for the one
on the prow of her parents' boat. Her dread was the one morning
her parents' cumbersome, leaky vessel wouldn't return. Their
bodies would be found washed up on the beach and covered
with a shifting crust of crabs. The broken planks of their boat
would be scavenged to form part of some villager's hut.

Kasane trembled inside the wet silk robe that clung to her
like another skin. She closed her eyes against the stinging spray
of a breaker. She tried to ignore the pain radiating up from her
ankle. She tried to ignore the longing for her parents and her
village and the sonorous call of the evening bell.

CHAPTER 44
A FAST BUSY SPIRIT

Okitsu's Pine Beach was as lovely as the guidebook claimed.
Cat and Kasane waited in the sand among the children who had
gathered to watch the ceremony to appease the restless spirit of
the homeless ghost. The old priest stood at the water's edge. He
gazed past Suruga Bay and its jagged, dark green rim, the forested mountains of the Izu peninsula to the southwest.

The calm waters of the bay had been burnished by the rays of
the setting sun. The late-afternoon light gilded the fishermen's
sails as the last of them dipped and bowed in the wind. Behind
him, Mount Fuji's slopes glowed copper.

The priest was chanting softly to himself. When he finished,
Cat waded out into the icy surf. She carried the small boat
Kasane had made of straw and loaded with a paper flower, a
bundle of burning incense, and a lighted candle. She waited
until a wave was retreating, then set the boat afloat and gave it
a careful push. The priest intoned scriptures and tapped on his
bowl-shaped bell while the small craft bobbed on the low swells.

When a wave finally swamped the boat, the priest bowed,
turned, and headed up the beach, still chanting. His feet sank
into the soft sand, which flowed into his straw sandals, slowing
his progress almost as much as the children who swarmed around
him. The children gave Cat an idea.

She walked alongside the priest. "Thank you, holy one." She unobtrusively placed a packet of coins into his begging bowl.

"If life comes, this is life. If death comes, this is death." It wasn't the response Cat expected, but in the short time since Kasane had hobbled up with this priest in tow, Cat had come to realize he never said the expected.

"Holy one, I want to buy your talismans."

The old man opened the drawstring of the pouch around his neck and with the long, tapering nails of his first and second fingers extracted a folded slip of paper. "When one passes through the gateless gate . . ." He handed it to her gravely. "One walks freely between heaven and earth."

"Excuse my rudeness, holy one, but I need all your talismans."

He took the pouch from around his neck, but he paused before he gave it to her. His eyes were as remote as a corpse's, and yet Cat felt as though he were speaking directly to her inner thoughts. "If someone hesitates," he said, "he is like a person watching from a window. Life will pass by the window and be gone, and he will not see it."

The priest bowed and with both hands held out the bag. "That which is form is emptiness. . . ." He began chanting again, turning away from Cat as though she had ceased to exist. "That which is emptiness is form."

Cat fingered the soft, much-worn cloth of the sack as she watched his progress through the wind-gnarled pines that grew almost to the water's edge. The trees rose from a haze of smoke from the piles of seaweed that were being burned for salt. Clusters of drying octopi dangled from long poles stuck in the sand. Brown swags of nets hung from tall bamboo racks.

The children returned to their play and to their chores, separating the day's catch from the nets or bailing out the boats. Fathers sat under the pines and dandled their little ones, as they did every evening.

A line of women balanced shallow wooden tubs on their heads as they walked along the shoreline. They wore their sashes brashly tied in front. The well-side gossip was that men who bought their flatfish, mollusks, and seaweed could also rent their clams.

It was a lovely scene, but Cat wasn't in a mood to appreciate it. She had money now, but it wouldn't buy her peace of mind in a public accommodation. Kira's men were probably checking them all.

"We can't stay at an inn, elder sister," Cat said. "Enemies are still searching for me."

"Then we can sleep on the beach like a pair of gulls." Kasane smiled happily at her.

"Where?" *The blind fear no snakes,* Cat thought again.

"About sea matters, ask a fisherman." Kasane was almost elated at being able to provide shelter for her mistress and protector.

Cat had purchased a crude crutch in Yui. Kasane used it as she led the way past the fishermen's tiny reed shacks and open-air tea shops to a deserted, marshy part of the beach where the river emptied into the bay. With Cat's help she cut a few saplings and propped them against two pines to make the sloping roof of a lean-to. She used the tough river reeds to lash fallen branches across them as a framework.

With her crutch under one arm, she waded into the marsh at the river's mouth and began cutting the long reeds that grew there. She showed Cat how to use single stems to tie them into bundles, then split the bundles and slide them over the poles, forming a simple thatch.

Cat had always assumed that it was the nature of peasants to be clever with their hands. However, she was beginning to think that Kasane, if given time, could fabricate from bamboo and straw and river grass anything they might need.

While Cat walked down the darkling beach to buy bream from the day's catch, Kasane laid out the sleeping mats, cut grass for pillows, and started a fire of pine needles. As they ate Okitsu's famous bean flower dumplings and the bream, broiled on a driftwood plank, Cat watched the lights across the curve of the bay. They were from the fishing village of Ejiri, nestled among the dark folds of the foothills.

Ejiri was only a *ri* away. Even after buying secondhand clothes and mats and other necessities in Okitsu, they could have rented a horse and traveled at least that far tonight. But for the first time Kasane had balked, and not because of her injured ankle.

"It will be dark before the ceremony for the restless spirit can be completed, mistress," she had said.

"It can be done in the dark."

"Please, couldn't it be done here? Now?"

There had been a tremor in Kasane's voice. She feared that the homeless soul of the dead man might have fixed on her and

Cat. She was terrified that the ghost would catch them in the dark before it had been appeased. Cat had agreed to stay.

Now Cat concentrated on mending the drawstring on her bag of patience, as the old saying went. So far today her heedlessness had not only slowed her down, it had injured Kasane. Musashi said that speed was not part of the Way and that the truly skilled never appeared busy. Musashi said that a fast, busy spirit was undesirable.

"The bream is delicious," Cat said.

Kasane ducked her head shyly. "It seems too dry. I must have foolishly overcooked it."

"It's perfect." With her chopsticks Cat picked up the last crisp curl of skin and savored it. "And it certainly doesn't lack seasoning." She grinned at Kasane over her hand as she put her tongue to it to taste the salt left by the seawater. Then she cleansed her mouth with pale tea.

The lopsided moon wouldn't rise for hours yet, but stars spangled the night robe of heaven. Their light outlined the wind-sculpted forms of the pines and twinkled like fireflies among the needles. Cat closed her eyes and inhaled the fragrance of pine resin.

"Your pipe, mistress."

Cat bowed in thanks. "Hold out your leg, elder sister," she said.

"It's better now." Kasane was disconcerted by the attention, but she put her foot near the fire so Cat could see the bruised, distended ankle. She winced when Cat probed it with her fingers. "Surely it will be much better tomorrow."

"Tomorrow blows tomorrow's wind." Cat opened the prettily packaged clamshell that held the medicine. "Let's see if the Maru-ichi shop's Salve-Conveyed-in-a-Dream is worthy of its repute."

She put a dab of the thick black paste onto one of her paper handkerchiefs laid out on a flat rock. She took a glowing pair of brass chopsticks from the fire and smeared it around. The heat released an odor so pungent, Cat's nose wrinkled as though in retreat from it, but she gently placed the medicated paper onto the ankle. Cat felt as responsible for the sprain as if she herself had taken Kasane's foot in her hands and twisted it.

"The young women who sold the salve were very beautiful." Kasane leaned forward to watch Cat wrap her towel tightly around the ankle and the paper.

"Dear Kasane, you're as ignorant of the world as a frog in a well." Cat laughed. "They aren't women."

"They aren't?"

"Of course not. They're boys."

"Is that right?"

"Yes." Cat tucked in the end of the bandage and eased Kasane's foot down in the cushioning sand.

Then she lit the pinch of Okitsu's famous Dragon King tobacco and looked out at the starlight on the bay while she smoked it. Kasane used a twig to write in the sand by the light of their small fire. "A very foolish person tried to compose a poem," she said.

"Please recite it."

"It's unfinished." Kasane deeply regretted mentioning it. "It's clumsy and vulgar."

Cat leaned forward to read what Kasane had written. " 'Your look, a silk robe . . .' "

Kasane turned bright pink and hastily smoothed the sand, erasing her words.

"It's a good start," Cat said. "When you think of an ending line, you can write to your pilgrim yourself."

"Excuse my rudeness, mistress, but he already knows your hand. He'll be looking for it."

"That's true." Cat remembered that the last letter from Kasane's pilgrim had said he would check the notice board of each temple for word from her. "We'll think of a finish to your poem, and I'll write it for you."

"He must be very handsome," Kasane murmured.

"Who?" Then Cat realized that Kasane was referring to the fictional lover waiting on the southern island. "Some people say he's fair of face," she admitted.

A long silence followed, and Cat knew Kasane longed for details of Cat's affair but was far too shy and polite to ask.

"We met in the springtime while my maids and I were on an outing to the countryside to hear the first song of the cuckoo." Cat remembered an incident from Lady Shōnagon's *Pillow Book* and revised it to suit her purposes. "We picked branches of saxifrage, all covered with white flowers. We wove them into the wickerwork of our palanquins until they looked as though white quilts had been thrown over them. We were so pleased with the effect, we ordered the bearers to take us to the country house of my mother's first cousin.

"We arrived at his gate, all of us laughing and shouting for him to come see. My beloved happened to be visiting. When I saw him I knew I would never be happy with anyone else.''

"How wonderful.'' Kasane sighed at the prospect of actually loving the man with whom she shared her life. "My husband-to-be was born in the year of the Rat.''

"That's good,'' Cat said. "That means he's thrifty and will prosper.''

"But I don't know which year of the Rat.''

"Ah.'' Cat sighed in sympathy. Kasane's groom could be twenty or thirty-two or forty-four or fifty-six. She and Kasane were silent for a long time, each with her own bitter thoughts.

Kasane remembered sitting, head bowed, while her parents and the go-between haggled over her and the gifts to be given the groom's family. Kasane knew that even if she could return home, even if the groom's family accepted her, she would only have to leave again. She would become the servant of her mother-in-law. She would live out her days among strangers.

Cat remembered the first man she had known. There had been nothing romantic about it. He had paid Old Jug Face a great deal for the privilege of being the first. As she sat waiting for him Cat had almost regretted her decision to enter the Yoshi-wara. But she had reminded herself that she would have had to pillow with a stranger in any case, even if she had married.

The night wind carried the sound of a drum and *samisen* and voices singing in one of Okitsu's many inns. Okitsu was a popular resort. The partying would go on most of the night.

Cat recognized the song. It was from a play about this beach.

"At a time now past,'' Cat said, "a fisherman found a robe of feathers hanging in one of these pine trees.''

"Who did the robe belong to?''

"A beautiful princess. She appeared to the fisherman and pleaded with him to give it back to her. Without it she couldn't fly to the moon where her home was.'' Cat put down her pipe, draped her new travel cloak over her shoulders, and moved out onto the beach.

"She promised the fisherman that she would perform for him a dance known only to the immortals.''

With the bay and its reflected glitter of stars behind her, Cat danced in time to the distant music. As she bent and swayed she wove an intricate pattern in the air with a pair of folding fans.

"She danced under the pines to a heavenly music until the wind caught her robe and lifted her. She flew past Mount Ashi-taka. Past Mount Fuji. She was never seen again.'' Cat ended her performance by kneeling. She extended her arms behind her and fluttered the fans as she bowed until her forehead almost touched the sand.

Kasane clapped her hands. "You dance like a princess, mistress."

Cat returned to her seat by the fire. She pulled the cloak close around her. They were almost into the twelfth month, and the wind was cold.

As the wind shifted, the music and laughter from Okitsu faded. They were replaced by the steady murmur of the surf and the low rustling of the pine boughs overhead. Tomorrow, Cat vowed, tomorrow they would be on the road before dawn.

She had already set her plan in motion by dropping some of the priest's paper talismans on the beach where the children would find them. The charms were of the simplest sort, slips of paper inscribed with an invocation to the Fox god. The poor folk pasted them above their doorways as protection against robbers.

While Kasane cooked supper, Cat had cut her paper handkerchiefs into strips and written out fifty or sixty more of them. She hoped the Lord Buddha would understand her desperation and forgive the sacrilege.

Tomorrow she would leave the papers along the road. She would surreptitiously tuck them into the loads of passing pack horses. She would plant a rumor to go with them. The chances of the ruse working were slim; but if she couldn't lose the *rōnin* from Tosa, at least she could try to make his job more difficult.

Hanshiro was proving difficult to lose, and not just because he was as persistent as boiled rice on the sole of her foot. His face and his presence were beginning to haunt Cat. Someone, somewhere, was playing a bamboo flute. Perhaps it had summoned the memory of him.

As Cat lay on her narrow mat with her head cradled on her arm and listened to the melancholy song and to the constant rush and murmur of the waves, Hanshiro returned. His dark face, shaded with the stubble of his beard, was almost gaunt.

Tosa dog! Cat thought.

She remembered him as he had looked in the lantern light of the abbot's poetry gathering. Shadows lay under the arches of his prominent cheekbones and in the deep hollows around eyes that glittered like ice on obsidian. His face was rugged, cold, ruthless as the mountains. And like the mountains he was remote, mysterious, and beautiful.

CHAPTER 45
CROSSING AT A FORD

"Ditch planks!" By the time Cat arrived at the edge of the river outside Okitsu, the two porters were wading the swift, shallow current as it meandered through the boulders and across the shingle of the riverbed.

"Wooden privy shoes!" She raged at their naked, *moxa*-scarred backs and their buttocks, which were clad only in faded gray cotton loincloths.

She would have waded in after them had not Kasane held on firmly to her sleeve. Cat jerked it from her grasp.

"I would rather be attacked with swords than made a fool of." Cat hitched up her own loincloth under her trousers, as though about to go after them anyway. "Robbers in every country, rats in every house," she muttered.

"For a warrior of your skill to attack them would be like skinning a louse with a spear, Hachibei." Kasane was diplomatic, but surprisingly firm. She feared her mistress's aristocratic temper would draw attention.

The porters had demanded seventy coppers each, thirty over the usual rate, to carry Cat and Kasane across the river. The river was deep and treacherous, they said. They deserved the extra pay, they said. And the river had been deep. Kasane had been terrified as the man carrying her on his back struggled against the rushing water. The cold water had pushed past her thighs, soaking her to her waist.

Shrouded in gray clouds, the sun had just risen above the horizon when they reached the shore. The porters had found no return fares at such an early hour, so they had wandered upstream, around a sharp curve. Cat had grown suspicious and followed them. She'd arrived at the bank as they were wading across the real ford, which was much shallower. The river had shifted in its bed recently, moving the sand bank away from the highway's crossing. Cat had been gulled.

"Cockroaches!" Cat shouted one more imprecation at them

while she untied the sandals hanging from her belt and put them on. She pulled the left front opening of her jacket farther across the right and tightened her sash. *"Baka!"* she muttered.

"We're on our way back, Your Honor," a voice called from above. "We can take you cheap as far as Mariko."

The two hostlers were the ones who had sold their hats to Cat and Kasane at the base of the climb to Satta Pass. Now they were sitting on a bench in front of an open-air tea stand among booths selling sugared rice cakes, ear shellfish, and gift-wrapped packages of dried bonito and papery seaweed. The tea stand and the bench were on a rise, commanding a view of both the actual and extortionary fords. The postboys' mare was tied to one of the shop's front corner posts.

Cat knew Kira's men were questioning all the hostlers and *kago* bearers. Traveling back and forth as they did, they were in the best possible position to act as spies and informers. These two had big grins on their faces, which made Cat even warier. Oishi had always said a laughing person could not be estimated.

"Your offer is kind." Cat bowed politely. "But we shall ride the knee chestnut-haired horse."

"Well, then, walk if that suits you."

The hostlers looked so much alike, they must have been brothers. They had thick mustaches and goatees. A disorderly fringe of dusty hair stood out around the shaved crowns of their heads. They wore the small topknots of laborers. Their patched and faded blue jackets were dirty at the collars and frayed at the sleeve hems. Curly black hair showed at the diagonal front openings of the jackets.

"Walking is very good for the circulation." The second man grimaced in ecstatic concentration as he dug in his left ear with a long-handled, ladle-shaped ear pick.

Cat glanced at Kasane. The swelling in her ankle had gone down some, and she was maneuvering well with her crutch; but Cat still felt terrible about making her walk.

"You understand why we can't hire a horse, don't you?" she said in a low voice.

"Yes. Don't worry about me."

"Boss Viper sends greetings," one of the men called out as Cat and Kasane started back toward the main road.

"The *kago* man?"

"The very one."

Cat took a firm grip on her staff, looked around for trouble, then climbed the steep path to the tea stand. Once she got closer she could see that the two men had drawn a grid in the dirt. While they drank their morning tea, they used river pebbles as markers for a game of Six Musashi. One moved the "parent" stones with a long bamboo withe. The other had removed one of his sandals and was using his toes to grip and move the "child" pieces.

"I'm Bōshū." The stouter one bowed as he sat cross-legged with his feet tucked under his thighs. Cat knew that Bōshū wasn't his name, of course, but the province from which he came.

"This hirsute love child of a bow-legged badger," Bōshū continued, "is my brother, Hairy."

Cat was in no mood for what passed as wit among the laboring class. "How do you know Viper?" she asked.

"He's Boss." Bōshū seemed surprised Cat didn't know that.

"Everyone knows Boss Viper," Hairy added.

"He instructed us to look out for you," his brother said. "Though he wears rags, Viper has a heart of brocade."

Cat beckoned with her staff to a tall thicket of bamboo. The Bōshū brothers abandoned their game and untied their shaggy chestnut pony. As the mare followed them her hoofs clattered on the stony path.

Cat looked around to make sure no one else was close by. "What did he tell you about me?"

"It's as they say, honorable sir," Bōshū said. " 'Word of an evil deed travels a thousand *ri* before good news leaves the gate.' " Boss Viper sent word to those he trusts that you're the son of a poor but honorable warrior confined to his bed by a lingering illness. You're on a quest to recover a treasured pair of swords stolen from your father's house by his evil steward. The steward has since fled to the Western Capital. The thief's henchmen are pursuing you to keep you from recovering what's rightfully yours."

Kasane listened attentively to this latest version of her mistress's adventures. Cat wore a neutral expression, but she was impressed with Viper's creativity. Whether he and the Bōshū brothers knew Cat's real identity was a mystery, however.

"How did you like the view from Satta Pass?" Bōshū untied the straw horseshoes from the saddle and began tying them on the mare's feet. It wasn't an easy task. The pony stamped and fidgeted. She drew her purple lips up over her long yellow teeth, twisted her neck sideways, and nipped at him as he worked.

"So you were the ones who left the barring-stone," Cat said.

And tied the crossed feathers of my father's crest to it, she thought.

"We noticed the Edo sharks swimming upstream." Bōshū and Hairy managed to look both noncommittal and conspiratorial.

"How much would you charge to take us to Mariko?" Cat asked.

"Because you're the first customers of the day and we're going that way anyway, we'll give you a bargain for luck. Only two hundred coppers each."

"Two hundred coppers!" Cat narrowed her eyes and shifted the staff she was leaning on, a warning not to cheat her. "You said Father Viper told you to watch out for me."

"He didn't say we had to starve doing it." Hairy led the mare in front of the stone wall that kept the hillside from sliding onto the road. With a merry jingling of the brass bells on her bridle, the pony turned to glare balefully at Cat through her long, disheveled forelock, white as mulberry threads.

Cat felt a tug on her sleeve.

"Please, Hachibei," Kasane said. "You ride. I'll walk."

Cat handed her bundle to Hairy and climbed onto the retaining wall. "We should take advantage of this opportunity to wash our clothes while the devil's away." She held out a hand to pull Kasane up.

The saddle was a rickety affair consisting of two oaken arches front and rear with two thick pads of cloth-covered straw between them. A pair of open wooden frames large enough to hold one passenger each hung on either side of it. The panniers' bottoms, with their bars and knobs and the ridges formed by the rope lashing them together, were padded with a pair of shabby, thin quilts, folded to fit. The horse's blanket was decorated with large black characters spelling "good luck." From the looks of the saddle, "good luck" was an appropriate sentiment.

With a great deal of chivvying and clucking and whipping of his bamboo rod, Bōshū kept the mare in one place long enough for Cat to lower herself into the nearest box. Then he turned the horse so Kasane could clamber into the one on the other side. He tightened the straw rope that served as a cinch and compensated for the differences in the passengers' weight by dangling stones from Cat's pannier. But the entire contrivance looked as if it might come apart or slide under the horse's belly at any moment.

Hairy tied Cat's and Kasane's bundles across the mare's

haunches, but Cat rested her staff along the rim of the box so it would be close at hand. She wedged the soles of her sandals against the corner pieces to brace herself for the jolts to come. She shifted about gingerly in a futile effort to fit her shoulder blades under the frame's crosspiece.

Bōshū jerked on the nose rope, and the mare lurched forward with a tinkling of bells and a great explosion of wind. As Cat's pannier rolled and pitched to the rhythmic jingle of the pony's brass bells, she thought of the river porters again. Musashi wrote of crossing at a ford in his *Fire Book*.

Crossing at a ford occurs often in a lifetime, he had written. *It means setting sail even though your friends stay in harbor. It means discerning the enemy's capabilities and attacking at his weak point. If you succeed in crossing at the best place,* Musashi had said, *you may take your ease.*

"Bōshū," Cat said, "do you know of a maker of weapons between here and Mariko?"

CHAPTER 46

HE WONDERS IF HE OUGHT TO WASH HIS CLOTHES

Shichisaburo's assistant was waiting for Hanshiro when he left the police office and walked out into the dawn's pale light. The troupe was packed and waiting to leave when he arrived at their quarters on the temple grounds. Shichisaburo was understandably nervous. He knew that Hanshiro knew he had been sheltering a miscreant, a crime for which he could be severely punished.

Even if Hanshiro didn't inform on him, Shichisaburo expected the magistrate to change his mind and throw them all in jail until the officials in Edo gave a ruling. That could take a very long time, and conditions in the jail were worse than execrable.

While his people waited anxiously outside, Shichisaburo presided at a hasty meal of tea and cold rice. "I so much regret the inconvenience you have suffered," he said as he poured the tea.

Hanshiro leaned forward. Walls had ears. "No one need be

inconvenienced any more"—his calm voice contained a calculated menace—"if you tell me how that person escaped and where that one's going next."

Shichisaburo blanched under his light, daytime makeup. "An old tunnel." His hand shook, spilling a few drops of tea, which he hastily mopped up with one of his embossed paper napkins. "I truly don't know where the person plans to go, other than up to the Western Capital."

"Don't worry." Hanshiro took pity on him. After all, Shichisaburo had, at great risk to himself, helped the woman who had snatched away Hanshiro's heart. "I wish to serve the person's cause."

Shichisaburo regarded him so warily, Hanshiro laughed out loud. "You think that's setting a cat to guard dried bonito, don't you."

"I'm only a wretched riverbed beggar, honorable sir. My opinions are worth nothing."

"But your help is worth something."

"We are in trouble already." Shichisaburo's voice held an entreaty. He had more than discharged his obligation to Lady Asano. He didn't want to live out his life in exile for a woman with whom he hadn't even pillowed. "We must be beyond the town borders before the hour of the Dragon or face penalties."

"If you won't intercede with our mutual acquaintance on my behalf, at least allow me to accompany you. Seeing me in your company might help persuade the person of my honorable intentions."

Shichisaburo bowed an unhappy acquiescence.

"Of course, I can count on your discretion in this matter," Hanshiro added.

" 'If a thing is said' "—in a voice barely above a murmur, Shichisaburo quoted Bashō—" 'the lips become very cold, like the autumn wind.' "

By the time the troupe reached Okitsu, Hanshiro was beginning to regret his decision to travel with them. The members of the Nakamura-za trailed for nine *cho* behind Hanshiro and Dragonfly. They were all afoot. Because of government restrictions on those they called riverbed beggars, not even Shichisaburo, the head of the most popular theater in the Eastern Capital, could legally hire a horse or a *kago*.

Shichisaburo was about halfway back in the long line of actors and their apprentices and servants. He was followed by musicians, carpenters, wig makers, shampooers, tailors, dressers, stagehands, and almost a hundred porters. He was keeping a close eye on the man carrying the lacquered box that held his carved head. During the riot at Kambara he had rescued it at some peril to himself.

Like the other actors, Dragonfly was hidden beneath the huge rush hat he was required to wear when mingling with people on the road. His wadded silk travel robe, the color of cloves, was covered by a drab, rusty-black paper cloak. His paulownia wood *geta* were of a utilitarian height, which made life easier for the servant who walked behind him, holding a paper umbrella over his head. His son, identically dressed, was at his side as always.

Dragonfly was possessed by curiosity about the handsome boy he had helped escape. He had spent most of the trip trying to wheedle information from the taciturn *rōnin* of Tosa. Hanshiro had replied only in noncommittal grunts. He himself had learned that rumors abounded among the members of the company. The one closest to the truth said the young stranger was an Asano retainer, trying to deliver a message to the councilor, Oishi Kuranosuke.

As Dragonfly walked he held a small piece of sandalwood to his nose, to mask the mélange of odors around him. He stepped delicately around a pile of horse dung that hadn't been collected yet by some enterprising farmer's child.

"Travel is a gloomy and trying experience." He waved a limp hand at the passing throng, which, strangely enough, seemed to include more than the usual number of children. "Candles exhaust themselves to give light to men." He sighed the words in a wan, melancholy tone.

"If I had known you were going to rest your head so uneasily on your pillow last night," Hanshiro said, "I would have invited you to share my accommodations." He was amused to discover that he liked the actor. He found him easy to talk to. Dragonfly had the sensitive nature of a cultured woman, yet he wasn't bent on seduction for profit.

Hanshiro suspected that Dragonfly's complaints masked the real cause of his unhappiness. He missed the loving wife and three young daughters waiting for him in Ōsaka.

"Oh, hideous!" Dragonfly tilted up his chin so he could give Hanshiro a look of sympathy from under his hat brim. "I pity you. Spending all night in that police office with those ruffians."

"It was very instructive," Hanshiro said.

The police had deftly chain-tied all the offending farmers together and herded them into a small outer room. By nightfall they had sobered up and were quite chastened. But because Hanshiro had been kept in a separate room with the others of his class, he had been able to listen to Kira's men talk among themselves. He hadn't learned much that he hadn't been able to guess already, however.

Bureaucracy wasn't to be hurried. The magistrate had spent most of the afternoon listening to the complaints of exasperated farmers from a nearby village. The headman's grandmother had been stealing again. Because everyone in the village knew of her predilection, the only thing she had found to take were buckets of night soil. She had collected quite a hoard of them before the stench revealed her crime. The story was a complicated one, entailing a series of events that went back years. The magistrate listened patiently to all of it.

He was probably avoiding the larger problem that filled the police office and overflowed into the yard, where the rioting farmers' families had set up camp. So many people had been involved in the artistic debate at the Nakamura-za's performance, the magistrate had insisted on sending to Edo for advice.

The young westcountryman who called himself Nameless had sat silently in a corner throughout the night as, one by one, men were called in to present their cases. He was still sitting there when Hanshiro finally left at dawn. Like Hanshiro, he seemed to be considering the consequences of his own folly.

The hunter pursuing the prey sees not the mountains, as the old saying went. Hanshiro had been so intent on his fight with Nameless that the police had been able to twist their blunt pitchforks into his sleeves, immobilizing his arms. It had been humiliating. As Hanshiro had sat, straight upright, through the night, he had thought of the ancient poem:

> Beautiful lady, standing alone,
> None in the world like her,
> A single glance and she upsets a city,
> A second glance, she upsets the state.

She had certainly upset him. The prospect of seeing Lady Asano was still distracting him. He was even conscious of the shabbiness of his appearance for the first time since he had left Tosa.

" 'He wonders if he ought to wash his clothes,' " he recited aloud.

" 'Having lived with them for a while . . .' " Dragonfly continued the old poem. " 'He now loves the lice.' "

Dragonfly smiled to himself under his big hat. He understood now the purpose of the stoical *rōnin*'s quest. He was in love with the fugitive lad from Edo.

As they passed the salve shops clustered outside the big gates of Seiken temple, Dragonfly studied the bright robes and broad sashes of the lads who sold the wonderful salve that was Okitsu's most famous *meibutsu*, "name thing." The painted boys themselves were Okitsu's second most famous product. They didn't impress Dragonfly, though. He slanted his brim up again to share a look of disdain with Hanshiro.

Okitsu boasted over two hundred houses, and the shopping district around the temple was always busy. But the activity today seemed even more frenetic than usual. Laughing, shouting children dodged among the two-wheeled handcarts and the stacks of vegetables and goods. The adults' voices were loud. An almost palpable excitement shimmered in the air, which was already charged with an oncoming storm.

Hanshiro and Dragonfly and his son passed between the old plum trees outside the temple gate. The trees' limbs had grown so heavy that they crept along the ground. A child stood sobbing among them as people brushed past him.

He was very young. His head was shaved except for a round patch of hair gathered into a bunch on his crown. He wore a bib and loincloth and quilted jacket and a small damask bag at his side for the amulet that would protect him from childhood's calamities.

Hanshiro crouched in front of him. "What's the matter?"

"My brother went to the shrine of the Sun Goddess without me."

"You're too young to travel so far." Hanshiro wiped the boy's eyes and nose with one of his paper handkerchiefs.

"But I found one, too." The child opened his bag and drew out a wrinkled scrap of paper.

"Where did you get it?"

"They rained down during the night. We've been finding them everywhere. Everyone says they're a holy sign. The other children are going. I want to go, too."

Hanshiro studied the smudged writing on the paper. It was hastily done, but even though he knew it was highly unlikely, Hanshiro thought he recognized Lady Asano's hand. *Fool*, he thought. *You imagine her everywhere*.

"*Dame!* Impossible child!" A frantic woman scooped up the boy and hoisted him onto her back. He clung to her neck while she supported his small bottom with her forearms crossed behind her. He bounced along as, without a glance at Hanshiro or Dragonfly, his mother trotted off through the crowd.

Hanshiro stood and looked around. The clerks of a nearby thread shop were writing names and addresses on wooden tickets to hang around the young pilgrims' necks. Another merchant was giving them straw sandals. Beside the gate a woman was passing out oranges from a large basket.

Was this the beginning of something like the mysterious mass pilgrimage to Ise that had happened almost sixty years ago? And could Cat have started it? As Hanshiro entered the temple's grounds behind Dragonfly, he stopped to look over the hundreds of messages, invocations, and pleas written on wooden tags and hung from the message board near the massive gate. He did it at each big temple or shrine he encountered.

"Anything there from someone you know?" Dragonfly asked.

Hanshiro grunted noncommittally. But he stayed where he was as Dragonfly swept on through the gate with his son, his servants, and the Nakamura troupe after him.

The bold, black calligraphy of one letter was unmistakably Lady Asano's. "To the Traveler," it said. "From the Floating Weed."

Hanshiro knew the reference, of course. It was from a poem written nine centuries earlier by Lady Ono no Komachi, one of the six poetical geniuses. "So forlorn am I, that my body is like a floating weed." "Floating weed" had come to symbolize a precarious, uprooted existence.

For the briefest of instants Hanshiro imagined the letter was addressed to him. While people streamed past him he reached out and touched it lightly with his fingertips. His heart, his soul, his marrow, ached to open it.

But as surely as he knew the calligraphy was Lady Asano's, he also knew the letter's contents were not meant for him. Even if it could tell him her whereabouts, honor would not allow him to take it down and read it.

There is no medicine that will cure a fool, he thought. *You aspired to break off the flower, but the branch is too high for the likes of you.*

CHAPTER 47
IF ONE EATS POISON

"Your five-*fun* strumpet looks like a rice mortar wearing a *kimono*." As the wind blew swirls of dust around him, Bōshū continued an argument that had been meandering along since he and his brother left Fuchu.

"Yours has a face worn down in the middle like a mounting block." Hairy turned away from the gusts to light his pipe. He puffed on it as he walked on the other side of the mare's nose from his brother.

"Remember when the sandal bearer got drunk and annoyed the women of the Three Gate House, and they dared him to screw a sea urchin?"

"It stung him until his stalk swelled up like a paper lantern." Hairy waddled a few paces. "For two days he walked like a duck visiting fire victims."

"That's the only time his stalk was ever thicker than a dumpling skewer."

Even though it was only midday, the Bōshū brothers had rested several times along the way. At each stop they had washed down the dust of the road with cheap wine. After each stop they had become more waggish. By the time the first of the many stands selling Mariko's famous sweet-potato stew came into view, they were laughing uproariously. They were boiling tea in their navels, as Kasane put it.

They were also wearing a hole in Cat's bag of patience. Fortunately the double gates to Fuchu's pleasure district had been closed when they passed through the town, or the brothers would surely have found an excuse to detour by way of it. As it was, for the one and a half *ri* to Mariko they had regaled each other with stories of their past adventures there.

Cat was worried. Viper trusted this pair, but wine jugs had mouths. "We've hired a pair of oil sellers," she muttered.

Kasane gave her a sympathetic glance. Door-to-door oil vendors even made their way to her village from time to time. Their

304

habit of stopping to gossip with the housewives had earned them a reputation as laggards.

The journey to Mariko may have taken longer than Cat had anticipated, but the frequent stops hadn't been wasted. She and Kasane had been grateful for the chance to stretch their cramped legs each time the dust clogged the hostlers' throats and they stopped for a drink. And thanks to the two Bōshū, they had new travel permits bought from a forger at a hundred and fifty coppers each.

Cat's name was now Jimbei and Kasane was Sugi. As their home they named Kururi, the capital of Kasane's home province of Kazusa. There would be a mix of dialects there, and even if they encountered an official who could distinguish accents from individual villages, they might be able to pass. It was risky, but not as risky as trying to use their old permits.

Better than the permits, though, was Cat's new staff, also purchased in Fuchu. It looked harmless enough. It was a wooden pilgrim's staff with a pointed iron cap that fitted tightly over the shaft. Six iron rings, three on each side, dangled from the two filigreed loops.

It looked very much like the first staff Cat had carried when she left Edo. But the cap on this one could be lifted off to reveal a straight, double-edged blade, sharp enough to shave a nun's head. The decorative bands of beaten brass around the shaft added strength to the places most likely to be struck with a sword or staff.

Kasane had been too preoccupied to notice the mare's slow pace. With her legs dangling from the front of the open pannier frame, she had leaned her elbows on the rim. When she wasn't glancing behind her, looking for her pilgrim, she gazed dreamily into the future. Cat could guess what she was thinking.

Kasane had passed the hours singing old tunes softly to herself. Her voice was full and pleasant, and all her songs had been about love. So was the one she was singing now.

> Time cannot alter
> The flow of water,
> Or love's strange, sweet way.

Bōshū dropped back to walk alongside Cat's pannier. "For five hundred more coppers, Your Honor, we'll take you over the Utsu-no-yama trail."

"That's too much money."

"The pass is dangerous. A murder was committed there just last month."

"Surely you two fierce men aren't afraid?"

"Of course not. But even in daytime the trees make the road so dark that if someone were to pinch your nose, you wouldn't see him. Besides, the nag wears out a bale of sandals on the rocks."

"Looks like we can't go with you for any price." Hairy pointed his pipe at the mob of porters, hostlers, horses, and *kago* bearers milling about in the yard of Mariko's transport office.

With a rolled scroll, probably a labor requisition, a minor transport official waved the brothers over to the side of the road. "Excuse the inconvenience," he called out.

Cat slumped in her seat, lowered her head so her face was hidden by her hat, and pretended to be dozing. Her hand rested casually on her staff.

"How fares your saintly mother, Bōshū-san?" the official asked politely.

"Still waiting for good fortune, Your Honor." Bōshū squinted into the blowing dust.

"Fortune and misfortune are entwined like the strands of a rope." The official sucked air through his teeth philosophically. The amenities observed, he brandished the scroll. "Lord Hino's councillor is on his way to Edo and will stay here tomorrow night," he said. "Lord Wakizaka will be here tonight on his way back to Harima." With the processions of two lords arriving, the official had reason to look harried. "The members of the two trains are like the teeth of a comb in number. Lord Wakizaka must have your steed."

Cat stiffened. Lord Hino had been an ally of Cat's father. Wakizaka, lord of Tatsuno, was from Harima, the same province as her father. His warriors had accompanied the government's agents when they took possession of the Asano castle and lands.

"Lord Wakizaka!" Hairy grumbled from behind Cat's pannier. "Lord Wakizaka tries to pay with promissory notes or samples of his poetry. He's pawned his genitals to the money lenders."

"We are at the august lord's service." Bōshū bowed sardonically.

"Report this afternoon for your assignment." As the official walked away the wind whipped his *hakama* about his thin legs.

Bōshū turned to face Cat. "Forgive my rudeness, Your Honor, but may I suggest you wait until tomorrow and follow Lord Wakizaka's procession? Your safety will be assured on the Utsu-no-yama road."

"Thank you for your concern," Cat said. "But my sister and I will go on alone."

"It's a risky undertaking," said Bōshū.

"A teacup on the edge of a well," Hairy added.

The Bōshō brothers were right. The Utsu-no-yama trail was steep and rocky and lonely and dark. And though it was early afternoon, a coming storm made the road even gloomier than usual.

Thunder grumbled among the peaks. Wind moaned through the tops of the towering cedars, causing their trunks to creak. It rustled the dense undergrowth ominously.

The *kagos* and horses for hire had all been detained at the transport office in Mariko. Most foot travelers had already taken refuge. The road was almost deserted. Cat knew she was being followed, though. She had looked over the edge and counted five men coming up the narrow switchback below.

She used a long cord to tie her sleeves back out of the way with the warrior's dragonfly knot. She rolled her towel into a band and tied it around her head to keep tendrils of hair from blowing in her eyes. When she finished she did indeed look like the young lord Yoshitsune, trained in the warrior's Way by mountain demons.

She waited at the far side of two huge rock formations flanking the road. The trail narrowed here until only one person at a time could pass comfortably between them. The outcropping on her right jutted out from the cliff at the top of the pass. Behind the one to her left was a drop-off into a narrow gorge three *cho* deep. Mist rose from the river that foamed and tumbled over the rocks at the bottom of it.

"Elder sister," Cat said, "go on ahead. You can catch up with the pilgrims who passed a while ago. Wait for me across from the gate of the Wisteria Inn in Okabe."

"We could hide until they pass, younger brother." Kasane had seen the five men, too.

"They must know I'm here. They'd find me eventually." Cat had decided that if she must fight, this was the best possible place. "Even if they try to kill me, I won't die until I'm fated to."

"Then I'll stay with you." Kasane was still using her crutch, but the swelling in her ankle had gone down. She could walk with a slight limp. "I won't die until I'm fated to, either."

Cat sighed at the obstinacy of peasants. "Stay out of sight."

Cat heard the men's voices before they rounded the corner. When they saw her they stopped to confer and tie back their own sleeves. Even though there were five of them, they would have to run at Cat one at a time. And each attacker's sword arm would be constricted in the narrow defile.

"Give up and we won't hurt you." The leader of the group swaggered out in front of the others. He was powerful and ugly. He wasn't much taller than Cat, but he had long arms.

"You must enter the tiger's den to catch the cub," Cat taunted. She assumed a fighting stance, with the spear held close to her side, the blade pointed up at an angle.

Ragged strands of lightning illuminated the pass in an explosion of light. The ensuing thunder resonated in Cat's chest, which felt taut as a drumhead. She remembered Oishi's advice, *"Move calmly, like a lotus flower in the middle of a raging fire."*

Kira's retainers drew their swords and advanced with a caution Cat found flattering. She faced them with a cool, remote stare. She regretted only that she had no helmet in which to burn incense so that if her head were taken, it would be perfumed and presentable.

"I am Asano no Kinume." To be heard above the wind, Cat had to shout her challenge. "I am the daughter of Asano Takumi-no-Kami Naganori, lord of Akō castle and third master of the Banshu-Akō clan."

Cat took a deep breath. She felt as though she were part of the storm rising around her. "I am a person of little merit," she continued, "but it's a matter of indifference to me if I live or die here today. If you care to test my arm, step forward."

The leader of the group refused to lower himself by answering a woman's challenge. With the flat of his blade held carelessly against his shoulder, he strode forward as though Cat were unarmed. As he cleared the narrow passageway he brought up his sword to parry her blow and disarm her, but he was too late.

Cat used the blow Oishi had taught her and that had served her in the fight at the ferry near Kawasaki. Her spear moved in a blurred, precise arc. It sliced deep into the forearm. Then she lunged, driving the blade through the man's jacket and into his chest, pushing him back against the rock. She heard the muffled scrape of metal on stone as the blade passed through him.

The weight of his body pulled the spear downward as he slid into a crouching position at the base of the rock face. Cat put a foot against his chest and yanked the blade out. She could see he was dead, and she turned her attention to the next man.

Holding the spear horizontally above her head, she dropped onto her left knee with her right leg out in front of her, the knee bent, the foot braced. She swung the butt section around to parry the second man's downward blow, then dispatched him with a sweeping strike that opened his stomach. When he fell she stabbed the point into his ear, finishing him.

His corpse lay in the opening between the rocks, making a third attack even more difficult. While two of the survivors tried to hold Cat's attention with feints and threats, the third clambered up into the wind-sculptured hollows and crevices of the huge outcrop to her left.

He planned to get above or behind her, but Kasane was hidden and waiting for him. She hadn't room to swing her crutch in the narrow defile, so she had tied a fist-size stone into one end of her towel. As the man passed below her she whirled it three times, then slammed it down on the shaved crown of his head.

He slumped, but his body was too tightly wedged in the crack to fall. Kasane hit him until splinters of bone drove into his brain.

Panting and shaking, Kasane lay stomach down across the boulder above him and peered over the edge at the two remaining *samurai*. She ducked out of sight when they scanned the rocks for their missing comrade.

"Shirō," one of them called out. "Where are you?"

"In hell!" Kasane shrieked with laughter so demonic even Cat shivered, and wisps of hair stirred at the nape of her neck.

The men turned and ran, stumbling in their haste to get away from a place that was clearly haunted.

Kasane scrambled down from her perch and ran to the heap of stones generations of travelers had left next to a small statue of Jizō. She moved several of them to the edge of the cliff. Cat realized what she had in mind and helped her. They each found a rock that took both hands to lift. As they waited with them poised over their heads, they smiled grimly at each other.

When Kira's two retainers came into sight on the switchback below, Cat and Kasane threw the rocks down on them. Most missed, although Kasane, who had thrown rocks at crows in the fields, had the better aim. Her second stone hit one where his neck joined his shoulder. He pitched sideways, rolled headlong down the steep incline, and hurtled over the side. The other man rounded the corner at a run and disappeared from sight.

Kasane helped Cat heave the two bodies over the edge of the mountainside and into the river far below. Cat knew she couldn't keep the men's swords, but she considered ramming their points into the ground so they stood upright in the middle of the road.

It would have been an act of defiance, a message to Lord Kira. But she thought better of it. The wisest course was to leave behind as little evidence as possible. The swords followed the bodies over the side.

"Where's the other one, elder sister?" Cat stuck her hands in her sleeves to hide the fact that they were shaking.

Together they pulled out the body and disposed of it, too. They had just finished when the first large, cold raindrops hit their faces and bare arms so hard that they smarted. Then the rain began to fall in torrents. It diluted the blood on the rocks and the ground, tinting it pink before washing it away.

Cat and Kasane stood in the shelter of the outcrop while they caught their breaths, and Cat put the iron cap back on her spear's blade.

Already rivulets were turning to streams and wearing new channels as they rushed down the steep road. They carried first pebbles, then larger and larger rocks, with them.

"You did well, elder sister." Cat held up her staff in salute. "I'm proud of you."

"Your Ladyship has taught this unworthy person to do everything thoroughly. You have taught her that if one eats poison, one should lick even the dish."

The rain splattered on Kasane's back as she bowed very low, to the proper level for addressing the daughter of a *diamyō*. She had heard Cat call out her real name. "She is honored that Your Ladyship looks on her miserable person with favor."

Cat smiled ruefully as she took Kasane's arm to help her along the treacherous path. Kasane had risked her life for her again. She had proven herself not only courageous and loyal, but resourceful as well. She deserved to see the bottom to the bottom. She deserved to know the real story.

CHAPTER 48

SOMETIMES A TRICKLE, SOMETIMES A WILD SEA

The Oi River lay just beyond Shimada, the twenty-third post station. It was always treacherous. In flood it was deadly, the worst of the many rivers that flowed down from the mountains and cleaved the Tōkaidō.

The Oi wasn't usually flooded at this time of year, but the weather had been unusually warm. Melted snow from the mountains covered the wide floodplain. It carved steep banks and formed deeps where shallows had been before. The rains washed away mountainsides. The trees that had grown there rode the flood's crest. Rocks and gravel and mud traveled downstream, to be deposited near the river's mouth.

Cat stood in the mire at the river's edge while Kasane read the government order on the sign posted there.

"It says we mustn't cross." Kasane slowly sounded out the characters. "It says the transport office will advise all travelers when the way is safe so that 'they may proceed according to their rank.' "

"Even if the water recedes today," Cat said, "the lords' processions will require all the available boats and porters to cross. We would still be delayed for days."

Cat and Kasane glanced back at the thatched roofs of Shimada. The rain had turned the town into a quagmire. Muddy sandals were heaped at the doors of any establishment that could provide lodging. Layers of sodden straw raincoats hung dripping from the eaves.

The inns were filled with the retainers and porters and attendants of Lord Hino's councilor, who was traveling to Edo. Half his people had crossed the river and were waiting for the rest, stranded on the far side. Lord Wakizaka's retinue hadn't arrived yet, but already those without the privileged status of *daimyō* were sleeping under roofed gates and verandas, chapels and bridges.

Cat knew she had to keep in front of Lord Wakizaka, who

was heading in the same direction she was. He was allowed to take a thousand men when he traveled. Even if he only had a fraction of that with him, he would cause long delays at every river ford.

"What shall we do?" Kasane followed Cat, who was already slogging along the path that led upriver.

"Find a boat."

The boat groaned and shuddered. For what seemed forever it hung motionless in the maelstrom, suspended from the boatmen's poles. Then its stern flipped up, plunging the long, flattened prow into an eddy that spun it around.

Cat and Kasane and the tubs and bales that made up the cargo slid down the shallow bilge, ending in a heap in the bow. Cat grabbed Kasane's legs in time to keep her from pitching over the low gunwale and into the clay-colored water surging and heaving around them.

Cat lay sprawled among the straw-wrapped bales of rice. She was prepared to die, but she resented being seasick. She hauled herself up, rested her chin on the downwind gunwale, and vomited into the waves. She sighed with relief and slumped back down.

Cat had seen carpenters and porters, coopers and gardeners and stonemasons, perform tasks that seemed much too strenuous for the fragile apparatus of muscles, tendons, and bones. She had seen peasants carrying their own weight and more in the loads on their backs. But she had never seen anyone work as hard as the three men in this boat.

For the last half of the hour of the Monkey they had been struggling to reach the opposite shore, still five *cho* away. With feet braced, they stood at the stern and wrestled with the sweep and the poles that usually propelled their battered old dory. The poles were bending like bamboo in a typhoon. The sinews on the men's arms and backs and the veins on their foreheads bulged until Cat thought they surely would break.

Kasane grabbed Cat's arm. "Look!"

Cat turned to see a barge broach in a whirlpool upstream. Sideways and out of control, it raced toward them through the gathering darkness. It seemed to swallow up the scenery as it came.

Cat held Kasane close and stroked her wet hair as though she were a child. "None of us is destined to live forever," she said.

Kasane didn't seem terribly comforted. She would have liked

to live long enough to hear her suitor's voice. And she was terrified of river demons dragging her under and ripping out her liver.

"*Namu Amida Butsu.*" Kasane's chanting was muffled because she had buried her face in Cat's jacket. "Homage to Amida Buddha." The drone of her chant sent up tickling vibrations in Cat's chest.

With her arms around Kasane, Cat watched the barge angle in on its disastrous course. The slimy black planks of its side loomed over them, filling her field of vision. She could see the terror on the bargemen's pale faces as they clung to whatever handholds they could find. They were shouting, but they couldn't be heard over the roar of the water.

Cat didn't flinch when the barge hit the bow, knocking it aside with a bone-rattling jolt. The wet wood shrieked as the barge scraped its entire length along the smaller boat's forward section.

The huge sweep, chiseled from the trunk of a cypress, slammed back and forth in its cradle. With each swing it thumped the side of the boat until Cat was sure it would shatter it. Then the barge was clear of them.

It hit a submerged boulder with a grinding crash that sent its crew flying. When they landed the water closed in over their heads. The barge split apart as if it were a toy.

In its fatal journey it must have gathered to itself all the malevolent spirits of the flood, because the rest of the passage was uneventful. Cat had prepared herself so well for death that she was surprised when the keel plowed into the mud of the Oi's western shore. Two of the crew helped Cat and Kasane across the sagging gangplank and up the slippery bank. After the plunging and surging of the boat, the ground seemed to rise too solidly to meet Cat's feet, and she walked stiff-legged.

While the men secured the line, Cat and Kasane stood shivering among pyramidal stacks of the river porters' ladderlike pallets. They were surrounded by fish weirs, algae nets, discarded wooden lunch boxes and wrappings, straw raincoats, and broken sandals, the detritus of commerce and travel.

"We are mortified at the discomfort you have suffered in our poor craft." The owner and captain of the boat bowed apologetically. Ashore he was much smaller than he had seemed at the sweep.

"The blame is ours for inconveniencing you in such weather." Cat slipped a paper packet into the captain's sleeve. It contained all the silver coins she had left. "Please honor us by accepting this insignificant token."

The boat's owner slid his hand tactfully into his sleeve and hefted it. "It's rude of me to disagree, but this is too much."

He bowed until Cat could see only his back, the black whisk of a topknot, and the long, wet hanks of hair that had escaped it and clung to his neck. "Our fee is one hundred and sixty coppers for each passenger."

"But the river is so dangerous . . ."

"Please . . ." While he talked and bowed, the captain separated out the equivalent of three hundred and twenty coppers and rewrapped the rest, all without taking his hand out of his sleeve. "We could not cheat you by asking for more." He returned the packet.

"An honest man's head is the seat of the gods." Cat and Kasane bowed low. "The Lord of Immeasurable Light will bless you."

With wishes for a safe journey, the three boatmen trotted off into the dusk toward Kanaya. The town's main street was marked by a string of lights snaking up into a narrow, tree-choked cleft in the foothills.

Now that the danger was past, Cat stood on the bank and watched the water rush by. Musashi said the spirit was like water. It adopted the shape of its receptacle. It was sometimes a trickle and sometimes a wild sea. Both in fighting and in everyday life, Musashi said, one's spirit must be calm yet determined.

Cat stood there until her legs had stopped trembling and her spirit had calmed. By the time she and Kasane reached Kanaya, the watchman was making the first of his night's rounds. He clapped his wooden blocks, and in a lilting chant he warned householders about the dangers of untended hearths.

"How does your ankle feel?" Cat asked.

"Much better. The Okitsu medicine is as good as it's claimed to be."

"Mitsuke lies about seven *ri* ahead, and there are no rivers that require porters between here and there. Can you walk that far tonight?"

"The crossroad ogres might wish us harm, my lady," Kasane murmured.

"I'll warn them away with my staff." Cat pounded her pilgrim's staff thrice on the road, setting the iron rings to jangling.

"And if they don't heed the warning, I'll skewer them like dumplings." She flourished the staff and made a comic face.

"Let's go, then." Kasane smiled gamely.

Kasane was uncertain about traveling at night. On the one hand she was terrified of the evil beings that lurked in the dark, especially at the meeting of the roads. But Mitsuke was where she hoped to find a message from her pilgrim.

She knew he himself was probably somewhere behind her, but she was learning the ways of the road. She knew he could pay a messenger to carry the letter ahead and post it on the temple gate. Since Okitsu she had studied each messenger jogging past with his wooden letter box on his back. Perhaps in one of them lay a poem written in her lover's strong, simple hand.

CHAPTER 49
DRAWN ON BY MOONLIGHT

A line of singing children danced past Hanshiro and his new traveling companion, the pilgrim who had been following Kasane. The children were calligraphy students from a school on Tub Makers' Street in Mariko. They wore identical white robes and bamboo hats, each inscribed with an inspirational verse painted by their teacher. To keep their group together they held on to a straw rope that caused frequent entanglements on the crowded road.

Now that the rain had stopped, the muddy Tōkaidō was a-swarm with youthful pilgrims again. The urge to go to Ise had reached at least as far as here. Hanshiro's companion smiled at the noisy children as though they were innocent, poppy-cheeked Buddhas. In fact, everything seemed to cause him delight.

"They say that what with this holy call to the children and the arrival of Lord Wakizaka and Hino's men, Shimada looks like an earthquake in a thread shop," he said.

Hanshiro grunted in reply.

The young man called himself Traveler. He had an angular face, a wide mouth, squared jaw, and narrow black eyes. His high nose belied his peasant origins. He wore brown leggings and brown cloth arm coverings with flaps that extended to the first knuckles of his callused fingers. He had on a wide-brimmed pilgrim's hat with the shallow rim that shielded his face. He wore a pilgrim's robe and trousers of cheap white cotton. He carried a wicker pack on his back. His pilgrim's scroll was rolled into his straw sleeping mat to keep it dry.

The lad was a relentless optimist. As far as Hanshiro could tell, he was a model of his class. He extolled hard work and the nobler virtues. He was friendly, earnest, honest, cheerful, and candid. He was almost handsome. Hanshiro wanted nothing more than to run his sword through him and leave him squirming in the mud.

For Hanshiro, emotions of all sorts were infrequent and unwelcome guests, but he had never experienced jealousy before. He had gone back on his resolve to ignore Lady Asano's vulgar indiscretion, and he was furious with himself. Instead of continuing his journey, he had waited for the recipient of her letter to retrieve it from the temple message board in Okitsu. The discovery that Lady Asano was carrying on a flirtation with a peasant had Hanshiro almost speechless with rage.

Never turn loose the reins of the wild colt of the heart, he thought bitterly.

Traveler was such a simple, countrified sort that Hanshiro suspected a ruse. He was too innocent to be plausible. Maybe he was putting on a cat show, feigning innocence.

Hanshiro preferred to think so. He wanted to believe Traveler was not a suitor, but a conspirator in the Asano cause. The love letter was only a subterfuge, a way of passing messages.

Traveler wasn't behaving like a conspirator, though. He was behaving like a man addled by love. He looked like a pigeon that had swallowed a peashooter.

For the past five *ri* Hanshiro had listened carefully for mistakes in his speech, but his dialect was flawless. Either he was a superb actor, or he was what he appeared, a rice farmer from the province of Kazusa. And he was receiving love poems from the most beautiful, ferocious, accomplished woman Hanshiro had ever known. The woman who called herself the Floating Weed.

"I haven't spoken to her yet, but when I saw her with the actors in Kambara, she was dressed as a boy." The worst of it was that Traveler insisted on discussing his dalliance. "She looked charming, really charming. And she's so cultured for someone of her class. She writes the most exquisite poetry."

"Umh." Hanshiro was appalled by the possibility that with very little encouragement this bumpkin would recite Lady Asano's amorous poetry.

Hanshiro had coaxed from the young man the information he wanted. Now he was ready to quit his maddeningly genial company. Traveler was to leave his reply to Lady Asano's last letter on the board near the east gate of the main temple in Mitsuke. He already had bargained with a messenger to run ahead with it, but he was hopeful of finally speaking face to face with his beloved there. That explained his ebullience.

Unless, of course, the whole story was a fiction.

"Bow down! Bow down!" A liveried runner trotted along the road, scattering people in front of him.

Behind him Hanshiro heard the calls of Lord Wakizaka's shouters. Above the dispersing crowd he could see the rhythmic shiver of the plumed fringes on the heralds' tall staffs. The rear of the procession wound up the slope and out of sight around the crest of a hill. Pedestrians were either disappearing into the refuge of tea houses to wait out the train's passing or they were kneeling by the side of the road and bowing until their heads touched the ground.

Hanshiro sighed. No wonder the Tokugawa family had held on to power for a hundred years. The mandatory annual visits to Edo drained the provincial lords' coffers. And when Wakizaka traveled he insisted on making a display of every sandal bearer and armor polisher he was allowed.

Hanshiro didn't much care that the expense was ruining Wakizaka and adding to the influence of the money lenders. He did care that the Tōkaidō would be clogged for days. Unless he stayed ahead of Wakizaka, he wouldn't be able to find a bed or a river porter or a decent meal anywhere. Fortunately, staying ahead wouldn't be too difficult since *daimyō* trains only averaged four or five *ri* a day.

Traveler, however, was awed by the ranks of banners, emblazoned with Wakizaka's crest and snapping in the breeze. He gaped at the guards in their matching jackets and *hakama* and wide-winged vests. The pike bearers and bowmen and the caparisoned horses bearing the swordsmen were followed by clerks, grooms, footmen, sandal bearers, and servants of all varieties.

Just coming into view on the slope were the women's black-lacquered palanquins with their swaying gauze curtains. Walking beside them were maids and ladies-in-waiting wearing bright cloaks and veils and twirling their parasols. Still out of sight behind the hill's crest was the baggage train that extended back a *ri*.

They entered the town limits of Mariko in a silence that intensified the solemnity and splendor. The heralds twirled and tossed their tall, feather-decked staffs in rhythm with their stride. Behind them the footmen drew their left feet up to their lower backs in unison and extended their right arms, then reversed the order. As they advanced they appeared to be swimming through the air. Hats and umbrellas and banners and feather-fringed pikes danced with the motion of the march.

The government that required travel of the *daimyō* tried to deny it to the peasantry. Government edicts forbade "sight-seeing and rambling over the hillsides." As with most edicts, this one was often ignored, but Traveler had never in his nineteen years seen such a sight. He prostrated himself in the mud but indiscreetly tilted his chin so he could peek at the marchers as they approached.

With legs astraddle and his hands on his hips, Hanshiro looked down at him. If the fool weren't careful, some fifty-*koku* field warrior with rice paddy manure still between his toes would catch his eye, take offense, and lop off his head as though it were a cabbage.

Hanshiro didn't consider Traveler's well-being his concern, however. He took a few quiet steps backward, turned, and joined the people ducking into side streets.

By nightfall he reached Fujieda and found it crowded, too. The *daimyō*'s retinues were augmented by youthful pilgrims who slept everywhere. He read a note pinned to a door: "We have gone to give thanks at Ise."

The word of the holy signs found in Okitsu had surged on ahead of Hanshiro. People were camping in courtyards and under the roofs of well sheds. Charitable merchants were offering free food and tea and towels and sandals. As the town watchman made his rounds, he called for a lost child.

The horde of pilgrims was wonderful cover for someone passing as a pilgrim herself. If Cat had started this flood, she could now lose herself in it. She would be the translucent fish, the white-bait. "The white-bait, just like the color of water, itself moving," as the poem said.

Hanshiro knew he could find lodging and a warm welcome at the Iris inn no matter how crowded the Fujieda might be. The Iris's gentle, soft-spoken proprietor would serve him herself.

She would ladle scalding water over him in the bath. She would laugh softly behind her hand as she caught him up on the gossip since his last visit. When the night lantern burned low, she would slide under Hanshiro's covers.

When he left the next day she would demonstrate her love. She would leave her gate and come out barefoot into the cold dew and the public's gaze. She would wave to him until he was out of sight.

Hanshiro had never felt worthy of such affection, bestowed like a gift, without thought of thanks or repayment. He certainly had never encouraged it, except to treat her with the grace and affection he accorded all the women he admired. Her silent, enduring devotion had always mystified him, but it had been as comfortable and warm and all-enveloping as the Iris's satin quilts.

Thoughts of the Iris's cooking and quilts would have to suffice for now. Hanshiro only paused to look through the gate and into the inn's small garden. He knew the Oi River was in flood and Shimada was jammed with people; but he would not stop. He would use a ruse that was risky but had worked for him before.

He had supplied himself with a lantern on which was painted "official business." It was the sort carried by the men escorting government messengers. It would get him across the river ahead of the processions of Hino and Wakizaka.

The moon rose late, halfway to morning; but it was worth the wait. Even in its last quarter it was so bright that it threw shadows from the rocks in the road. The silvery light gave a soft, spectral glow to the houses and trees and signposts. It gleamed from the bald heads of the Jizō statues in the stone niches along the roadside.

As he strode through the light, Hanshiro savored the elegant syllables of an old poem.

> Drawn on by moonlight
> He passes right by the inn
> Where he meant to stay;
> A traveler in the night
> Is walking tomorrow's road.

"Ssst. Your Excellency . . ." The nighthawk stood in the shadow of a wooden bridge that arched over a stream. She was careful not to let the moon's beams fall on her face and expose the wrinkles there. "For a trifling thirty *mon* I shall play your flute as it's never been played," she whispered hoarsely.

"I'm grateful for your kindness, auntie," Hanshiro said good-naturedly. The moonlight and the solitude had restored his composure. "But I haven't time for heavenly music tonight."

CHAPTER 50
A BELL ON THE END OF A POLE

On the road to Nissaka, at the pass called the Middle Mountain of Little Night, a cluster of tiny shops sold the sweet rice cakes that were the local specialty. The hour was late, and all the shops had closed but this one. Its lantern was a welcome beacon in the darkness.

As Cat bought the rice cakes, wrapped in bamboo sheaths, she could see the proprietress's children sitting around a small firewell in the platform at the rear of the single room. Their belongings hung on pegs or lay scattered about. The exposed and homey clutter of the shop seemed especially poignant against the wilderness that surrounded it.

As Cat and Kasane left, the proprietress extinguished the flame in the lantern out front. Then she slid the heavy wooden shutters across the shop's wide front opening, leaving Cat and Kasane feeling alone and abandoned. But the light from their small travel lantern cheered them as it skipped and slid along the rocky path. The lantern's glow threw into relief portions of the huge cryptomeria trees around them. The deep shadows just beyond the trees made them seem even more immense and mysterious.

Kasane peered nervously into the darkness beyond the massive trunks. She knew of an astonishing array of supernatural beings. To pass the long miles she had told Cat stories of those who lived in rivers and streams and wells or who lurked around bridges and gates and even privies. But according to Kasane, more varieties of demons, ogres, and ghosts lived in the mountains than everywhere else put together. On this particular stretch of mountain road Kasane was apprehensive about *tengu*, the long-nosed devils who inhabited cryptomeria trees.

"Teach me a song." Cat didn't want to hear any of Kasane's terrifying stories here.

Kasane thought a moment. "They sing this one in my village." She gathered her confidence, then sang in her high, sweet tremolo.

> There are men you marry
> And life is boring.
> There are men you don't marry
> And love consumes you.

"Shame is thrown aside when one travels." Cat smiled at her. "You must be thinking of your Traveler and not the man you're betrothed to."

Kasane blushed.

"Beware of men who want a marriage not entered in the temple registry, elder sister."

"I've met some of them." Kasane's breath caught in her chest at the thought of them.

She remembered the procurer peddling her from inn to inn. She remembered men poking her and pinching her as though she were a fish for the table. She remembered the pirate, probing to feel if she was intact, and her face grew hot.

They walked a while in silence, then Cat sang softly.

> The loves of a short time ago
> And the smoke of tobacco
> After a while leave only ashes.

Its plaintive notes lingered in the stillness.

"It's lovely, mistress. Did you learn it . . ." Kasane paused shyly. "In that place?"

"Yes." When Cat told Kasane the story of her father's death and her mother's ruin, she had included her decision to sell herself into the pleasure district and Kira's attempt to murder her there. Cat was amused by the fact that Kasane, who a day ago had known nothing about the Yoshiwara, was now as avid for fashionable gossip, Floating World–talk, as any jaded Edokko.

"Are the young men handsome in that place?" Kasane asked.

"Some of them are, I suppose." Cat thought back on the

many men she had entertained and the very few for whom she had consented to loosen her sash. She couldn't recall a single face. It was as though they had never existed. "Lust is applauded in the Floating World," she said. "But love is not permitted." She thought of the other connotation of "Floating World," an existence of suffering and impermanence. "If I could have supported my mother from hell, I would have preferred to go there."

"Higher than the mountain, deeper than the sea." Kasane didn't have to elaborate. All children, high and low, learned the saying as soon as they could speak. It described the height, depth, and breadth of their obligation to their parents.

Cat also knew that Kasane must be unhappy about failing her own mother and father. "If fate allows it," Cat said, "you will see your parents again."

"The fallen blossom never returns to the branch," Kasane murmured sadly.

When they came to a clearing in the trees, they sat on a large flat stone in the brilliant starlight. A shallow depression had been worn in the stone by the countless other travelers who had rested there. Kasane put out the flame to save oil, and soon their eyes became accustomed to the light from the stars. As they cooled down after the exertion of walking, they doubled their travel cloaks and sat under them, shoulder to shoulder, to share their body heat. Cat unwrapped a rice cake and handed half to Kasane.

In a niche cut in the rock face beside them stood a weathered stone statue of Jizō, the guardian of travelers, pregnant women, and children. Jizō-sama was a comfort in such a lonely place. Some grieving mother who had lost a child had supplied him with a new bib and infant's cap of red cloth. Worshipers had put pebbles on his shoulders and arms and heaped them at his feet.

In the afterlife, a hag-like demon stood at Sanzu, the River of the Three Ways, and reviled sinners crossing over to hell. She stole the clothes from the deceased children who came within her grasp. She forced them to pile stones endlessly on the river's banks. To help Jizō-sama ease the children's terrible burden, travelers had piled up the pebbles.

In the road in front of Cat and Kasane stood a rounded boulder, about head high and firmly planted. The boulder was spectral in the starlight, as though awash with silver made molten in cold fires.

"The guidebook says it's called the Night-Weeping Stone."

Cat spoke in a hushed voice. The starlit scene was too chimerical to disturb with loud talk.

"Does it really weep?"

"So they say." Cat divided a second rice cake with Kasane.

"One night, long ago, a woman heavy with child set out from Nissaka. She was headed for Kanaya to find her husband. At this very spot bandits attacked her and killed her." Cat lowered her voice even further. "Blood fell on the stone, and it has wept ever since. They say it's the dwelling place of the woman's spirit."

"Did they catch the murderers?"

"The merciful goddess Kannon-sama passed by disguised as a priest. She took the child from the dead woman's body and raised him. Years later the son took revenge for his mother's murder."

"As you will avenge the spirit of your father, mistress."

Cat stared at the haunted rock standing so lonely and eloquent in this desolate place. She savored the taste of sweet rice cakes shared with a young peasant woman who had become, she realized, a beloved companion.

"Sea Weed," Cat said suddenly, softly. "My father called my mother Sea Weed."

Kasane said nothing. Cat's confession of something so personal was too astonishing for a reply.

"The name comes from his favorite poem." Cat recited part of it in a voice strained with grief.

> Pliant as the swaying sea tangle
> She lies beside me,
> The woman I love with a love
> Deep as the ocean.

The ensuing silence was broken by the sound of running footsteps, a rhythmic crunch in the darkness on the road behind them. Maybe the steps belonged to a courier. Maybe they didn't.

Cat tied her towel over her head and knotted it under her lower lip. She tugged the fold at her brow low to shroud her face in shadow. She loosened the iron cap over the blade of her spear but left it in place.

"We can hide in the bushes, mistress," Kasane whispered. "They'll pass without seeing us."

"They'll only meet us somewhere ahead, in a place not so

secluded.'' Cat moved to stand facing the northeast, with the Night-Weeping Stone at her back. She held her staff ready.

''You have a higher purpose.'' Kasane was bolder now that Cat had entrusted her with the secret of her mission. A straightforward, albeit dangerous, elopement had turned into something much greater. And in any case, a good servant took an active interest in her mistress's affairs. ''Do not throw your life away before you've achieved it, my lady.''

''The warrior-priest Saigyo once asked, 'Why regret leaving a world that merits no regrets?' '' Cat smiled sadly at Kasane. ''He said we save ourselves only when we cast ourselves away.''

Kasane sighed. She selected a rock from the road and twisted it into her towel. She swung it to test its heft and balance. She picked up another rock to throw and waited for an enemy to come within range.

They heard loud, rhythmic panting, then a lone figure rounded the bend. His face was shrouded by shadow and by the towel he wore low on his forehead. Cat couldn't see that he was the young *rōnin* who called himself Nameless, the one whose nose she had broken at the ferry. He had exchanged his clothes for those of a nondescript underling of the merchant class. His sword was inside the rolled sleeping mat on his back.

When Nameless saw Cat standing in the road, staff poised, he improvised. He yelped in surprise and dropped to his knees. Before he prostrated himself he yanked on the paper cord that suspended the cloth purse inside the front of his torn and faded jacket. He broke the cord and shied the clinking bag ahead of him. It skidded to a halt not far from Cat's feet.

''In the name of the Merciful Buddha, most kind sir, have pity on me.'' He had learned to disguise his west country dialect, but he hadn't quite gotten the Edo accent right. His face was so low to the ground, though, that his body muffled his voice, which was trembling with exertion. ''A thousand apologies for the thinness of my purse. May those few miserable coins help you in your time of need.''

''What are you doing on the road at night?'' Cat asked sternly. ''When honest folk are in their beds.''

''I'm just a miserable, poorly paid dry-goods clerk, Your Honor.'' Nameless adopted the manner of a clerk who seemed to think he would be safe as long as he kept talking. ''I heard the mysterious call to Ise and dropped the abacus and account book. My master was generous with his blessings, but he withheld aid of a more fiscal nature. I calculated that my finances would not fit around a leisurely journey to the holy shrine, so I decided to shrink the journey to accommodate my finances.''

''You're traveling night and day?''

''As long as the moon and stars provide light, Your Honor. By running I'll spend fewer days on the road, thereby eating less and requiring fewer nights' lodging.''

''And has there been a holy call to Ise?''

''Oh, yes, Your Honor. The road to the east is as crowded with pilgrims as sardines in a tub. If you wait, you'll soon meet far richer''—Nameless searched for a polite term for his situation— ''clients than the poverty-stricken wretch you see before you.''

''I'm not a bandit, you simpleton,'' Cat growled.

''Oh, I could tell you weren't, kind sir.''

''No.'' Cat smiled mischievously at his supine back. ''I'm an ogre in disguise. And I have a particular fondness for the taste of human flesh.'' She paused to see what effect that would have.

''We are not destined to live forever, Your Honor.'' Nameless shook as though afflicted with ague.

''You've run so far already, you look stringy.'' Cat poked his side with the butt of her staff. He curled up tighter. ''I could boil you a year and still wear out my teeth on you.'' As she talked Cat motioned for Kasane to hide in the bushes. ''Can you count, Dry-Goods Clerk?''

''Surely, Your Honor. Counting is my speciality. It's the only thing I *can* do.''

''Count slowly to eighty-eight in a loud voice.'' Cat was becoming tired of his chatter. ''Then pick up your purse and go. If you look up while you're counting, I'll shave your scrawny limbs into flakes like dried bonito and make soup of you.''

Nameless started counting, but he interrupted himself continually with pleas for mercy and sad stories of all the people who were depending on him and the intense grief his master would suffer if he didn't return. Cat slipped a pilgrim's gift of a small silver coin into his bag. On top of the bag she set the last rice cake wrapped in a bamboo sheath. Then she joined Kasane in the underbrush.

They stifled their laughter as they watched Nameless reach fifty, raise his head slightly, and look up. He stood cautiously and stared up the road. He turned and stared down it. Then he picked up his purse and retreated back the way he came.

''He's a chatterer,'' Kasane managed to gasp through her laughter. ''A bell on the end of a pole.''

Cat and Kasane added pebbles to the piles at Jizō's stubby bare feet. They each pressed their palms together in front of their faces, bowed low, and prayed to the smiling god for protection on the dark road across the mountain. Then, laughing softly, they continued their journey.

CHAPTER 51
BOILS AND TUMORS

Cat and Kasane reached Mitsuke when everything was still tightly shuttered against the eleventh-month wind and the night. With their travel cloaks blowing about their legs, they limped wearily down the empty main street. They sat on a pile of poles and watched the sky lighten and the mist rise from the fast-flowing Tenryu River.

Cat had wanted to cross the river, but a pack driver had already hired the only ferryman awake. Cat could see that loading and ferrying the horses two by two would take a long time. Besides, Kasane was nodding where she sat, and she had begun limping badly the last *ri*.

Cat put an arm around Kasane's waist. She helped her back to the lane that crossed a red-painted bridge over a ditch, then meandered off between the hedges of bush clover through the dark forest. Faded characters on a small wooden sign promised an inn at the end of the lane.

A servant was just opening the shutters. In the dawn's light the place seemed secluded and tranquil. Cat and Kasane were grateful for the tiny, cluttered room they were given.

The tranquillity didn't last long. The roosters were the first to shatter the silence, then the wood seller with her shrill, monotonous song. A rice huller started up somewhere with a low, hollow thud that vibrated the floor and walls like a heartbeat. Only thin sliding screens divided Cat and Kasane's room from the inn's usual morning exuberance.

Most of the overnight guests were preparing to leave, and they were discussing the packing arrangements with their servants. The *kago* bearers and porters laughed loudly outside.

Horses neighed. A shrill quarrel erupted in the kitchen, where pots and tubs and ladles rattled as though a minor tremor had settled there on a semipermanent basis. A baby was crying, and someone was beating a hand drum and chanting his morning devotions at full volume.

The proprietress was a big woman with a capacious blue apron. She had tied back the wide sleeves of her *kimono*. She had wrapped a thin blue towel around her hair. She followed the maids around, shouting instructions and remonstrances at them as they shook and flailed the bedding. Over it all was the steady *patta, patta, patta* of paper-strip dusters against the panes of the wall screens.

Cat wasn't used to the noise necessary to running a large household. The rooms where she and her mother had slept had always been serene. She had wakened most mornings to the soft rustle of the servants' robes and *tabi* socks, to the song of birds in the plum tree outside her veranda, and to the splash of water falling into the carp pond.

"Don't grasp the brush as though it were a rice mortar." Cat rolled over so her back was to Kasane. She covered her head with the thin quilt that was molting gray cotton wadding, and she tried to ignore the cacophony. "Hold it lightly between your thumb and first two fingers," she added. "Keep your wrist limber. Move the brush from your elbow."

Kasane continued covering the cheap sheet of paper with tiny black characters of the *hiragana* syllabary. When she came to the left-hand side she began again, filling in the spaces from right to left, top to bottom.

She had found the letter from Traveler on the temple message board. She was composing a reply. Even though she was as exhausted as Cat, even though her remaining pair of straw sandals, like Cat's, was in tatters and she had walked the last *ri* limping with the pain in her ankle, love was an elixir. She was wide awake. She cheerfully offered to keep watch while Cat slept.

More than anything, Cat wanted to sleep. She had crossed the raging Oi River and come eleven and a half *ri* since the previous morning. She had walked all night to do it.

Cat felt disoriented in time as well as in place. The rhythm of her life had been disrupted. She was trying to sleep while the world went about its business. Finally exhaustion overcame the uproar. She slept for hours.

She awoke to a man's voice that sounded as though its owner were at her bedside.

"In this age work and ingenuity don't count. Only money makes more money." The man was in the next room. He spoke with a thick Ōsaka accent.

A pair of maids tittered. Men's voices growled in agreement. The proprietress, suddenly demure, murmured in admiration of her wealthy, uncultured guest.

Cat reached from under the quilt and found the staff she had left by the lumpy pallet. Kasane was asleep on her own bed. The paper on which she had been practicing still lay on the low writing stand. It was black. When she filled it she had written over the previous characters, until they could only be distinguished by the shininess of the wet ink.

"One press of my seal can open chests of gold," the merchant said.

Cat relaxed. She laid her head back on the hard cylindrical cushion of the pillow stand and closed her eyes. In the House of the Perfumed Lotus she had heard this sort of boasting many times. The women listened dewy-eyed until such guests left. Then they bet on how long the wastrels would take to spill their fortunes with a winnowing fan in the pleasure districts. They joked about how soon the men would be reduced to cooking their millet gruel over a fire of broken chopsticks and fingernail parings.

Cat glanced out the round window at the roof. She assessed the angle of shadow on the thatch and sagging eaves and bamboo gutters where weeds had sprouted. She realized she must have slept most of the day away. The house was quieter now. Kasane was breathing evenly. Her face was young and peaceful in sleep. Cat lay still, floating in the sluggish river of her exhaustion.

"I have my sources of private rice, you know." The merchant in the next room lowered his voice conspiratorially, although it was still perfectly audible. "I'm on my way back from the tenth-month distribution in Edo. I have warrants to collect for three lords and seventy-two *samurai*." He tapped the mouthpiece of his brass pipe on a locked document box.

Rats and rice brokers multiply at harvest time, Cat thought.

She knew what he was. In the early days of the Tokugawa family's rule, officials had collected their own rice stipend. But as peace continued and the bureaucracy grew, lowly government positions were filled by low-ranking *samurai* or *rōnin*. Unable to live on their meager annual salaries of twenty *koku* or less, they borrowed from the merchants against the three yearly distributions. They gave them warrants to collect the rice on their behalf, thus saving themselves the trouble and indignity of waiting in line.

Cat remembered them, the threadbare warriors, waiting in the tea houses near the government storehouses. With ivory toothpicks they probed meditatively between their teeth as though they had just eaten, when in fact they hadn't money to buy bean paste or a bowl of pickled vegetables.

Government officials were assigned payment dates according to rank or, for those of equal standing, by lottery. The system was so complex, the men often waited for days before the broker brought them the monetary equivalent of their rice allotment. After the go-between subtracted his fees and commission, as well as the amount of the original debt and its exorbitant interest, his clients were usually indigent again.

"What use are the *samurai* and their arts of war?" Food had been served in a hollow clatter of lacquered bowls and cups and trays. The merchant talked with his mouth full. "Their swords are only good for paring radishes. Their skill with the *naginata* might scare off the occasional burglar. They could shoot their cats with arrows for stealing their fish."

He slurped his soup loudly as everyone laughed politely at his wit. "The *daimyō* owe a hundred times more money than exists in the country. They do no work, yet their retainers swagger through the streets as though they owned even the maggots in the piles of horse dung."

Once—only days ago, in fact—Cat would have slammed aside the sliding screen and served him up a bitter course of her fury. Now she almost smiled. He was his own punishment. All the money in the country wouldn't expand his soul or make him a whit less vulgar.

She remembered what her father had told her. *"Others deal in visible things,"* he had said. *"We deal in the invisible. The only business of the* bushi, *the warrior, is to maintain 'rightness.' If we didn't exist, right would disappear, the sense of shame would be lost, and injustice would prevail."*

"The *rōnin* are the worst." The proprietress sounded as though she had been tasting some of her own *sake*.

"The *rōnin* are a plague in the country," someone agreed.

"Take Asano's man, the coward Oishi, for example." The rice broker sucked his teeth and belched. "He's so cautious he carries a lantern in daytime."

Everyone in the next room laughed. Cat stiffened. The fact that Oishi hadn't registered a vendetta had made him the object of ridicule from one end of the country to the other.

"Last month, at the hour of the Tiger, I was returning from the House of the Maple Leaf," the broker continued.

"Where is that?" asked the proprietress.

"Shimabara. Kyōto's paradise." He must have leered because the maids giggled again. "There by the light of my servant's lantern I saw Oishi lying in the road."

"Was he hurt?" the proprietress asked.

"He was drunk. He was covered with his own vomit and singing abominably."

"Disgraceful."

" 'You're a boneless man,' I said to him. He only babbled stupidly. I was so disgusted I kicked him. He didn't move. So I spat on him. I couldn't be bothered circling around him. I stepped on his hand and continued on my way. I may only be a wretched townsman, but I have more heart than Asano's councilor."

The screen slid open next door. "Does anyone want tobacco or tooth powder?" a youthful voice said. "I have here the finest nose papers from my master's shop on High Street."

The conversation turned to the clerk's selection of wares, but Cat didn't hear it. She lay with her eyes closed. A hot tear ran down her cheek, and sorrow burned inside her.

Kasane reached across the *tatami* between the pallets and took Cat's hand. She rested her upper body's weight on one elbow, leaned close, and whispered, "Pay no attention to him, mistress. Like boils and tumors, tactless people don't care where they appear." Kasane's hand was warm and callused and strong. "Oishi-sama will help you," she whispered.

CHAPTER 52
A STONE BOAT

Just inside the big gate of Mitsuke's main temple, the priests had set up a long counter for feeding the hordes of young pilgrims. Three men were heating mason's trowels over a brazier until they glowed red. Then they used them to scorch parboiled fish laid out on planks. Two other men used rakes to stir vegetables in a huge tub. Hungry pilgrims swarmed around them or squatted on their heels while they ate.

With his knees spread, a man sat on a stool under the wide eaves of the temple gate. He had stuck a bamboo pole into the ground next to him. The pole sported a vertical cloth banner with a comic picture of Daikoku, the plump, smiling god of wealth, painted on it.

"Personal finances are my specialty," he informed the throng of people passing in and out the gate.

At first glance the financial adviser seemed prosperous enough, but Hanshiro noted that his topknot smelled of an inferior grade of hair oil. The collar of his yellow-and-white-checked robe and the hems of his black *hakama* were almost imperceptibly frayed. His black camlet jacket displayed the crest of no particular clan. Hanshiro suspected that inside it and the robe was the rental shop's cipher embroidered in white cotton floss. Even the *inro*, the nested medicine box suspended from his sash, was the cheap type rented at ten *mon* a week.

To get Hanshiro's attention the adviser slid the back of the long nail of his middle finger across his abacus, producing a clicking whir like insects in an autumn meadow at night.

"You too can hear the crickets' song of wealth, honorable sir," he said. "My rates are reasonable. If money is troubling you, let's talk it over. I can help you sort it all out."

Hanshiro ignored him. He stared at the letter pinned to the temple gate among the prayers and messages and petitions. He pulled one hand back through his wide sleeve and inside his jacket. He poked it up through the neck opening and rubbed the stubble on his chin. He had made a decision about the letter, but it was troubling him.

"*Kamiko-rōnin,*" the adviser muttered contemptuously. "Paper-clothing drifter. Pauper."

Hanshiro turned his head to flash him a brief, wolfish smile from under his wide-brimmed rush hat. "The general of a defeated army should not talk tactics," he said softly.

He carefully unpinned the letter and tucked it between the overlapping front flaps of his jacket, under his sash. He strode through the crowd toward a small tea house in the licensed quarter that had sprung up to serve the more secular needs of temple visitors. Devils live in front of the temple gate, as the old saying went.

He was in no hurry. The farmer to whom this letter was addressed was at least half a day behind him and more likely two or three days. If Hanshiro noticed the pair of rough-looking men who followed him at a distance, he gave no indication.

The children's religious fervor had spread to the adults. Parents were closing their houses and setting out after their offspring. Masters were laying down their account books and tools and following their clerks and apprentices. The tea shop, like all the restaurants in Mitsuke, was packed with pilgrims.

The racks for the customers' sandals and *geta* and swords were full. Footwear was stacked on the packed earth of the entryway. The management had run out of wooden redemption tickets for them and was using chips of bamboo with numbers hastily painted on them.

Steam rose in warm, moist clouds from the big kettles on the clay stoves. The aroma of a vat of cooked rice competed with the smell of roasted eel. The waitresses glistened with perspiration even though the entire front of the house was open to the winter air.

The waitresses all wore identical blue aprons, robes the deep blue of a winter's night sky, and wide yellow headbands charmingly tied in mannish style above their right ears. They shrilled their customers' orders at the harried cooks. Their wooden *geta* made a cheerful din as they hurried back and forth along the bare earth runways between the raised platforms where the customers sat.

An extra silver piece rented Hanshiro a tiny room to himself in the wing at the rear of the garden. At night the rooms there served for assignations with courtesans from the House of the Trout next door. Now they offered solitude to customers willing to pay for it.

Hanshiro had made no move to surrender his long blade so it could be hung with the others at the entryway. And no one had dared ask him for it. The tea shop's owner had been relieved to usher him and his swords out of sight.

Hanshiro looked around the tiny room. Several of the paper panes in the sliding screens were ripped. The high shelf to the gods was dusty. The picture scroll in the alcove was faded. But the room opened onto a corner of the garden, and the embers in the firewell gave off a comforting warmth. Hanshiro took his long-sword from his sash and sat cross-legged on the *tatami* next to the well. He laid the sword on a silk cloth at his right side with the honed edge facing outward. He put Cat's letter next to it.

The kneeling waitress slid open the paper wall panel facing the garden. She stood, carried in the footed tray, knelt, and set it down. "Eels eaten on the Ox's day are good for your health." She fanned the embers and added a few pieces of charcoal. Then she poured a cup of tea, bowed, and retreated, sliding the door closed behind her.

Hanshiro left the letter on the floor, a mute and puzzling companion for his meal. He ate three steaming helpings of rice from the large covered dish and three skewers of eel grilled with sweet soy sauce to a dark, glossy brown.

When he poured the last of the tea into his rice bowl, the water was almost clear from passing so often through the leaves. He stirred the remaining few grains of rice into it and drank it. He wiped his mouth and fingers with one of the paper napkins in his wallet, folded the napkin into a tiny packet, and slipped it into his sleeve.

Only then did he pick up the letter and hold it in his big, square hands. The ideograms that spelled "To Traveler" had been drawn by a calm hand. Even after all Lady Asano had been through, she betrayed no fear or excitement in the subtleties of the strokes that made each character.

Hanshiro closed his eyes, concentrating all his senses into the tips of his fingers. He imagined the warmth of Lady Asano's touch on the paper. He felt himself melt into her body as she wrote. For an instant he looked out from her eyes. His hands were shaking when he unfolded it.

He had rationalized that reading the letter would lead him quickly to Lady Asano so he could protect her from her enemies; but he felt like a thief. He felt like an impotent man who pays to watch from behind a screen the pillowing of others. His face grew hot as he read what Cat had written.

> Oh, to be the moon
> shining in the still of night
> On my lover's bed.

And then, "Prayers to Inari. The Floating Weed."

He understood the message in "Prayers to Inari, the Rice God," but the poem seemed to be no more than the insipid peasant verse it was. Was she indeed carrying on a flirtation with a farmer? Had grief driven her mad? Had he misjudged her completely?

He carefully refolded the letter and retied it in the flat knot. A woman would detect the tampering immediately, but Hanshiro was sure Traveler wouldn't notice.

When he heard the whispers in the next room, they were a welcome diversion. He had expected the thieves to wait until he stopped for the night and was asleep, but they looked the type to be short of patience as well as cunning.

He pretended to study the refolded letter as he listened. He distinguished at least five voices. The two who had been eyeing his swords since he'd entered the outskirts of Mitsuke were *machi yakko*, town underlings. They were almost certainly intent on illicit gain. Each carried a single sword of his own. Hanshiro assumed their accomplices did, too.

As a rule, swords were paid for not by quality or decoration, but by the inch. Kanesada blades were another matter, however. The price these thieves could receive for Hanshiro's matched pair would either support their families for life or make quite an impression at the brothels and card games for a much shorter time.

While Hanshiro waited for the whispering to stop, he thought of *sensei*, his teacher. He remembered him as he had last seen him, silhouetted by the sun shining through the paper screen of the tiny tea house in his garden. That was the day *sensei* had given Hanshiro the swords.

They both had known that the tea ceremony would be the last time they would see each other, yet neither had spoken of parting. And although *sensei* had intended to award a certificate of mastery to Hanshiro, he made no comment about his favorite student's decision to leave.

"The sword of the New Shadow school is the sword that gives life." *Sensei* had spoken in his usual soft voice. He had looked with affection at the blades resting on their low ebony stand. They had shone softly in the sunlight filtering through the paper screens. *"Its purpose is defense, not offense,"* *sensei* had continued. *"The New Shadow school aims not to slash, not to take, not to win, not to lose."*

Sensei had always seemed so old, possessed of a wisdom that could only have come from a long life. Hanshiro realized with a start that twenty-three years ago, when he had become *sensei*'s disciple, the master had only been as old as Hanshiro was now.

Two of the men next door raised their voices as though in

argument. Hanshiro knew the others were using the noise to cover their approach. He sensed the change in the pressure of air in his room as they lifted a panel from its tracks behind him and slid it silently open. He felt them watching him. He had met their sort before. He knew they were likely to be crude but vicious fighters.

As he sat, Hanshiro wove his hands through the intricacies of the nine-symbols-cutting, the esoteric hand signs affected by *ninja*, or ''warrior wizards.'' He knew it would impress them. Then he picked up the three slender skewers that had held the grilled eel and tossed them into the air. With a move too fast for the eye to follow, he drew the short-sword from the scabbard in his sash and struck. The skewers dropped to the *tatami*, each in two pieces, sliced lengthwise. He gathered the six pieces, threw them up, and cut each one in half as they fell.

He solemnly replaced his sword in the sheath. He rested his hands on his thighs with his elbows out and continued staring straight ahead while the men next door left quietly and quickly.

Yagyū Muneyoshi, the founder of the New Shadow school, had written more than a hundred poems about being a swordsman. As Hanshiro thought about Cat, he remembered the one that seemed most appropriate.

> Though I may win fights with a sword
> I'm but a stone boat on the sea called life.

When he left the inn he returned to the temple and replaced the letter exactly where he had found it. Then he went to the transport office. He had to dicker and cajole and pay a high price, but he managed to rent a horse without a postboy to lead it at a walk. He mounted and set off at a brisk canter for Futagawa and the famous temple to Inari.

CHAPTER 53
CLOUDS OF BEWILDERMENT

Because Cat and Kasane started from Mitsuke late in the afternoon, the hour of the Dog was half over by the time they were approaching Maisaka. Cat could see the lanterns of travelers, though. They were taking advantage of the level terrain and hurrying to reach the ferry at the treacherous stretch of water called Now Broken.

When she reached a fairly deserted area of the highway, Cat showed Kasane the "floating step." The courtesans had originally used it, but it had caught on among women of fashion in both capitals. Cat was still trying to teach Kasane the various arts of attracting a man. She was hoping Kasane's suitor would become so taken with her that he would lure her away from Cat's dangerous company.

"Turn your body like this." Cat swiveled slightly at the waist. "Move your feet as though you're kicking sand with your toes."

Kasane laughed behind her sleeve as she minced along. Cat put her hands on Kasane's shoulders and turned them a bit more.

"Stand as though you're about to glance back over your shoulder at your lover," she said. "Your body should express your melancholy at leaving him. Or you can look as though you're inviting him to follow you." Cat stood back to assess the effect. "It's more effective if you're wearing *geta*."

The hollow *whap* of a hand drum interrupted them. It was being played by a woman who stood near a red *torii* gate leading to a small Shintō shrine.

"Stop here. Stop here," she called. "Learn what the Love-Knowing Bird predicts for your future." She rattled a narrow wooden box with a hole at one end. "All my fortunes concern love."

Kasane slowed as she passed and glanced wistfully back over her shoulder. Cat recognized the look. Diviners lined the steps of every temple and shrine and haunted most street corners.

336

From time to time Cat herself had been tempted to pay for a glimpse at fate's plans.

Cat held out a ten-*mon* piece. The woman took it, drew her hand into her wide sleeve, and deposited it. Then she shook the box until a narrow strip of bamboo slid from the hole.

Kasane pulled it out and read the number painted on it. "Sixty-four."

Cat sighed. The number was an unlucky one. Cat feared Kasane was in for disappointment. The woman searched through her basket of paper fortunes until she found one, folded lengthwise, with "sixty-four" written on it.

Kasane unfolded it, but all she could see was the shadowy hint of a drawing.

"The ink is invisible until you hold it up against the light." The woman held out her lantern.

"Look!" Kasane moved aside so Cat could see the characters emerging, pale and spidery, next to the darkening picture of a crudely drawn bird.

" 'The person who draws this paper,' " Kasane read, " 'let that one live by the heavenly law and worship the blessed Kannon. As for love, the one desired is betrothed.' " Kasane looked at Cat, alarm and despair in her eyes.

Cat started to tell her that the woman was a fraud, that her foolish fortunes meant nothing. But she thought better of it. She gave the woman another ten-*mon* coin. "Try another, elder sister." She smiled at Kasane, who looked as though she feared the bamboo marker would sting her.

Cat noticed that the woman tilted the box so a bamboo slip from the other side fell out. Cat was sure the box had a partition inside, separating the good from the bad. She was also sure the diviner regularly gave her customers a bad fortune first. Few people would walk away without trying for a better one.

" 'Ninety-nine.' " Kasane looked at Cat for reassurance. Cat smiled. Ninety-nine was propitious.

" 'The person who draws this paper,' " Kasane read, " 'let that one worship the gods of prosperity. If anything is lost, it will be found. If one is sick, recovery is certain. If one loves, she will win the affection of her beloved.' "

Kasane beamed as Cat steered her back onto the road. The drumming took up again behind them.

"Ei-sassa, ei-sassa, ei-sassa." A mail carrier trotted by chanting in rhythm to his footsteps. As usual, Kasane stared after him longingly. Maybe he was the one carrying her lover's

next letter to Futagawa. *"Ei-korya, sassa, sassa."* He disappeared into the darkness.

"Have you thought about what you'll do if you find Traveler himself at the temple gate instead of just his sentiments?"

"No, mistress." Kasane blushed. "The petty affairs of such a one as I merit no thought until you've found Oishi-sama. Until the great wrong done your father is avenged."

"Do you love him?"

Kasane blushed a deeper crimson and ducked behind her sleeve. "I don't know," she murmured.

"What if he turns out to be a disastrous character?"

"It's impertinent of me to disagree, mistress, but he couldn't. His poems are so heartfelt."

"I don't mean to be cruel, elder sister, but the poems of men are usually prompted by a part of them that's quite distant from their hearts."

"A flute."

Cat laughed. "Yes, the part that rules them resembles a flute, but they prefer to have someone else play it for them."

Then Cat heard the music. The flute player's only audience was an old man with a pilgrim's staff, bell, and pack and a small satchel of food around his neck. The two of them were standing next to a roadside shrine under a few gnarled pines on a small knoll. Behind the trees stretched rice paddies.

"Why is he playing in the dark?" Kasane asked.

"Night and day are the same to him," Cat whispered. "He's blind."

The flute player finished his piece and slid the flute into a sack.

"There's no rush to reach Maisaka," he said.

Cat almost jumped when he spoke to her. His sightless eyes stared straight at her.

"Why?" she asked.

"They're all running around as if their heads were on fire."

The musician was a young man with a shaved head. He was dressed in a faded *hakama* and robe and a torn black coat of wadded cotton. He chuckled. "A delegation of red-haired barbarians is on its way to the Eastern Capital and has reached Maisaka. The populace is in a frenzy to catch a glimpse of them. And others are possessed by Ise fever." He took his fan and a chopstick from his sash. "Bide a while and hear the story of Yoshitsune and Benkei at the barrier."

"Clearly we were born at an auspicious hour," the old pilgrim said. "To partake of such an august talent as yours."

The old man's shabby paper robe and cloak were covered with dust. His tiny topknot was thin and gray. He stood with a rapturous look on his face while the minstrel chanted, marking the rhythm of his lay by scratching the chopstick across the ribs of the fan. Cat waited politely, and Kasane listened spellbound.

When the minstrel finished Cat bowed and put paper-wrapped coppers into his bowl. The old pilgrim did the same.

"I give thanks that destiny has allowed us the privilege of hearing you, honorable sir," he said. Then he hurried after Cat and Kasane.

"Are you pious folk bound for the Sun Goddess's holy shrine?"

"Yes," Cat answered.

"Ah, how fine! So are we." He smiled brightly at them.

Kasane looked around for the old man's companion but saw no one. Cat assumed he was possessed of a gentle madness.

"For thirty-eight years my wife and I would go arm in arm to look at the cherry trees growing on the embankment near our humble house." He seemed serenely unembarrassed by this self-indulgent talk of affection for the woman he had married. For him, shame had indeed been left behind when he traveled. "We sat under the trees at sunset and dreamed of visiting the sacred shrine.

"My wife collected discarded mussel shells and sold them at the lime kiln. She saved in a tea canister the coppers she earned. At planting time I cleaned the other farmers' ditches. I earned a copper for every six feet cleared. I added the coins to the canister. Then, when the children were grown, my dear wife became ill. And so we had to postpone the pilgrimage until now."

His eyes sparkled in the moonlight. "But what a marvelous journey it's been for us. We've enjoyed sitting in the shade of a pine and opening our little tub of *sake*. We watch the pilgrims go by singing and ringing their bells, *tan, tan, tan*."

"Excuse my rudeness, sir." Kasane blurted it out before Cat could nudge her into silence. Cat had noticed the brocade bag hanging around his neck. It was the kind that usually contained wooden mortuary tablets. "Is your wife waiting for you in Maisaka?"

"My wife is here, dear child." He held up the stoppered bamboo tube that hung on a cord next to the bag. "When we have seen the shrine of the Heaven-Shining-Great-August-Deity together, we'll go to Mount Koya. I'll beseech the monks there to bury her ashes'' —he tapped the bamboo tube—''and add her memory to the prayers they raise from the altars. The Buddhas will usher her spirit into the bliss of Amida's Pure Land.''

''My sister and I would be honored by your company and that of your wife,'' Cat said.

The blind musician had been right. Maisaka was in chaos. All the lodgings were full. Travelers' belongings filled the court-yards and overflowed into the streets. The crowd, however, was concentrated around the inn where the delegation of Dutch traders was staying.

Normally the folk who lived along the Tōkaidō were too worldly to become excited about the unusual. The road, after all, provided a daily parade of the unusual. Many people had seen the two elephants that passed through a decade ago, with all the pomp and status of the most powerful *daimyō*.

The red-haired foreigners traveled the road twice a year on their way to and from Edo and their audience with the *shōgun*. But now Maisaka was filled with simple pilgrims from the out-lying hamlets and from the villages between the official post stations. To make matters worse, a *sake* shortage had caused a shortage of goodwill as well.

The Dutch traveled in palanquins that were carried into the wide entryways of the first-class inns before unloading so the occupants couldn't be seen from the street. The foreigners were forbidden by law to show themselves once they stopped for the night. But that didn't stop the populace from trying to see them.

In spite of the police's efforts to disperse them, people had climbed onto the roofs of the buildings around the Dutchmen's inn. Cat and Kasane and the old pilgrim stopped to listen to an altercation between a policeman and a group of indignant farmers.

''Our miserable lives will pass without once seeing a foreign devil,'' a woman shouted. ''It's most unkind of you to keep this great sight to yourself.''

The argument was interrupted by a loud crash and screams. A roof had collapsed under the weight of the people on top of it. The owners of the other shops and houses ran into the street, shouting pleas and threats to those on their own roofs. Cat and her companions hurried through the turmoil.

''My cousin's house is not far,'' the old man said. ''It's on the old road around the bay. It's a humble place, but you can stay there with me tonight. Walking around is better for the young lady anyway. Crossing this particular stretch of water is bad luck for marriages.''

Cat was quite willing to avoid the ferry. She feared that Kira's men might be watching for her there. She didn't realize that as she traveled farther from Edo their threat lessened. Kira had more difficulty communicating with them. The description of Cat grew more and more vague with time and distance. The men who had survived earlier encounters with her had exaggerated the circumstances until it was impossible to say what they had been.

Those in the fight at the *kabuki* performance in Kambara said Lady Asano had a gang of fierce swordsmen with her. The man who lived through the attack at Satta Pass wrote in his report that she was defended by a spear player the size and ferocity of Benkei and a shrieking female demon in the shape of a green ball of fire.

Kira had come to distrust all the messages he received from his retainers on the road. Besides, he had troubles of a much more serious nature than a runaway woman. The rumors in Edo of Cat's escape and flight had been replaced by gossip of a revenge plot against him. Kira stayed behind the walls of his mansion and called back most of the men he had sent after her. He kept secret the fact that many of them had returned in casket tubs slung from poles and carried by porters. The casualties confirmed his belief that Lady Asano wasn't acting alone and that her father's retainers were finally rising against him.

Halfway through the hour of the Boar, Cat and Kasane and the pilgrim came to a double row of houses perched on a ledge between the side of a hill and the river below. The single street through the hamlet was so narrow, the eaves almost met over it. No lights shone from the open spaces between the mud-plastered walls and the roofs. Several houses were propped up with poles that extended into the narrow roadway, and the three travelers had to pick their way around them.

The pilgrim's cousin's house was the most prosperous of the lot. He pounded on the shutters and called to those inside. Then the three of them stood among the large cylindrical open-weave baskets in the darkness under the eaves and waited. They could hear voices and footsteps inside, but they also heard a faint rustling and creaking much closer.

"Ma!" Kasane jumped and squealed and grabbed Cat's arm. "Something touched me."

"Cormorants," the old pilgrim said. "My cousin fishes with them."

The storm shutter slid open with a loud squeal. When a lantern's light shone on the baskets with their hinged wooden lids, the birds inside stirred and muttered. They poked their bills through the weave and nattered for fish.

The house was a single room occupied by the aged cousin and his wife, their son, daughter-in-law, and three grandchildren. They moved to make room for Cat and Kasane and the pilgrim. Kasane piled their sleeping mats one on top of the other, and she and Cat lay curled together for warmth. Cat could feel Kasane shaking.

"Are you cold, elder sister?" Cat whispered.

"No." Kasane snuffled. She hesitated before giving in to a personal confession. "This house reminds me of the one where I used to live."

Cat held her close to comfort her. She lay awake after Kasane finally cried herself to sleep and looked up at the bunches of long white radishes hanging like ghostly, rat-gnawed stalactites from rafters black and shiny with soot. She was still awake when the family's questions and conversation ceased and the room was filled with the sound of heavy breathing.

She heard a low shudder nearby.

"Grandfather," she whispered, "are you ill?"

The old man let out a long, tremulous sigh. "Once I stepped on my dead wife's comb," the old pilgrim murmured. "The chill of it under my bare heel pierced my heart. At night she used to comb her hair with it."

"You know as I . . ." Cat softly recited the ancient poem:

> The nature of this illusory world,
>   How nothing stays—
> Endeavor to be brave and stalwart,
> Do not wear out that heart in grief.

But the old man lay awake a long time, stifling quiet sobs in the crook of his arm. Cat lay awake, too, with tears running silently down her cheeks. The weight of sorrow seemed enough to wear out her heart. She cried for herself and for her parents and for Kasane, an exile, too. And even though she knew her mother's faithful servants were only living out their *karma*, she cried for them, turned out into the world with neither rice nor protector. She cried for Oishi Kuranosuke, the once proud warrior lying in the gutter. And for his abandoned wife and children.

She wondered what Musashi would have had to say about the tears. Would he have considered them clouds of bewilderment? *When your spirit is not in the least clouded*, he wrote. *When the clouds of bewilderment clear away, there is the true void. In the void is virtue and no evil.* And no tears, she thought.

Cat stiffened once when a horse's hooves echoed between the walls of the houses lining the hamlet's only street. The sound roused the cormorants, which clucked and murmured and shook themselves restlessly. As the hoofbeats faded Cat slipped, finally, into sad dreams, and Hanshiro continued on through the night, toward Futagawa.

CHAPTER 54

ONE DAY A THOUSAND AUTUMNS

Hanshiro's new clothes hung over a lacquered rack in the room next to the bathing area of Futagawa's public bathhouse. The two side sections of the rack were hinged to stand, as a sheet of paper will stand if folded in half vertically. The clothes were draped to form a sort of tent over the brass incense pot that squatted in the angle. From its openwork lid issued clouds of aromatic sandalwood smoke to perfume the silk undershirt, the black-and-white tile-design wadded-silk *kimono*, and the formal black *hakama*, and *haori* jacket.

Hanshiro had bought the clothes after he decided to pledge himself to Lady Asano's cause. They were the first such he had had in fifteen years. To buy them he had pawned his great grandfather's cloisonné medicine case and, for the first time in his life, borrowed from a money lender. While rain held him up he had had his family's crest, a graceful spray of wisteria bent in a circle, embroidered in gold on the *haori*.

The new loincloth, black silk waist cord, and stiff red sash lay folded on a high-rimmed clothing tray. On the raised floor of the alcove, below a scroll painting of the Amida waterfall, Hanshiro's swords rested on a low stand. Hanshiro himself was still in the steam-filled room that housed the cypress tub, but he had left the sliding door panel open so he could keep an eye on his swords.

From the neck down his skin was bright red. The line where the blush began was as sharp as if bounded by a thread. It marked where the scalding water had reached while he soaked. His body still tingled from the scouring the bath attendants had given it with loofah pads before he had climbed into the tub.

The priests said bathing symbolized the scrubbing away of evil. It cleansed the soul as well as the body. But Hanshiro had seen the latest letter to Cat posted at the shrine to Inari, the Rice God. He was wishing he could wash away lust and longing and jealousy as easily as he had washed away the dust of the road.

With one bare leg tucked under him and the other extended, he sat naked on a large cloth on the damp, polished boards of the bathhouse. One of the attendants had just finished cutting and polishing his fingernails. Now her shiny, triple chignon was bobbing over his toenails. Her elbow was a blur as she buffed them vigorously with pumice, then wood sorrel. Her other hand massaged his foot sensuously as she held it.

A second woman knelt behind him. She had slipped her arms out of her cotton bath robe so that it hung around the sash at her waist. She had trimmed his sidelocks and rubbed fragrant camellia oil into his long black hair and was arranging it in a topknot.

With one hand she held the thick hank so tightly that it pulled at the skin of Hanshiro's temples. She leaned forward, brushing her bare breasts slowly along his neck and shoulders as she reached for a flat paper cord. She tickled his ear with the cord on the way back.

Her teasing roused the desired response in him. He tried to redirect his restive thoughts, but for an instant the breasts were Cat's. The cord brushing his earlobe was Cat's tongue.

A third woman entered with more tobacco for the canister on the wooden tray at Hanshiro's side. A fourth arrived with tea.

"*Ma!*" The tea server regarded Hanshiro's crotch admiringly as she fanned the coals in the portable earthenware brazier. "A warrior of the school of the one-inch advantage."

The other three burst into gales of laughter. Musashi had written that those who sought to own swords longer than their opponents', to have the one-inch advantage, were deluded. These four might have disagreed with his premise.

" 'Five feet of blade lose to one inch of tongue.' " Hanshiro smiled at them roguishly. "I surrender to your wit."

"Put away your sword, then," giggled the manicurist. "I know of a snug scabbard."

The hairdresser finished and held up a pair of mirrors so Hanshiro could see the full effect of her work. He grunted his approval.

It didn't occur to Hanshiro to wonder if he was handsome. He only wanted to be presentable. Looking shabby when he offered his sword to Lady Asano would have been shameful. Just as carnal thoughts of her were shameful. And weakness besides.

The hairdresser began massaging Hanshiro's neck and shoulders. The manicurist looked up coquettishly from his foot. Her face was a mask of white powder.

"He has two of the three sacred treasures," she said. "The jewels and the sword."

" 'In the Floating World,' " Hanshiro recited, " 'the way of the warrior cannot conquer.' "

"A brilliant versifier, too!" The manicurist finished her task with a flourish. Hanshiro's neatly trimmed nails glowed.

She added water to the ink stone on the low writing stand. Then she slipped her robe off her shoulders and presented him with her plump, mottled back. The powdery white paste of her makeup formed a neat crescent, a chalky moon under her neck and shoulders. Her skin was pocked with *moxa* scars.

"Why don't you inscribe the poem using the implement that accompanied you into this fleeting world?" She pursed her red-painted lips and looked seductively over her shoulder. "It would rival Ikkyu's broom."

The others laughed behind their sleeves and tapped her playfully with their fans. Ikkyu had been known for using a broom to paint enormous characters.

To everyone's disappointment Hanshiro used the bamboo brush instead as he solemnly painted the poem onto her back. While the others fanned the ink dry, they exclaimed over the strength and refinement of Hanshiro's calligraphy. They argued about which of the six great calligraphers his hand most resembled.

Hanshiro knew this was professional gaiety. It was an old, old game of flirtatious pun and sexual ambiguity. It was a form of verbal fencing in which Hanshiro had indulged more times than he could remember.

He was amused by the fact that these women recognized him as a dangerous man, but they didn't fear him. They were like the teasing magpie that knew it was safe from the tiger. He also sensed a genuine longing in their banter.

Under the bathhouse attendants' hands, Hanshiro had cleaned up quite nicely. Beneath the dust and whisker stubble, the power in the set of his jaw excited the women. They were drawn to the ferocious sensuality of his angular cheekbones and his dark, remote eyes. Hanshiro had the eyes of a tiger in a cave.

Even these *jigoku-onna*, these bathhouse-hell-women, recognized the worldly quality that was called *sui* in the pleasure districts. In Hanshiro *sui* was more than mere sophistication. It was elegance. It was the artless grace of a wild animal.

The women were also responding to something subtler still. They could not have defined it, but they sensed in him a rare, pensive sort of sympathy. Hanshiro thought about their kind more than they would have supposed. He pitied them as caged birds who feigned their songs of passion in the night. He could not change their fate, but he could ease their lot with a jest and a kind word.

He bowed gallantly, lower than he needed to, but not low enough to risk disdain. "Both my heart and my insignificant sword of flesh regret that duty summons me from your luminous presence."

"We'll dress you, then." They rose like a flock of wagtails startled into sudden flight and headed for the room where his clothes were.

"Please." He knew he was about to offend them. "To ready the spirit as well as the body, I must not be disturbed. But if you would move my clothing to the upstairs room facing the street, I would be grateful."

It was midmorning. There were no other customers yet, and the prospect of the long afternoon was burdensome. The women had been looking forward to spending it in Hanshiro's company, but they heard the unspoken command in his request. They bowed quietly, picked up the tea things and the food trays, and left in a muffled patter of bare feet on glossy boards.

Hanshiro put on a cotton robe and tied it with a sash set low on his hips. Then he bowed to his swords and picked them up. He walked up the narrow staircase to the room where the attendants had taken his clothes. He carefully set his swords and their stand in the alcove and slid the door panel closed behind him.

He dressed with as much care as if he were going into battle. Before the day ended he would offer his fealty, his life, and his sword, which was his soul, to Lady Asano. *One day a thousand autumns,* he thought, *when spent in anticipation.*

The frivolity with the bathhouse attendants hadn't distracted Hanshiro. Over the years he had developed the released mind that his *sensei* likened to an empty gourd floating in water. If touched, the gourd slipped aside. By its nature it evaded being grasped. So it was with the mind of someone who perceived everything but lingered on nothing.

When he finished dressing, Hanshiro opened the outer screen and took his swords onto the balcony. He knelt on the boards and assumed the formal position, sitting back on his crossed ankles. While he polished the swords he could watch-without-watching the busy street below and the temple gate on the other side of it. He would know when a certain handsome boy and his sister arrived.

Holding the blade with a silk cloth, he placed his short-sword in front of him and bowed to it. He moved even more deliberately than usual to still the emotions churning inside him. He was worried about Lady Asano. She was suspended from his heart. His mind was no longer released. It was lingering on her and on the danger that surrounded her.

He held the hilt in his left hand with the sharp edge of the blade up. He took a sheet of special paper from his cleaning kit and folded it over the blade just beyond the ornate bronze hilt guard. He wiped the softly glowing curve with a single long stroke that flowed from the guard to the angled tip.

He repeated the process twice more. Then he rapped a small red cloth bag of limestone powder along the sinuous length of the temper line. It left patterns like delicate chrysanthemums. He wiped the blade with forty more smooth strokes to rid the surface of body oils. He finished by spreading a thin film of aromatic clove oil over it. As he worked he concentrated on freeing his mind of the doubts threatening to immobilize it. He concentrated on not-concentrating.

When he had rented the horse in Mitsuke, he had bought the postboy *sake* in the shop next to the transport office. He had learned that four of the five Edo *samurai* who had been waiting in town all month had disappeared. The remaining man had hired several members of Mitsuke's lower order. The hostlers didn't know what he had hired them to do, but Hanshiro could guess. The story had been the same in the other post stations between Mitsuke and Futagawa. Lord Kira was recalling his retainers to Edo. Something must be brewing there.

Don't despise your enemy though you take him to be small, nor fear your enemy though you take him to be great. Hanshiro was beginning to wonder if he had underestimated Kira's remaining men. He had assumed they and their local thugs wouldn't try to attack Lady Asano on the crowded road between Mitsuke and here. He had assumed they would wait until nightfall and that she would be in Futagawa and in his care before then. But what if he were wrong?

Hanshiro felt a shiver of dread and, worse, doubt. He should have waited for Lady Asano at the Arai barrier. He could have had a message delivered to her offering his services. If she had refused his help, he could have followed her. He could have protected her.

Instead, he had tempted fate. He had decided to test her, perhaps out of jealousy at her frivolous flirtation with the farmer or pique at her failure to meet his standards of proper behavior. If she passed the barrier at Arai, if she eluded Kira's men and reached Futagawa, she was worthy of his loyalty, if not his respect.

Mostly, however, he knew now he had been testing himself. By postponing the meeting, he was trying to prove that his foolish passion wasn't leading him like the hostlers led their shockheaded mares. He was trying to deny that he felt a kinship with the poet who wrote, "That such a one could be so longed for— Today I spent the whole day hopelessly gazing."

"Idiot!" He returned the gleaming short-sword to its scabbard. He could not polish his long-sword while in this state.

He placed his hands on his thighs, closed his eyes, and began to breathe deeply. His consciousness sank to the center of the center behind his navel. After a long while he heard the sound of rushing water, distant but approaching. Finally the torrent washed through his skull, flushing away thoughts and doubts. It left behind a welcome emptiness and a roaring, like a waterfall.

CHAPTER 55
SHOUT AGAINST THE FIRE

The old pilgrim decided to spend the day visiting with his cousin, so Cat and Kasane left him behind. The detour around the bay was long and arduous. Then they had to wait at the Arai barrier through the hours of the Snake and Horse because of a *daimyō*'s procession and the number of pilgrims trying to pass through.

The wait was tense. The Arai barrier marked the boundary of the province of Mikawa. Lord Kira's closest allies were in Mikawa. Once Cat and Kasane reached the head of the line, however, they found that the harried officials weren't checking commoners' papers very thoroughly.

By the time they reached Futagawa the sun had almost set. They ignored the shouts and the tugs on their sleeves as the waitresses tried to pull them into the tea houses for *sake* and raw fish. Instead they bought hot chestnuts from a street vendor and peeled and ate them as they followed the people heading toward the temple gates.

Once inside they found the compound mobbed. The noise of drums and bells and the loud, eerie moan of conch trumpets drowned out everything else. After hours of chanting and preparation, priests of the Shingon sect were about to perform the fire-walking ritual.

"Where is Inari-sama?" Kasane had to put her mouth to Cat's ear and shout to be heard.

"I don't know." Cat tried to get her bearings as the faithful surged past her. This was a Buddhist temple compound, but the guidebook said the shrine dedicated to Inari, the Shintō god of rice, swordsmiths, and fishermen, would be found here.

Cat checked her wallet, fastened to a cord around her neck and stuck deep inside her jacket. This crowd was a paradise for cutpurses. She held out a short straw rope, and Kasane caught the other end of it. They didn't so much follow the crowd as allow themselves to be carried by it.

They moved past the temple's drum tower toward the center

of the compound where a huge pile of burning logs was spewing flames and sparks. The ceremony had started hours ago, but as the climax approached, more and more people swarmed through the gates and added to the press. As Cat and Kasane pushed forward, the drone of chanting grew louder.

It filled the compound and resonated in Cat's chest and skull. From the sound of it a hundred or more priests must have been reciting *sutras* to Fudo, the fiery god of immovable strength. Cat glimpsed their orange and yellow robes through the crowd as she worked her way around the open square cordoned off by straw ropes.

Even as far back as she was, Cat began to perspire. The holy men standing within arm's length of the flames didn't seem to notice the heat, though. And here toward the center of the crowd the faithful were calm, their eyes fixed on the sacred fire.

Even so, everyone shrank back when the priests scattered the huge pile of embers. Sprays of sparks shot into the darkening sky, arced, and fell in a glittering rain. With long-handled rakes the priests began spreading the glowing coals into a path about twenty feet long and wide enough for two or three people to walk abreast.

"Over there." Cat gestured to a chapel set in a grove of trees away from the cluster of buildings around the main temple.

Now that the pyre had been leveled, the red *torii* gate and the distinctive thatch and uncluttered roofline of the Shintō building were visible beyond the roped-off area. As Cat got closer she could see the two slender stone foxes sitting on pedestals on either side of the entrance.

Cat and Kasane slipped through the crowd, moving outward, until they reached the chapel. Looking back across the path of embers, Cat could see a solid mass of worshipers filling the compound. Here, however, only scattered groups of people moved among the deep shadows cast by the trees and the buildings.

Up close, the stone foxes and their massive granite bases were taller than Cat. Their backs were covered with dark green moss. Their legs were dappled with silvery lichens. Their pointed muzzles had broken off, giving them a raffish look. Their long, oblique green quartz eyes seemed to regard her mischievously.

Cat searched among the charms and invocations and notes written on wooden tags and hung on the roofed message board. Two letters addressed to the Floating Weed had also been hung there. Traveler's was folded as usual. The other had been knotted elegantly.

"Two letters, younger brother?"

"So it seems." Cat regarded the two pieces of paper as if she expected them to grow the wings and claws of a long-nosed mountain demon and leap at her.

The letters were side by side. Both were addressed to the Floating Weed, but the writing had been done by two different hands. Cat recognized the earnest, childlike strokes of Kasane's pilgrim. She recognized the other, too. She remembered Hanshiro's calligraphy from when he and the monks and Musui had composed poetry that night so very long ago.

As Cat handed the pilgrim's letter to Kasane, she studied the dark forms of the people around her. Suddenly they looked sinister. With shaking hands she opened the second letter. It contained the first part of a linked verse written by the master Shōhaku over two hundred years earlier. She read it quickly by the dim light of the lantern next to the stone fox.

> Now is not the time
> To be thinking of yourself
> As one all alone.

He had signed it, "One who asks to serve you."

As Cat folded it quickly and stuffed it into the front of her jacket, she saw Hanshiro approaching.

"My lady," Hanshiro said.

In the noise of the nearby ceremony, in the rush of fear and rage that roared through Cat, Hanshiro's words and the nuances of his gesture were lost to her.

In his *Fire Book* Musashi said the voice was a thing of life. He said to shout against the fire, against the wind, against the waves. He said to shout before one flourished one's sword and after cutting down the enemy.

Cat shouted, then she charged Hanshiro. He hardly moved to avoid the thrust of her spear. The passing blade riffled his side-lock. He stepped aside as the force behind the blow carried Cat past him.

"Well done, my lady." Hanshiro had seen Cat pass the pilgrim's letter to her companion, the young peasant woman. Maybe Lady Asano was only serving as scribe for another's affair. Hanshiro didn't smile, of course, but joy shone in his eyes. Given the circumstances, it made him look triumphant.

"Burei-mon!" Cat said. "Impudent wretch! Kill me, but do not mock me!"

As though to oblige her, Hanshiro raised his sword and assumed the fighting stance. He had seen the ruffians closing in. He knew Kira's man had been in the drum tower directing them with hand signals, but they had arrived sooner than he expected. The bystanders had prudently disappeared.

"Younger brother," Kasane cried. "Behind you!"

Cat slid sideways, ducking behind the stone fox where Kasane was hiding. She hadn't much time to observe or to plan. The Tosa bounty hunter was on one side. From the other came a group of men armed with knives and staves. And she couldn't be sure, but she thought she saw in the shadows a young *rōnin* who looked familiar. He too was advancing with sword raised.

"Take off your sandals," Cat muttered to Kasane.

Kasane didn't question the command. Crouched behind the statue, she could hear the shouts of the men and the clash of steel and wood over the din of the drums and cymbals, conchs, rattles, bells, and the priests' chanting. She yanked off her sandals and hastily crammed them into her sleeves. Taking advantage of the shadows and with Kasane close behind her, Cat ran toward the only path of escape.

"The holy men haven't drawn out the heat," Kasane shouted when she realized what Cat had in mind.

She was right. The priests were lined up at the far end of the fiery path of glowing coals. They seemed to shimmer and dance in the rising waves of heat and smoke. Only after they had walked across, neutralizing the fire's effect, would the faithful follow.

"No time." Cat took Kasane's hand, lifted the straw rope, and ducked under, pulling Kasane after her. The priests' chanting faltered, and they looked at her in horror. A groan went up from the crowd.

Cat heard Hanshiro shout, "Stay away from the drum tower!" Then she took the first step onto the coals.

CHAPTER 56
THE WHOLE TIGER

"Walk slowly." Cat ignored the thousands of eyes fixed on her. "Put your heel down firmly and roll forward smoothly. Push off with the ball of your foot."

Cat tried to catch her breath. She had seen this done, but she'd never walked herself. Her mother had once told her that when walking on fire the innocent and the serene needn't fear. But what about the harried and the frightened?

Cat set her bare heel down in the deep bed of coals, pulsing with heat and light. Kasane did the same. The two of them took one step, then another. They felt only a pleasant warmth underfoot as they walked, hand in hand, the length of the path.

The head priest looked inclined to berate them, but he was reluctant to further disrupt the ceremony. He glowered at them as they murmured apologies and slipped through the ranks of brightly robed bonzes lined up to walk across the fire pit. They ducked into the crowd and disappeared.

Cat pulled Kasane behind a tall stone lantern and studied the roofed-over two-story gate and the drum tower near it. A shadow moved in the tower. Someone there was watching the compound and the gate. Cat would have been willing to wager that men were waiting outside the gate to catch her if she tried to leave by it.

Kasane held up a straw cord broken in her haste to strip off her sandals. Breaking a sandal tie was very bad luck.

"Buddha will protect us." Cat gave her another sandal from the pair tied to her sash.

She put on her own muddy sandals and began working her way along the high wall. She dodged among the people and used the huge cryptomeria trees and the stone lanterns and monuments as cover. Her mouth was dry as silk floss, and she stopped at the stone cistern so she and Kasane could rinse their mouths and drink from the bronze, dolphin-shaped spout.

As Cat gulped the cold water from her palm, she kept watch.

She had no trouble picturing the bounty hunter striding after her across the coals. She wouldn't have been surprised to find him close behind her.

The faithful had pressed into the center of the compound to take their turns at fire walking. That made the going easier here at the fringe. It was also darker away from the lights of the ceremony.

Cat followed a path into the blackness of the cryptomeria grove. She passed the Revolving Library, the Hall of Bones, and the Founder's Hall. Beyond them was the temple's kitchen. Cat and Kasane picked their way through the usual debris discarded behind it. From there three paths branched off. Cat chose the one without a marker of any kind.

She took Kasane's hand, and going by the feel of the stone paving through the soles of her sandals, she groped toward a distant light. When they reached the end of the lane, they stayed in the shadow of the trees and surveyed the thorn hedge in front of them.

It was twice as tall as they were. The thorns were as long as Cat's thumb. The only opening was a wooden gate flanked by lanterns and two red-painted wooden statues of the ferocious guardian kings who frightened away demons. Sitting at the gate was a small group of black-robed bonzes, their shaven heads gleaming in the lantern light. They seemed to be keeping a vigil as they rattled their rosaries and intoned the *sutra* of the Jewel in the Lotus. Above the hedge Cat could see the roof tiles of a building.

She considered the situation. Getting over the roofed, two-story-high wall around the temple compound would have been very difficult, if not impossible. The grounds were vast. Finding another way out in the dark might take all night. This was the time of the new moon, a "moon-hidden" day, and they could expect no light from above.

If Cat returned to the main area, the crowds would provide some protection, but she was sure the *rōnin* from Tosa would find a way to capture her, witnesses or no. He had plenty of help, and he was better than good at his job. He was supernatural. The fact that he had anticipated her arrival at the temple, then had had the effrontery to taunt her with a letter, had unnerved her. As for his warning about the drum tower, she was sure it was a trick of some sort.

If Cat stayed in the forest, she risked his finding her and capturing her with no one but Kasane to see him do it. With no witnesses there was no telling what the beast would do. He might force himself on her. He might kill Kasane to ensure her silence.

However, whatever was beyond that hedge seemed to be off limits to the laity. If she and Kasane could sneak inside, they might be safe for the time being.

With her flint, Cat lit their collapsible travel lantern and trimmed the wick as low as it would go. She tugged Kasane's sleeve, dragging her back up the path. When they came to the kitchen, Cat searched stealthily through piles of broken tools and utensils. Kasane gave a little squeak when Cat disturbed some roosting chickens and they flapped away. Cat felt around until she found what she needed.

"Catch hold of that end of the tub," she whispered.

"It has no bottom." Kasane peered through the wooden cylinder. The fitted staves were still held together by twisted bamboo strips, but it was missing a bottom.

"I know." Cat blew the lantern out again and waited until her eyes adjusted as much as possible to the darkness.

The two of them carried the cumbersome tub back toward the end of the path. Cat stubbed her toe and bit her lip to hold back tears. The pain was intense, but she knew if she started crying, she might not be able to stop.

She and Kasane hauled the tub around the outer perimeter of the hedge, feeling their way through the deep underbrush. Every time the leaves rustled, Cat held her breath and waited for someone to shout, "Halt!"

Finally Cat thought they had gone far enough. The darkness here was almost complete.

"Set it down," she whispered.

"What will we do now?"

"Help me shove it into the base of the hedge." Cat lined up the tub with one of the open ends facing outward. "Keep your head down so no thorns stick you in the face. And keep your eyes closed."

She rolled the cylinder back and forth until she found a spot between the individual stalks of the plants. She and Kasane pushed the tub into the hedge until it formed a sort of tunnel to the other side. Cat took off her bundle and pushed it and her staff through the opening. Then she dropped to her stomach and wriggled after it.

"It's safe." The tub amplified and distorted Cat's voice. It startled Kasane, but she hastily put her *furoshiki* into the hole and pushed it ahead of her.

When they stood and looked around, they saw they were at the rear of a chapel. Stone lanterns lit patches of the bare ground in front of the building, but not much of their light reached here. A mist rose from the damp earth. The building had a forsaken, haunted look about it.

"We shouldn't be here," Kasane whispered.

In the darkness under the broad, low-hanging eaves, Cat felt along the back wall for a door.

"We'll get into trouble," Kasane whispered.

Cat almost laughed out loud. Irritating officialdom was not Cat's definition of trouble. "Stop grazing on the roadside grass and help me find a way inside."

"Avoiding the fire, they leap into the water," Kasane muttered. But she dutifully began fumbling among the water barrels, door frames, and stacks of poles and shingles. "Here, mistress," she called softly.

The bottom of the window was about chest height. The pale light coming through perforations in the cedar shutter looked like constellations of stars. Kasane and Cat heaved up the shutter that was suspended over the window casing by iron hooks.

While Kasane held it, Cat propped it open with a pole. She looped her waist cord through the tied ends of her *furoshiki* with her narrow straw mat attached and lowered it quietly through the window. When it was resting on the floor inside, she let loose one end of the cord, retrieved it, and used it to put Kasane's bundle and mat inside. She poked her staff through last.

Cat climbed onto a barrel and ducked under the shutter. She threw a leg across the bottom of the casing and eased herself over. Then she helped Kasane in.

They were in the area behind an altar set on a platform approached by wooden stairs at the front. Light filtered through the altar curtain, once dark red but now faded to a streaked and dingy gray. The light illuminated a jumble of dusty statuary, portable altars, chests, draperies, scrolls, and screens leaning at angles against the wall. They could hear chanting from the chapel beyond.

They knelt on the floor. Each licked the pad of a middle finger and tapped it lightly against a rice paper pane of the screen beyond the curtain. They wet their fingers and tapped again, repeating the process until they each had made a small hole.

They put their eyes to them and peered into the main hall of the chapel.

The room was lit as bright as midday by hundreds of lanterns crowded among the rafters. It was hazy from the smoke spewed by bundles of incense sticks in large brass urns. A few priests sat on the floor with legs crossed and palms together, fingers pointed upward. They were facing Cat and Kasane, but their eyes were closed. They held their rosaries draped over their hands as they chanted.

Cat and Kasane moved away from the curtains and screens and into the shadows.

"We can spend the night here," Cat whispered.

She edged around the corner of a panel of the altar shrine to see which form of Buddha was being venerated. Instead of a statue of Amida, serene and inanimate, she saw a mummy. He was dressed in the tall conical hat and brilliantly colored robes of an abbot. His brown skin was so desiccated, it stretched over the bones of his face, drawing his mouth into a hideous, toothless grin.

His eyelid twitched.

Cat clamped her hand over Kasane's mouth before she could scream. "Don't be afraid," she murmured in her ear. "He's an honorable tree-eater." She removed her hand.

"He's alive," Kasane whispered.

"He's probably at the end of his fast."

Cat and Kasane retreated as far as they could get from the living corpse. They sat huddled against the rear wall, under the window.

"Tree-eaters subsist on nuts and berries and bark for a thousand days or more," Cat whispered. "At the end of their alotted time they eat only pine needles. Their flesh and organs wither away, leaving only skin and bones. If this one is truly blessed, he'll expire on the last day of his fast and his body won't decay."

"Why do they do it?"

"They believe they won't really die. Their souls can stay in their bodies and wait for the coming of the Blessed Buddha."

Cat and Kasane spread their mats where they could find room and lay close so they could whisper to each other. Each drew comfort from the other's presence.

"My foolish letters caused your enemies to find us." Kasane sighed. "The mouth is the front gate of all misfortune."

"Don't dwell on what's past." Cat spoke gently, although

she had already rebuked herself for being so careless as to leave traces of her presence in public places.

"Who wrote the other letter?" Kasane whispered. She hadn't had time to spell out the contents of her own letter, and it was too dark to do it now. She was consumed with curiosity about the second message.

"He's a filthy wretch, a hireling of my father's enemy. He's chased me from the Eastern Capital."

"The *rōnin* you tried to stab?"

"Yes."

"He looked like he was trying to help you."

"By seeing one stripe you know the whole tiger. He had no intention of helping me."

"But he warned you about the man in the drum tower."

"It was a trick, a needle concealed in a mass of silk floss."

For a while they lay in silence in the mustiness of the old draperies and straw matting and scrolls around them. Cat was bothered by the fact that Hanshiro hadn't tried to capture her. Had he been toying with her?

"Even his poem was deceptive," she said finally.

"Is that so?" Kasane tried to sound noncommittal.

" 'Now is not the time,' " Cat recited, " 'to be thinking of yourself as one all alone.' "

"Maybe he means he wants to help you."

"He's mocking me. He's telling me I can't escape him. But I'll travel the Three Paths before I'll allow him to take me."

Her anger discouraged further conversation. Kasane tumbled quickly into an exhausted sleep. Cat sat up and tried to keep watch, but eventually she could fight off fatigue no longer.

She awoke stiff and sore, curled up next to Kasane. She looked up into the rays of sun shining through the holes in the cedar shutter of the window. In the daylight she could see that the holes formed a graceful pattern of waves.

"Did you sleep well, my lady?" Hanshiro asked politely.

Cat sat up and gathered her legs under her in a crouch. She grabbed for her staff, but it was gone. Hanshiro was kneeling in the formal position, sitting back on his heels, his palms resting on his thighs. Cat looked into his tiger eyes.

Cat was incensed that Hanshiro had seen her asleep like some servant or peasant or outcast under a bridge. She pulled the knife from her jacket and heard Kasane scream as she lunged at him with it. He barely swiveled sideways, but Cat's blade stabbed emptiness where his chest had been.

Cat knew there was no use continuing. She could not harm him. She could not escape him. She turned her blade around and would have stabbed it into her own breast if he had not reached out faster than she could see. He held her wrist in a grip gentle but strong as an iron band.

"Kill me if you will, my lady," he said. "I will not try to prevent it. Only grant me the favor of hearing me out."

"Mannerless wretch!"

"You have reason to think so." He handed her a brocade bag. "But accept this as a token of my sincerity."

Cat opened it as though it contained a snake. She shook the contents onto her cotton towel. With the point of her knife, she separated the topknots and laid them in a line. There were eight of them.

"They belonged to your enemies, Your Ladyship," Hanshiro said. "I have named my sword the Barber." If Hanshiro was making fun of himself, Cat couldn't tell. His face was perfectly solemn. "I apologize that I couldn't catch the man in the drum tower."

"Are the owners of these dead?" she asked.

"Worse. They're shamed. The magistrate detained them for public brawling. They won't bother you again." Hanshiro took a long, slow breath to compose himself.

Even now, her eyes heavy with sleep and her hair disheveled, Lady Asano was lovelier than anyone he had ever seen. Teeth like pasania nuts. Dark, perfectly arched eyebrows. Strong chin and the high, narrow nose of a warrior. Arms white as mulberry ropes. A perfect hairline, each hair strong and glossy as black silk thread and growing from skin smooth as pale jade. Hanshiro longed to trace with his finger the contour that marked the wilderness of Cat's hair.

"I have something that will be of use to you, Your Ladyship." Hanshiro laid a folded letter on his open fan and offered it to her. The wax seal bore the crest of her father's ally, Lord Hino.

CHAPTER 57
THE BLADE THAT DEALS DEATH

Hanshiro sat at the writing stand in Futagawa's shrine to Hachi-man, the Shintō god of warriors. With a dagger he sliced the tip of the fourth finger of his right hand. He squeezed the finger until a puddle of blood formed in the bottom of a small bowl. He dipped a fine-haired brush into it, put it to the thick sheet of white paper, and began writing an oath of loyalty.

Cat watched him warily. She was seated on a pile of cushions that raised her head above his. The position symbolized that Hanshiro was below-the-eyes, a subordinate.

The abbot gestured to an acolyte, who brought forward a small brazier, set it down near Hanshiro, and fanned the coals. When the blood had dried, Hanshiro lit the paper and held it over another bowl while it burned. A second acolyte added hot water to the ashes, and Hanshiro swirled the bowl to dissolve them. Then he drank the mixture.

When he finished, the abbot and his assistants discreetly rose, bowed, and left. Kasane started to leave, too, but Cat motioned her to stay. She remained kneeling unobtrusively in a corner, but in effect Cat was alone with the bounty hunter.

"That was an impressive performance." Cat's voice was chilly and remote. "Did you drink a similar oath in the service of Kira?"

"No, my lady."

"Then why have you pursued me?"

"The mistress of the Perfumed Lotus wanted you found." Hanshiro knew that fact certainly wouldn't raise him in Lady Asano's esteem. "My sword would never have harmed you."

"Crows circle your sword guard. Are you of the New Shadow school?"

"Yes." Hanshiro was impressed. Lady Asano was a keen observer.

"Doesn't the New Shadow school teach that weapons are unfortunate instruments hated by Heaven's Way?"

"Heaven's Way is to maintain life."

"Then why do you offer to kill my enemies?"

"When one man's evil causes suffering for thousands of people and that man is killed, then the blade that deals death is the one that also gives life." Hanshiro could see that Lady Asano still distrusted him. "Perhaps time will convince you of my sincerity."

"I don't have time." Cat tugged at the front hem of her secondhand jacket. She pulled the overlapping flaps tight so they wouldn't bag open when she stood up. Under his steady gaze she had become acutely aware of her shabby traveling clothes. "All I wanted from your oath was your promise not to betray me." She bowed curtly. "Now my companion and I must start. We have far to go, and the sun's already high."

"Your Ladyship . . ."

"I do not have the right to be referred to in that way," Cat was irritated. *If you weren't an ignorant provincial, you'd know that,* her silence said. She motioned to Kasane, who rose and gathered up their two bundles.

"Then what shall I call you?" This interview wasn't going as Hanshiro had planned it.

"You have no need to call me anything." Cat hardly glanced at him as she took her *furoshiki* from Kasane, who helped adjust it on her back. "Our paths fork here."

Hanshiro didn't show his surprise, but he had assumed she would be grateful to have his sword and his arm as protection.

"Lady Asano . . ." The command in Hanshiro's voice was subtle, but so compelling that Cat hesitated at the door. In spite of her reproof he called her by the title her father's death had stolen from her. "I know you must be on your way, but grant me a few moments."

Cat returned to the cushions. She regarded him with a neutral, unreadable expression.

Hanshiro was more pleased than if she had meekly accepted his offer. She had heart. She had spirit. She had dignity. She was a mistress he could be proud to serve. And he would serve her, no matter what she said now.

"The travel permit from Lord Hino's councilor is for me and my disciple and a servant," Hanshiro said.

"Yes. You might as well take it back." Cat drew the letter from the front of her jacket and held it out. "It won't help me, but I thank you for your trouble."

Cat knew her behavior was rude, but she was angry. He had

harried her and frightened her and now thought he could make amends with a prick of the finger.

"At least allow me to present you with a small token, as an apology for the anxiety I've caused you." Hanshiro pushed a new wicker traveling box across the *tatami*. Then he bowed and left so Cat could open it.

A gift. Cat drew the box to her and stared at it. Gifts could be very expensive for the recipient. What price would the Tosa *rōnin* try to extract for this one?

When Cat took the lid off the box, Kasane moved close to see the contents. "It's beautiful," she breathed.

Cat held up the garment on top of the pile of folded clothes. It was a pale chrysanthemum-colored robe of wadded silk lined with striped satin. Pine trees, each needle embroidered, bordered a rushing blue river. The river started at the left front hem, spiraled to the right and around the side. On the back a huge carp the color of cedar bark leaped upstream against the rapids. It was the design invariably worn by actors portraying the youngest Soga brother in his struggle to avenge his father.

Under the robe were a hempen *hakama* and formal *haori* jacket the color of cedar and the accessories to make up a young warrior's traveling outfit. At the bottom of the box was a servant's livery of the same color with a horizontal stripe of dark rust.

"I'll give them to the abbot." Cat folded them neatly and replaced them in the box. "He can sell them to raise money for the temple."

Kasane made no argument, but Cat could see she was crestfallen.

"These clothes will make us conspicuous," Cat said. "At the very least they'll attract thieves."

Kasane read her suitor's poem aloud to Cat.

> Alone in the night
> I visit you by dream paths—
> There's no blame in that.

"He's a bold, romantic rogue, Kasane." Cat laughed.

"Here's my answer." Kasane was shy and proud. She had written this one herself. In her letter she confessed that someone else had copied the earlier poems for her.

I would read your words by moonlight
Or by the reflection of the snow
Or by the glow of the fireflies.
And if there were no moon or snow or fireflies
I would read it by the light of my heart.

"He'll like it, I'm sure." Cat curbed her impatience to get started. Thick gray clouds were moving in overhead, and she could hear distant thunder. Cat felt Hanshiro's letter under her jacket. " 'Now is not the time to be thinking of yourself as one all alone.' " Surely the lowering sky was what was making her so melancholy.

Kasane hung her letter to the Traveler on the big wooden message board near Inari's shrine. Cat whirled when someone spoke from close by.

"Forgive me, my lady." Nameless bowed low.

"You're the lantern painter." Cat raised her staff, ready to strike. She recognized the young warrior from the attack at the ferry on the Tama River, and she was ready to break his nose again.

He looked much younger than Cat remembered him, probably no more than fifteen or sixteen. The bruise across his nose and under his eyes had faded to lavender. The nose itself was misshapen from her blow.

"Forgive me, Your Ladyship, for failing you."

"What do you mean?"

"Didn't Hanshiro-san tell you?"

"No."

"I was trying to guard you, but I failed. In the fight last night he took all the topknots, *shu, shu, shu.* He prevented me from killing your enemies."

"Who ordered you to follow me?"

"No one." The boy looked thoroughly dejected. "I was a page in Akō when the news of your father's shameful betrayal arrived. We all wept bitter tears. I swore with the others to defend our lord's castle to the death or wreak vengeance on his enemy.

"But the councilor betrayed us. He meekly handed over the keys to the *shōgun*'s agents. Then he became a profligate in the brothels, probably with the money he stole from your father's estate."

"And are there no plans to avenge the Asano name?"

"None that I know of, my lady. I went to Edo to try to kill

Kira myself, for one cannot live under the same heaven with the slayer of one's lord. But I was unsuccessful. Kira's house is a fortress. His son, Lord Uesugi, has stationed extra bowmen there. I had decided to follow my lord in death when I heard you had escaped. I set out to find you and try my insignificant best to guard you against your enemies.''

The lad had also hoped that if some of Lord Asano's former retainers were plotting revenge, Cat would lead him to them. He'd been disappointed all around.

"What have you been doing between Kawasaki and here?''

"I was in the scuffle at the theater in Kambara, and I joined the fray behind the pilgrims' inn in Mishima.''

"You were there?''

"You almost broke my nose again.'' In spite of his misery, Nameless smiled shyly. "Forgive the impertinence of a humble boy, my lady, but you were magnificent. You were also very difficult to follow.'' He didn't mention that he had blundered into Cat at the mountain pass near Nissaka and had pretended to be a babbling dry-goods clerk.

"And the Tosa *rōnin*, what do you make of him?'' Cat despised herself for asking, but she couldn't help it. She wanted to hear everything she could about Hanshiro.

"He can drink a great deal, my lady.'' The boy grimaced at the memory of trying to match Hanshiro at draining *sake* jars. "At first I thought he was one of Kira's hirelings, but he's on your side after all. That's a great stroke of fortune for you. He's an accomplished swordsman.''

"Thank you for your help.'' When Cat picked up her bundle the boy tried to take it from her. Cat gently pulled it away. "Kasane and I will continue to travel alone,'' she said.

"I can carry your things and protect you from ruffians and make arrangements at the inns. I'll bargain with the river porters and the ferrymen and heat water for your tea at night.''

"We'll get along by ourselves.'' Cat wished she were as sure of that as she sounded. "We prefer to travel as we have been.''

She was half tempted to accept his offer; but after watching Hanshiro's sure, graceful movements, after looking into his dark, gold-flecked eyes and reading his poetry, she couldn't bear the thought of spending her days in the company of this boy.

She rationalized that she didn't know anything about the boy except that he was persistent. She couldn't trust him any more than she could trust the dangerous, taciturn *rōnin* from Tosa. Yet how to refuse without wounding his pride?

"I have an important, personal favor to ask of you," Cat said. "It will require great discretion, cunning, and courage."

"Anything, my lady."

"I want you to take a message to my mother."

The boy's eager expression faltered. "Back to Edo?"

"Yes. It grieves me to think how worried she must be. But the task is a dangerous one. My enemies will try to intercept you if they find you have word of me. You understand, don't you?"

Cat told the absolute truth, but her face lied artfully. Her face said the letter would contain a message of far greater moment than reassurances to her mother. She let the boy think it would be the final link in a plot to avenge her father.

"Your wish is my will, my lady." The boy wasn't entirely fooled.

CHAPTER 58

THE MUTUAL EMBRACE OF STINKING BONES

"Look at him," Cat muttered. "Planted like a willow in the road."

Cat and Kasane stood elbow to elbow with the other travelers crowded under the wide eaves fronting on the Tōkaidō, which was also Akasaka's main street. Rain cascaded in a silvery sheet from the edge of the roof. They would have waited out the icy downpour inside the tea house just behind them, but it was filled beyond capacity. The entryway was heaped with tall rain *geta* and straw and paper raincoats. The mass pilgrimage that Cat had started was still crowding the road to Ise. Akasaka's famous pleasure district was thriving.

In the middle of the river of mud that was the Tōkaidō, Hanshiro sat on the wicker box he had tried to give Cat. He had offered to buy the box and its contents from the abbot in Futagawa to whom Cat had donated it. But the abbot had insisted on giving it to him. Like most people who knew about Lord Asano's tragic fate, the abbot's sympathies lay with the lord's daughter and the man who seemed determined to help her.

In spite of the rain, Hanshiro hadn't bothered to open his umbrella. His feet were planted firmly in the brown water that flowed past his ankles. He stared ahead stolidly as the rain thrummed on his broad-brimmed bamboo hat and splattered his leggings with mud. The hat and the oiled-paper raincape were keeping him neither dry nor warm.

"He looks cold," Kasane said. She and Cat had been carrying on their conversation sotto voce.

"He looks smug as a snake that's swallowed a mosquito."

Over the roar of the rain on the roof, Cat could hear the speculation going on around her. Everyone was curious about the *rōnin*. Most people had concluded he was mad. In any case, he was drawing unwelcome attention.

"He'll surely catch cold." Kasane shivered in the wind that whined around the corner of the building and whipped her rain cloak against her legs.

"He doesn't have to sit there," Cat said. "He didn't have to follow us for the past four *ri*."

"Couldn't we let him walk with us?"

Cat exhaled loudly in exasperation. "Tell him I request that he get under shelter. Tell him I said his stubbornness is drawing attention to us and putting us in danger. Tell him I'll hear his plan."

Cat watched Kasane wrap her cloak about her, pull down her hat brim, and splash out into the rain. After she spoke to Hanshiro, he turned and bowed to Cat. Then he stood, stuck the carrying pole through the loops on the box, and shouldered it.

Instead of coming to where Cat huddled against the cold, however, he made his way through the press in the tea house. Cat frowned. What was the madman up to now?

In a few moments a maid arrived.

"Follow me, please," she said.

She managed to find space to wash Cat's and Kasane's muddy feet in the cluttered entryway. Then she led them through a side corridor that skirted the rear garden. She slid open a door panel and bowed them into a small room. When she left, Cat could hear her calling out orders.

Soon a procession of waitresses and maids arrived. Two of them carried in a brazier filled with coals. Another delivered a tall-handled tray of pipes, tobacco, and smoking accessories. The rest brought in high-rimmed lacquered trays containing heated towels and soft, wadded cotton robes and jackets. They poured hot tea into narrow winter cups that warmed the hands that held them.

As the heavy robe enveloped Cat in warmth and the chills that had racked her faded, Cat felt a pleasant lassitude settle over her. So far on this trip, whenever she was being discussed out of earshot, trouble followed. The relief of having tobacco and hot tea and dry clothes arrive instead of armed attackers was almost overwhelming.

Cat succumbed to the luxury of being taken care of instead of shifting for herself. She knew it was a pernicious weakness, but she indulged it. She had a feeling it would be as brief as it was glorious. It was glorious enough, in fact, to make her feel a bit more tolerant of the surly *rōnin* from Tosa.

As a grand finale, waitresses carried in a wooden frame that stood almost waist high. It contained matching nested picnic boxes lacquered in black with an allover design of golden cart-wheels in a golden stream. The boxes were filled with such delicacies as broiled abalone, raw sea bream and garnishes, roasted gingko nuts, and red bean paste soup with freshly picked mushrooms. There were imperial persimmons, Chinese walnuts, and falling-goose candies.

"Ma!" Kasane stared, wide-eyed, as the waitresses unpacked more varieties of food than she would have seen in a lifetime in her village.

Hanshiro followed the food in and slid the door closed behind the departing waitresses. He had changed into his formal clothes, and Cat caught her breath at the sight of him. He was undeniably handsome, and his eyes were hypnotic in their intensity. That, along with his air of elegant menace and offhand competence with a blade, made her wary.

Enemies might be listening beyond the thin wall panels, so Cat had to lean close to Hanshiro to talk. When she did she could smell the lingering scent of sandalwood and camellia oil and cloves. Her chest felt tight, and heat spread up from her neck. She almost feared to breathe, as if even so slight a movement might break the fragile bonds that kept danger and passion pent up in this man.

"Do you think you can bribe me, Tosa," she murmured. "Clubs have not caught me, nor will chopsticks."

"It is I who have been caught, my lady."

"Tell me, then, this plan of yours."

"Your companion can dress as our servant, and you will pose as my page. . . ."

"To serve you." Cat's voice plainly showed how little she thought of that idea.

"Unless you have been a retainer, you cannot use a retainer." There was irony in Hanshiro's bow as he recited the old proverb. "By obeying we learn to command."

Cat felt a shy tug at her sleeve. "What is it, Kasane?"

"Remember Benkei-san and Yoshitsune-sama at the barrier?"

Kasane was happy to be in the company of a man who had a strong arm and a sharp sword and who wasn't trying to kill her. Fear that her mistress's stubbornness would lose them their champion, their Buddha in hell, made her bold. She struck the pose of the blind minstrel outside of Maisaka. She recited, almost word for word, the part of the story where Benkei struck his lord to prove to the barrier guards that Yoshitsune was only a humble porter.

"Well done!" Cat lit her pipe and drew in a mouthful of warm smoke. It calmed her and slowed her racing heart. "But Benkei had already proved his loyalty."

Hanshiro threw the die he knew would win the game. "As my disciple you can carry two swords openly." The rain had stopped drumming on the roof overhead, and he lowered his voice further.

"Or a *naginata*?" Cat whispered.

"Yes."

Cat lifted the sack of coins Hanshiro had delivered as a gift from Lord Hino's steward. "I'll pay for it," she said. She wanted to keep her debt to the Tosa *rōnin* to a minimum.

"As you wish, my lady."

"Sword master and pupil are often lovers." Now that Cat had decided Hanshiro was probably trustworthy, this was the part of his scheme that worried her.

Hanshiro drew from his sleeve a copy of *An Evening Waiting for a Pair of Sleeve,* a treatise on the love of boys. He unwrapped the oiled paper that had protected it from the rain and tucked it in the front of his jacket so the title could be read by anyone passing by. He had bought it as part of the masquerade, but it had the added effect of placating Cat.

" 'A woman adorns her fair skin with powder,' " Hanshiro recited. " 'Reddens her lips, blackens her eyebrows . . .' "

" 'Yet carnal pleasure between man and woman is but the mutual embrace of stinking bones.' " Cat finished the old Chinese poem.

"To carry this off we should pretend to be lovers," Hanshiro said. "But it will be only an act. And you have proven yourself an excellent actor, my lady."

CHAPTER 59

IT SHOULD SOFTEN RELATIONS BETWEEN MAN AND WOMAN

The Persimmon Inn was as crowded as all the others in Okazaki. There was a constant scrape of wall panels being slid back and forth in their wooden tracks and glimpses of merriment in the rooms behind them. Maids and servants laden with food and *sake* and bedding scurried to and fro. Blind shampooers and masseurs plied their trade. Choruses of the Ise song sounded from all corners of the Persimmon as pilgrims settled in for an evening of revelry.

The room next to the one Hanshiro shared with Cat and Kasane was lit bright as day. Four drapers were throwing a party there, and a *geisha* was dancing to the rhythm of his own hand drum.

The drapers called themselves the Four Heavenly Kings, and they boasted that they were experts at libertinage. To prove it they had hired a covey of women who specialized in entertaining travelers.

Because Cat could hear every word they said, she knew more than she cared to about three of the Kings. The fourth man was already slurring his words too badly for her to understand what he was saying.

Cat and Hanshiro had had their baths and now wore the indigo cotton robes and tie-dyed crepe sashes supplied by the Persimmon. By the light of a single lantern, Hanshiro was teaching Cat to play *go*. As he sat studying the board he seemed oblivious to the racket nearby. When the *geisha* finished her bawdy dance, a *samisen* player struck up "Shallow River."

Cat had heard the song many times in the Perfumed Lotus, and she began humming along absentmindedly. When she realized what she was doing, she fell silent and stared down at the board. She was appalled that her embarrassment must be evident on her face.

The song was about wading into shallow, then deeper and deeper water. Cat knew that as the women danced they lifted their robes to expose more of themselves. She could tell from the giggles and shouts that they were complying with the last verse and that the water had risen quite high.

Cat glanced toward the door.

"She'll be safe." Hanshiro didn't look up from the *go* board. Normally he wouldn't have spoken at all until the game was over; but he was teaching, not competing, and he was trying to put Cat at ease.

"She's a simple country woman." Cat had misgivings about allowing Kasane to go out by herself, especially at night.

"She seems able to take care of herself. I'd venture to say you've taught her a great deal in the time you've spent together."

Cat didn't trust herself to answer. Hanshiro made her feel as awkward as a child, until even her silence seemed foolish to her. She was flattered, though. The *rōnin* didn't seem the type to scatter compliments about with a winnowing fan. And what he said about Kasane was true enough. She looked dashing in the stiff new livery.

Cat had gathered Kasane's hair into a boy's whisk on top of her head and tied a headband jauntily above her left ear. Kasane had carried the travel box effortlessly the four *ri* from Akasaka to Okazaki. She was strong anyway, and Hanshiro had transferred the heavier items to the *furoshiki* slung across his own back. Kasane had sung to herself as she marched along behind Cat and Hanshiro.

Now she was at the temple looking for another letter from her suitor. She carried Cat's spear disguised as a staff, but Cat was worried about her. She feared that if Kasane got into a situation where she needed the spear, she'd only hurt herself with it.

Cat heard a polite cough and a shuffling of feet at the door.

"Come in." She called out the invitation before she remembered that she wasn't supposed to be in charge here.

When the panel slid open a cloud dweller, a member of the nobility, entered. He was thin and stooped. He had the face of a crane, and he wore the outmoded fashions of the emperor's court. His wrists and hands extended like talons from the wide, layered sleeves of his robes. He had stained his teeth black in the old-fashioned way and had powdered and rouged his face.

"Good evening, sirs. Forgive the intrusion." His smile was brittle. Conspiratorial. His painted face was a grotesque caricature of beauty and refinement. "My name is Nakajo, chamberlain of the fifth rank. Retired." His bleary eyes restlessly searched the corners of the room, as though he expected an enemy, or at least a rat, to be lurking there. He made Cat nervous.

"It is no intrusion." Hanshiro bowed. "My companion is merely learning the game."

"I was told that two supreme examples of manly beauty were gracing this worthy establishment, men with souls as fearless as the god of war." The old man turned aside. He hawked and spat into an embossed paper he took from his wallet. "But the stories fall far short of the truth." He folded the paper into the figure of an iris and tucked it into his sleeve. "Your young companion has a countenance like the moon, serene in the autumn sky." The chamberlain nodded toward Cat, who bowed low in return.

"How can we help you?" Hanshiro tried to hurry the old man along in his pitch. The emperor himself received an annual stipend less than that of the lowest-ranking *daimyō*. His courtiers had little except time; but they had plenty of that.

"It is I who desire to help you, kind sir." The chamberlain lowered his voice and leaned forward, although the Four Kings and their guests were making so much noise, no one could have heard him. "It is said that 'dallying with youths is like consorting with wolves beneath scattering cherry blossoms.' "

" 'Whereas pillowing with prostitutes is like groping in the dark without a lantern beneath a new moon.' " Hanshiro finished the quote, but he was surprised the old aristocrat knew the works of Saikaku, the commoner and townsman.

"Coupling with wolves requires energy." From the depths of his many robes the chamberlain produced a small, stoppered earthenware jar and held it up. "I have here the elixir that will ensure that each night of love lasts as long as autumn itself. One need only mix a drop of it with water and bathe in it."

"What does this miraculous potion consist of?" Hanshiro offered a pipe, which the old nobleman accepted with an alacrity that bordered on the indecorous. Cat lit it for him and tended it while he went on with his story.

"Do you remember the elephant delivered to the dog *shōgun* as a present from the most august emperor of China?"

"The huge, gray, wing-eared beast that was all the talk ten years ago." Hanshiro remembered it well.

He had found the towns along the Tōkaidō in an uproar because of the elephant and its entourage. Local officials were recruiting farmers to clean the highway even more thoroughly than usual. They had drafted all available laborers to build earthen bridges over the rivers. The *shōgun* banned all cattle and horses from the vicinity of the road so they wouldn't frighten the huge beast. Citizens had been ordered to keep silent so they wouldn't disturb its sleep.

Yes, Hanshiro remembered the elephant. It was still living on the grounds of Tokugawa Tsunayoshi's palace in Edo.

"A most uncommon animal. . . ." As the cloud of tobacco smoke enveloped the chamberlain, Cat thought he looked as close to contented as he ever had or ever would. In a way she could empathize with him. She had learned that deprivation raised the simplest pleasures to the extraordinary.

"The beast's urine is collected and saved." The chamberlain shared the confidence as though it were a state secret.

When Cat glanced at Hanshiro she detected a glimmer of amusement in his stoic expression. It was as surprising as a wasp's sting getting a reaction from a stone Jizō. Hanshiro too must have been imagining the unfortunate underling who had the job of holding the tub each time the elephant emptied its bladder.

"The elephant's proper-thing is as big as a fishing boat's mast," the chamberlain said. "So it is no surprise that its urine has a potency unparalleled in this fleeting world."

"Are we to assume that you have some of that marvelous liquid?"

"As you can imagine, it is in great demand. Those of the highest rank covet it. But because you are such a rare and refined pair of individuals, I am going to part with the very last vial in my possession."

"Your generosity far exceeds our slight merit."

The chamberlain made a deprecating gesture with his sleeve. He jumped when someone fell in the next room and rattled the wall panels in their tracks. A bathtub must have been delivered there because the sound of splashing joined the gales of laughter and loud music.

"The four jovial townsmen next door would be most disappointed to miss the opportunity you so generously offer," Hanshiro said. "The god of wealth has smiled on them. They would be able to express their gratitude far more suitably than a pair of humble and poverty-stricken wanderers.''

''I'm grateful to you for the suggestion.'' The chamberlain understood that Hanshiro had just refused him, but he stayed through the hour of the Dog anyway. He realized that Hanshiro was the only truly educated person in the inn. He discussed the classics with him as though that were the sole purpose of his visit.

Cat didn't mind. She preferred having the chamberlain there to spending the time alone with the *rōnin*. She would have gone with Kasane to explore Okazaki, but that would have started speculation among those who assumed she and Hanshiro were lovers.

When the old man finally left, Cat couldn't help looking impishly over her sleeve. She was astonished to see a smile flicker across Hanshiro's face in return. For a moment, in the shadowy room, across the dimly lit *go* board, Nakajo's foolishness made them comrades.

''The bag of cupidity has no bottom,'' Hanshiro murmured as he made one more move toward the inevitable downfall of Cat's *go* pieces, although the most satisfying conclusion to a game of *go* was always a draw. He snapped the stone down with a satisfying click that was amplified by the hollow sounding-box under the board.

''*Tenjo bito,*'' Cat whispered. The words meant ''cloud dweller,'' but they could also mean ''ceiling person,'' a euphemism for rat.

Kasane slid the door open, bowed, and entered.

''I was worried about you.'' Anxiety put an edge to Cat's voice.

''I'm very sorry, young master.'' Kasane glanced toward the far wall, beyond which the Four Kings' party was reaching a crescendo of splashes and squeals. ''I went looking for paper at a night market.''

Cat started to remind her that the Persimmon's management had provided writing materials. Then she realized that Kasane probably wanted paper of a higher quality. Next she would insist on fresh spring water to mix with her ink. She was developing sensibilities beyond her station. Cat should have disapproved, but she couldn't manage it. She knew Kasane couldn't help herself. For lovesickness there was no cure.

''Did you find a letter from Traveler?''

Kasane looked at Hanshiro and blushed a bright scarlet.

"Yes," she murmured. "He's been hurrying. He's not far behind us."

"No wonder you're radiating joy from the tip of your nose." Cat nodded toward the writing stand and the box with ink stone, brush, and water pot. "Use the writing things if you wish."

"Thank you." Kasane carried the stand and a floor lantern behind the four-panel folding screen set up in the corner. Against the painted paper surface of the screen, Cat could see her shadow bent over the desk. Like Hanshiro, she seemed oblivious to the uproar next door. She was absorbed with the task of composing a poem in reply to her suitor's.

" 'Poetry should move heaven and earth. . . .' " Hanshiro glanced at the screen as he quoted from the preface to the *Kokinshu*. It was an anthology of thousands of ancient poems that every educated person knew by heart. He paused to let Cat continue.

" 'It should soften relations between man and woman, and soothe the heart of the fierce warrior.' "

The inn's maids arrived, hidden behind towering stacks of folded bedding. They laid out Kasane's thin pallet behind the screen. Then they sneaked flirtatious glances at Cat as they made up a pile of three thick mattresses.

Cat realized, to her horror, that the bed was for her and Hanshiro to share. When the maids left she could hear their whispers and muted laughter diminishing down the corridor. She knew they were discussing her and the *rōnin*. She felt her face grow hot again.

"I'll sleep with Kasane," she said.

"As you wish, my lady." Hanshiro didn't take his eyes from the *go* board. "But people will notice."

Privacy was not possible. The maids and servants might bustle in at any moment to trim lamps, deliver tea, or replenish the tobacco supply. A masseur might drop by to offer his services or a priest to request donations to his temple.

"*Shiri sumo!* Buttocks wrestling!" A woman next door shouted it, and the others took up the cry.

Hanshiro made such a droll face that Cat laughed out loud in spite of herself.

Everyone at the party had reached the stage of inebriation where nothing would do but that the Kings pair off and engage in the contest of buttocks wrestling. Each pair stood back to back on two large, flat, square cushions. They bent over and grabbed their own ankles. The women threw the skirts of the inn's blue robes up over their heads, exposing their bare rear ends. Then each combatant tried to knock his opponent off his cushion using the most prominent part of his anatomy.

It wasn't hard to do. They had been drinking a long time, and they were having difficulty just remaining upright. Even before they were hit they would stumble off the small, lumpy field of battle or fall sprawling.

The women helped them up. The men got back into position. The women raised their robes over their heads and slapped their bare cheeks by way of encouragement. They supported the men as they swayed and urged them on.

Hanshiro was just getting ready to clear the stones off the *go* board when the inevitable happened. One of the Kings crashed headfirst through the flimsy wall. Cat and Hanshiro leaped clear, but the black and white *go* stones scattered to the four corners of the room. The tipsy partygoers crowded around the opening and stared in at them.

"It must be the New Year," one of the women shouted. "They're throwing beans to cast out demons."

Everyone laughed uproariously. Two of the women, still laughing, stepped over the shattered frame to rescue the draper, who was tangled up in his blue robe with the Persimmon's crest on it.

Hanshiro put up a hand, and the women stopped. He bent down, took the fallen man by the arm, and helped him gently but firmly to his feet.

"The hour is late." Hanshiro's quiet voice silenced the giddy intruders. "We must be on the road early tomorrow." He guided the draper through the opening and into his room. "We are most grateful for your consideration."

Chastened, they retreated. A pair of servants brought a new wall panel. In a few moments they had installed it in the tracks and cleared away the debris. They apologized profusely before leaving Cat and Hanshiro to work out their sleeping arrangements.

The drapers and their one-night wives whispered and giggled for a while. The lights dimmed. Eventually the only sounds were the usual rustling and murmurs of couples pillowing.

Kasane picked up the *go* stones and replaced them in their box. Then she retreated discreetly behind her screen.

Cat tightened the sash of her sleeping robe. She lay down facing outward on the far side of the bed and moved as close to the edge as she could. Hanshiro sat reading by the dim light of the night lamp.

Cat knew he was sparing her the embarrassment of having a stranger lie down beside her. She knew that he would probably slip under the quilt when he thought she was asleep. She was sure she could trust him not to try to make a fool of her, as Kasane would have put it. Yet still her heart pounded.

Cat closed her eyes and concentrated on breathing deeply. She drew in long, even breaths until air seemed to fill her down to her toes. Then she exhaled until she felt completely empty. But sleep wouldn't come.

She heard Hanshiro turning the pages of his book until he closed it and put it away. She heard the grinding of an ink stone and the clink of a bamboo brush handle against the side of a porcelain water pot and knew he must be writing something.

Finally, halfway through the hour of the Rat, the quilt stirred and a draft briefly chilled Cat's back. The mattress shifted as Hanshiro lay down. Cat continued taking the steady breaths of someone deep in sleep, but she listened, tense and intent. Judging from Hanshiro's breathing, he seemed to fall asleep with maddening ease.

Brute! she thought.

The two of them lay, back to back and wide awake, until the first crowing of the cock.

CHAPTER 60
ONE WHO LIVES BEYOND MY WORLD

The shoreline of Miya's waterfront was lined with fishing smacks, excursion boats, and trading scows. Shouts of "Who's for the boat?" could be heard from the ferry landing. Miya was the largest town between Edo and Kyōto, and today it was particularly busy with pilgrims. Cat was glad she and Kasane and the *rōnin* had left Okazaki at the first ringing of the dawn bell. As it was, they would be lucky to obtain passage on a ferry at all, much less soon.

Ise Bay at this point was six and a half *ri* across. Unless they left soon, darkness would fall long before they arrived at Kuwano. At Yokkaichi, the post station after Kuwano, the road branched off toward the great shrine at Ise, so the Tōkaidō should be less crowded beyond there.

Cat and Hanshiro sat on a bench in front of a small tea stall near the bay. Hanshiro seemed to be idly observing the maelstrom of activity, but Cat knew he had drawn into himself. He had the look she had come to recognize while walking with him from Okazaki. He had an impressive and irritating way of appearing at once remote from and aware of absolutely everything. Cat wasn't used to being ignored.

Glancing sideways at him now, Cat had difficulty imagining him smiling. If she hadn't seen him do it, she wouldn't have believed him capable of it. He looked as austere as a stone Buddha.

She turned her attention back to Kasane, who was making her way around the waiting *kago* and pack horses and stacks of freight on the broad beach. Her progress was slow. She kept appearing and disappearing among the travelers and porters and inn touts, the merchants and vendors and beggars.

The name on the papers Hanshiro had gotten for Kasane was Hachibei, and she was now dressed in the livery of his servant. Cat worried that Kasane wouldn't be able to carry off her disguise as a young man. Maybe she would be overcharged by the ferrymen. Maybe something terrible would happen to her for which Cat would feel forever responsible.

"She'll make a mistake." When Cat leaned over to whisper to Hanshiro, her shoulder brushed his. To anyone passing by, they looked like a pair of lovers exchanging surreptitious endearments.

"The servant's job is to bargain with porters and ferrymen," Hanshiro answered. "If she's to pass as a servant, she has to behave as one."

"You're asking too much of her," Cat muttered.

"And you expect too little." Hanshiro finished his tea. He rose, bowed, and retired to the dense stand of bushes next to the tea house.

He was relieving himself when three young *samurai* swaggered toward him. They wore the wide sashes of dandies and wastrels. They had put lead weights in the padded hems of their quilted robes to make them swing. Their swords were longer than the average. That they had been drinking was evident. Their faces were florid, their talk was loud, and their gait was wobbly.

Without glancing at them, Hanshiro reflexively checked the angle of the long-sword in his sash. He wasn't surprised when one of them managed to brush it with his own scabbard anyway. *Rōnin* had no association with a clan that could exact vengeance for their deaths. That made them the preferred targets for brash young men trying to establish reputations as swordsmen. Hanshiro had been accosted many times.

"*Saya-ate!*" the young ruffian cried. "Scabbard striking!" He and his friends formed a semicircle around Hanshiro.

With his back to them Hanshiro calmly adjusted his clothing. Finally he turned to face the three and nodded ever so slightly. "I apologize for any offense I may unwittingly have committed."

He made a slight gesture to restrain Cat, who had unsheathed the blade of her new *naginata* and was standing, narrow-eyed and at attention.

"The affront was too egregious." The dandy spoke so loudly, people stopped to watch. Soon a ring of spectators had formed around the four men. "The only apology that will satisfy such a breach of etiquette is your blood flowing onto the ground."

"I do not care to duel with you."

"Coward!" Rage deepened the red of the young man's face. "This country beast is afraid of a real warrior," he informed the crowd. Then he turned on Hanshiro. "My name is Tamagawa Seijuro of the Itto school. Prepare to defend yourself if you can."

His companions shouted their names, too. All three pulled their right arms out of the sleeves of their jackets, robes, and undershirts, exposing the smooth, unblemished chests of youth. They drew their swords and raised them, ready to strike. The afternoon sun flashed off the blades.

Hanshiro sighed. Best to get this over with before Lady Asano lost her temper and decided to test her *naginata* and cause annoyance and delay. He left his sword in its scabbard.

Empty-handed and apparently indifferent to the other two, he strode directly at the one who had called him out. The young man retreated slowly before Hanshiro's steady advance. He was wondering if he had challenged a madman. Then he gathered his resolve.

With eyes bulging he shouted his name and clan and struck. Hanshiro moved his head out of the sword's path at the last instant. With the edge of his hand he struck the wrist, causing him to release the hilt. In a transfer too deft to see, Hanshiro ended up holding the sword casually in his right hand.

When the man on the left attacked, Hanshiro pivoted, reversed, and shot out his left arm. His opponent flipped over backward, and his sword flew into the air. When it landed Cat moved over and stepped on it.

Hanshiro drew his iron fan from his sash. He stepped into the reach of the third assailant and rapped his right shoulder at the base of the neck. The man dropped his sword, his arm and hand temporarily paralyzed. Hanshiro picked it up and retrieved the third sword from Cat. Then he disappeared into the nearby convenience. He returned without the swords.

With her *naginata* Cat held the young men at bay while the bystanders taunted them. Hanshiro walked over to them and spoke softly. They retreated to the *sake* shop across the street, where they watched Hanshiro warily.

"You didn't spare them shame by finishing them." Cat slid the blade back into its curved wooden sheath.

Hanshiro resumed his seat at the tea shop. The waitress refilled his cup and bowed lower than she had before.

"Remember what Lao Tzu said," Hanshiro said.

" 'Weapons are unfortunate instruments. Using them when there is no other choice, that is Heaven's Way.'

"Besides, if I had killed them, I would have had to fill out papers at the magistrate's office."

"I've heard of *muto*, of fighting unarmed an armed opponent, but I've never seen it done."

"Youth and wine are like a whip to a galloping horse." Hanshiro wrapped coins in a paper to pay the waitress. "Shall we see what bargain our man Hachibei has struck with the redoubtable ferrymen?"

"Eels! Try our eels," the captain of the trading boat shouted. "They'll make you fertile."

His wife smiled shyly at Cat as she passed the longitudinal section of dark green bamboo across the gunwale to her and received the wrapped coins in return. Cat took off the top half of the bamboo, revealing the long brown slab of eel resting on a bed of white rice in the bottom half. The aroma set Cat's stomach to rumbling. She pulled off the long slivers that had been sliced into the bamboo's edge to serve as chopsticks.

"Itami *sake*! The very best made!" Another boat had pulled

up at the ferry's starboard side. Its owner was selling rice wine and pickles.

Here in the middle of the bay, enterprising peddlers were doing a brisk business with the ferry's passengers. A forest of hands waved money, received food, and passed it along to whomever had ordered it. When the vendors had taken care of everyone, they cast off and sailed away to intercept the next boatload of customers.

The waters were calm. A fair wind filled the ferry's sail and kept it steadily on course. The passengers sat on straw mats spread in the broad bilge. They and their belongings were packed side by side like dumplings strung on skewers, but they talked good-naturedly as they ate. They entertained the children headed for Ise and shared food with them.

A group of women known euphemistically as "shampooers" were on their way to Ise, too. "A body that loves is fragile and uncertain," they sang. Their voices were sweet and wild and strangely fitting here, as though capable of calming a restless sea. Their song brought sudden, stinging tears to Cat's eyes.

> The body that loves
> Is fragile and uncertain,
> A floating boat.
> The fires in the fishing smacks at night
>   burn red,
> My heart burns red.
> Wooden stakes hold up the nets
> Against the tide of Uji.
> The tide is against me.

When they finished their performance, a doctor from Echigo prescribed his special powder for seasickness. A diviner began casting fortunes for a price.

The captain was not the wild-haired pirate Kasane now connected with every vessel. Still, she had become increasingly anxious as the thatched roofs of Miya dwindled, then disappeared. One who had been bitten by a snake feared even a rotted rope.

Kasane had gone pale when the captain asked for a donation to the Sea God and a crewman with a bamboo ladle made his way through the press to collect it. She had been sure they all would be robbed and thrown overboard.

"Does your eyebrow itch?" Hanshiro seemed to enjoy teasing Kasane. "If so, it means your lover must be about to visit you."

"No, Your Honor."

"It should itch. Traveler must be close behind us now."

He was making a gallant effort to calm Kasane's fears, but he was only partially successful. Having him as a bad dog at her side on shore was reassuring. But even he couldn't appease the Sea God if he decided to sink the boat.

"Traveler is a firm-grained individual," Hanshiro added.

The lack of gender in the language aided Kasane's masquerade. A listener could not tell from the conversation if Hanshiro's servant's admirer was male or female. And Kasane was doing rather well at imitating a boy. She had been watching Cat do it for the past ninety *ri*.

"Do you know the individual?" she asked.

"I had the privilege of traveling a short way with the person. Seemed quite taken with you."

Kasane leaned against the travel box, which was wedged among the equipment in the stern of the boat. Lost in her own thoughts, she withdrew into herself. A smile played across her face now and then, like a riffle of wind on still water.

Cat hadn't slept at all the night before, and she was exhausted. But she sat stiffly. Hanshiro had arranged a place for her next to the gunwale so she could have an unobstructed view and fresh air. He was on her other side, however, and forced by circumstance to sit pressed tightly against her. She had been aware of his warmth, the hardness of his body, and the steady rise and fall of his breathing since they'd left port.

The sun disappeared behind mountains stark against a sky ablaze with color. The sliver of the new moon was setting with the sun.

The passengers finished their meals and settled down for the voyage. Some of them dozed off, their chins dropping onto their chests. Kasane slept with her head back and her mouth slightly open. Cat blinked and pinched her arm to keep herself awake. She was mortified to think that, asleep, she might do something hideously vulgar, like drool or snore or let her mouth hang open.

As the sky darkened Cat realized they still had a long way to go. The crewmen lit fires in the metal baskets that hung out over the long, pointed prow of the boat. Other points of light, the cold luminescence of shrimp, glittered in the black water around them. Cat dozed, and the rocking of the boat carried her back to the evening excursions she had enjoyed with her mother in the waters off Akō.

"Those are the lanterns of the Dragon God." Cat heard her mother's sweet voice. She remembered the feel of her mother's heavy silk brocade coat sleeve brushing against her cheek as she pointed to the lights on the black water.

". . . the spirits of the Taira warriors." Hanshiro's voice sounded distant, hollow in the darkness. Cat realized she must have fallen asleep.

"Where?" She sat up straighter and took deep gulps of the cold, damp air. The boat was quiet now, except for the creaking of the rigging and of the rudder in its cradle. She could see the dark forms of the sleeping passengers silhouetted against the starlit sky.

"There." He leaned partly across her to point at the lights moving through the mist in the distance.

"They're only fishing boats."

"Are you sure?"

" 'Since I am convinced,' " Cat recited the poet-priest Saigyo's poem. " 'That reality is in no way real, how am I to admit that dreams are dreams?' Or spirits are spirits?" she added. "Or fishing boats are fishing boats?"

" 'A sunset with clouds like the Sea God's banners.' " Hanshiro recited.

Cat was almost asleep. She murmured something, a recognition of the poem, perhaps, that was between a sigh and a sleepy moan. Her head fell back against Hanshiro's arm until it was cradled in the crook of his shoulder. His hand trembled as he wrapped that side of his cloak around her to keep her warm. He laid his cheek gently on the shiny fragrance of her hair.

At the sunset hour . . . As the words echoed in his thoughts, he felt a kinship with the nameless poet who had suffered five hundred years ago as he did now.

> At the sunset hour
> The clouds are ranged like banners
> And I think of this:
> Think of what it means to love
> One who lives beyond my world.

CHAPTER 61
AN EFFICIENT HAWK

As soon as Hanshiro stepped off the ferry at Kuwano, he spotted the *rōnin*. He looked to be the sort who hired himself out as a bodyguard for rich merchants. He was dressed in shabby gray trousers, a laborer's short blue jacket with cotton wadding showing from rips, and a faded green-and-black-striped coat. He wore a blue cotton towel draped over his head and tied under his chin. Hanshiro couldn't read the white lettering on the towel, but it probably advertised some inn or a shop's specialty.

The bodyguard was sitting on a straw-wrapped *sake* tub and lounging against a stack of boxes. He had crossed one leg over the knee of the other, and his *geta* dangled from the knob between his bare toes. The pairs of slats on the bottom of the *geta* had worn down almost to the nub. The *rōnin* seemed to be absorbed in watching the stars' reflection on the bay and in cleaning the wax from his ears with a long bamboo pick.

"Someone to be wary of," Hanshiro said. *A thousand years in the sea and a thousand years in the mountains,* he thought. The bodyguard had the air of a man made cunning by hard experience.

"Uhm." Cat had noticed him, too. In spite of his ragged clothes he had an air about him. "You said Kira was hiring dregs to track me."

"Dogs and hawks work for the same master." Hanshiro reached up a hand for Kasane to hold.

She used it for balance as she shouldered the pole of the travel box and carried it down the board that served as a gangplank. She smiled a shy thanks. Hanshiro was as at ease with Kasane as he was stiff and formal with Cat. Kasane was quite charmed by him.

"Perhaps Kira hired this one as the final fart of a weasel," Hanshiro said.

"Who?" Alarmed, Kasane looked around.

"Don't look at him." Cat pretended to check the baggage. "Tosa thinks the *rōnin* sitting off to the right is waiting for us."

"Will he attack us here?" Kasane asked.

"No." Hanshiro shouldered his bundle. "He's the type to despise filling out official papers. He'll ambush us at a crossroad distinguished by an absence of witnesses."

"How many others do you think there are?" Cat surveyed the crowded beach in an offhand way.

"He's alone."

"What makes you think so?"

"I would be if I were him. Too many sailors drive the boat up the mountain."

"Then let's sample some of Kuwano's famous clams." Cat strode across the littered beach toward the brightly lit shops facing the bay from the other side of the wide floodplain. "I'm hungry."

Kuwano's waterfront was busy. The big round lanterns glowed, and banners fluttered in the wind. The shutters of the tea shops and souvenir stands were open, exposing the interiors to view. The occupants were industriously vying for the business of the passengers disembarking from the late ferries. For the nonce, however, most of the passengers were intent on finding a spot to relieve themselves.

"The disciple always follows three steps behind his master." Hanshiro caught up with Cat.

Cat scowled at him, but she slowed her pace to walk behind him.

"Are you tired, Hachibei?" Cat asked.

"No, young master." Kasane knew that meant they'd walk a while before they stopped for the night. "I slept on the boat."

"We can use the lantern to light our way as far as Yokkaichi. The inns will all be full here anyway."

"As you wish." Hanshiro understood her eagerness to push on. They were within twenty-six *ri* of Kyōto and Oishi Kuranosuke and the vengeance for which she had struggled so valiantly.

Hanshiro read the shops' signs. "I'll meet you at the Clam House."

Cat almost panicked at the thought of his leaving. She had a sudden fear that if left alone with the shabby bodyguard, still picking his teeth, she would be as helpless as a carp on a chopping block. "Where are you going?"

"Nature makes demands that even a student of the New

Shadow school can't ignore." Hanshiro's sardonic bow included a gibe at his own dignity.

He angled off toward the privy, where a line of people were waiting. They were mostly women and a few men for whom a short pause by the roadside wouldn't suffice. Hanshiro stepped into the shadows of a bamboo thicket where he could keep an eye on the Clam House and Lady Asano.

The bodyguard ambled up beside him and arched his back as he too relieved himself. He stared out at the bay and gave a long, satisfied sigh.

"Beaten to the privy," he recited. "He praises the stars." The poem was droll, but artful and spare. Hanshiro expected no less.

"Who scattered the stars so carelessly in the sea?" Hanshiro composed a *haiku* using the last word of the bodyguard's as a pivot. "Now they sparkle there."

"Traveling far?"

"In this fleeting world one never knows how far one will travel." Hanshiro bowed politely. " 'Rosy cheeks in the morning, white bones at night.' " He left the *rōnin* and walked through the flocks of travelers whose inn *geta* made a merry clatter on the stones of the road and the slate entryways of the tea houses.

The Clam House's customers were clustered around the braziers, watching the clams bake in the hot ashes. Inside the shop, square platforms stood like islands surrounded by earthen passageways where the waitresses passed back and forth.

Hanshiro stepped out of his sandals at the flat boulder that served as a stoop. He drew his long-sword, in its scabbard, from his sash and knelt on the platform. He laid the sword on a silk cloth on his left side, with its cutting edge facing him to show he had no hostile intentions. Then he crossed his legs and sat at the low table across from Cat and Kasane. He unwrapped the bamboo sheath from around a serving of clams, picked up a pair of chopsticks, and selected a plump one that steamed fragrantly.

Cat and Kasane were discussing Yokkaichi. From there a road led south to Ise and the great shrine that had been Kasane's original destination.

"I prefer to go with you up to the capital, young master," Kasane was saying.

"What of Traveler? He's going to Ise."

"I'll leave a message in Yokkaichi." Kasane's unspoken

thought was that if he really cared for her, he would change his plans.

From the corner of her eye Cat saw the bodyguard enter the shop and take a seat on a platform at the rear. He roared jovially for service.

"I'm an ordinary man," he shouted to the world at large. "I neither burn incense nor fart."

Cat also saw a smile flicker so quickly across Hanshiro's face, it could have been mistaken for a tic. Could the impudent wretch from Tosa be happy to see the hired thug?

"What did he say?" Cat spoke in a low voice, but she needn't have bothered. The waitresses were buzzing around the bodyguard and laughing at his jokes.

"He praised the stars." Hanshiro's mood was approaching elation at the prospect of a contest to the death with a worthy adversary. He ate with gusto.

"He looks so harmless," Kasane said hopefully.

"He's not," Cat answered.

Kasane sneaked a look at the bodyguard.

" 'Who came along with his auger,' " the *rōnin* recited loudly, " 'and drilled these nine holes in us?' " He grabbed at a passing waitress, who shrieked and laughed and slapped his hand. " 'Year after year we fret over taxes,' " he continued. " 'By the thousands we knock our heads together and yell as we scramble for coppers.' "

"He's hiding his talons," Cat murmured.

" 'An efficient hawk hides its talons.' " Kasane had learned the saying from Cat.

"Exactly so." Hanshiro scooped a mound of sticky rice onto the chopsticks and ate it.

Hanshiro guarded the small procession's rear while Kasane walked ahead, carrying the wicker travel box and the travel lantern. There was always the possibility of a bandit ambush from the front, but Hanshiro knew that tonight an attack from behind was more likely.

"Forgive my rudeness, Your Honor . . ." For probably the hundredth time since leaving Kuwano, Kasane stared into the darkness behind her. "But how could you tell the bodyguard's dangerous? He seemed so good-natured."

"Scoundrels know each other."

"Pardon my contradicting you, sir, but you're not a scoundrel."

"He carries himself a certain way."

"Oishi-san once told me a story his *sensei* told him." As Cat spoke she kept watch over her shoulder, too. She expected an attack from the shadows. "A young man who was orphaned and masterless and desperately poor came to the master asking for instruction. The master glanced at him and said, 'You might as well go your way. There is nothing I can teach you.'

"The man was so desperate, he cared not if he lived or died. He was already living as though he were dead. He had attained what students of the warrior's Way seek. A master of the arts of war can recognize the attitude just by looking at how someone carries himself."

For a while the three of them walked in silence along the dark road, deserted now and cloaked in a cold, ghostly mist. Kasane continued to look back over her shoulder. Cat was absorbed with thoughts of Oishi and what would happen when she reached Kyōto.

Hanshiro too was preoccupied. He wondered if he had lost the transcendence of regard for life and death he had had when he'd left Edo. Had his spirit been dangerously affected by the haughty, willow-hipped beauty who now made life enticing and wretched?

"I'll wait for him here." Hanshiro lowered his *furoshiki* to the ground at the crossroad. He folded his towel into a cylinder and tied it around his forehead to catch the sweat of a duel. He tied back his sleeves and made himself comfortable on the stone step of a roadside chapel to Jizō.

"The two of you can meet me in Yokkaichi," he said. "Go to the Nightingale Inn on South Street, across from the distillery. Tell the master there that I sent you. You can trust him."

"You go ahead, Kasane," Cat said. "I'll stay here."

"You both must go." Hanshiro took out his tobacco and began filling his pipe.

"This is my fight, not yours. I won't go."

"Yes, you shall."

" 'My will is not a mat to be rolled up.' " Cat crossed her arms around her *naginata* and glared at Hanshiro. Then she remembered the end of the poem, and her blunder confounded her. The poem finished with "My heart is not a stone to be tumbled about." Its meaning included much more than Cat had intended. She knew from the heat in her neck and cheeks that she was blushing like a child.

"My lady . . ." Hanshiro bowed low, then looked up into Cat's face. "I can fight effectively only if I know you're safe."

Cat stared into his eyes and into the dark vortices of regret and longing and resolve that swirled there.

"Please, my lady," he said softly. "If you seek to fool me and hide nearby, I will sense your presence." *I will always sense your presence,* he thought. *And if I die tonight, my spirit will cling to you.*

Cat picked up her pack, turned, and walked away as though in a trance. Kasane followed, walking backward until Hanshiro was swallowed up in darkness.

"He'll kill the bodyguard, won't he?" Kasane whispered. She had to trot to keep up with Cat.

"I don't know." Cat was distracted. She was calculating how far Hanshiro's inner senses could reach and how far she must walk before she reached their limits. She was wondering how even a match this would be. She was swimming upstream against the emotions that swept over her.

She walked another half a *ri* or so before she left the road and began scrambling up the steep hillside to an outcropping of rock. She put out the light, then she and Kasane lay on their stomachs and surveyed the road.

"Surely he'll win," Kasane whispered. "He was born in a Tiger year. The holy Kokuzo watches over those born in the Tiger years."

"Hush." Cat stayed silent and unmoving for what seemed an eternity.

She didn't plan to flee up the Tōkaidō with the bodyguard on her trail. She knew she wouldn't get far. She also had no illusions that she would be able to surprise and kill the *rōnin* if he won the contest with Hanshiro and passed under her perch. He was too well trained to be ambushed, but at least she could make his job more difficult.

Cat tried to gauge the passage of time by the thumping of her own heart. Hours must have passed since she had left Hanshiro at the crossroads. The thought of him lying dead, his blood draining into the dust, filled her with despair.

"If the bodyguard comes, I'll meet him," she whispered finally.

"Do you have a plan?"

"Musashi says that if one sacrifices one's life, one must make the fullest use of one's weapon. It's false to die with a weapon undrawn."

"I'll join you in the Western Land." Kasane laid her knife within reach on the rock.

"You must not," Cat said. "Find Traveler. Go with him and bear children to care for your spirit when you die."

Cat looked over at Kasane. By the brilliant starlight she could see that Kasane's face was set. She'd seen that look before. Kasane had no intention of leaving here if Cat didn't. Cat sighed.

"Do you know how to do it?" she asked.

"No."

Cat took Kasane's hand and placed it against her chest. "With your palm, measure from this bone here, in the center. Put the point where the tip of this finger lies." Cat tapped a spot under the swell of Kasane's breast. "Hold the hilt firmly in both hands like this." With her arms outstretched and elbows slightly bent, Cat grasped the knife and pointed it at her own breast. "Or you can cut your throat," she said. "Although that way is messier."

"Should I tie my legs together?" In Kasane's village the women had whispered about a young woman who had been clumsy and left her legs untied. They had sprawled in an unseemly way in her death throes.

"If you have time."

Cat heard the crunch of gravel. She held her *naginata* ready and stared down, trying to identify the dark figure walking slowly toward her. A chill racked her when she recognized the bodyguard's blue towel, blood-soaked now, wrapped around the man's head. He stopped beneath her rock and looked up, his face shrouded in shadow.

Cat stood up and Kasane moved back to give her room. Kasane took the cap off the spearhead of Cat's old staff. She had changed her mind about suicide. She was resolved to follow Musashi's advice and die with her weapon drawn.

Cat walked to the edge of the rock ledge. Hanshiro was dead, and she soon would follow him. She was filled with a strange euphoria. "I am Asano no Kinume of the Banshu-Akō clan," she shouted. "I intend to kill you."

CHAPTER 62

SHE LIES IN THE DARKENING WIND

"My lady," Hanshiro answered, "if I have offended you that deeply, I shall take my own life and save you the inconvenience."

Cat was grateful to the night. It hid the tears she couldn't keep back. "Don't laugh at me." She scowled down at him.

"No one ever suffered loss because of laughter," he said.

"I saw the towel." Cat surreptitiously wiped her eyes on her sleeve as she slid down the rocky hillside. "I thought you were the bodyguard."

"There was no sense in sullying my own towel when he wouldn't be needing his any longer."

"He cut you." When Cat came closer she could see the wound that the *rōnin*'s blade had laid open in Hanshiro's cheek.

"He was very good."

"But you were better, Hanshiro-san." Kasane followed Cat down the hillside.

"My fate was not to leave this burning house today." With a slight wave of his hand Hanshiro indicated the world at large, starlit and silent.

The three of them resumed their journey. Kasane led the way with the lantern. She still looked back over her shoulder, but now she feared that the bodyguard's vengeful spirit would pursue her. Cat trailed at Hanshiro's right elbow, just far enough behind to be considered following, but not far enough to qualify as respectful.

Hanshiro's feet moved as though they belonged to someone else. His head rang and his cheek throbbed. He was ashamed of the elation he had felt at the prospect of a duel. It had been childish of him to relish another's death.

The outcome of the fight had been uncertain until Hanshiro dodged the downswing that would have sliced his head diagonally like a melon had it connected. Instead it opened the cut that reached from the corner of his left eye to his chin. Almost blinded by his own blood, he had feinted with a flower wheel maneuver and driven his sword into the bodyguard's chest. He and the bodyguard had crossed swords less than ten times, but their duel had seemed to last a lifetime.

"Where is he?" Cat asked.

"I laid him out by Jizō-san with a note saying the priests would come for him. He had war funds. I'll leave the money at the temple in Yokkaichi."

Hanshiro hadn't been surprised to find a small bag with coins and a letter inside. No matter how poor a warrior might be, he always carried "war funds," money enough to bury him.

The bodyguard's note read, "If I should die, do not trouble yourself trying to locate my family. I have none. I shall be grateful if my bones are disposed of in the manner customary for a man of no great merit."

Hanshiro had also found a poem and a cylindrical ivory chop with Kira's seal carved into the end of it, both of which he kept. The bodyguard probably had written the poem in the Clam House before he'd set out after Cat, for Cat was surely the object of his pursuit.

Hanshiro planned to leave the poem with the priests to inscribe on the nameless *rōnin*'s funerary tablet.

> My time here is up.
> I will challenge Lord Emma
> To a duel in Hell.

"Did you leave his swords?" Cat asked.

Hanshiro nodded over his shoulder, indicating that the swords were in the rolled sleeping mat he carried there. "I'll give them to the priests."

Hanshiro walked in silence while he phrased the question that had been on his mind. "My lady," he said finally, "if I am to be of any use to you, I should know as much as possible about the councilor."

Cat almost retorted that details about her father's councilor were none of his concern. But she knew he was right. If she was going to accept his services, she would have to surrender information, some of it personal.

"Please allow me time to consider an answer," she said.

Cat wondered how she could describe Oishi. He had always been a quiet, solid presence in her life, but she knew less about him personally than she did about the lowliest privy cleaner in her mother's mansion. Instructing Cat in the *naginata* and the warrior's Way had been only a minor function in Oishi's years of service to Lord Asano.

His skill as Asano's adviser was already well known, but Cat was not about to tell this surly stranger about Oishi's other role. For twenty years he had acted as go-between for Lord Asano and his beloved outside-wife, Cat's mother. As the years passed and Lord Asano's legal wife bore no children, Oishi's job became more difficult.

Cat would not speak of the occasions Oishi had taken her and her mother to temple festivals or special outings because her father's duties, official and conjugal, kept him away. Oishi, not Lord Asano, had accompanied Cat to the ceremony marking the entry of her name on the temple rolls. And more years than not, at the festival of the Weaver Maiden, Oishi was the one who held her up so she could tie brightly colored silk threads and examples of her best calligraphy to the branches of the cherry tree in the garden.

One of Cat's most vivid childhood memories was the grip of his strong hands on her waist. Of being lifted high into the air as though suddenly weightless as a kite. She remembered being held aloft by that unwavering grip as her small fingers fumbled with the knots tying the threads and the fluttering strips of paper containing her childish poems.

With a rush of awareness that left a hollow, churning sensation in the pit of her stomach, Cat realized that she felt betrayed as well as abandoned by Oishi. She had trusted him as she had trusted her father. She had assumed he would always protect her and guide her along the Way. His feet would always follow the honorable path. If, as rumor asserted, he was carousing in the Shimabara while his lord's spirit remained unavenged, then he was making a mockery of everything he had taught her about life and honor.

Cat sorted through a lifetime of memories and picked out the two facts most relevant about her *sensei*. "Oishi Kuranosuke is a master of the Yamaga school of strategy," she said. "He served my father for twenty years."

"Did you receive instruction from him?"

"Yes."

Hanshiro grunted pensively. Actually he didn't need any more information. He could tell from Cat's bearing and the disarray of her enemies that the man who had taught her was an exceptional fighter and *sensei*. *One day with a great teacher,* he thought, *is better than a thousand days of study.*

"The councilor has not betrayed you," he said.

Cat stiffened as though he could read her mind. "How do you know?"

Hanshiro stopped and turned to face Cat. He knew from her long silence that she had traveled into the past. He knew the journey must have been a sorrowful one.

"Consider Oishi's actions." As Hanshiro stared into her eyes, he thought how easily he could be hypnotized by them. "Until six months ago he did everything possible to convince the government to reinstate your father's brother. He would not attack Kira for fear of ruining his chances. Since your uncle was sent to Hiroshima, Oishi has been offered employment by several lords, yet he accepted none. I do not know what his plan is, my lady, but I can assure you that he has one."

"Dare I hope that?" Cat whispered.

"Yes, my lady."

They walked through the sleeping town of Yokkaichi and pounded on the shutters of the Nightingale Inn. When the sleepy proprietress showed them to their room, Kasane disappeared behind the screen set up for her. She fell asleep on her hard pallet almost instantly. Cat, however, sat wide awake and restless. She could not, even at risk of starting inquisitive tongues to wagging, lie down next to Hanshiro. She excused herself on the pretext of "going somewhere."

When she didn't return Hanshiro became alarmed. He padded in his stockinged feet down the quiet corridors and woke the ancient servant sleeping on a mat in the vestibule. He handed him his wooden chit to retrieve his swords from the rack, tipped the old man to let him out, put on his sandals and went in search of her.

He found her beyond the wind-mauled pines on the beach behind the inn. She was kneeling in the sand near the water's edge. She held her *naginata* across her thighs. The starlight that tipped the gentle waves of the bay glowed on her head and shoulders. It outlined her sloping forehead, her high nose, strong chin, and the sensuous curve of her nape. Hanshiro studied her as he would an exquisite painting or a statue of Kannon-sama, the lovely goddess of mercy.

"How I waste away . . . ." He thought of the old poem. *"I who thought myself so strong, now feeble with love."*

Cat was obviously deep in reflection, but she glanced up at the shadows of the pine grove where Hanshiro thought himself hidden. She too was developing the sight beyond sight, the sense that transcended hearing, touch, and smell. In her case, the ability had been sharpened by the fact that she was pursued night and day by enemies. And perhaps because Hanshiro's spirit called to hers.

For more freedom of movement, Cat ignored the cold and pulled her right arm out of her robes, exposing her breast. She tied back her left sleeve with a long cord. She crossed it in the middle of her back and knotted the ends. She folded her towel diagonally into a strip and tied it around her head. Then she rose in a whisper of russet-colored *hakama* skirts.

She stood facing Hanshiro. Her expression was remote, haughty. She held the *naginata* over her head with the curved blade behind her. The stance was an invitation to join her in performing *kata*, the warrior's ritualized series of thrusts and cuts, evasions and parries.

Hanshiro took off his cloak and pulled his arms out of his sleeves, letting the top half of his robe fall down around his waist. He drew his long-sword, held it with both hands in front of him, and stepped out of the shadows to share the chilly starlight with her.

They began with the simplest forms and increased the pace slightly with each succeeding set of motions. Cat knew that Hanshiro wasn't expending himself fully, but she was keeping him on the defensive a respectable part of the time. She closed in with small, fast steps, spinning the *naginata* in its powerful, deadly circles as she came. Hanshiro parried and leapt and barely avoided a slash to his shins.

Cat moved a fraction too slowly in the follow-through, and Hanshiro's sword swooped down in a blur. It stopped with the blade resting on the nexus of Cat's neck and shoulder. She neither flinched nor changed the imperious look in her dark eyes.

In the next form she used her front hand as a fulcrum and pivoted the blade upward, forcing Hanshiro to release his right hand from his sword to keep his forearm from being severed. Cat whirled again. She stamped for momentum, and the blade flashed through an overhand arc and came to rest against his inner thigh.

They advanced and retreated and circled, Cat hissing now and then with the effort and the concentration. Their movements were reciprocal and restrained and palpable with danger. The slightest error in reflex or judgment would have killed or maimed one or the other of them.

As they fell into the rhythm of the *kata*, their dance became an affirmation of trust that went far beyond the words of an oath, even one written in blood. Surrounded by the aura of eternal present, they moved to the pulse of life and death and rebirth. They were invulnerable. Time slowed for them until each could clearly see, even in midstroke, the temper marks on the other's blade.

When they finished they were panting from the exertion. Hanshiro sheathed his sword, and Cat held her *naginata* off to one side. They stood so close that Hanshiro could feel Cat's breath stirring the dark hairs on his bare chest. She looked up into the shadows and lights of his face, ravaged in defense of her. She could hear his harsh breathing over the sigh of the spent waves brushing the sand nearby. Nothing held Cat there except Hanshiro's tiger's eyes and the sea mist that wound around the two of them.

Hanshiro lightly touched her mouth with the tips of his fingers. He cradled her pale face in his scarred hands, leaned down, and gently brushed her temples with his lips. Cat trembled under his touch. A plover cried mournfully from the river shoals.

"The bridge, my lady," Hanshiro murmured.

Cat walked with him to the massive stone pylon supporting the arch of the wooden bridge nearby. Hanshiro spread his cloak on the sand. The air was cold, but that wasn't why Cat trembled.

" 'For her straw mat bedding . . .' " As he recited the ancient poem, Hanshiro untied the cords of Cat's *hakama* so that it fell around her feet.

" 'The Lady of the Bridge spreads the starlight out . . .' " He unwound her sash.

" 'And in the waiting night . . .' " With the palms of his hands he pushed back the front edges of her robe and undershirt. As he did so he caressed her breasts, taut and satiny as the buds of cherry blossoms. He bent his head and touched each nipple with the tip of his tongue.

" 'She lies in the darkening wind.' " He knelt with her on the cloak and laid her gently back.

CHAPTER 63

PASSIONATE LOVE AND
A COUGH

Cat and Hanshiro lay entwined on top of Cat's travel cloak and under Hanshiro's. Over them arched the intricate wooden corbelings and underpinnings of the bridge. The river murmured nearby. Plovers cried plaintively from the shallows. Cat pressed harder against Hanshiro and drew in long, slow breaths of contentment. So this was what all the courtesan's songs and stories were about.

Hanshiro himself was stunned with joy. Years of sorrows and disappointments had fallen away. He felt as giddy and carefree as a child at a temple fair.

"I was so cruel to you." Cat rubbed her cheek in the thick hair of his chest. "Making you sit in the rain."

"To serve when the master treats you well is not to be a retainer." Hanshiro ran his hand along the sinuosity of her side and hip. He kissed her bare shoulder, then pulled the cloak up to cover it. "To obey a master who's heartless and cold, that's true service."

"Do you think me heartless and cold?"

"I thought you had neither blood nor tears." He brushed unruly wisps of hair from her eyes.

"Why did you persist?"

"I knew you would relent. You returned Lord Hino's letter of safe passage to me instead of tearing it up." Hanshiro's smile stretched the torn skin and muscles of his cheek, but he hardly felt the pain. "By giving me the letter to hold, you made me the pawnbroker of your fate."

"I thought you cold and cruel, too." Cat touched his lacerated cheek tenderly with the tips of her fingers. "I was frightened of you."

"Not as frightened as I was of you, my sweet lady."

"You're making fun of me again."

"I'm not." Hanshiro threw aside the cloak and reached between Cat's legs for the end of the red silk loincloth she had worn. " 'More fearful than a tiger,' " he whispered in her ear, " 'is a length of scarlet crepe.' "

Half of the cloth lay under Cat. Hanshiro drifted the other end lightly along her thigh and across the dark thicket that sheltered the confluence of desire. He increased the pressure, drawing the silk into the swollen folds and pulling it between them until it glistened with a satiny moisture. Cat moaned as it pressed against the hidden kernel, the core of her delight, and tugged it tantalizingly upward. She could also feel the other half of the cloth sliding forward, tight and insistent, along the crevice of her buttocks.

The long silken caress sent Cat soaring in a tightening spiral toward the bursting. When the cloth pulled free of her weight, Hanshiro teased it lightly across her belly and breasts. Using knots reserved for one's most beloved, he wound it around her neck and wrists. He tied it so that by pulling her wrists Cat could tighten the cloth's pressure on her neck and increase her own pleasure.

As she writhed in Hanshiro's tender bonds, he licked her breasts and throat, her chin and mouth. The heat of his tongue and mouth and the chill of the night air on Cat's wet skin concentrated her entire awareness to the surface of her body. Bared to the indifferent night, to the stars, to any passerby, Cat, though bound, felt a wild freedom.

She pulled on the silken manacles until her head spun and light exploded into incandescent copper dust behind her eyelids. She increased the pressure until she was gasping for air. As though he were traveling with her, Hanshiro knew when she reached the peak and hovered there. He knew the exact instant between soaring and falling, and he spread the soft folds of her groin and touched her once, lightly, with the tip of his finger. She cried out, a single descending note that set off alone into the darkness. A plover answered with its mournful cry.

Hanshiro untied her wrists and cradled her as she floated back to him. In the distance a wakeful rooster crowed.

" 'If I were to make this night into a thousand nights . . .' " Hanshiro murmured into the tumbled fragrance of Cat's hair. " 'Many a sweet word would remain unsaid when the cock heralded the dawn.' "

Kasane awoke before the rooster crowed. The twisted rush wick of the night lantern had burned out, and the room, an inner one, was dark. She dressed quietly in her servant's livery and sneaked past the mattress and quilts, still as unrumpled as when the maids made it up for Hanshiro and his disciple. But the quilts were heaped high, and in the dark Kasane couldn't tell if they were occupied or not.

When she reached the front of the Nightingale, she found the old servant sitting, stark naked, in the wan light of a rush lamp. He was mending his worn loincloth.

"More traffic," he grumbled when Kasane handed him the wooden ticket for her sandals and her pilgrim's staff. "In and out, all night. A body can't get any sleep."

Kasane refrained from pointing out that he hadn't been asleep. With much mumbling and wheezing and creaking of leathery joints, the old man produced her sandals from among the fifty or so pair stored neatly on shelves against the wall.

Kasane stepped from the raised floor of the entryway onto the big flat boulder, then into her sandals. She lit the small travel lantern with the inn's name on it and hung it from the end of its pole. She pulled her cloak about her and ducked out the small side door into the darkness of the sleeping town.

The eaves of the two rows of buildings almost met over the narrow street. The cold wind from the bay blew down it as though through a tube. The scuffle of Kasane's soles reverberated off the rows of heavy wooden shutters.

Kasane passed through the large open market for which Yokkaichi, Fourth Day Market, was named. The small stands were shuttered with screens of woven bamboo or with straw matting. A few booths and two-wheeled carts sheltered their owners, who slept curled up on matting with other ragged mats pulled over them. A scrawny dog growled at her. Sleepy chickens stirred on their roosts along the rooflines of the sheds.

Kasane approached the transport office, where a pale necklace of bare male nates ringed the fire in the trampled yard. The hostlers, porters, couriers, and *kago* bearers were warming themselves. Kasane could hear their slang and their laughter when she stopped to read the official notices on the bulletin board. They were only the usual edicts and admonishments, though, none of which concerned her mistress.

Kasane turned onto the lane leading to the local temple and walked between the shuttered souvenir stands that linked it. Doves cooed and fluttered among the massive, ornate eaves of the roof over the temple's wooden gate. Kasane was disappointed to find no letter addressed to the Floating Weed among the posted notices, the *sutras*, and the pleas for health or the return of wayward mates. She began scanning the message board again.

"Forgive my rudeness. . . ." The voice was diffident, but it startled Kasane. She took a firmer grip on her staff and whirled to face the speaker. The accent identified him as being from Kazusa, her home province.

Traveler stood in the shadow of the eaves of a shuttered noodle stand across the way. His face was hidden by the square straw hood on his head and by the towel pulled low over his eyes and tied under his mouth. He wore used clothes, the fringed apron and ragged jacket of a low-class ne'er-do-well for hire.

He didn't know what had become of the shy young maiden who had stolen his heart at the See No Evil in Oiso, but by now he was sure she was embarked on a venture sown with peril. He had decided to go into the disguise business himself until he solved the mystery.

"I was instructed to give this to the one serving the Tosa *rōnin* and his disciple." The young man bowed deeply as he held out a thin bamboo pole with his latest letter wedged into the slit in the end. The letter was on the finest pale yellow Sugiwara stock. It was adorned with a single sprig of pine.

"Where is the one who asked you to deliver this?"

"Not far away, Your Excellency." Traveler backed deeper into the shadows. He was sure Kasane could hear his heart thumping like a hand drum. *Truly,* he thought, *one sight is worth a thousand hearings.*

"Did the sender give you any verbal message to accompany this?" Kasane had been waiting for ten days to meet her suitor face to face. She didn't know whether to be despondent or relieved or angry that he hadn't arrived yet. *He's as slow as a centipede tying on sandals,* she thought.

"The author of this letter said only that I would know the object of his regard by beauty of form and tenderness of expression."

Embarrassment warmed Kasane's face. "Are you to deliver my reply also?"

"I can be here when the fifth bell sounds and receive a reply if Your Excellency so desires."

"My two masters may have offices for me to perform. Meet me instead at the Nightingale inn." Kasane bowed. "Ask for Hachibei of Kazusa."

"As you wish, Your Excellency."

Traveler was in a turmoil. Swinging between despair and a

most uncharacteristic rage, he watched Kasane tuck the letter into the front of her jacket and walk back toward the town.

He was confused by the gender change his beloved had undergone along the road. He was no longer sure if he had begun by loving a man dressed as a woman or if he was now in love with a woman disguised as a man. Whichever she was, he was distressed to find her in the company of the taciturn Tosa *rōnin* who had walked with him for part of his journey. Ever since he had seen the three together in Miya he had been racked by jealousy.

He was suffering from the usual lover's delusion. Because he loved Kasane he assumed everyone found her as irresistible as he did. To make matters worse, he wondered if his own praise of her had brought her to Tosa's attention.

Even if Kasane had still been the shy young peasant woman on pilgrimage with her brother, as when Traveler first saw her, he would have been cautious. He may have thrown himself into this affair with reckless abandon, but he was not interested in the usual roadside romance. Whoever this exciting and enchanting enigma was, he had decided he couldn't go on with his life unless she shared it. He would have to approach her with respect and decorum.

The decision was as daring as it was irresponsible. A suitable marriage had already been arranged for Traveler with a woman he had never seen. He was about to abandon his duty, fail his parents, and risk exile from the village of his birth. He was about to become the worst possible creature, one without a sense of obligation.

At a distance he followed Kasane into the market, where people were stirring now in the dawn's ashen light. Women were wetting down the dust with gourds of water or arranging vegetables in artistic stacks. Men were rolling out tubs and kegs. Children swept the ground around their parents' booths or raced about on errands. Chickens scratched for scattered rice and millet grains. They dodged reluctantly from in front of Kasane's feet.

Kasane made several purchases, her cloth bundle growing larger with each one. Then Traveler watched her disappear into the Nightingale, through the big wooden shutter that the old servant was shoving open with his bony shoulder. The young man crouched behind a stack of empty tubs in the alley next to the distillery to wait and to speculate on the entire bewildering affair.

Since Hanshiro had given Kasane the responsibilities of a servant, she had developed a determined, capable air. She had begun taking care of the details of travel. In her dealings with porters and innkeepers, she no longer bowed as low as she once had.

Now she went directly to the tiny room the master of the Nightingale used as an office. After exchanging the usual pleasantries with him, Kasane handed over the delicacies she had bought and left instructions for breakfast. When she finished there she strode, flat-footed and formidable, down the halls. She acknowledged almost curtly the obeisances of the inn's staff.

In the morning light filtering through the paper walls, she could see that the pile of mattresses was occupied. Cat and Hanshiro were lying on their left sides under the quilt. Cat was curled against Hanshiro's chest, and he slept with an arm thrown over her protectively, his cheek against her hair.

Kasane smiled to herself. Like as not Hanshiro-san's bridge to heaven was snug inside her ladyship's royal gate and his heart was beating fast against her shoulder blade. *Passionate love and a cough,* Kasane thought, *cannot be concealed.*

When she knelt at the foot of the bed, she saw Hanshiro's hand tighten on the wooden staff he had left there. Kasane knew the movement was reflexive and that he wouldn't strike her. Hanshiro had an uncanny ability to identify people by their footsteps. Kasane was sure he knew she was the intruder.

Kasane found Cat's ankle under the quilt and gently shook it. "Young master," she said, "the hour is late. The road is calling."

CHAPTER 64
WOLVES OF PRETEXT

The yard of Yokkaichi's transport agency was stacked with bales and crates to be loaded. The patient pack mares stamped and flicked their tails. Postboys and bearers and drivers dickered with prospective customers over fares to the next post station.

Children circulated with tea and snacks for sale. The few women travelers were admiring the wares of a traveling seller of dildos.

The wooden shutters of the transport office had been slid back in their wooden tracks, exposing the high platform where the officials knelt at their writing stands. The wall behind them was papered with work rosters for the maintenance of their section of the Tōkaidō and the labor requisitions of traveling *daimyō*. A disheveled line had formed, but even the richest rice broker moved quickly out of Hanshiro's way. Cat wasn't surprised. People respected those born in the year of the Tiger. The tiger had the power to chase away thieves, fire, and ghosts. *And merchants,* Cat thought.

From the yard Cat watched Hanshiro talk to the official in charge. Her love formed an aura around him that blurred and muted everything else. She hardly heard the hubbub in the yard. A cryptic smile flickered across her face.

"I suppose Traveler will turn off here for Ise." Kasane broke into Cat's reverie.

Traveler hadn't shown up at the Nightingale Inn at the appointed hour that morning. Kasane had had to entrust the old servant with delivering her letter to the man she thought was her suitor's messenger. She didn't know that in the alley across the way Traveler had lost his nerve and had watched her go. Now she was preoccupied with the thought that her pilgrim would disappear without her ever seeing him again.

"You told him you had to go up to the capital." Cat had read the letter and the poem, of course. Poetry was meant to be recited aloud; and Kasane wouldn't send it without asking her to correct any errors in form or vulgarity in style. The *tanka* had been charming. Unpretentious but heartfelt.

> Tossing and turning
> Morning comes, hair in tangles.
> Part it with fingers
> As though plaiting a straw rope.
> Wondering, will I see you?

"You could go on a secret pilgrimage to Ise with him," Cat said. "Traveling alone together, you would become fast friends. You could spend every night with your hearts murmuring to each other."

"I couldn't leave you, young master!" Kasane was horrified at the thought of such disloyalty. That Cat might prefer to be alone with Hanshiro didn't occur to her. "He'll do the sleeve. He'll jilt me." Kasane had picked up some of the courtesan's slang from Cat. "It's said that the women of Ise are pretty and agreeable and plentiful." Kasane kept her voice low. It wouldn't do to be overheard speaking as women.

"Added to all your other virtues, elder sister, you have one that every woman at Ise lacks where the pilgrim is concerned."

"What is that, mistress?"

"Propinquity."

Kasane laughed behind her sleeve. Then she drew from it a small packet formed by folding a bamboo leaf into a tetrahedron and tucking in the ends.

"Hanshiro-san gave me money. He ordered me to spend it on myself." Kasane was ashamed of her self-indulgence but pleased with her purchase. "I bought this in the market this morning."

"What is it?"

"The ashes of a lizard." Kasane lowered her voice even further. Tokugawa Tsunayoshi forbade the killing of even a mosquito. There was no telling what the punishment would be for trafficking in lizard remains. "The holy woman who sold them to me said that if I sprinkle them into the hair of the person I love, he'll love me in return."

" 'Lust will not keep . . .' " Cat laughed as she recited one of Kasane's aphorisms. " 'Something must be done about it.' "

Cat had more to say on that subject, but she didn't get a chance. Two guards bustled from the side door of the agency. They held the old courtier, the purveyor of elephant urine philters, by the arms. Activity in the yard ceased as people turned to stare.

The old cloud dweller wasn't going quietly. He flailed and shrieked as the guards stuffed him into a waiting palanquin. Before the sliding door slammed closed, he managed to land a mortal insult. He hit one of the guards on the head with his run-down *geta*.

"We aren't rubes." The guard rubbed the shaved strip up the center of his skull where a lump was already forming. He opened the door just wide enough to poke an errant corner of the old man's travel cloak inside. For good measure, he borrowed a bearer's stick and thumped the top of the palanquin with it. "Your tricks won't work here."

The four bearers had been standing by, grinning broadly and

holding a long rope. They had been in this situation before. They passed the rope around the basket, lashing the doors shut.

"When I report this outrage, my august lord, the emperor, the son of heaven, will have your heads!" the old man shouted. "Your entrails will be food for the crows of the river bank."

With a grunt and a shout the bearers heaved the palanquin onto their shoulders and began marking time in rhythm to their chant. A mother whispered to her child, then shoved him forward. The boy darted toward the palanquin, dropped to his knees, and scuttled under it and out the other side. Assured of long life by proximity to one who had served his august majesty, the boy threw a clod of dirt at the palanquin.

Through the thin bars in the palanquin's window, Cat could see the veins, purple as eggplants, standing out on the cloud dweller's temples. His beak of a nose jutted from between the bars. When he screamed he sprayed spittle.

Hanshiro looked amused by it all when he joined Cat and Kasane. "If they aren't careful," he said, "they'll have a worse problem than the one they're trying to avoid."

"What crime did he commit?" Kasane asked.

"The magistrate here heard that all along the road he's been pretending to fall from the palanquins provided by the government and demanding compensation." Hanshiro actually chuckled. "But if the old man has apoplexy and dies in a government-supplied palanquin, the transport officials will be filling out papers until their retirement."

With his fan Hanshiro beckoned to the hostlers who were bringing three horses from the stable next door. Then he led the way to the mounting block. Hanshiro was pleased to see how well Cat sat her shaggy little mount. Since the saddle was raised more than a foot from the horse's back, staying on it required skill and balance. Kasane rode in a pannier, balanced on the other side by their baggage and by stones dangling as ballast. The postboy walked ahead of her, leading the pack horse by a rope.

Kasane opened the white paper wrapping from the present Cat had given her. Kasane had found it on her bed when she'd returned to the Nightingale that morning. The book was called *An Illustrated Manual of Eroticism,* and it was much more informative than the pillow book Kasane had traded for firewood at the pilgrim's inn in Mishima. This book had text in *hiragana* script as well as pictures.

It was divided into four sections—"Heaven and Earth,"

"Animals," "Human Beings," and "Instruments." Kasane turned to "Human Beings" and the essay called "Sensuous Women."

If you possess one of the following characteristics, you are a sensuous woman. Kasane ran her finger down the page, and her lips moved as she silently formed the words. *You have a gentle voice. You cough softly when you speak to a man. This means you have an adventurous heart.* Kasane practiced coughing softly behind her sleeve.

"Are you pursuing your studies by the light of fireflies and snow, Hachibei?" Hanshiro called over his shoulder.

"Yes, master." Kasane blushed and shielded the book with her sleeve. *Your eyes are very narrow, but you open them wide when you look at a man.* She read on silently. *This is extremely seductive.*

Hanshiro pulled farther ahead of the pack horse and guided his mount up close to Cat's. With his knee touching hers he spoke in a low voice so the hostler wouldn't overhear. "I left the notice with the transport officer. He agreed to post it right away."

"Do you think it will throw off the dogs?"

"It should. It says that a certain retired official no longer wishes the capture of the clerk who stole from him. I signed it with the seal I took from the bodyguard. I stamped extra sheets and paid a clerk to make copies. He'll send them off with the next government courier. We should find them posted on bulletin boards between here and the capital. By the time Kira finds out about it we'll be in Kyōto."

"I want to keep going until we reach there."

Hanshiro looked up at the gray clouds rolling over the mountains to the west. A chill gust shivered the pines and whispered of rain.

"There may be a delay at the Seki barrier," he said. "And Suzuka Pass lies ahead. It's a treacherous climb. The peasants say the demons who live there crush the bones of evildoers. But I think the demons have an interest in people's purses and not their sins."

"Even so . . ."

Cat didn't have to elaborate. Hanshiro understood her anxiety. If Oishi refused to help her, her arduous, dangerous journey would have been for nothing.

"All of Edo sympathizes with your father's case," Hanshiro said. "Everyone's waiting for his retainers to take a just revenge.

The rumor is that even Kira's wife has advised him to commit suicide. They say she wants to avoid the shame of seeing him fall into his enemies' hands.''

"He mustn't!" Cat was horrified that Kira might kill himself and deprive her of the satisfaction of arranging his death herself.

"You needn't fear, my lady." He smiled at her. "In Kira's house his wife is the only one with the fortitude to end her life by her own hand. And as you know, Kira's son hasn't moved his father to the safety of his villa, much less to his estate in the north country. I would guess that even he's reluctant to become too involved in the affair.

"The *shōgun* has shown his displeasure with Kira by forcing him to move out of his house behind the castle walls. All in all, I would say that if Oishi chooses to attack, he'll meet with little opposition."

"But no vendetta has been registered for my father." Cat rode in silence for several long moments. Then she recited the words of Ieyasu, the first Tokugawa *shōgun*. " 'Persons who neglect to give notice of their intended revenge are like wolves of pretext.' ''

"But there's more, my lady."

" 'And their punishment or pardon,' '' she went on, " 'should depend upon the circumstances of the case.' ''

"Whether registered or not," Hanshino said softly, "a vendetta is still possible.''

CHAPTER 65
ONE DAY IN THIS WORLD

Cat and Hanshiro and Kasane stopped only to visit the wayside privies, change hostlers in Ishiyakushi and Kameyama, and buy food to eat as they rode. High in her rocking pannier, Kasane read her new manual of love.

Cat and Hanshiro rode in silence. They had no need for words. They were experiencing *yoin*, resonance. Pulses from their lovemaking still reverberated through them like the aftertones of a temple bell. A glance, a sigh, a wisp of a smile, began the sweet throbbing again.

A cold rain began to fall after they passed the government checkpoint in Seki early in the afternoon. The postboy put on his straw raincoat and hat. Kasane made a tent of her oiled-paper cloak and a straw mat and went on reading under it. She had progressed to the "Instruments" section, and only a typhoon could have distracted her. Cat and Hanshiro rode with their thighs touching so they could share Hanshiro's big red umbrella.

The road wound upward into steep green mountains. At Saka-noshita they had to turn in the horses and proceed on foot. Beyond there, an avalanche had covered a section of the Tō-kaidō, and travelers had to take a detour. The new route included a bridge suspended over the deepest gorge. It was a swaying, precarious affair of bamboo poles and hawsers. Horses could not cross it.

While Hanshiro returned the mounts, Kasane read under the wide eaves of Sakanoshita's transport office. She had come to the part of the manual that described types of vaginas. She was wondering if hers was one of those "moist and snug and lined with bumps like herring roe."

When Hanshiro returned she reluctantly wrapped the book in paper treated with persimmon juice. She put the package in a bag and looped the long cord around her neck. Then she stuck the bag and its contents into her jacket. She shouldered the carrying pole and travel box and set out behind Hanshiro and Cat.

By midafternoon they were well into the highest of the mountains, the upper fringes of the wild Kinki region to the south. Far below, muddy rivers, pale as liquid plaster, filled the sharp clefts of the gorges. Mist from them snaked among the trees and undergrowth. Silver waterfalls plunged into the layers of mist, only to reappear farther down the slopes. Hanshiro took the travel box to ease Kasane's burden.

By the time they were nearing Suzuka Pass, the day was as dark as late twilight and the rain was still falling. The gloominess was heightened by the overhanging cedars. The road went from precipitous to perilous. Torrents of water and slick gray mud cascaded down the slope.

At a narrow defile Kasane strayed too near the edge of the road, and the saturated ground gave way under her feet. She screamed and plummeted straight down.

"Kasane!" Cat flung herself onto her stomach at the rim of the gaping hole. "Kasane!" She was oblivious to the water rushing past her and into the funnel formed by the cave-in. Kasane clawed at the rocky slope as she slid down it. Cat could see the terror on her receding face. She came to a stop with a jolt, her feet hitting a small outcropping of rock. She grabbed the stem of a stunted bush and barely saved herself from falling over backward and onto the boulders in the river below. Her face looked small and pale and indistinct in the mist.

Hanshiro always carried a hempen rope. In his profession ropes and the tying of specialized knots often came in handy. But when he threw one end to Kasane, it fell far short. He retrieved it and knotted both his and Cat's sashes and then their loincloths. It still dangled just above Kasane's outstretched hand. She tried to scramble to it and almost fell again.

Cat and Hanshiro looked around for another traveler who might have a rope. The road was empty, the rain relentless.

Hanshiro was in a quandary. He could reach Kasane if he were lowered down, but Cat couldn't pull both of them back up.

"I'll go." Cat tried to take the rope from Hanshiro's hand, but he held it tightly. She stared up at him as the rain pelted her face. "If she dies while we argue"—she had to shout to be heard over the roar of a sudden gust of wind—"I shall throw myself after her."

Hanshiro had no doubt she meant it. Cat could see the flash of despair in his eyes.

"Sleeve touches sleeve," she said. She did not have to finish the saying: *Because it was fated in a former life.* If they were meant to be together, nothing would part them.

Hanshiro tied the rope around her chest above her breasts and under her arms. He tugged on it to check the knot. "Wrap it around your arm and hold it like this." He pulled on it again to test her grip, then he helped her coil the trailing end. "I'll hold your ankles."

Even if fate meant for them to be together, he couldn't bear to test it by lowering her over a cliff on the end of a rope. He had to keep her in his grasp. He lay on his stomach and gripped her ankles as she inched over the precipice. She braced herself with her elbows to keep from scraping her face on the rocks. Gravel and larger stones hit her on their way to the bottom of the gorge. The water rushing over the edge flowed into her eyes, making it impossible to see. Perhaps that was just as well.

Even with Hanshiro's fingers digging painfully hard into her ankles, she felt as though she were falling already. She concentrated on Kasane and not on the dizziness that swept over her. She didn't see the young man, hidden under a sodden straw hood and cape, who kneeled to help Hanshiro. Hanshiro saw that the man was Traveler, but he was too preoccupied to acknowledge it.

"Drop the rope directly beneath you," Hanshiro called.

"I have it," Kasane shouted. She tied it around one wrist and held on with the other.

Cat braced the rope against the palm of her hand as Hanshiro and Traveler began pulling her back. Even though Kasane tried to help, pushing off with her feet where she could, her weight made Cat's arms feel as though they were being wrenched from the sockets. The rough hemp and the rocks of the slope bloodied her hands.

As soon as they had Cat safely back on the road, Hanshiro and Traveler grabbed the rope and heaved while Cat tried to wipe the mud and water from her eyes. When Kasane was close to the edge, her young suitor backed away and trotted off without waiting for thanks or recognition. He was too embarrassed about missing his meeting with her that morning to face her now.

Cat and Hanshiro each took one of Kasane's hands and hauled her up. Hanshiro didn't know how things stood between Kasane and Traveler and decided not to mention him. Panting and laughing, he and Cat and Kasane sat in the mud and the rain. Then, on trembling legs, they walked the half a *ri* to the dank hamlet of Tsuchiyama and stopped to warm themselves at the thatched hovel that served as its only tea house. Kasane's blue fingers shook as she sipped the hot cup of pale mushroom tea and watched the rain pour off the eaves.

Cat wiggled her bare toes, tingling with cold, even after the maid had washed them in scalding water. The owner of the tea house claimed to have a room where they could sleep, but Cat could see it would be tiny and roach-infested. "We can spend the night here."

"Please don't stop on my account, young master." Kasane had long since made Cat's mission her own. "I can walk all night."

"Just don't try to fly again, Hachibei." Hanshiro grinned at Kasane through the steam rising from his teacup. "The rest of us can't keep up with you."

"Yes, master." Kasane smiled shyly into her own cup. She

had to agree with the old saying. Truly, one day in this world was more pleasurable than a thousand in the next.

Minakuchi's night market was noisy and reckless as a country fair. Groups of town lads strolled among the booths. They flirted with the young peasant women selling produce and loudly discussed the best ways to win favor with courtesans.

A gang of them brushed by Cat, who had stopped to look over the display of dildos. The itinerant peddler was the same one she had seen in the yard of Yokkaichi's transport office. Now he had turned his big wooden traveling case into a makeshift kiosk by spreading a square of black silk over the top of it. He had arranged his wood and lacquered papier-mâché phalluses on the cloth.

"Something for your wife, governor?" The man caught Cat's eye. "I have a wide assortment of finely crafted instruments to console her when business compels you to be absent from her bed."

"Fate has not plagued me with a wife." Cat had paused here to see if the man following her would pass on by. He didn't. Instead, he pretended to inspect the bunches of straw horseshoes, hanging like shaggy fruit from the pole of a vendor nearby.

He had been behaving suspiciously. He wore a towel tied to cover most of his face, and he kept his head down except for furtive glances at her.

Hanshiro had wandered off mysteriously, and Cat suspected he was looking for a present for her. She considered setting out to find him. Hanshiro's strength and skill tempted her to let him do everything for her. But this, she decided, was something she could do for herself.

The man seemed to be alone and inept at knavery. He was probably some small-time hireling who hadn't read or heard of Hanshiro's letter, signed with Kira's crest, countermanding the order for Cat's capture. His hands were empty. His only likely weapon would be a knife or truncheon hidden in his sleeve or legging or jacket.

From the corner of her eye Cat watched him sneak up on her. When he reached out to grab her sleeve, she picked up the biggest dildo from those on display. She had been hefting them on the pretext of shopping, and she knew this one was of dense, hard ebony.

Cat whirled with it and hit the man just above his ear. His

eyes flew open in surprise, then closed as he pitched forward. Cat knelt and pulled back the towel covering his face.

"Traveler!"

CHAPTER 66

LEAVING THE MOON AS A KEEPSAKE

The inn in Minakuchi was full of travelers, so Hanshiro and Cat couldn't linger in the bath. Still, the hot water and the steam washed off the cares of the road along with the mud. The easy intimacy made them feel as though they had been lovers a long time. They crouched on the wooden grid across the floor and scrubbed each other with bags of rice bran. They laughed and splashed basins of water over each other, as carefree as children.

When they finished washing they took the wooden cover off the tall, round cedar tub and climbed in. They lowered themselves through the cloud of steam and into the scalding water. The tub was just big enough for the two of them. The water came almost to Cat's chin.

Cat sat with her knees pulled up and her toes pressed against the far side. The sleek curve of her back and hips nestled against Hanshiro's chest and groin. She put her arms around his muscular thighs, which were drawn up at her sides, and draped her palms over his knees. She leaned her head against his chest.

He crossed his arms over her breasts and laid his head back until his neck rested on the rim of the tub. They both sighed, then took long, slow breaths, their chests rising and falling in unison. They closed their eyes and sat motionless and absolutely, completely happy.

Finally they could no longer ignore the loud coughing of the maids outside, reminding them that others were waiting to bathe. Hanshiro helped Cat out of the tub. They wiped each other off with their small towels, then put on the blue-and-white-striped wadded cotton robes supplied by the inn.

When they returned to their room, it had been prepared for them. Coals glowed in the firewell, and a small brass brazier gave off additional heat. A long-handled box of smoking utensils sat on the floor. A pair of pillow stands had been set side by side at the head of the pile of mattresses. The servants had put two low tables next to it. Tea and sweet bean cakes were laid out on one. Writing materials sat on the other. Words meant only for one other pair of ears were better written than spoken in a crowded inn.

"I'll return as soon as I can." Cat started to rise to leave, but Hanshiro held her tight against him while their hearts beat together.

"I'll be waiting," he whispered.

Cat pulled away reluctantly. She opened the sliding panel and stepped into the passageway. She turned and knelt facing Hanshiro, who sat in the glow from the firewell. Cat laid one hand on top of the other, palm down on the floor, and bowed, then she closed the door, stood, and walked to the room next to hers.

Inside, Kasane was sitting back on her haunches next to a low, freestanding shelf littered with cosmetics. She was naked from the waist up, and her cotton robe hung down around her sash. Her rented silk robes were draped over a rack in the corner. Cat breathed in the incense that was burning there to perfume the clothes. She had picked it out and was reassured that it was just the right combination of scents for the occasion.

Cat supervised the shampooer's work. Because Kasane's hair had been cut to shoulder length, the woman added switches of long black hair and rats of bear fur to fill it out. When she finished, the shampooer used a bag of rice powder to whiten Kasane's body as far down as the nipples. For her face she rubbed on a base of sticky camellia oil. Then she moistened white powdered lead with perfumed water and brushed it into a smooth mask.

After the shampooer had put on the foundation, Cat dismissed her so she could do the rest herself. She used a thin brush dipped in black dye to emphasize Kasane's hairline. She outlined her eyes in red, then black. As she worked she gave some final advice.

"Remember, elder sister, don't crack your knuckles or adjust the floor lantern while you're standing up. Above all, don't scratch your head with the dumpling skewer."

"I won't." Kasane's whitened hands trembled so badly, she had to hide them in her sleeves. She had studied the forty-eight positions illustrated in her manual, but much as she yearned to pillow with her lover, the thought of actually doing it terrified her.

"Remember to move slowly," Cat said. "Moving slowly lends dignity and grace and minimizes blunders." She chose another brush from the low shelf and dipped it into a clamshell of rouge. She frowned with concentration as she painted a tiny bow of a mouth over Kasane's natural lip line. "Untie your sash to let him know you're ready to accept him, but do not practice the artifice of foolish whores who pretend their sashes came undone by accident. Do remember to stick in some cries. They'll give him confidence." With both hands Cat extended a stiffened silk case with a packet of folded paper handkerchiefs and bowed slightly over it. "For the pledging liquid."

Kasane knew that. Her manual emphasized that the success of a pillowing was marked by the number of paper napkins required afterward.

Still on her knees, Cat moved around Kasane, arranging the folds of the silk robes she had rented for the occasion. She tugged at the back of the collar to expose more of the seductive line of Kasane's nape and back. She had Kasane sit at just the right angle to the door. She gently but firmly adjusted her upper body and shoulders, her neck and chin, into the most alluring curve. Then she placed the night lantern to take full advantage of the lights and shadows on Kasane's tranquil form.

When she was satisfied that Kasane looked her best, she knelt in front of her.

"I spoke sternly to the young man." Cat didn't mention that Traveler had been sprawled and groaning in the dust and debris of the marketplace when she had interviewed him. Because he thought Cat was Kasane's brother, he had been gathering the nerve to speak to her. Before he approached Hanshiro, he had intended to ask Cat's permission to accompany them on their journey.

"I wanted to be sure he would be kind to you," Cat said. "He answered me candidly. He began his pilgrimage with a friend, but the friend wandered into the pleasure district of the first post town they came to and refused to leave it. He seems sincere, and he has good prospects. He swears he wants to marry you."

Kasane blushed, but she was too worried about disturbing her hair and robe to even hide her face behind her sleeve. She had to resist the urge to pull her collar forward to hide the indecent display of the nape of her neck.

"Your first joining might be awkward and even painful, but with time you'll learn to give each other joy." Cat reached out to smooth Kasane's already sleek hair. Her voice was hoarse from holding back tears of joy for Kasane's good fortune and her own. "You have been a brave and true comrade, elder sister. Now if it's fated to be, you will have the greatest of gifts, a heart's companion on life's road."

"Thank you, mistress. You have been very kind to one of small merit."

As the white space of a painting intimated mountains and mists, oceans and infinite possibilities, so the words Kasane did not say spoke volumes. Her lips, which Cat had painted with a false line, red and round as a peony bud, trembled.

Cat turned in the doorway to look once more at her. She smiled reassurance before she knelt and slid the panel closed. She went to find a servant and slip him thanks money. She instructed him to lead Traveler discreetly in through a rear entrance after the thin, perforated wooden shades had been lowered over the night lanterns. She was sure Kasane would sit without twitching an eyelid until he arrived.

Cat returned to her room to find Hanshiro reading by the light of the night lantern. He put down the book and sat cross-legged with eyes closed as Cat knelt behind him and kneaded and rubbed his shoulders and back. She had moved down to his hands and was gently tugging his fingers, one by one, when she heard the creak of footsteps on the *tatami* in Kasane's room. A man spoke, his voice too low to be distinguished.

Cat moved to the writing table and sat so that her sleeping robes fell into graceful folds around her. She took up the brush, dipped it into the well of the ink stone, and wrote, "He must have a terrible headache." She was feeling remorse for the blow she'd given Traveler.

She passed the paper to Hanshiro, who wrote, "If you gave him a headache, you also gave him a cure."

Hanshiro had given the lad a pinch of powdered ginseng from his stock of medicines, but he was certain Cat's medicine would be much more effective.

Cat and Hanshiro could hear the chime of a porcelain *sake* jar against a cup, the rustle of clothing, and a riffle of laughter. Cat wrote, then held the paper out on her fan for Hanshiro to read.

A pair of noisy sparrows
Bamboo thicket, moon rising.

For the first time Cat saw him smile without the enigmatic sadness that had always veiled his eyes. She saw the pale flecks in them shift and brighten as yellow silk would shimmer gold in sunlight.

He linked his verse to hers in an admission of love's effect on him.

> A rising lark, lost
> In the mist of winter hills,
> As baffled as I.

Watching him write, Cat thought her passion too great to be contained. Surely it would burst from her heart and scatter as wantonly as silk floss on the wind.

Cat and Hanshiro dared not provoke fate by discussing the future, but hungrily they questioned each other about the past. In a few hours they tried to recover the lifetime they had spent apart. Long into the night, while the storm of passion rose and swirled in Kasane's room, they wrote. They filled the thick, pliant sheets of lavender-tinted paper with graceful characters and with the secrets of their hearts.

"Lotus-eyed one, sweet of touch," Hanshiro wrote. "Hair iridescent as a wet crow's wing."

It was a form of communication as sensual as a whisper in the ear. Cat felt as though each stroke of Hanshiro's brush, lingering and supple on the paper, were inscribing his love on her skin. They discreetly ignored the muted laughter next door, but it added to the witchery.

"Oh, when you do that," they heard Kasane murmur. The rhythmic whisper of bedclothes grew more urgent until finally Kasane's impassioned cry sounded through the inn. She must have thrown a pillow because something crashed into a screen. The usual late-night music and laughter and talk ceased for several beats, then took up again.

Cat and Hanshiro knew their time of love would be brief and they must live in the moment. The future was uncertain at best, and in their case they would have to devote themselves to the vengeance to which Cat was sworn. They could have written all night, but they knew they must try to sleep. The days ahead would be arduous.

They burned their love letters one at a time in the brazier. Then they untied each other's sashes, and as Cat's robe fell away Hanshiro kissed each of the bruises left by the rocks of the mountain. He held Cat to him, and when he trailed his fingers down her spine he drew out any fatigue or tension that might have remained there.

They both knew that they could not enjoy the usual lovers' courtship. They might never view the cherry blossoms at Asukayama or walk along the seaside at Shinagawa or go into the mountains to hear the first lark in the springtime.

Knowing that this might be the last time they would hold each other gave their passion a tender urgency. Silently, languorously, they traveled the silken road. They caressed and entered into the caressing until the lantern they carried became the brilliance of the moon. Then they lay with their arms around each other and their legs entwined until the dawn bells rang.

" 'Coming to an end,' " Hanshiro whispered. " 'And leaving the moon as a keepsake.' "

"Tonight." Cat looked up at him and smiled sadly. If fate willed it, that night they would enter the Western Capital. Perhaps then they would find Oishi Kuranosuke. They would end their quest and begin their vengeance.

CHAPTER 67
HEAVEN'S NET IS WIDE

Even before Cat and Hanshiro, Kasane and Traveler, reached Kusatsu they knew Kyōto wasn't far beyond. Buildings had shallower eaves and less steeply pitched roofs. Porters and *kago* bearers were more polite and better dressed. People spoke in the more cultured accents of the west, and westbound travelers had a gay air of anticipation about them.

Kasane had left her rented finery behind. She was again dressed as a *samurai*'s box bearer. Her lover walked with her behind Cat and Hanshiro and helped her with the load.

Dressing in men's clothing was all the rage with the women of Edo, and Traveler thought Kasane's costume stylish and brash and irresistibly appealing. She wore her stiff new cedar-colored robe tucked up in back, showing tight trousers underneath. Her narrow sash was tied low on her hips, and the thick tassel of her hair stood out jauntily from the crown of her head.

Traveler himself still wore the clothes he had bought as a disguise. He had sewed Kasane's letters into the lining of the jacket so that they might warm his body as well as his spirit.

As Kasane invented her work of fiction, she had to speak loudly enough for Cat to hear, so she would know the details should they come up later. But whenever other travelers passed she fell silent, as though her story were a shameful family secret. Her tale had entertained Cat and Hanshiro and fascinated Traveler all the way from Minakuchi to Kusatsu.

Kasane had no intention of trusting her lover with a true account of her mistress's quest. Lovers were the pleasantest of indulgences, but they could hardly expect the loyalty one owed one's lord or lady. Besides, the real story of how she and Lady Asano came to be companions included Kasane's being kidnapped and pandered as a harlot. It involved forgery, theft, murder, and the fact that Kasane was betrothed to a man from Traveler's own village.

Cat was amused and impressed with Kasane's creativity. Her tale went back several generations and meandered down numerous side paths. She suspected that Kasane had recycled the histories of the more prominent families of her village. She also had thrown in elements from the *kabuki* plays of Shichisaburo's troupe.

Traveler listened with a dazed expression. The occasional twitch of a smile at the corners of his mouth had nothing to do with the story he was hearing. He was a sensible lad, but the calm waters of his intellect had been considerably muddied by the erotic adventures of the previous night. Kasane could have told him anything, and he would have believed it.

Kasane had finally arrived at the more immediate past. "As you know, for one general to succeed, the bones of ten thousand men must lie bleaching under heaven. And so the wars and intrigues of long ago reduced our family to poverty." Kasane's sigh was so poignant, Cat was impressed. Besides combat and acting, poetry and love, what other talents did she harbor?

"Our father was a poor but honest *rōnin* who fished to eke out the meager harvest from his stony fields." Kasane thought of her parents, caught in the net of poverty. She thought of them working in their rock-strewn field by day, then fishing all night. The tear that slid over her lower eyelid and down her cheek was not feigned. "His boyhood friend, who was also a *samurai* and the son of the magistrate, developed a passion for our mother."

At a gesture from Hanshiro, Kasane stopped to buy some of Kusatsu's famous rice cakes. She shared them with her companions, then went on with her story.

"One evening, while Father was away, his friend drank too much. He tried to seduce Mother as she walked home from the well. She struggled and protested, but besotted with wine and passion, he forced himself on her."

"The beast!" Since Traveler still only knew Kasane by her alias, Hachibei, he kept his own name to himself and listened. He didn't mention that the bride his parents had chosen for him was from his beloved's own village. The coincidence was unsettling, and Traveler didn't know how to proceed.

"She hid her shame from us, but when Father came home he found her torn and muddy clothes. Sobbing, she confessed. Father went looking for his friend. They quarreled, and the man Father loved as a brother killed him, then fled. Mother shaved her head; but before she withdrew into a life of contemplation, younger brother and I made her a most solemn vow. We are pledged to find the villain and take revenge."

"Is that so?" Traveler was intrigued and perplexed. The marriage broker had said nothing of rape and murder in his fiancée's village. Maybe she had feared it would interfere with negotiations and she wouldn't be able to collect her fee.

"I must warn you." Kasane lowered her voice. "The murderer's father is influential. He has hired men to stop us, which is why we travel in disguise. Our situation is as uncertain as a candle's light before the wind. Hanshiro-san took pity on us and agreed to help. But he is trained in the warrior's arts. You would be held blameless if you decided to continue your pious journey to the shrine of the Sun Goddess."

"The flow of water and the destiny of human beings are uncertain," Traveler said. "No matter if it rains fire or spears, I'm coming with you."

Kasane bowed, making of it a remarkably subtle gesture of gratitude, pleasure, and promise. Somewhere along the road, she had mastered more wiles than the ones Cat had taught her. Her grace entranced Traveler. The secret he harbored stirred restlessly in him, like a meal of bad fish. As he walked he tried to think of words to explain his situation to her.

After Kusatsu the Tōkaidō climbed into the mountains again. Even though it was midday and the sun was shining, the four passed into the stillness of trees, into the sharply fragrant twilight trapped beneath the dense canopy of cryptomeria and pine.

Kasane slowed her pace so she and Traveler could walk farther behind and not be overheard. Their voices formed a murmuring background for Cat's and Hanshiro's silence.

Oishi had tried to teach Cat to live with all her strength of will in the present moment. So she tried not to think of the past, not even of the night she had just spent with Hanshiro. She tried not to worry about the future and what she would accomplish in Kyōto.

Kasane's anguished wail startled her from the ringing stillness of no-thought. She turned and saw abject despair in Kasane's eyes. Traveler looked thoroughly miserable.

"What is it, elder sister?"

"The diviner was right," Kasane said. "He's promised to another."

Hanshiro decided this was a good time to stop for tea and a very small helping of truth. He steered them all to a bench outside an open-air tea stall. Arms akimbo, he stood facing Kasane and her lover, who sat on the edge of the bench, their legs dangling.

"Remember that 'sleeve touches sleeve because it is predestined,' " Hanshiro said. "The two of you are together because you're fated to be." He rubbed his chin as he considered the improbabilities of their situation. He didn't believe in coincidence. He turned to Traveler. "What's your name, and to whom are you promised?"

"Shintarō." Shintarō was embarrassed to discover that he couldn't remember his future wife's name. "I'm supposed to wed the daughter of Saburō of Pine village before the spring planting."

Kasane turned so pale, Cat feared she would faint. She put a hand on Kasane's arm to steady her.

"I'm the daughter of Saburō," Kasane said. "My name is Kasane. I'm betrothed to Shintarō of Shadow Pond."

Shintarō's mouth dropped open, and his face turned bright red. "I'm such a fool." He bowed into his fists and knocked his forehead against them. "My callous disregard for your tragic situation is unforgivable. You and your brother must think me a heartless wretch."

"There's no reason for you to be anxious about it." Cat answered for Kasane, who sat speechless as joy and alarm scuffled in her eyes. "You didn't know our story."

A waitress arrived with tea, and everyone drank in silence. Hanshiro and Cat were trying to calculate just how much this new turn of events would complicate their quest. Kasane was reviewing the complexity of lies she had just told to see if Shintarō's revelation would affect it. Shintarō simply was stunned by the idea that he was in love with the woman he was to marry.

Cat drank her tea quickly and stood. In spite of all the admonishments of her mother, her father, her nurse, and Oishi, impatience was still her biggest fault.

"Shall we go?" She shouldered her sheathed *naginata* and waited while Kasane paid the bill. Then she set a fast pace into Otsu, the last post station before Kyōto.

Otsu was a cheerful, bustling place. Its shops and inns clung so closely to the shore of Lake Biwa that the masts of the fishing smacks, the pleasure boats, and the ferries beached there seemed to sprout from thatched roofs. Caricatures of imps in priests' robes grinned down from the shops' curtains and banners.

The demon priest carried an umbrella on his back, a wooden staff in his right hand, and a temple subscription list in his left. A bowl-shaped bell dangled on his chest. The paintings were bold and primitive and droll, and Otsu was famous for them.

Kasane and Shintarō stopped to buy food for the night while Hanshiro and Cat climbed the long flight of stone steps to Midera temple. Over the centuries the steps had settled until they tilted at different angles. The feet of countless worshipers had worn down broad concavities in them. Dark green moss grew where feet didn't disturb it. The trees along the route had sent roots into the cracks and corners of the steps. The roots had grown gnarled and twisted until they seemed fused with the stone.

On a hill high above Lake Biwa, Cat and Hanshiro left their own calligraphy brushes in the earthenware container full of those left by worshipers. Now that the brushes had shared the secrets of their hearts, they could hardly be used for anything else. The priests would burn them along with the others, out of respect for the services they had performed.

The wind billowed Cat's and Hanshiro's jackets and *hakama* as they stood on a promontory overlooking the calm blue waters far below. The boats bobbing there looked like toys in a tub.

"Hard to imagine a storm." Cat thought of the legend of the woman who had fallen in love with a monk. He had told her that if she rowed in a washtub across Lake Biwa seven nights in a row, he would give in to her desires.

Hanshiro knew what Cat was thinking. The woman in the old tale had almost succeeded. But on the seventh night a violent storm had risen suddenly and drowned her. People living around the lake claimed that on the anniversary of her death a storm always raged there. Hanshiro knew Cat feared she too might die before she achieved her goal.

"Heaven's net is wide and coarse," he said gently. "But it catches everything eventually. Kira will be punished."

"I fear," Cat said, "that I'm trying to catch the moon in the water."

CHAPTER 68
RULED BY EVIL STARS

Cat and Hanshiro, Kasane and Shintarō, crossed the high pass beyond Otsu. On the far side they began to see the tiled roofs of villas and temples above the treetops on the steep slopes. Soon they could see glimpses of the city, nestled in the bowl formed by the surrounding mountains. But not until they stepped onto the long arc of the Sanjō bridge did the full magnificence of the nine-hundred-year-old Capital of Peace and Tranquillity reveal itself.

The bridge was thronged with pedestrians. A procession of sumptuously dressed attendants walked beside their mistress's lacquered palanquin. The women carried yellow paper umbrellas to match the billowing gauze curtains of the palanquin. A group of nuns with white scarves covering their shaved heads sang as they walked along. A *samurai* cantered by, bells ringing from the bright trappings of his horse. The porters and merchants and *kago* bearers bowed low as he passed.

Ducks and geese swarmed among the barges and pleasure boats on the Kamo River. Downriver, lengths of newly dyed scarlet silk rode the current as its clear waters rinsed them. Between the river bank and Mount Hiei, with its sprawling temple complex, lay a flat expanse of tiled roofs.

On the other side of the bridge the Tōkaidō merged with Sanjō, Third Avenue, the broad tree-lined thoroughfare that divided the rectangular city from east to west. To the north of it lay the vast, walled compound of the Imperial Palace.

"The houses are thick as frogs' eggs!" Kasane exclaimed.

"Hanshiro-san, do you know the way to the Shimabara?" From what Cat had heard, she assumed the best place to seek Oishi would be in the pleasure district.

"Perhaps I can find it." Hanshiro affected an air of innocence, and Cat gave him a wry, sidelong glance.

While Kasane and Shintarō went to arrange for the night's lodging, Hanshiro and Cat found a secondhand clothing store on Hemp Alley, just outside the eastern gate of the Shimabara. They rented robes of a plain, dark nubbly blue silk with the matching reinforced collar bands worn by folk from the outlying provinces. The skirts were too tight and the sleeves too short to be fashionable. They added heavy cotton leggings and cloaks of a striped pongee so stout it was called "three linings" because that was how many it could wear out.

They debated which paper handkerchiefs to buy before settling on an inexpensive but respectable brand. They wanted to look as though they had just arrived from Tosa, but if they seemed too poor and countrified, they would be denied entrance to the better establishments in the pleasure district.

Gaining entrance to the brothels of the Shimabara was a complicated process. As in Edo's Yoshiwara, the custom was to stop at an introduction tea house. Clients changed there from travel clothes to their town outfits and waited for an escort to the assignation house. The procedure was a time-consuming one. It also limited Hanshiro's and Cat's choices since each of the hundreds of introduction houses tended to be associated with one or two specific houses of assignation.

Hanshiro knew that if he went to the tea house he usually frequented on his trips here, the proprietor would know his story was fabricated. He and Cat decided to play dumb instead. They changed into their rented clothes at a tea shop and followed the custom of renting broad sedge hats and a lantern, all with the name of the shop written on them in bold, black characters. Then, like a pair of bumpkins ignorant of big-city ways, they set out on their own.

Twilight had fallen by the time they joined the throngs in the Shimabara. Servants were lighting the strings of lanterns strung from the first- and second-story eaves of the establishments on Trysting House Way. The lower-class courtesans sat behind the wooden latticework facades of their brothels. They smoked their tiny brass pipes and preened and flirted with passing men or played fling tunes on their *samisens*.

Cat couldn't help staring at the parade of courtesans and their entourages of maids and servants and lantern bearers. She had always heard that the people of the Western Capital would spend their last coppers on clothes rather than food. Now she believed it. The Shimabara's higher-class courtesans and their young maids wore silks and satins and brocades more opulent than any she had seen. As they minced through the crowded streets on their way to the evening's assignations, their tall lacquered *geta* made a cheerful clatter.

The magnificent plumage of caged birds, Cat thought.

The days when she had been one of them seemed like a former life, remembered as though in a dream. She thought of the time when the lot of a courtesan had seemed the best she could hope for. Now she was so happy to be free of that servitude, she didn't even mind the derisive sidelong looks the women gave her or the little maids' snickers as they passed. Cat's rustic clothes were being noticed.

Hanshiro was amused by the fact that the lower the brothel they stopped at, the higher Cat lifted her nose. At the House of the Wave, Lady Asano's nose was quite high, but at least the smiling, gap-toothed auntie in charge admitted knowing the former chief councilor of the Akō-Asano family. Hanshiro was sure everyone in the Shimabara knew the houses Oishi frequented, but no one had been willing to say so. Even if they believed Hanshiro's story that he had been sent by his lord in Tosa to hire Oishi, they refused to become involved. Oishi's reputation was bad, even for the pleasure district.

It was barely the mouth of the evening, but a raucous party was already under way in a back room of the House of the Wave. Since the guest of honor was advanced in years, the courtesans and jesters were performing an indelicate burlesque of the ceremony for the dead. Their chanting was punctuated by laughter, the hollow tap of hand drums, and the clink of *sake* jars.

When they finished the rite they decided to bestow on their victim his *kaimyo*, his death name. Their suggestions were full of puns and double meanings.

"Honorable Noodle," someone shouted.

"Old Draggin'."

"Badger Dumplings."

"We should call you Lord Asane, Lord Morning Sleeper," a woman said. Taken literally, the word meant "late rising."

Everyone laughed and shouted, ''That's it! That's it!''

When Cat heard ''Asane'' she almost reached for the dagger in her jacket. Hanshiro glanced at her in warning, but she already had realized the partygoers weren't talking about her. She returned her attention to the Badger, the *geisha* Hanshiro was questioning.

''In the pleasure districts of Kyōto, Fushimi, and Ōsaka, Oishi Kuranosuke is known as the Master Floater of the Floating World.'' The Badger wore a dark brown *hakama* over a robe of heron's egg–green crepe.

He had a habit of patting out rhythms on his paunch, like his mythical namesake. His narrow eyes formed slits in the cushions of flesh around them. Over his pipe he assessed them professionally. He was calculating how much thanks money they would leave for him.

''He favored us here for a brief time,'' the Badger said. ''He said he admired my wit, although it's inadequate at best. But he hasn't been here in such a long time mice have made nests in the topknots of Kira's spies at the front gate.''

''Perhaps we should go to his house,'' Cat said to Hanshiro.

''You won't find him there.'' The Badger filled their *sake* cups to the polite level, a bit above the halfway mark. ''Foxes with their wives and kits have moved into Oishi's house, and owls drop by to do their laundry. The men assigned by Kira's son to watch its gates have achieved self-mummification without the inconvenience of the seven austerities.''

The Badger leaned close, and Cat could smell the cheap incense in the small bag he wore around his neck to ward off evil spirits. ''I hear that when Oishi stopped coming here he began spending his nights at the Sumi-ya on Ageyamachi Street.''

From the back room, cries of ''Take it off! Take it off!'' and shrieks of laughter made conversation difficult, and the Badger paused to see if the uproar would quiet down. A boy of about fourteen bowed and entered the room.

''My name is Shigamori Sambei.'' He didn't waste much time with amenities. ''I clean privies at the House of the Dragon Gate next door. I hear you're looking for the Akō *rōnin* Oishi Kuranosuke.''

Cat shifted slightly so her face was hidden behind Hanshiro's shoulder. She had known Sambei as a small child in Akō. She feared he might recognize her. And she was distressed to hear that one of her father's retainers had been reduced to such straits.

''Do you know the councilor?'' Hanshiro asked.

"I was a page in the Asano household in Akō," Sambei said. "I was present when Oishi-san discussed the options with the men of the estate."

"Can you tell us where he is now?"

"In hell, if there is justice in this fleeting world." Shigamori spoke with the bitterness of one betrayed by a beloved uncle. "Forgive my bluntness, Your Honor, but your lord would be well advised to reject Oishi as a retainer. He's a base, treacherous coward. He's shamed his lord and forgotten his duty. He pawned his honor for the favors of actors and riverbed-strumpets. He deserted his wife and children and squandered the money from the Asano coffers that was entrusted to him. He's used it to wade up to his ears in the sea of debauchery."

Cat felt suddenly very cold. A wintry hollowness seemed to expand in the pit of her stomach until it pushed against her ribs and spine. A wind roared in her ears, and she feared she would tumble inward, into despair. She thought of the end of a poem by the Mad Poet of Cold Mountain.

> All my life is ruled by evil stars.
> If only I could be like the tree at the
>   river's edge
> Every year turning green again.

CHAPTER 69
A STEADY SPIRIT

"I have not seen him." Yoshino of the Sumi-ya spoke in a soft, neutral voice, but Cat could detect the grief in it nonetheless. After a year in the Yoshiwara she could always detect the grief in a woman's voice.

"However, you might ask at the Amagawa-ya, the Celestial River, in Sakai," Yoshino continued. "It is owned by Gihei, a former retainer of the Asano family."

There were no loud parties at the Sumi-ya. The house's main reception hall, the Paulownia Room, was quiet and large—ten by fifteen mats. Except for the scroll of classic verse and the arrangement of winter grasses in the alcove, the shelves that seemed to float on the wall next to it, and the two low trays of cakes and tea, the room was empty of objects. It was furnished instead by shadows.

The darkness there seemed to have mass that absorbed the scent of paulownia flowers from the incense burning on the small altar shelf high up on the wall. The darkness hung over Cat and Hanshiro and Yoshino as though pressing down from the ceiling. It swayed and pulsed slowly just beyond the pale nimbus of the floor lantern. It seemed to absorb Yoshino's voice as well as veiling her face, ghostly in its mask of white powder.

"I fear he died of a broken heart." Yoshino's magnificent control was as understated as the dark gray satin robes she wore and the plain, rust-colored outer wall and polished corridors of the Sumi-ya. Her hair was impeccably oiled and dressed in a simple style befitting her forty years. Like the assignation house she ran, she had become more beautiful and elegant and expensive with age.

"Humans are weak vessels." Yoshino's voice was so low, she seemed to be talking to herself. "Perhaps Kuranosuke could no longer contain his grief. Perhaps it finally killed him."

"Then you do not think he abandoned his duty?" Hanshiro asked gently. Direct questions were rude, but he had the feeling Yoshino wanted to talk about the man who had obviously been her lover.

Yoshino was silent for a long time, and Hanshiro and Cat waited patiently. "No," she said finally.

"And you do not know where he is?"

"No."

"But Gihei in Sakai might know?"

"Yes. The night ferry has left Kyo bridge in Fushimi, just south of here. But a barge departs at midnight for Ōsaka, then on to Sakai. They take passengers. You should arrive by midday tomorrow."

The evening bells were ringing at Konryu temple when the Sumi-ya's steward arrived to escort Cat and Hanshiro out. They left Yoshino sitting alone in the darkness of that vast, empty room. The track of a single tear formed a shining thread on her powdered white cheek.

From the kitchen of the Amagawa-ya came the clamor of chopping and shouting and the banging of pots. The cooks were preparing a feast for their distinguished guest. Cat and Hanshiro, Kasane and Shintarō, had arrived, rumpled and muddy and smelling of the fermented bean paste that had traveled with them on the river barge.

After Cat and Hanshiro had bathed and changed into the inn's robes, they were shown to the inner reception room. Three flat, square cushions had been piled up for Cat to sit on, to raise her to a height suitable for her station.

"My lady, you gave me such a start!" Gihei wept openly as he knelt. He bowed until his forehead rested on the *tatami*, but his protruding stomach made the maneuver difficult. "In those clothes you resemble so remarkably your father as a boy, I thought his ghost had come to rebuke me." He wiped his eyes on the lining of his sleeve and blew his nose loudly.

Gihei was a rotund man with a face round and ruddy as a ripe peach. He wore a formal black *hakama* and *kataginu*, the starched, winged vest, and the flat cloth cap that marked him as master of the House of the Celestial River.

"I come in my father's stead, Gihei." Cat stared down at him with her old, imperious look. She was once again the *daimyō*'s daughter, and Hanshiro sat respectfully in the shadows.

"I will not clothe the tongue in silk," she said sternly. "I am disappointed that not one of the men of Akō has sought to make Lord Kira pay for his evil deed."

"Your ladyship . . ." Gihei waved a pudgy hand at his crippled right leg, which he stretched in front of him as he sat. "As you see, I'm too short for a sash, too long for a sleeve tie. I'm not suitable for much of anything, even less so for strenuous deeds."

"Then tell me what you know. And do not cloud the tea," Cat snapped. "If you lie to me, I shall cut you down."

"You would honor me by releasing me from this sad, onerous wheel of existence." Gihei bowed again, as though baring the rolls of his thick neck to her blade. "Without my kind and bountiful lord, life is not worth living."

But you live it anyway and prosper, Cat thought bitterly.

"The first messenger reached us at the hour of the Boar four and a half days after our lord's lamentable death." Gihei began his account of the events at Akō castle. "But not until the second messenger arrived did we know Kira had survived our lord's righteous attack. The councilor called all of us together to discuss what to do, although the noise of our weeping almost drowned out his voice.

"We divided into two camps—those who wanted to commit

suicide immediately and those resolved to barricade themselves in the castle. We knew the forces of the neighboring lords would be massed against us, and I stood with the warriors determined to fight.''

The months following Lord Asano's suicide had been full of difficult decisions. Gihei took most of the afternoon to detail them. Oishi and the majority had decided to send a messenger to Edo with a plea for the restoration of the family name and estate under Lord Asano's younger brother, Daigaku. While they waited for a reply, the men of Akō cleaned the castle and grounds, the moat and the roads leading in. They took inventory and made sure the account books were in order. Oishi hurriedly redeemed the estate's currency notes at sixty percent so that people could recover something before the confiscation order was carried out.

''Then the councilor surrendered the castle to Tsunayoshi's representatives,'' Gihei said.

Cat remembered Gihei as a huge, jolly man with a loud laugh and an inexhaustible bag of jokes about his withered leg. Now, as he talked, Cat noted how events had changed him. He seemed to have shrunk to fit his leg, with only his stomach and face retaining something of their old robustness.

''I remember the last night as though it were yesterday.'' Gihei's voice broke, and he stopped to collect himself. ''We kept watch on the ramparts, so that no fire or disturbance might threaten it. It is said that one must not regret one's fate, my lady, but we men of Akō begrudged each moment as it slipped away, never to be retrieved. As dawn began to bleach the eastern sky, we went up into the highest towers to look out hungrily over the roofs of the sleeping village below. A last look at our beloved country.''

Gihei stopped talking, and the room was silent but for his weeping.

''Then we heard the call of a conch trumpet,'' he said finally. ''And we saw the line of torches winding their way down from Takatori Pass and crossing Chigusa River. They were the soldiers, come to make sure we left peaceably.

''For a year, until Tsunayoshi-sama made a decision about your uncle,'' Gihei said in a tired voice, ''we were neither in this world nor the next. Our lord was dead, which made us *rōnin*, but the family name hadn't been officially stricken from the records, so we were still Akō retainers. Then, five months ago, came word that our petition had been denied and your uncle was to be sent to Hiroshima, to live in his cousin's custody. We were without lord or livelihood in this fleeting world.''

"Why did no one take action then?''

"A few tried, but of course Kira and his son, Lord Uesugi, were expecting an attack. The men were arrested at the barriers before they could reach Edo. After surrendering the castle, Oishi tried to retire to the country, but Kira's spies were so thick he tripped over them going to the well. The bean curd salesman, the ditch cleaner, the paperer, the almanac seller, even the man who offered to rid Oishi's house of rats was himself a black-headed rat.

"Oishi divorced his wife and sent her back to her parents' house so she would not be implicated in the vengeance he planned. He sold all his belongings and mortgaged his house so his children would be taken care of. Then he proceeded to throw the hounds off the scent.

"It's true he has immersed himself in the Floating World, but the flame of a warrior's spirit cannot be drowned or snuffed out. He was so successful that most of Kira's spies left by the end of the summer.''

"Then his behavior was only an act?''

For a moment Gihei's old humor returned. He smiled slyly at Cat. "A man who is prepared to die has more zest for life than one who thinks his days are as numerous as the leaves on the maple.''

"Where is *sensei* now?''

"Ah, my lady, I do not know.'' Gihei looked apologetic. His nose was wet and shining from his weeping. He wiped it discreetly. "Perhaps Lord Hino can give you more information. I'll engage horses to take you there tomorrow.''

Hanshiro saw the anger and frustration in Cat's eyes and the set of her mouth. Reaching Hino's estate near Nara would require another long day's journey.

"My lady . . .'' As Hanshiro wiped the stem of a fresh pipe in a fold of his sleeve and handed it to her, he contrived to brush her hand with the tips of his fingers.

"Patience is bitter,'' he murmured. "But its fruit is sweet. Musashi says one must be calm. One must have a steady spirit.''

CHAPTER 70

THE SOUL CAN JOURNEY
A THOUSAND *RI*

The floor at the far end of the inner audience chamber was raised
a foot above the rest of the room. Lord Hino sat cross-legged
there, as though he were part of the clouds of cherry blossoms
and peacocks painted on the gilt sliding panels of the wall behind him. He wore a stiff, formal black *hakama* and *haori* coat
over a black-and-white-checked robe with the red satin underrobe showing at the collar. He sucked in his breath politely as
he bowed to Cat and Hanshiro kneeling on the *tatami* below.

So the rumors were true, he thought. Asano did have a daughter. The resemblance was remarkable. Unsettling, actually. Hino
had the feeling he was holding audience with Lord Asano's
ghost. Fate had delivered the young woman here, and Lord Hino
wondered what other improbable surprises it might be about to
spring on him.

"I see that Hanshiro of Tosa persuaded you to accept his
services." Hino was a small, dapper man, as trim and well
tended as the garden beyond the open hallway at the end of the
audience chamber.

"He did, sir."

"And now you seek information about the councilor."

"We do."

"You have overcome great obstacles to get here," Hino said.
"I will open my heart and speak frankly." He paused as he
considered where to start this complicated story. "First, you
should know that Oishi-san always intended to avenge the injustice done his lord."

"But he handed over the castle without a protest." Cat's outrage overcame her breeding. She allowed her anger to show.
"He didn't register a vendetta."

Hino held up a calming hand and gave her an indulgent smile.
Lady Asano had inherited her father's temper as well as his
looks.

"If he had filed a notification of his intentions, Kira's son

430

would have taken his father to his estate in Yonezawa, out of Oishi's reach. Besides, Lord Asano's closest relatives had the duty of registering the vendetta, and we know your father's younger brother lacks"—Hino tried to be diplomatic—"resolve."

"But to do nothing . . ."

"Oishi maneuvered brilliantly through those tumultuous days. He sent a petition asking for reinstatement of the family name under Lord Asano's brother. While he waited for a reply he shamed even the most reluctant of the retainers into vowing to defend the castle."

Hino sucked on his teeth reflectively. "But he knew that in these times of ease and peace many warriors lack the courage to die for a cause. He knew that when the day came to fight the armies that would undoubtedly be raised against them, most of the men would decide to flee."

"Gihei said only sixty appeared to defend the estate."

Hino nodded ruefully. The behavior of the Akō retainers had shown all the *daimyō* what they could expect of their own men in a crisis. "Oishi then proposed that those who did assemble form a vengeance league. He even had the papers with the pledge already written on them."

"He was right about the cowardice of the others."

"Of course, my lady. He proposed defending the castle as a way of separating out the cowardly and the disloyal. From the first, Oishi was half a *ri* down the road while the others were still trying on their sandals. That's why several of us tried to persuade him to enter our service once it became evident . . ." Hino trailed off when he realized he had blundered into a discussion of the obliteration of young Lady Asano's father's family.

"Still, after he vowed to hold the castle, how could he give it up so easily?" Cat diverted the subject without changing it.

"Oishi made sure Lord Asano's brother heard of the plan to withstand a siege. As he expected, Asano Daigaku sent a letter ordering him to turn over the holdings."

"Gihei said Oishi-san's behavior these past months was a ploy."

"Gihei." Hino chuckled. "Did he tell you he's been supplying the league?"

"No."

"As you know, Kira's spies settled on everyone like flies on fresh bean paste. To throw off suspicion, the loyal *rōnin* sold everything, including their armor and weapons. But Gihei secretly bought a great deal of it back through agents and hid it for them.''

"One wonders where one might find the councilor." Cat was almost too excited by this news to sit still.

''He left for Edo more than a month ago. I gave him false papers and an escort so he could pass as one of my men. He had bought uniforms, and my servants carried them and his armor in two large boxes with my crest on them. He arrived at an inn near Nihon Bridge the night you fled Edo.'' Lord Hino's bow expressed genuine regret. ''Your quest has been in vain.''

Cat sat in stunned silence.

''A pity time was wasted.'' Hanshiro was so angry that he allowed the reproach to escape unchecked.

''In keeping the information from you, Hanshiro, my councilor obeyed my orders not to tell anyone of Oishi's whereabouts.'' With hooded eyes Hino regarded Hanshiro. He recognized him as dangerous. ''He saved Lady Asano from being connected with a plot that will certainly mean the death of everyone involved.''

Cat knew that to be angry with Hino was ungracious. She was kicking up sand with the hind legs, as Kasane would so eloquently have put it. She should be grateful to Hino for aiding the Akō men at some peril to himself. But she was furious with him for gulling her into continuing a fruitless chase. He sat there so sleek and smug and condescending. How dare he talk of saving her from danger?

Cat wanted to leap up and flee back down the long corridor. She wanted to run to Lord Hino's stable, order the grooms to saddle the fastest horse, and start at a gallop for Edo. Instead she kept her voice calm and low and almost, but not quite, respectful.

''When is Oishi planning to take revenge?''

''He has taken it already.''

''What!'' Trembling with rage at Hino's trickery, Cat leaped to her feet.

Hanshiro stood just behind her and to her left. He rested his hand on the hilt of his short-sword. He was prepared to defend her if her impetuous nature got her into serious trouble. And it well might. Obstinacy and impulsiveness had caused her father's death.

From behind the nearby wall screens they heard the dry, cool sigh of honed steel sliding across lacquer. In the adjoining anteroom Hino's bodyguards were drawing their swords from their scabbards. Hino made a slight gesture with his pipe, and Hanshiro sensed the guards relaxing.

"The attack on Kira's mansion was planned for yesterday," Hino said. "The loyal retainers left as warriors. They shall return as buddhas."

Cat sank to the floor. She buried her face in her arms and sobbed until the hot, bitter tears soaked her sleeves. Hanshiro gently put his stack of paper handkerchiefs in her hand, then looked on helplessly.

Cat struggled to control the sobs that shuddered through her. She took a long, deep breath before she spoke.

"I used to watch my father, standing with his tall bow in the snow on the archery range," she said. "He shone like a mirror in the sun. I trusted in my father as a sailor trusts in his ship. And I used to wish that those days would endure with heaven and earth." She fell silent again until she could speak without tears causing her voice to waver. "But my greatest sorrow under heaven, my wildest grief in this world, is that I have failed him. I did not witness the destruction of his enemy."

"My lady . . ." Hino came down from his platform and knelt in front of Cat. "You may stay here with us as long as you like. The servants will see to your every need." He glanced at Hanshiro. "And I would be pleased to accept you into my service, Tosa."

"Thank you for your generosity," Cat said. "But when word comes that Oishi has accomplished his duty, I shall join my father." She looked up at Hanshiro. "Will you honor me?"

Hanshiro bowed his assent. He knew she was asking him to sever her head with his long-sword once she had driven the knife into her breast.

"I also thank you for your offer, Lord Hino," Hanshiro said. "But I will accompany my lady on the Three Paths."

He helped Cat to her feet and walked with her out of the chamber, followed by Lord Hino. Cat was in a daze. She didn't see the artful arrangement of ponds and rocks and trees in the garden just beyond the open corridor. She didn't hear the chirping from the strategically placed nails and metal cramps under the polished cherrywood planks of Lord Hino's nightingale floor, his melodious alarm against intruders.

They passed the first and second Great Chambers where the most important visitors were received. They passed the ornate waiting rooms and the offices of Lord Hino's administrative staff.

At the doorway of the messengers' room stood the steward. Beyond him a dusty figure knelt on the *tatami*. He was obviously exhausted by the ordeal of five sleepless days and nights in a *kago*. His hands were still bloody from clutching the strap to keep himself from pitching about in the jolting basket.

"A messenger has just arrived, my lord." The steward bowed low. "From Edo."

Lord Hino accepted the letter, then he led Cat and Hanshiro into a small, inner audience chamber safe from curious ears. He seemed to while away an eternity slitting the wax seal with his long thumbnail, unfolding the heavy outer paper, taking out the letter inside, and reading it.

"The attack must have been called off," he said finally. "Though of course the councilor gives no names or details. He writes only that the tea ceremony was canceled." He handed the letter to his steward, who in turn passed it to Cat.

"He says the 'forgetting the year' tea ceremony has been rescheduled for the fourteenth." Cat looked at Hanshiro. "The fourteenth!"

"The monthly anniversary of Lord Asano's death." Hino bowed to acknowledge the ironic turn fate had taken.

"It hardly seems possible that Oishi and sixty Akō men could have been in Edo all this time without the authorities being aware of them," Hanshiro said.

"Indeed!" Hino smiled. "Rumors of their presence have been abundant, yet Tsunayoshi has taken no action to stop them."

"Even he must realize the justice of their cause," Cat said.

"I would not be surprised." Hino filled his pipe with threads of tobacco. Usually a servant was on hand to do it, but he had dispensed with servants in the interests of secrecy. "Lord Uesugi provided his father with a bodyguard of his finest archers, but he has not offered him sanctuary at his mountain retreat. It seems that Kira's son wants to protect the reputation of his clan's retainers as warriors, but doesn't intend to interfere otherwise. He too must agree with the virtue of the Akō men's quest for vengeance." Hino smiled at Cat. "Do you remember Kanzaki Yogoro?"

"Of course."

"He disguised himself as a rich rice dealer from Kyōto, and gained entrance to Kira's mansion. He made a detailed plan of the house, the guard posts, and the retainers' barracks. But the problem remained of learning Kira's schedule. He had been spending time at his son's mansion near the *shōgun's* palace. There's no sense attacking the hole when the fox is away, is there?''

"You speak wisely, my lord." Cat wished Lord Hino would get to the point. Patience was proving bitter indeed.

"Another Akō man, Otaka Gengo, disguised himself as a rich draper and was accepted as a student of Kira's tea master. He learned of the tea ceremony Kira had planned for the morning of the sixth, which meant that the evening before he would surely be at home making preparations.''

"But it was rescheduled. I can still reach Edo in time." Cat half rose, but Hino gestured for her to sit.

"You would only be carrying water to the river," he said. "The councilor will do his duty. Members of the league believe it far better to die with their names on everyone's lips than to live out inglorious lives. It's doubtful you could arrive in time. And if you did, you would jeopardize their undertaking.''

Cat kept her anger in check. She knew that Hino could not understand how determined she was. When he looked at her he saw a girl, and girls were by nature weak and irresolute. But that was due to his lack of perception, not hers.

She also knew that if he decided to hold her here behind the walls and moat of his castle, neither she nor Hanshiro could escape. She bent gracefully, like a willow in the winds of circumstance. And like a willow, she would not break.

"You are right, of course, my lord," she murmured. "Time is short, and my arm is weak. The spirit, however, is invincible. And a soul can travel a thousand *ri* in a day."

Hino bowed in gracious defeat. Her unspoken threat was plain. If he held her against her will, she would kill herself. Hino didn't believe that her resentful ghost would haunt his corridors, alarming the chambermaids and disturbing sleep, but the scandal would linger for a long time.

"Judging by your past accomplishments, my lady, your endurance is admirable. But you might find it difficult to stay in the saddle for so many days and nights. I will arrange for a relay of *kagos* to take you to Edo." *Besides,* Hino thought, *I can also arrange for the* kago *bearers to arrive after the fourteenth.*

A page arrived with a message, which Hino gave to Cat.

"Most honorable mistress," Kasane wrote:

There is talk in the servants' quarters. For the safety of your exalted person and the success of your most worthy cause, blessed by Buddha and approved by all the gods, you should know of it.

Your humblest, but most devoted servant,

Kasane of Pine village

Hino sent for Kasane, who came at a run and entered on her knees. She touched the floor three times with her head and on the third time left her forehead resting there. She was trembling. She was sure Lord Hino would be angered by her news.

"Speak up, girl," Hino said. "No one will harm you."

"A certain scullery maid . . ." Kasane searched for the words that would minimize Hino's wrath at the intrigue in his house. "Grants her favors to an apprentice stable groom whose cousin is a courier married to the sister of the third assistant clerk in the armory at Lord Kira's estate in Mikawa."

Hino scowled because it wouldn't do for him to appear to condone such goings-on. He was chagrined that a stranger in his house, and a servant at that, had learned so much in a day's time. But he was secretly amused, too. A courier! No wonder secrets passed so quickly. "And what did the scullery maid tell you?"

"She heard that Kira's chief councilor in Mikawa knows of Her Ladyship's arrival in Kyōto. He knows she was coming here. The third assistant armory clerk says an unusually large number of weapons have been withdrawn from the inventory. He heard that Kira's councilor plans to ask his lord's son's allies to ambush Her Ladyship should she try to reach Edo. Her life is in peril if she leaves the shelter of your castle walls."

Hino considered the information. Kira had few friends and almost no influence, but his third son, the powerful Lord Uesugi, could call in favors. Hino suspected that Uesugi's steward, a man noted for his cunning, was behind any plans to stop Asano's daughter.

Hino couldn't imagine one young woman being worth so much trouble, but he didn't know about the litter of dead bodies Lady Asano had left behind her. He did know that if Lord Asano's daughter reached Edo, she would certainly be an embarrassment and possibly a threat to Uesugi's father. However, if Asano's illegitimate offspring disappeared on the road, no one would be likely to come looking for her. The most widely believed rumor was that she was dead already.

Kasane's news didn't surprise Hino, but it did complicate matters. One of the lords who might help Uesugi lived nearby.

"We could divert them," Hanshiro said.

Cat felt a shy tug at the trailing end of her long sleeve. Kasane leaned close to whisper in her ear.

"She says she would be honored to commit suicide in my stead so you could claim I was dead." Cat's calm face showed no trace of what she was feeling. "Then I could escape in disguise."

"We must regretfully decline your generous offer." Hino graced Kasane with a nod. "Only a head inspection would satisfy Lady Asano's enemies that she is truly dead. But your idea of falsifying her death is a good one. Perhaps a lingering illness."

"We haven't time for a lingering illness." Cat's face was still impassive, but she was almost mad with impatience. Each beat of her heart marked that much less time left to reach Edo and the league of loyal Akō men.

"When in a hurry, make a detour," Hino said. "I have an idea that's a bit *kabuki*, outlandish, but it should work." He looked pleased with himself. "Lady Asano, you don't fear heights, do you?"

CHAPTER 71

A STRANGER LIKE A CLOUD OF HEAVEN

As Cat lay in the darkness beyond the night lantern's pale sway she thought about Lord Hino's plan. Only six days were left before Oishi would carry out his revenge. She had lost another day while Hino made arrangements with the captain of his guard and a few of his most trusted men.

It was a preposterous plan, but if it worked, it would be worth the delay. And it might work. By the time couriers circulated among Lord Uesugi's allies and they figured out that none of them had sent attackers to Hino's castle, Cat and Hanshiro would be in Edo. Kira would be ashes and smoke and a bitter memory. Cat's father's spirit would rest peacefully in the Western Paradise.

From the gate house, the nightwatchman's wooden blocks

clapped out the hour of the Rat. The time had come. Cat sensed
the stealthy forms moving down the castle's corridors. Even
though she knew they were Hino's own men, her heart fluttered
with fear. To calm herself she went over again in her mind the
escape route she was to take.

She wished Hanshiro were with her instead of in the room
next to this one. But under Hino's roof Hanshiro and Cat had to
pretend to be no more than mistress and bodyguard. In fact,
Hanshiro had to affect cynicism and disregard for the noblewoman who paid him. That way, when she was declared dead,
he could leave without arousing suspicion.

For this ruse to work, he also had to pretend to be drugged.
The guards at Cat's door really had been slipped a sleeping draft
in their tea, and Cat felt exposed and defenseless. For comfort,
she slid her hand under the edge of the mattress and touched the
short oaken staff Hanshiro had provided.

As he had been instructed, the captain of the guard allowed
the door to the outer room of Cat's chambers to squeak when he
slid it open. By the time the disguised captain and his two men
crowded through the door separating the dressing room from
the one where Cat slept, she had grabbed her staff and disappeared through the sliding panel of the room's back wall.

Barefoot, and with the hems of her voluminous pale blue silk
sleeping robes tucked up into her sash, she hurried down the
narrow, secret maze of passageways connecting Lord Hino's
mansion with the castle's enormous keep and with the battlements and walls that surrounded it. Hino had seen to it that
candles burned in sconces set far apart. They barely lit Cat's
way along the twists and turns of the route, and she blew out
each one as she passed it, leaving Hino's phony *ninja* in the
dark.

A young guardsman dressed in robes like Cat's was supposed
to be waiting at the foot of the series of ladders that rose through
square openings in each ceiling and into the upper reaches of
the five-storied keep. He was to lead the attackers on a chase
across the curved tile roofs of the castle's bastions and battlements. Cat called softly, but he wasn't there. She would have to
carry out the ruse herself.

Cat could hear grunts and scuffling and the muted scurry of
cloth-swathed feet behind her. "Idiots!" she muttered. Even for
fake *ninja* they were unusually noisy.

With her heavy staff in one hand she started up the steep pitch
of the first ladder. As she climbed she had to duck under cob-

webs draped from the great dusty diagonals of the massive beams supporting the ceilings and the thick, white-plastered outer walls. She braced her shoulder against the heavy wooden trapdoor at the top of the last ladder and heaved it open. Bats fluttered about her head. And in the rush of their wings she could imagine the murmur of cloth-covered shoulders brushing the beams below her.

Panting, she crawled out onto a narrow ledge scoured by a cold, wailing wind that blew her robes about her. The tiers of blue-tiled, upswept roofs of the towers and battlements were arranged in zigzag fashion so that an object thrown from the barred windows and arrow slits at any corner would have an unobstructed path to the ground. Clinging to the ornate eaves and guided only by starlight, she made her way along the ledge and dropped onto a lower roof.

Cat fell and slid on the steep angle. As she bumped over the rough corrugations of the tiles, she grasped at the dirt and moss that had taken hold in the troughs between the tile courses. She saved herself from plummeting over the edge by grabbing on to a bronze dolphin ornamenting the end of the ridge pole. She climbed back up and sat on the ridge to catch her breath. She saw the silhouette of a man pass on the spine of the roof above and to the left of her. She was sure he could hear her heart pounding as she ducked under the wide eaves of a battlement.

"Idiot!" she muttered to herself. She was a fool to let her imagination run wild. She had no cause to be frightened. Through some mix-up, the guardsman who was supposed to take her place hadn't been at his post; but the men following her were Hino's.

Cat figured that as long as she was here she might as well make the act more believable. She stood up so her pale, flapping robes were visible from the ground, and she screamed. Soon she could hear excited voices in the courtyard far below. Hino was rousing his soldiers and household staff for the climax of his scheme. She screamed again, and her cry was answered by a satisfying increase in the tumult in the courtyard.

She backed out of sight of those below and turned to face the first of the *ninja*. He wore a gray towel draped over his head and tied under his mouth. The shadow it threw made him seem to have no face at all. He was supposed to have the dummy, also clad in pale blue robes, that was to be pitched off the roof into a deserted part of the garden. Hino's steward and a few loyal servants were waiting there to whisk it away in the darkness and confusion before anyone realized it wasn't Lord Hino's guest.

Instead of producing the dummy, the man lunged at Cat. Instinctively she turned sideways to him and with all her strength brought the staff down across the top of his shoulders. He hadn't been expecting her to move as fast as any well-trained warrior. He certainly hadn't been expecting the staff. He toppled and slid, his fingernails grating across the tiles as he went. He managed to stop his fall as he hung half over the edge, and he began heaving himself back up.

Cat crouched so as not to hit her head on overhanging eaves. Going mainly by feel, she ducked into the tiered jumble of blue-tiled roofs. Another slender shadow dropped from the roof behind her and grabbed for her foot as she scrambled up onto a level above him. Something was terribly wrong. These men were trying to kill her.

"Help me!" Cat reached a windswept ledge at the top of the keep and screamed like a woman in panic. When she screamed, she could sense the change in her attacker's stance.

Expecting to find a weak, frightened victim, he came straight at her. She let him grab her and shove her toward the rim of the roof before she dropped to her knee. Instead of resisting, she clung to one of the iron bars in the window for balance and with her other arm used the force of his own attack to pull him onto his back. He clawed futilely for a handhold as with her staff she hit him on the head and pushed him over the edge.

Cat was now backed up against the side of the keep with only a black emptiness at the corner of the wall and a wind moaning around it. She could hear Hino's soldiers pounding on the trapdoor leading into the keep's attic. The _ninja_ must have closed and barred it.

Cat could see them rising like lithe scraps of darkness over the roof ridges or sliding around corners. She tried to count them but couldn't. They appeared as silently as if shreds of a shadow had separated from the rest. They vanished just as effortlessly.

Cat soon realized, though, that they were no longer heading toward her. They were converging on a roof separated from her by a deep, rectangular well of blackness, enclosed by bastions and turrets, bulwarks and battlements. With his wooden practice sword drawn, Hanshiro stood silhouetted there against the starlit sky. His _tabi_-clad feet gripped the arced line of ridge tiles as he ran lightly along the roof peak.

He leaped from that roof down onto another. He teetered for

just an instant before he regained his balance, and Cat's breath caught in her chest. Using their hands to steady themselves, the attackers climbed up the slope toward him. Steel rang against the wood of Hanshiro's sword. One man plummeted over the edge, two rolled down the roofs to lie crumpled on a lower level.

"Above you!" Cat screamed.

Hanshiro whirled and ducked under the spidery form that dropped down on him. He stood and, using the man's own weight and momentum, threw his attacker over the side. As Cat scrambled toward him, she ripped her robes, tore her fingers, and scraped her knees and elbows on the rough tiles. Suddenly a man loomed up in front of her. Cat and her staff had lost the advantage of surprise, but she raised it anyway. She had little room to swing here under the wide eaves.

Before she could strike, a curved, sword-shaped length of loquat wood hit the man at the base of his neck and shoulder. Hanshiro caught him as he fell and eased him down so he wouldn't slip over the edge.

Hanshiro was spattered with blood. "Help me undress him. Then take off your robes."

"How did you get here?" Cat untied the man's dark gray leggings and cotton trousers. The *ninja* was dressed in the nondescript clothes of a farmer.

"I felt uneasy about Hino's plan. I left a rolled-up quilt under the covers and waited in the attic of the keep. When I saw the men fasten down the trapdoor, I suspected something was wrong. But you led us all on quite a chase."

Hanshiro smiled to himself. How fortunate Cat was to be a woman. All her enemies automatically underestimated her. She went into every fight with an advantage.

"Hino's trying to kill me." Cat shivered as the icy wind washed around her bare body.

"Perhaps." Hanshiro hastily pulled Cat's torn blue robes over the unconscious man's arms. He rolled him over to wrap the long sash around his waist. "Scream," he said.

Cat obliged while she dressed in the *ninja*'s clothes. The man's disguise was good. Cat could even smell the field manure and the dust of rice chaff in them.

Together they hauled him to the agreed-on corner. They laid him on the sloping roof far enough back so they weren't visible from the ground and pushed him. Cat screamed again as he rolled to the edge and over, the blue robes flapping like a loosened sail in the wind. They heard the shrieks of the maids and the female attendants in the courtyard below while the figure fell, tumbling with a peculiar grace.

With the cold wind blowing and the stars so close Cat felt as though she could reach out and gather a handful, Hanshiro encircled her with his arms. They felt their hearts pounding in unison as they held each other. They stood among the bronze fish and the blue, upswept eaves, as though in a stormy sea frozen in time.

" 'I saw you on the road,' " Hanshiro murmured into her ear as long strands of her hair whipped across his face. He didn't have to finish the thousand-year-old words. She already knew them by heart.

> I saw you on the road,
> A stranger to me like a cloud of heaven:
> And the words I could not speak to you,
> Quite choked my heart.
> Yet we two, by the mercy of the gods,
> Are now united in love and trust.

"Now, my beautiful ghost," Hanshiro said, "hide where Hino told you to."

"But what if he's the one who's trying to kill me?"

"I won't be far. I will never be far. Not in this world or the next."

CHAPTER 72

DOESN'T IT MAKE THE CROWS SNEEZE?

With eyes closed Cat sat in her huge, round coffin tub of aromatic cypress on the raised section of flooring at the far end of Hino's Great Chamber. Around her neck hung a brocade bag containing the lineage of the transmitters of Buddhism. Clouds of incense, the clamor of bells, and the chants of the priests swirled about her. She had been sitting this way for hours, meditating until she had fallen into a trance. Her expression had the remoteness of death in it. Her breathing was too shallow to be detected.

Kasane had shaved Cat's head so she would look the part of a corpse. Hair had an unpleasant odor when burned, so it was removed from bodies bound for the crematorium. Lord Hino's provincial consort had artfully rubbed charcoal under Cat's eyes and blended in a large patch of rouge on her cheek. Under the shrouds and the white face powder and in the dim candlelight, the makeup looked like the bruises of someone who had fallen from a great height. Finally, Kasane had helped Cat dress in the white hempen robes and veils of the dead.

The robes hid the fact that Cat's arms and legs were not the broken limbs of the man who fell from the top of the keep in her place. At the hour of the Tiger, while the morning was still dark, Lord Hino's laborers had loaded the assassins into handcarts. With a servant trotting ahead with a lantern, they had wheeled them to the execution ground by the river where the corpses of criminals were exposed. They had dumped them there. Among them was the man caught spying. He had managed to cut his throat before details of the plot could be extracted from him.

Nor was there to be an elaborate funeral ceremony for the captain of the guard. Mats had been spread in the garden at dawn, and he had committed *seppuku* there shortly after sunrise. Officially he was atoning for the attack that ended in the murder of his lord's guest. Unofficially the captain was expressing his shame at allowing a spy to infiltrate the elite corps and humiliate Lord Hino.

The spy had alerted the *ninja* who had tied and gagged the guardsman waiting in the back passageway to take Cat's place. They had let Cat pass, then they had ambushed the captain and his two men. They had knocked them out, tied them up, and continued the chase. Lord Hino had not yet discovered who had sent them, but he had apologized profusely to Cat.

The wild, mountainous region lying just to the north was famous for its *ninja*, it's "warrior wizards." Their feats of cunning and combat were more myth than reality, but they were inclined to believe their own propaganda. Lord Hino thought it a sad state of affairs when they had little better to do than go after one lone woman.

His usually mild expression had been replaced by a dark glower. His face was florid with rage at the penetration of his stronghold by enemy agents. He sat at the head of his highest-ranking retainers and the members of his household and staff. They all wore the plain, uncrested silk robes of mourning, and they filled the fifty-six-mat room called the Great Chamber. They had gathered to pay their respects. They were also serving as witnesses to the fact that Lady Asano was indeed dead.

At the rear of the chamber Kasane sobbed and moaned into her sleeves. Her lover, Shintarō's, main task was to keep a steady supply of paper handkerchiefs ready for her, and she was going through them at a prodigious rate. When Lord Hino bowed low before the coffin and put in six coppers to pay Lady Asano's passage across the River of Three Ways, Kasane threw back her head and wailed like a stricken animal.

Four servants carried a six-panel set of folding screens onto the dais and arranged them discreetly in front of the coffin. Hino's master carpenter and his first apprentice, laden with the heavy, circular coffin lid, disappeared behind the screens. The sound of hammering rose over the drone of the priests' chanting as the carpenters used mallets to fit the lid in tightly, then tied straw ropes around it.

"Ahhhhh!" Kasane wailed. "All one gets from life is sorrow and disappointment!" She began clawing at her face and tearing out strands of her hair until poor Shintarō looked quite alarmed.

Her grief became so impassioned, the other guests swiveled their bowed heads sideways to look at her. Blushing and bowing his apologies, Shintarō helped her up and led her from the room. In the Great Chamber the sound of her cries faded as she stumbled away down the long outer corridor.

Kasane's keening drowned out the noise of the trapdoor opening behind the screens. Cat's coffin was lowered through it, and a duplicate was hoisted up to stand in its stead. In the secret room under the floor, Hanshiro anxiously supervised the men who ran a carrying pole under the straw rope. The coffin was airtight, and Hanshiro feared Cat would suffocate before he could get the lid off.

Crouching to keep their heads from hitting the low wooden ceiling that was the floor above, they carried it along a series of narrow passages. When they were too far from the chamber for the people there to hear the noise of wood scraping against wood, Hanshiro pried open the lid.

He helped Cat out of the coffin, but she had lost the feeling in her legs and slumped against him. He carried her through back corridors to a room hidden among the inner apartments of

Hino's private living quarters. He tried to set her gently on the thick silk quilts covering a pile of mattresses.

"No." Cat wobbled and almost fell. She clung to Hanshiro's heavy wadded coat, the deep red uniform worn by Hino's foot soldiers. "We haven't time to tarry." She smiled up at him, a calm, serene smile, as though while attending her own funeral she had come to know death as a friend. "Please, help me walk. It'll return the use of my legs faster."

She put her arm across Hanshiro's shoulders, and he held her around the waist. Together they paced back and forth in the small room while the men who had carried the coffin knelt at the perimeter. They were dressed in the dark-red-and-yellow-striped livery of Hino's palanquin bearers.

Kasane slid open the door and slipped inside. Shintarō stood behind her. Cat had given Kasane permission to tell him the true story of their mission.

"Are you well, mistress?" Kasane asked. In her mourning she had pulled her hair out of the carefully arranged loops of her *shimada*. It now framed her face in a wild tangle.

"Yes." Cat beckoned for her to come closer. "You had no trouble finding the fish?"

"No, mistress." Kasane's brief smile looked out of place under her disheveled hairdo, red-rimmed eyes, and crimson nose. "The other coffin is full of it."

Buying Cat's weight in the small fish called "In Place of a Child" had been Kasane's idea. When burned it smelled like human flesh being cremated.

Kasane picked up the clothes hanging on a lacquered stand and followed Cat behind a screen. Cat held the end of the *haramaki* to her abdomen, while Kasane, pulling it taut, wound it in place. It would ease the terrible jolting her organs would receive during the next five days. Then Kasane helped Cat change into the white traveling robes of a Buddhist nun.

"I've arranged with Lord Hino for your trousseau," Cat said in a low voice as she dressed.

When Kasane started to protest, Cat put her fingers to her lips to silence her.

"I asked Lord Hino to provide you with a chest with natural finish. In it I've instructed him to put a writing case, plain lacquerware, and cooking utensils. In a cedar trunk he's to include two gowns of first-grade cotton, quilted bedding of Chinese flower design, and a mosquito netting with a green lining, as well as numerous other things. He's also promised to give you

a generous dowry and provide you and Shintarō with employment in Edo if you desire it.''

Cat knew that Kasane would need work. Once peasants had
been to either capital, government edicts discouraged them from
returning to their villages. Officials feared they would infect
others with their prodigal city ways.

''But, mistress . . .''

''Elder sister,'' Cat said gently as Kasane tied the sash, ''I
can never thank you or repay you for the aid and companionship
you've given me.''

''But won't . . . ? Can't . . . ?'' Tears welled up in Kasane's
eyes when she realized she was about to be abandoned. ''Please,
mistress . . .'' Her voice was barely audible. ''Take me with
you.''

''Lord Hino's palanquins are waiting, and time is short.'' Cat
had dreaded telling Kasane she must stay behind. ''I ask you to
mourn that tub of fish until the kites and the crows sneeze.''

Cat smiled sadly at her, and Kasane tried to smile back. She
knew the poem. It was one of the many Cat had taught her to
make the long Tōkaidō pass more quickly under their tired feet.

> At Toribeno,
> The smoke never ceases
> Over the funeral pyres.
> Doesn't it make the kites
>   and crows sneeze?

''How long must Shintarō and I stay here?'' Kasane asked.
''And should we burn incense and chant *sutras* for the honorable
fish?''

''If you leave before your mistress is buried, you'll raise suspicions. You would do me a great favor if you mourned those
fish as though they were your sainted parents.'' Cat tenderly
smoothed Kasane's unruly hair. ''But you need tarry only until
tomorrow night when the fish are carried in their coffin to the
burning grounds and turned into smoke.''

''To make the crows sneeze.''

''Yes.''

''Then may we follow you to Edo?''

''Yes. By tomorrow night, even if my enemies learn they've
been tricked, they'll be too late to stop us. But your trousseau
and dowry and position in Lord Hino's household will be wait-

ing for you when you want them. And if I live, I will leave a message for you at Lord Hino's house in Edo.''

"We've come so far together.'' Kasane didn't mean either her words or her tears as a reproach, but Cat began to cry, too. She held Kasane as though she were comforting a disconsolate child, but she was seeking comfort herself.

"Something might happen to you while we're apart.'' Kasane buried her face in Cat's robes, and her sobs distorted her voice. The thought of Cat's dying far from her was almost more than she could bear.

"Sweet, brave, loyal Kasane,'' Cat murmured. "In this world, we leave no trace more enduring than the tracks of the plover in the sand.'' Cat held Kasane's face in her hands and tilted it so she could look into her eyes. "If fate wills it, we will see each other again.''

"As you say, mistress.'' Kasane wiped her eyes on her sleeve.

"Lord Hino has one of these. . . .'' Cat held out a small brocade bag. Inside was the lacquered strip of wood with her *kaimyo*, her death name, written on it. "I want you to keep this one.''

Kasane bowed and slipped the bag into her sleeve.

"You have the money I gave you?''

"Yes.''

"Then we must go.'' Cat adjusted the nun's veil on her shaven head. She laid her palms together, and Kasane draped the big rosary over her hands and hooked it under her thumbs.

"You look very holy.'' Kasane tried to smile in encouragement. She knew her outburst had been unseemly for the servant of a warrior.

"My lady,'' Hanshiro called softly.

"I'm coming.''

With Hanshiro, Kasane, and Shintarō and several guards behind her, Cat followed the bearers, hand-picked by Lord Hino, through the dark garden to a hidden door in the rear castle wall. In a covered entryway stood Hino's portly factotum. He would see them to the borders of the fiefdom. With him were two *samurai* who would pose as criers and clear the roadway for Cat and Hanshiro to pass. Nearby, two palanquins rested on frames that raised them to a convenient height for the passengers to enter them.

These were not the flimsy, rude *kago* of the Tōkaidō's lower-class travelers. These were *norimon*, the transport of nobility. Crosspieces had been lashed to the ends of the long, hollow, arched carrying pole so that two pairs of bearers, front and rear, could run side by side. Lashed with slipknots alongside the pole on Cat's palanquin was a *naginata*, its long blade encased in its wooden sheath.

The black lacquer of the palanquins gleamed softly in the lamplight, and Cat could see that both were decorated with an interlaced pattern of Lord Hino's crest and wisteria vines worked in gold powder. Yellow silk curtains covered the barred windows. The doors were slid aside, and two huge red silk tassels dangled from the corners of each doorway.

"My lady . . ." Hino and his steward hurried along behind their lantern bearer.

"Yes, my lord." Cat bowed low.

"I can't leave the vigil for long or someone will become suspicious." Hino bowed as he handed her a brocade amulet bag. "This is from Ise. It will protect you."

"Your kindness is beyond measure, my lord."

"I would send a larger escort and baggage to make your journey easier . . ." Hino was mortified at the meager show he was making.

"A retinue would only slow us." Cat smiled up at him from behind her sleeve as she slid gracefully into the palanquin and settled down on the thick, dark green silk cushions.

Hanshiro climbed gingerly into the one behind her. He despised traveling in a palanquin, no matter how big. The tiny compartment hampered his sword arm and made him feel like a caged cricket.

"A courier has gone ahead to see that bearers are ready when needed." Hino had to raise his voice because these bearers had already hoisted the poles onto their shoulders and were marking time. The steward had instructed them to make a show of being in a hurry.

"Thank you, my lord, for all you've done."

"Ya-en-sa!" With a muted shout the men started forward in the stiff-legged gait peculiar to their trade. It made the journey more unpleasant for their passengers, but it enabled them to cover great distances in little time. As they moved away, grunting in unison, their straw-clad heels flashing in the moonlight, Hino heaved a sigh of relief. The night's hail of *ninja* littering his garden would make him the subject of ridicule and conjecture, and he was glad to have Lady Asano outside his walls. He would be even more relieved when she was beyond the bounds of his lands.

Lord Hino knew that this mock funeral for a tub of fish was going to cost him more than a real one would have. To insure the head priest's silence, Hino's contributions to the temple would have to be generous to the point of ruin. And the timing was bad. The New Year would soon be upon him, bringing with it the annual plague of creditors swarming about his house.

Hino felt embarrassed to be fretting about money. Warriors didn't besmirch themselves with the coins that passed from hand to hand, among commoners and the ruling class alike. Besides, the young Lady Asano was the daughter of his old friend. Digging the pit of his debt deeper on her behalf was the least he could do. Hino even felt a bit bad about the fact that he had seen to it that she and her surly paladin would not reach Edo in time.

CHAPTER 73
CAN THEY SLEEP PEACEFULLY?

Night filled Cat's palanquin as though it had seeped out from the black peaks surrounding her, had flowed inside and solidified. She could feel the sides of the box closing in, pressing the darkness into a denser and denser block. She drew her elbows close to her body in anticipation of being crushed. The darkness was forcing the air out through the barred and curtained windows, and Cat began gasping, desperately drawing breath into her lungs.

Cat always got sick in *kagos* and palanquins, but never this sick. Cold, hunger, exhaustion, nausea, and the spikes of pain in her skull begot hallucinations. The long night became death itself. The palanquin turned into a coffin. The hissing, grunting bearers were paired demons carrying her to Yomi, the Land of the Dead. The white nun's robes were the shrouds of a corpse.

Maggots. Cat could feel them wriggling under the *haramaki* wrapped tightly around her abdomen. She bit down on her knuckles to keep from screaming. No purpose would be served by it. She knew she was imagining the maggots. She knew that in the darkness her exhausted mind had tricked her into thinking she was the goddess Izanami traveling to the netherworld. Maggots were part of Izanami's legend.

The vision of Izanagi, Izanami's husband and brother, floated, shimmering and transparent, as though trapped like a delicate insect in the amber of night.

"I have eaten of the furnace of hell." She clearly heard Izanami's voice pleading with her brother when he followed her into the land of death. "Do not look at me."

But Izanagi *had* looked at his beloved sister. He had seen the maggots squirming in her body. And so Cat could feel them now. Bile rose again in her mouth at the thought. She fought the need to claw at the tight wrapping around her stomach. *I have eaten of the furnace of hell.* Perspiration beaded on her forehead and turned chill in the frigid mountain air.

The narrow road had become steeper and rougher as it led into the rugged mountains north of Nara. Dense stands of cryptomeria blocked the light of the stars, and the moon had already set. Only the flickering lanterns lit the rocky track and reflected back from the arch of trees overhead. They caused the lantern bearers' shadows to loom over them like dark ghosts, following. In spite of the darkness, the bearers kept up an astonishing pace.

That was probably because when only the peak of the highest roof of Lord Hino's keep had been visible in the moonlight, Hanshiro had ordered the men to stop. He paced along the line of march and spoke with each pair of them.

He didn't mention that he suspected Lord Hino of ordering them to set a slower pace. He offered them a bonus if they arrived in Tsuchiyama ahead of time. And he assured them that if they tried to impede Lady Asano's progress, they would begin their next incarnation as food for the fish in the river at the bottom of the first deep gorge. The bearers knew they would be trotting along the rims of many gorges.

The road wound upward into the remote fastness of the narrow valley of Kizugawa, Scar River. Perhaps it was just as well that night hid the scenery outside the palanquin's curtained windows. The cliffs that towered over the trail were so precipitous, they seemed about to tumble forward under their own weight. They dwarfed the men and their burdens and their petty concerns with life and death, honor and shame and bonuses.

The bearers' eagerness to accommodate Hanshiro kept the palanquins bouncing and lurching violently. Cat's sedan was big enough for her to lie down in if she curled up tightly, but she dared not sleep. All night she rode with her hand wound tightly into the cloth loop tied to the frame of the ceiling, but it wasn't much use. Her shoulders and knees were bruised from hitting the sides. Her tensed stomach muscles ached from trying to maintain an upright position. Her feet and legs rested like fallen stone columns under her.

And there was the delirium, the visions that came unbidden and unwelcome into her thoughts. Izanami. Izanagi. The maggots.

At first Cat thought the loud panting just outside her window was more of the same. Then a more rational sort of irrationality took over. Lord Hino was a liar. He had planned all along to have her killed. When the rooftop plot failed he'd decided to do away with her in this demon-infested wilderness. Even now his assassins were chasing her.

Cat rested her free hand on the butt of her sheathed dirk and tensed. She concentrated on opening her eyes. She had shut them in an attempt to banish the specters from her mind's eye. When she finally coaxed them open, she saw that morning had come. The sun hadn't risen above the mountains yet, but the darkness had receded, had itself drained out the windows. It left exposed the rich green of the palanquin's silken upholstery. In the pale dawn light the silk gleamed softly like algae under water.

Cat wanted to cry with relief. If she was going to die, she much preferred to do it in daylight.

"A message, Your Ladyship." A bamboo pole with a letter appeared through the center opening of the curtains. Lord Hino's factotum trotted alongside the palanquin. He was carrying too much of his own weight, and his was the panting that had alarmed Cat.

Cat took the sheets of paper, one folded inside the other, and the pole disappeared. The man stopped to catch his breath. When he did, the cold wind chilled the sweat on his body. Shivering, he resumed his dogged pace.

Soon the small procession would reach the village that marked the farthest limits of the lands of Lord Hino's closest neighbor and ally, and he could turn back. The servant thought wistfully of his tiny house backed up against Lord Hino's castle wall and his bed piled with thick quilts. Before he slept he would have his wife bring him tea and rice and rub balm into his abraded and aching feet.

Cat pressed the folded envelope against her thigh and tried to slide her nail under the wax seal, but the letter slipped back and forth with the motion of the palanquin. Disengaging her other hand from the strap would be useless. It had been wound into the loop long enough for her fingers to have stiffened into claws.

Cat's fingers trembled with the cold as she patiently unfolded the thick, pliant paper envelope. She pushed back the curtain to let in more of the dawn's light. The letter contained a poem.

Hanshiro must have written it before leaving Lord Hino's castle. He must have been waiting until the last quarter of the hour of the Tiger brought enough light to read it. The effort of concentrating on the characters in the violent tossing of the palanquin sent bolts of pain into her eyes.

> Travelers shelter
> At the pass of Suzuka,
> Can they sleep in peace,
> Remembering days gone by?

The poem was a thousand years old, composed on the occasion of Prince Karu's night sojourn to this province. Hanshiro had made one change in it, though. He had substituted "pass of Suzuka" for "plain of Aki." Cat closed her eyes again to relieve the pain behind them as she tried to follow Hanshiro's reasoning.

If Hino had wanted to kill them, he could have ordered the bearers to dump them into a gorge. Not many people knew Cat existed. Most of those who did believed she was dead already, so he could have done it with impunity. Yet the dawn had found Cat only wishing she were dead. But Hino had given in too easily to Cat's demands for transport to Edo. Both she and Hanshiro suspected him of trickery.

If Hino wanted to keep Cat from becoming involved with Oishi's plot, he would try to delay her. And he would have planned for the delay to happen as soon as possible. The farther Cat traveled from the center of his influence, the more difficulty he would have in arranging a mishap.

Not providing fresh bearers at Tsuchiyama, where Cat would enter the Tōkaidō, would be one way to do it. However, failure to have men standing by when palanquins arrived with Lord Hino's crest on them would be a public humiliation. Lord Hino had already invited ridicule by staging a *ninja* raid. Cat doubted he would subject himself to another such loss of face.

Causing problems at the barrier at Seki was another tactic. But that would mean involving the government, as well as losing face. Lord Hino was too smart for that.

Staging a robbery to frighten off the bearers and leave her stranded was the most likely possibility. The Tōkaidō was crowded this time of year. Many *daimyō* and their huge retinues would be trying to reach Edo to spend the New Year's holidays with their families. Bearers and porters would be in short supply.

Cat figured she was safe from a staged attack as long as she was on Hino's neighbor's land. Hino wouldn't risk further criticism that he wasn't in control of his own estate, nor would he call it down on his friends. Bandits were known to haunt the Tōkaidō Road at Suzuka Pass, though, and no blame would fall on Hino if the mysterious nun and her companion were waylaid there.

"Bow down. Bow down," the crier in front shouted. The bearers slowed their headlong pace. The palanquin settled into a rhythmic jouncing that merely made Cat's teeth ache.

The edge of the sun finally rose above the peaks. It caused the yellow silk gauze curtains to glow the same pale gold as thin barley tea in firelight. Cat lifted the curtain so she could look out.

During the night, snow had dusted the trees and massive outcroppings of rock. The jagged peaks of the Kasuga range, white as monkeys' teeth, loomed on all sides. The village was a poor one. Very little smoke rose from the roofs of the flimsy hovels tottering up the steep hillside. They seemed about to slide down from their perches, across the narrow trail, and over the cliff to the river far below. If they stayed where they were, they would soon be covered to their eaves in snow. Straw-covered stacks of firewood towered above the rooflines.

The road curved here, and Cat could see her escort's slow, elaborate dance, alternating one arm out, opposite leg back, body horizontal with the ground as though swimming through the thin mountain air. He entered the forlorn hamlet as though he were passing through the gates of the Imperial Palace. He scattered chickens and brought to their knees the few sleepy inhabitants who happened to be caught outside with nowhere to hide.

He twirled his long pole of office as he tossed it high in the air. As it rose, whirling, the thick ring of horsehair fringe at the top flowed like an eddy around it, then rose and quivered when he caught it. Hino's factotum hustled forward to greet the hamlet's headman, who was facedown in the snow, and to arrange a quick meal of cold barley gruel and millet tea.

The bearers set down their burdens in the grove of trees that sheltered a shrine to Inari-sama, the Rice God. Drenched in sweat and shivering in the icy mountain wind, they squatted on their heels and wrapped their arms around themselves. The ropy muscles of their calves trembled. The strain of the night's run contorted their faces. And they still had two *ri* to go before reaching the Tōkaidō and their replacements at Tsuchiyama's transport office.

"Can you walk, my lady?" Hanshiro bowed as he slid open the palanquin's door.

"I wouldn't notice if you carved my legs into chopsticks." Cat held her sleeve in front of her face and managed to smile with her eyes above it. But she was struggling against the nausea that sent a vile-tasting tide up into her throat.

She put her arm around Hanshiro's neck. On legs heavy and ungainly as kindling, she hobbled into the bushes. The cold air revived her somewhat, but not enough. Hanshiro laid a gentle hand on her back as she heaved and gagged, vomiting up strings of acid and bile. When she finished he gave her his packet of paper handkerchiefs.

"Can you go on?" he asked softly.

"Yes." She leaned against a cedar and panted for breath. She gulped the cold air as though it were water from a mountain freshet.

The headman's wife arrived with the millet tea, which Cat used to rinse out her mouth. Then Hanshiro left Cat to take care of her morning needs in private. He walked to the edge of the gorge, loosened his clothing, and urinated into the abyss.

As Cat crouched, she saw the ice leaves under the nearby clump of bamboo. Rime had formed on the leaves. It had been imprinted with each threadlike vein and then had fallen away. The perfect, fragile copies, translucent and glittering, littered the ground. Cat wept at the intensity and transience of their beauty.

CHAPTER 74
TIME TO BEAT THE GRASS

Hanshiro rested his right hand on the Barber's hilt. He pulled his left hand back through his wide sleeve and out the neck of his jacket. He rubbed the dark stubble on his chin and stroked the long, ugly scab over the gash on his cheek. The sleepless night had left his eyes red-rimmed and puffy and particularly menacing.

Like a falcon surveying plump mice from a great height, he stared around at the semicircle of fresh bearers who squatted on their dirty heels before him. Behind the bearers, the front and rear criers stood leaning on their poles. Beyond them rose the ascent to Suzuka Pass. The Tōkaidō was crowded with early-morning traffic. The bells on the pack horses made a merry noise.

"If any of you bolt"—Hanshiro's tone, barely above a whisper, was far more effective than a harangue—"I will widow your wives and orphan your children."

He waited a few beats to let the message register. These were the men who had been waiting in the yard of the transport office in Tsuchiyama. Lord Hino's advance man had hired them from the pool of local laborers. They weren't Hino's retainers, nor were the criers his warriors in disguise. In matters of defense Cat and Hanshiro were now on their own.

"But if we reach Kameyama by midday," Hanshiro added, "you'll each receive a bonus."

From the corner of his eye Hanshiro saw Cat return from the roadside convenience. Her nun's scarf hid her face and shaved head as she lowered herself into the rear palanquin sitting beside the road. Hanshiro grunted, and the men rose and trotted to their places at the carrying poles.

"Ho-yoi-yoi." The bearers used their sticks to heave the poles onto their callused shoulders, and the palanquins lurched forward. Only one of them held a passenger, though. Hanshiro chose to jog just behind the front crier.

By the time Hanshiro had run one of the two nearly vertical *ri* separating Tsuchiyama and Sakanoshita, his heart was thumping like a frantic animal in his chest. His calves cramped with pain, but he was so relieved to be free of the confines of the palanquin that he didn't care.

The mist that had reached tentative wisps out onto the low lands had thickened into a dense fog by the time the bearers reached the suspension bridge, the detour over the deepest gorge. The crier gave his usual shout. The line of travelers waiting their turn to cross the narrow, swaying span parted and bowed. Looking out into the fog, Cat had the feeling that the rest of the world had disappeared. That these were the survivors, the last of earth's mortals.

The bearers stopped at the entrance of the bridge so Cat could get out. She untied her wide-brimmed hat from the side of the palanquin and put it on over her veil. Then she retrieved the *naginata* from the carrying pole and walked back to stand behind the rear crier. Hanshiro gave her the briefest of looks, but it sufficed. He was counting on her to help him keep the bearers from deserting.

Hanshiro led the way out onto the lengths of bamboo lashed together to form the bridge's floor. Five farmers had already started across carrying heavy wooden frames loaded with bales of rice and towering bundles of firewood. They were followed by a lightweight *kago* carried by two men. Their passenger followed them on foot. A large party of pilgrims, several of them women, approached, single file, from Sakanoshita. The bamboo flooring clattered incessantly, and the woven bamboo hawsers creaked with the travelers' weight and tread and the wind that blew in the gorge.

The bridge's concave arc hung below the tops of the cliffs on either side, and the chasm looked as though it had been filled to overflowing with thin, steaming rice gruel. When Hanshiro had almost reached the middle of the bridge, he could just make out the five disreputable-looking *rōnin* lounging at the other side. He smiled to himself. Hino was so predictable.

But there were only five swordsmen. Hanshiro was offended that Hino thought so little of his skill and that of Lady Asano. Apparently Hino thought she had insisted on the *naginata* only as some foolish female whim, as an accessory, like a mirror or a tortoiseshell comb. Perhaps he thought that because she wasn't a legitimate daughter, Lord Asano had neglected her training in self-defense.

"Halt!" The leader of the *rōnin* moved to the entrance of the bridge.

Suzuka Pass was famous for bandits. The people heading toward the *rōnin* wasted no time. They turned and began pushing back through those behind them. Those already moving away from the ruffians increased their pace.

"We have a quarrel with the hirelings of the traitor Hino," the man shouted. "The rest of you may cross in peace."

No one believed him for an instant. The women began screaming. Everyone bunched up ahead of Hanshiro as they tried to crowd past the *kago*. The *kago*'s bearers, however, were also trying to turn around, and their carrying pole had become entangled in the woven ropework that formed the sides of the bridge.

The fact that Hanshiro and the white-robed nun and their men didn't retreat seemed to infuriate the *rōnin*. He made a great show of drawing his short-sword and sawing at one of the two main hawsers supporting the bridge.

The travelers' fright turned to panic. Men and women clawed at each other's clothing as they tried to force their way through the press. The *kago*'s owners cut the ropes holding the pole to the top of the basket and pushed it through the mesh of ropes and out into space. The fog swallowed it. One of the bearers almost fell after it as he tried to hoist the flimsy bamboo *kago* onto his back while the other travelers shoved past him.

Hanshiro motioned for his own men to move to one side so people could hurry by. And still the *rōnin* sawed at the hawser.

"He's bluffing." Hanshiro could tell the bearers didn't believe him. "And even if he weren't, you can cling to the bridge if it falls, but you cannot escape the Barber." With one hand he slid his long-sword a few fingers' width from its scabbard. When he pushed it back in, the iron sword guard hit the sheath's lacquered rim with a hollow, ominous click. The click's echo seemed amplified by the fog.

Finally everyone had passed Hanshiro but the unfortunate *kago* bearer, deserted by his partner and fare. He stood, mouth agape and eyes bulging, as Hanshiro strode toward him. When he realized that with such a bulky load he could not pass the palanquins, he looked back over his shoulder. The *rōnin* was still sawing on the hawser.

"Homage to Amida Butsu." Hardly pausing to take breath, the bearer muttered the sacred phrase over and over. With his immortal soul taken care of, he tried to figure out how to save his *kago* and his livelihood.

Cat disdained letting go of the *naginata* to grab the ropework that formed the side of the dancing bridge. She planted her feet firmly about a shoulder's width apart on the corrugated bamboo surface. She flexed her knees so her legs moved easily in response to the bridge's gyrations. She stood like a sailor on the deck of a storm-tossed boat as the wind whipped her white robes and scarves about her.

From habit, she turned to reassure Kasane, who had always stood behind her. And she remembered the poem a courier had handed through the bars of her window when she'd reached Tsuchiyama. It had been written in Kasane's childish hand.

> The mist that rises
> On the far-flung mountaintops
> where morning finds you
> Is but the breath of the sighs
> Of one who remains behind.

The ancients believed that the thoughts of those at home accompanied loved ones on their journeys. Cat felt Kasane's presence now. *I welcome your spirit, elder sister,* Cat thought.

She was glad Kasane was safe. Her young man would marry her. She would bear children noisy as summer's flies. In time she would remember her former mistress only on the prescribed days of mourning.

Cat watched the desperate *kago* man suspend his flimsy basket over the side. Leaning his chest against the cables, he sidestepped along, carrying it past the terrified palanquin bearers. The *rōnin* cut through the hawser, and that side of the bridge dropped with a sickening lurch. The sudden fall and shift in the cant of the bridge's floor threw the bearers and Cat against the cable webbing that formed the handhold on the lower side. Cat recovered first.

When the palanquin bearers turned to flee, they saw her kneeling on one knee. She had braced her other leg in front of her. She held the *naginata* over her head and aimed at them. Behind the flapping ends of the scarf she was grinning like a madwoman. Oishi had been right when he'd told her that swordsmanship led one to the center to confront life and death.

Cat realized that perhaps Hino planned to kill her after all, but she wasn't afraid. She was exhilarated by the prospect of falling into the swirling void below her. She and her beloved would die together, to live forever in Paradise.

Her men were convinced, however, that they were in the employ of a particularly deranged pair of demons. Wide-eyed, babbling in terror, they struggled to carry the palanquins forward on the tilting bridge.

Cat decided that the bearers had come too far to try to retreat. She could pass them now to be at Hanshiro's side. As good as Hanshiro was, he would need her help against five men. She began toiling up the tilting, sloping, swaying span. The bearers looked back at the yawning expanse of the abyss behind them and hurried after her.

The *rōnin* was sawing at the second cable as Hanshiro closed in on him. He looked murderous, but he didn't fool Hanshiro. Even though the man himself had obviously fallen on hard times, his short-sword was of a superior quality and finely honed. He could have cut through the cable in one stroke of his long-sword instead of making all this show.

Hanshiro remembered Kasane's endless store of peasant aphorisms. *Time to beat the grass and scare the snake,* he thought. Time to do the unexpected.

He crossed his arms on his chest, threw back his head, and laughed. He laughed heartily, joyously. He laughed louder than he had laughed in ten years.

"*Baka!*" The leader of the *rōnin* glowered at him. Hanshiro could see the thoughts going on behind those squinting, venal eyes as plainly as if they were written on a scroll being slowly unrolled. The *rōnin* hadn't been instructed to kill Hanshiro, but even if he had, he wouldn't have been able to bring himself to attack a laughing opponent.

Hanshiro's laughter was so infectious, Cat began laughing, too. Helpless with it, she braced the butt of her *naginata* and hung on it. She laughed until her sides ached and tears ran down her cheeks.

CHAPTER 75

THEY REFUSE TO HELP
A TRAVELER

Cat lay curled up tightly on her side among the cushions of the palanquin. The pounding of the bearers' feet across the wooden bridge woke her from the anxious sleep into which she had plummeted. The drumming scattered the memories and dreams swarming about her.

She tried to stretch to relieve the cramps in her legs and feet but came up against the sides of the palanquin. Still disoriented and anxious from the imaginary voices that had been shrilling for her attention, she thought of the poet-priest Musui, Dream Besotted. His kind eyes and lopsided smile comforted her, and she wondered, briefly, where he was this cold winter morning. Probably on the road somewhere, she thought, in a hovel sharing a cracked cup of millet tea with some peasant whose load he had carried.

She remembered Musui lifting his staff when crossing bridges so as not to disturb Kōbō Daishi's sleep. She remembered him reciting Daishi's poem.

> They refuse to help
> A traveler in trouble.
> One night seems like ten.

In spite of her own troubles, or maybe because of them, the tattoo of feet on a wooden bridge at night had distressed Cat ever since her brief time with Musui. It distressed her now, at dawn, just outside Totsuka.

She wanted to tell the bearers to stop. To walk softly. People might be sleeping underneath. A young outcast woman and her children and their grandfather might be huddled there, seeking shelter from the long cold nights. Travelers in trouble, whom no one would help. Whom Cat had been unable to help.

In the past five nights and four days, Cat had had time to remember the outcast family and a great deal more. The world

460

had shrunk to the interior of the palanquin. She could close her eyes and visualize every stitch and stain and wrinkle in the silk upholstery. She had memorized every brush stroke of the illustration from *The Tale of Genji*, painted on the gilt walls.

She had tried to read but had become too sick. So she had folded a piece of paper several times to stiffen it. She had stuck it vertically between two thin reed slats of the blind covering the window. It was a vulgar practice, a casual disregard for propriety that her nurse had always deplored as a sign of society's decay. Cat remembered her scoldings fondly.

Cat had spent the past four days gazing out through the narrow opening at the procession of muddy brown rice fields. She'd watched the same straw and mud-plastered hovels of the villages and the backs of the bowing populace, endlessly repeated. She'd felt helpless and detached as the relays of bearers changed without a word from her. She'd felt like a stone on a *go* board, being moved by a greater hand.

As she passed each village and town, she tried to remember what had happened to her there, but she found it difficult. Those things had happened to someone else. The Tōkaidō itself was completely different when experienced from inside a palanquin. Once removed from the company of the people who traveled the road and lived along it, the danger, the romance, the singular excitement of the great highway, ceased to exist.

The nights were the worst. That was when Cat shivered in a frigid darkness clamorous with memories and regrets. At night she babbled incoherently to her nurse. She sobbed with longing for her mother and father. She held long, silent conversations with Kasane. She dreamed of boarding a boat with Hanshiro and sailing into the rising sun, toward the far green land of Tosa.

Toward the end of her journey she screamed silently for the bearers to stop torturing her with their cruel, steady, bone-shaking pace. The only relief had been on the second night. She had spent much of it on the boat from Kuwana to Miya. She had been lulled by the drone of the boatmen's talk, by the flap and hum of the sails, and by the crackle of fire in the big iron basket that hung out over the prow. She had slept curled with Hanshiro under a tattered rented quilt in the bottom of the boat. Now she tried to imagine his arms around her again, his body warm against hers.

She knew that boat ride might be the last time she would feel the strength of his arms encircling her. If fate willed it, she would be in Edo tonight. She would find Oishi. She would avenge her father. Then she would die.

The palanquin jerked to a halt, and Cat heard the familiar morning garble of a transport office yard. She heard the shouts of her own bearers, who, somewhere in the long, grueling journey, had ceased to be human. They had become apparatuses like the wheels that lifted water into the irrigation ditches, or the stone disks and wooden cranks that hulled rice.

The palanquin lurched forward, then back, as the bearers set it down. While they went off to report to the transport officials, Cat sat relishing the few moments of peace and anticipating the chance to stretch her cramped legs. Hanshiro slid open the door.

"My lady." As he bowed, Cat detected a conspiratorial smile.

She pulled her scarf across her face. The rowdy crowd of men in the transport office yards was always ready to have a look at the occupants of palanquins, especially if they were women. Hanshiro stood between them and Cat as he helped her out into a world transformed by a thick white quilt of snow.

As he walked with her to a grove of pines across the road, their sandals crunched in the deep fluffy powder. Beyond the trees a narrow river coiled like a black snake through the white expanse of rice paddies. Hanshiro turned Cat so she faced south and west.

"Ma!" Kasane's favorite phrase escaped before Cat could stop it. No wonder Hanshiro had been smiling.

The gently curving slopes of Mount Fuji were covered in snow tinted mauve against a golden-pink sky. A spindrift of windblown snow floated eastward from the peak. The lower peaks around Fuji seemed to float on a tinted ocean of mist.

" 'One never tires of gazing upon the face of Fuji,' " Cat murmured.

They both stared at the volcano, watching the subtle shifts in color on its slopes. Finally Hanshiro reluctantly broke the silence. "Lord Tōdō travels ahead of us, my lady."

Cat grimaced. Lord Tōdō's retinue would number in the hundreds, and it would be moving extremely slowly. To try to pass him on the road would be more than rude, it would probably be suicidal. A lord's retainers had the right to cut down anyone of lower rank who disrupted their procession.

"Move smartly, Cold Rice!"

The shout from the yard startled Cat from her gloomy calculation. She turned to see Viper trotting in place at the front of her palanquin. She pulled her scarf farther down over her face and sidled over to stand behind Hanshiro.

"Do you know him?"

"He and his wife sheltered me." *In another life*, Cat thought.

"It would be best if he didn't see you."

"Yes. That would be best." Cat had to smile behind her scarf.

Given Viper's reckless determination to help her, that indeed would be best. Viper surreptitiously tried to see who his mysterious fare was, but Cat held her scarf in place as she ducked into the palanquin. Viper and Cold Rice grunted in unison as they lifted the front of the large carrying pole and two other men held up the rear.

When Hanshiro gave the new bearers the usual promise of a bonus, he also tipped them in advance, to ensure that their songs wouldn't be insulting. So for the next *ri* Viper exchanged ripostes with passing *kago* men and sang his bawdy ditties to entertain his veiled passenger. Cat wasn't amused, though. With a lump of dread heavy in the pit of her stomach, she watched for the criers and liveried porters who would be bringing up the rear of Lord Tōdō's procession. She watched the sun climb higher in the sky.

Then a courier Viper had just good-naturedly insulted called back over his shoulder as he trotted away, "I hear they hung Sakuta out like a shop banner."

Viper didn't answer, but Cat felt an almost indiscernible falter in his stride.

Sakuta. Cat concentrated until she remembered where she had heard the name. Sakuta was the headman of Viper's village. He had been such a mild, honest-seeming man. Even when he'd drunk too much at the celebration in Viper's kitchen after the exorcism of the homeless ghost, he had been soft-spoken. She remembered that he'd been worried about the welfare of his people. Cat wondered what he could have done to deserve execution, for that was surely what the courier had meant.

Cat raised the blind, held her fan out the window, and gestured with it. The four bearers moved to the side of the road and set the palanquin down near an open-air tea shop. They lined up, knelt in the snow, and bowed until flakes of it powdered their foreheads.

"I wish to speak privately with the two forward *kago* men," Cat said.

The other two joined the crier and box bearer and Hanshiro's four *kago* men, who crowded around a roadside stand to order a bit of *sake* for warmth. Viper and Cold Rice remained prostrate next to the palanquin. Hanshiro, ready for trouble, stood behind them.

Viper and Cold Rice both wore baggy trousers and leggings and jackets with the skirts tucked up into their sashes. Their jackets and trousers had started out dark indigo, but they had been patched and repatched with whatever cloth was available. They were so worn, frayed, and covered with stitching and patches that they were hardly recognizable as specific articles of clothing. The towel Viper wore over his head and tied under his chin hid most of the gaudy tattoo.

"Are you in good health, Boss of the *kago* men?" Cat drew back the yellow gauze curtain with two pale, slender fingers and allowed Viper to catch a glimpse of her face. She almost laughed at his astonished expression. "Do you remember me?" she asked.

"Yes, Your Lordship." Viper hastened to correct himself. "Your Ladyship."

"Do you still think me the ghost of Lord Yoshitsune?"

"Forgive my stupidity for thinking that, Your Ladyship. Wisdom can't circulate in the body of a big man. A fool at thirty is a fool for life."

"What happened to Sakuta?"

"A farmer's lot is to have just enough to live on and no more. But our lord didn't leave us even that much. Sakuta delivered our petition for lower taxes to Lord Katsugawa's bailiff, but he was refused. Sakuta became very sad. He said that if he ignored the pain of the villagers, it was like leaving his own wounds untended. So he went to Edo, to the palace of O-Kubo-sama himself. He waited at the Tiger Gate until O-Kubo-sama's chamberlain passed. Then he ran past the guards and stuck the petition in through the palanquin window."

Cat took a deep breath of anguish. She knew what must have happened next. Sakuta also must have known what would happen. "He was executed?"

"Crucified. His body was left hanging for the crows to dine on."

"I'm so sorry."

"It was his duty. And O-Kubo-sama did reduce our taxes by forty-five bales, so Sakuta was successful in his mission." Viper's voice faltered. "But his family—his wife and children and parents—were made outcasts."

"They will all surely be reborn higher on the Wheel."

"Thank you, Your Ladyship. But on death all accounts are canceled, and we shouldn't trouble you with our petty problems. You must reach Edo tonight, is that correct?"

"Yes."

"Tōdō is ahead of us with a train of five hundred. His movements are as drawn out as an ox urinating. If we have to follow him, we won't reach the Shinagawa barrier by sundown."

They all knew the barriers closed at sundown.

"Do you know a detour?"

"It's a long one. But if you hire extra bearers in Kanagawa, Cold Rice and I can slide the palanquin door off its tracks and run ahead with it."

"With the door?"

"If the door arrives at the barrier by sunset," Hanshiro broke in, "the officials are required to wait for the rest of the palanquin."

Hanshiro sensed the affection between Lady Asano and this outlandish commoner. He wondered, briefly, what had formed the bond. And he realized that his beloved mistress still had her secrets.

"If you get us to Edo tonight, I will be in your debt," Cat said.

"The debt is mine, my lady." Viper dallied while Cold Rice went back to his place at the carrying pole and began gulping down the rice and tea the other bearers had brought him. Then he spoke in a low voice. "The cloud didn't cover the moon this month."

"Congratulations!" Cat knew Viper was saying that his wife's monthly bleeding hadn't arrived.

Viper actually blushed. "It's too early to know for certain, of course. But my foolish, inconsequential wife is very happy."

CHAPTER 76

THE TROUBLED WATERS ARE FROZEN FAST

When Cat and Hanshiro arrived at the government barrier in Shinagawa, Viper and Cold Rice were jogging in place. Viper held the palanquin door balanced on his head. They were both shouting, "Go on! Go on!" in rhythm with their feet, as though they were carrying the whole conveyance.

The sun had set long before, and underlings had lit the lanterns. They had slid the big shutters partway across the open front of the building and stood ready to close the narrow opening they had left. Inside, wrapped in a cocoon of lantern light and secure in the prerogatives of government service, clerks were finishing the day's paperwork. They sat on the *tatami* and leaned over their low desks, their brushes flying. Rolls of paper lay piled up around them.

Cat could tell that the barrier official's impassive expression was only masking his exasperation, but he let the small procession pass with little trouble. The travel papers Lord Hino had supplied were all in order. Cat's pass gave her mother's family name of Suzuki. Besides, a highborn woman entering Edo didn't require the scrutiny of one leaving.

Hanshiro knew that the guards and clerks and the officials themselves assumed Cat was Lord Hino's consort, his woman of the provinces. The silent affront set him to seething with a fury that surprised him, but he matched their polite hisses and bows.

On the other side of the barrier, Hanshiro dismissed the two criers, the box bearer, and the men carrying his palanquin. He arranged for the officials to have it returned to Lord Hino. Viper and Cold Rice insisted they could carry Cat's palanquin themselves, and the extra men were paid off, too.

From here Hanshiro would trot along behind and act the part of a servant, carrying the clothing box on its pole across his shoulder. He looked as stalwart as always, but the long, rough ride had made him ill. He ached in every joint. The exercise and the cold air would do him good.

Cat directed Viper and Cold Rice to turn off at Sengakuji, Spring Hill Temple. Whatever happened, she couldn't pass by her father's grave without honoring him, especially now, on the eve of the monthly anniversary of his death. Viper and Cold Rice passed through the big, ornate wooden gate, turned left, and set down the palanquin among the gravestones in the grove of trees.

Hanshiro helped Cat out into snow that came above her ankles. In the moonlight, her white robes seemed to be part of the soft white landscape around her. To Hanshiro she looked like the mythical Lady of the Snows, who would fade into mist in a man's arms.

Cat turned to Viper and Cold Rice, who had folded into tight obeisances in the snow. Only the ragged patchwork humps of their jackets and the cheerful sparrows on their blue head towels were visible.

"I thank you both for your great efforts on my behalf. Amida will bless you," Cat said. "And please, Boss Viper, give my greetings to your honorable wife." She shivered and pulled her cloak about her. "We'll continue on foot, so you can leave the palanquin. Hanshiro-san will arrange with the priests here for its return to Hino-sama."

"Your Ladyship . . ." Viper looked up at her from the snow. "We're ready to carry you to your final destination. And we might be of some further, though humble, use to you."

"That wouldn't be prudent. And please stand up before your hands freeze."

"At least let us take you to Nihon Bridge," Viper persisted doggedly. "You can travel faster with us carrying you."

"Lord Hino's palanquin would draw attention to us." Cat was used to Viper's impertinent habit of arguing with his superiors, but Hanshiro marveled at her patience with him. Someday, if they survived the night, he would ask her about it.

"How's this for a bargain, my lady?" Viper adopted his favorite expression, somewhere between cunning and irony. "If, when you finish here, Cold Rice and I are waiting with a *kago*, a nondescript, lowly, and completely unworthy affair, would you honor us by riding in it?"

Cat had to smile to herself. Viper and Kasane were chiseled from the same rough-hewn, cross-grained stuff. "We're not sure where we'll go from here, but perhaps we'll have need of your services, if you can find a *kago* in such a short time.''

In fact, Cat didn't know where to look for Oishi and the Akō men. She planned to begin at the inn where Oishi and his son had stayed near the Nihon Bridge. It was the same one that received the red-haired barbarians on their annual visits to Edo.

If he wasn't there, she would go to the drapers' district and ask for the shop of Otaka Gengo, the Akō retainer who took lessons from Kira's tea master. Then she would try to find the shop of Kanzaki Yogoro, who had posed as a rich Kyōto rice merchant and had gained access to Kira's mansion. There were thousands of rice shops scattered throughout Edo, though, and finding Yogoro's would be difficult. The thought of knocking at shuttered doors in deserted streets and finding no one there filled Cat with despair.

When Viper and Cold Rice trotted off into the darkening night, Cat leaned against Hanshiro. She drew comfort from his warmth and solidity. He put an arm around her shoulder and held her close to shelter her from the cold. Then he prayed with her at the statue of Kannon-sama, the smiling goddess of mercy.

Snow had been falling in Edo for three days, and a thick covering of it lay over everything on the temple grounds. The full moon had risen. The snow mounded on the gravestones and statues and tall granite lanterns glowed in its light. Long black shadows flowed away from the buildings and monuments and trees.

The full moon hung low in the eastern sky like the tip of a fat, badger-hair brush dipped in light. Cat's exhaustion made her weak and dizzy, and she succumbed to the moon's spell. As she stared, it pulsed and shimmered, growing and receding. No wonder the peasants believed that to gaze on the moon in solitude was to risk enchantment. Cat had to shake her head to break its hold.

''Everything looks different from the last time I was here.'' Cat thought back to the morning she had awakened in the chapel to Kannon-sama so very long ago. She remembered how ignorant and foolish she had been. ''It seems so peaceful. As though there could be no sorrow in all the world.''

'' 'The troubled waters are frozen fast under clear heaven,' '' Hanshiro recited.

'' 'Moonlight and shadow ebb and flow.' '' Cat finished Lady Murasaki's poem.

They walked to Lord Asano's grave. Fresh incense was still

burning there as Cat unwrapped the food and joss sticks she had bought as an offering. She lit the incense in the coals that burned for that purpose. Hanshiro took out the scarf, still wrapped around the coil of Cat's hair. He laid it on the grave as his own offering. Then he and Cat bowed their heads and prayed.

A pale moon shadow fell across the grave, and Hanshiro leaped back, his hand on his sword hilt.

"My lady." The plump-faced man on the other side of the grave had slightly bulging eyes and a mild expression. He folded his hands together and bowed. Several gray-headed men, all in formal black clothes, stood behind him like a gathering of sages.

"Good evening, *sensei*." Cat bowed low. "Are you in good health?"

"Yes, *hime*, princess. And you?"

"I am well." Cat turned to Hanshiro. "This is the councilor, Oishi Kuranosuke," she said.

As the abbot ended the purification ceremony in a rear reception chamber of the monks' quarters, Hanshiro sat silent in the corner with Cat. He had never been in a room so suffused with warrior spirit. These were the old men, the leaders, the planners of the vengeance league.

One was seventy-seven. Five were in their sixties and four in their fifties. Except for his sixteen-year-old son Chikara, Oishi, at forty-five, was the youngest of the Akō retainers there.

Several of the temple's acolytes served tea and tobacco. Then, when the abbot withdrew to let the men discuss their plans, Oishi turned to Cat. She still wore the nun's clothes, and the white scarf framed her oval face. She was even more beautiful than Oishi remembered her.

His large, sad eyes sparkled with tears in the lantern light. He had heard that the young Lady Asano had been killed somewhere along the Tōkaidō Road. It had been one more care added to the terrible burden he had carried for two years.

"*Hime*, we've been worried about you." He used the affectionate term from Cat's childhood. "It eases our hearts to see you safe and in the shade of such a strong tree as Hanshiro of Tosa."

Hanshiro caught the brief glance Oishi gave him. It was a request to continue looking after Lady Asano no Kinume. Hanshiro nodded slightly, in acceptance of the charge.

The sight of her father's oldest and most trusted retainers almost made Cat forget the tragedy that brought them here. The occasion seemed like a reunion of loved ones after a long separation.

But she knew that soon all these men would be dead. Chikara, with whom she had hunted fireflies and explored the rocks and beaches of Akō, would be dead. Oishi would be dead. Surely a heart was too small a vessel to contain so much grief.

"How many men are in the league?" she asked.

"Forty-seven."

"Forty-seven," Cat murmured. Lord Hino had said there were sixty. Could forty-seven men overcome the small army living in barracks on the grounds of Kira's mansion?

"A number of them fell away." Onodera Jūnai, Oishi's sixty-one-year-old chief of staff, spoke up. "People nowadays have lost the perseverance of their ancestors."

"One cannot weigh honor on a merchant's scale," added Yoshida Chūzayemon. "And so it has been discarded as worthless."

"How will you manage it, with so few?"

"It's best, mistress, that you know as little as possible about the plan," Oishi said.

"I have a right to know."

Oishi smiled. That was true. She was her father's daughter in spirit as well as in beauty. Oishi had heard of the troubles Kira's men had experienced on the Tōkaidō. He could easily believe she and her companion from Tosa had taken such a toll on their enemies.

Besides, he recognized the look on her face. He had seen her narrow those swallow's eyes, flare her nostrils, and set her jaw since before she had been old enough to speak the word *no*. He gave in gracefully.

"Dressed as tradesmen and laborers and priests, the young men have been mapping the area around Kira's mansion on Matsuzaka Street, Honjō-chōnai, Honjō ward. Tonight we will all meet at the hour of the Ox at Yogoro's rice shop north of the Ryōgoku Bridge. It's close to the mansion." Oishi paused to light his pipe and take a puff. He was terribly weary, but he knew the end was near now. "I'll take half the men to the front gate. Chikara, with Jūnai and Chūza, will lead the rest around behind the mansion. While Kira's men try to stop the tiger at the front gate, the wolf will enter at the rear."

Chikara nodded politely. To Cat he looked hardly older than when she last had seen him, a laughing, naked boy of nine wading in the surf at Akō.

"The young men will enter and fight," Oishi said. "A few of them will rush the armory and cut the bowstrings and break the spear shafts. Hara, Mase, and I, we old ones, will guard the gate, to cut off the enemy's retreat and repel reinforcements."

"Lord Uesugi's bowmen?"

"Yes. Lord Uesugi has loaned his father some of them. We think the rest are quartered at Uesugi's villa in Azabu, all the way across the city. Unless we can find Kira quickly, we expect them to come to his aid as soon as they hear of the attack."

"If we fail to find him, mistress," Jūnai said, "we will set fire to the house and commit *seppuku*."

"*Sensei . . .*" Cat began.

Oishi raised a few fingers in a gesture of restraint, and Cat fell silent.

He knew that she had been about to ask to go with them. The silence in the room became strained. Hanshiro understood it. He knew he had no place here. Even Lady Asano, for all her determination and skill and noble blood, had no part in this.

For almost two years these men had lived only for this night. They had abandoned their families and destroyed their good names. They were risking the ignominious death of criminals and perhaps subjecting their families to the same fate. They had given up everything to keep faith with their honor. In the process, they had become a unit with a single mind and arm and purpose. They could admit no one else.

Oishi lifted his right leg from under him and by dropping it forward, shifting his weight, lifting the other, and pivoting, he moved along the mat. In his full black *hakama* he seemed to glide across the floor until, almost knee to knee with Cat, he put his legs under him and settled back on his ankles.

"Whether we find our enemy tonight or not," he said gently, "all who embark on this will die as a result of it."

"I'm not afraid to die, *sensei*."

"I would expect no less of you, my lady. But true courage is in living when it is time to live and dying when it is time to die. In your veins alone flows the blood of your father. If you die before bearing an heir, your father truly dies. While you live, his spirit lives. Future generations depend on you." Oishi paused to give Cat time to think about his words.

"For me there will be no moment like this one, *sensei*." Cat's grief threatened to overwhelm her, so she retreated behind the barrier of decorum. "None of us can hope to live forever," she said. "But your names and your devotion will live in the hearts of those to come." She bowed low. "On behalf of my mother I thank you. I will pray for your success."

"We are grateful, my lady, that Amida of Immeasurable Light has spared us to see this night. And to see you before we follow our liege on the dark path." Almost as though he were talking to himself, Oishi quoted Li Po. " 'Heaven and earth,' the poets say, 'are but a roadside inn for Time, a traveler on a journey through the ages, and our fleeting lives are but phantoms in Time's dreams.' "

Oishi was silent for a moment, and when he spoke again his voice for the first time betrayed his weariness. "Please, *hime*, when you see your mother, tell her I deeply regret the sorrow my actions must have caused her. Tell her she has always been in my thoughts."

"I will, *sensei*." Cat knew the time had come for her to go.

Hanshiro held a brief, whispered conference with Oishi, then he and Cat left the room. As they walked down the quiet corridor, the voices of the men faded behind them. *As though but phantoms in Time's dream*, Cat thought.

She and Hanshiro tied on their sandals at the stone stoop of the veranda and walked out into the night. The temple bell tolled five times, marking the hour of the Dog. They had three long hours until the watch of the Tiger and the raid on Kira's mansion.

"What did *sensei* say to you?" Cat asked.

"I volunteered to perform a service."

Cat was about to ask what service when she saw Viper and his partner. They were standing next to a battered open wickerwork *kago*, and though they were suitably solemn, the expression in their eyes was triumphant.

Suddenly Cat was exhausted. The temple bell had stopped ringing, but the sound continued to reverberate in her skull. The strain of speaking with her father's men for the last time had used up the strength that had brought her through the long ordeal of the trip. When Hanshiro helped her into the basket, he was alarmed at how cold her hands were. She settled back against the worn cushions and closed her eyes. Viper draped a ragged quilt over the *kago* to keep out the worst of the wind.

"The Circle Inn." Hanshiro's voice seemed far away to her. "Honjō-chōnai, Honjō ward."

Cat imagined she was a snowflake, whirling on a high wind before gently dissolving into nothingness.

CHAPTER 77

A DREAM, AN ILLUSION, A BUBBLE

The seven-foot scroll hanging in the *tokonoma* contained a single ideogram as long as Hanshiro's arm. At the serifs of its bold black strokes, splatters of ink arced out onto the white paper, testimony to the calligrapher's vigor. The character spelled "DREAM," the single word the priest and swordsman Takuan was to have written just before he died.

Hanshiro lay on his side with his arm across Cat's waist and studied the scroll by the dim light of the night lantern. As he stared at it, the ideogram seemed to separate from the soft rice paper and brocade of the scroll and float in the clouds of incense from the bronze pot nearby. It was a universe in itself. Hanshiro knew that each angle of the strokes, each irregularity left by the calligrapher's brush, had meaning, if he could only interpret it.

The midnight tolling of a distant temple bell told him the time had come to get up. He lay still a few moments longer, breathing in rhythm with Cat and savoring the feel of her body pressed against him. As he lifted his arm off her and eased away, he tucked the quilt around her bare back so the cold air wouldn't waken her.

His good clothes and the ones Cat had worn as his disciple were draped on racks. Fragrant smoke drifted up from the incense pot under them. Hanshiro's swords, helmet, long-bow, and quiver of arrows and Cat's *naginata* rested on racks in front of the *tokonoma*.

To retrieve his helmet and bow, Hanshiro had detoured by the tenement where he rented a tiny room. Viper and Cold Rice had waited in the street, standing guard over their borrowed *kago* and its sleeping occupant while Hanshiro hurried inside. He had been relieved that Cat had been asleep and didn't see the shabby neighborhood where he lived.

Then they had trotted through the throngs on the tall arc of the Ryōgoku Bridge. The Sumida River below had been crowded with boatloads of partygoers eating and drinking and enjoying the moonlight on the snowy landscape. The boat's strings of lanterns spangled the night. The aroma of broiling eel and the sounds of hand drums and *samisens* and laughter drifted upward.

They had made their way through the busy, brightly lit district of stores and *sake* shops and riverfront restaurants around the bridge. They had passed the gate into Honjō ward and walked down the quiet, residential streets to the Circle Inn. Hanshiro had carried Cat, still sleeping, through the small side door in the front gate.

Now it was time for him to prepare for the night ahead.

He ignored the new clothes he had bought when he intended to pledge his sword to Lady Asano's cause. Instead he put on his old *hakama* and jacket and wadded coat. He wrote a message for Cat should she wake up, although that didn't seem likely. She had been sleeping so soundly when they arrived, he had felt as though he were carrying a body from which the spirit had fled. She had barely awakened long enough to bathe.

Hanshiro settled his swords precisely in his sash. When he left, his stockinged feet made no noise on the boards of the corridor.

Viper was waiting for him outside. He was flanked by a merry band of carpenters and roofers, plasterers and stonemasons. They appeared to have been celebrating early the arrival of the New Year.

At Spring Hill Temple Hanshiro had realized that Viper was determined to help Cat whether she wanted him to or not. So he wasn't surprised to see that while he and Cat had been sleeping Viper had been enlisting the aid of men from Honjō ward's *otokodate*, the society of "brave men." Hanshiro, however, thought of them by the less flattering name of *machi yakko*, town underlings. For Hanshiro, an alliance with Viper and his friends was as cautious as it was temporary.

Many of the *shōgun*'s bannermen entertained themselves by roaming about the city and brutalizing merchants and laborers. For protection, some of the merchants funded societies formed by the local artisans and guild bosses. Sometimes the *otokodate* also fought with low-ranking *samurai* and *rōnin*, many of whom now made their living by theft and extortion.

To *otokodate*, a *rōnin* like Hanshiro was a potential enemy. And to those of the *samurai* class, common street brawlers like Viper and his friends were beneath contempt. But the *otokodate* were skilled with a variety of weapons, many fashioned from the tools of their trade. They asked no member about his past, which was just as well, since many were gamblers and men with stained histories.

The *otokodate* claimed that they were sworn to help the downtrodden. Hanshiro, however, had often found them to be disposed to violence for its own sake and to be dishonest when it profited them. He also knew that among the various leaders of *otokodate*, Chubei of Honjō was one of the most powerful.

There must have been thirty or forty of Chubei's men here now. Their small topknots were fashionably askew, and their sidelocks stood out in disorderly fringes from their florid faces. The reinforced linings of their collars were stained, their cuffs frayed, and their jackets much mended and patched. A few carried ladders or used their long rules as walking sticks. Others had stuck their hands into the fronts of their jackets to warm them. Most carried their tools—mallets and planes, chisels and adzes—dangling from their sashes.

"Propitious dreams," they shouted as they bowed to Viper and Hanshiro. They went off discussing where they could buy *sake* and women at this hour. Their straw sandals squeaked in the snow. They left a wake of laughter in the quiet of the street.

Hanshiro turned to Viper. He knew he would have to be diplomatic in rejecting the *kago* man's help and that of his friends. They were an unpredictable lot. Insulting them would surely cause trouble for Cat and Oishi and his men.

"Regulations forbid that the 'chastisement of an enemy be attended with riot,' " he said.

"Everything will be done with discretion, Your Honor." Viper gave his sly, ingenuous smile. He was a bit more circumspect with Hanshiro than with Lady Asano, but not much.

"Good evening." The man who joined them from a side street was dressed in the dark blue trousers and tight-sleeved wadded jacket of an artisan.

He carried a carpenter's long-handled adze with a mattock-shaped steel blade. His short legs were bowed, but his chest was round and solid as a rice bale. He had big, callused hands, and his arms strained the black canvas arm guards. His bushy brows almost met at the concave bridge of his nose. A shaggy mustache sprouted from under the lumpy end of that nose like rank grass from under a boulder.

"Good evening," he said.

Hanshiro nodded in reply to Chubei's bow. He had met the

boss once, many years ago, while intervening for a young wastrel in debt to a gambling boss in Honjō.

"So, Tosa, tonight you're not here to bargain for the balls of a young dandy."

"No." Hanshiro was impressed with Chubei's memory. The affair had happened long ago.

"It grieves me to observe," Chubei said with a smile, "that sons are quite inferior to their fathers these days and that grandsons rarely offer hope for improvement."

"Just so," Hanshiro said politely. "As for what brings me to Honjō, Viper and I were just discussing the regulations concerning the proper conduct of a vendetta."

"Ah, yes. The dog *shōgun*'s regulations." Chubei's grin widened. " 'The chastisement of an enemy may not be attended with riot.' " He spoke in a low voice, but it carried in the silent street. From somewhere behind a nearby wall a dog began barking.

"Is there a place we can talk in private?" Hanshiro asked.

"Certainly."

Chubei lit a lantern and led Viper and Hanshiro through the narrow back streets to the large shed, open on two sides, that sheltered his cluttered workshop. Hanshiro sat on the rough-hewn surface of a huge cypress log that was being dressed as a beam. Viper and Chubei sat cross-legged among the fragrant curls of wood that the apprentices' adzes had shaved off the log. Around them were stacked the beams and posts of the house Chubei had been engaged to build.

"This is no ordinary street brawl," Hanshiro said. "It involves men of great honor who are determined to right an infamous wrong."

"I'm not a fool, Tosa." Chubei's voice was still cordial, to show he meant no real offense. But he was no longer smiling. "I know who is involved."

"Who else knows?"

Chubei chuckled. "Viper told only me, but everyone suspects. Edo has been waiting two years for this night."

"Then the object of the endeavor might suspect, too."

"No more than usual. For two years Kira's been as suspicious as a cat with its head in a bag. He rarely peeks out from behind his walls." Chubei stroked his mustache lovingly. "My wife's cousin is a rice dealer. He says the food bills for Kira's extra bodyguards are ruinous. He's only recently sent some of Uesugi's bowmen back to Azabu, probably so his son can feed them for a while.''

"If Kira had done the honorable thing and opened his belly," Viper said, "or even shaved his head in penance and taken holy orders, folk might have felt more kindly toward him.''

"It's more important to shave the heart than to shave the head," Chubei said. "And Kira's heart is as hard as ever. Many's the man, even among us wretched Edokko, who would like to see him pay.''

"This isn't a matter for commoners." Hanshiro looked hard at Chubei. He had to make this very clear. "For them to participate would sully the honor of the men involved. Is that understood?''

"Yes, Tosa," Chubei said. "It's understood.''

Chubei rose and walked to the open side of the shed. He stood in the rectangle of moonlight and looked up. "My old and tender friend Viper has suggested an evening stroll to view the moon.'' He threw open his arms, as if to embrace the full moon, which was almost directly overhead. Then he turned to face Viper and Hanshiro. "*Mairimasho ka?* Shall we go?''

For the next hour Chubei showed Hanshiro which street gates would be open and which would be locked. He showed him where the vantage points would be and where the blind alleys were. He introduced him to the gate guards and to the men of the fire watch. And when Hanshiro parted company with him he gave him two brown canvas firemen's coats.

When Hanshiro returned to the inn he slipped in the small side door that he had paid the night attendant to leave open for him. He padded down the dimly lit hall to the room he shared with Cat.

He took off his old clothes and put on the white satin loin-cloth, the new undershirt of wadded *habutae* silk, and the black-and-white wadded silk robe and black *hakama*. An undertaking such as tonight's required purity of heart and mind, body and dress.

He knelt and shook Cat's hip gently.

"Is it time?" Cat sleepily ran a hand over her skull, fuzzy now with a six-day growth of dark hair.

"Yes.''

She rose and pulled her quilted sleeping robe closer around her. She went to the low desk, mixed ink, and wrote what she dared not say aloud. "What did you speak to *sensei* about?''

While Hanshiro wrote a reply, she knelt and tied on his leggings.

"I offered to watch for messengers trying to reach Uesugi to ask for reinforcements."

"Viper is plotting something." Cat's nervousness showed in her calligraphy, but her only fear was that some outsider would interfere with Oishi's plan.

"I know." Hanshiro put down the brush and helped Cat tie her *hakama* cords. Then he wrapped her long sash three times around her waist. As he bent down to tie it in a warrior's dragonfly knot, he leaned over her shoulder and whispered in her ear. "He and Honjō's boss showed me the area while you slept. But they understand that they must not interfere."

When Cat had dressed she draped a large cloth over her bare head. She folded the sides down along her cheeks and tied it under her chin. Hanshiro lit incense in his shallow, bowl-shaped black-lacquer helmet. If things went awry tonight, if warfare broke out in Honjō and his head were taken, it would be fragrant.

He and Cat lit more incense in front of the ornate lacquered cupboard that housed the altar. They each put their palms together, bowed their heads, and prayed to Amida Buddha and to the god of warriors. In unison they softly chanted the Diamond *sutra*.

> Every phenomenon is like a dream,
>   an illusion, a bubble, a shadow;
> It is like dew and also like lightning.
> So is all to be seen.

They burned their messages to each other. Hanshiro stuck his swords into his sash and put his coat over them. He hung his helmet from the sash. He tied the quiver on his back so the fan of arrows stood up over his head. He picked up his long bow.

When he gave Cat the heavy fireman's coat, tears welled up suddenly in her eyes. She stroked the stiff canvas.

"My father . . ." She paused until her voice was steady enough to go on. "My father took great care with his fire brigade."

Lord Asano's fire company had numbered more than fifty men, picked from the strongest and handsomest of the Akō-Asano retainers. They were better equipped and trained than any in their part of Edo. Cat remembered how proud she had always felt when she had watched them drill. They had looked so impressive in their leather coats, with their pikes and fire hooks on their shoulders.

Hanshiro helped Cat adjust the hood of the coat. He held her face in his big hands and laid his forehead against hers. He brushed her lips with his. She picked up the *naginata*, and they went out into the silence of the snowy street.

CHAPTER 78

THE ULTIMATE OF SWORDSMANSHIP

As in all of Edo, gates shut off most of Honjō's narrow side streets. The gatekeepers slept inside the small gate houses. Those of the main street, a thoroughfare that ran north from the Ryōgoku Bridge, were open to facilitate movement in case of fire. Hanshiro and Cat strode down the center of it. A light snow earlier in the evening had covered the layer dirtied by the day's traffic. It silenced the tread of their sandals, but they made no special effort to be quiet.

They had no need to skulk. They were going about their duties as part of Honjō's latest innovation, a merchants' fire brigade. Of course, paired swords, a *naginata*, a seven-foot bow, and a quiver full of arrows weren't standard fire-fighting equipment, but Chubei had assured Hanshiro that no one would interfere with him and Lady Asano.

They entered Honjō's commercial district. The streets were lined with the dark wooden shutters of shops and tenements. Hanshiro led the way past fire buckets stacked against a large house. Like the others here, the house fronted directly on the roadway. The ladder to the fire watch's rooftop lookout leaned against the first-floor overhang.

Cat started up it. She climbed past the first- and second-story eaves to the small platform built above the roof peak. This was Chubei's house. Between it and the open workshop behind it was a small garden, exquisitely designed and ethereally beautiful in the moonlight. Cat was astonished to find it attached to a carpenter's house.

Edo was built on low land that was fairly level. For as far as Cat could see stretched the jumble of snow-covered roofs, none more than two stories high. Except for a distant five-storied pagoda, only rooftop drying racks and spindly fire towers rose above the undulating expanse of white.

When Cat turned around, her *naginata* hit the bronze bell hanging from the center of the platform's roof. In the stillness it set up a metallic rumble that seemed loud enough to wake the whole district or at least the household sleeping below her.

"I'm sorry," she whispered as Hanshiro's head appeared. Her breath formed a cloud in the cold air, and she shivered.

"Don't worry," Hanshiro said. "It could hardly be heard from below."

The full moon seemed inordinately large and almost close enough to touch. It was beginning to descend in the southern sky, but it lit everything with a silvery clarity. The snow reflected and intensified the light. From the platform, Cat and Hanshiro could see the Sumida River and the Ryōgoku Bridge to the west.

To the north and east were the residences of the lords. Their walled compounds of gardens and outbuildings, servants' quarters, family shrines, and rambling houses were scattered among the pines. In Edo's crowded center near the walls of the *shōgun*'s castle, the lords' "upper" mansions were set one against each other. That was why so many of the government's retired officials had chosen to build their "middle" mansions here.

The middle mansions were where the lords' families lived and where they had room to quarter their retainers in barracks along the inner side of the wall facing the street. Kira's middle mansion only had two small rooms next to the armory near the gate. His guards were crowded into them.

"Which is Kira's?" Cat asked.

Hanshiro pointed with his fan. "Where the branches of the pine hang over the wall."

Cat found the gate of Kira's compound. She studied the barracks roofs and the inner courtyard where the palanquins and carriages of guests were received. Beyond the courtyard's low wall lay Kira's garden and private quarters.

Cat followed the angular meandering of the mansion's rooflines. She memorized the wings and ells, the verandas and covered corridors, connecting the main part of the house with the family's rooms at the rear of it. Somewhere under those roofs Lord Kira was sleeping.

"The men should pass by here," Hanshiro said. "Yogoro's rice shop is past the brewery, three blocks down and across the street."

The brewery was easy to distinguish from the other shops. Its symbol, a huge brown globe of dried cypress needles, hung from the second-story gable. Nothing stirred in the streets except the occasional cat and a rat that scuttled along the white plaster walls of a warehouse. But Cat stared as though she could have looked through the roof of the rice shop and seen the men inside. She tried to imagine what they were doing, what they were saying. What they were feeling.

Cat and Hanshiro stood with their hands on the railing and their sleeves touching and surveyed the moonlit, snow-shrouded walls and houses and trees below. The streets and rooftops seemed empty, but they weren't.

Cat walked around the platform looking for signs of Viper and his friends. She knew they must be hiding behind the big tubs of water on the roofs or behind fences or in the narrow side streets, but she could see no one.

"They're very good," she whispered. Perhaps some of the stories she had heard about the *machi yakko* hadn't been exaggerated after all.

"There." Hanshiro pointed with his iron fan to a roof several blocks away.

Moon shadow faintly outlined footprints leading up the roof's slope to the huge wooden barrel of water, stored there in case of fire. Cat realized that what few traces of the *machi yakko* she could detect were in the area around Kira's mansion.

"Chubei swore his men wouldn't interfere." Hanshiro answered Cat's unspoken doubt. He expected Chubei to keep his word, but he wasn't surprised to see the *machi yakko* keeping watch. They wouldn't miss the chance to see this night's battle.

Cat and Hanshiro looked down the street toward the bridge and canal that separated Honjō from Fukagawa, the next ward to the south. If Lord Uesugi sent reinforcements, they would most likely approach from that direction.

"We're to ring the fire bell once if we see them coming," Hanshiro said.

A temple bell began tolling the seventh watch, the hour of the Tiger. Its notes hung, expectant, on the air. Cat gripped Hanshiro's arm to keep her own hands from trembling. The hairs on the back of her neck stirred, and her heart pounded. She felt transcendently aware, as though through the walls of Yogoro's rice shop she could hear the forty-seven men breathe. As though she could smell the incense with which they had perfumed their helmets.

The last note had faded when Cat heard the faint rasp of a wooden shutter being slid back. The Akō *rōnin* began fanning out from the front door of the shop. Cat strained to distinguish individuals as they formed into a double line. When they moved out from under the eaves, they and their weapons threw a bristling shadow, like a long, spiked dragon, onto the snow.

For more freedom of movement, they had wrapped leggings around the bottoms of their *hakama*. As a disguise they wore the heavy canvas hooded capes of a warriors' fire brigade. Their sleeves were tied back to reveal mail gauntlets under matching black broadcloth coats with large white triangles around the cuffs and hems. The white design would be easier to see in the dark corridors of Kira's mansion and would identify the men to each other.

Some men had on helmets. Others had tied cloth bands around their heads. They carried paired swords in their sashes, of course, but they were also armed with spears and *naginata*, bows, arrows, and staffs. Rust on a man's weapon indicated corrosion of his spirit, and every blade had been polished until the moonlight glinted off it.

Some of the men had stuck thin poles into the backs of their sashes so that the small cloth banners attached to them waved above their heads. They had written their death names on the banners.

A few men carried bamboo ladders and heavy, long-handled mallets. Several held large, truncated cones of blackened cypress veneer with handles at the narrow ends. The cones were lanterns with gimballed candles that could direct a beam of light at the enemy while leaving the bearer in shadow.

Kanzaki Yogoro led the procession. He was followed by a man holding up a pole with a small box on the end of it. Cat knew the box must contain the Akō *rōnin*'s statement of purpose.

Oishi walked behind the box bearer. He carried a battle drum by a cord loop. The drum's head was painted with the twin red *yin* and *yang* symbols, the crest of the Yamaga school of strategy. His expression was calm.

As Cat watched him approach she murmured the ancient poem.

> Yamato is a land
> Where the word-spirit aids us.
> Be happy. Fare you well!

When she saw Oishi look around she started, even though she knew that spoken words possessed a spirit of their own. They could carry out the speaker's wishes, and perhaps Cat's words had made themselves felt.

The moonlight was so bright that the men had no need of lanterns. No one spoke. Their presence was announced only by the crunch of their straw sandals in the fresh snow and by the muted rattle of metal and wood. It was an archaic noise, an echo from the centuries of warfare that had preceded this one. It was a sound not often heard in the streets of Edo.

Hanshiro had been raised as a warrior, but he had never seen men march into battle. He had thought the warrior spirit extinguished by the corrupting influence of money and the decadence of his generation. He knew the Edo had never seen the equal of this procession, nor would it be likely to again.

Cat and Hanshiro watched the double column move down the empty street. Then it turned a corner and was lost to sight. Cat stared, rapt, at the buildings hiding her father's men until they reappeared at the head of Matsuzaka Street. When the procession reached the corner of Kira's wall, it divided, like a stream flowing around a boulder. Chikara and his men separated and headed for the rear of the compound.

Oishi and the rest walked to the front gate. The warriors crouched in the snow while those with the ladders leaned them against the eaves of the gate's wide roof. Men climbed the ladders and eased up the slope of the gate roof until they could look over the peak into the compound beyond. As Cat watched them, the silence of their movements gave the scene the quality of a dream.

A few of Oishi's men scrambled up over the gate roof and dropped into the courtyard below. Cat couldn't see them there, but they must have overpowered the night watch huddled around their brazier in the gate house, because soon the heavy doors swung slowly open. Those with the gimballed lanterns lit them.

Oishi raised the war drum and held it poised and silent until Cat wanted to shout to him to give the signal. Finally he hit the drum sharply with the drumstick. A heartbeat later Cat heard the hollow report. It was followed by the faint crash of huge wooden mallets against the smaller back gate. Oishi's men crowded through the front gate. Oishi and two of his older lieutenants, Hara Soyemon and Mase Kyudaiyu, stationed themselves outside to repel reinforcements and to stop those inside from escaping.

Cat leaned out from the railing, as though she could fly to join her father's men. She heard shouting and saw Kira's guards burst from their tiny rooms along the front wall. They were barefoot and half-dressed. Their uncombed hair hung down around their shoulders, but most of them had their swords drawn. The clash of blades rang out over the men's shouts.

Long beams from the lanterns flashed and swooped. Their light caught parts of the combatants—a leg, an arm, a face contorted with rage—and froze them for an instant like some artist's depiction of war. Some of the Akō rōnin held off the guards in the courtyard while the rest charged up the steps onto the veranda. They battered down the door of the entrance hall, and women began screaming from inside the house.

"They're getting away." Cat pointed to two men running across the garden. The men threw a gardener's ladder against the wall on the far side and climbed over. They dropped to the street below and raced for the Sumida River. "We should warn Oishi." Cat started for the ladder, but Hanshiro held her arm.

"Remember the words of one wiser than we," he said. " 'Do not fight with another's bow. Do not ride another's horse. Do not discuss another's faults. . . .' " He paused to let her finish.

" 'Do not interfere with another's work.' " Her voice was low and bitter. *But this* is *my work*, she thought.

She strained to make sense of the confusion in Kira's compound, of bodies in motion, of light and shadow, flashing steel, and the high whine of bowstrings discharging their arrows. The sounds of shrieking and crashing and ripping rose and fell inside the house as Oishi's men searched for Kira. The fight spilled over the courtyard wall and into the garden beyond.

Lights came on in the nearby compounds, and soon people appeared on the roofs. Most of them were afraid a fire had broken out. Men slipped out the smaller doors set in the main gates and ran to see what was happening.

Oishi had unfolded a stool and sat calmly in front of the gate while his two gray-haired companions, Hara and Mase, paced. When a small crowd gathered, Hara and Mase conferred with the men sent by neighboring lords. The messengers dispersed, scattering back to their masters' compounds and disappearing through the side doors.

Mase unfolded a stool and sat next to Oishi. Hara went back to pacing. Cat and Hanshiro waited for Kira's neighbors to send men to aid him, but the gates of the surrounding mansions stayed discreetly shut.

About halfway through the hour of the Tiger the noise of fighting finally quieted. Cat could see bodies scattered about the courtyard and the garden. They sprawled across the steps and the verandas. She could hear the sound of women wailing and the noise of destruction. In their search for their lord's enemy the Akō men were breaking open chests, pulling down ceiling panels, and slashing bedding. Kira's mansion was modest, but even in a modest mansion there were lots of places for a man to hide.

The moon had almost set. In the east a band of pale light lay along the horizon, but no whistle signaled that Kira had been found. Cat thought she would go mad with the waiting. To reassure her Hanshiro allowed his sleeve to brush hers. He moved his hand so that it rested lightly against hers on the railing.

After a long discussion Hara and Mase finally persuaded Oishi to let them go inside. They left him sitting alone on the stool in the trampled snow outside the gate. He seemed as calm as a buddha, but he looked forlorn, abandoned, left out of the vengeance he had planned. Cat wondered what he was thinking. Had Kira escaped? Had all Oishi's effort and suffering been for nothing?

"They're coming," Hanshiro said.

Cat turned to look. A bristle of bows moved across the bridge into Honjō from Fukagawa. The thirteen archers were a token force, but they were reputed to be the best in the country. And the Akō *rōnin* must be exhausted by now.

Cat reached for the iron rod that hung near the big bell, but Hanshiro put a hand on her arm.

"If we ring the bell, Uesugi's men and Oishi's will clash," he said. "The master of the New Shadow school wrote that if your mind reaches the ultimate of swordsmanship, the sword will have no place."

"What do you propose?"

"Persuasion. It would be best if you stay here while I go down and talk to them."

Cat just looked at him, and he smiled ruefully. He hadn't

really thought she would agree to stay behind. "If they kill us, we will at least have delayed them," he said.

Chubei's *machi yakko* appeared suddenly, as if on cue, on the rooftops lining the bowmen's route.

"You said Chubei promised that his men wouldn't interfere."

"They're not there to fight." Hanshiro started down the ladder. "We'll use them as *go* stones, surrounding the enemy and ending the game in a draw."

He led Cat at a run through back alleys reeking of garbage and sewage. They came out on the main street a few blocks in front of Uesugi's bowmen. With their faces hidden in the shadows of their hoods, they waited.

Hanshiro's bow was unstrung and slung across his back. His swords were in their scabbards. Cat's *naginata* blade was sheathed, and she held it vertically, with the butt resting in the snow.

"Comrades," Hanshiro said when the archers drew close, "this quarrel is not with you or your master."

"We have our orders." The captain was in his middle years and obviously very well trained. He was from Yonezawa to the north, and he had little regard for city warriors. In Hanshiro he recognized an equal, something he hadn't found often in Edo.

Hanshiro approached close enough to speak softly. He nodded toward the rooftops, where almost a hundred men were clearly outlined against the pale gray sky. They stood so that their mattocks and adzes and scythes were silhouetted, too. From side streets came the creak of gates closing.

The captain knew his men could be trapped here between the unbroken facade of the buildings, with no room to maneuver while they were attacked from above. He realized his choices would be to engage in a brawl with commoners or retreat from them. He didn't relish either alternative.

"Your orders were to come to the aid of a certain lord," Hanshiro said. "Surely your master didn't mean for you to sully your weapons with the likes of them."

"True." The captain had been instructed, in fact, not to cause a disturbance in the streets.

"The ignorant rabble of Honjō are an impulsive and irrational lot. And they've taken an insolent interest in this case. If you continue, I fear they'll attack."

Hanshiro knew the captain wasn't afraid of a gang of commoners, and the captain knew Hanshiro knew it. They both also knew that the government forbade interference in private disputes. And then there was the edict about the chastisement of an enemy not being attended by riot. The *machi yakko* excelled at riot.

"I . . ." The captain stopped. He sighed. He bowed.

Cat and Hanshiro bowed lower to lend dignity to his retreat as he spun on his heel and strode off the way he had come. His men wheeled and followed him.

Cat turned and ran north, toward Kira's mansion. She was only a block away when she heard the shrill call of a whistle, then another. A shout went up. Oishi's men had found Lord Kira.

CHAPTER 79
SPRING DWELLS INSIDE THE STRUGGLING BUDS

When Cat arrived at the gate, a crowd of the neighboring lords' servants and retainers stood in front of it, craning to see inside. Oishi and his stool had disappeared. Cat set her *naginata* against the wall and walked without hesitation through the heavy wooden doors.

Hanshiro started to call her back, then thought better of it. A month ago Lady Asano had set out on her journey alone. It was only right that she finish it alone. Hanshiro tried neither to stop her nor follow her.

Cat stopped just inside the gate and looked around. The courtyard was quiet. It was empty except for the bodies. The predawn light revealed the dead and wounded everywhere, but she was relieved to see that none wore the black-and-white coat of the Akō men. On the other side of the yard the offices and front reception rooms of Kira's mansion lay open to view. The inner wall panels all had been smashed or toppled, exposing room after room, receding into the night that lingered there.

A warrior-priest lay sprawled in the shadow of the gate, his sword still clutched in his hand. He must have been one of the first to die. Perhaps he had been performing his morning devotions and so had been awake at the hour of the Tiger.

Cat had no time to ponder what his relationship to Kira might have been. She stripped off her fireman's coat and put on the man's outer robe. She took the cloth off her shaved head, transforming herself into a young bonze. She pulled the rosary from under the dead priest's sash and draped it over her hands.

Fingering the beads and chanting *sutras* for the repose of the spirits of the dead, she walked slowly across the courtyard and up the steps. She was concentrating so intently on the interior of the house and the enemies who might be lurking there that when she passed the slain warrior on the veranda she stepped into the pool of his blood. Her sandals left crimson tracks behind her on the *tatami* as she walked into the devastation.

She walked around the heaps of broken ceiling panels and painted screens and powdered plaster. She surveyed the scattered account books and abacuses and the upturned writing tables of the steward's office. She saw the scroll torn from the wall of the reception hall's *tokonoma*. A lacquered altar cupboard had been toppled and the articles inside smashed underfoot.

As Cat walked through the ruin of Kira's mansion, it seemed like a lovely garden to her. A paradise of retribution. It soothed her angry spirit as water running over the rocks in her mother's garden once had.

She headed toward the sound of women sobbing. They were in the family's private quarters, and that was where Kira most likely would be. But the corridor leading to the inner rooms at the rear of the house was empty, and Cat wondered where her father's men had gone.

At the other end of the hallway the damage was even worse. Cat waded through torn robes and mattresses and gossamer drifts of silk floss wadding. She stepped over scattered porcelain and lacquerware, smoking utensils, lanterns, and works of art. Storage chests big enough to hide a man had been smashed and the contents strewn about. Bedding had been pulled from the cupboards and ripped open. Draped over a broken rack was a torn purple satin quilt with arrows bristling from it.

In the next room, long smears and splatters of fresh blood glistened on the wall like the calligraphy of a death poem in an alien language. Braziers had been knocked over, but Cat noticed that someone had doused the embers in them. Wet charcoal and floods of ash-thick water had flowed out across the floors. Oishi's men had seen to it that fire didn't destroy Kira's house before they found him.

The outer wooden shutters had been knocked from their tracks along the corridor facing the garden. Cat could imagine the Akō men kicking them out at the top so that they lay in a row, in a long uneven slope from the raised floor of the corridor down to the ground. As she followed the hallway to the back of the mansion, she began to hear men's voices. When she reached the end of it she stood in the shadows and looked past the family shrine with its small *torii* gate.

Oishi and his men were gathered there around a small shed near the rear wall of the compound. The shed was the sort used to store charcoal. It stood near the kitchen in the midst of the gardeners' clutter—ladders and poles, dusty baskets, mats, and heaps of straw rope. It was a contemptible place for someone of Kira's position to hide.

Cat could feel her heart pounding as she tried to see what was happening there. The men all moved back when those inside the shed came out. Someone raised a spear, and everyone cheered. Stuck onto the willow-leaf-shaped blade was a bloody head. Cat had no doubt it was Kira's. The ferocity of her joy was so intense, her ears rang with it.

She drew back into the darkness of the house and retraced her route through the blood and the desolation. She had seen no one inside, but she still heard women wailing in a distant room.

When she walked out through the front gate, Hanshiro was surprised to see his beloved, who had entered as a fireman, emerge as a priest. Her face was impassive, but he recognized the look of triumph in her eyes. She retrieved her *naginata* and stood quietly next to him in front of the crowd. Together they waited for the forty-seven *rōnin* of Akō to appear.

When Oishi finally led his weary men through the gate, a murmur went up from the people outside. The warriors' clothes were torn and bloody. Several of the wounded leaned on their comrades. Some of the older men staggered from exhaustion. Onodera Jūnai, a blood-soaked rag wrapped around his gray hair, stepped away from the others.

"Lord Kira Kozuke-no-suke Yoshinaka is dead," he announced. "We have satisfied the restless spirit of our master, Asano Takumi-no-Kami. We mean no harm to anyone else."

He moved to join the others, who were forming a double column behind two spearmen and a man bearing a box on a pole. Inside the box was Kira's head wrapped in a wide sleeve torn from a silk robe. Several warriors moved in as a guard behind the box bearer. They were followed by Oishi walking alone, then Chikara, supporting his seventy-seven-year-old comrade. The rest of the forty-seven fell in line at the rear. A bell from the nearby temple began sounding the hour of the Hare.

Oishi stopped in front of Cat. *"Hime."* He smiled at her. "Never have I seen you look so saintly."

The rosary rattled as Cat reached up to touch with the tips of her fingers the soft black fuzz that covered her head. "Where will you go now, *sensei*?"

"If no one stops us, we'll walk to Sengakuji, to Spring Hill Temple. We'll burn incense and leave this offering on our lord's grave. We'll tell him of our insignificant efforts to repay some small part of our debt to him." Oishi reached into his jacket and drew out two folded pieces of paper. He hadn't expected to be able to give them to her in person. "I regret most deeply that I cannot stop to see your mother." He held out the letters. "One is for you. Will you please deliver the other to her?"

Cat accepted them with both hands and bowed low over them. She was still bowing when Oishi took his place in the procession and the forty-seven men began walking through the snow toward the setting moon. When Cat looked up she watched their receding backs until they were out of sight.

Only when the last man turned a corner and the crunch of sandals and the rattle of weapons faded away did she look at the letters. The sight of her mother's name on one of them created a longing so intense, her chest ached with it. She realized she was free to see her mother and her nurse.

The tiny house where they were living seemed as great as a mansion to her now. On the way there she would buy charcoal to fill the braziers and warm every corner of it. And she would write Kasane a message and send it to Lord Hino's upper mansion.

She looked at the second letter. It was addressed to "One who desires flowers." Cat had almost forgotten the nickname, taken from the opening line of an old poem. Oishi had called her that when she was a child and used to beg him every spring to take her to see the cherry blossoms at Mukojima on the banks of the Sumida.

Cat opened the letter with trembling fingers and held it so Hanshiro could read it, too. The familiar calligraphy of Oishi's poem was like a dear friend she hadn't seen in a long time but whom she could now keep with her for as long as she lived.

"Remember," he wrote, "that spring dwells inside the struggling buds of snow-covered hills."

"My lady . . ." The familiar voice sounded just behind her.

Cat turned to see Viper and Cold Rice standing next to their borrowed *kago*. They bowed low. "We're at your service to carry you anywhere."

"Where do you want to go?" Hanshiro asked softly.

"Home," Cat said.

EPILOGUE

After spending the day at Sengakuji, then being questioned by a government inspector, Oishi, his son Chikara, and fourteen of his men were put in Lord Hosokawa's care. The rest of the Akō retainers were divided among three other lords while the government deliberated their fate. They were treated as honored guests while controversy raged through Edo. Because they had acted in the true spirit of the warrior's Way, petitions were raised asking the government to spare them. Finally, after six weeks, an envoy delivered the verdict.

The government's Great Council had been lenient. It had decided that the forty-seven loyal *rōnin* of Akō should be granted the deaths of *samurai* instead of criminals. Apparently they agreed with the powerful abbot of Ueno who pointed out that if the Akō *rōnin* lived, they might do something later that would sully the purity of their deed. The greatest lords in the country gathered in Lord Hosokawa's garden to see the sentence carried out.

Cat and Hanshiro came early, before the others arrived. A bamboo screen hid them, but they could watch the sad proceedings through the latticework woven into the screen. The cherry tree nearby was white with blossoms, but their fragrance was too faint to be detected over the metallic scent of blood pervading the garden.

Cat wore the unadorned *kimono* of mourning. Hanshiro was dressed in formal robes, *hakama*, and winged vest bearing the crest of Matsudaira Aki-no-Kami. Lord Asano's family had been a minor branch of Aki-no-Kami's clan, and at Oishi's request he had discreetly offered Cat and Hanshiro, and their loyal servants, Kasane and Shintarō, places in his Edo household. But when Cat and Hanshiro married, they held the ceremony at Lord Hosokawa's mansion so Oishi could be there.

Beyond the screen shielding Cat and Hanshiro was a corner of bare ground. It was bordered on two sides by the raised floor of the veranda of Hosokawa's mansion. Lining the veranda and seated in rows on *tatami* mats on the ground were the lords. In the center of the open space three mats had been turned upside down and laid side by side. A white cloth had been spread in the middle of them, but it didn't completely cover the smears of fresh blood.

Behind the low dais, a curtain of white silk hung from ropes stretched between poles. The silk billowed gently in a light spring breeze. It hid the platform from the view of the fifteen men who had approached it, one by one, this morning. The executions had been carried out according to rank, and only one man was left.

Cat had bid Oishi good-bye the night before, but she wished she could have told him today that his son had died well. She saw the man who would serve as second approach the dais. He drew his sword and took his stance behind the white cloth.

Hanshiro glanced over at Cat. ''Victor and vanquished,'' he murmured.

Cat finished the poem silently. *Victor and vanquished are but drops of dew, bolts of lightning, illusion.*

The silent men in the garden seemed to give a collective sigh as Oishi strode out from the door of the mansion. He turned at the end of the curtain, stepped onto the dais, bowed, and knelt. As Cat watched him through her tears, his figure seemed to shimmer there.

Fare you well, sensei, she thought. And she knew the ancients were right. Her thoughts and her love would accompany him on his long journey.

AUTHOR'S NOTE

A book could be written about the eccentricities of the fifth Tokugawa *shōgun*, Tsunayoshi, known as the dog *shōgun*. The years of his rule were called the Genroku period. Genroku officially lasted from 1688 to 1703, but its flowering of art and literature and drama extended into the next two decades of the two hundred and fifty years known as the Tokugawa or Edo period.

Saikaku Ihara, the son of a seventeenth-century merchant, wrote many entertaining novels detailing life and love among the common people of that time. His works, such as *Five Women Who Loved Love*, *Some Final Words of Advice*, *The Life of an Amorous Man*, *This Scheming World*, and *Comrade Loves of the Samurai* are available in paperback editions.

Howard Hibbert's work, *The Floating World in Japanese Fiction*, and Stephen and Ethel Longstreet's *Yoshiwara* give a good account of the demimonde of Tokugawa, Japan's pleasure districts and *kabuki* theaters. Charles Dunn's *Everyday Life in Traditional Japan* is also a wealth of detail about the period.

Jippensha Ikku's comic novel *Shank's Mare*, translated by Thomas Satchell, follows two picaresque vagabonds down the Tōkaidō. Hiroshige Ando's famous series of woodblock prints depicting the fifty-three post stations of the Tōkaidō Road are also available in book form. Because of the Tokugawas' resistance to change and their refusal to allow foreign commerce, both Jippensha's and Hiroshige's works, although done over a hundred years after this story, impart the ambience of the time.

Various nonfiction accounts, with embellishments, have been written in English about the Akō-Asano affair. The two most widely read are found in A. B. Mitford's *Tales of Old Japan* and John Allyn's *The Forty-Seven Rōnin Story*.

One study mentions that Lord Asano Takumi-no-Kami had a daughter and that Oishi Kuranosuke tried to arrange an adoption for her. Other research indicates that Lord Asano had no offspring. I chose the middle ground, postulating that he had a child by a secondary wife. This was a common occurrence and the children of such unions were often adopted.

The Akō *rōnin's* loyalty raised the issue of civil law versus a higher moral imperative. The common folk were loud in their support of the forty-seven and scholars argued the case at great length. As a consequence, almost more has been written about the aftermath of the vendetta than about the raid itself.

Oishi Kuranosuke and his men walked five miles through the center of Edo and no one interfered with them. After washing Kira's head in the well at Sengakuji and visiting Lord Asano's tomb, they surrendered to the abbot there. Sentence was passed on the fourth day of the second lunar month, about the third week in March by the Gregorian calendar. In the mansions of the lords who had hosted them, forty-six of the *rōnin*, including Oishi's sixteen-year-old son, committed *seppuku* on the same day. They were buried with their lord at Sengakuji.

After the raid on Lord Kira's mansion, the lowest ranking member of the league was dispatched to Hiroshima to take the news to Lord Asano's brother. Two years later the messenger surrendered and begged to be allowed to commit *seppuku* and join his comrades. The *shōgun*, perhaps unwilling to reawaken the whole tumultuous affair, denied his request and he lived to be eighty-three years old.

Within two weeks of the incident, the first play about the heroic forty-seven appeared. The events in it were only thinly disguised as having happened in an earlier century. Since then hundreds of plays, books, essays, and movies about the story have been produced. The version written in 1748, by the famous playwright Chikamatsu, is still performed every year on the anniversary of the raid. The two movies, called *Chushingura*, about the forty-seven loyal retainers, are broadcast nationwide on that same day.

At the quiet temple of Sengakuji, near the subway stop by that name on the outskirts of Tokyo, their graves are still visited by those who honor them. Clouds of incense burned in their memory always hang over them. Their names have become immortalized in Japan, and each of them is a national hero.

Be sure to read the complete collection of

Lucia St. Clair Robson
Native American historicals
from Ballantine Books

LIGHT A DISTANT FIRE

Osceola had no illusions that the struggle would be an easy one. But after years of humbly acquiescing to the white man's demands, he was ready to fight, no matter what the cost. The young men would have the chance to earn war honors. Their women would have reason to be proud of them again. But when "Old Mad" Jackson declared war on the Seminole, he never envisioned battling a people who would become symbols of courage, loyalty, and patriotism.

RIDE THE WIND

In 1836, when she was nine years old, Cynthia Ann Parker was kidnapped by Comanche Indians from her family's settlement. She grew up with them, mastered their ways, and married one of their leaders. Except for her brilliant blue eyes and golden mane, she was in every way a Comanche woman. This is the story of Cynthia Ann Parker and the last days of the Comanche.

WALK IN MY SOUL

Tiana of the Cherokee grew up learning the magic, spells, and the nature religion of the Cherokee. Sam Houston was known to all as the father of Texas, but the young Sam ran away from his family's general store to live among the Cherokee. He came to love Tiana. And as the Cherokee would say, she walked in his soul.

LUCIA ST. CLAIR ROBSON